# The Purest Gold

by

Heather Starsong

This is a work of fiction. Names, characters, and events described herein are imaginary. Any resemblance to actual events, locations, organizations, or persons, living or dead, is entirely coincidental. The towns of Gold Creek, Montview, and Coal City are also fictitious.

*The Purest Gold*
Copyright © 2017 Heather Starsong (www.heatherstarsong.com)
All rights reserved. No part of this book may be used or reproduced in any manner whatsoever without written permission, except in the case of brief quotations embodied in critical articles or reviews.

Edited by Gifford Keen and Susan Ring-deRosset
Cover art by Stephen Clay Elliott
Design and layout by Ann Erwin
Proofread by Margaret Pevec

Names: Starsong, Heather.
Title: The purest gold / by Heather Starsong.
Description: First edition | Boulder, CO: Dancing Aspen Press [2017]
Identifiers: ISBN: 978-0-997545-04-3 (paperback) | 978-0-997545-05-0
     (ebook) | LCCN: 2016909670
Subjects: LCSH: Teenage girls--United States--1865–1898--Fiction. | Twins--
     United States--1865–1898--Fiction. | Clergy--United States--1865–1898
     --Fiction. | Wagon trains--United States--Fiction. | Frontier and pioneer
     life--Colorado Territory--Fiction. | Pioneers--Colorado Territory--Fiction.
     | Colorado Territory--Fiction. | Romance fiction, American. | LCGFT:
     Historical fiction. | Romance fiction. | BISAC: FICTION / Historical. |
     FICTION / Romance / Historical / General.
Classification: LCC: PS3619.T3767 P87 2017 | DDC: 813/.6--dc23

1 3 5 7 9 10 8 6 4 2

Printed in the United States of America

*Throw now your heart in the flame.*
*From the ashes gleams the purest gold.*

*– Author Unknown*

~

# Table of Contents

## Part 4 ~ The New Life



## Epilogue

# Characters

~

## Boston

Reverend Daniel Wright . . . . . . . . . . minister
Lily . . . . . . . . . . . . . . . . . . . . . . . . . Daniel's daughter, twin to Rose
Rose . . . . . . . . . . . . . . . . . . . . . . . . Daniel's daughter, twin to Lily
Becky . . . . . . . . . . . . . . . . . . . . . . . Daniel's housekeeper
Thomas Peabody . . . . . . . . . . . . . . . elder in the church
Ebenezer Decker . . . . . . . . . . . . . . . church member
Rachel Decker . . . . . . . . . . . . . . . . . his wife
Nell . . . . . . . . . . . . . . . . . . . . . . . . . Ebenezer's housekeeper
John . . . . . . . . . . . . . . . . . . . . . . . . Ebenezer's hired man
Mrs Lowell . . . . . . . . . . . . . . . . . . . maternal grandmother of the twins
Mrs Lowell's servants:
    Jackson . . . . . . . . . . . . . . . . . . . . butler
    Flora . . . . . . . . . . . . . . . . . . . . . housekeeper
    Abel . . . . . . . . . . . . . . . . . . . . . . coachman
    Cora . . . . . . . . . . . . . . . . . . . . . . cook
Eli Erickson . . . . . . . . . . . . . . . . . . . man who had been to Gold Creek

## Council Bluffs

Mr and Mrs Grundy . . . . . . . . . . . . . boarding house keepers
Jeff Jerome . . . . . . . . . . . . . . . . . . . wagon crafter
Mrs Garland . . . . . . . . . . . . . . . . . . seamstress
Miss Towry . . . . . . . . . . . . . . . . . . . rancher

## People of the Wagon Train

Jake Abrams . . . . . . . . . . . . . . . . . . wagon master
Stephen . . . . . . . . . . . . . . . . . . . . . outrider
Ben . . . . . . . . . . . . . . . . . . . . . . . . . outrider
Gabe Archen
Nathan and Mattie Hollis
    Their children: Amelia, Little Nate, Baby Beth

Bill and Lydia Merrill
    Their children: Cindy, Willy
The Cohen Brothers: Abe, Enoch, Manny
Dr. Franz
    His sons: Noah and Sam
Clay and Evelyn Dunin
Mr and Mrs Shively
Randall, Jim, and Mark . . . . . . . . . . men from the Ohio Wagons
Seth Mooreman
Brad and Regina Bradley

## *Robinson's Road Ranch*

Mr Robinson . . . . . . . . . . . . . . . . . . owner of the ranch
Mr Smythe . . . . . . . . . . . . . . . . . . . visitor
Laura. . . . . . . . . . . . . . . . . . . . . . . shop girl

## *Gold Creek*

Jeremy Wilgus. . . . . . . . . . . . . . . . . mayor
Ken Hill . . . . . . . . . . . . . . . . . . . . . lawyer
Aaron Jenkins . . . . . . . . . . . . . . . . . runs the sawmill
Bud Budke . . . . . . . . . . . . . . . . . . . butcher and barber
Hannah Anderson. . . . . . . . . . . . . . runs boarding house
    Her sons: Ned, Jim
Isabel Flanagan . . . . . . . . . . . . . . . . becomes Daniel's housekeeper
    Her son, Ed
    Ed's wife, Lucinda
Burt and Elsie Martin . . . . . . . . . . . . own the store
    Their children: Al, Joe, Billy, Tessy
Dwight and Dolly Dodge . . . . . . . . . run the bank and the post office
    Their children: Gerald and Annabelle
Widow Marlow. . . . . . . . . . . . . . . . seamstress
Moses Sachs . . . . . . . . . . . . . . . . . . runs the printing press
The Saloon and Brothel
    Smythe. . . . . . . . . . . . . . . . . . . owner
    Brick . . . . . . . . . . . . . . . . . . . . bartender
    Fancy Women: Lisbeth, Ella, Belle, Suzy, Kitty, Candy

Gabe Archen . . . . . . . . . . . . . . . . . . . carpenter
Nathan Hollis . . . . . . . . . . . . . . . . . takes over the sawmill
    His wife, Mattie
    Their children: Amelia, Little Nate, Baby Beth
Shanty Town men: Marcus, Benedict, Harry, George

## *Fairdale Ranch*

Andrew and Kate Fairdale . . . . . . . . . owners
    Their children: Jonathan, Julia, Amy
Bernie . . . . . . . . . . . . . . . . . . . . . . . foreman
James and Sophia . . . . . . . . . . . . . . hired hand and wife
Luke and Molly . . . . . . . . . . . . . . . . hired hand and wife
    Their son, Johnny

## *Montview*

Rev. Caldwell . . . . . . . . . . . . . . . . . Presbyterian minister
Rev. Haywood . . . . . . . . . . . . . . . . . Methodist minister

# Part 1

# UPHEAVAL

*Boston 1866*

# Chapter 1

# *Exposed*

Clouds hung heavy over the city of Boston, over the cobblestone streets cluttered with wagons and carriages hurrying home as the cold February afternoon faded into dusk. Like a long finger pointing heavenward, the white steeple of the River View Presbyterian Church stood out against the gray of the darkening sky.

In the elegant manse next door to the church, Lily stood outside the closed door of her father's study, her hand pressed over her heart, her eyes wide with shock. Her father, the stern and perfectly controlled Reverend Daniel Wright, was crying. She could hear him gasping, choking on his sobs.

Upstairs, in the spacious bedroom at the front of the manse, her sister, Rose, lifted her head from her embroidery and stood, spilling her work from her lap. *Lily?* she called inwardly. A moment later she heard footsteps quick and light on the long spiral staircase, then the door flew open and Lily burst in.

"Papa's crying," she said.

"Crying!" Rose exclaimed. She held out her arms, and Lily rushed into them. Rose took her hand and led her to the wide four-poster bed.

They sat down, put their arms around each other, and leaned their heads together so their foreheads touched. A shiver of fear moved between them. Their father paid little attention to them; most of the time he barely seemed to notice them. But still he was their papa, their anchor.

They spoke softly, words and thoughts flowing between them, as they always had, so fluidly that it hardly mattered who spoke and who listened.

"This morning," Rose said, "when he came in from his calls, he didn't see me or answer when I greeted him, just went straight to his study and shut the door. And now he's crying? Papa never cries."

"He cried when Mama and the baby were buried."

"I remember."

They were silent, holding each other a little closer, sharing the memory of the day when they had huddled by the open grave, watching the first shovel-full of earth fall on the casket. Their father stood beside them, weeping openly in front of all his congregation. It had been ten years since that day, and they had been only five, but the memory was still vivid.

"What could be so wrong that he would cry now?" Rose asked.

"I don't know," Lily answered. "We have to find out."

The rattle of a buggy and the sound of horse hooves on the curved cobblestone drive in front of the manse startled them.

Catching each other's hands, they ran to the window and looked out.

"It's Mr. Peabody," Lily said.

They watched as Thomas Peabody, elder in the church and their father's closest friend, climbed down from his buggy.

"Maybe he knows what's wrong."

"There might be trouble in the church."

"We could hide."

"Where?"

"That table in the corner of Papa's study with the red cloth over it."

"Quick!"

They ran—down the long corridor to the back stairway, down the narrow, dark stairs. The housekeeper, Becky, had gone to answer the front door bell. They flashed through the kitchen and the dining room and hovered outside the sliding door to their father's study until they heard him go out the other door to the parlor. They slid the door open, silently closed it behind them, and dived under the table in the corner.

"Straighten the cloth," Lily whispered.

"Pull your foot in."

After a moment of breathless scuffle, they settled in the dim, reddish light behind the heavy red cloth. It was a tight squeeze for their full-grown young bodies, but they wedged themselves in, pressed close against each other. They were used to being close, had been close in every way since their beginnings, curled together in their mother's womb.

The parlor door opened. They heard their father's voice. It was husky but warm and cordial.

"Thomas, it is always a pleasure to have a visit with you. Come in. Come in, let me take your coat and hat. Have a seat. Can I offer you any refreshment?"

"No. No, thank you."

The twins felt footsteps through the floor. They heard their father's chair creak and Mr. Peabody's chair scuff against the carpet as the two men sat down. There was a moment's silence.

Mr. Peabody said, "Daniel, I am here with a troublesome matter. I hope you can put my concern to rest and help me decide how to handle a difficult situation."

"I hope so, too. What is it?"

"Ebenezer Decker came to me this morning, beside himself with rage and jealousy, telling me he had discovered yesterday his wife was with child. Ordinarily this would be a cause for rejoicing, but he claims he has not touched her for more than a year, seeking to subdue his unseemly passion for her—"

"Oh, he has touched her!" their father's voice broke in. "Not to cherish her as a husband ought, but to beat her whenever his 'unseemly passion' arose. So severely that his housekeeper Nell—she is sister to our Becky—came to me last summer, pleading with me to intervene lest he kill her in one of his fits of violence."

"That's shocking! I didn't know that."

Behind the red cloth, the twins' eyes met, wide with horror.

"So I went to talk with him," their father continued, "to dissuade him from abusing her. I persuaded him to give her her own room so she would not be a temptation to him. But still she sometimes comes to church veiled, as I learned later, to hide her bruises."

"He is a strict and pious man," Mr. Peabody said. "I've heard he has a temper, but I did not know he took it to such extremes. Until this morning—and now, hearing what you say. He is convinced that his wife carries the child of adultery. He said he beat her, but she would not tell him who the father was."

"He beat her, knowing she was with child?"

"With the child of adultery, so he believes."

The twins heard their father's chair creak, then felt his footsteps shake the floor as he paced, his voice raised in anger.

"She never should have married him. Oh, he can be charming, I know. They told her he was a good match, a wealthy banker, a lucky chance for an orphan, never mind he was twice her age. Little did she know what a monster he was."

"I have never heard you speak this way before! About anyone. He's not a monster, just a poor wretched sinner, struggling to be good, but out of control of his passions."

"An evil man."

"Daniel, please sit down. There's more." The pacing footsteps stopped, the chair creaked again. "Mr. Decker told me he came home this morning at a time when he is usually at work, hoping to catch the culprit. He said he found your horse and buggy tied up in front of his house, and upon stealthily entering, saw his wife in your arms. He watched until you left, then confronted her, locked her in her room and came straightaway to me with his accusation. He believes you to be the father of her child. I know this cannot be true …"

Under the table, the twins tightened their arms around each other.

Their father's voice broke in, sharp, urgent. "Mr. Decker—what did he do after he made his accusation?"

"I forbade him to speak of it until it could be investigated according to the rules of our church. Then he left, still in a rage."

"You let him go? Thomas, I fear for her life!"

"As did I. I tried to restrain him. Though he is thin, he was strong in his passion, and broke away. But he was back in an hour, saying she had fled."

"Thank God!"

"He was beside himself the second time he came, insane, saying she must be at the manse and we should search it, that you should be tarred and feathered and run out of town on a rail, that she should be stoned. Suddenly he clutched at his heart, turned white, and passed out on the floor. I sent the office boy for the doctor, who came immediately and managed to revive Mr. Decker. We took him to the hospital, where he is now, heavily sedated. The doctor says he has had these spells before."

"God strikes him."

"He must have imagined in his hysteria that you were holding her in your arms, that you're the father of her child. He has always been critical of you, saying you spoke too much of God's love and not enough of His vengeance. But this is going too far, to make such a outrageous accusation."

Their father coughed, cleared his throat. "It is."

Mr. Peabody went on. "I am concerned about Mrs. Decker fleeing alone in the winter. I don't know if it is true she is with child. You have been counseling her. Do you have any idea where she went?"

"She had planned to go to her aunt in New Hampshire for her confinement. She was to take the train today. I went to say good-bye to her and found her all bruised and battered … But if he locked her in her room, how could she get away?"

"Bruised and battered!" The twins could hear the shock in Mr. Peabody's voice. "So she *is* with child? That much is true?"

"Yes … yes it is."

"She confided in you? Do you know then who the father is?"

"Yes … I … It's confidential."

Lily pulled the edge of the curtain aside, and the twins peered through the narrow space between the edge of the red cloth and the table leg.

Their father started to get up from his chair, sat down again, fumbled with some papers on his desk. Mr. Peabody leaned forward, a strange expression on his face.

Their father began speaking fast. "It must be Mr. Decker's child. He didn't want children, she told me that. Maybe that's why he got so upset and made such accusations. He said he hadn't touched her, but he beat her. Who knows what else he might have done when overwhelmed with his 'unseemly passion'?"

Mr. Peabody was slowly standing. "But you just said she confided in you. That you know who the father is. Don't you understand? He has accused *you*. We must get to the bottom of this, to clear you…. Daniel, why won't you look at me?"

The twins watched their father twist in his chair and bend forward over his desk, his head turned aside.

Mr. Peabody came around the desk and gripped his shoulders. "Daniel, what is it?"

Their father's voice was husky, choking. "I cannot hide from you, my closest friend … or from God … any longer … It is I … I am the father."

There was a terrible silence in the room.

Then Mr. Peabody spoke. "I cannot believe you. Tell me I misheard."

Their father's voice was almost a sob. "You did not."

There was another silence. The twins could barely breathe. Their father spoke again, his voice breaking.

"I never intended … I went to minister to her, for she was so desperate as to be at the point of suicide. She is so young, so vulnerable, to be faced with such an intolerable situation … I went to speak to her of the love of Christ … and found that I, too, loved her."

"And led her into adultery."

Mr. Peabody strode across the room, coming dangerously near the table in the corner. Lily hastily let the red cloth drop into place.

Mr. Peabody's voice was anguished. "It *is* you then? How could you? Daniel, you of all people, who have nourished this church faultlessly for all these years, who are beloved and honored by your congregation like no other pastor in all the city of Boston, whose sermons, in their beauty and inspiration, open the hearts of all who hear you. How could *you* do such a thing?"

There was no sound from their father.

Anger came into Mr. Peabody's voice. "Do you have any idea what this will do to our congregation? You have betrayed us, disgraced the church. Some may turn away from Christ because of what you have done. And what of Mrs. Decker, cast adrift in the world so near her time?" Mr. Peabody paused in his pacing. Lily pulled the edge of the curtain aside again.

Their father was gripping the arms of his chair. "I urged her to leave earlier. I feared Mr. Decker would discover her condition and harm her. But she didn't want to be parted from me. She didn't plan to ever return. We hoped that after a while he would divorce her and …"

"Say no more! Your soul is in mortal danger. You must never see her or communicate with her again. Your only path to salvation after this is to repent and pray for forgiveness."

Their father bent his head. "I do repent. I have sinned most grievously. I could have comforted her without … Pray God she is safe!"

His head came up again. "But Thomas, it wasn't all evil. She blossomed with my love, after her loveless orphan childhood, and then Ebenezer Decker. You should have seen her, how her face opened, like dawn coming, like the sunrise … her smile …"

"Hush! You must never speak of her again. Pray, pray, repent!" Mr. Peabody paced again. "What's to be done?

"That's for the Presbytery to decide."

"Yes, that's true. There's no need for an investigation, because you have confessed…. . If only this need not come out, be a public disgrace."

Again Mr. Peabody came near the corner table, but this time, abandoning all caution, Lily left the edge of the curtain pulled aside, and the twins peered through, riveted by the scene before them.

"No one knows but you and I and Ebenezer Decker," their father murmured.

"True. I do not know what the Presbytery will decide. But surely you cannot stay in your present position. You will have to leave. And who could ever replace you?" Mr. Peabody stopped by their father's chair and laid a hand on his shoulder. His voice softened. "What will I do without you? You have been like a brother to me as we've worked together all these years to build our church." He took a deep breath and straightened. "I will call an emergency meeting of the Presbytery. Perhaps this does not need to come out, if we deal with it speedily. We will pray for guidance, and you—pray, pray for forgiveness. I must go now."

Mr. Peabody hastily gathered up his great coat and hat and moved toward the parlor door. Their father left with him.

"Quick!" whispered Lily.

They burst out of their hiding place, ran to the sliding door, and slipped into the dining room. At the door to the kitchen, they paused, pushed it open a crack.

Becky was poking at the coals in the stove. Her apron was tied high under her abundant bosom. Wisps of gray hair, broken loose from her bun, hung around her face.

"That Mr. Peabody," she was muttering, "comes just at suppertime and stays as long as he pleases. The soup's gotten too thick, and the bread is cold, and the stove's nearly out. Well, he's gone now."

She bent to add more coal to the fire, her broad back to the dining room door. The twins slipped through the corner of the kitchen and up the back stairs, down the long corridor to their room. Lily shut the door and leaned back against it.

"Oh, my goodness!" she gasped.

"Oh, my goodness!" Rose echoed.

They stared at each other.

"I don't understand," Rose said. "What did Papa do?"

"He led her into adultery."

"But what's adultery?"

"I asked Grandmama when we were learning the Ten Commandments." Lily shook her head. "And she rapped the back of my hand with her fan, like she does, and said it wasn't to be spoken of."

"You're not supposed to commit it."

"I *know*. That's why I asked Grandmama. How are you supposed to not commit it if you don't know what it is?"

"Papa is the father of Mrs. Decker's child?" Rose asked.

"A child of adultery, Mr. Peabody said. She must be—we're not supposed to speak of that either."

"How could he be?"

"He was holding her in his arms."

"He loves her. He said her face was like the sunrise. And she loves him." There were tears in Rose's eyes. "She didn't want to leave him, even to escape Mr. Decker's beating. How could he be so mean? To beat her when she was … How could it be Papa's child?"

Lily shook her head. "It's so confusing. But it's clear Papa has done something with Mrs. Decker that would disgrace the whole church if it came out. And now she's gone away. That must be why he was crying when I came by his study."

Rose's tears spilled over. "Poor Papa. How can it be so bad to love someone?"

"Maybe because she's married to Mr. Decker … Maybe adultery is loving someone who is married to someone else."

"What will happen? Mr. Peabody said Papa would have to leave. Where will he go?"

"Where will *we* go?"

A bell rang in the downstairs hall. Becky called up the stairs, "Lily, Rose, come to supper. Hurry up, it's late."

The twins hugged each other.

"We must never tell that we know," Lily said.

"Never."

∽

Daniel heard the bell for supper as he sat, slumped over his desk, in his dark study. He couldn't eat. He was sick, sick with shame and despair. His thoughts tumbled in a downward spiral. To have Thomas know … to have the whole church know …

I will have to go away. Where can I go? Not back to the farm. When my mother hears what I have done …

Maybe it won't have to come out. Thomas wants to prevent that for the sake of the church. But Ebenezer is bent on revenge …

Rachel. If only she'd left before Ebenezer found out. But we clung to each other. Too long. Where is she? He beat her again, even as far along as she is. Beast! How did she escape, locked in a second-story room? How badly is she hurt? I can't bear not to know where she is, how she is … Did she get to the train? How could she, alone, big with child?

What if she dies in childbirth, as Grace did? … Rachel, what have I done to you?

There was a knock on the study door.

"Reverend Wright, supper's ready," Becky called through the door.

Daniel controlled his voice with difficulty. "Thank you, Becky. I'm not going to eat tonight."

"You're not eating? I have a good soup ready, and hot bread."

"Not tonight, Becky."

"You all right, Reverend?"

"I'm fine. I just have a lot of work to do."

"Come on out if you change your mind." He heard Becky's footsteps retreating.

Daniel sat a moment, then straightened, arrested by a thought. Nell. Becky's sister. Maybe Nell helped her.

He got up and strode back and forth across the room. Maybe that's how Rachel got away. Nell would have a key to her room. Nell loved her. Who could not? Nell knew about us and protected us, though she never let on. That must be how she got away … I need to talk with Nell.

He started toward the door to put his thought into immediate action, but was arrested by another knock.

"Who's there?" he asked.

"Papa, may I come in?"

Daniel opened the door. Light poured in from the dining room. One of the twins stood in the doorway with a tray in her hands.

"Becky said you couldn't come to supper because you had too much work to do. But you need to eat. I brought you some soup and bread. It's really good." She looked into his face. "I thought you could eat while you work." She came in and set the tray on his desk. "Shall I light the lamp?" She lit it as she spoke.

Daniel sat down and lifted the cover off the soup bowl. It did smell good. He looked up at his daughter.

"Thank you … Which one are you?"

"I'm Rose."

"Thank you, Rose. That's very kind. The sort of thing your mother would have done."

Rose bent and kissed the top of his head. "I hope your work goes well, Papa." She turned and left, sliding the door closed behind her.

After all he was hungry. Rose is kind, he thought. She looks so much like Grace. They both do. There must be a way to tell them apart. Becky can. What will become of them when I am sent away? I hardly know them, what they would want.

When he finished eating, he pushed the tray back, got up and paced again. Nell. I have to talk with Nell. He stopped by the window and looked out. It was fully dark, snow falling thinly in front of the gas street lamp. He drew the curtain. Then he realized, I can't go over there. Ebenezer might be home from the hospital.

His stomach churned as the immensity of the day's events assailed him.

On the floor by the window seat was a worn, red cushion on which it was his habit to kneel in prayer. Numb, he sank to his knees there, bent his forehead to the cool, smooth wood.

I should pray. But how could even God forgive me?

# Chapter 2

# *The Broom Closet*

It snowed all night and was still snowing in the morning. Abel, Mrs. Lowell's footman, tramped over to tell the twins the snow was too deep to get the carriage out, so they had an unexpected free day. They loved their lessons at their Grandmama's house, but today they would have found it difficult to concentrate on French and music. The night before, they had lain awake late, curled together in their curtained, four-poster bed, whispering, trying to comprehend the implications of all they had heard.

Now they stood at the window of their bedroom, watching the snow drift down. The driveway was a pure white half moon in front of the manse. The street lamps, standing tall over the empty street, wore drooping white caps. There was no one stirring except a sturdy-looking woman, her head wrapped in a green scarf, trudging toward the manse.

"Here comes Nell," Rose remarked. "Even the snow doesn't keep her from her Wednesday morning coffee with Becky."

"Nell!" Lily exclaimed. "Maybe she'll tell Becky something about Mrs. Decker."

"The broom closet."

They ran down the long corridor to the back of the house, down the back stairs. The broom closet, adjacent to the kitchen but opening off the back hall, was a favorite hiding place for the twins. There were long cracks in the wall between the closet and the kitchen through which they could both peer and hear. Becky was sociable and often had a guest at her kitchen table. Throughout their childhood, the twins had hidden there whenever Becky had an interesting visitor, garnering family gossip and information of events outside their sheltered world, often information Becky would not have considered proper for little girls.

"Quick! Nell comes in the back door."

They reached the hall and crowded into the broom closet just in time. A moment later Nell rapped on the back door and Becky came through the hall to meet her. Rose hadn't had time to latch the closet door and it was open a crack. The twins held their breath.

Becky kicked it shut as she passed. "Fool thing never latches properly," she muttered. She opened the back door. "Morning, Nell. Come on in. The kitchen's warm and the coffee's hot."

Nell stamped the snow off her feet. "Sounds good. It's cold."

The twins shifted in the broom closet, careful to avoid rattling the brooms, mops, and buckets surrounding them. They settled, hand in hand, each with an eye to one of the long cracks in the wall.

In the kitchen, Becky poured coffee. Soon she and Nell were settled at the kitchen table.

"What's the news of your house?" Nell asked.

"Things are a bit strange," Becky answered. "The Reverend's been upset the last few days. He had a long conversation with Mr. Peabody last evening and then wouldn't even come to supper. Must be some trouble in the church."

Nell set down her coffee cup and nodded, pushing out her lower lip.

"And the twins are up to something," Becky went on. "A mischievous pair they are. Mrs. Lowell says I've spoiled them, like I did Grace when she was little. Now they're near grown, though they're so protected and innocent they still seem like children. All the same, they do bear keeping track of."

In the closet, the twins grinned at each other.

"What's happening at your house?" Becky asked. "I heard Mr. Peabody and the Reverend speaking of Mr. Decker in the hall last night. Maybe Mr. Decker brought a complaint again. He harasses the Reverend something awful. Do you know anything about it?"

"Oh …" Nell's voice was rich with portent. "There's been terrible goings on."

"What?" Becky leaned forward. In the closet the twins tightened their grip on each other's hands.

"Terrible," Nell repeated. "Now I've told you as how Mrs. Decker is with child and didn't want Mr. Decker to know, 'cause he didn't want any babies. And how she was planning to go visit her aunt till her time, for fear he would beat her like he used to and harm the child. She was set to go yesterday, had her bag packed and all. She was just gonna take the train and go."

"Just leave?"

"She couldn't tell him, 'cause then he'd want to know why. The night before she was to go—that was day before yesterday—I heard Mr. Decker screaming at her and her crying and knew he was beating her again. I called to John, and we ran upstairs. The door was open to her room and he was in there, tearing off her clothes—you could see then how big she was with the babe—and yelling over and over, 'Tell me who it is. I'll kill him! Tell me.' And with each 'tell me' he was banging her up against the wall."

Becky put her hand to her face. "Against the wall! What did you do?"

"We rushed in. John grabbed him from behind, pinning his arms. 'Mr. Decker,' John says, 'you'll harm her, knocking her around like that,' and he pulled him back. Mr. Decker struggled. Even though he's a skinny little man, he fought hard. But my John is big and took him on out of the room. He's done that before, you know, when Mr. Decker loses control. Mr. Decker is grateful, but not until later. That night he struggled worse than usual, yelling at Mrs. Decker as John dragged him away, 'I'll find out who. You just wait. I'll find out, and I'll kill him!'"

"That's awful!" Becky's gasped. "Poor Mrs. Decker. She'll lose the child if he bangs her around like that."

"That's what she's afraid of. And she wants that child. My, how she wants it. She told me her secret long ago and was so happy. 'I'll have someone to love,' she said to me. Poor dear. After John dragged Mr. Decker off of her, she just sank to the floor, pulling the rags of her clothes around her, shaking and sobbing. I took care of her as best I could, got her to bed, put some salve on her face—all bruised she was. She wanted to run away that night, but there was no train until the next day."

"That man should be committed!" Becky exclaimed. "Before he does kill her or someone else. He puts on such a pious act in church, so righteous—and doing that at home. What's he think she's done?"

"He thinks someone else is the father. Someone should tell him the facts of life, that when he does what he does with his wife ..." Nell shook her head and took a sip of coffee.

"Men," Becky snorted. "I'm glad I'm not married."

"Now they're not all bad," Nell said. "My John's a good one." She took another sip of coffee. "But that's only the beginning of the goings on. Yesterday was worse. Mrs. Decker was up in the morning, all packed. John was to take her to the train at noon in the wagon. Mr. Decker was real quiet, and went off to the bank in his buggy. Gave me chills how quiet and tense he was."

Becky put down her coffee cup and leaned forward.

"The Reverend came over to say good-bye to Mrs. Decker," Nell went on. "He knew she was going; he'd helped her plan her escape, fearing, as we all did, that Mr. Decker would harm her if he found out about her condition. I let him in. He was real upset when he saw her so bruised. They were in the parlor, and I in the kitchen when I heard footsteps in the back entry, and there was Mr. Decker coming in, all stealthy. He went to the parlor door and saw the Reverend in there with Mrs. Decker, but he didn't do anything. Just hid behind the door and watched. Then when the Reverend left, he jumped out and grabbed her. I didn't know what to do. John was way out in the carriage house getting the wagon ready.

"It was horrible! He took to hitting her again, screaming, 'So he's the one! Your pious little pastor, so pretty and preaching love with his evil, black heart, creeping around *ministering* to you! I'll deal with him! He'll never show his face in the city of Boston again!'"

Becky clenched her fists on the table. "How could he think that about the Reverend?"

"Who knows? He kept on yelling at her, all the time shaking her back and forth. He dragged her up the stairs to her room. I didn't know whether to run after or go for John. I ran after. I heard a thud. It made me sick to hear that thud. Then he came out again, locking the door of her room behind him. He pushed past me in the hall, never seeing me, screaming back at her, 'You stay there. I'll be back to deal with you and that bastard child. It'll never see the light of day.' Then he tore down the stairs and out the door, and drove off. I could hear him lashing his horse."

"Lordy!" Becky exclaimed.

Inside the closet, the twins clutched each other.

"The minute he was gone I rushed to Mrs. Decker's room. He thought he'd locked her in, but forgot I have a key. She was lying on the floor, awful still, dead white. The poor dear soul, so sweet and good as she is, being treated like that. When I came to her, she stirred and said, 'Nell, the train. I've got to get to the train or he will kill my baby.' She tried to get up, but fell back. I got her onto her bed. It was quarter past eleven and the train leaving at noon all the way across the city. 'I'm going to get John,' I told her. I ran, calling John, and he came. Quick as we could, we got her up and into her cloak, the hat with the veil to cover her face, and John carried her down to the wagon.

"I stayed behind, sick with fear they would miss the train, and then where could she go? Then I got an idea. I ran back to Mrs. Decker's room, opened the window. There's a big evergreen tree right outside. I took my broom and knocked snow off the branches. Ran out, leaving the window open and locking the door behind me. Then outside under the tree, I knocked more snow off, stirred up the snow under the tree, and made footprints out to the street.

"I was back in the kitchen when he came storming in. Straight up to her room he went. I heard him unlock the door. Silence. I could hear him walking around. Then he let out a terrible cry, 'Rachel, Rachel, where are you?' and he didn't sound angry anymore, but desolate, as if he knew then he'd lost her.

"He came to the kitchen. 'Where is she? Nell, where is she?'

"I was shaking in my shoes, but said, real innocent-like, 'She must be in her room, sir. You locked her in.'

"'She's not there.'

"'She must be,' I said, and went upstairs with him. He stared at the open window and the tree. 'She must have climbed out the window and run away,' I told him. 'You scared her,' I dared to say.

"He ran down the stairs, went outside. When he saw the footprints going away, he started trembling something awful, white, choking, could hardly talk. I got worried he'd have one of his spells. Then he was off in his buggy, whipping his horse again."

"But what about Mrs. Decker?" Becky broke in. "Did she make the train?"

"She did."

Inside the broom closet, the twins let out their breath.

"John said they barely got there in time. Pray God, her aunt sent someone to meet her. Mrs. Decker wasn't hardly fit to stand."

"She'll not come back, will she?"

"No indeed! But she gave me a hug when we put her in the wagon, and said she would write to me. I'll miss her. She brightened up the house."

"What of Mr. Decker?"

"I haven't seen him since. Mr. Peabody came 'round late, and told me Mr. Decker had one of his spells, worse than usual, and was in the hospital. Mr. Peabody was real concerned about Mrs. Decker. I told him the story of the window and the tree, and he went away. I hated to deceive him—he's a kind, good man—but if Mr. Decker knew how me and John helped her get away …"

"You did right," Becky said, "and were very brave. I don't know how you can stand to work for such a man. Do you want more coffee?"

"Yes, thanks. He's really not all bad. Just when he gets upset and loses control. It's not that often. He's been good to me and John."

Becky brought the coffee pot to the table and refilled their cups.

"It's really sad," Nell went on. "Remember when Mr. Decker first married her, how I came and told you how in love he was? I've never seen a man so much in love. It was almost too much, really. Then only a month after their wedding he takes to beating her. I never could figure out why. She was so good and sweet and did whatever he wanted. Maybe he just couldn't stand loving like that, and had to spoil it."

"I've heard"—Becky lowered her voice—"that some men are like that, get their thrills from beating their wives instead of hugging them. It's awful perverted."

Inside the broom closet, the twins looked at each other, pulling down the corners of their mouths.

"But what about Mr. Decker saying the Reverend was the father?" Becky put the coffee pot back on the stove, came to the table and stood with her hands on her hips. "That couldn't be. Reverend Wright is the most moral man I know."

Nell was silent a moment, then said, "That he is."

"If Mr. Decker starts spreading that story around …" Becky sat down and struck the table with the flat of her hand. "No wonder he wouldn't come to supper. That's dreadful, to malign an honest man like that. That must be what Mr. Peabody was here for last night. What will happen, Nell?"

"I don't know." Nell took a last sip of coffee and got up from her chair. "I've got to go. If Mr. Decker gets out of the hospital, I'll need to have his dinner ready. He never did eat what I fixed him yesterday."

Becky brought Nell her coat and scarf. "Be sure and let me know if you get a letter from Mrs. Decker," she said. "I'm not going to be able to stop thinking about her, poor lamb."

"And you tell me what happens with Reverend Wright."

"I will. You take care of yourself. I'm worried about you being around such a violent man."

"Don't worry. He's never laid a hand on me all these years. And he's always real quiet and drained after one of his spells. They take him hard. I'm afraid one day they'll kill him."

"All the same, you be careful." Becky helped Nell into her coat, hugged her, and walked with her into the back hall.

The twins heard the back door opening. "The snow's stopped and the plow's coming," Nell said. "Good-bye now."

"Good-bye." Becky closed the back door and went into the kitchen, muttering, "No one would believe such a thing of the Reverend."

As soon as the kitchen door closed, the twins extricated themselves from the broom closet and ran swiftly up the back stairs, down the hall to their room, and tumbled onto the four-poster bed.

"You were right," Rose gasped. "Nell did have something to tell Becky about Mrs. Decker!"

"I'm glad she got away."

"Nell is brave—and clever, too, to think of that part about the tree."

"I hope she doesn't lose her baby," Lily said.

"We should pray for her."

"Yes, let's."

The twins knelt down on the floor by their bed, side by side, palms together over their hearts. A ray of sunlight broke through the clouds outside, and slanted in through the window, touching their bent heads. The sound of Becky bustling around in the kitchen floated up the stairwell. In the study below, their father, too, was praying.

After a while Rose whispered, "Jesus is with her. I think she's safe."

"I do, too."

"I wish it had been Papa who found her at the orphanage and married her," Rose sighed. "She is so pretty and kind. I'd love to have her for our stepmother. And then the baby would be our little brother or sister."

Lily gave Rose a shake. "Rose, if Papa is the father, then the baby *is* our little brother or sister."

Rose looked startled. "Oh! But I still don't understand how Papa could be the father."

"I don't either. We're not supposed to know about those things."

"Or even wonder."

"But we're going to have to figure it out. You know how Grandmama has big plans for us to marry"—Lily imitated her grandmother's voice—"into the best families of Boston."

"What if we got someone like Mr. Decker?"

Lily frowned. "I don't think most men are like that. Papa would never have hit Mama."

She stood and walked to the window. "We have to get married. It's expected of us. Otherwise we'll be old maids."

"But I don't want to." Rose sat on the bed looking at Lily, half turned away from her at the window. "Then we'd be separated, and have to live with our husbands instead of each other. It wouldn't be so bad to be old maids."

Lily turned to her. "But then we couldn't have babies."

"We could adopt some from the orphanage."

The dinner bell rang and Becky called up to them, "Rose, Lily. Dinner."

They took hands and went out into the hall.

"She could *either* ring the bell *or* call us," Lily commented, "but she always does both. Come on, let's slide down the banister."

She let go of Rose's hand, dashed ahead, and seated herself sideways on the smooth, curved railing. Rose was right behind her. They slid down and landed lightly on their feet in the hallway below.

Chapter 3

# *The Verdict of the Presbytery*

Late that afternoon, Daniel and Thomas came down the wide steps of the First Presbyterian Church of Boston. They walked across the square in front and around to where the horses and buggies were hitched.

"Where did you leave your buggy?" Thomas asked.

"I didn't bring it. I walked, seeking to calm myself before the meeting."

"That's a long walk. Let me give you a ride home."

"Thank you. It would be good to talk with you. It has been an overwhelming day."

Thomas touched Daniel's shoulder. "They gave you another chance."

"I know. I can't believe it yet."

The two men climbed onto the seat of the buggy. Thomas slapped the reins and drove out onto the cobbled street, still wet with snow. A chill wind blew off the bay. Daniel turned up the collar of his great coat.

"Another chance," he said. "But what a chance! To travel so far I can't comprehend it, to the wild frontier to minister to a parish of miners, drunkards, and prostitutes ..."

"And twelve good people who earnestly desire a pastor to bring the Gospel to that parish."

"Twelve! Here we have a church of three hundred."

"Don't forget. We were only forty when you came to us. And see what you have built in these years—a strong congregation, a beautiful sanctuary. You can do it again. And the parish you go to is blessed to have you."

Daniel turned to Thomas. "Forgive me. I have no right to complain."

They rode in silence for a while, the horse's hooves clattering on the cobbled street.

"What happened before I got there?" Daniel asked. "What about Mr. Decker? Jonas said there would be no problem with him. That's hard to believe."

"I met with the Presbytery first and told them what happened yesterday—how Mr. Decker came to me with his accusation, the flight of his wife, your confession. You can believe they were all shocked. There was much heated discussion about what to do. They finally agreed with me that it would be best for our congregation, and the church as a whole, if this did not come out." Thomas turned to look at Daniel. "You are much honored, and they feared, as I did, that your fall would be damaging. They also agreed that you must go away as soon as possible. Then they wished to speak with Mr. Decker. I went to the hospital and picked him up. He was pale, but calmer."

"How in the world did they persuade him to stay silent, if that's what they did?"

Thomas returned his gaze to the road. "Well," he said quietly, "the Presbytery was quite upset about you, but they also didn't take kindly to a Christian man beating his wife so severely that she fled for fear he would kill her child. They told him you would be leaving, and if he did not hold his tongue, his abusive ways would be made known and he would be suspended from the church. His image of a good, pious man and his place in the church are crucial to him. He agreed. It was blackmail, I confess."

"Amazing."

Again they were silent. Dusk deepened. Thomas turned his horse off the road onto the soft dirt of the track that crossed the Commons. The buggy slowed as its wheels sank into the slush. They stopped at the top of a rise and sat looking down over the Commons and the city, its lights sparkling in the bay.

"And the part about sending me to the Colorado Territory?"

"There's been talk for some time, as you know, about the importance of getting the Protestant message out West to prevent those vast regions, which will be settled eventually, from turning to Papism or Mormonism, or worse yet, Rationalism. Home Missions has grown increasingly urgent about the necessity of following up on the work of the itinerant preachers. You are a gifted minister and still young enough to brave the rigors of the frontier. Jonas had recently received a request from the Missouri Synod for a preacher for Gold Creek. It fit perfectly into our dilemma about what to do with you."

"I am humbled—and grateful. I thought surely they would defrock me and send me away in disgrace. They are sending me away, indeed, far, far away, but not in disgrace. I need only say I am called to this mission. And I do not have to give up my ministry. It is my life, sinner that I am, to serve Christ, to bring the lost to Him, to care for his flock. I do not know how I could go on if this were taken from me, as I have feared it would be. I did not think that God, much less my fellow ministers, could ever forgive me."

"The mercy of the Lord is from everlasting to everlasting," Thomas said, "and we who serve Him seek to live in His image." He picked up the reins and set the buggy moving again, down the hill.

"They said I need to be out of the manse in two weeks, to make space for the next minister. That is harsh. It has been my home ever since I carried Grace over the threshold on our wedding day. How can I move everything in two weeks? They said I will have to wait for spring before I can start on my journey. Where can I and my family go?"

"The Lord will provide a place for you. And you will need to leave most of your possessions behind. It is a long journey; you can't take much with you."

They had crossed the Commons, and the horse's hooves were loud on the cobbled street by the river.

"I know nothing," Daniel said after a while, "except what they told me briefly about Gold Creek. I don't know what to bring besides my Bible."

"My wife knows of a man who has recently returned from the frontier. I will try to locate him. He should be able to give you the information you need."

"You are a true friend. Indeed these last two days, you have been the minister to me, I the lost sinner. How can I thank you? It could have gone ill for me without your intervention."

Thomas turned the buggy into the curved driveway in front of the manse.

"Will you come in?" Daniel asked.

"For a little while," Thomas replied. "Then I must get home to my family. It is near suppertime."

In the front hall, Daniel helped Thomas off with his coat.

"How I will miss you," he said. "In all the Colorado Territory, where will I find a friend such as you?"

They moved through the parlor into the study. Neither of them noticed two shadows cast across the top of the stairwell by the lamp in the upstairs hall.

The gas street lamp shone dimly into the upstairs bedroom. It was late, but the twins were far from sleep. They were sitting up in their long nightgowns amidst the tumbled quilts of their four-poster bed, facing each other, hugging their pillows.

"The Colorado Territory," Lily breathed. "Do you know how far away that is?"

"Past Pennsylvania where Uncle Benjamin lives," Rose said.

"Past the Mississippi River and way past that. There are the Great Plains—"

"And the Rocky Mountains." Rose hugged her pillow tighter. "Lots of people die on the journey. Remember that newspaper article Grandmama showed us about all the graves along the trail?"

Lily pushed back a long lock of hair. "We have to decide if we're going to stay here or go with Papa."

"Papa will just order us."

"Of course." Lily gestured impatiently. "But we know how to get our way."

Rose nodded. They exchanged a smile.

"So," Lily went on, "we could probably stay here with Grandmama. She would want us to. Or maybe we could go to Grandma and Grandpa Wright on the farm."

"But if we don't go with Papa," Rose interrupted, "then he'll be all alone in all those dangers, with no one to take care of him. I don't think Becky would go with him."

"Hardly! Can you see Becky bumping along in a covered wagon?"

They giggled.

"If we go and she doesn't, she won't be able to take care of us anymore," Lily pointed out.

"No, we'll have to learn to take care of ourselves."

"And Papa."

"We have to go with him," Rose said. "I can't bear to think of him going all alone. He is so sad and worried about Mrs. Decker."

"Let's not call her Mrs. Decker. She isn't going to be married to Mr. Decker anymore. Let's call her Rachel. She told us once at church that we could. Remember? She said she wasn't that much older than we are, and we could be friends."

"I remember. I like her so much, but we still didn't dare call her Rachel."

"Well, we can now," Lily said. "And we should pray for her every night and for our baby brother."

"How do you know it's a boy?"

"I just think it is."

"Let's pray for them now."

The twins climbed off the bed, knelt beside it, and bowed their heads. When they lifted them again, Rose said, "I think she's sleeping."

"We should sleep, too. And I'm cold."

They climbed back into the big bed, arranged their pillows, and pulled up the quilts.

"We'll go with him," Lily said, as as they nestled down. "I'm glad that's settled. Now we just need to make sure Papa wants to take us."

"I'm kind of scared," Rose whispered. "People die."

"We won't die."

"And sometimes the Indians kidnap young girls."

"They won't kidnap us," Lily declared. "Just let them try."

Rose gave a hesitant giggle.

Lily hugged her tight. "Just think how exciting it will be," she said. "Maybe we'll even have our own horse."

# Chapter 4

# Daniel Wavers

Daniel barely slept that night, his heart a turmoil of fears, grief, relief, guilt, excitement. He was tormented with worry about Rachel. At the thought of her, he ached with desire. *Dear Lord, take this sinful passion from me!* he prayed in agony. He wept, turned his pillow, seeking sleep in vain. Toward dawn he gave up and made his way downstairs to his study. Wrapped in a blanket, he knelt on the red cushion by the window, bowed his head and prayed.

Worn out, he slept at last, still kneeling, slumped over the window sill. The sound of Becky slamming around in the kitchen as she fired up the cookstove woke him. He got up, stiff and aching, and hurried upstairs to dress, then returned to his study and sat staring blankly at the pages of his next sermon scattered across his desk.

Upstairs he heard his daughters moving around. Their voices and laughter floating down to him set off a new round of worry. Rose and Lily. What shall I do with them? They can't come with me. The frontier is no place for young girls, rough and immoral as it is. And the journey is dangerous. I could leave them with Mrs. Lowell. She has brought them up these last ten years. She and Becky.

I don't know my daughters. I have neglected them. I assume Becky and Mrs. Lowell have attended to their Christian education—I should have done it myself. And now I'll be leaving them.

I need to talk with Mrs. Lowell today. If she can take the girls—

Becky banged open the door between the kitchen and the front hall, rang her bell vigorously, and called, "Rose, Lily, Reverend—breakfast!"

She's a good woman, Daniel thought, rubbing his head. Salt of the earth, but loud. As he walked through the parlor into the front hall, he heard a burst of laughter. Lily and Rose came sliding down the banister and landed in the hallway in front of him.

"Morning, Papa," they chanted in unison and came to each side of him to kiss his cheeks.

"Good morning, Lily, Rose," he responded. "Stand here a moment. I want to look at you."

They stood before him, hand in hand, dressed alike in modest blue gowns. Their gold-brown hair clung in ripples around their faces and tumbled in ringlets over their shoulders and down their backs. They were slender and shapely with wide white brows, sparkling blue-gray eyes, and rosy mouths.

"Aren't you too old to be sliding down the banister?" he asked. "Isn't it time for more ladylike deportment?"

"Oh, no, Papa! We'll never be too old to slide down the banister," one of them laughed. "It's so much fun."

"You should try it," the other one said.

"We know how to have ladylike deportment—"

"But we don't need it to come to breakfast."

Their words came fast, tumbling out from first one and then the other. Daniel felt confused, bewildered by their pertness, their beauty.

He gathered his sternness. "How old are you? Shouldn't you be wearing your hair up by now?"

"We're fifteen. And we do."

"We'll put it up before we go to Grandmama's. She insists."

Becky stuck her head through the kitchen door. "Breakfast's *ready!*"

"We're coming, Becky," one twin answered.

They whirled ahead of him into the kitchen, and were kissing Becky good morning when he came in. The kitchen, warmed by the glowing cookstove, was filled with the aroma of fresh-baked bread, coffee, and bacon. I have such comfort and plenty, Daniel thought. What will it be like in Gold Creek?

Becky bustled and scolded, calling one twin Lily and the other Rose, seeming to have no difficulty telling them apart. Daniel ate in silence, studying them. They were indistinguishable as far as he could see. I never even tried to tell them apart before, he realized. They have just been the twins.

"Hurry up, now," Becky was ordering them. "Go on upstairs, put your hair up and get your books. Abel will be here any minute and you know your Grandmama doesn't tolerate your being late."

Daniel finished eating and took a cup of coffee to his study. He heard the carriage arrive, the twins laughing. They probably slid down the banister again. He heard the front door bang and the sound of the carriage pulling away.

His head ached. He looked around his study at his bookcases, filled with his beloved books. He stroked the smooth wood of his desk, gazed at the comfortable leather chair where he liked to read, the deep red curtains, the oriental carpet. I must leave it all, he thought. No. Not my books. I must take at least some of my books with me. How will I travel? By train at first—but then? There's no train west of the Missouri River. Stage coach? Is there one? I don't know … I don't know.

He groaned, weary from his sleepless night. I must begin, he thought. I will go and call on Mrs. Lowell.

An hour later he rang the bell of Mrs. Lowell's tall brownstone house on Beacon Hill. The butler opened the door. He was thin and stooped with a wispy white goatee and an air of irrefutable propriety.

"Good morning, Jackson," Daniel greeted him. "Is Mrs. Lowell in?"

"Come in, Reverend Wright." Jackson held the door open. "I will let her know you are here." He hung Daniel's coat on the coat tree, and led him up the wide steps to the parlor.

Daniel settled into a dark, leather chair. A moment later the door opened between the parlor and the library, and Mrs. Lowell entered. Daniel composed himself and stood. Through the open door, he saw his daughters seated at a long table reading, their hair now neatly coifed. Mrs. Lowell closed the library door and came to greet him.

She was small, slender, and upright, stylishly attired in an elegant dark-red dress with a high lace collar. Around her neck she wore a gold locket that Daniel knew contained the picture of her late husband. Her grey hair was arranged in the latest fashion, and she carried a furled fan.

"Daniel, what a pleasant surprise," she greeted him. She seated herself in a high-backed rocking chair. "Please sit down. Would you like some tea?"

"Yes. Thank you." Daniel lowered himself back into the leather chair.

Mrs. Lowell turned to Jackson who was still waiting by the door. "Ask Flora to bring us tea."

"Yes, ma'am." He inclined his head and disappeared.

"What brings you out so early?" Mrs. Lowell asked.

She helps me get right to the point, Daniel thought. He cleared his throat. "Well … I have just made a decision that will involve a big change in my life."

"Change?"

"I met with the Presbytery yesterday. They have given me a call to minister to a fledgling church on the frontier, in the Colorado Territory."

"Indeed!"

"So I will be leaving, within the month, and I need to make a decision about the future of Rose and Lily."

"They must stay with me, of course. The frontier is no place for innocent young girls. It's a lawless den of iniquity, from all I've heard." Mrs. Lowell drew in her chin and frowned at him. "The Colorado Territory. Whatever came over you to take on such a call?"

"There is great need, as you yourself have just said, to bring the Gospel and civilization to such places." Daniel cleared his throat. "The settlement of Gold Creek, north of Denver City, has a small church in need of guidance. The Home Mission especially wanted me because of my success in building the congregation of River View."

What a story you're telling her, he thought guiltily.

Jackson entered, followed by a white-haired lady carrying a tea tray. Jackson pulled a small table up between Daniel and Mrs. Lowell. Flora's hands trembled as she laid out the fine china. She straightened stiffly. "Is there anything else, ma'am?"

"No thank you, Flora." Mrs. Lowell nodded to them, and the two old servants departed.

Mrs. Lowell picked up the tea pot. "Would you like cream or sugar?"

"Both, please."

"You look pale. Are you ill?"

"No, no, not ill, but I have been sleepless thinking of this decision, especially as it affects my daughters."

"Do not be concerned." Mrs. Lowell handed him his tea and poured her own. "They will do well here. I have been preparing them to enter society. Soon after their sixteenth birthday, I will have a coming-out ball for them."

"A ball? You would not have them dance!" Daniel set down his tea cup and gripped the arms of the leather chair.

"Of course they will dance. They dance beautifully. They cannot succeed in society without knowing how to dance."

"I didn't know they danced."

"I can see you don't approve. But you gave them to me to educate when Grace passed away and have not directed me further in all these years. They have become accomplished young ladies and will be very successful in society. In a few years I will have them well married into good families."

Daniel felt a wave of panic. Dancing! What else have they been learning?

"I'm grateful for your care of them all these years," he managed to say. "I fear I have neglected them … They are so like Grace. Sometimes I think I am seeing her double when I look at them… . and then feel the pain of her loss."

"I know." Mrs. Lowell's voice softened. "They are very like her, but taller and fuller. I think your farmer stock has made them stronger than Grace was. Perhaps they need not die so young."

Daniel picked up his cup. "Tell me, what are they reading there in the library?"

"The essays of Ralph Waldo Emerson."

"Emerson! He is a deist, a rebel against the Gospel and the church! Why are you filling their young minds with such rubbish?"

Mrs. Lowell lifted her chin. "Emerson and the other Transcendentalists are much spoken of in society." Her voice was no longer soft. "Your daughters need to be able to carry on an intelligent conversation."

"But what of their *Christian* education?" Daniel was almost trembling, overwhelmed by the guilt of neglecting his daughters in addition to the stress and exhaustion of the last two days.

"Of course I have attended to that. We begin each day's lessons with Bible study. Becky has taught them their prayers, and they are in church every Sunday, as you know."

"Yes, yes, I know." Daniel set down his tea cup because his hand was beginning to shake.

Mrs. Lowell shifted in her chair. "You said you were leaving within the month?"

"Yes, but we must be out of the manse in two weeks, so it can be prepared for the new pastor. I do not know yet where we will go, or what to do with our possessions."

"You must come here, of course, all of you. I will be glad to have Becky back. Flora is getting too old to manage the household. This is a big house with many empty rooms. You can store your belongings here. There will be a train out to Denver, they say, in a few years, and you can have your possessions shipped to you then. Or perhaps by then you will return."

"I do not think I will return."

Mrs. Lowell gave him a sharp glance. "I suspect there is more to this sudden decision than meets the eye."

Daniel's stomach lurched. "No more than I will speak of."

"I see."

She picked up the tea pot. "More tea?"

"Yes, thank you."

They sipped in silence.

Mrs. Lowell continued to observe him. "Your daughters will miss you. They quite adore you, you know."

"I didn't know that."

"They do. And it will be hard for them to lose you after losing their mother."

Daniel's head was swimming. They adored him? What had seemed perfectly clear a few hours ago was now becoming a question. "Perhaps, after all, I should take them with me," he ventured.

"Nonsense." Mrs. Lowell rapped her fan on the arm of her rocking chair. "As I said before, the frontier is no place for innocent young girls. In most settlements, I hear, there are a hundred men to only ten or twelve women. They would not be safe. To say nothing of the dangers of the journey. And all their education would be wasted in such a harsh environment."

"Maybe it would be welcome."

"Do not even think of such a thing. You must leave them—unless you change your mind about this call."

"That's impossible."

Mrs. Lowell folded her lips together, her gray eyes piercing.

Dear God, Daniel agonized inwardly. Does she suspect?

"You might not find it so easy to have them along," Mrs. Lowell went on. "They can be a handful, mischievous. Especially that Lily. Becky has spoiled them. They are not always … biddable."

"I confess I have difficulty telling them apart. Becky seems to have no trouble."

"Nor do I. They are alike, to be sure, but if you observe them closely, it is easy to see the difference."

Daniel leaned forward in his chair. "Tell me."

"You need only notice their deportment, their manner of speaking. Lily is more forward, too pert sometimes, though that is part of her charm. If there is mischief afoot, she'll be at the root of it. Rose is more soft-spoken, compassionate, aware if anyone around her has pain or sorrow."

Daniel listened intently. I want to know them, he realized, and make up for my neglect. The idea of leaving them behind began to feel as impossible as taking them with him had felt only a few hours earlier.

"Maybe we should ask them what they want," he suggested.

"We can ask them, but, of course, *we* shall make the decision."

"*I* shall."

Mrs. Lowell leaned back slowly into her chair, snapped her fan open and fanned herself. Daniel picked up his tea cup and tilted it to his lips. It was empty. He set it down.

"I have not spoken to Rose and Lily about my plans," Daniel said after a pause. "I fear it will be a shock for them."

"Perhaps not. They observe you far more closely than you do them. Also, you should know"—she got up from her chair and moved quietly toward the library door— "they have a habit of eavesdropping."

She opened the door suddenly. The twins were almost too quick for her, back at the table, heads bent, but Daniel could see through the open door that their skirts were still settling and their bodies tense with suppressed giggles.

Mrs. Lowell stood in the doorway a moment regarding them. Daniel could see her stern mouth soften and turn up in a half-smile, her sharp eyes misting.

She loves them, he realized, even if she is misguided in educating them.

"Lily, Rose," she said.

The twins turned to her, their eyes wide with innocence.

Mrs. Lowell controlled her smile.

"Your father is here." She was stern again. "We wish to speak with you. Please come and join us."

The twins closed their books, stood gracefully, and came into the parlor. When they were seated, they turned to him expectantly.

He cleared his throat, returning their gaze. I must learn to see them for who they are, not always Grace in them. What Mrs. Lowell said is true; they are taller and fuller than Grace was.

"Your father has some important news for you," Mrs. Lowell said.

"Yes." Daniel cleared his throat again. "I met with the Presbytery yesterday. They gave me a call to minister to a new church on the frontier. This means we will be moving from the manse in the next two weeks. Your grandmother has invited us to stay with her until my departure. We have been discussing what is best for your future in light of these changes."

The twins reached across the space between their chairs to clasp hands.

"You spoke of *your* departure," one of them said. "Do you plan to leave us behind?"

"That is not yet decided," Daniel answered. "Your grandmother would like you to stay with her to continue your education—"

"But Papa," the other twin broke in, "we might never see you again—"

"And you are our only Papa—"

"If you leave us behind, you'll have no one to take care of you on that long journey."

Their words came fast, from first one and then the other. Bewildered, Daniel tried to remember what Mrs. Lowell had told him about telling them apart. It was no use.

"How could you take care of him?" Mrs. Lowell demanded. "You can't even take care of yourselves. You have been brought up to be ladies, not to cook and clean and sew and do laundry."

"We could learn."

"Don't leave us behind, Papa."

"We can learn to take care of you."

"Becky can teach us."

Both twins now had tears in their eyes.

Daniel was touched. "You mean you want to go with me? Do you realize it is a long and difficult journey? And when we arrive we'll be living roughly? There are few luxuries on the frontier."

"We know. It doesn't matter."

"We don't want you to leave us behind."

"We're strong. We can help."

"You shouldn't go alone."

"Nonsense!" Mrs. Lowell cut in. "You have no idea what the journey would entail. And the frontier is no place for young ladies. It is dangerous and wicked."

"There's a church."

"Papa's going to build a church."

"There must be good people if they want a church."

Mrs. Lowell tightened her lips and fanned herself. She took a deep breath and spoke more gently.

"I think it would be best for you to stay. Here, you will be safe and can continue your education, and in a few years move into society where all you have learned will be appreciated. Your father will find help along the way."

The twins were silent. Daniel saw that they had tightened their grip on each other's hands.

Finally one asked him, "Papa, don't you want us to go with you?"

Daniel glanced at Mrs. Lowell, still fanning herself, then turned to the twins.

"This is a difficult and important decision," he said. "I need to give it thought and prayer. We will not decide today."

One of the twins turned to Mrs. Lowell. "Grandmama, we love you, too, and will miss you very much. But do not think that all you have taught us will go to waste. Maybe we can teach the children there, start a school."

The other spoke up. "Certainly people there will want music. We can't take the piano, but I can take my violin and Rose can take her flute."

There, Daniel thought. That's Rose who is comforting her grandmother. She's the compassionate one. That's Lily who just spoke. Lily plays the violin, Rose the flute. Remember that.

Mrs. Lowell was silent. Daniel stood.

"I must go," he said. "I have much to attend to. Mrs. Lowell, I am most grateful for your offer to store our possessions and host us until our departure. You have taken a great load off my mind. Lily, Rose, return to your studies. We'll speak more of this matter later."

The twins rose, bent their heads in acknowledgment, and returned quietly to the library.

They do know ladylike deportment, Daniel noted.

Mrs. Lowell had risen also. "Please consider this matter carefully, Daniel. Your daughters' entire future depends on a wise decision. Do not be overly moved by their pleas and tears. They are too young to know what is best for them." She took a breath. "Understand that my home and all its resources are available to you. Abel will help you with the move."

"Thank you. You are very kind and generous." Daniel bowed. "We will speak again soon."

~

That afternoon the twins sat at their grandmother's grand piano. They were playing, four hands, a Schubert sonata they knew well enough to keep playing as they whispered to each other under cover of the music. "We're going," Lily murmured. "Did you hear Papa say 'until *our* departure'? It's settled. He's just saying that about thinking and praying to pacify Grandmama."

"Grandmama took care of it for us—Emerson and dancing," Rose whispered back. "We didn't have to do a thing. It's kind of scary, though." Her right hand stumbled, and they stopped playing.

"Let's take that part again," Lily said aloud. Their eyes met as they shared a smile, then began the phrase again.

## Chapter 5

# *Transitions*

Daniel announced his decision the next day, first to Mrs. Lowell and then to Becky. Mrs. Lowell was bitterly disappointed that he was taking the twins away from her, but, being a true lady, she swallowed her dissent and set Flora to work preparing rooms for the Wright family.

Becky was taken completely by surprise. The twins came into the kitchen shortly after their father had spoken to her and found her sitting at the kitchen table, her face in her apron, sobbing. They rushed to her sides.

"Becky, Becky, what's wrong?" Rose asked.

Becky lifted her head, tears streaming down her face. "Your papa's taking you away. Did you know? Way out West where there's wolves and Indians and no safe house to live in, and who knows what will happen to you. I'll never see you again, my lambs, my little ones!"

"Oh, Becky, don't cry." Lily stroked her back.

The twins kissed away her tears, then pulled up chairs and sat down on either side of her.

"We'll write to you."

"And maybe in a few years, when the railroad comes through, we can come visit you."

"Or you can come visit us."

Becky's eyes grew wide with terror. "No! No! I'd be scared to death!" She wiped her face with the corner of her apron, but tears filled her eyes again as she looked from one twin to the other.

"We need to learn to cook so we can take care of Papa," Rose said. "Will you teach us?"

"And to clean and sew and wash clothes," Lily added, remembering all the things their grandmama had said they didn't know how to do.

"Will you?"

"'Course I'll teach you." Becky heaved a sigh and wiped her face again. "But it's a crying shame, you brought up to be fine ladies and now having to learn to do what the likes of me do."

She pushed back her chair and blew her nose on the handkerchief she kept in her bosom. "Okay, you can start by helping me peel potatoes for dinner."

The twins followed her as she pulled a bag of potatoes out of the pantry, took a big pot out of the cupboard, filled it with water, and set it on counter.

"You wash 'em in here, peel 'em with these knives, cut 'em up, and put 'em in this pot." She banged a second pot onto the counter. "Dear God, do you know how to use a knife? Don't cut yourselves now."

The next two weeks passed in a blur for the family at the River View manse. Thomas Peabody stopped by often to talk with Daniel and help, especially with the painful task of deciding which books should go, and which stay behind. On one such visit he said, as he stacked books into a crate, "I located the man I spoke of earlier, who has been out to the frontier. His name is Eli Erickson, and he said he would be glad to come and talk with you. It turns out he has actually been through Gold Creek."

Daniel looked up from the book in his hands. "Thank you. I will talk with Mrs. Lowell and see if we can arrange a dinner party for him. I'm eager to hear what he has to say."

News of Daniel's imminent departure, somehow leaked, spread like a wind storm through the congregation of River View. On the Sunday of Daniel's last service, the sanctuary was packed. His final sermon was passionate, eloquent. His voice broke more than once as he spoke of his love for his congregation and exhorted them to carry on the work of Christ under the guidance of their new pastor. He spoke of his call to serve the new territory in the West and the importance of bringing these vast new regions into Christ's fold. Following the service, his parishioners pressed around him, some weeping, touching him, all blessing him and wishing him well in his new life. Only Ebenezer Decker was not there, having been forbidden by the Presbytery to attend church until Daniel departed.

Abel came each day with the carriage and hauled boxes and trunks to the house on Beacon Hill. The manse grew emptier and emptier.

The day before the move, Nell came to help Becky pack her personal belongings. In the midst of the bustle of packing, Nell caught Daniel alone for a moment.

"Sir," she said, "she did get the train. I had the keys and let her out of her room where he had locked her up, and John got her there in time. I thought you'd want to know."

Daniel's heart raced until he was almost dizzy.

"Thank you! Thank you for telling me." He grasped Nell's hand. "Thank you for helping her. I am very relieved. Have you heard from her?"

"Not yet."

"When you do, please let me know how she is. If I've already gone, Becky will have my address in Gold Creek."

"I will, sir, I'll write to you once I hear."

Becky called to her, and Nell hurried out.

Daniel stood, head bent, hand to his brow. *Dear Lord,* he prayed, *watch over her, bless and protect her and the child. Forgive us our sin. Grant us Thy mercy.*

Mrs. Lowell's house on Beacon Hill was four stories high. On the first floor were the entry, the kitchen, and the servants' quarters; on the second floor the parlor, the library, and the dining room; on the third floor Mrs. Lowell's bedroom and sitting room at the front of the house, and a spacious bedroom at the back where Daniel was settled. Rose and Lily were given a big room under the eaves on the fourth floor. Across the hall was a room packed full with trunks and boxes from the River View manse. A spiral staircase wound through the center of the house connecting the entry on the first floor to the hall on the fourth. When their grandmama wasn't looking, the twins used the smooth banister as their expressway from their room at the top to the floors below.

Becky took the responsibility of teaching the twins seriously. They learned to clean their room—mop the floor, beat the carpet, dust, wash the window. "This is like training a new maid," Becky muttered under her breath. "No, Lily! You don't *blow* the dust off; it'll just land somewhere else. Here, use this damp rag."

There were sewing and laundry lessons. "Fancy needle work's fine," Becky said, "and you both know how to do it beautiful, but you're going to need to make clothes. We'll start with aprons." She found them sturdy cloth, and taught them how to shape and cut and sew strong seams. They stood at the wash tubs behind the kitchen and washed their father's clothes, heated the heavy iron on the cook stove, and pressed his shirts.

Cooking lessons continued. At first Mrs. Lowell's cook, Cora, was grumpy at having her domain invaded. She sat at the table drinking coffee and glared at Becky and the twins. Then after a while she got interested and offered her own tips. Under the guidance of Becky and Cora, the twins learned to prepare vegetables, make a hearty soup, pick and roast a chicken.

They entered into the new learning with buoyant, youthful energy, laughing and teasing each other and Becky, and overall did well. They had some struggles learning to manage the cookstove, and Rose burned a hole in one of their father's shirts when she got the iron too hot. Lily seared the back of her hand taking bread out of the oven, and for a while Daniel had only to look at the bandage to know which twin was which.

～

February turned to March. The sun shone warmer, and the snow began to melt. One evening a soft rain fell.

Lily and Rose, lying in bed in their attic room, heard the sound of rain on the roof.

"Spring's coming," Lily whispered. "We'll be leaving soon.

# Chapter 6

# *News of Gold Creek*

The evening Mr. Erickson came to dinner the twins dressed with special care. They wore rose-colored damask gowns, their slender waists cinched by tight corsets and emphasized by their swaying hoop skirts. Rose was straightening a rosebud in Lily's hair when a bell rang in the hall below, Becky calling them for dinner.

The twins rustled out of their room, full of anticipation, because Mr. Erickson was the man who had been to Gold Creek, and they were eager to hear what their new home would be like. As they came to the top of the stairs, they saw Becky, two stories down, looking up at them with the bell in her hand. Their hoop skirts forbad the use of the banister, so they descended the stairs decorously. Becky beamed at them. "Pretty as a picture, you two are," she said. "Go on in now. Mr. Erickson's already here."

In the parlor, Mr. Erickson stood with his back to the fireplace, engaged in conversation with Daniel. Mr. Erickson was tall, fair-haired, broad-shouldered, wearing a fringed leather jacket. He waved his arms as he spoke, his manner large and expansive, making the parlor seem small by comparison. Mrs. Lowell sat in her high-backed rocker, listening.

They all turned as the twins entered. Daniel introduced them. "Mr. Erickson, meet my daughters, Miss Lily Wright and Miss Rose Wright." The twins bent their heads in acknowledgment. "Lily, Rose, Mr. Erickson."

Mr. Erickson stood back and surveyed the twins slowly from head to foot. "Are these young ladies going with you?"

"Yes," Daniel answered.

"Twins are they? They'll sure brighten up that little mining town." Mr. Erickson looked them over again. Mrs. Lowell frowned and tensed in her chair.

The door from the dining room opened. Flora, wearing her best black dress, invited them in.

In the dining room, Mrs. Lowell directed the seating—Daniel at the foot of the table facing her, the twins on one side, Mr. Erickson on the other. Flora served the soup.

"Tell me more of the route we must travel." Daniel said.

"The railroad goes as far as St. Joseph," Mr. Erickson answered. "That's about a week's travel from here. Then you can get a steamboat up the Missouri River to Council Bluffs. You need to arrive there no later than April first to allow time to equip yourself before the wagon trains leave around the middle of April. You can get your oxen and wagon there, and the other equipment you'll need. You'll want to wrap everything in India rubber sheets."

"Why," Lily asked. "Won't our things stay dry in our wagon?"

"Sometimes you get water in the wagons, crossing the rivers."

"Oh." Rose caught her breath.

Mr. Erickson looked over at her. "Yep. Can happen. Depends on the river, how high it's running. Can be tricky. Once in a while a man gets drowned swimming across, or some livestock get lost."

"It's dangerous, then, crossing the rivers?" Mrs. Lowell turned her sharp gaze on Mr. Erickson.

"Whole trip's dangerous, ma'am. People die for all kinds of reasons. Disease, Indians, accidents. But most people make it."

Mrs. Lowell laid down her soup spoon and sat straight in her chair.

"Is Council Bluffs where we connect to a wagon train?" Daniel asked.

"That's where they gather. You want to look out for a man named Jacob Abrams. I traveled with him going out. If you can find him, you'll be in good hands. Leading wagon trains is what he does. Big man. Goes by Jake. Ask around for him when you get to Council Bluffs.

"You young ladies, now," Mr. Erickson said to the twins. "You leave those hoop skirts at home. One girl in the wagon train I traveled in went to jump out of the wagon—it was moving slow so she thought she could just jump— caught her hoops on the wagon tongue, fell under the wheels and was crushed to death."

"Really!" Mrs. Lowell exclaimed.

"And leave those corsets home, too," Mr. Erickson went on.

The twins gasped and put their fingertips to their lips. Mrs. Lowell rapped the edge of the table with her fan.

Mr. Erickson turned to her. "Sorry, ma'am. But these young ladies need to know that every one on the frontier, man, woman and child, spends most of their day doing heavy labor. They've got to be able to breathe. Fainting women aren't much use out there."

"I think *that* is sufficient discussion of clothing." Mrs. Lowell's voice was icy cold.

She snapped her fan open and fanned herself for a moment, then said more cordially, "Tell us about Gold Creek, where Reverend Wright will be starting his church. I understand you have been there."

Daniel leaned forward. "What sort of town is it? What kind of people?"

"Well, it *is* a town. They've incorporated it, platted it out. There's a saloon, of course, at the mouth of the canyon, usually the first institution in these mining towns. Run by a man named Smythe. I met him. A good-looking man, Smythe, except for a scar on his cheek." Mr. Erickson traced a line from the corner of his left eye to his ear. "But the decent folks in town don't like him. He's got a brothel upstairs, and does too well selling drink and women."

Mrs. Lowell rapped her fan again. "Mr. Erickson! Please remember you are in the presence of young ladies."

The twins exchanged a quick glance.

Mr. Erickson nodded. "Yes, ma'am. But you'll want to watch out for Smythe," he said to Daniel. "He won't be wanting a church. Christian morals and his business don't mix. There's a boarding house," he went on. "I stayed there. It's a clean, decent place. There's a general store. A sawmill just opened. The houses are mostly log cabins. Now the sawmill's there, some of those cabins'll be getting board floors."

"What kind of floors do they have now?" Mrs. Lowell inquired.

"Dirt."

"Dirt!" she exclaimed.

"Yes, ma'am. Most of those cabins are pretty basic. Folks spend all their money getting out there, and then don't strike it rich as soon as they expect. They get together what they can to protect themselves from the elements, hauling logs down out of the mountains. Often it's just a one-room cabin without windows for the whole family to sleep and eat and live in." He looked around at the elegant dining room, the white damask table cloth, the fine china and crystal, the silver candlesticks, the heavy pale-gold drapes covering the windows. "It's a different world," he said. "A different world than this one here."

"And the church?" Daniel asked.

"Don't know of a church. There's no church building. That'll be one of your projects, I suppose."

"What kind of people?" Daniel persisted.

"There's the miners, of course. They're up on the mountain during the week, but pour into town over the weekend. There's the townspeople and homesteaders farming in the river valley. Some of them have wives and kids. Out on the plains there's ranches and more homesteaders. There's one bank with a telegraph station. Mr. Dodge, Derrick Dodge, is the banker. I think he has a wife. Didn't meet her."

"Who are the people who want a church?" Daniel wondered.

"Don't know. I just passed through, stayed only two nights in Gold Creek. Spent one day up at the mine and most of the next with Mr. Dodge."

"Is there a school for the children?" Rose asked.

"Don't think so. The kids I saw were working as hard as their parents. Not much time for education, I'd imagine."

"A church and a school are needed," Daniel said emphatically.

"Probably help to calm the place down," Mr. Erickson agreed. "It can get pretty rough, especially on weekends."

Mrs. Lowell stiffened in her chair. Under the table the twins gripped each other's hands.

Becky came in to clear the soup dishes and Flora followed with the main course. The conversation paused as Mrs. Lowell served.

After everyone was served, Lily asked, "Is it true there are bears and lions out there?"

"Not in the towns, but in the mountains. There's wolves, too. Sometimes you can hear 'em howling at night. In the towns there's all kinds of animals—foxes, rabbits, coyotes. And deer. You'll need to put a high fence around your garden, or the deer will eat it right down to the root. Lots of birds. Wild geese come through there in the fall. Now there's a sight—all of 'em lifting off in a swoop, flying in a V, honking… I miss being out there. It's rough and hard, to be sure, but wide and open."

The twins looked at each other, sharing a rush of excitement.

As the meal progressed, there were many more eager questions from Daniel and the twins. Mr. Erickson grew expansive, sometimes gesturing with his fork as he described life in the wagon train and in the mining towns along the foothills of the Rocky Mountains. Mrs. Lowell sat in silence, her lips folded together, her sharp eyes moving from one speaker to the next.

Soon after the meal, Mr. Erickson expressed his thanks, made his farewells, and was escorted out by Jackson.

Mrs. Lowell turned to the twins. The knuckles of the hand holding her furled fan were white with tension. "It's time for you to retire now," she said.

The twins came to either side of her to kiss her cheeks. "Goodnight, Grandmama." They kissed their father, "Goodnight, Papa."

As they went out the parlor door, Lily left it open a crack. She caught Rose's hand. "Grandmama's really upset," she whispered.

Rose nodded. They leaned close to the crack in the door.

"Daniel," they heard Mrs. Lowell exclaim, "I beg you to reconsider. Did you hear? Did you see the way he looked at your daughters, spoke to them? Is this the etiquette of the West that you would expose them to? And the living conditions, the dangers of the journey—they might not make it to Gold Creek alive! What are you thinking of, to take them on such an escapade?"

"Oh no," Lily breathed.

Silence. Daniel cleared his throat. "The decision has been made," he said. "The Lord will protect us."

## Chapter 7

# *Departure*

Daniel and Abel carried two big empty trunks up the stairs to the twins' room.

"I've been to visit Mr. Erickson again," Daniel told the twins. "He said we'd do best to keep our wagon light. So I have purchased a trunk for each of us. Everything you are taking with you, except for what you carry in your carpet bag for the train, must fit in your trunk."

"Everything?" Lily asked, her eyes widening.

Rose put her hands to her face. "Even our dishes and cooking pots?"

"Everything." Daniel turned to Abel. "There's one more trunk, to go to my room."

After Daniel and Abel left, the twins surveyed the two trunks. They were about four feet long and three feet high, brown, with a heavy metal clasp at the center, and a wide leather handle on each end.

"They're pretty big," Lily said. "We'll manage."

Rose nodded. "We'd better get busy."

For the rest of the afternoon, they rummaged through their wardrobe and bureau drawers. They made a pile of dresses on the bed.

"It's hard to know which ones to take," Rose said, separating them and laying them out.

Lily pulled out two blue-gray gowns with lace collars. "We'll need these for church."

"We can't take the damask rose ones." Rose stroked the bright cloth. "They don't look right without the hoop skirts and the corsets."

"No hoop skirts," Lily said. "Not after what Mr. Erickson told us."

"What about the corsets?"

"No. They're uncomfortable. Anyway it sounds like we'll be working hard and not dressing up much." Lily tossed the corsets on the floor.

"But let's take our pink silks just in case," Rose said. "There surely will be parties, church socials."

"We really don't know." Lily's eyes were dreamy. "It's all unknown. But I'm glad we're going. I never liked the idea of being a Boston lady. It felt stifling. I think things will be much more fun on the frontier."

"I'm not sure." Rose shook her head. "Papa's going to be quite strict. Not as easy as Becky or even Grandmama. No dancing."

"I know. The main reason he's taking us is to see to our Christian development. But I'm not giving up dancing."

"He can be determined."

"So can we."

~

The next day the twins packed and repacked their trunks, opened the boxes in the room across the hall and dug around to retrieve treasures that, after all, could not be left behind. Their room was scattered with piles of clothing, jewelry and hair ornaments, a box of writing materials, books, music.

Becky came huffing up the four flights of stairs with a box of kitchen supplies.

"Heavy," she gasped as she dropped it on the floor by the trunks. "There's a soup pot in there, tin plates and cups. Not fancy, but they won't break. I put in three crockery mugs for your coffee. They're wrapped in dish clothes, 'cause they can break. But tin cups'll burn your hands with anything hot. There's pot holders and a table cloth." She straightened, her hands on her low back. "How are you going to cook without a cookstove?"

"Mr. Erickson said the women make a fire in a trench on the ground," Lily answered.

"Like them Indian women? Lordy, what would your mama say, you coming to this after all your fine upbringing?" Becky's eyes filled with tears.

Rose put her arm around her. "She'd want us to take care of Papa. It'll be all right. We'll get a stove when we have our new home."

Becky wiped her eyes with the corner of her apron. "I'm going to get you some towels and soap." She bustled out.

The twins continued packing, dividing the kitchenware between their two trunks.

"The quilts go," Rose said, "even if we have no bed to put them on."

"Absolutely," Lily agreed. "We'll get a mattress in Council Bluffs. Mr. Erickson said there were lots of stores there to supply people for the wagon trains."

"I'll put that box from Grandma Wright with seeds and dried food in my trunk," Lily said.

"I've got our embroidery materials." Rose wrapped hoops and bright thread in a fold of cloth.

"I'll take the sewing kit. Where is it?" Lily searched around. "Here it is. We mustn't forget our hymnbooks. We can play for Papa's services."

"And our Bibles." Rose picked up her Bible and opened it. Inside the front cover was a card with a picture of Jesus. He had a halo of light around His head, and His dark eyes seemed to look straight into hers. She paused a moment, stroked the picture with her fingertip, then closed the Bible and laid it in her trunk.

~

The evening before their departure, Mrs. Lowell called Daniel into her sitting room and stood facing him.

"I'll not have you and Rose and Lily living in a one-room cabin with a dirt floor. It's not proper for you to share a room with them. You'll need a cook stove, and glass for your windows as well." She handed him a packet of papers. "I've set up an account for you at First Bank. Mr. Erickson said there was a telegraph at the bank in Gold Creek. Promise me you will get or build yourself a decent house."

"But Mrs. Lowell," Daniel stammered. "This is very generous of you. I never expected …"

"It's nothing." Mrs. Lowell opened her fan and waved it in short, quick strokes. "I'm a wealthy woman, Daniel, and have no heirs beyond Benjamin and the twins. They may as well have some of their share now when they need it. I looked into the amount of severance pay you got from River View. It is not sufficient for you to make the journey, create a home, and start a church."

She turned partly away from him to look out the window. "You know, I did not approve of Grace marrying you—she, the most beautiful and sought-after debutante, falling for a young assistant minister. But she loved you, and you ended up after all doing well. I don't understand why you are giving up all you have built here and taking your daughters into such a dangerous and harsh environment. But you are clearly set on it. Please allow me to offer what assistance I can."

Daniel passed his hand over his brow. "I don't know how to thank you. They have promised me a year's salary from the Missouri Synod, but I have no information about when that will come to me. Knowing there will be money for us there when we arrive is ..."

"Say no more." Mrs. Lowell snapped her fan shut and turned back from the window. "I'm sure you have more preparations to make."

～

The morning was gray and chill. Abel and Daniel loaded the three trunks into the carriage at the back of the house.

Lily and Rose stood at the top of the stairs, dressed in simple dark-blue gowns, covered by gray hooded cloaks, each carrying a big carpet bag. Lily's violin case stuck out of the top of hers.

"One last time," Lily said.

Lily went first, sitting sideways, her carpet bag in her lap, one hand behind her on the banister. Rose followed. They went fast, in spite of slowing themselves with the hand behind them. Mrs. Lowell was just stepping out onto the second floor landing as they went whizzing by, bubbling with laughter.

"Lily! Rose!" she exclaimed. She hurried down the stairs after them. They had already landed, stumbling a little as their feet hit the first-floor entry way. "It's time for you to grow up. Don't you realize ..."

But her words were cut off by their hugs.

Becky met them in the kitchen with a big lunch box. She was sobbing and scolding, "You behave yourselves now. Don't let the wolves get you. You write to me."

Both twins dropped their carpet bags and wrapped their arms around Becky.

"We'll be okay."

"Of course we'll write to you."

Daniel came in the back door. "It's time now. The train won't wait."

The twins picked up their bags. Daniel carried the lunch box. Mrs. Lowell preceded them out the back door to the carriage.

As the carriage pulled out of the courtyard, the twins turned back to see Becky standing in the doorway, pressing the hem of her apron against her wet cheeks, waving.

～

The sun broke through the clouds as they stood on the platform at the train station, the three trunks and carpet bags piled beside them. Mrs. Lowell held herself stiff and straight. Daniel tapped his foot and looked down the track. The twins, standing one on each side of their grandmama, shivered with excitement. From far down the track came the whistle of the train.

Mr. Peabody burst out of the station door and hurried toward them. Daniel ran to meet him. They held each other by the shoulders, looked into each other's eyes, then embraced.

The whistle of the train drew nearer.

Daniel looked around, suddenly frantic. "Do we have everything?"

"The lunch box!" Rose exclaimed.

"I'll get it." Lily picked up her skirts and ran toward the station.

"Come back," Daniel called. "The train's almost here."

Lily kept running, but she hadn't gone far when Abel came out of the station with the lunch box in his hands. Lily grabbed it and ran back.

The train roared into the station, the engine huge and black, smelling of coal smoke, screeching as it came to a halt.

The conductor swung down the metal steps of the passenger car. "*Boston*," he chanted. He turned to assist the passengers getting off—three men in business suits and a woman with a baby in her arms. Thomas and Daniel carried the trunks to the baggage car, where the baggage man lifted them and swung them in. The twins hugged and kissed their grandmama one last time. "All aboard," the conductor called.

Daniel kissed Mrs. Lowell on the cheek, clapped Thomas on the shoulder.

The twins gathered up their bags and the lunch box. The conductor helped them up the metal steps. Daniel followed. At the top of the steps, the twins turned back. "Good-bye, Grandmama," they called. "Good-bye, good-bye." Daniel stood behind them, silent, his eyes meeting Thomas's.

The conductor grabbed the hand rail, swung up onto the steps.

The whistle blew. The engine belched steam and sparks. Slowly at first, then faster, the pistons moved the wheels, and the train roared out of the station.

With another long, lonely whistle, it picked up speed and disappeared around a bend in the track, leaving behind only a trail of black smoke in the gray morning sky.

The station platform was empty and suddenly quiet. Mrs. Lowell and Thomas Peabody stood silent, looking down the track. Thomas's jaw was tight. Mrs. Lowell made a small, incoherent sound and turned away from the empty track, her shoulders folding in, her head bent into her hand. Thomas looked around at her.

"Mrs. Lowell," he said extending his arm, "may I escort you to your carriage?"

She straightened her shoulders, drew in her breath, and lifted her chin. "Thank you, Mr. Peabody."

She placed her small gloved hand in the bend of his elbow. They turned together and went back through the station to where Abel waited with the carriage.

# Part 2

# THE JOURNEY

Chapter 8

# The Train

The first day of the journey was a day of many changes, full of wonder for the twins, but stressful and exhausting for Daniel. The train went only as far as Fall River. Shortly after eating their lunch from Becky's big box, they got off the train and found a cab that took them to the wharf. There they boarded a steam ship for New York City. The twins were delighted with the ocean journey, lifting up their arms to the seabirds, hanging over the railing to watch the wake, exclaiming with awe when twilight tinged the clouds pink over the towers of New York. In the city, they caught another cab to the ferry across the Hudson.

With every change of conveyance, Daniel had to deal with their heavy trunks. They had become infinitely precious to him, as they contained all that remained of their former life. As the day went on, he became obsessed with the fear of losing them.

He was equally anxious about letting the twins out of his sight. He could get help with the trunks from the baggage men and cabbies, but he was reluctant to leave the twins standing alone on the station platform or wharf. Although they were modestly dressed, their refinement was unmistakable. That, coupled with their beauty and their unusual likeness to each other, elicited stares and comment wherever they went. They were innocently friendly, striking up conversations with everyone around. Each time he left them, Daniel feared he would not find them when he returned.

It was almost dark when they disembarked from the ferry across the Hudson. Daniel left the twins with the bags as he had done with each change all day, but this time when he returned, with a baggage man carrying the other end of a trunk, there was only one twin standing by the pile of bags. His anxiety, building and held in all day, erupted.

"Where is—?" he shouted. He didn't even know which one was missing.

"Lily went to get a cab," Rose explained.

"I told you both to stay right here!" he bellowed. He set down his end of the trunk. The baggage man wiped his brow and watched with amusement. "Bring the other two," Daniel ordered him. "I've got to find my daughter. Rose, don't you move from this spot. Don't let anyone take that trunk."

"I'll sit on it, Papa."

Daniel looked around wildly. "Which way did she go? I told you"— to the baggage man— "bring the other two trunks."

The baggage man shifted his weight into one hip, tucked a thumb under his suspender, and pushed back his hat. "Can't carry 'em alone, sir."

Just as Daniel drew in his breath to shout another order, Lily appeared, walking calmly across the wharf, followed by a young man who was eyeing her with obvious appreciation.

"Lily, where have you been?" Daniel roared.

"I got us a cab, Papa. This gentleman has one waiting for us and he can help you carry the trunks."

"I told you to stay right here! Don't you understand that you can't just go wandering about on your own?" Veins stood out in Daniel's brow. "You have to learn to obey me. Now sit down on that trunk, and don't budge until I come back."

Lily lifted her chin. "You should thank me for getting a cab, not yell at me." She turned to smile at the young cabby. "Could you please help my Papa with the other two trunks?"

"I told you to sit down."

Lily remained standing.

The baggage man looked over at the cabby, tilted his head, and the two turned back toward the ferry. Daniel stood a moment, his head swiveling back and forth between Lily, still standing with her chin lifted, and the two men walking away. After a moment he turned and raced after them.

Lily sulked briefly, but apparently let it go after Rose whispered to her in the cab, "He didn't mean it. He was just so scared something bad had happened to you."

When they reached the train station in Hoboken, they found they'd missed their connection. "Next train doesn't leave till midnight," the station master told them. He helped Daniel drag the trunks inside. The station was dingy and grubby, infused with the acrid smell of coal smoke. Wads of chewing tobacco were splattered on the floor. Daniel could barely curb his frustration. One of the twins, he thought it must have been Rose, opened the lunch box on the dusty bench, and took out carefully wrapped packets of Becky's delicious meat pie and cornbread, apples and carrots.

"It's okay, Papa," she said. "We can have supper while we're waiting. You'll feel better after you eat."

~

Night. The train roared through the darkness. Daniel sat with his back to its forward motion. The twins slept, wrapped in their cloaks, curled up together on the seat across from him. Lily lay with her head on a pillow next to the window, Rose with her head on Lily's hip. When Rose discovered he had not brought a pillow, she had given him hers.

A baby, a few seats behind him, fussed. Cigar smoke drifted in gray spirals under the swinging lamp. The rattling roar of the train was constant.

Daniel propped Rose's pillow against the window and leaned his head against it. He was weary and wretchedly uncomfortable. He marveled at his daughters. Once they were settled on the midnight train, the twins knelt in the narrow space between the seats, silently said their prayers, then curled up together and slept. He couldn't figure out how they'd both managed to lie down on that narrow wooden bench and sleep so peacefully, in spite of the noise and motion of the train.

He sighed and twisted, trying in vain to find a comfortable position. Memories arose of his last visit to his family on the farm, less than week ago, though it seemed as if it were already folded into the far past. He and the twins had gone to say goodbye and stayed only two days. Only two days rooted one last time in the devout, hardworking rhythms of his childhood and his mother's love.

He groaned. If she knew …

His last look as he drove the buggy away from the farm, just before turning the bend in the lane. His father's arm around his mother, his mother weeping. His brothers with their arms crossed on their chests, the women and children waving. Behind them, the gray weathered farmhouse.

The train rounded a corner, jerking his head. The pillow slipped to the floor. As he bent to pick it up, he glanced over at the twins.

Their faces were soft with sleep and looked very young. Rose's cloak had slipped partway off and trailed on the floor. Moving carefully, he picked it up and tucked it around her. She gave a small sigh and nestled her cheek into Lily's skirts. Daniel's heart swelled with a confusion of protectiveness and helpless trepidation.

He ached all over. The wooden seat, when he sat down again, felt harder than ever. Propping Rose's pillow against the window, he gazed out. In the darkness, fleeing away from him, was all he loved.

His church. The beautiful sanctuary with the pipe organ, the stained glass windows, his pulpit. Faces of his parishioners. Thomas. His study at the manse, breakfasts in the warm kitchen …

He arched his back, pounded the pillow, leaned his head against it again.

Rachel … What has happened to her? Where is she? Is she safe? It's nearing time for her child to be born. My child. I want to be with her when her time comes, to hold our child in my arms. I want to be with her.

Overwhelmed by longing, he twisted on the hard bench, remembering her shining dark hair, her wide dark eyes, her soft yielding body, her love cries. Passion, shame, and guilt flamed through him. *Christ have mercy on me!* he prayed.

He sat hunched, his face in his hands, trying to still the agony in his heart. Finally he flipped around, facing the aisle, and pushed the pillow against the back of the seat.

Two men across the way glanced at him curiously over their cigars. He turned back again, pillow against the window.

I must not cry. Not in front of those men.

～

At five in the morning, the conductor strode through the car, calling out, "Phila*del*phia, Phila*del*phia. End of the line. Everybody out."

Daniel woke startled. The twins stirred, sat up, and rubbed their eyes. "We have to get off here," Daniel told them. They gathered the bags and lunch box and followed him drowsily through the car. He helped them down the metal steps and found them a bench on the cold, drafty station platform. They sat down, wrapped their cloaks around themselves, leaned their heads together, and closed their eyes.

All around was bustle and confusion, the roar of the engine, the black smoke falling. Daniel stopped a station attendant who was passing by. "Where do we get the train for Pittsburgh?"

"Right here, sir. Five-thirty sharp." He hurried on past.

The train they had arrived on began backing up. Panic seized Daniel. "Wait!" he shouted. He ran after the station attendant and caught his arm. "My trunks are still on that train!"

"Naw, they're all unloaded." He pointed to a pile of baggage farther down the platform. There was a crowd around it, baggage men with carts moving bags and trunks off in several directions.

Daniel ran.

At first he could find only one trunk. He looked around frantically. A second trunk was at the far side of the heap. He pushed through the crowd, grabbed the handle, and dragged it next to the first one. He couldn't see the third one. His heart pounded. A stout woman shoved by him and pulled two suitcases out of the pile. The third trunk was underneath. Daniel's legs shook as he retrieved it. Panting and shivering in the predawn cold, he looked down the platform at the twins, innocent and vulnerable, dozing on their bench. People flowed by them. A tall man in a ragged coat stopped and bent over to peer into their faces. Daniel gathered himself. The man moved on.

Daniel turned to one of the baggage men. "Where should I take these trunks to get them on the train to Pittsburgh?"

"Just leave them right here, sir. The Pittsburgh train'll be around in about fifteen minutes. I'll see they get loaded on for you." He took a long look at Daniel. "There's coffee in the station, sir."

"Thank you." Daniel went back to the twins. "Would you girls like some coffee?"

They lifted their heads. "No, thank you, Papa," one murmured.

One answers for both of them. He shook his head slightly, went into the station, and got coffee, hurrying, still fearful. He was standing by the twins, sipping his coffee, with an eye on the trunks down the platform, when the Pittsburgh train pulled up. A young conductor leaned out from the steps of the passenger car chanting, "Harrisburg, Altoona, Johnstown, *Pitts*burgh. All aboard!"

In the bustle of boarding, Daniel lost sight of the trunks. The whistle blew, the train lurched into motion. He and the twins found seats and stowed their bags. The twins curled up on their seat and went back to sleep. Daniel fidgeted. Had the trunks really gotten loaded? What if they hadn't? Panic washed through him. He hesitated, tense, then abruptly got up, and walked through the train to the baggage car. The space between the cars was dark and windy, rocking precariously. He pushed open the door to the baggage car and stepped in. One lamp swung from the ceiling. The baggage man was slouched on the floor, leaning back against the mail bags, dozing. He sat up.

"What're you doing?"

"I'm looking for my trunks. I want to be sure they got loaded on."

The baggage man scratched his beard, spat a wad of tobacco at Daniel's feet, and grinned. His left eye tooth was missing and the rest of his teeth were yellow. "And what if they didn't? Can't turn the train back, ya know."

Daniel stepped back and stiffened. "Nonetheless, I need to know if they are here. In what part of this car"—he looked around, inwardly despairing, at the confusion of crates, bags, and luggage—"would trunks bound for Pittsburgh be stored?"

"Pittsburgh, eh?" The man got to his feet and ambled toward the back of the car.

Daniel followed. The trunks were there.

The twins slept until the train rounded a curve heading north and the morning sun shone through the window into their faces. They stirred, sat up, and smiled at Daniel.

"Good morning, Papa."

"Where are we?"

"Somewhere in Pennsylvania," he answered. "Are you ready for breakfast?"

They got the lunch box down and shared out the packets Becky had labeled for breakfast—more cornbread, applesauce, cold bacon.

After breakfast, Daniel began to relax. He sat watching the twins, who were pressed together looking out the window. They were used to being physically close, he noticed, almost always touching, leaning against each other, holding hands. He remembered how Becky had said to him once, "There's no getting so much as a blade of grass between those two."

All through the day before, he'd thought at times he could tell them apart from their attitudes and way of speaking, but then he became confused again. Now, as he observed them, he was pretty sure that Rose was the one closest to the window, and Lily the one leaning around her to look out.

"Lily, Rose," he said aloud, musing. They turned their heads to smile at him.

"You know, it was your mother who named you. Usually the father names the children. I remember her holding you and saying you were her little blossoms. I wanted to give you names of Christian virtues, like your mother's name, Grace, but she insisted on flower names. So Lily and Rose you became."

"What would you have named us, Papa?" asked the one he thought was Lily.

"Prudence and Charity were the names I had in mind."

"Prudence and Charity!" they exclaimed in horrified unison, the corners of their mouths turned down.

"I'm glad it was Mama who named us," said the one he thought was Rose.

After a pause, Lily said, "Well, even if we don't have names of Christian virtues, we do have Biblical names."

Daniel frowned. "How's that?"

Lily tilted her head and looked at him mischievously. "Consider the lilies of the field, and Jesus rose from the dead."

"Lily, you're being flippant," Daniel admonished.

"I'm not Lily, I'm Rose."

Daniel looked from one to the other, confused again. The twin by the window met the eyes of the one who had just spoken, and shook her head slightly. They both started laughing.

"What's so funny?" Daniel asked, annoyed.

They didn't answer. The whistle blew as the train passed through a village. The twin by the window exclaimed, "Look, Lily. They're waving at us!"

Daniel tightened his jaw. That *was* Lily. She lied to me.

The whistle blew again and the train picked up speed as it left the village behind. The young conductor, coming through the car, winked at the twins.

"Lily," Daniel said sternly, "you lied to me."

Lily bit her lower lip and bent her head, lifting only her eyes to look up at him. "It wasn't really lying, Papa. I was just teasing you. You get such a funny look on your face when you can't figure out who is who."

They giggled. Rose said, "It *is* a funny look. You get your brow all scrunched up."

More giggles. Daniel didn't know whether to laugh with them, or be angry.

"It's not just you," Rose added. "We've always had fun confusing people. Becky would just laugh."

"Well, I'll not have it. It's disrespectful. I want to know to whom I am speaking. Do you understand?"

"Yes, Papa," they said in unison.

Daniel reached into his bag and pulled out his book. *How do they do that, speak at the same time, as if they were one person? Well, I hope that's settled. I need to teach them respect.* A moment later, he glanced up. They were looking at each other, dimpling, eyes dancing, sharing wordlessly some mischievous secret.

~

Later, after a short stop in Harrisburg, one of the twins stood to pull the lunch box down. She handed out the packets Becky had labeled for lunch of the second day.

"Thank you, Lily," Daniel said.

"I'm Rose." The twins giggled. "Really," Rose said.

Lily chuckled. "Oh, Papa, your face is all scrunched up again."

Their giggles bubbled up and spilled over, so infectious that Daniel couldn't help smiling. "All right, all right." He put his hand up to feel his brow, setting off another round of hilarity.

Finally, after a few gasps and sighs, they settled down.

As they ate, Rose said, "Papa, it's not really so hard to tell us apart. We each have a swirl here in our hair." She pointed to the center of her forehead. "Mine goes to the left and Lily's goes to the right."

"Of course," Lily put in, "it would be easier if mine went to the left and Rose's went to the right—"

"Then you could remember because it would be alliterated—"

"Left for Lily, right for Rose—"

"But it isn't—"

"It's opposite—"

Daniel's brow scrunched even deeper. The rapidity of their words, coming from first one and then the other, and the bewildering way they interrupted each other to finish each other's sentences completely confused him. He'd always had trouble telling left from right, ever since he had started writing with his left hand when he was five and been sternly admonished to use his right.

The twins had stopped talking and were looking at him, struggling not to laugh again.

"I'll remember that," was all he could say. *They giggle all the time, he thought. Do all young girls do that?*

~

Daniel dozed off and on through the afternoon. He waked when the door of the car slammed open and the conductor called "Al*too*na."

As the train slowed the young conductor came and leaned against the corner of their seat. Daniel watched him suspiciously. His cap was set at an angle on his russet curls. He had stopped by during the day, more often than his duties demanded, Daniel thought, and his roguish amber eyes rested all too freely on the twins.

"We'll be stopping here in Altoona to add another engine to the back of the train, to push it up the mountain," he informed them. "It's a steep climb and we need the extra power to get up there. If you get out when we stop, you can see the mountains, the Alleghenies they're called, just ahead of us in the west."

Lily jumped up. "Let's get out and see." The train jerked to a stop, throwing her against the young conductor.

Daniel leaped up and grabbed her arm. "Lily, sit down."

The young conductor recovered himself, went on down the car, and swung out onto the metal steps.

Departing passengers filled the aisle. Daniel and the twins followed the last one out. As the young conductor helped the twins down the steps, his hand lingered on Lily's elbow. Daniel, watching, bristled.

The mountains were aglow in late afternoon sunshine.

"We're going up there?" Rose breathed.

"So wild and high!" Lily exclaimed.

Daniel stood behind them, his heart sinking, seeing only another barrier, soon to be crossed, between him and all he loved and knew.

The next two days passed like an endless dream—the stopping, the starting again, the passengers moving out and on, the roaring, rattling rocking of the train, the long, lonely whistle. Pastures, farmlands, woodlands, villages, the back yards of cities flashed by the window.

Daniel slept little, tormented at night by longings, memories, regrets. Days were easier. The twins' delight in all their experiences rubbed off on him, and he found himself forgetting his homesickness at times and entering into their spirit of adventure.

There were more train changes. Somehow, miraculously Daniel felt, the trunks were still with them. The last change was in Hannibal. It was evening.

They were to travel across Missouri that night and arrive in the morning at St. Joseph on the Missouri River, the westernmost end of the railroad.

Once they were settled in their new seats, Rose opened the lunch box. "It's almost gone, just the packets for tonight and breakfast tomorrow."

"Becky has taken good care of us," Daniel said.

"I miss her." Lily had sudden tears in her eyes.

"I do, too." Rose put her arms around Lily.

"She was like our mother, after Mama died—"

"Tucked us in at night. Kissed us and hugged us—"

"Combed our hair and told us stories—"

"Scolded us and made us laugh—"

The twins leaned their heads together, holding each other tight.

Daniel's heart ached in sympathy. "How about your grandmama?" he asked. "Was she like a mother to you, too?"

"She was like a grandmother."

"She taught us."

"She loved us, we know, but she didn't like to show it."

"Not like Becky."

Rose sighed, kissed Lily, and turned back to the lunch box to hand out the packets for their supper. After they had blessed the food and eaten, the twins repacked the box and put it overhead again. The three of them sat in silence, rocking with the motion of the train.

"Papa," Lily said after a while. "We want to ask you something."

"What is it?"

The twins looked at each other for a moment. Rose reached out and took Lily's hand.

"Why …?" she started. She looked over at Lily.

"After Mama died," Lily picked up. "You didn't play with us anymore. Remember how you used to hold us on your knee and sing to us—"

"And chase us around the house, playing hide and seek—"

"And toss us in the air?"

"Then Mama died, and we were all so sad, and you never played with us again."

"Or even looked at us, or spoke to us."

"Why?"

They looked across at him, tears in their eyes.

Daniel shut his eyes. His stomach clenched. The wheels of the train screeched as it rounded a curve.

He opened his eyes again to look into their eyes. "I ... I couldn't. You look so much like her. I couldn't bear to see you. Every time I saw you, you reminded me ... I missed her very much. I'm sorry. I shouldn't have abandoned you." He struggled with his own tears. Closed his eyes again.

In a swift movement, the twins came to sit on either side of him.

"Papa, it's okay."

"It's okay now."

They kissed his cheeks. Daniel sighed and opened his eyes, shifted to put his arms around them. They rested their heads on his shoulders.

The train roared on into the darkness.

## Chapter 9

# *Council Bluffs*

I wish Papa would hurry up and come back." Lily stood at the window of their small boardinghouse room in Council Bluffs. "I'm tired of being cooped up here; I want to go out and see the town."

They had arrived the night before, after their steamboat trip up the river from St. Joseph. Daniel had left after breakfast, served downstairs in the dining room by their dour landlady, Mrs. Grundy. He'd told them to stay in the room until he got back.

They had ordered hot water and bathed, opened their trunks and found clean clothes, washed the railroad soot out of their traveling clothes, and hung them on a rope across one end of the room. They'd even written a long letter to Becky and their grandmama—and still Daniel had not returned.

"I hope he's all right." Rose joined Lily at the window. "He's been gone a long time."

"Don't worry. He's okay." Lily took Rose's hand. "I just wonder what he's been doing."

They stood together gazing out. From their window they could look down on the river, the ferry, the wagons lined up on the road to the ferry, and the river valley overflowing with wagons, tents, carts, and cattle.

"The river looks wild," Rose said. "It didn't seem so bad when we were coming up it yesterday in the big steamboat. But that ferry doesn't look very substantial. I guess we'll be going across on it soon."

"Not until we get our wagon and supplies."

"Then we'll be in the midst of all that down there." Rose leaned her forehead against the window. "All those people going west. It looks like more people than in the whole city of Boston."

"I know. It's chaotic, except for over there." Lily pointed. "Those wagons are all in a circle. I wonder what kind of group that is."

"There's Papa!" Rose exclaimed. "Coming up the hill."

They dashed out of the room and down the stairs. Daniel was just coming in the door.

"Papa!" they called, and ran to kiss him. "Where have you been?"

Daniel took off his hat and wiped his muddy feet on the doormat. "I've been looking for Jake Abrams all morning, but no luck in finding him. There are so many men and wagons … The blacksmith said he keeps his wagons in a circle, but I couldn't see a circle anywhere, just total confusion. People yelling, a gun fight—"

"We know where the circle is," Lily interrupted.

"We saw it from our window. Come and see."

The twins caught his hands and pulled him up the stairs. At the window of their room they pointed out the circled wagons.

"Sure enough." Daniel blew out his breath. "Easier to see from up here."

"Let's go find him." Lily danced from one foot to the other.

"I'll go. You girls stay here. It's too rough out there."

Lily stamped her foot. "We've *been* staying here."

"Please, Papa." Rose kissed his cheek. "We'll stay close by you. We can help."

Daniel looked from one to the other and sighed. "All right. But you must stay right beside me. No running off."

"We promise."

"Let's look at the circle one more time from here," Rose suggested, "and note some landmarks. We might lose it again when we're down below in the middle of all the people and wagons."

"Good idea." Daniel went to the window again. The twins came to either side of him.

After figuring out the best route to the circle, they set out. The road in front of the boarding house led to the ferry road, which wound down the steep bluff to the river. It was clogged with wagons and cattle waiting their turn for the ferry. Daniel and the twins had to walk along the very edge of the road to avoid being trampled.

Near the river, a narrow muddy track went off to the left and led down into the midst of the tents and wagons. Daniel stopped and turned back to the twins. "Stay close behind me."

"We're right here, Papa."

The path was too narrow for them to walk side by side, but the twins clung to each other's hands, Lily walking in front. Over the underlying hubbub of many living beings crammed close together, they could hear men's voices arguing, children crying, a gun shot, donkeys braying. The smell of manure, leather, human sweat filled their nostrils.

Before long they came to the edge of the circle of wagons and stepped inside. It was quieter there, somehow, with a sense of order. They approached a small man in a wide-brimmed black hat, who was bending over, examining his mule's hoof.

"Good day," Daniel greeted him. "Could you tell me where I could find Mr. Jacob Abrams?"

The man stood up, smiled a wide, snaggletoothed smile and held out his hand. "Name's Gabe," he said. "Gabe Archen, but most folks just call me Gabe." The brim of his hat was frayed; threads dangled down to mingle with his straight black hair.

Daniel shook his hand. "Reverend Daniel Wright."

Gabe peered around Daniel to look at the twins. "And who we got here?"

"These are my daughters, Miss Lily Wright and Miss Rose Wright."

"Pleased to meet you, Lily, Rose." He held out a lean brown hand. His black eyes were so bright, his smile so engaging, his whole air so enchantingly rakish, that the twins dimpled, holding in their delighted laughter.

"Pleased to meet you, Mr. Gabe." They each shook his hand, suddenly feeling happier than they had all day.

Gabe turned to Daniel. "Did'y say you're a preacher? Are you wanting to go West with Jake?"

"Yes and yes." Daniel was smiling, too.

"Thanks be to sweet Jesus. We done got us a doctor for the bodies, but we ain't got no preacher for the souls. Jake's over yonder." Gabe pointed across the circle. "That tall fellow in the red shirt, a'giving grief to poor Mr. Dunin 'cause his wagon's so rickety."

"Thanks." Daniel nodded to Gabe. Gabe nodded back, smiling his gap-toothed smile.

Daniel and the twins crossed the circle and approached the man Gabe had pointed out. To say that Jake Abrams was tall was an understatement. He was a giant of a man, bearded and barrel-chested. In spite of the cold, his shirt sleeves were rolled up, and his head and huge muscular arms were bare. His long hair blew loose in the wind.

He was examining the wheels on a run-down covered wagon. A sallow-faced woman looked out from inside. A thin gray-haired man slouched against the side of the wagon and whined, "It'll cost a lot of money."

"Don't argue with me." Jake's voice was as big as his body. "You need new wheels, that's flat. Look at the cracks in the rims, here and here. These ones'll never make it to Denver City."

He turned to Daniel. "Hey, there. Who're you?" Piercing blue eyes shone out above his bushy brown beard.

"Daniel Wright. Are you Mr. Jacob Abrams?"

"Jake, I go by. What can I do for you?"

"I'm heading out to the Colorado Territory. Eli Erickson gave me your name and recommended I travel with you."

"Eli." Jake's white teeth flashed in a smile. "I remember him. Good man, Eli. Helped me pull a drowning man out of the Elkhorn last summer. But this wagon train's full, mister. Got fifteen wagons. That's all I take."

"But …" Daniel stammered.

"Do you have a preacher in your wagon train?" Lily stepped out from behind Daniel. "Mr. Gabe said you didn't and you need one. Our Papa's a preacher."

Jake seemed to notice the twins for the first time. "What's this?" He put his hands on his hips and stepped back, surveying them. "Twins? How do you tell 'em apart?"

"I sometimes have trouble," Daniel acknowledged.

Jake slapped his thigh and laughed. "Even their own pa can't tell?" He sobered. "Is she right? You're a preacher?"

"Yes. I'm Reverend Daniel Wright, an ordained Presbyterian minister, recently from Boston, on my way to serve a new parish in Gold Creek in the Colorado Territory."

"Hmm. So Gabe thinks we need a preacher. How big's your party?"

"Just myself and my two daughters."

"How many wagons?"

"Just one. I don't have it yet. We got here only yesterday."

"One wagon, eh?" Jake sighed and rubbed his beard the wrong way up the side of his face. "Well … I guess I could stretch it for one more wagon, one with a preacher and twins their pa can't tell apart." He laughed and winked at Lily. "Perky little lady you got there."

Jake turned to the man leaning on the wagon. "Get those wheels replaced and a spare as well, or you don't travel with me. I don't want you breaking down in the middle of nowhere. There's a wheelwright up in town, right on the main road. Caulk the bottom, too. We've got rivers to cross."

Daniel looked at the twins, and let out his breath. "Thanks, Lily."

Jake turned back to Daniel. "We need to talk. Follow me." He led them to the middle of the wagon circle where logs were arranged around a fire pit. He gestured. "Have a seat."

Lily and Rose gathered their cloaks around them and sat down beside their father.

"My price is one hundred dollars a wagon. That's for guiding and protecting you, and to pay two outriders who'll help with that." Jake looked a question at Daniel.

Daniel nodded. "That's okay."

"Now I don't take anyone who's not well equipped. What you got?"

"Not much yet. Just three trunks with our personal belongings. Mr. Erickson said it was best to travel light."

"Right. We'll start from scratch then."

Rose took a pad and pencil out of her apron pocket.

"A wagon. There's a wagon crafter at the far end of town. Get a spare wheel and have him attach it on the underside of the wagon. Be sure the floor is caulked. Two yoke of oxen. Towry Ranch down river has good oxen and horses. You'll want a horse for hunting. You got a gun?"

Daniel shook his head.

"You'll need one. Boston, did you say? Are you a city boy?"

Daniel straightened his shoulders and lifted his chin just slightly. "I've lived in Boston recently, serving a church there, but I grew up on a farm. I can hunt. I know how to handle oxen and horses."

"How about your girls?"

"They grew up in the city, but they've spent their summers on the farm."

"Grandpa says we have a way with animals," Lily put in.

"We've had riding lessons," Rose added.

Jake looked from one twin to the other. "That's good," he said. "You'll need tools," he went on addressing Daniel. "A pick and shovel, an ax, an awl and a ball of rawhide string for making repairs. Rope, lots of rope. Replacement harnesses, a bucket of grease for the wagon ..." It was a long list.

Rose wrote busily.

"Food for eight weeks. If all goes well, we'll make it in six, but things can come up. Sometimes we can buy supplies at the ranches along the road, and usually we can get some game, but you can't count on it. Flour, bacon, rice, coffee, dried apples, dried beans, baking powder, dried meat. Whatever else you can find that you like to eat, as long as it isn't perishable. You girls have cooking equipment?"

"We have a soup pot, bread pans—"

"A coffee pot, plates, cups and utensils."

"You got a dutch oven?"

The twins shook their heads.

"You might want to get one." Jake glanced at the twins' shoes. "You'll need good boots. Not fancy ones, but sturdy comfortable ones. High tops protect from snake bites. Two pairs each. You'll go through 'em. You'll be walking over five hundred miles in the next couple of months."

"Five hundred miles!" Lily exclaimed.

"Won't we be riding in the wagon?" Rose asked.

"Maybe some of the time, if you get tired. But even the weight of you two young ladies makes a difference to the oxen. They have the hardest job, pulling the wagons; we got to make it as easy as we can for them… You'll all need hats with big brims to protect from the sun."

He shifted his huge frame on the log and scratched his beard. "I think that's it. There's a ladies' apparel shop on the main street. Mrs. Garland there can advise you girls. A cobbler two doors down for your boots. You can get your tools at the trading post. Come back down here tonight at dusk. I've called a meeting for the whole train. In the meantime, start getting your gear together. We're on the ferry register to cross the river in five days."

"All right." Daniel stood. "Thank you."

"See you tonight." Jake clapped Daniel on the shoulder with his massive hand, nodded to the twins, and strode off.

The town of Council Bluffs sat above the river, wedged between two high bluffs. The main street was muddy and deeply rutted. As Daniel and the twins walked through town to find the wagon crafter, they noted Mrs. Garland's shingle and, a little farther on, the cobbler shop.

"We'll come back to those," Daniel said as they passed. "The wagon's first."

At the far end of town, down a narrow road that led off to the left, they saw a small log cabin with a long board building beside it, nestled up against the foot of the bluff. In the field surrounding it, there were numerous wagons, some with white covers.

"That looks like the place." Daniel lengthened his stride.

The door to the long building stood open. They could hear the sound of hammering and men's voices.

Daniel walked to the door and called, "Hello."

A short pot-bellied man came to meet them. He held a stubby black pipe in his teeth and wore his pants, held up by bright blue suspenders, high over his round belly.

"G'd afternoon," he said. "You looking for a wagon?"

"Yes," Daniel answered. "We're heading out to the Colorado Territory in a few days."

"Well, you've come to the right place. Jeff Jerome's my name. Best wagon crafter on the Missouri River."

"Daniel Wright." They shook hands.

"I've got 'em four-by-ten and six-by-twelve. All made of oak. All my covers are sturdy canvas, waterproofed with linseed oil, pockets built into the inside. Have a look at this one."

He led Daniel to a covered wagon at the end of the building. The twins followed close behind.

"This one here's a six-by-twelve. Your girls going with you?"

"Yes," Daniel answered. The twins were already peeking into the end of the wagon.

"Then you'll probably want a six-by-twelve." He gestured toward the front of the wagon. "I built a box under the jockey seat for storing your tools. I can add a water barrel with a spigot to hang on the side." He moved to the back of the wagon. "This here's the hand brake. You lean on it like this when you want to go slower downhill. This here's the chuck box. Metal. Latches tight. Keeps the varmints out. The side panel folds out to make a table." He demonstrated. "It's extra."

The twins had crowded close. "Look at that!" Lily exclaimed.

Rose opened and closed the side. "We should get one of these, Papa." She peered inside. "Look, there's cubby holes to keep everything organized."

"Can we go inside the wagon?" Rose asked.

"I want to see the pockets," Lily said.

"Lively crew you got there." Mr. Jerome shifted his pipe to the other side of his mouth. It was out, but he didn't seem to care. "Wait a minute, little miss. There's a step here by the tongue." He took Lily's elbow as she climbed up, then helped Rose up after her.

Mr. Jerome turned back to Daniel. "You want the chuck box? Your girls seem to, and I reckon they'll be doing the cooking."

"Okay … The chuck box is probably a good idea. I want the floor caulked and a spare wheel."

"My wagon bottoms are all caulked. I can hang a spare wheel underneath. How about the water barrel?"

"Probably should get that."

Mr. Jerome tilted his head toward the log cabin. "The wife makes mattresses, straw and corn husk with a sturdy cover."

"Look, Papa." Rose stuck her head out the back of the wagon. "You can close the end all the way by pulling these ropes like this." The end closed, she disappeared, and immediately reappeared. "Let's get the mattresses."

Lily's head popped out beside hers. "One for us and one for you."

Daniel rubbed his brow. "How much will all this cost?"

"Let's see." Mr. Jerome took a pad out of his back pocket and jotted. "Six-by-twelve wagon, cover, water barrel, chuck box, spare wheel … You want the mattresses?"

Daniel nodded.

"Two mattresses… . That'll come to two hundred seventy dollars."

Daniel drew in his breath. "All right," he said after a moment. "When can you have it all ready?"

Mr. Jerome shifted his pipe again. "Tomorrow afternoon. I'll fix up this one for you, and you'll be set to go."

The twins jumped down from the tongue of the wagon, and came to Daniel.

"We can put the trunks along the sides with the mattresses on top during the daytime—"

"Spread them out on the floor in between at night."

"It will be so cozy."

"We can keep our instruments, and our hair brushes in the pockets."

"You didn't see the pockets, Papa."

"They're very handy."

"All right, girls." Daniel turned to Mr. Jerome. "We'll be by tomorrow afternoon, after we get our oxen."

As they walked away, Daniel muttered under his breath. "Two seventy for the wagon, sixty or seventy each for two yoke of oxen, two hundred or more for a horse, tools, gun, food …"

The twins, who had been walking behind him, came to either side of him.

"Are you worried about money, Papa?" Rose asked.

"Don't worry," Lily said. "We have money."

"Grandmama gave us each a lot of money—"

"In case something happened and we were separated from you."

"We can help with the expenses."

Daniel stopped in the middle of the road. "Your grandmama gave you money? Where is it?"

Lily patted her apron. "Right here. We each have a little belt with a pocket that we wear under our skirts."

"Really!" Daniel looked from one to the other. "Your grandmama is very generous. But I have enough to get us supplied. You keep your money safe for emergencies, as she intended."

The cobbler shop was busy with four men seated at benches, cutting and sewing. Daniel found ready-made boots that fit him and ordered another pair. The proprietor measured the twins, and promised two pairs of boots would be ready for each of them in two days.

"Now." Lily gave a little skip. "Mrs. Garland's."

Mrs. Garland's shop had lace curtains at the window, a carpet on the floor, comfortable chairs, and a big mirror on one wall. Mrs. Garland was pink-cheeked and plump, wearing a white ruffled apron over her gray gown. When Daniel and the twins entered, she had pins in her mouth and was adjusting the waist of a short red skirt worn by a young woman in bloomers. She looked up at them as they hesitated by the door, took the pins out of her mouth, and said, "Hello. I'll be with you in just a moment."

Daniel and the twins stared at the bloomers.

"There now, Mrs. Bradley," Mrs. Garland said, "how does that look to you?"

Mrs. Bradley turned sideways to the mirror to survey her back view, tossed her long black curls, and said, "I like it."

"Very well. We'll make these adjustments for you and you can pick up your order tomorrow morning."

"*Mrs.* Bradley!" Lily whispered. "She doesn't look even as old as we are."

"And wearing her hair loose," Rose whispered back.

Daniel shifted from one foot to the other. "I think I'll go to the trading post and look at tools while you girls do your business here. Just don't leave until I come back."

"We won't, Papa."

"And *no bloomers*!" he said, his voice low and intense.

The twins dimpled. "Okay, Papa."

Daniel left. Mrs. Bradley tossed her curls again and went out through a door at the back of the room. When the door opened, the twins could see two young women sitting at a work table, sewing.

Mrs. Garland smiled at the twins. "What can I do for you today? You must be twins. How pretty you are."

"Thank you," Rose said, smiling back at her. "We've come for travel clothes."

"We're going to the Colorado Territory in a few days."

"Traveling with Mr. Abrams."

Mrs. Garland nodded. "Jake takes good care of his folks. He probably told you you needed sunbonnets."

"Yes, two each."

"And we each want a traveling dress."

"He said you could advise us."

"Of course." Mrs. Garland beamed at them. "What are your names, dears?"

"Lily."

"And Rose."

"Lily and Rose. How lovely. Now then, linsey-woolsey's best, for durability and protecting you from the wind and sun. I have several designs I can make up for you. You saw Mrs. Bradley just now in bloomers. They're very practical."

"Papa said—"

"The last thing he said was—"

"No bloomers."

Mrs. Garland chuckled. "Aren't you cute, the way you finish each other's sentences. Now I can make you a simple practical gown of linsey-woolsey like the ones you're wearing, but I have another design that perhaps your papa wouldn't object to. It's a split skirt."

Mrs. Bradley emerged from the back room. "I heard you say you are going with Jake," she said to the twins. "We are too, me and my husband. We just got married. Isn't it exciting?"

"Yes." The twins smiled at her.

She flounced out the door calling back, "I'll be seeing you."

"A split skirt?" Lily asked Mrs. Garland.

"Yes. You can't really tell that it's split unless you sit astride a horse, but it's easier to walk in. You'll be walking a long way in the next couple of months. I really recommend the split skirt if your papa won't allow bloomers."

The twins looked at each other. "Let's," Lily said.

"I wonder how long it will take Papa to notice."

"Probably a long time. He's not too observant."

"We'll do it."

"Fine." Mrs. Garland nodded. "I know you'll appreciate the freedom. Come here now. Let's choose what color you'd like." She took down several bolts of cloth from a shelf in the corner.

After much discussion, the twins decided on green linsey-woolsey gowns with split skirts.

"You'll look lovely in the green," Mrs. Garland beamed. "Let me measure you now."

As she measured she said, "I can make you a little woolen vest to go under the bodice. The wind blows cold on the plains this time of year. You would be glad of it."

"That sounds like a good idea." Lily said. Rose nodded.

"All right. My girls will get to work on your dresses and vests right away," Mrs. Garland said. "We can have them for you day after tomorrow. Now sunbonnets. I have some ready-made." She pulled out a box from under the shelf. "There are colors here that should go well with your green."

The twins had finished selecting their bonnets and were paying for them when Daniel returned, wearing a new, wide-brimmed black hat.

"Don't tell," Rose whispered to Mrs. Garland.

Mrs. Garland smiled and nodded.

"Hi, Papa," Lily greeted him. "You have a new hat."

"Yes." Daniel turned his head to the side. "What do you think?"

"Very distinguished," Rose said. "Papa, this is Mrs. Garland. She's been helping us plan travel clothes."

"Pleased to meet you." Daniel nodded.

"And these are our new hats." Rose put on one of the sunbonnets. The brim extended four inches in front of her face. "They give you a very narrow perspective."

Daniel studied the sunbonnet. "So I see."

"Never mind," Mrs. Garland said. "They will protect you well from the sun. That's what they're for."

The twins thanked Mrs. Garland and followed Daniel out the door.

As they approached the trading post, they had to step around two dogs playing in the road. One mounted the other and began rutting. The twins stopped to stare.

"Lily, Rose, come!" Daniel grabbed them roughly by the arms and almost dragged them through the trading-post door.

∾

There was a fire burning in the center of the wagon circle when Daniel and the twins returned that evening. The people of the wagon train gathered, settling themselves on the logs that surrounded the fire. The twins, wrapped in their cloaks, sat on either side of Daniel and looked around the circle. There were two young couples with small children nestled in their laps. Three middle-sized boys scuffled on the ground at the edge of the fire, poking it with sticks. Mrs. Bradley waved to the twins as she emerged from the biggest and fanciest wagon with her handsome young husband. Gabe nodded and smiled at the twins. Across the circle, Mr. Dunin, dragging his sallow-faced wife, stumbled and almost fell onto the log next to another older couple with pinched faces and tight lips. All the rest were men, some young, some with gray in their hair.

Jake strode into the center of the circle. The firelight flickered on his massive frame and cast a long shadow behind him. "Stephen," he said, "do a head count."

A lean young man, with brown curls spilling out from under his faded blue hat, stepped up beside him and counted. "All here," he reported.

"All right," Jake said. "I've called you together because I want you to understand the rules of this wagon train. Anyone who doesn't agree with these rules can still leave before we cross the river on Monday." He looked around the circle with his piercing blue eyes. At his glance, the young boys sat still and fell silent.

"Rules one through three: no gambling, no fighting, no drinking—no exceptions. Anyone with whiskey will give it to Dr. Franz, who will keep it for medicinal purposes.

"I've been taking two trains each season, Council Bluffs to Denver City, since they first found gold there. I know the path and the dangers. You've hired me to guide you. So, rule four. When I give an order to move or to stop or to circle up, or any other command, you do it. If we're in an emergency, I don't want to waste time arguing. Any problem with that?" He looked around. The circle was silent.

"Okay. Of all the dangers on this journey, the worst is not Indians or wolves or rivers, but people shooting themselves or each other with firearms they don't know how to handle. Rule number five—never keep caps in your gun unless you're going to shoot, and take your caps out when you come back from the hunt. Pay attention to what you're doing whenever you have a gun in your hands. If you all do that, we might make it to Denver City without any of you killing a member of your family or shooting your own foot off.

"Rule number six concerns Indians."

"Savages," the pinch-faced woman muttered.

Jake turned to her, frowning. "Mrs. Shively, they are people. A different culture, but otherwise people like us. We're crossing their land. It is their custom to offer a gift when they cross another tribe's land. I've asked all of you to have gifts for them. We give them gifts and treat them with respect, and then hopefully they don't bother us."

"Respect!" Mrs. Shively exclaimed.

Jake raised his voice slightly. "Yes, respect. It just takes one person being disrespectful to put the whole train in danger. Do you understand?"

Mrs. Shively did not answer. Her husband sat beside her, stony-faced. Jake continued looking at her for a long moment, his eyes fierce.

He lifted his gaze to address the whole circle. "Those are the rules," he said. "Any problems?"

A man stood up in the back. "No whiskey? Not even a little nip at the end of the day?"

"No drinking any time of day." Jake brought his hand down in a decisive gesture. "Drink causes trouble." He paused a moment, regarding the man, then said more gently, "If you can't do without your nip, this isn't the wagon train for you."

The man sat down. There were mutterings in the group near him, then silence.

A gust of wind blew in from the river. The waning moon, just past full, rose orange above the bluffs. Jake looked over the circle again. "Any other questions?"

Mrs. Shively stood. "Will we be resting on the Sabbath, as the Lord commanded?"

"Probably. We'll all need a day of rest, oxen and mules as well as people, and we'll do it on the Sabbath if possible. But if there's a danger near, or a river that must be crossed before a storm, or any other threat to your safety, we'll travel whatever the day. Rule number four."

Mrs. Shively sat down and mumbled something to her husband. A ripple of conversation went around the circle.

"Anything else?" The rising wind blew Jake's hair back from his face and fluttered the fringe on his jacket. There was no response.

"Ben, Stephen," he said, "come up here."

A short dark man, stocky and muscular, wearing a red bandana around his brow, came to stand beside Jake. Stephen came to his other side.

Jake clapped them on the shoulder as he named them. "This is Stephen, this is Ben. They're our outriders. They'll ride ahead to find campgrounds, game, and water. Or be available if help is needed. They're good men, have traveled with me before. In any emergency, obey them as you would me.

"We're lucky to have a doctor in our train. Dr. Franz, would you stand up?"

Dr. Franz stood with quiet grace. The firelight flickered on his kindly face, glinted on the gray in his hair. He nodded to the circle and sat down again.

"We're also fortunate to have a preacher," Jake said. He gestured to Daniel. Daniel stood, tall and elegant in the firelight. "Reverend Wright will be giving us some prayers as we travel, leading services on Sundays. Everyone is invited to attend, no one is required."

The wind blew stronger. The twins shivered in their cloaks and pressed close to Daniel when he sat down again. Clouds raced across the moon.

"I think that's it," Jake said. "We're on the ferry register to cross the river on Monday. Everyone must be in camp before dark on Sunday night. We'll pull out of here at dawn and line up on the ferry road. Once we're across, the journey begins."

～

The next morning Daniel and the twins were up early for their trip downriver to Towry Ranch, where they hoped to find oxen and a good saddle horse for Daniel. Daniel hired a cab, a dilapidated buggy with an elderly, bewhiskered driver.

The cabby dropped them off at a big rambling barn where several men and a tall lean woman wearing a man's brown leather hat were bringing the horses out for the day.

"Who's in charge here?" Daniel asked a short, burly man.

"She is." He jerked his head toward the woman.

The twins watched with amusement as Daniel swallowed his surprise. He beckoned to them and approached the woman. "Morning ma'am. I'm Reverend Wright. These are my daughters, Lily and Rose. We're heading out West in a couple of days and looking for two yoke of oxen and a good saddle horse."

The woman held out a leather-gloved hand. "Zena Towry," she said. "I've got some oxen left. Come and see." As she strode toward the corral, the twins saw that her skirt was split. They nudged each other and watched to see if Daniel would notice. He was oblivious, focused on oxen.

For the next half hour, he and Zena Towry examined the oxen, discussing their attributes. The twins followed close behind, adding their opinions about which ones he should choose.

"These white ones have good coats."

"That means they're healthy."

"Don't get that one. These ones over here look sturdier."

Finally Daniel settled on a pair of white and a pair of brown steers with white faces, apparently unaware of how much the twins had influenced his selection.

"Do they have names, Mrs. Towry?" Rose asked.

"*Miss* Towry. No, I haven't named them." A thin-lipped smile touched her stern, tanned face. "That'll be for you to do."

The twins scratched the heads of the brown steers, stroked the sides of the white ones. "We'll give you good names," Lily promised.

Miss Towry did not allow the twins into the horse pasture. She and Daniel walked among the horses, while the twins leaned on the fence.

At length Daniel chose a tall mare, coal black except for a white blaze on her chest.

"Her name's Shadow," Miss Towry said, as she slipped a halter over Shadow's head.

"Shadow?" Daniel frowned.

"That's her name. She's a sturdy one. She'll get you there, and she's gentle enough for your girls to ride. She's a good cattle horse, too. I've used her the last few years for round-up." Miss Towry saddled her up, and Daniel rode her around the pasture.

"She looks like a good horse," Lily said to Rose.

Rose nodded. "I think so, too. I hope he'll let us ride her."

Daniel rode back to the fence. "All right. I'll take her."

He and Miss Towry bargained over prices for the horse and the oxen. Miss Towry threw in a saddle and bridle and yokes for the oxen, and invited them to the noonday meal at the ranch. "It's a long hike back up to Council Bluffs," she said. "You'll need some vittles."

"Thank you, Miss Towry," Lily said.

"We *are* hungry," Rose added.

"That's quite a pair you've got there," Miss Towry commented to Daniel. "A yoke of girls. Plenty of opinions about everything. And pretty enough to be trouble. Have they set Council Bluffs on its ear yet?"

"No. Nor shall they," Daniel replied.

It was early afternoon when Daniel and the twins set out along the rough river road toward Council Bluffs. Daniel had yoked the oxen together, the brown ones in front and the white ones behind, and walked beside them leading Shadow with one hand, the oxen with the other.

The twins stepped up to either side of the oxen. "We can lead the oxen if you'd like," Lily said. "We used to help Grandpa with oxen on the farm."

"We drove the ox cart, too," Rose said. "We can probably drive the wagon sometimes if you want us to."

"Really." Daniel stopped and looked at the twins. "That would be very helpful." He handed the ox lead to Lily. "Let's see how you do."

Lily stroked the neck of the lead steer and gave a gentle tug on the ox lead. The oxen moved forward.

Rose rested her hand lightly on the neck of the other brown steer. "We need to think of names for them. Is it okay if we name them, Papa?"

Daniel glanced over at her. "As long as I approve of the names you choose."

The twins exchanged a glance. Their dimples deepened as they pressed their lips together, suppressing laughter.

"Their names need to be easy to say," Rose said.

"It's usual in a pair to have them start with the same letter," Lily added.

They continued to discuss possibilities as they walked.

After a while, Rose announced to Daniel, "We've decided what to name them. The white ones are Lad and Lucky."

"We could have named them—" Giggles bubbled up.

"Prudence and Charity—" Their giggles spilled over.

Daniel stopped walking and glared at the twins. "That's enough. You're being impertinent."

"Sorry, Papa." Rose contained herself with difficulty. Lily was still out of control, not even trying to stop laughing.

Daniel set his jaw. "I said, that's enough." He walked ahead, his back stiff. They went on a while in silence.

"Do you want to know what we named the brown ones?" Rose ventured.

"I'm not sure."

Rose came up beside him and took his hand. "Nothing impertinent."

"Well, what?"

Lily started laughing again. Rose looked over at her and shook her head. "We named them Bo and Buff," she said. "Do you like those names, Papa?"

Daniel softened a little. "I guess they're okay."

They reached Council Bluffs in the late afternoon and went straight through town to the wagon crafter. Their wagon was ready.

The twins drove the new wagon back through town, perched proudly on the jockey box. Daniel walked beside the oxen, leading Shadow. When they pulled up to the boarding house, Mr. Grundy was sitting on a bench outside the stable. He stood up, spat a wad of tobacco, and surveyed their rig.

"There's extra charge for the animals," he said. "Put those oxen in the corral. I'll take the horse."

"No, thank you." Daniel held firmly to Shadow's halter. "I'll take care of her myself."

While Daniel settled Shadow in the stable, the twins took the oxen to the corral, fetched fresh water from the pump for the watering trough, and brought hay from the stable. They scratched the oxen around the ears. "Good-night Lad and Lucky, good-night Bo and Buff."

Inside Mrs. Grundy informed them they were late for supper. "Five o'clock is when I serve and it's six-thirty now." After some persuasion, she produced some cornbread and beans. The cornbread was cold, the beans greasy and sour.

The twins wrinkled their noses. "We can't cook as well as Becky, but we can sure do better than this."

"I'm glad we got a good meal at the ranch."

Daniel set his mouth. "Never mind. This will be our last night here. Tomorrow we start living in our wagon."

## Chapter 10

# *Easter*

Daniel ran. Out of the wagon circle, weaving between cattle, wagons, and campfires, to the river. On the river bank children played, women washed clothes and filled their water buckets, men strolled and talked.

Daniel ran on, away from them all, his heart a chaos of grief and guilt.

Easter! How could I have not known? So separated I have become. Holy Week and I was traveling, Good Friday I was buying a horse and oxen, never remembering. And on this day, when Christ lay in his tomb, I haggled at the trading post.

At last he came to a deserted curve in the river bank where a huge old cottonwood reached out its trunk toward the water, then straightened and grew upward. He fell to his knees, bent his brow against the curve of the trunk. *Christ forgive me,* he prayed.

Memories of Holy Week at River View Church poured through him. Palm Sunday, the procession of children in white robes carrying palm branches up to the altar. Good Friday, the sound of the organ, the hymns of lamentation. Then Easter, the light through the stained glass windows, the joy and exaltation. All his people were there before him in the pews, dressed in their celebratory best—Thomas with his family, the other elders who had prayed and worked with him for years, Mrs. Lowell sitting straight and stiff, Becky and Nell and Nell's John. And sitting next to Ebenezer near the front, Rachel, her wide dark eyes meeting his with love.

Rachel … He crumpled to the ground and lay face down, his head in his arms. All the grief and loss, held back for weeks, overtook him. He sobbed and prayed, *Father, care for her as I cannot. Watch over her and protect her and the child. Forgive us, forgive us, do not hold thine anger against us …*

The great river gurgled near his feet. Above him a light wind whispered. At last he rolled onto his back, wiped the tears from his face with his sleeve, and looked up at the sunlight dancing in the leaves of the wind-rippled cottonwood.

I have left everything I loved, he thought, lost everything … except two mischievous young girls whom I have no idea how to father. How in the world can I bring them up? See to the salvation of their souls?

He had left them to organize the wagon, full and cluttered with the three trunks, and all the tools and supplies they'd gathered that morning. They were delighted with the project; he'd heard them chattering and planning as he walked away.

He had intended to walk around the circle of wagons and meet the people of the wagon train whom he already thought of as his new parish. The first person he encountered was Gabe, who, after greeting him, asked if he would be leading an Easter service tomorrow. Daniel had no idea what he had replied. He had just run.

The wind moved in the cottonwood. The tree praises God, he thought, in the dance of its leaves and its song. A gentle serenity descended as if from the tree itself, and it seemed he heard his Lord's voice saying, *Be at peace, my son. You are loved and forgiven. And now arise. I have work for you to do.*

Daniel sat up. By long habit, he kept a pad and pencil in the inner pocket of his jacket. He pulled them out, nibbled at the end of the pencil. An Easter Service. An Easter sermon for those who, like me, have left everything behind for a new adventure. He began to jot.

An hour later he returned to the wagon train. As he approached he heard music, an Easter hymn. He paused at the edge of the circle and glanced around.

Two young mothers, one big with child, sat together chatting and watching over their small children, two little girls playing with their rag dolls and two little boys, just toddlers, scratching lines in the dirt with sticks. A group of men was clustered around a horse, examining its points. The three middle-sized boys competed, throwing knives at a target on a stump. Mrs. Shively and Mrs. Dunin were trying to start a cook fire in a trench near one of their wagons.

In the center of the circle, sitting on the logs around the fire pit, were the musicians—Gabe with a violin, Lily with her violin, Rose with her flute, and a tall loose-limbed man with a big drooping mustache playing an accordion. They were belting out a lively version of "Christ the Lord Is Risen Today." Daniel approached them.

As they finished the last "Alleluia," Lily lowered her violin. "Hi, Papa. We're practicing some hymns for Easter. Mr. Gabe said you're going to lead an Easter service tomorrow."

"What a good idea." Daniel said. "You sound fine. Gabe, I didn't know you had a violin tucked away with everything else in that cart of yours."

Gabe smiled. "I don't go nowhere without my fiddle."

Rose turned a few pages in the hymnbook on her lap. "We thought we'd do that one at the end of the service, and begin with 'Come Ye Faithful, Raise the Strain.' How does that sound to you? And Papa, this is Mr. Seth."

Seth unwound his lanky form to shake hands with Daniel. "Seth Mooreman. Glad to meet you, Preacher. You've got some pretty talented girls here."

"Do you want to hear 'Come Ye Faithful'?" Lily asked.

"Sure." Daniel sat down on a log.

Seth picked up his accordion and tapped a beat with his foot. The other three raised their instruments. Lily nodded, and they began, but ran into a moment of discord. Rose lowered her flute and glanced at the hymnbook. "The violins came in too soon there. Let's take it again."

The second try went smoothly. Daniel was impressed. "Very nice," he said. "It's going to add a lot to have music. Thank you."

He walked away toward his wagon. Mrs. Lowell was right, he thought. They really are accomplished young ladies. He was touched that they were preparing for the Easter service without his even asking. They're basically good girls; their mischief isn't bad, it's even funny sometimes. Maybe I don't need to worry about the salvation of their souls.

Stephen, one of the outriders, greeted him. "Good day, Reverend Wright. I'm looking forward to your service tomorrow."

"Thank you. I'm glad." Daniel watched as Stephen approached the musicians. That's a very nice-looking young man, he thought. What if he starts to flirt with one of the twins, like that young conductor did? His anxiety about fathering them flared up again. How do I keep them safe? They are so pretty. All the men in the wagon train will be after them.

As night fell, Daniel and the twins walked to their wagon.

"This is our first night in our new home." Rose said. "It's going to be really comfy."

"Much better than that boarding house room," Lily agreed.

Daniel helped the twins up the step, then climbed in after them. The moon was just rising and shone in the open end of the wagon. Everything was neatly arranged.

"Shall I light the lantern?" Daniel asked.

"I don't think we'll need it," Lily said. "We have the moonlight."

"We've got it all planned," Rose said. "We'll put your mattress crosswise at the front of the wagon, and ours lengthwise between the trunks."

The corn husks rustled as Lily unrolled the mattresses. She handed one to Rose, who laid it out across the front of the wagon for Daniel. "And here's your blanket and pillow, Papa."

Daniel sat down on his mattress and took off his boots. He watched as the twins arranged their mattress, talking softly to each other. Lily lifted the lid of one of the trunks.

"Here's our quilts. We'll put one under and one over us."

"I have our pillows."

"We can put our hair pins in this pocket with our brushes."

He turned away as they began to slip off their gowns, then could not resist glancing back. They stood in their shimmies in the moonlight, letting their hair down. He quickly looked away again, heard rustlings and soft murmurings as they settled. When he looked back, they lay on their mattress snuggled together under their quilt. He sighed as he lay down and pulled up his blanket. "Good night, Lily. Good night, Rose."

"Good night, Papa."

Easter morning dawned clear and chilly. The twins, Gabe, and Seth got together early to practice their hymns. The sound of their music and word that there would be an Easter service at ten o'clock spread into the camps around Jake's wagon circle. When the time came, a large group had gathered. They sat in the dust, leaned on wagons, perched on logs, or just stood.

Gabe had somewhere found a buckboard for Daniel to stand on. As he emerged from his wagon, dressed in his Sunday best, the musicians played one verse of "Christ the Lord Is Risen Today." The people hushed as Daniel climbed onto the buckboard. He lifted his arms. "The Lord is in His holy temple; let all the Earth keep silence before Him." He lowered his arms and gazed out over the congregation. "We are gathered this joyful morning to celebrate the resurrection of Jesus Christ our Lord and Savior. Let us begin by singing 'Come Ye Faithful.' If you don't know the words, join in as you can, hum along with us."

He nodded to the musicians who were seated on a log by his feet. The people sitting down in the front stood. Gabe, Seth, Rose, and Lily played an opening phrase, then moved into the hymn. Daniel sang, his clear, strong voice leading as the others joined in.

"Come ye faithful, raise the strain of triumphant gladness,

God has brought his people forth into joy from sadness."

Their voices rose in the fresh spring morning, filling the valley and floating out over the river that they were all soon to cross.

When the song ended, Daniel spoke. "Our scripture this morning is from First Corinthians 15: 20-22." He did not read from his Bible, but looked out into the faces of the people, speaking from memory:

"Now is Christ risen from the dead and become the first fruits of them that slept. For since by man came death, by man came also the resurrection of the dead. For as in Adam all die, even so in Christ shall all be made alive."

He paused. In the silence, a meadowlark sang.

"My sermon today is on the new life. All of us here, preparing to cross this great river, seek a new life. And indeed we shall find it, far from this riverside campground. But the true new life is not to be found in the gold fields or homesteads of the vast West, but in Christ. Some of you seek gold, but remember that the purest gold is the redeeming love of God …"

Daniel had no pulpit to rest his notes on, but stood before the people on the rough buckboard, speaking from his heart. The gathering was spellbound by his strong, musical voice, his dynamic presence, the power of his words, the passion of his eloquence.

"Look at him," Lily whispered to Rose. "He is so handsome."

"And they love him," Rose whispered back. "See how still they are. Just like in Boston."

The twins gazed up at their father. All traces of the grief they had seen so often on his face were gone. The wind ruffled his dark wavy hair; his blue eyes shone. He glowed with the joy of his message.

When the sermon was over, he bent his head. "Let us pray." His prayer was a fervent call to come to the new life in Christ. In the silence after his "Amen," the twins heard someone weeping softly in the crowd.

Daniel lifted his head. "Let us close by singing 'Christ the Lord is Risen Today.'" More people knew the words to this hymn and the singing was strong and exuberant. When it ended, Gabe leaped up, threw his hat in the air, and shouted "Alleluia!"

"Alleluia!" the crowd responded. More hats flew into the air and alleluias rang all through the valley. Daniel looked startled at first, then laughed. When the alleluias died down, he raised his arms again for the benediction.

"May the Lord bless you and keep you …"

The congregation was silent for a moment after his last "Amen." Then they stirred, and murmured. Daniel jumped lightly down from the buckboard, and the people pressed around him.

## Chapter 11

# *On the Overland Trail*

At dawn the next morning, Jake's wagon train unwound from its circle and snaked its way along the narrow track through the sleeping camps and down the steep ferry road to the river. It took three ferry trips to get all the wagons in Jake's train across the Missouri. By that time, it was noon. Jake led them aside to a shady place on the river bank for rest and lunch. Then they climbed the steep bluff out of the river valley onto the wagon road west.

The afternoon was cool, the sun in and out of the moving clouds, the wind blowing from the west. Jake led the train, Ben brought up the rear, and Stephen rode alongside. Daniel told the twins he was going to ride up and down the wagon train and bring the Gospel to those who traveled with them. He mounted Shadow and rode off. The twins walked side by side, holding hands, Lily's other hand guiding the oxen.

Toward mid-afternoon Stephen rode up beside them, dismounted, and walked with them.

"Your pa's a mighty fine preacher," he said.

"He really is." Rose turned her head so she could see Stephen out of her deep bonnet.

"He seemed kind of surprised when Gabe shouted out 'Alleluia.'"

Lily laughed. "He was."

"But I think he liked it," Rose said.

"Gabe must be a Baptist," Lily said. "Baptists shout a lot."

"We're Presbyterians," Rose explained. "Presbyterians never shout."

Stephen laughed with them. "But even if your pa doesn't shout, he sure can preach the Gospel. Did he have a church before you came here?"

"He had a big church in Boston."

"Why did he leave?"

The twins looked at each other for a moment. "He got a strong call to serve in the West," Lily answered.

"And you came with him. What about your ma?"

"She died a long time ago … Do you have a family?" Lily asked.

"My folks have a farm back in Pennsylvania. I've got three brothers and two sisters to help with the farm, so I took off. I've always wanted to see the West. This is the second year I've traveled with Jake. He only goes as far as Denver City, though. I'd really like to see California. Maybe I'll do that some day."

"Did you go home in the winter?"

"No. It's too far. I stayed with my uncle. He's got a dairy ranch north of Denver City, near a little mining town called Gold Creek."

"Gold Creek!" Rose exclaimed. "That's where we're going. They have a new church there that Papa's going to serve."

"Oh!" Stephen stopped a moment in the road. "You'll have to look up my family, the Fairdales. I've got three cousins close to our age—Jonathan, Amy, and Julia. Uncle Andrew has been there seven years now and has done very well. He has a real nice place, a big house, lots of books, and a piano. Stuff most folks out there don't have."

"A piano!" Rose exclaimed.

"Yes, and I'm sure my cousins would be glad to have you come and make music with them. You were great yesterday."

"We really miss our piano," Lily said.

"Where did you learn your music?"

"Before we knew we were going out West," Rose answered, "we had lessons with our grandmama—French, literature, mathematics, philosophy. A music tutor came once a week, and we practiced every day."

"Then when we knew we were going with Papa," Lily added, "we had to give it all up and learn to cook and sew and take care of him. But we miss our music the most."

The afternoon passed quickly as they walked and talked together. When Daniel came in sight, riding back from the front of the train, Rose called to him, "Stephen's been to Gold Creek. He's been telling us all about it."

"You don't say!" Daniel reined in, dismounted, and turned to Stephen. "I'd like to hear about it, too."

～

The sun was low in the sky when Jake called out the order to circle up. Stephen split the train in the middle; one half followed Jake, the other half followed Ben until the circle was formed.

After the oxen had been unhitched and tethered, Jake gathered everyone at the center. "We've done well today. Conditions have been good. We've made almost eight miles and the elephant didn't even flip his tail."

"The elephant?" Lily interrupted. "There's no elephants here, only in India."

A ripple of conversation went around the circle, some laughter.

Jake turned to Lily. "It's a different kind of elephant. The elephant that lurks here on the Great Plains is all the dangers of the trail. Watch for him." Jake grinned as he looked around the circle. "Let me know if you see him wiggle his ears. Stay clear of his big feet." He turned back to Lily and raised an eyebrow.

"We'll stop here for the night," he went on. "Tomorrow morning at dawn Ben'll blow a horn. Loudly. It'll wake you up. Then you've got an hour to get your coffee and bacon and get your teams hitched. He'll blow it again when it's time to start. The wagon at the end of the train eats the most dust, so we'll rotate; each morning, whoever was first in line the day before, goes last. Tomorrow that'll be you and your brothers, Abe. Fuel is scarce, so share your cook fires. Have a good night."

When the people dispersed to fix their evening meal, the young mother big with child approached the twins. "Hi," she said. "I'm Mattie Hollis. My husband, Nathan, is building a fire over by our wagon. Would you like to share our fire with us?"

"Thank you," Rose said. "We'd love to."

The twins gathered their food and cooking equipment and went to where Nathan had a small blaze going. Nathan and Mattie's two little ones sat in the dust, watching the fire. The twins learned that the little girl was three and named Amelia, and the boy, Little Nate, was just one and a half. Amelia smiled shyly at the twins. Little Nate hid his face against his mother's skirt, then emerged to play peek-a-boo. Daniel soon joined them. In the cooking and sharing of the meal, in the conversation that followed, a warm friendship began between the two families.

It was fully dark when Lily, Rose, and Daniel gathered up their dishes and returned to their wagon. Rose packed the dishes into the chuck box.

Daniel stretched and sighed. "Well, we're really on our way now."

The twins came to either side of him. He put his arms around them.

Lily rested her head back against his shoulder. "Look at the stars!"

The deep night sky was vast, the stars thick and brilliant. The three stood, heads tilted back, in silent awe.

"When I consider thy heavens, the work of thy fingers," Daniel murmured, "the moon and the stars which thou hast ordained, what is man that thou art mindful of him …"

"And yet," Rose whispered, "He knows when even a sparrow falls."

At dawn the next morning, the twins woke to the sound of Ben's horn. It *was* loud. They rubbed their eyes, snuggled one moment longer in the warmth of their quilts, then scrambled up, pulled on their gowns, twisted up their hair, and climbed out over the chuck box at the back of the wagon so as not to disturb Daniel. They gathered coffee and bacon and went to help Nathan start the fire. When Daniel emerged and joined them, they had his coffee ready and were cooking bacon and biscuits. Rose went back to the wagon and brought dried apples to share with the Hollis family.

As the sun rose, Ben blew the horn again, and Daniel and the twins hitched up their oxen. There was a commotion across the circle. Jake strode over to Mr. Dunin's wagon. "Come on, Clay, what's holding you up? Everybody else is ready to go."

"Got my harness tangled," Mr. Dunin whined.

Jake took the harness, straightened it out, and handed it back to Mr. Dunin. Mr. Dunin dropped it, then stumbled over it as he went to climb in his wagon. Dr. Franz's boys snickered. Jake waited, hands on hips, until Mr. Dunin was settled on his jockey box.

Then he called to Daniel. "Can you give us a prayer for the road, Preacher?"

"Gladly." Daniel stood up on the front of his wagon and bowed his head. "Dear God, our Father," his musical voice rang out. "We give Thee thanks for this day and the journey before us. Like the children of Israel, we set out into the wilderness in search of a new land. Guide and protect us as Thou didst them, open the way before us, keep us from false idols, feed our souls with Thy manna from heaven. And let us remember always, that no matter what befalls us, we are in Thy hands, we trust in Thy mercy and rest in the assurance of our salvation through Jesus Christ our Lord. Amen."

"Amen!" shouted Gabe.

"Amen!" echoed around the circle.

"Thank you, Preacher. All right, let's roll." Jake swung onto his horse and led the train out of the circle and onto the trail.

Once they were rolling, Daniel rode off again on Shadow. The twins jumped down to walk beside the oxen. Mattie, with Little Nate on her hip and Amelia by the hand, came to walk with them, and soon they were joined by the other young mother with her children.

She introduced herself to the twins. "I'm Lydia Merrill. This is Cindy and Willy. She's four and he's two. They're a handful," she sighed.

"They're very cute," Rose told her.

Cindy caught hold of Amelia's hand and they skipped along together. Willy ran in circles, his little legs moving so fast they were almost a blur. He ran dangerously close to Lucky's hooves.

"Willy, come back." Lydia dashed after him and grabbed him. He set up a howl of protest. "You have to stay away from the oxen. You could get hurt." She held him firmly by the hand. "I don't know how we're going to get through this trip alive," she worried. "There are so many dangers for the little ones."

Mattie patted her shoulder. "We have to trust in God."

The four young women walked together and chatted for a while, with frequent interruptions from the children. When the little ones were tired, their mothers took them back to their wagons.

Lily and Rose continued walking, hand in hand. The wagon bumped along the rough road.

The Bradley wagon was two ahead of theirs, higher and wider than any of the other wagons. Mrs. Bradley jumped down off the wagon tongue.

"It makes me nervous to see her jump off the wagon tongue," Rose said. "I can't help but think of that poor woman in hoop skirts that Mr. Erickson told us about."

"Not to worry about Mrs. Bradley; she's wearing bloomers," Lily pointed out.

Mrs. Bradley walked toward them. Over her bloomers, she was wearing the short red skirt she had been trying on at Mrs. Garland's. Her long, glossy black curls tumbled loose out of her bonnet. She approached the twins a little shyly.

"Can I walk with you?"

"Of course, Mrs. Bradley," Rose said warmly. "I'm Rose."

"And I'm Lily."

"You don't need to call me Mrs. Bradley. We're about the same age, even if I'm married. My name's Regina."

It turned out Regina was younger than the twins, just barely fourteen.

"Didn't your parents think you were too young to get married?" Rose asked her.

"My ma did, but my pa said I was grown enough and one less mouth to feed." Regina frowned and bit her lower lip, then brightened. "So my ma had to say yes, and Brad was impatient and wanted me to go with him—so we got married."

"What's it like to be married?" Lily asked. She and Rose exchanged a quick glance that contained all their questions.

"It's okay." Regina tossed her curls. "Brad's rich and gives me anything I want. We have a very nice wagon. Do you want to come and see?"

"Maybe when we stop," Rose said. "We have to lead the oxen now."

When the sun was overhead, Jake called a halt. "Nooning," he said. "Time to eat and rest. Unhitch your teams and let them graze, but don't unyoke the oxen. We're only stopping for an hour."

They pulled off the track. Another wagon train passed them as they rested. Daniel rode up to get his lunch, then stretched out in the wagon while Lily and Rose cleaned up.

As they set out again, the sky grew cloudy and the wind picked up. The twins were glad of the woolen vests under their gowns. By mid-afternoon, weary of fighting the wind, their legs and feet aching, they gave up walking and guided the oxen from the jockey box.

The clouds had grown heavier by the time the train circled up at the end of the afternoon. Jake called the evening meeting. "We've done well today, almost sixteen miles. That's very good for our first full day." Lily and Rose glanced around the circle. Everyone looked as tired as they felt. The cold wind carried a few spatters of rain. "Looks like rain," Jake went on. "Cook for two days tonight. We may not be able to have fires tomorrow."

As soon as the evening meal was over, the twins crawled into the wagon, took off their boots, and rubbed each other's tired feet.

"Five hundred miles," Rose moaned.

"We can ride sometimes," Lily comforted her.

Lily unrolled the mattresses, and Rose laid out their father's blanket and pillow. They found their quilts and nestled down to the sound of rain drumming on the canvas cover. The wagon rocked as Daniel climbed in.

"Lily? Rose?" he asked softly.

"We're here, Papa."

They heard him sigh as he sat down; then they were asleep.

~

The first day set the pattern for the days that followed. Each morning the people of the wagon train woke at dawn to the sound of Ben's horn. They cooked their breakfast and hitched up their teams. Daniel offered a brief prayer service before they started out. He read from scripture, Rose brought the hymn book and led a hymn, and Daniel prayed. Most of the people came. Then Ben blew the horn again, and the train uncurled and moved out onto the trail.

Each noon they rested for an hour. The rest of the day, morning and afternoon, they walked or rode, driving their teams across the wide endless plains. Each evening, after they had circled up, Jake gathered them at the center of the circle to comment on the day's progress and listen to any complaints or difficulties that had arisen during the day.

As Jake had predicted, it did rain on the second day. The twins pulled out their India rubber ponchos and slogged along beside the oxen. The trail grew muddy, and the wagons moved more slowly, but still they made ten miles that day; and the next morning the sun was out.

The third evening, after supper, Gabe settled himself on a bucket in the center of the circle and tuned up his fiddle. The twins hurried to join him with their instruments. Then Seth came with his accordion and two other men joined in, one with a banjo and one with a tambourine. They played hymns and popular songs, and a group gathered around singing and clapping hands until darkness fell.

Another evening Stephen offered to teach knots. Brad and Regina, Daniel and the twins, and the three young boys came to learn.

"This one's for tying onto something you need to pull," Stephen said as he demonstrated. "It's a good secure one. We'll be using it to pull the wagons across the river in a few days."

Others who had been watching joined in. Stephen taught three basic knots, then set up a contest to see who could tie them the fastest. Rose won every time, with Lily coming in a close second. "Rosie has the most dexterous fingers," Stephen said, smiling at her.

Early on the fourth morning, the wagon train passed into an area that was trampled and scattered with manure.

"Buffalo passed here a while ago," Jake told the twins as he rode beside them. "Lots of buffalo chips. Gather them up. They're good fuel."

"Buffalo chips?" Lily asked. "You mean their … manure?"

"*Gather* them?" Rose wrinkled her nose.

"Yup." Jake laughed at their disgusted expressions. "There's no trees out here, you may have noticed. If you want a fire, pick up those buffalo chips… . Just the dry ones." He chuckled and rode on down the train.

"Nathan was worrying we were almost out of wood," Rose said.

"But buffalo … *manure!*" Lily turned down the corners of her mouth.

Mattie came to join them. "Did you hear what Jake was saying? Buffalo chips for fuel? We're almost out of wood. I was afraid we wouldn't be able to have a fire much longer. So maybe we should gather them."

"Okay. Ugh. We'll do it," Lily agreed.

"We can put them in that empty flour sack," Rose suggested.

"And tie them on the *outside* of the wagon."

As Jake passed the word along, people emerged from their wagons to gather up buffalo chips. The men laughed and called back and forth. Some of it was not at all what Mrs. Lowell would have considered fit for the twins' ears.

All day they rode through the trampled area where the buffalo had passed. Toward the end of the afternoon, Lily commented, "Think how many buffalo there must have been to trample all this land."

Rose nodded. "I'm glad we weren't here with the wagon train when they came through."

As the days passed, Daniel visited the people of each wagon, dismounting and walking beside them, or riding alongside those who were driving.

Mrs. Shively sat on the jockey box beside her taciturn husband. She had lots to say to the preacher, suggestions about what scripture he should read in the morning and concerns that the rules of the wagon train were not strict enough.

Lydia Merrill and her husband, Bill, rode together up front while Cindy and Willy played behind them in the wagon. Lydia shared her worries about the dangers of the trail, and Daniel assured her God was watching over them.

Mrs. Dunin hid in her wagon and would not respond when Daniel called a greeting to her. Mr. Dunin whined and complained, stumbled and dropped things.

Daniel rode beside the older Cohen brothers, Abe and Enoch. He learned they were Jews. When he started to speak to them of Christ, Abe said firmly that they had their faith and did not want to be converted. Daniel moved on, saddened, understanding he could only pray for them.

He walked with Dr. Franz as Dr. Franz taught his older son, Noah, to guide the oxen. The younger son, Sam, ran free with Manny, the youngest Cohen brother. Noah, who had been part of their mischievous trio only days before, seemed to mature before Daniel's eyes as he took on his new role. As they walked together, Dr. Franz shared how his wife had died only three months ago, and he and his sons had decided to leave the scene of their grief to seek a new life.

Daniel always enjoyed walking with the Hollis family. Nathan and Mattie spoke of their former life in Pennsylvania. Nathan had worked with his brothers at a sawmill, and it had gone well enough, but he had been inspired by tales of the West and decided to find a homestead in the Colorado Territory. The children were shy of Daniel at first, but before long came to trust him. Amelia would slip her small hand into his, and sometimes he gave Little Nate a ride on his shoulders. All the delight he'd had in the twins when they were little, too soon buried in grief, reemerged as he delighted in the Hollis children. He watched Mattie with concern, thinking of Rachel, and how she, too, must be near her time.

The Bradleys were very proud of their wagon. They invited him in and showed him the platform with a feather bed, the rocking chair, the gilt-framed mirror, the table and chairs where they could sit comfortably inside. The wagon was high enough for even Daniel to stand upright. They had three yoke of oxen to pull it and a fine thoroughbred saddle horse. "Lay not up for yourselves treasures upon earth," Daniel quoted to them, "but lay up for yourselves treasures in heaven … for where your treasure is, there will your heart be also."

Brad frowned and said nothing. Regina tossed her curls. "Don't worry, Preacher, we know about Jesus. We got married in church."

Three of the wagons, all from the same town in Ohio, held four men each. All twelve men were focused on the riches they hoped to gain from finding gold in the mountains around Denver City. Daniel spoke to them also about treasure in heaven, but without much effect.

Sometimes Daniel rode with Jake at the head of the column.

"I'm worried about my daughters," he confessed one day. "I'm afraid all these men will bother them. They've been protected and are innocent. They're so pretty …"

"Pretty!" Jake snorted. "They sure are. And bright and sweet and perky. Hard-working, too. I've been watching how they take care of you and the wagon and the beasts. Any man's dream. After I said you could join us, I was slapping my brow worrying about that very thing—all those men and two lovely, unattached young ladies. Last thing we need is fighting over them. So I told all the single men, hands off the preacher's daughters or you're out. I'm not expecting there'll be any trouble. You let me know if there is."

Every day, sometimes twice in a day, Daniel walked with Gabe. Gabe's rig was the simplest in the wagon train, only a two-wheeled cart drawn by one mule.

"Where do you sleep?" Daniel asked him.

"Under the sky. Ain't no roof more beautiful than God's heaven."

"And if it rains?"

"Under the cart."

Little by little, Daniel learned Gabe's story. His father had disappeared before he was born. His mother raised him alone, then died when he was only twelve. Before she died, she apprenticed him to a carpenter. He grew up under the carpenter's tutelage and opened his own shop. "Ain't no trade better than what Jesus had," he said. He'd felt called to go West for several years, but had waited until the war was over. Then he sold his shop, packed up his fiddle and his few belongings, hitched up his mule, and started out. He walked from eastern Tennessee to the Mississippi, took the steam boat up the river, and met up with Jake in Council Bluffs.

"Why?" Daniel asked him.

"Jesus called me. Me and Sadie." Gabe patted his mule. "Don't know yet what He wants me to do, but He'll show me the way."

Daniel was touched by Gabe—his unquestioning faith, his childlike simplicity and exuberance, though clearly Gabe was no longer young. A few white hairs streaked his straight black hair, and deep laugh wrinkles radiated from the corners of his eyes. If Daniel were weary or worried or weighed down with sorrow, walking with Gabe always lightened his heart.

Chapter 12

# The Elephant Stamps His Foot

It happened at the end of nooning on the fifth day as Jake led the first wagon back onto the trail.

A wild shriek echoed the length of the wagon train. Jake spun around, held up his hand to stop the first wagon, and galloped back along the train.

Clay Dunin lay on the ground, under his wagon, his foot a bloody pulp, shrieking. Mrs. Dunin hung over the edge of the jockey box wailing, "He's dying, my husband is dying." People poured out of their wagons and crowded around. Lydia Merrill fainted. Daniel caught her. Willy ran away and Bill Merrill chased after him. Rose dropped to her knees beside Mr. Dunin and took his hand. Lily stood looking at the mangled foot, her stomach turning.

"Where's Dr. Franz?" Jake bellowed.

Dr. Franz ran up. "I'm here." He took a quick look at Mr. Dunin and turned to Noah behind him. "Bring me my bag."

"He's dying." Mrs. Dunin wailed.

"What happened?" Jake demanded of her.

"He was climbing onto the wagon and he fell and the wagon ran over him and he's dying. Oh, we should never have left home. What will I do?"

Mr. Dunin was still screaming, writhing on the ground. "He's not dying." Jake raised his voice to be heard over Mr. Dunin's screams. "If he were, he couldn't yell like that."

Dr. Franz knelt on the ground beside Mr. Dunin. "Disperse this crowd," he ordered Jake. "Lily, take Mrs. Dunin for a walk. Get her out of here." He looked over at Rose, still kneeling by Mr. Dunin's head, holding his hand, talking to him, though she could not be heard over the din. "Rose, stay where you are. I need you."

A few sharp orders from Jake scattered the crowd. Daniel carried Lydia to her wagon with Cindy crying and clinging to her mother's skirt. Nathan turned Mattie around before she could see Mr. Dunin's foot.

"What will become of me, abandoned in the wilderness?"

"Stop your wailing!" Jake bellowed at Mrs. Dunin. She gulped and was silent. "Get down off of there and go with Lily." He lifted her bodily down. Lily took her hand and led her away.

Jake stood over Mr. Dunin. "Clay, stop yelling and flipping around. Dr. Franz is here to help you, but he can't do anything until you quiet down." Such was the power of his presence, that Mr. Dunin's screams subsided into gasping weeping. It was suddenly quiet.

Dr. Franz looked up from where he knelt by Mr. Dunin. "Jake, help me get him out of there." The two men lifted him and slid him out from under the wagon. Rose stood by, her heart pounding. *He needs me? What can I do?*

Mr. Dunin screamed again when they moved him. Dr. Franz knelt by his head. "Listen, Clay. Your foot is crushed. If you can lie quiet, I will try to set it. With luck, you may be able to bear weight on it again. But I can't do anything unless you lie still. You hear?"

Mr. Dunin gulped and gasped and nodded.

Dr. Franz reached into his bag. "Here, have a swig of whiskey … and another." He lifted Mr. Dunin's head and held the bottle to his lips. "No more screaming now. Lie still. Rose, stay by him, talk to him like you were. Comfort him."

Rose knelt by Mr. Dunin again and took his hand. "No." Dr. Franz pushed her hand away. "Don't hold his hand. He'll crush it once I start working. But touch him. Talk to him. Help him stay quiet."

Torn between terror and pity, Rose prayed, *Jesus, help me. Thou canst heal. Help me. Show me what to do.*

A gentle quietness came over her. She felt her breathing slow, and her heart stopped pounding. She laid her hand on Mr. Dunin's chest and bent to look into his eyes. They were hazel, and crazed with fear and pain. Her own eyes were full of tears. Mr. Dunin gasped and sobbed, but lay still.

"Don't be afraid," she said softly. "Jesus will help us. He's here with us. He'll help Dr. Franz set your foot. You just need to lie quiet." She felt within herself the peace that slowing her breath had brought her. "Slow your breath. That will help you. Breathe with me." She kept her right hand on his chest. With her left she smoothed his brow.

Dr. Franz spread a cloth on the ground by the mangled foot and laid out his instruments. "Okay," he said to Mr. Dunin, "I'm ready to start work. It will hurt. But don't move. Rose, do all you can to calm him."

The first time Dr. Franz touched his foot, Mr. Dunin screamed again. Dr. Franz gave him more whiskey.

Rose continued smoothing his brow. "Look in my eyes, breathe with me." She held his eyes with her own and kept talking to him. She could never remember afterward what she said, but words of comfort and courage poured through her. Gradually she felt Mr. Dunin's breath slow to match hers. She held his eyes and breathed prayer. Wave after wave of peace poured through her, even as she felt his pain.

After an hour, Dr. Franz lifted his head, his brow beaded with sweat. "We've done it, Rose," he said. He turned to Jake, who had been standing guard. "Help me get him into the wagon." Mr. Dunin groaned as they lifted and carried him. Dr. Franz gave him another swig of whiskey and settled him on a mat in the back of the wagon. Rose stood outside, holding onto a wagon wheel, pale and trembling.

"Is he okay to travel?" Jake asked Dr. Franz. "I'd planned to reach the river today. We still can, if we start now."

"He'll be okay. I've bound and splinted the foot. The jogging of the wagon shouldn't harm it."

"Where's my angel?" Mr. Dunin called from within the wagon. Rose looked up, startled. Just then Lily returned with Mrs. Dunin.

"Where's my blue-eyed angel? I want her."

"Hush!" Dr. Franz looked back into the wagon. "Your wife is here."

"My wife." Mr. Dunin was yelling. "She's no wife."

"One swig too much whiskey," Dr. Franz muttered.

"No wife," Mr. Dunin yelled. "A dried-up prune is what she is. So dry I can't get it in her."

A crowd had gathered again. Some of the men started snickering. Lily went to Rose and took her hand.

"Can't get it in her. Too dry." Mr. Dunin yelled louder. "Where's my little angel. Bet she's not dry."

Ben rode up. The men were laughing out loud now, making their own remarks. Mrs. Dunin stood by the wagon, stricken.

"Ben," Jake ordered. "Blow your horn. I want this wagon train in motion in three minutes flat."

He glared at the laughing men, and they scattered to their wagons. Lily and Rose still stood by the Dunin's wagon, clinging to each other.

Mr. Dunin's yelling became more ribald and profane.

Daniel came running. "Lily, Rose!" he shouted at them. "Get back to the wagon." They fled.

"Lydia?" Jake asked Daniel.

"She came around. Bill caught Willy and he's with her."

"Help Mrs. Dunin, then. We need to move."

Ben's horn sounded. Daniel took Mrs. Dunin's arm. "Come. Let me help you up. I'll drive the oxen."

Mr. Dunin had subsided to muttering, but his language was no cleaner. Mrs. Dunin was flushed, the corners of her mouth pulled down. The wagon train began to move. Daniel flicked the reins, setting the oxen in motion. He turned to Mrs. Dunin. "He's crazed with pain and shock, and drunk with the whiskey. Don't take his ravings to heart."

"He's always drunk," she said through clenched teeth. "He has his nip every day. Secretly. Jake doesn't know. That's why he's so clumsy. He's half-drunk all the time… But now he's done it. And I'll have to hold the pot for him and tend his stinking wound. I wish he *had* died."

She grabbed the whip out of its holder and lashed the oxen. The wagon lurched, almost throwing her off her seat.

"Easy." Daniel reached out to restrain her hand. "I know you're angry. I don't blame you. But don't take it out on the oxen. You need them."

"How can I face anyone? I'll die of shame. And I can't hide in the wagon anymore, because *he's* there."

"You'll need to drive the wagon."

"I can't. I don't know how."

"You can learn. I'll teach you."

~

Lily and Rose walked hand in hand beside the oxen. Rose was still trembling. "What happened?" Lily asked.

Little by little Rose told her, her words broken by sobs as she remembered the sweet presence of Jesus and the terrible pain Mr. Dunin had suffered, that she had suffered with him.

"It's so strange to have to tell you," she said at the end, "because you weren't there. We've always been together before."

"I know." Lily squeezed her hand. "But this time we had different jobs to do. You were so brave and good. You *are* an angel. I'm not. I wanted to smack that Mrs. Dunin. Her husband is injured and all she can think of is herself, moaning on and on what would become of her, who would drive the wagon because she can't, and how she'd have to take care of him… In a way I don't blame her. I wouldn't want that man for a husband."

"No. He would be hard." Rose reached into her bonnet to wipe away her tears. She tightened her clasp on Lily's hand. "I'm glad you're with me now. I don't like us to be apart."

"I'm here."

After a while, Dr. Franz came to walk with them. "Thank you, Rose. You were a huge help. I don't know what I would've done without you. I don't know how you calmed him so, but I was able to set his foot far better than I thought I could. He may yet walk on that foot, if he doesn't get an infection. What did you do?"

"It wasn't me. It was Jesus." Rose's tears welled up again. She pushed back her bonnet so she could see Dr. Franz. "He told me what to do. He spoke through me… but I'm afraid I did something wrong. I didn't understand what Mr. Dunin was yelling about at the end, and why the men were laughing. And Mrs. Dunin was really upset."

"You did nothing wrong. Poor Mr. Dunin is so mixed up he confused the love of Christ with lust."

They walked a while in silence. Dr. Franz touched Rose's shoulder. "You are blessed," he said softly. "Blessed with a healing touch. Blessed that you knew to call on Jesus, and even more blessed that you could hear His voice."

# Chapter 13

# *River Crossing*

It was late afternoon when they reached the river. The flat land gave way to low hills that descended into a wide river valley with trees and lush grass. After the train had circled up, Jake went to the edge of the water. The people gathered around him. The river was wide and dark. An occasional piece of driftwood swirled swiftly by.

Jake rubbed his beard. "I think there's enough light left. Stephen, Ben … I need two more strong swimmers." He looked around. Two men from one of the Ohio wagons stepped forward. "Randall, Mark …Good. I want you four to swim across. Each with a rope. We made a sturdy raft last year and with any luck it's still there. Ben, Stephen, you remember where we stashed it?"

Ben nodded.

"Okay. Tie yourselves in well. We'll hold you from this side. When you get across, tie your rope to the raft if you find it, and we'll haul you back over."

The young men went to get ropes and soon returned, barefoot and stripped down to their drawers. The group watched silently as they waded in, watched in silence as they swam. Wrapped in their cloaks, Lily and Rose shivered beside Daniel. The swimmers landed far downstream from where they started and looked small and distant as they scrambled up the opposite bank.

"Current's stronger than last year," Jake muttered. He looked up at the sky. Long thin clouds veiled the late afternoon sun. He turned to Daniel. "A few prayers wouldn't hurt, Preacher. Pray that we get across tomorrow before the rain comes." He gestured to the rest of the people. "Go get your supper. It'll be a while before those boys get back."

The people scattered to their wagons. Jake stayed by the riverbank, ropes wrapped around his waist, searching the opposite shore. After a while the twins brought him a steaming bowl of bean soup. "Mattie sent this," they told him.

"Thanks." Jake ate hungrily. The twins were still beside him when they saw a tug on the ropes around his waist.

"There they are," he exclaimed. He handed Lily the bowl and took hold of the ropes. On the far shore, way upstream, the twins could see four small figures lowering a big raft into the water. "They found it." Jake slapped his thigh. He turned to the twins. "Quick. Go get Nathan, Bill, Brad, and your pa."

Lily and Rose ran. In no time, the river bank was crowded, the men clustered around Jake. The four across the river climbed onto the raft and pushed it off. It swung wildly downstream before the men could gather enough tension on the ropes to steady it. Slowly they pulled it across. Everyone cheered when it landed.

"Here's our raft," Jake said, waving his arm to the crowd. "Tomorrow we'll haul it back across with a wagon on it. Back and forth, till we're all on the other side."

～

It was barely dawn, the light still dim and gray, mist drifting over the river, when Ben blew his horn.

Jake gathered the people at the edge of the river. "We're starting right away. First couple of wagons over will have time to get their breakfast on the other side. Men, you'll swim with your oxen to keep them from panicking. Horses will also have to be swum or ridden across. Women and children will ride in the center of the wagon. You ladies with little ones, *hold onto them*. Tie up your valuables in India rubber, or hang them high in your wagons."

Jake gazed out over the river. "The best beaching place is between those two cottonwoods." He pointed. "Gradual slope, gravel so the wheels don't sink in. Only there's a nasty rock a bit farther downstream you need to keep clear of. Ben, Stephen, swim your horses over there and show the first men over how to handle the ropes. I'll need men to hold the ropes on this side to steady the raft. You fellows from Ohio want to go first? The rest of you, go get your breakfast."

No one left. They watched in tense silence as Ben and Stephen, each with a coil of rope, rode their horses into the swift current. A rough wind stirred the water. They stayed to watch as Mark and Randall guided their oxen into the river and swam with them, as their wagon mates helped Jake load their wagon and lash it onto the raft. Ben and Stephen reached the opposite shore and secured the ropes. Four men pushed the raft into the river. It moved slowly, rocking in the waves, ropes stretched across the water, men on the west side pulling, men on the east side steadying, straining against the current.

The crowd shouted when the raft safely reached the western shore. It took a while to unload the wagon from the raft, hitch it to the wet and frightened oxen, and pull it up onto the bank. As the raft was hauled back across the river, Jake turned to the crowd again. "That's how it goes," he said. "You other two Ohio wagons stay here; you're next. The rest of you go eat and prepare your wagons."

One by one the wagons were hauled across. Once a spinning driftwood log hit the corner of the raft when it was midstream. The wagon tipped precariously; men leaned on the ropes. After a breathless moment the wagon righted itself and the raft continued safely across.

When it was their turn, the twins climbed onto one of the trunks and clung to each other as the wagon rocked and swayed. Daniel had ridden Shadow over and returned on the empty raft to swim with the oxen. The twins knew he was swimming near them, wished they could see him, but dared not move from their trunk. On the far side, they jumped out into the shallow water to help Daniel hitch up the oxen. Once the wagon was safely ashore, they unhitched the oxen, and led them to graze on the rich green grass of the river valley. Daniel went back on the empty raft to help with loading, and holding the ropes on the east bank.

Clouds gathered as the afternoon wore on. The men were exhausted. The last wagon across was the Merrill's. Daniel swam with their oxen while Bill rode their horse. The twins stood on the bank, watching the wagon come to shore. As the oxen pulled the wagon up onto the bank, Willy broke free of his mother's grasp and leaned out the back. The wagon lurched. Willy teetered, clutched at the edge of the wagon cover, hung a moment, then fell into the river.

Daniel and Bill were behind the wagon, pushing it, when Willy's little body hit the water. Daniel spun and grabbed the child, pulled him out, wet and screaming, and passed him to Bill. Whether from exhaustion, or loss of balance from his swift spin, Daniel stumbled, staggered and fell backward. The current caught him. As he struggled to right himself, the river flung him against a rock whose top jutted just above the surface. His head struck the rock; he went limp, and the current spun him away.

"Papa!" Lily screamed. She turned and raced after him along the river's edge. Rose grabbed a coil of rope that lay by her feet and ran after her. In just a few steps, they were out of the area that had been tamed by many wagon trains. They leaped over logs, pushed through underbrush, stumbled over stones, running, running to keep Daniel's body in sight.

But the current was faster than they were. They lost sight of him as the river curved. Still they ran. Suddenly they came to a place where the river bank had caved in, creating a tiny cove. A driftwood log had lodged against the edge of the cove, and branches and debris had piled up against it. Into this nest of flotsam, the river had flung Daniel's limp body. He hung there, his face in the water. "Papa!" Lily screamed again, and tore down the bank.

"Wait!" Rose caught her around the waist. Swiftly she tied the knot. "Wait." She ran up the bank with the rope, twice around an old tree that leaned over the water, tied the other end of the rope around her own waist, and stumbled back down the bank to Lily's side.

Lily plunged into the water. There was no current in the little cove, but the bottom dropped off steeply. In three steps, Lily was up to her waist, her wet skirts heavy around her legs. Rose stayed behind her, knee deep in the water, bracing her feet against the gravel bottom, holding the rope. Two more steps, chest deep, Lily reached her father and wrapped her arms tightly around his chest. The tangle of flotsam broke loose and swirled away. The current tugged at Daniel's body. Lily went under, still clinging to Daniel. Rose's feet slipped and she fell to her knees. She struggled to her feet again and pulled with all her strength. Inch by inch she pulled Lily and Daniel toward her.

Then Jake was beside her, taking the rope. In one long stride he reached Daniel and Lily, flung Daniel over his shoulders and gripped Lily's arm. Rose stumbled again and fell forward into the shallow water. Strong arms lifted her from behind. "Rosie. I've got you, Rosie." It was Stephen. He picked her up in his arms, carried her up the bank, set her on her feet and held her close, cradling her head against his shoulder. "It's okay now. You're safe, and Jake's taking care of your pa." Rose trembled and wept; yet in the midst of it all she felt a moment of unexpected sweetness resting in his gentle embrace.

Then she heard Lily crying, "Papa, Papa," and broke loose. Jake had lain Daniel face down on the ground and was straddling him, frowning, pumping his back rhythmically. Water poured from Daniel's mouth. Lily knelt by his head, crying. Rose ran and knelt beside her.

Daniel coughed and struggled. "That's it," Jake said, his brow smoothing. "That's it. You're gonna make it." Daniel gasped, coughed again, spat more water, and lay still—breathing.

Jake looked up at the twins, his blue eyes intense under his bushy eyebrows. "Good work." He nodded to them, then turned back to Daniel, resting his hand on Daniel's back, watching him breathe.

Slowly Daniel sat up, his eyes dark and unfocused. The twins realized that Nathan and Dr. Franz were there also.

"May I have a look at him?" Dr. Franz knelt beside Daniel, looked into his face, and ran his hands over Daniel's head. "Looks like he's had a concussion. We need to get him back to his wagon, get him warm and dry. Daniel, can you walk?" Daniel nodded, mute. Dr. Franz helped him stand.

Stephen took Rose's hands and pulled her to her feet.

"I think we'd better untie these girls," he said. Rose felt his fingers at her waist, untying the knot. "You tied it well, and I bet you did it fast."

Rose looked up at him, her face still wet with tears. "I'm glad you taught me how."

Upstream, thunder rumbled. The clouds were low and dark. It began to spatter rain. Jake looked up at the sky. "It all comes at once," he muttered. "Dr. Franz, can you get Daniel back okay?

Dr. Franz nodded.

"We'll stay with him, too," Lily said.

"Good." Jake gave the twins a glance of approval. "Stephen, Nathan, come with me. I need your help. There's wagons and beasts all over the valley. Got to get them up to high ground. This storm—could be a flash flood." He broke into a run.

"Tell Noah to take care of our wagon," Dr. Franz called after them.

Daniel could only go slowly. The logs and stones the twins had leaped over so swiftly were cumbersome obstacles that he could barely manage, even with the support of Dr. Franz and the twins. The scattered rain turned into a downpour.

When they reached the wagon train, the river valley was in chaos. Men who had dropped to the ground exhausted, stumbled to their feet, searching for their oxen. Thunder and lightning came closer. The wind picked up. The river roared. Horses reared and neighed. In the midst of it all, Jake was a whirlwind of orders and action. A few wagons lurched up the steep bank out of the valley.

The twins helped Dr. Franz boost Daniel into their wagon, then dashed off to find their oxen. Shadow, tied to a tree, neighed and pawed the ground. Lily brought her to the wagon, stroked her nose and soothed her. Rose found their oxen. Together the twins lifted the heavy yokes and hitched the oxen up.

Lily called into the wagon. "Dr. Franz, is it okay if we move now?"

"Yes. Do you see Noah?"

"He just passed us with your wagon, on his way up."

"Good. Where are your pa's dry clothes?"

"In the trunk to your left. His blanket is there, too."

The oxen were frightened by the storm, but when Rose talked to them, urging them, they lowered their heads and pulled the wagon up out of the valley onto the flat plains. Lily walked beside Rose, leading Shadow. As soon as they reached the top, the wind hit them, sweeping across the open space. Rain beat horizontally into their faces so they could hardly see where Stephen was circling up the wagons. Dr. Franz climbed out. The wind snatched at his hat. He barely caught it.

"Your pa is resting now. I'll check on him in the morning. Which way did Noah go?" Rose pointed and Dr. Franz hurried off.

Once their wagon was in its place in the circle and Shadow and the oxen securely picketed, the twins climbed wearily up over the chuck box and into the back of the wagon. The wind beat against it and the rain drummed loudly on the canvas roof, but Jeff Jerome had done his job well, and inside all was dry and snug. Rose pulled the ropes to close the back tight, causing the dim light inside to become darkness.

"Let's take our wet stuff off here, so we don't drip all over," Lily whispered. "I'm soaked to the skin."

"But Papa's here."

"I think he's asleep. Papa?"

There was no answer. The twins struggled out of their wet gowns and piled them on the metal chuck box. They pulled off their boots and squeezed out their wet hair, wriggled out of their shimmies. Both of them were shivering.

"Do you think it would wake Papa if we lit the lantern?" Lily asked.

"I think it would be okay. We need to find dry clothes. I'm really cold."

"Me, too."

Lily found the lantern and lit it.

Daniel lay drifting in and out of sleep in the dim light of the wagon. His head ached. His mind whirled in confusion. He knew he was on his mattress in the wagon, his blanket over him, and that he was warm. He vaguely remembered being cold. That loud noise was rain on the wagon cover. He remembered falling backward into the river, then nothing until he lay vomiting water with Jake pressing on his back and the twins weeping by his head. His memory of walking back to the wagon was jumbled. He only knew it had been difficult and he had needed Dr. Franz's support. Why? He remembered the twins walking with him, and Dr. Franz telling him they had saved his life. From what? How? He drifted back into sleep.

He woke when Lily lit the lantern. He lay still, watching the shadows on the wagon cover, hearing the twins whispering. Slowly he turned his head. His eyes started wide open. They were naked, one drying the other with a towel.

Daniel had never seen a naked woman before. He had been celibate until his marriage to Grace, and Grace had been very modest, dressing under her voluminous nightgown. He had made love to Rachel under her clothes. Only once, when he was in seminary and had borrowed a history book from the university library, had he seen a photograph of a statue of a naked Greek goddess. He had quickly turned the page so as not to be tempted to sin.

Now he could not tear his eyes away from his naked daughters. The lantern light flickered on their full round breasts, the nipples erect with cold, the curve of their buttocks, their wet hair tumbling over their white shoulders, the tangle of blond curls at the base of their abdomens, their long fine limbs. When one, her back to him, bent to dry the other's legs, Daniel caught a glimpse of her mysterious crevice.

He turned his head away then. He was erect, his loins on fire. Guilt seized him with red-hot tongs. No! No! No! he cried inwardly. They are my daughters. How could I sink so low? He could feel the twins near him, hear them whispering to each other. He wanted to writhe and toss, cry out in his torment of shame and longing, but dared not move or utter a sound.

*Dear Lord, help me, help me,* he prayed. *Uproot this wicked passion out of me. I cannot subdue it alone, I cannot. I am lost… Oh why hast thou made so beautiful what it is sin to look upon?… Do not cast me off… I love thee more than life… forgive me… lead me in the paths of righteousness… do not turn thy face from me …*

He heard the twins' mattress rustle as they settled. The rain pounded on the wagon cover. At last, exhausted by his anguished prayers, he slept again.

Rose and Lily snuggled down together in their quilts. Lily, curled around Rose, felt her shivering. "Are you still cold?"

"No, I'm getting warm. But I'm scared."

"We're safe now. Why are you scared?"

"I don't know. When it was all happening, I was too busy to be scared. But now … Lily, what if we had lost him?"

At the thought, Lily, too, felt a wave of fear. "But we didn't. Dr. Franz said we saved his life, and I think that's true. You were so quick to grab the rope."

"You were so brave to plunge in after him."

"I knew you were holding me."

"I don't know that we were the ones who saved him," Rose said. "I think God did. If Papa hadn't gotten caught in that pile of brush … "

"And the moment I put my arms around him, the brush washed away."

"That was the scariest moment." Rose shivered again.

"We're all right now." Lily held her close.

"And then Jake came."

"Even if he hadn't, we would have gotten Papa out. You were pulling us. I had my feet on the bottom again."

"But Jake knew how to help him breathe. We must be sure to remember what he did, in case we ever have to help someone drowning."

"Yes." Lily nestled her cheek into Rose's damp curls, thinking, I may forget, but Rose never will. In that moment she understood for the first time, with a pang, that she and Rose were different.

They were awakened in the dark by a crashing roaring sound, terrifying, thunderous. The twins sat bolt upright, clinging to each other. Daniel staggered to his feet, bumped his head on the wagon bow.

"What?" he cried.

Lily scrambled onto the chuck box and opened the back end of the wagon cover. The rain had stopped and the sky was clear. The light of the waning moon, hanging low over the eastern river bank, flowed into the wagon. The roar was deafening. A horse neighed. Oxen bellowed. There were shouts and cries from the other wagons.

Jake's huge voice boomed over the roar. "It's okay. Calm down. It's the river cresting. We're safe up here. I need a few folks to help quiet the beasts."

"I'll go. Stay with Papa." Lily grabbed her cloak, swung her legs over the edge of the chuck box, and dropped out of sight.

Daniel stumbled and fell to his knees. Rose crawled to him. "Papa, it's okay. Please lie down."

"The river's cresting?"

"Yes, Jake was worried about a flash flood. I guess it's happening. It's a good thing he made us all come up out of the valley. What a terrible sound!"

The crashing sound moved on down the river. The roar continued.

"Come on, Papa. Jake says it's okay. Lie down again."

"My head hurts."

"Yes, you hit it awful hard. Dr. Franz says you have a concussion and you need to rest. Lie down now. Everything's okay. The beasts are quieting, hear? Lily's taking care of ours."

Daniel sighed and lay down. Rose covered him with his blanket, smoothed his brow, bent to kiss his cheek. She made her way back through the wagon and climbed up on the chuck box. There she sat, shivering in her shimmy, looking out into the moonlight, waiting for Lily to return.

# Chapter 14

# *Sabbath*

When Daniel woke, his head still ached, but his mind was clear—except for the vague memory of an upsetting dream.

It was early. He could see the gray dawn light through the open end of the wagon and the twins nestled in their quilts, still asleep. He thought it must be time for Ben's horn, but instead he heard voices. Throwing back his blanket, he sat up and looked out. People were climbing down from their wagons and following Jake.

He pulled on his jacket and joined the flow of people moving to the bank that overlooked the river. There they stood huddled around Jake, staring down in awe. The valley, where they'd pulled their wagons out of the river and rested from their exertions only the afternoon before, was overflowing with a dark raging torrent, swirling with flotsam.

"It's good we got out of there when we did," Jake commented.

"Thanks for seeing it coming," a man said.

Barefoot, wrapped in their cloaks, the twins came to stand on either side of Daniel. He shivered and put his arms around them.

Jake gestured with a sweep of his arm. "Let's gather in the circle. Ben, blow your horn and get the rest of the sleepyheads up."

When they were gathered, Jake said, "Hitch up your teams. There's a place only a half mile from here. Would've taken you there last night but for the storm. A little stream, maybe bigger after the rain, trees, clean water, good grass. We'll rest there for the day."

"It's the Sabbath," Mrs. Shively spoke up, "We shouldn't be traveling."

Jake gave her a long look, then turned to Daniel. "Preacher, you up to giving us a service today?" Daniel nodded. "Well," Jake said to Mrs. Shively, "Sunday service will be by the little stream. Far as I know, the Lord allows people to travel on Sunday if they're going to service." Mrs. Shively was silent. "So," Jake went on, "hitch up. When we get there we'll have lots of leisure for fires and breakfast." He glanced up at the dawning sky. "Looks like we'll also have some sun to dry us out."

As the sun rose out of the plains, the wagons wound their way north to the creek and spread out under the trees. Soon the aroma of coffee and bacon and woodsmoke mingled with the scent of wet warming earth and trampled grass.

Daniel sat leaning against a wagon wheel, sipping coffee, watching Mattie and the twins cook breakfast. Dr. Franz and Jake came over.

"How're you doing this morning?" Dr. Franz asked.

"Pretty good. My head aches, but it's getting better with coffee."

Dr. Franz squatted down in front of Daniel and looked into his eyes. "You look better." He explored the back of Daniel's head with gentle fingers. "You've got a knot back there, big as a goose egg. I've brought you some white willow bark." He pulled a small packet out of his pocket.

Rose looked up from the fire. "White willow bark?"

"Yes, we use it for pain." He handed her the packet. "Boil up some water, put in a teaspoon or two, and let it steep. It should help your pa's headache."

"Okay." Rose opened the packet and sniffed it, then folded it and put it in her apron pocket.

Daniel touched Dr. Franz on the shoulder. "Thank you for taking care of me yesterday. But what's bothering me more than my headache is that I have only the vaguest idea what happened to me. I've heard bits and pieces that only leave me more confused. Could you please tell me the whole story, in order?"

"It's quite a tale. Jake can tell you. I need to go check on Clay's foot." Dr. Franz went off, and Jake sat down in the grass beside Daniel.

"Coffee, Jake?" Mattie asked.

"Sure." Jake took the cup Mattie offered. "Where's your small fry?"

"Running everywhere, glad to be out of the wagon. Nathan's with them. Tell us the story. I'm not clear what happened either. There was so much going on with Willy, and then the storm."

"Somebody ought to put a leash on that boy," Jake commented. "I wasn't there when it started. I got the first part from Lydia when I could finally get her calm enough to tell me. Seems Willy fell out of the wagon just as you and Bill were pushing it up out of the river. You grabbed him."

"I remember that part," said Daniel.

"Then you lost your balance and fell back into the current and it whipped you away and whacked your head up against that rock I was telling everyone to watch out for. Lydia and your girls here were the only ones who saw. Everyone else was so taken up with Willy and his screaming that they didn't get that Lydia was screaming about you. The way that current was moving, you'd be flotsam half way to the Mississippi by now if your girls hadn't taken off after you so quick. It would've been far too late by the time the rest of us realized what was happening."

He went on to tell the rest of the story, including the twins in the telling. When he finished, Daniel looked over at them as they sat by the fire. "You were very brave."

"We had to be, Papa."

"We couldn't bear to lose you."

It was a quintessential spring day, the earth washed clean by the rain, the trees budding, the little stream singing its gurgling song. After the people finished eating, they strung ropes between the wagons and the trees and hung out their wet belongings to dry in the warm sun and the light lively breeze. Lily and Rose found the clothes their father had worn the day before in a sodden pile on the jockey box, then pulled out their own wet garments.

"Let's wash them," Rose said. "The stream is clean and clear and who knows when we'll get a chance again."

Daniel found a quiet place to prepare for the Sunday service, grateful that his jacket with his notebook of sermon ideas had been safe in the wagon when he fell in the river.

Later he walked over to see how the Dunins were doing. Mr. Dunin sprawled on the jockey seat of his wagon, silent, his bandaged foot stretched out. In the grass nearby, Gabe sat carving crutches for him out of sturdy tree branches. Jim, a tall dark-haired man with large, patient hands, was showing Mrs. Dunin how the ox harness went together. Something had shifted in Mrs. Dunin. She was no longer moaning, but listening and learning. Daniel thought, observing her, that the Dunins' marriage was about to change radically.

Earlier that day she had said privately to Daniel, with a gleam of angry vengeance in her eye, "I poured out all his whiskey. It's gone. And he can't get any more out here."

"He'll have a hard time coming off it."

"Serves him right."

~

Toward noon, the twins and Seth and Gabe settled in a wide space under the trees playing hymns, and the people gathered for Sunday service. Daniel preached on the children of Israel crossing the Red Sea with the message that God watches over his chosen people, and closed with prayers of thanksgiving for their own safe crossing.

Afterwards he was tired and the bright noon-time sun had made his headache worse. He retreated to the wagon and slept.

When he woke it was mid-afternoon. He climbed out of the wagon, stretched, and looked around. Except for the sound of Seth's accordion playing a low minor melody, the camp was quiet. Many of the men lay sleeping, scattered across the grass under the trees. Mattie sat in the shade of their wagon playing with her little ones. Her time will come soon, Daniel noted. His heart contracted. Rachel's will come soon, too. *Dear God, watch over her.*

Nearby he saw the twins sitting by a small fire, watching over their Dutch oven. They sat side by side, in their customary pose, arms linked around each other's waists, heads leaning together so that their brows touched. Daniel walked over to them.

They looked up and smiled. "Hi, Papa."

"How's your head?" That was Rose.

"Pretty good. I think your tea helped." He squatted beside them. "What are you cooking?"

"We're making cornbread."

"Mattie gave us a recipe that doesn't need milk and eggs."

Rose picked up a shovel and scooped more coals onto the top of the Dutch oven. "Randall shot an antelope and is going to share the meat with everyone, so we're all going to eat together tonight."

"And everyone's going to bring something to share."

Mrs. Shively walked toward them, purpose in her stride. Daniel rose to meet her. She stood over the twins, her lips thin.

"What are you girls doing?"

"We're making cornbread for tonight."

"Baking on the Sabbath! And earlier today I saw you washing clothes." She turned to Daniel. "Reverend Wright, I'm surprised at you. How can you allow your daughters such flagrant disregard of the Sabbath? I know the others ..." She waved her hand. "But your own daughters should set a better example. The Sabbath, as you must well know, is for praying and resting, as it says in the holy writ."

"We're resting." Daniel knew it was Lily speaking by the angle of her chin. "Just sitting here by the fire, resting."

"And praying," Rose added, "that our bread will rise."

They looked up at Mrs. Shively, blue eyes wide and innocent. Daniel stifled a chuckle. Though heaven help me, he thought with a touch of trepidation, if ever I am the recipient of such a gaze.

"Under normal circumstances," he said to Mrs. Shively, "I would quite agree with you, but traveling as we are, the Sabbath is the only time we can tend to some of these tasks. People *are* resting. It seems the spirit of the commandment is being honored."

"Humph. I didn't think you would be so lax." Mrs. Shively stalked off in the direction of the stream where Jake was sitting with Ben and Stephen.

Daniel sat down again beside the twins. "I don't know how to thank you." His voice broke. "You saved my life. If it hadn't been for your quickness and courage …"

"We did pull you out," Lily said.

Rose touched his hand. "But it was really God who saved you."

"You were snagged in a pile of brush. If you hadn't been, we couldn't have caught up with you."

"I didn't hear about that."

"God wanted you to live." Rose leaned her head against his shoulder.

"And we did, too." Lily came to his other side.

He put his arms around them, his heart aching. Guilt swept through him. If they knew … But God knew. Is it true He saved me? How could He find me worthy?

Jake came storming up. "Daniel, can't you do something about that woman? She's been driving people crazy all day. There's such good morale in camp after we survived the crossing and the flood, and she's doing her best to ruin it. Look at her now—harassing Jim, who couldn't be more Christian, sitting over there mending a harness for the Dunins." Jake rubbed his beard up the wrong way.

Daniel sighed and stood up. "There's one in every parish. I'll go see if I can get her to pray for all these Sabbath-breakers instead of lecturing them."

As the sun slanted low across the plains, backlighting the grasses and sending long shadows eastward, Daniel strolled over to where the people of the wagon train were busy around a central fire. Jake and some of the other men had dragged logs over to create a circle around it. Numerous pots sat in the coals, and an enticing aroma filled the air from the spits of fresh antelope meat roasting over the flames.

Daniel sat down on one of the logs. His head still ached and he was weary from a long conversation and prayer session with Mrs. Shively. Slightly dizzy. He closed his eyes and rubbed the back of his head. Something teased at the edges of his memory, troubling him. Jake's voice brought him back. "Preacher, can you give us a blessing for this feast?"

He stood, took a breath, and felt with gratitude God's holy presence with him, pouring through his words, as he gave thanks.

The meal was lively with lots of jokes and laughter and retellings of the preceding day's adventures. When Jake stood, the circle quieted. He hooked his thumbs in his suspenders. "Well," he said, "the elephant's come by, no question."

A murmur of agreement ran through the circle.

"Flicked his tail at Mr. Dunin two days back," Jake went on. "But thanks to Dr. Franz, he's healing, and thanks to Gabe he's got new crutches to get around on."

Everyone turned to look at Mr. Dunin. He sat silent, his head down.

Jake continued. "The current was swift in our crossing yesterday. But we made it, not even one beast lost. We almost lost one harum-scarum boy and our preacher, but thanks to our preacher pulling the boy out, and the preacher's girls pulling him out, we're all here. Thanks to the good Lord, we got up out of that river valley before the flood came. So even though the elephant came by, he didn't get us this time." He looked around the circle, nodding. "You all worked hard and helped each other, and that's turned us from a string of wagons into a tribe. Good. The more we act like a tribe and look after each other, the safer we'll be."

Later Gabe tuned up his fiddle and started playing a hymn. The twins gathered up their dishes and hurried to the wagon for their instruments. When they returned, Seth had his accordion out, Randall his banjo. The wagon tribe lingered around the fire, singing until dark.

On the way back to his wagon, Daniel stopped to speak to Gabe, who was unrolling his blanket beside his cart.

"Where did you sleep last night?" Daniel asked him. "The way it was raining, it must have been a river under your cart."

"I was fixing to sleep there anyway. I was so wet I didn't figure I could get any wetter. But then this big hand come down on my shoulder and Seth hauled me up into his wagon. Gave me a dry blanket. So I slept warm. But tonight" — Gabe looked up at the starry sky, smiling— "Ain't no better place to sleep than right here under God's heaven."

"It's a fine night," Daniel agreed. He touched Gabe on the shoulder and turned toward his wagon.

The twins had gone ahead of him and lighted the lantern. He could dimly see their shadows through the canvas cover.

Suddenly his head ached, his stomach clenched. He stopped, passed his hand across his brow. He felt dizzy again. I guess it was a bad blow, he thought, moving his hand around to the back of his head, touching the lump there. The thought of his bed in the wagon felt stifling. He sat down in the grass. Maybe I should sleep outside like Gabe, he thought. I could go get my mattress and spread it out by the wagon. But he didn't move. The dizziness intensified. He sat with his head in his hand until the lantern went out. He got up then, feeling sick and exhausted, and went to the wagon.

"Papa?"

"We have your bed all ready."

"Where have you been?"

Starlight shone in through the open end of the wagon. In its dim light, Daniel could see the twins sitting on their mat, wrapped in their quilts.

"I've been talking to Gabe," he answered. "He has a good idea. I'm going to sleep outside tonight." He reached into the front of the wagon and pulled out his mattress and blanket.

"You forgot your pillow." One of the twins, slender in her shimmy, emerged from the quilts and bent to hand it to him, her long curls falling forward around her face.

Daniel turned his head away. "Thanks. Good night now."

"Good night, Papa."

"Sleep well."

## Chapter 15

# *The Great Platte River Road*

The next morning the wagon train set out again, the people much refreshed by their day of rest. By evening they had reached a land of sandy hillocks, covered by sparse, coarse grass. After they circled up, Jake led them to a place where they could look out. The Platte River spread below them, so wide they could not see across it, a river of many channels separated by long, low islands. The late sun glinted on the water. On the near side of the river was a wide trampled track. East and west, as far as they could see, were trains of wagons and cattle, some resting, some in motion.

"Tomorrow we join the great Platte River road," Jake announced, waving his arm out over the expanse below. "Along with thousands of others. We'll be following the Platte now for a couple of weeks till it joins the South Platte. Then we'll follow that all the way to Denver City. We'll have water near, but it's thick with sand. You'll have to strain it."

A murmur of conversation ran through the crowd.

"So many wagons. It looks like everyone in the East is going West."

"Never saw a river like that. No valley, no banks. Just flat with the ground."

"And no trees, except on the islands."

"We'll need to gather more of those buffalo chips."

"How will we strain the water?"

"We'll be meeting some Indians," Jake went on. "Remember, we're crossing their land. Give them gifts, share your food, that's their custom. And be respectful. It's also a good idea to keep your valuables out of sight. Sometimes they prefer something other than what you choose to give them and help themselves."

"Thieving savages," Mrs. Shively muttered.

Jake turned and glared at her. "Mrs. Shively, when we meet Indians, you'll stay out of sight in your wagon. And keep your mouth buttoned. That's an order. I'll not have you endangering the whole train with your attitude."

"I'll be glad to." Both Mr. and Mrs. Shively glared back. There was a tense silence.

"Okay." Jake turned and beckoned. "Back to the wagons now. Get some food and rest. We'll start early tomorrow. Getting down through this sand will take some time."

～

Their first encounter with Indians came the next day at nooning. A whole village, it seemed, flowed around them as they rested and cooked their meal. There were women with babies strapped on their backs, a horde of half-naked children, tall men in fringed buckskin clothing and beaded moccasins. The people of the wagon train gave gifts, shared food, gestured in sign language, did some trading. When they moved on after a longer than usual nooning, the Indians flowed over to the train behind them.

The second encounter came two days later, in the middle of a warm, sunny morning.

Lily and Rose and Regina, chatting quietly together, walked beside the oxen.

The wagon in front of them suddenly halted. Jake came galloping up.

"Get in the wagon. Quick!"

Lily pulled the oxen to a stop. "What's wrong?"

"There's trouble ahead, a band of Pawnee braves. I want all women and children out of sight. *Especially you three.* Get in. No arguing."

The three girls scrambled into the wagon.

"Close it up tight. Not a sound."

Rose closed the back. As Lily started to close the front, she heard Ben farther down the train repeating Jake's orders, a brief scream from Lydia. Daniel rode up.

"What's happening?"

Jake rubbed his beard up. "A few trains ahead, Pawnee braves kidnapped two women and a child, and killed three men who were defending them. Some of their band is coming this way. Keep your gun at hand, but don't shoot unless attacked." He galloped off.

Daniel tied Shadow to the wagon and jumped onto the jockey seat. He spun around to look inside. "Are you both there?"

"Yes. Regina's here, too."

"Give me my gun."

Lily grabbed it from where it hung on the wagon bow, handed it out to Daniel, and then pulled the ropes to shut the front. The wagon began to move again.

The three girls huddled together. It was dim and stuffy inside. There was no sound but the creaking and jolting of the wagon.

"They kidnapped two women," Lily said, her eyes wide.

Rose clung to her. "What if they kidnap us?"

"They'd rape us," Regina said.

"What's rape?" Lily asked.

"Hush!" Rose squeezed Lily tighter. "They're coming."

They heard galloping hooves approaching, whooping calls, the snorts of horses.

"I want to see," Regina whispered.

"Me, too." Lily shifted out of Rose's arms.

"Shh. No! We mustn't," Rose breathed.

"It's okay. I'll make just a teeny crack." Lily crawled to the side of the wagon bed. Silently she lifted the bottom edge of the canvas, just an inch. The three girls lay flat on the wagon floor, almost on top of each other, peering through.

The wagon stopped. Outside there was a swirl of dust as four braves pulled up their horses right outside the wagon. They were almost naked, dressed only in breech cloths and moccasins, their long black hair braided and adorned with feathers. The one closest to the wagon dismounted. As he swung his leg across his horse, his breech cloth slipped to one side, revealing for a second what hung beneath it.

The three girls froze, their breath stopped. There were more whooping cries, then Jake's voice. Another voice answered in strange accents. The four braves moved out of sight. For a long tense time, the three lay there, hearing Jake's voice and the other strange voice, talking back and forth. It seemed as if there were many horses all around the wagon. There was no word from Daniel.

Finally the voices ceased, and the sounds of horses moved away and off into the distance. The wagon moved forward.

"Do you think they're gone?" Regina shifted a little.

The creaking and jolting of the wagon covered their whispers.

"I think so." Lily let out her breath.

"But they might come back." Rose clung to Lily. "I hope Papa's okay."

Lily smoothed Rose's hair. "He must be. He's driving the wagon."

Regina wiggled over to sit against a trunk. "Did you see that Injun's seed planter?"

"His *what?*" Lily sat up straight.

"His seed planter. That's what my husband calls it. That thing dangling down, when his breech cloth slipped."

Rose was still curled up on the floor, her face hidden in her hands.

"I guess all men have them." Regina said. "Even Injuns. Did you ever see one before, like on your pa?"

"No!" Lily's whisper exploded.

Rose sat up beside her. "Never!"

Regina looked at them for a moment, lifted her chin. "We had ten kids in a two-room cabin. I saw it plenty, even before I was married. My brother liked to show his off, make it stand up straight. Till Pa caught him and beat him, and he ran away."

The twins stared at her, eyes round with shock and fascination.

Regina tossed her black curls back. "I bet you had a big house before you got the covered wagon."

"Bigger than two rooms," Lily said.

"We have the biggest wagon in the whole wagon train. And it's just me and Brad. I got out from under all those snot-nosed kids climbing all over me."

"Shh!" Rose put up her hand.

They heard a horse approaching their wagon. They tensed again, clutched each other.

"Hey, Daniel. Everything okay?" It was Jake. "You girls all right in there?"

The three let out their breath. "Yes," Lily called.

"Good. I want you to stay hidden a little longer. Ben's following the braves to see where they go. I want to be sure they don't circle around again. You can give yourselves a little air."

"Thank you." Lily got up to open the front. "Papa? We were scared for you. What happened?"

Daniel looked back at Lily. "There were some tense moments when they stopped the wagon and were all around us. I did a lot of praying. What did you do, Jake, to get them to go on?"

"I gave their leader some silver," Jake said. "He remembered me from last summer. I gave him silver then, too, and he let us alone. I'm trusting it will work as well this year." He rode off down the train.

Jake set guards all around the camp for nooning, then allowed the women and children out. They had just finished their meal and were preparing to start moving again, when Ben came back. Everyone gathered around for the news. The Pawnee braves had ridden off to the north, Ben reported, and it did not look as if they were coming back. A posse of men had ridden after the kidnapped women and child. They'd been unable to retrieve the child, but found the women, some distance from the trail, apparently abandoned when the braves realized they were being followed.

"Had they been …?" Mrs. Shively asked.

"They were frightened and shaken up, but otherwise unharmed," Ben said. "The husband of one of the women was killed defending them, and the other woman was the mother of the stolen child. A boy of six. Some men are still out searching for him." Ben turned to Daniel. "They have no preacher. They asked if you could come comfort the women and do a funeral for the men who were killed."

"Of course," Daniel responded. He looked at the twins who stood near him. "Are the women still to be hidden?" he asked Jake.

"Yes, for a day or so, until we are sure all this has settled down."

"Then I will need someone to drive my wagon and protect my daughters while I am gone."

Randall stepped forward. "I will."

"Good." Jake nodded. "Ben, go with our preacher. You guards, keep your positions. We'll trade off guard duty tonight. Let's get rolling."

The following morning, the wagon train came to the graves of the men shot by Indians. Daniel and Ben were waiting there for them. Jake stopped the train for the people to get out and pay their respects, and Daniel led a prayer for the souls of the slaughtered men, the grieving women, and the lost child who still had not been found.

The next few days were tense. Everyone was on edge, the men constantly wary, the women and children cooped up in the stuffy, jolting wagons. Finally, Jake called all clear.

"I never thought I'd be so glad to walk all day," Lily said to Rose, as they took their accustomed place at Bo's head.

∼

The Platte River valley was a source of continual wonder for the twins. The track was broader than any road they'd ever known, running sometimes close to the river, sometimes a mile or more away to avoid mud pits and sloughs. Behind them and before them, wagon trains stretched out as far as they could see. On their left flowed the wide river without banks, flat with the land, sparkling in the sun, gold and silver with mica and sand. Islands filled the river, like green jewels on the shining water. Willow and cottonwood grew there, and often the men would wade through the shallow water and shifting sand to gather wood for the their campfires.

There was no vegetation around the Platte River road; all had been laid bare by the passage of thousands of emigrants before them. Often Jake would have to lead the wagon train a mile or more off the trail for their evening camp in order to find grass for the beasts.

At times the sun shimmering on the bare ground of the valley created mirages. It looked to the twins as if the islands in the river floated above it, or as if a wide lake lay before them, only to become dry trail as they grew closer.

On their right the sand hills rose up, blown into strange shapes by the wind. Regina rode to the top of them on Brad's horse and came back with glowing reports of the view. The twins longed to go up there, too, but Daniel had not yet let them ride Shadow.

There were hardships as well as wonders. The wind was relentless, sometimes biting coldly through their cloaks, other times hot and dry, whirling dust into their faces as they pushed against it. There were days of chilly rain creating deep mud that bogged the wagons down. The trail was frequently cut through by grooves as much as four inches deep and more than a foot wide.

"Buffalo tracks," said Jake. "They come down from the sand hills to the river, thousands of them, walking single file, carving out the earth. Take it slow going through those ruts. They're deep enough to break an axle."

The river water was thick with sand, and straining it through flour sacking was a daily chore. Even then it never was clear.

The hardest part for the twins was passing all the graves at the sides of the trail. The women often stopped to read the rough wooden plaques that marked them. A baby girl only a few days old. Farther along, the grave of her mother. A man shot by Indians. Another who died of fever. Many who died of dysentery. Some graves had been torn open by wolves and the bones scattered about.

"It's like that newspaper article Grandmama showed us," Rose said through her tears, as she and Lily bent over an inscription on the grave of a child who had been trampled by oxen.

After they passed nine graves in one morning, Lydia became hysterical.

At nooning Jake said, "No more stopping at the graves. It slows us down, and we've got a long way to go. If you wish, say a prayer for those souls as you pass. But don't dwell on the dead. Look around you." He waved his arm at the wagon trains behind and before them. "There's plenty of folks living and on their way. Like us."

# Chapter 16

# *Dancing*

April opened into May. The days lengthened and grew warmer. Indians came and went around the wagon train, but there was no further threat of violence.

One evening Daniel sat with Mr. Dunin outside the wagon circle. Clay was depressed over being without his alcohol, being crippled, and having his wife take over, not so kindly. His misery was making him more open to Daniel's message. Daniel had hope that he would soon come into Christ's fold.

In the background, Daniel could hear laughter and music. He had just come to a sensitive and promising place in the conversation, when Mrs. Shively stalked up.

"Reverend Wright."

Daniel curbed his exasperation. "Yes."

"I thought you'd want to know that they're dancing, all coupled up, even some of the men pretending to be women. Your daughters, too. That Randall came up to Lily and held out his hand, and she's up and dancing with the rest. Looks like she's done it before. Then Stephen asked Rose, and now she's dancing. Disgraceful, the whole scene. That Gabe, for all he shouts 'Amen,' is making the music for it. Him and Seth."

Daniel stood up. "My girls are dancing? I've forbidden them. Are you sure?"

"Go see for yourself."

Daniel bent to touch Clay's shoulder. "Excuse me, Clay. We'll talk more later."

He hurried around the wagons, between the tethered oxen, and into the circle. It was true. They were dancing, the young wives with their husbands, and four couples of men, each with one man wearing a bandana on his head to signify his feminine role. The rest of the men were sitting around the circle, clapping and stamping, and calling out teasing remarks to the men dancing as women. Lily and Rose were dancing, too. For a moment he just watched them, seeing how beautifully they danced, their feet quick and light, their slender bodies swaying with the music, their faces aglow.

Then, at a shift in the dance, the men put an arm around the women's waists and walked with them down the set. Lily tipped her head back to smile into handsome Randall's dark eyes; Rose leaned her head against Stephen's shoulder.

Rage surged up in Daniel. They are flaunting their disobedience, he thought, and disgracing me. I'll not have it.

Just as the couples turned, he strode across the circle, right into the dance. He grabbed Lily by the arm, then Rose, and jerked them away from their partners. The music faltered. The dance stopped. Everyone stared at Daniel and his daughters.

"I have told you"—his voice was low and fierce— "no dancing." A hot flush suffused his face as he felt all eyes on him. "Go to the wagon."

Lily and Rose caught hold of each other's hands. He saw bewilderment, then defiance cross their faces.

"Go!" he ordered.

The twins ran to the wagon and disappeared inside. Daniel looked around the silent circle, started to speak, gestured wordlessly, then followed his daughters to their wagon.

They were sitting side by side on the chuck box, holding hands, facing him as he climbed in the front end. He couldn't tell them apart. They both held their chins at the defiant angle he associated with Lily. Both pairs of blue eyes were blazing.

"Well," he said, "what do you have to say for yourselves?"

"What do you have to say for *yourself*?"

He couldn't tell whether that was Lily or Rose.

"You spoiled the whole dance—"

"Barging in like that."

"Everyone was having fun—"

"Till *you* came along."

Their words came fast and angry, from one and then the other. It was infuriating, not knowing which one was speaking.

"I have told you," he said, slowly and evenly, a space between each word, "you are forbidden to dance."

"Why?"

"Those men had their arms around your waists."

"But that's how you dance."

"My point exactly."

"What's wrong with that?"

"It leads to sin."

"Papa, we're not going to be ravished, right in the middle of the circle."

"Ravished! Where did you learn that word?"

"Papa, we read."

"What are you reading? I'll not have you reading dime novels, filling your minds with nonsense no young girls should be thinking of. Do you know what that word means?"

"Not exactly," one said.

"Something bad men do to women," the other said.

Daniel groaned and bent his brow into his hand.

"We have *not* been reading dime novels."

"Grandmama would never allow it."

"Then where did you learn that word?"

"Probably from Shakespeare."

Daniel was silent, glaring at the twins. They glared back. Tension zinged from one end of the wagon to the other. He picked up his rolled mattress from the top of his trunk, opened the lid and pulled out his blanket and pillow. He climbed out of the wagon, looked back inside.

"I want you to consider the fifth commandment and pray that you may be forgiven for your disobedience."

Twilight folded around him as he unrolled his mattress and laid it on the ground outside the wagon. The wagon circle was quiet; the dancers and musicians had dispersed. Daniel sat on his mattress and pulled off his boots. His head ached and he felt like weeping with anger and helpless frustration. He was aware of the twins moving around inside the wagon, heard their voices, but could not make out their words. Finally he lay down and pulled up his blanket. Above him the stars came out in the vast night sky.

He awoke with first light. Now that the days were longer, Ben's horn no longer came at dawn. He lay thinking of his daughters. Maybe I was too harsh. But I'm responsible for them. I have to keep them safe. I know too well how men think and what they do. His own guilt assailed him. He rolled onto his side with a groan.

After a while he got up and peered into the wagon. He had expected to see Lily and Rose still asleep. To his surprise he saw that they were sitting together with a quilt wrapped around them, brows touching, reading their Bible. He drew away without speaking. *Maybe they are penitent,* he thought. *Maybe they've been praying and are now studying their Bible. Maybe they are looking up the fifth commandment, though they ought to know it.*

He walked away from the wagon, out of the circle, taking in the beauty of the dawn, feeling relieved and calm. *They're good girls, after all. Just high-spirited.*

The camp began to stir. Daniel returned to the wagon and looked in. One of the twins lifted her head from the Bible. "Good morning, Papa."

"Good morning."

"Papa," the other said, "we'd like to read the scripture for the prayer meeting this morning. May we?"

Daniel was touched. "That would be very nice."

They looked up at him, smiling, blue eyes wide and sweet. He realized later he should have recognized that look, but he was too relieved by their apparent penitence to be warned.

After breakfast and morning preparations, the people gathered for prayer.

"Lily and Rose are going to read the scripture this morning," Daniel said, when all were assembled.

Lily opened the Bible. "Our theme this morning is praising God. I will read from Psalm 149. 'Praise ye the Lord. Sing unto the Lord a new song and His praise in the congregation of saints. Let Israel rejoice in him that made him: let the children of Zion be joyful in their King. Let them praise his name in the *dance*: Let them sing praises unto him with the timbrel and the harp.'"

There was a slight movement in the circle, all eyes on the twins. Daniel's neck tightened.

Lily passed the Bible to Rose. Rose turned a page.

"And I will read from the 150th Psalm. 'Praise ye the Lord. Praise God in his sanctuary; praise him in the firmament of his power. Praise him for his mighty acts according to his excellent greatness. Praise him with the sound of the trumpet: praise him with the psaltery and harp. Praise him with the timbrel and the dance ... Let everything that hath breath praise the Lord. Praise ye the Lord.'"

"Amen!" Gabe shouted.

Scattered laughter, quickly stifled, rippled around the circle. Rose shut the Bible and both twins looked up at Daniel. Oh, he recognized that look now! He felt his color rise. Somehow he stumbled through a prayer. As soon as the wagon train was in motion, he mounted Shadow and galloped away, burning with shame and confusion. Under the sound of Shadow's hooves pounding the hard sand, he thought he heard God laughing.

## Chapter 17

# *Birth*

When the twins went to the Hollis's wagon to share the cook fire one morning, Mattie did not come out. Nathan looked tired and worried. He told the twins that Mattie's time had come and asked them if they could look after Amelia and Little Nate.

"Of course," Lily answered.

When Daniel joined them, Nathan asked him to say a prayer for Mattie. Daniel looked at Nathan's anxious face and remembered sitting in the parlor while Grace was in labor with their son—and the loss. His heart ached with compassion.

"I will pray," he said. "And have faith. She's in God's hands."

After the breakfast dishes were cleared and the fire put out, the twins took charge of Little Nate and Amelia. The children loved the twins, as they had often played with them, so there was no fussing, though Amelia was old enough to be worried about her mother. All morning the twins took turns, one guiding the oxen, the other playing with the children in the wagon. When it was Rose's turn to ride, she noticed how rough the road was, how much they were jostled around. She knew nothing of birthing, only rumors of terrible pain, but thought it must be hard for Mattie to be shaken around so.

When they stopped for nooning, the twins prepared food for the Hollis family as well as their own. Nathan was sitting by their wagon, bouncing Little Nate on his knee, when Jake came by. Nathan got up and drew him aside.

Rose heard fragments of their conversation: "It's hard for her."

"Of course … Maybe you should get Dr. Franz."

Nathan went off to look for Dr. Franz. Jake stood in the middle of the circle and raised his big voice. "We'll be stopping here for the afternoon. Mid-week rest." People gathered around him, questioning. Jake said only, "Send Mrs. Hollis your prayers."

"Eve's curse," Mrs. Shively muttered as she walked away. "'In sorrow she shall bring forth children.'"

Lily took Little Nate into the wagon to settle him for his nap. Amelia was anxious. "Is my mommy sick?" she asked Rose.

"No, she's not sick. She just has hard work to do. Dr. Franz will help her."

"Will you tell me a story about my doll?"

Cindy wandered over, her rag doll dangling from her hand. "I want a story about my doll, too."

"I'll tell you one about both of them." Rose held out her arms and the two little girls came to nestle in her lap, their soft heads, one fair and one dark, resting against her shoulders.

She had taken the dolls through a series of adventures and Lily had emerged from the wagon to add to the story, when Daniel approached them. "Seth and I are going hunting. I'll be back in a while. Maybe we'll have fresh meat for dinner tonight. Any word about Mattie?"

"Not yet," Rose answered. "Dr. Franz is with her."

"That's good." Daniel reached into the wagon for his gun, mounted Shadow, and rode off.

A few minutes later Nathan came to them. "Rose, Dr. Franz wants you. If you can help …"

"Oh!" Rose looked up. "I don't know what I can do, but I'll come." She kissed the two little girls and lifted them out of her lap. "Lily can tell you the next story."

Her heart pounding, Rose followed Nathan to the Hollis's wagon. As she approached, she heard a low groan, then Dr. Franz's voice speaking quietly.

Nathan took her by the shoulders. "Help her," he begged.

Hours passed. Lily ran out of stories. Little Nate got up from his nap, and Lydia brought Willy over. The children played hide and seek around the wagons until they were tired, and Lydia took Cindy and Willy away. Lily was trying to think up the next diversion for Amelia and Little Nate when Daniel returned.

"I got two prairie chickens," he said proudly. "One for us and one for the Hollises. Where's Rose?"

"She's helping Dr. Franz."

"*What?*" Daniel swung down from Shadow. "She's in there with Mattie?"

"Yes."

"What is Dr. Franz thinking of? She shouldn't be in there!" Daniel tossed Shadow's reins to Lily and strode toward the Hollis wagon.

Lily ran after him and grabbed his arm. "Papa, you can't go in there. Mattie's … Not even Mr. Hollis is allowed in."

"But I have to get Rose. She mustn't be seeing that." Daniel almost ran, dragging Lily. "Why in the world didn't Dr. Franz get a married woman to help him?"

"Papa." Lily pulled harder on his arm. Daniel stopped and looked down at her. "There isn't anyone else really. Lydia faints, and Regina's just a scatter-brained child even if she's married. Anyway, she went off for a ride with Brad on their fancy horse. And would you want Mrs. Shively or Mrs. Dunin with you when you were … having a hard time?"

"No, I wouldn't."

"So there's just me and Rose. Dr. Franz wanted Rose because she helped with Mr. Dunin. She's helping Mattie, I know."

Daniel frowned. "How do you know?"

"I … we're twins … I can feel her."

"Can you?" Daniel's frown deepened.

"Papa, don't take her away from Mattie. Mattie needs her. Go sit with Mr. Hollis. He's having a hard time, too."

Daniel looked over at the Hollis's wagon. Nathan sat hunched on the ground outside. "Maybe I should do that. Take care of Shadow for me. The chickens are in the saddle bag."

When Rose climbed into the Hollis's wagon, the first thing she noticed was how hot and stuffy it was. The afternoon sun beat down on the canvas cover and created a dim diffused light inside. Mattie was propped up on pillows, sweating, her brown eyes dark with fear. Dr. Franz sat beside her with his stethoscope on her swollen belly. He looked up with a relieved smile when Rose entered.

Rose went straight to Mattie, kissed her, and took her hands. Inwardly she prayed: *Dear Jesus, come and help us. Come be with us.* Like a sweet light descending, she felt His presence fill the wagon. Her pounding heart quieted, and she took a long slow breath.

"What can I do?" she asked Dr. Franz.

"Try to calm her. She's fighting it."

Rose looked around. Both ends of the wagon were closed tight. "Dr. Franz, may I open the ends of the wagon a little to let some air in? I think it might be more comfortable for Mattie."

"We closed them for privacy."

"I could open them just a little at the top."

"I guess that would be okay. What do you think, Mattie?"

Mattie nodded, then grimaced and gasped, "It's coming again."

Rose knelt beside Mattie, still holding her hands. She felt herself breathing long slow breaths and remembered how it had been with Mr. Dunin. "Look in my eyes," she said. "Don't be afraid. Jesus is here. He'll help us. Breathe with me."

She held Mattie's eyes as the contraction swelled, crested, and subsided. "That helped," Mattie said in surprise.

"Rest now," Dr. Franz said. "That was a good one."

Rose got up to open the ends of the wagon, allowing a cool breeze to flow through. She found a jug of water and a cloth to wipe the sweat off Mattie's face.

"Thank you," Mattie whispered. "That feels better." She began to relax and the fear left her eyes.

For hours Rose breathed with Mattie, wiped her face with a cool cloth, dropped with her into the rhythm of contractions coming like ocean waves, and finally experienced with her the momentous miracle of birth.

A little girl! Her thin new-born wail filled the wagon. Mattie and Rose wept with her.

"Tell Nathan," Mattie said.

Rose opened the front of the wagon and looked out, her face glowing with joy. "Mr. Hollis, you have a beautiful little daughter, and Mattie is fine."

It was a long evening, full of celebration and hard work for the twins. Rose washed out the blood-stained linens in the river and hung them on ropes strung between the wagons. Lily made a fire and plucked and cooked the prairie chickens. People gathered around the fire to congratulate Nathan. Rose took a plate of food to Mattie in her wagon. Nathan took Amelia and Little Nate to see their mother and their new little sister, then brought them back with their mat and their blankets to spend the night with the twins.

At last, as dark fell, the chores were done. The little ones were tucked in, asleep in the front of the wagon. Rose and Lily slipped out of their gowns, unrolled their mattress, and lay down. They were weary from the long day, but too excited to sleep.

"Tell me about it," Lily whispered. "What I can't imagine is, how did the baby come out of her?"

"She pushed it out through her hole down there."

Under the quilt, Lily's hand went protectively to the space between her legs. "But that's only a *little* hole. How could a whole baby come out there?"

"She stretched and stretched. You couldn't believe how much she stretched. And then you could see just the top of the baby's head, then all at once all of her head, and then she just slipped out. Dr. Franz wiped off her face and she cried—such a funny little wail. Lily, it was the most miraculous thing. I felt like heaven opened for her to come to us. And Mattie was so happy holding her new baby. It seemed that she forgot all her pain in that moment."

"Did it hurt her a lot?"

"Yes, it did. But at the end, she didn't seem to care. She was just pushing so hard to get her baby out."

"I felt you. That you were scared at first and then … Did Jesus come, like He did with Mr. Dunin?"

"Yes. But you know, He's always with us. I guess I just listen better when someone needs my help."

Lily stroked Rose's hair, feeling again how different they really were. "You're so good," she said softly.

They lay quietly together. A coyote sang out on the plains. Another answered.

"You know," Rose said after a while, "all the time I was with Mattie, I kept thinking of Rachel. Sometimes I thought I was seeing her instead of Mattie, holding her hands. I think maybe Rachel's baby came today, too."

"Do you?" Lily sat up. "Maybe we should pray for her."

"Yes." Rose sat up, too. "We haven't for a long time."

"Let's do it right now."

They came to their knees, hands clasped over their hearts, heads bowed against the chuck box. The waxing moon shone in through the open canvas, touching their hair with pale light. When they lifted their heads, their eyes were shining.

"I think her baby did come," Lily said.

"I do, too."

"Our little brother!"

When they lay down again, Lily curled around Rose, nestling her cheek in Rose's soft curls. Her mind was racing.

"If the baby comes out the hole down there," she whispered, "then maybe that's where …"

But Rose was asleep.

## Chapter 18

# *Regina*

The next day the wagon train moved on. For several days the twins cared for the Hollis children so Mattie could rest. Every day Dr. Franz asked Rose to come with him when he checked on Mattie, teaching her what needed to be done after a birth. The baby thrived, and Mattie healed well under Dr. Franz's watchful care. Soon she was up and able to care for Amelia and Little Nate again. On the first Sunday after the birth, Daniel baptized the new baby Elizabeth Rose, though soon she came to be called simply Baby Beth.

Another week passed. A three-day rainstorm dampened everyone's spirits, but when the sun came out, the plains were bright with wild flowers.

One evening, when the wagons were circled up and the people of the wagon train gathered at the center, Jake announced, "Tomorrow we pass by the convergence of the South Platte and the North Platte where they join to become the Platte River. By evening we should come to a ford across the North Platte. We'll cross over—that'll be our last major river to cross—and head south-west along the South Platte to Denver City. This is the halfway point."

"Halfway!" exclaimed Mrs. Dunin. "After all this time, all this misery, only half way?"

Jake looked over at her. "It's a long journey. But we've done well. Three and a half weeks to get this far. Three more weeks, and, God willing, we should arrive in Denver City."

It was hard to tell exactly where the convergence was when they passed it the next day. The trail curved north around a large swampy area, and, when it returned to the river's edge, Jake informed them that the river they now traveled beside was the North Platte. The following day they crossed over. The river was wide and swift, but not so deep that they had to unhitch the oxen. They had to keep moving fast once they entered the water so the wheels of the wagons wouldn't sink into the quicksand. It was a long, hard day's work, but there were no mishaps. They circled up for the night on the peninsula between the two rivers, and the next morning took up their journey along the bank of the South Platte.

Regina walked often with the twins. She complained she wasn't feeling well, her stomach was upset. "It's probably that river water. For all we strain it, it tastes terrible, and I get sand in my teeth."

"It's bad," Rose sympathized, "but Lily and I don't feel sick. Maybe something else is wrong. Maybe you should talk with Dr. Franz."

"Won't catch me doing that. I'm not having any man, who's not my husband, poking around on my body. I get enough of that from Brad."

The twins glanced at each other, signaling a question back and forth, but they didn't ask.

Then one day Regina came to them in tears. "I was talking to Lydia, and she said it's clear I'm pregnant. She asked me how long since I had the curse, and I haven't since we got married, and she asked how long, and I said two months, and she said 'You have the look. Your bosom is bigger.' And it is and it hurts and I feel awful and I want to puke all the time, and I never would have let Brad poke me like he does if I knew it would make me feel like this ..." Her words trailed off into sobs.

Rose put her arm around Regina. "But aren't you happy you'll have a baby?"

"*No!*" Regina almost screamed. "No, no! I just got away from all those babies and snot-nosed toddlers and bratty kids. Someone always screaming. I was *free!* Just me and Brad, and our wagon is as big as my family's whole cabin. And we're going to Denver City to have fun, which I never had any before. Just work, work, and every year a new baby, and guess who has to clean their shitty bottoms and wipe their yellow-green snot and wash their napkins. And I say to my ma, 'Stop it!' but she says it's a man's pleasure and a woman's duty and the babies keep coming. And now I ..." Regina gasped and rubbed the back of her hand over her tear-stained face.

The twins' eyes met in shock. Rose took a handkerchief out of her apron pocket and offered it Regina. The oxen plodded along and the three girls kept walking, Rose with her arm around Regina.

After a while Lily asked cautiously, "But when you married ... well, didn't you know you might get ...?"

"Of course." Regina tossed her head. "Of course I knew. I'd been around my ma long enough to know what that 'man's pleasure' leads to. But I got a pisser."

"A what?"

"A pisser. The fancy name's 'pessary.' I paid a whole dollar for it. You put it inside and it's supposed to stop babies from being planted."

Lily puckered her brow. "Inside?"

"A whole dollar." Regina's voice rose. "And it didn't work."

She broke into sobs again. "I'm never gonna let Brad poke me again with his damned big seed planter. He pumps and pumps it and groans and shouts, but it's me that gets left with the mess and now this …"

The twins' eyes met again, sharing in an instant the image of the dogs outside the trading post in Council Bluffs.

Regina broke loose from Rose's arm and went to the side of the trail and threw up. Rose went after her, held her head, and wiped her face with a handkerchief. The wagon train moved on and Lily had to keep going with the oxen. Rose stayed with Regina. When the Hollis wagon came along, Mattie stopped by Rose and Regina.

"It's that way with you, is it?" she asked Regina, smiling. "How wonderful! The sickness will get better. It only lasts a little while." She patted Regina on the shoulder and walked on.

Regina was pale. "Let's catch up with Lily. Lydia's coming next, and I'll puke again if she tells me how wonderful."

Moonlight flowed into the wagon. Daniel had gone outside to sleep. The twins sat on their mattress, wrapped in their quilts, hugging their pillows, facing each other.

"I think we know now," Lily said. "Regina told us how she got with child."

Rose shuddered. "She shouldn't have said that word."

"No. Becky would wash her mouth out good, all the bad words she said, but at least she wasn't hiding everything, saying babies come from heaven and all that."

"Maybe they do come from heaven. It seemed like that when Baby Beth was born. Maybe having them come out of the mother down there is God's way of sending them to us."

"But it isn't true what they always made us think, that God just put the baby in the mother's tummy. It's the man that does, with his seed planter. I think he puts it in her down there because that's where the baby comes out, and he pumps it, like those dogs."

Rose drew her knees up and wrapped her arms around them. "Ugh!"

"That's the big secret we're not supposed to know."

Rose bent her head over her knees. "Lily, let's never get married. I couldn't stand that."

"Maybe we're like animals," Lily reflected. "Not so different after all."

"I don't want to be like animals." Rose's voice was muffled. She lifted her head. "What if we got married and didn't know anything?"

"We'd think our husband had gone crazy."

Rose moaned and buried her face in her knees again.

Lily put her arms around her. "Well, thanks to Regina, we do know."

"Poor Regina."

The twins sat in silence, thinking of Regina and all she had told them.

Rose lifted her head, eyes wide with a sudden thought. "Did Papa do that to Rachel? And to Mama?"

"He must have."

"Oh, we shouldn't speak of it. He's our papa."

Lily stroked Rose's hair. "Come on. Let's lie down now."

They rearranged their quilts and pillows and lay down. Lily curled around Rose. They lay quietly together, but neither was sleeping.

After a while, Lily whispered, "Remember that time when we were little, taking a bath in the big tin tub in the kitchen, and we were rubbing down there and it felt all tingly and we were laughing?"

"And Becky slapped our hands and said we shouldn't."

"Yes, but remember how it felt?"

Rose didn't answer.

"Maybe …" Lily's whisper was softer. "Maybe … if you loved someone a lot … maybe it wouldn't be so bad."

# Chapter 19

# *Astride*

Days passed. The people of the wagon train grew weary of the constant effort of living outdoors and keeping the wagons moving. For the twins, mid-afternoon was the hardest part of the day. Regina was too sick to walk with them, and Lydia and Mattie were in their wagons with their napping children, so there was no one to distract Rose and Lily from the wind and dust. Rose limped.

"What's wrong?" Lily asked her.

"I don't know. My foot hurts." Rose stopped and turned the bottom of her foot up to look at it. "No wonder. My boot is worn clean through. Look at that hole."

"Goodness!" Lily bent to look. "Let's see your other foot."

"No hole in that one," Rose noted. "But the sole is really thin."

The oxen, not being led, stopped and hung their heads. A space opened in front of them as the wagon train moved on.

"What are yours like?" Rose asked.

Lily turned one foot up. "Thin."

"Keep moving," Mrs. Dunin yelled from behind them. The twins looked back to see her glaring at them from the front of her wagon. She had her hand on the whip, as if she could whip the twins' oxen from there.

"Sorry, Mrs. Dunin," Lily called back. She picked up the ox lead and slapped it lightly on Bo and Buff's backs. The oxen sighed and started plodding again.

"She's gotten so pushy since she took over the reins," Lily muttered to Rose.

Rose glanced back. "Poor woman. I don't think Mr. Dunin loves her very much."

"It'd be hard to."

"We'll have to dig out our other pair of boots. It's good Jake made us get two pair."

Stephen rode up. "I saw your wagon stopped. Are you okay?"

"We're fine." Rose smiled up at him. "Only I have a hole in my boot. We just stopped to look at it."

Stephen dismounted. "Would you like to ride Fleet? I wouldn't mind walking for a while."

Rose's eyes widened. "I'd love to."

"Do you know how to ride? I notice your pa always rides his horse, but I've never seen either of you ride her."

"We can ride. We had riding lessons in Boston." Lily frowned. "But it was different."

"Did you ride side-saddle, English style?" The twins nodded. "You'll need to learn to ride astride. Side-saddle's hard if you have to go a long way and no good at all for rounding up cattle." He pushed his hat back and rubbed his brow. "My cousins and my aunt Kate do some trick with their skirts to ride, and then undo it with a flick of their hand when they arrive, but I don't know what they do."

"We have split skirts," Lily said, kicking one leg up to show him.

"Sure enough. Perfect. Come on then, Rose. I'll boost you up."

Stephen picked Rose up, his strong hands on her waist, and set her on Fleet. "Swing your leg over and hold on with your knees. Here, I'll adjust the stirrups."

Stephen walked beside Rose, giving her a few tips on riding astride. "You do know how to ride," he said approvingly. "Take him for a little trot."

Rose nudged Fleet into a trot and went ahead along the wagon train. After a while she circled back, eyes shining. "It's so much easier sitting astride. You don't get that crick in your back. Can Lily have a turn?"

"Of course." Stephen showed Rose how to swing her leg over to dismount, lifted her down, and boosted Lily up. Once Lily got the feel of riding astride, she took off, trotting then cantering all the way to the front of the train. Jake was sitting easy on his tall horse, leading.

"Hey there, look at you!" he called to her.

"Hi, Jake. Stephen let me ride Fleet."

"So I see. You're doing great."

Lily's bonnet had blown back, and she was flushed with exhilaration. She circled around Jake, then headed back down the train toward her wagon, kicking Fleet into a gallop. Part way back she met Daniel riding toward her.

"Hi, Papa," she called as she flew by.

"What in the world?" Daniel exclaimed. He spun Shadow around and rode after her. He caught up with her, reached out, and grabbed Fleet's reins.

"Don't, Papa." Lily tried to push his hand away. "You'll hurt his mouth."

Fleet, confused, halted abruptly, almost throwing Lily over his head.

"Papa, let go. You're hurting him."

"*What* are you doing riding like that? With your limbs … That's not ladylike. Whose horse is that?"

"It's Stephen's. He said we could."

"I did not give you permission. You're supposed to be leading the oxen."

"Rose is."

"Get down off that horse right now. I'll not have you riding like that."

Lily sat firmly on Fleet. Her chin came up. "Regina rides like this all the time."

"Regina wears bloomers and does a number of things I do not consider it proper for you to do. I told you to get down."

"No."

The wagon train moved slowly past them. Locked in their confrontation, neither noticed the amused glances coming their way.

"What do you mean, no? You obey me." Daniel swung down off Shadow and approached Lily. Fleet sidestepped away from him.

Lily's eyes were blazing. "I *do* obey you almost all the time, but you never ever let us have any fun. The one time we were dancing, you came and spoiled it. We do all the work—the cooking and cleanup, taking care of the oxen and Shadow, keeping the wagon in order, washing your clothes and all day leading the oxen walking, walking, while you do nothing but just ride around on Shadow …"

"I'm doing God's work when I 'just ride around on Shadow.'"

The wagon train flowed on by. Stephen approached, leading Bo. "How did it go, Lily?"

"Fine—until I met Papa."

Stephen glanced at Daniel standing beside Shadow, silent and glowering, then held up his hands to Lily. "Shall I help you down?"

"Thank you." Lily descended gracefully with Stephen's assistance. "Where's Rose?"

"She's in the wagon looking for her other pair of boots." Stephen turned to Daniel. "I hope it's all right with you, sir, that I let the twins take turns riding Fleet. They were tired of walking, and Rose had a hole in her boot."

"Well … I would have preferred that you ask my permission first. I am not pleased to see my daughter riding astride like a man."

Rose emerged from the wagon and sat on the jockey box to change her boots. Lily took Bo's lead back from Stephen. The two men led their horses.

"With your permission, sir," Stephen ventured, "I'd be glad to give your daughters lessons in Western riding. They both did very well with Fleet; they are clearly well-trained horse women. But riding astride is different. There are some tricks I could teach them that would help them be safer."

"I won't have them riding astride. No lady should."

Stephen was silent again. Rose finished lacing her boots and jumped down off the wagon.

"Be careful," Daniel snapped. "It's dangerous jumping off when the wagon's in motion."

"I'm careful, Papa." Rose came to walk beside him, slipping her hand into his. "Can we? Can Stephen teach us? He said we'll need to know. Everything is so spread out in Gold Creek and riding side-saddle always gives you a crick in your back if you go very far. Besides, we don't even have a side saddle."

"Sir," Stephen put in, "I know back East it wouldn't be considered proper for a lady to ride astride, but out West most do. There's no one in the whole valley more elegant and ladylike than my aunt Kate, and she always rides astride."

"But the skirts."

"We have split skirts." Rose swung her leg to show him.

"What!" Daniel stopped walking. "I said no bloomers."

"These aren't bloomers. They're split skirts. That's different. We got them from Mrs. Garland."

"Split skirts. I'll not allow it. It isn't proper."

"Papa," Rose said, "we've been wearing these gowns every day for weeks and you never even noticed, so they can't be too improper."

Lily had kept silent since getting down from Fleet, but inside her bonnet she was grinning.

"No… I guess I didn't notice." Daniel glanced over at Lily walking demurely beside Bo. It was all Rose could do to keep from bursting into giggles at the expression on his face.

"Can we, Papa?" she asked. "Can we ride Shadow sometimes? We can take turns so one of us leads the oxen. We'll need to learn to ride better so we can help you, run errands for you when we get to Gold Creek."

"Well …" Daniel's voice was gruff. "I need to think about it."

The next day at nooning, the twins came to Stephen. "Would you ask Papa again?"

"You'd do better to ask Jake. He has more influence than I do."

Jake was sitting on the ground nearby, packing up his mess kit. He looked up at them. "What are you two up to now?"

"We want Papa to let us ride again. He was upset about our riding astride. But Stephen says most ladies out West do. Have you seen that, too?"

Jake stood and stretched. "Some do, some don't. But there's no question sitting astride is safer, more secure."

"Tell Papa that."

Jake looked down into the twins' eager faces. "You want me to interfere with your pa's rules for you?"

Lily tilted her head up, smiling. "Would you?"

Jake set his hands on his hips. "Irresistible wench. Okay, I'll talk to him. But I wouldn't want to be the pa of you two. I'd go gray in a day."

Later, as Lily and Rose cleaned up the lunch dishes, they saw Jake talking to Daniel. They kept their heads bent to their task, but peeked out from time to time, sharing a secret, jubilant smile, well hidden in their deep bonnets.

The twins never knew what Jake had said to Daniel, but that afternoon, and most afternoons thereafter, Daniel relinquished Shadow for an hour, allowing the twins to take turns riding out with Stephen.

Daniel walked with Gabe. "Jake says it's safer for them to ride that way, but their mother would never have allowed it. In Boston. I always heard ladies shouldn't ride that way because it might … awaken them. It's so hard to know how to guide my daughters in this new world."

Under the wide brim of his hat, Gabe's black eyes were compassionate. "They say when you have you a high-strung young filly, or two, best not to keep the reins too short."

"It's such a responsibility."

"Remember, you ain't their only father. Their Heavenly Father watches over them, too."

As they walked and talked together, a mile or so away, out of sight of the wagon train, Stephen led Lily in a wild zigzag gallop along the flat edge of the river.

**Chapter 20**

# *The Road Ranch*

May merged into June, and the days became hotter and longer, although the nights were still cool. There were fewer wagon trains along the South Platte, the track less trampled. As they moved into the Colorado Territory, the landscape changed from the flatness of Nebraska to low rolling hills. Most of the time their trail went along the river bed where there was good grass and shade from the cottonwood groves, but occasionally, to avoid swampy areas, the trail went up and over one of the low hills.

One morning the trail took them up a fairly steep hill. Lily and Rose, walking with their oxen, were first in line that day, Jake riding beside them. As they topped the rise, Lily dropped the ox lead and lifted her arms.

"Look! Look!" she cried. "Rose, look!"

Far away across the plains, mountains rose majestic against the sky, blue in the distance, capped with white, purple shadows folded in the hollows of their slopes.

"Don't stop," Mrs. Dunin yelled from behind them. "*You* may be at the top, but the rest of us are still trying to get up this hill."

"Come aside," Jake said.

Rose took Bo's lead and led their wagon off the trail. Lily still stood staring. When the rest of the wagons had reached the top of the hill, the people of the wagon train gathered together, looking out in awe across the plains at the distant mountains.

"There they are," Jake said, with a wide sweep of his arm. "The Rocky Mountains. Beautiful to look at. Be glad we don't have to cross them."

At first the mountains could be glimpsed only from the high places, but soon they became part of the daily view, growing gradually closer. The sight of them filled the twins with awe and excitement. "Just think," Lily said to Rose. "When we get to Gold Creek, we'll be right at the foot of the mountains. Maybe when we get our own horse, we can ride up into them."

One day at nooning Jake announced, "There's a sizable road ranch a few miles ahead. We'll stop there for the afternoon. They have a grocery, a telegraph, and mail station, and the stagecoach stops there. You can pick up some fresh supplies, send off a letter if you wish."

There was an excited burst of conversation. They had stopped a few times before at small trading posts along the way, but never one with so many possibilities.

Rose and Lily stood listening, hands linked. "Maybe we can get some milk and eggs and make some real bread," Lily said. "I'm tired of biscuits."

An hour later the wagon train came to the top of a low rise. The road ranch lay below, sprawled untidily over an acre or so on the west side of the track.

"Robinson's Road Ranch," Jake said, as they paused to look down at it. "It's been here for the last five years. Robinson's a squaw man and some of his wife's kin live there. Probably that's why his place hasn't been burned down, like so many others have. Let's go."

The ranch was dominated by a long log building with elk horns hung over the door. On a rough bench in front, two men sat drinking and talking in loud voices. A stout squaw, followed by three small barefooted children, came out and headed toward a cluster of tepees in back. Behind and around the lodge, on bare trampled earth, were a large corral with a dozen or more horses, a stable, and a scattering of ill-kept outbuildings. A neat sod house stood a little apart.

Jake led the wagon train to a wide low area across from the ranch, between the track and the river. The earth was bare there, too, but some old cottonwoods shaded it. The wagon train circled up, and the people emerged from their wagons.

"No grass for oxen here," Mrs. Dunin muttered.

"Nope," Jake said. "Too many others've been here before us. You can buy feed across the way." He raised his voice to address the whole camp. "The grocery is in the log building, the telegraph and stagecoach station in the sod house. I want everyone back in camp before dark. We'll leave early in the morning as usual. Enjoy yourselves."

Mrs. Dunin jumped down from her wagon with Mr. Dunin's crutches under her arm, scuttled over to a clump of cottonwood trees, and hid them in the brush. As she hurried toward the lodge, Mr. Dunin emerged from the wagon bellowing, "Evelyn, what have you done with my crutches?" He pounded the jockey seat in frustration as she disappeared into the long log building.

Mattie and Lydia came by with their little ones in tow. "Are you coming?" they called to the twins.

Mrs. Shively peered out of her wagon. "You shouldn't. It's a sinful place. I'm surprised Jake had us stop here. Did you see those men drinking?"

"She's right," Daniel said, as he tied Shadow to one of the wagon wheels. "I want you girls to stay here. That's no place for young maidens like you."

"No, Papa," Lily protested. "We want to see it."

"We need to buy some supplies," Rose put in. "We want to get some milk and eggs so we can make real bread."

Lily stood silent, her chin up, her lips pressed together. Rose slipped her hand into Daniel's. "We'll stay right by you, Papa. You can protect us."

"Well …" Daniel rubbed his brow. "Real bread does sound good."

The inside of the lodge was dim, lit only by afternoon sunlight coming in the small square windows. The twins paused inside the door to look around. There were shelves of groceries along the wall on the right side, stocked with tins of sardines, bags of flour, jars of canned tomatoes and peaches, hanging strips of salted meat; farther back was an area with harnesses and hardware. On the left side of the lodge there was a bar and some plank tables. Three rough-looking men leaned on the bar, served by a tall, thin Indian woman, her long black braid hanging forward over her shoulder.

Two men sat at one of the tables, each with a bottle, their heads together. One had black shaggy hair and a black beard covering most of his face. His soiled deerskin vest stretched across his protruding abdomen, and he wore knee-high moccasins with fringe at the tops. The other man, handsome except for a white scar from his left eye to his ear, was clean-shaven and neatly dressed in blue denim pants, a yellow cloth shirt, and a leather vest. His back was broad and hard, his shoulders drawn slightly forward. As he talked to his companion, he glanced around the room with narrowed eyes.

Jake strode up to the table and clapped the black-bearded man on the shoulder. "Hey there, Robinson. I brought you a bunch of customers."

Robinson stood up to shake Jake's hand. As they greeted each other, the other man looked over at the twins with a sharp appraising glance.

Rose shivered. Lily caught her hand and stared back at the man. He shifted his gaze away.

"Come on," Lily said. "Let's get groceries."

The young girl behind the grocery counter was thin and pale, her pale brown hair pulled back in a tight bun, her pale blue eyes large and sad in her thin freckled face. Mrs. Dunin was keeping her busy, asking for one thing, then another, rejecting what she was given, demanding something else.

When Mrs. Dunin finally completed her purchases, Lily stepped up to the counter.

"Hi," she said smiling. "I'm Lily. This is my sister Rose. What's your name?"

The young girl looked startled, then smiled back shyly. "Laura."

"Do you have any milk or eggs?"

"Yes, we do. They're in the cold room. How much do you want?"

"A half dozen eggs and a quart of milk."

Laura went out a door between two shelves and came back with the milk and eggs.

"Let's get some peaches, too," Rose said.

As the twins continued their shopping they chatted with Laura. "Have you lived here long?" Lily asked.

"I don't live here," Laura answered. "I've just been here a few weeks. I was going to Denver with my family, but my mother got sick, and the wagon train went on without us." Tears filled her eyes. "Indians attacked, and my whole family, everyone … my parents and my brothers were all killed."

"Oh!" Rose reached across the counter to touch Laura's hand. "How awful! I'm so sorry."

"That wagon train shouldn't have left you!" Lily exclaimed. "Our wagon master would never have done that. How did you escape?"

"My mother had put me in a trunk. They didn't find me. Later another wagon train came along and brought me here. But I wish I could go home."

"Do you have family back East?"

"My uncle and aunt and cousins. They'd take me in, but I don't have money for the stagecoach. It's twenty-five dollars. Mr. Robinson said he would pay me ten cents an hour, but he hasn't yet. Then he said that man over there"—she gestured toward the man with the scar—"would give me a good job that would pay me lots, so I could buy a stagecoach ticket and telegraph my uncle. So I'm going with him tomorrow. I'm not sure where."

The twins exchanged a worried frown.

"You shouldn't go off unchaperoned with a man you don't know," Rose said.

Laura hunched her shoulders. "I don't know what else to do."

Lily leaned across the counter and whispered, "Is there a privy here?"

"Yes. It's out that door in back, past the stable. It has a half moon carved on the door."

"Thanks, we'll be back and pay for the groceries. Come on, Rose."

Rose pulled back on Lily's hand. "We told Papa we'd stay with him."

Lily glanced over at Daniel, absorbed in examining a bridle. "We'll be right back. He'll never miss us."

"Okay, but we must be quick."

They went out the door Laura had indicated, walked around the stable, holding up their skirts as they stepped around piles of manure and jagged pieces of junk metal. Behind a cluster of outbuildings, they found the shack with the half moon.

Rose wrinkled her nose. "Are you sure you want to go in there?"

"I have to."

Rose waited outside. The privy smelled atrocious. Lily was very quick. "Ick. That's the filthiest place I've ever been in. Do you need to go?"

"I'll wait. Let's hurry back now before Papa misses us."

The scattered outbuildings were confusing. The twins skirted a pile of broken wagon wheels and approached a leaning shed.

"Wait." Lily pulled Rose back. "There's voices."

The smell of cigar smoke drifted around the corner of the shed. Its door hung loose on its hinges, half open. It was empty, except for a few rusted tools leaning in one corner. The twins ducked inside.

One of the boards in the back wall was loose. The twins peered through the space around the edge of it. Only a few feet from the shed wall, Mr. Robinson and the man with the scar walked by, arguing.

The man with the scar was angry. "Your message said there were two."

"I told you," Mr. Robinson said, "the other one left yesterday. A train came through, heading for Denver. Had some women in it. She took up with them and off they went. I couldn't stop her. Those women were all over her, cooing and weeping over her bad luck." He shrugged.

The man with the scar pounded his fist into his palm. "I wouldn't have come all this way for just one, and she a scrawny little bitch. No bosom on her. And young. Probably the kind that will cry. Most of the men don't like that."

"Well, I kept her for you. Three weeks now. Feeding her and putting her up." Mr. Robinson waved his cigar. "Didn't pay her, so she'd be ripe for your deal."

"You had her working. You didn't come off too bad."

"That's as may be. You owe me twenty-five dollars for her, Smythe. That's our deal. Twenty-five dollars per girl."

"She's not worth it. I'll give you fifteen."

"Our deal is twenty-five. You want me to keep finding girls for you, you'd better keep your word. Hell, she's sure to be a virgin. You'll get a good price for that."

"Once."

They moved on out of sight around the corner of the stable, still arguing. The twins were shaking, clinging to each other.

"That's Laura they're talking about!" Rose whispered, pale with shock. "Mr. Robinson's *selling* her. Like a slave."

"For—" Lily drew in her breath. "He said he'd get a good price for … Rose this is terrible. We have to warn her."

"Hurry!" They scrambled out of the shed and hurried toward the lodge.

Lily pulled Rose back. "Wait a minute. We need to think. She needs to get away from those bad men."

"We could take her in our wagon, like that other girl who got away."

"But she wants to go home—only she doesn't have any money."

"We have money." Rose patted the front of her apron. "We can give her some to buy a stagecoach ticket. The stagecoach stops here."

"That's a *good* idea."

"Let's do it." Rose walked faster.

Lily strode along beside her. "But those are really bad men. They might stop her, take away her money. Mr. Smythe was really mad the other one got away."

They stopped short and turned to look at each other. "Mr. Smythe," they whispered in unison.

"Where did we hear that name before?" Rose asked.

"I can't remember." Lily frowned. "But it was something bad."

"Never mind. Maybe we can get Papa to help us," Rose said.

"No! If he knew we'd been near such bad men, he'd shut us up in the wagon for good."

"Jake."

"That's it. Jake. We'll give him the money and ask him to make sure she gets on the stagecoach. Nobody would dare argue with Jake. But first we have to tell Laura."

They ran to the lodge, opened the back door, and bumped smack into Daniel. He seized them, one with each hand, gripping their arms.

"Where have you been?" He gave them a shake. "You promised me you'd stay by me. I've been looking everywhere for you. You're going back to the wagon right now, and you'll stay there until we leave tomorrow."

He dragged them toward the front door.

"Please, Papa." Rose pulled back. "We need to get our groceries. Otherwise we can't make you bread."

Daniel let go of them. "All right. Pick up the groceries and pay. But don't move out of my sight."

He pulled out a chair by one of the tables and sat facing the grocery counter.

Laura was busy. Seth had a pile of groceries on the counter, and Gabe was behind him.

The twins waited in line, gripping each other's hands, until at last Laura was free.

Lily leaned across the counter. "Laura," she whispered, "don't go with that man with the scar, that Mr. Smythe. He's a very bad man."

Rose leaned over and whispered, "We heard him talking to Mr. Robinson. Mr. Robinson's *selling* you to him like a slave."

"That's why he isn't paying you."

"And Mr. Smythe said you would cry. Don't go with him."

Laura turned ashen. "What can I do?"

"We have money for your stage coach ticket."

Laura was trembling, her eyes filling with tears.

"Don't worry." Lily leaned across the counter. "Listen. See that big man over at the bar, the tallest one with the red shirt and loose brown hair? The really big man?"

Laura nodded.

"That's Jake, our wagon master." Rose reached across to take Laura's hand. "You can trust him. We'll give him the money and he'll buy your ticket and telegraph your uncle. And make sure those bad men let you go."

Laura looked as if she were going to faint, her cheeks flushing then turning pale. "Why would you do that for me?"

"We don't want to see you hurt. Take a deep breath," Rose urged her. "It's going to be all right."

"The stage comes by at eight o'clock tonight," Laura said.

"You'll be on it." Lily smiled at her and Laura smiled back, a wobbly, incredulous smile. "Okay." Lily became business like. "What do we owe you for these groceries?"

"Oh." Laura's hands trembled as she added up the tally. "Six dollars and twenty-five cents."

Daniel came up behind the twins. "Pay up. And then we go."

Lily leaned across the counter as she gave the money to Laura, whispering, "Remember, trust Jake."

Rose took her hand and squeezed it. "God bless you."

"How can I ever thank you?" Laura's eyes brimmed over.

"We're going *now*," Daniel said, turning the twins around and gripping their arms. He pulled them across the wide floor of the lodge toward the front door. "What are you up to? Why is she thanking you?"

"We did her a favor," Lily said, "just girl stuff. But, Papa, wait." She stopped, pulling back against his forward momentum. "Before we go back to the wagons, we need to speak to Jake."

Jake was talking to some men who were drinking at the bar.

"Absolutely not," Daniel said. "You're not going over there." He jerked them in the direction of the door.

"But it's important. Something dangerous." Rose looked up at him, her eyes pleading.

"Dangerous! Then you'd better tell me. What is it?"

The twins looked at each other and fell silent. Lily shook her arm, but Daniel didn't let go.

Daniel's brow darkened. "There's something dangerous you want to tell Jake that you can't tell your own father? That's enough of this foolishness." He dragged them again toward the door.

The twins struggled. Heads turned. The men at the bar looked over, laughing. "Got your hands full there?" one called. "Need some help?"

Daniel flushed. "Stop it," he muttered to the twins.

"Will you tell Jake to come talk to us?" Rose asked.

"Okay, I will. Come on now."

The twins stopped struggling. "We're coming," Lily said under her breath. "Let go of our arms."

"Come quietly then." He released them, and they followed him to the door. Rose looked back as they exited. Laura stood tense behind the counter, her eyes staring, her fists pressed against her chest.

The wagon circle was quiet. The Shivelys and Mr. Dunin were out of sight in their wagons. The oxen lay resting on the ground. The horses drowsed standing, switching the flies with their tails. Afternoon heat pressed down. The only person to be seen was Ben, sitting against a wagon wheel, whittling.

"Okay," Daniel said. "Here you are and here you stay. I've got work to do. Ben," he called, "these girls are to stay in the wagon circle. Keep an eye on them for me."

Ben looked up. "Yes, sir." As Daniel turned his back, Ben winked at the twins.

For the next hour the twins worked on the bread. Ben helped them make a fire in the shade of the cottonwoods.

"Let's send Laura a note," Lily said, "with our address in Gold Creek, so she can write us and let us know if she gets home okay."

"Good idea." Rose set the dough to rise on the chuck box and brought out paper and pen to write the note.

Lily paced, twisting a long lock of hair that had broken loose. "Papa didn't want to tell Jake."

Rose looked up from her writing. "But he said he would."

"Maybe not in time. Let's go look across the track. We can see the door of the lodge without leaving the circle."

"Let me finish the note, and we need to put more wood on the fire."

When the note was finished and the fire tended, they crossed the circle and slipped between the wagons.

Jake was talking to Mr. Robinson in front of the lodge, one foot up on the low bench.

Lily gave a little jump. "There's Jake."

The twins took a deep breath. "Jake," they yelled in unison. Jake looked up. The twins beckoned to him waving both arms, jumping up and down.

Jake turned briefly to Mr. Robinson, then came across the track. As soon as he reached the other side the twins ran to him.

"Oh, Jake."

"We're so glad you saw us."

"We need your help."

"Something really bad."

"Whoa, easy there." Jake touched their shoulders. "Let's go back inside the wagon circle." He glanced back at the lodge. Mr. Robinson had stood up and was watching them. Jake ushered the twins into the circle and over to the shade of the cottonwoods. "Let's sit down here. Tell me, what's wrong?"

Once they were settled, the twins poured out their story, speaking rapidly, one after the other, finishing each other's sentences as was their way. They told Jake about Laura's plight. Stumbling and hesitating, they groped for words to tell him what Mr. Robinson and Mr. Smythe were plotting. Their words still tumbling over each other, they told him Rose's idea of giving Laura money to get home, and their fear those bad men would prevent her.

"Will you help us?" they asked in unison.

They sat holding their breath, looking at him.

"Whew!" Jake let out a long breath, his expression a mixture of astonishment and concern. "Indeed I will." He frowned. "Tell me where you got this money."

"Our grandmama gave it to us for emergencies," Rose said.

"And you want to use it to help Laura?"

"Yes. And you should take the money now and buy a ticket for her and telegraph her uncle because it is getting late," Lily urged him. "The stagecoach comes at eight o'clock."

"I'll get it." Rose jumped up. She ran to the wagon, climbed in, pulled off her apron, and reached under the waist band of her skirt for the packet of money. She counted out thirty-five dollars, scooped up the note she had written, and ran back to Jake.

"Here. The ticket is twenty-five dollars. There's ten extra dollars for the telegraph, and money for food on the way, and a note from us."

Jake took the money and note and tucked them into his shirt pocket. His brow was deeply furrowed. "I'll take care of it right away. Now, there's danger here I was not aware of. You two stay here. Under no circumstances leave this wagon circle. You understand?"

The twins nodded. Jake strode off without another word. The twins watched until he disappeared around the wagon closest to the track, then turned and hugged each other.

"He'll take care of it," Lily said. "Laura will get away."

Rose was crying. Lily kissed her and wiped her cheeks. "Let's see what's happening to our bread."

"Oh, dear, the fire's probably gone out."

They found that Ben had kept the fire going with some drift wood he'd found down by the creek, and the dough had risen. Once they had the bread in the dutch oven, the coals piled on top, they sat together, suddenly exhausted, watching the fire, arms around each other, brows touching.

Soon the people of the wagon train came hurrying into the circle. There was a flurry of confusion, excitement, exclamations. The twins heard fragments of conversation—

"Danger."

"Especially for the women."

"He didn't say what."

The late afternoon shadows lengthened, and the people of the wagon train went about their evening chores, tending their beasts, preparing their evening meal. The twins' bread came out perfectly. They wanted to give Ben a slice, but Ben had gone across the road with Jake.

Daniel had not come back with the others. Rose and Lily prepared supper for him, set it aside, ate their own supper and cleaned up.

"It's almost eight o'clock," Lily said softly to Rose as they packed the dishes into the chuck box. "I want to see what's happening over there."

The wagon nearest the road was Seth's. He was across the circle, talking with Nathan.

The twins meandered toward his wagon. When they reached it, they glanced around, then scrambled underneath and crawled to where they could see the front of the lodge. They had not watched long before the door opened and Jake came out with Laura. He was carrying her bag, talking quietly with her as they headed toward the neat sod house. The twins couldn't hear what he was saying, but Laura looked happy, her thin body tense with excitement.

A moment later the door opened again, and Mr. Smythe charged out. In three long strides he caught up with Laura and grabbed her arm.

"Where are you going?" he shouted. The twins could hear that.

Jake spun. With one huge hand he twisted Mr. Smythe's wrist. Mr. Smythe swore and let go. Jake gave him a long look. "She's going back East on the stage coach. She's under my protection. Don't touch her again."

Mr. Smythe reached out. "She's mine. She's coming with me. It's all arranged."

"Arrangements change. I said, don't touch her."

But Mr. Smythe grabbed Laura anyway, this time around her waist, and yanked her backwards. Jake's big fist swung out. Mr. Smythe fell flat on his back, a puff of dust rising up around him as he landed.

Under the wagon, the twins gasped.

"Come, Laura," they heard Jake say, as he led her into the sod house. Mr. Smythe lay very still in the road.

A few minutes later the twins heard the sound of hooves and wheels, a jingle of bells, and the stage, drawn by four horses, rounded a bend in the road. It pulled up in front of the sod house, and came to an abrupt stop, throwing up a cloud of dust.

Mr. Robinson hurried out to meet it, but stopped when he saw Mr. Smythe lying in the road. He looked down at him for a moment, then grabbed him under the arms and dragged him to the bench in front of the lodge.

Meantime the driver of the coach jumped from his seat, opened the coach door and called in, "Ten minute stop here. There's food in the lodge." Two men and a middle-aged woman climbed stiffly out and followed him into the lodge.

Mr. Smythe sat up. He looked around, then across the road, straight at the twins where they crouched under Seth's wagon. Rose caught her breath, and both of them wiggled backwards away from his glance. When they dared to look again, he was rubbing his jaw and watching the men coming from the stables with fresh horses.

In no time, it seemed, the horses were changed, the passengers returned from the lodge. Jake and Laura came out of the sod house. The twins scrambled out from under the wagon and waved. "Bye, Laura," they called. Laura's face broke into a huge smile. She waved and called back, "Thank you!"

Jake looked across the road and glared at the twins. He helped Laura into the coach and threw her bag up on top, where one of the armed guards who rode there caught it and tied it down. Through the stagecoach window, the twins saw Laura sitting down, then turning to wave to them one more time. The driver leaped onto the front seat, cracked his whip, and the stagecoach tore off in another cloud of dust, soon disappearing over the brow of the hill.

Jake strode across the road. The twins hid behind Seth's wagon, but he found them. He towered over them. "I told you to stay *inside* the wagon circle." His voice was low, but huge and terrifying. "I did not want anyone, most especially Smythe, to know who bought Laura her ticket. So now he knows. Go get in your wagon and stay out of sight. Where's your pa?"

"We don't know. He didn't come for supper."

Jake rubbed his beard up the side of his face. "I'll go find him, but not until you're out of sight. Don't you understand you've just put yourself in danger?"

The twins scuttled to their wagon, scrambled in, and sat on the floor hugging each other.

"She's safe," Lily said. "Jake did handle it."

"I'm so glad it wasn't Papa with her when Mr. Smythe grabbed her."

They were both trembling.

Later Daniel came, ate his supper, and wandered off to talk to Gabe. Jake put a guard all around the wagon circle. As the long slow dusk of mid-summer deepened, the twins settled down into their quilts.

They woke a few hours later to the sound of men's voices approaching their wagon. It was dark. Stars shone through the opening in the wagon cover. In the front, Daniel snored. The twins sat up, tense.

"All quiet?" It was Jake. The twins let out their breath.

"So far." That was Ben's voice.

The twins slipped out of their quilts and leaned against the chuck box to peer out. Jake and Stephen and Ben stood close by.

"Good." Jake was turned away from them, his tall frame outlined against the night sky. "What a day," he sighed. "I've a half mind to go over and have a word with Robinson about this vile trade he's taken up. Brothels—it's bad enough if a woman chooses that life, but to sell off an orphan kid, who's under your protection, who's had more tragedy in the last month than anyone needs in a lifetime—I'd like to punch his face in."

Stephen laid a hand on Jake's arm. "Don't even consider it."

Jake clapped Stephen on the shoulder. "No, I won't. Of course. I'm needed here." He rubbed his fist. "I did get a good one in on that slime Smythe. I don't know what's happened to Robinson. I thought he was a decent man. We won't stop here again." He looked around at the quiet camp. A few men lingered by their fires. Mr. Dunin limped toward the edge of the circle on his crutches. "Is everyone accounted for?"

Ben nodded. "They're all here. I'll keep an eye on Clay. Guess he found his crutches, but I don't think he'll get far."

Jake rotated his shoulders. "Where did you find the preacher?"

"In one of the tepees, sitting on the ground in a circle of Indians, telling 'em about Jesus. They were all nodding and smiling, but I don't think they were buying."

"Such an innocent." Jake shook his head. "That whole family bears looking after. Those twins! But they did a mighty good deed today. Be sure and have an extra watch on their wagon. I saw in Smythe's eyes he'd like to get back double for the one he lost."

The twins shivered and drew back.

"I'll personally keep watch," Stephen offered.

"Thanks," Jake said. "Ben, you'd better follow Clay. He can probably smell the alcohol way over here."

The sound of their voices and footsteps faded away. The twins heard Stephen approach and felt the wagon shift slightly as he sat down and leaned against a wheel. They slipped silently back into their quilts.

"I'm glad Stephen's watching," Rose whispered. "It would be horrible to be kidnapped by that man."

"He wouldn't dare," Lily whispered back. "I'd bite and kick and scream."

Rose nestled back against Lily and drifted into slumber. But Lily lay awake, eyes open in the darkness.

# Chapter 21

## *Stampede*

It was a sunny morning, but there was more dust than usual in the air, and a low roar that was neither wind or water. The ground trembled under the twins' feet as they walked. The roar grew rapidly louder. The wagon train stopped.

Ben galloped up. "Turn back," he yelled. "Buffalo coming this way. Turn around and follow Stephen."

Chaos broke out as people began turning their wagons. Jake galloped by shouting, "Never mind turning. There's not time. Follow me." He led the train up a low hill to the north of the trail, beckoning with wide sweeps of his arm.

Daniel rode up, tossed Shadow's reins to Lily, climbed onto the jockey box, and set the wagon in motion. Rose and Lily ran beside it, leading Shadow. The other wagons followed Jake, scattering out on both sides of the hill.

"Stop here," Jake ordered. "Unhitch your oxen and tether them well. Stephen, Ben, stay here with the wagons. Randall, you too. All the rest of the men with horses, follow me. Bring your guns." He galloped over the hill to give orders to the wagons on the other side.

Daniel stopped the wagon, reached back for his gun, jumped out, and mounted Shadow. "Take care of the oxen."

Rose caught hold of his stirrup. "Papa, where are you going?"

"We're going to try to turn the buffalo aside. Keep the oxen calm." He galloped off with the other men toward the bottom of the hill.

"Take your stand here," Jake ordered the men. "Spread out in a line. When they come near, fire in the air. Turn them away from the wagons at all cost."

The buffalo were almost upon them. The thunder of their hooves was deafening. They snorted and bellowed as they ran, noses to the ground, tails in the air. Daniel sat astride Shadow, gun in hand, trembling with excitement. "Shoot now," Jake yelled. He rode between the line of men and the oncoming buffalo, hair flying, hat waving. Daniel raised his gun and began firing. The line of men seemed thin and fragile standing against the momentous onslaught, but the guns seemed to be working. The lead buffalo swerved away from them. The men cheered. "Keep firing." Jake spun back and forth along the foot of the hill that sheltered the wagons. More buffalo poured down toward them.

Suddenly a lone bull broke loose from the herd and charged straight toward Daniel. He lowered his gun and fired. A good shot, right between the eyes. But the bullet ricocheted off the buffalo's brow and into the earth between Shadow's feet. She reared and threw him. He landed hard on his back, still clutching his gun. As he rolled to his knee, he saw the buffalo, close by, shaking its head from side to side. Daniel fired three shots into its neck and heart. Just in time. It had turned to charge him again, horns lowered, when it fell.

Daniel scrambled to his feet. He stood for a moment breathing hard, then turned to mount Shadow. But Shadow had bolted and was racing up the hill toward the wagons.

～

The twins unhitched the oxen and tethered them. The trembling of the ground grew stronger, the roar louder. From their vantage point on the side of the hill, the twins could see the approach of the buffalo, like a great dark ocean, and the line of men spread out not far below.

Now the buffalo surrounded the base of the hill. The twins watched from above, clinging to each other. For a moment it looked as if the men would be overwhelmed. Then the dark mass swerved. A cheer from the men rose faintly up the hill. The twins searched for their father, but a cloud of dust obscured their view.

Above them, an ox bellowed. Others took it up. One of the Shivelys' oxen broke tether and ran. In a moment the wagon camp was a chaos of stampeding oxen. Stephen rode up to the twins. "Get out of their way," he shouted as first Buff broke loose, then Bo, Lad, and Lucky. The twins flattened themselves against their wagon.

Suddenly Shadow was there, empty saddle, stirrups flapping. Stephen jumped off his horse and caught Shadow's reins. "Quick! One of you. Ride Shadow and help me. We've got to keep the oxen from mixing with the buffalo."

"I will." Lily ran up to him. He caught her around the waist, lifted her up onto Shadow, swiftly shortened the stirrups.

"What about Papa?" Rose cried.

"I don't know. But we're lost without the oxen. Come on, Lily. Move with her like I taught you. Now!" They galloped off after the fleeing oxen.

Rose stared after them, her heart pounding with fear. All around her oxen bellowed, broke their tethers and fled down the hill, across the trampled track toward the river. She could see how easily their path could blend with the buffalo. Already far away, she saw the small figures of Stephen and Lily galloping furiously to hold the space between the two herds.

From the other side of the hill she heard a terrified scream. Lydia! She ran to the top of the hill just in time to see the Merrill's oxen tear loose the tongue of their wagon. Lydia had not unhitched them. Rose pressed her knuckles to her mouth as the scene below her unfolded like a slow-motion nightmare.

The Merrill's wagon teetered and fell onto its side. Willy careened out the open end, hit the ground and ran. Lydia scrambled out screaming, "Willy, Willy!" and ran after him. A moment later, Cindy tumbled out. "Mama," she called. She started after her mother, then stopped as an ox raced close in front of her. Rose ran as fast as she could, but not fast enough. Cindy stood bewildered, her doll dangling from her hand. More oxen charged toward her. Rose screamed, but no sound came from her throat. In slow motion she saw the oxen bear down on Cindy and pass over her. Willy was still running away from the wagon. Lydia tripped over her skirt and fell, scrambled to her feet, dodged a yoke of oxen, and ran on after him.

Cindy lay on the ground as limp as the rag doll beside her, her pale curls scattered in the dust. Rose reached her at last and fell on her knees beside her. Cindy's delicate little-girl chest was crushed, her head turned to the side. A trickle of blood ran out of her mouth.

Rose gathered her into her arms.

"Mama," Cindy gasped.

"Your mama's chasing Willy. She'll be right back."

Cindy drew in a gurgling breath, coughed. Blood poured out of her mouth. "Mama."

"She'll be back soon." Rose gathered the little girl closer, rocking her.

Cindy twitched, coughed again, and lay still, her blue eyes wide and blank, staring up at the blue sky.

Rose stopped breathing. Ice-cold panic poured through her. "Cindy?"

Cindy lay still, so still.

"Cindy!" Another wave of panic engulfed Rose. Her heart thundered in her ears. Her eyes went dark for a moment. When she could see again, she stared unbelieving at the fragile, broken child in her arms.

~

Lily rode Shadow at a full gallop after the stampeding oxen. Her bonnet blew back. She could feel the wind in her face. She was shouting, leaning with Shadow as Shadow darted and turned, driving the oxen away from the bellowing buffalo. All was speed and light of the dazzling sun, the thunder of hooves, the ripple of Shadow's muscles between her thighs.

Suddenly she hesitated, pulling back on the reins. Rose! Something had happened to Rose. Lily's body was shaken with Rose's terror, her shock. Shadow slowed, dancing with impatience. "Come on!" Stephen shouted to her. "We have to cut them off before they reach the river." Oxen streamed by her. Lily held the reins, wavering, looking back, then forward. A yoke of oxen shot out in front of her, heading toward the buffalo. She released the reins and was off again. Shadow turned and wove, and Lily could think of nothing but staying with her. She was ahead of all the oxen now, the river in front of her. Shadow turned, driving the oxen away from the water's edge. Stephen was beside her, shouting and waving his hat. As he spun in a sharp turn, Fleet stumbled, throwing Stephen down into the dust in front of the charging oxen. Lily screamed and cut between Stephen and the stampede. Stephen rolled and in an instant was on his feet and back on his horse. Ben galloped up on the other side of the herd.

The three of them held the milling, bawling herd as the oxen turning around mingled with those still racing for the river. Gradually they turned the oxen back toward the wagons, Ben driving from behind, Stephen and Lily on either side. Jake galloped up to join them. The oxen were exhausted, many still yoked in twos. They moved slowly, lowing. To the west the buffalo thundered by, into and across the river.

~

After what seemed an endless time, the last of the buffalo passed the edge of the hill. The dust began to settle, the roar of their passing diminished, leaving behind a strange quiet.

On either side of him, Daniel saw men turning their horses and riding up the hill to the wagons. All except Jake, who galloped off toward the river.

Daniel lowered his gun and stood up stiffly from behind the dead buffalo where he had hunkered down after Shadow ran away. Adrenalin rushed through him again as he looked down at the huge dead beast, then pride swelled his chest. He had killed the buffalo singlehandedly. Food for the whole wagon train.

Daniel trudged up the hill. The camp seemed deserted. There was no one in sight but Mr. Dunin, lounging on his jockey box with his bandaged foot stuck out in front of him. All the beasts were gone. The men who had ridden ahead passed him, riding out again at a gallop. He hurried to his wagon. Empty. Shadow was nowhere to be seen.

"What happened?" he asked Mr. Dunin.

"Well, as you can see, the oxen are gone, stampeded, all of 'em. Got excited by the buffalo, I guess."

"Gone? Do you know where Rose and Lily are?"

"Lily took off on your horse after the oxen. My wife, she's gone, too. When our oxen broke, she starts screaming at 'em." He raised his voice to imitate her. "'You come back here!'" He chuckled. "As if they'd listen to her yelling. And then off she goes, running after 'em—on foot. Maybe they'll run her down."

Daniel looked at him sternly. "Pray they don't. And Rose? Did you see where Rose went?"

Mr. Dunin's voice softened. "My little angel. There's some trouble back there over the hill. She went to help, like she always does if someone needs."

"Thanks." Daniel ran, his head spinning.

When he reached the top of the hill, he saw the Merrill's wagon on its side. All those left in the camp were gathered around. Their muted voices floated up to him. And another sound, a terrible sound. A woman's voice—screaming, sobbing, keening. His heart contracted.

He hurried down. "Ah, here comes the preacher," someone said. The circle opened to admit him.

Lydia sat on the ground beside the tilted wagon, wailing, rocking her dead child in her arms. Dr. Franz knelt beside her. Bill stood by, tears streaming down his face, holding Willy, white and wide-eyed, in his arms. Mattie sat behind Lydia, supporting her.

Dr. Franz looked up. "Daniel, see if you can get her to stop crying long enough to drink this laudanum. She's been hysterical too long."

"What happened to the child?"

"Run down by oxen."

Daniel knelt in front of Lydia and put his hands on her shoulders. His strong, resonant voice broke through her wails. "Lydia, the Lord is with you. Open your heart to the Comforter."

She gulped. Her cries trailed off.

"May I take her?" Daniel held out his arms. "I want to say a prayer for her."

Mutely, Lydia gave him the child. Daniel held her, head bowed, seeking the right words. The men standing around took off their hats.

"Dear Lord," Daniel prayed, "receive this little lamb into thy heavenly fold… ."

As he prayed, the wind sighed over the hill, stirring the rough grasses. The men bowed their heads. Clouds blew across the sun, darkening the afternoon, then passing. The sun shone out again.

Daniel lifted his head as he said, "Amen." He looked into Lydia's eyes. "Know for sure that at this moment your little one rests safe in the bosom of our Savior, enfolded in His love. And remember that you still have an earthly child who is very frightened right now and needs your comfort."

"Willy!" Lydia half stood, looking around wildly.

"He's here." Bill knelt beside her and put Willy in her arms.

Daniel looked up at the circle around him. "Surely there are enough men here to set the Merrill's wagon upright, so Mrs. Merrill will have a place to rest."

Randall stepped forward. "Let's go."

For the next hour, Daniel was so involved that he forgot to look for Rose. At last he saw her. She was lying curled up in the grass in a small hollow a short distance away from the Merrill's wagon. Gabe sat beside her, his lean brown hand resting on her back, his head bowed in prayer.

A wave of fear tore through Daniel. There was blood on her gown. She was lying so still. Why was Gabe praying by her?

He ran to kneel beside her. Gabe lifted his head. "She ain't injured," he said, answering the question in Daniel's eyes. "But she was a'holding the child when she died."

"Ah!" Daniel bent to look into Rose's face. Her eyes were closed. She was very pale. He touched her hand. "Rose?"

She opened her eyes. "Papa."

The sound of lowing oxen floated up the hill on the wind from the river.

"Lily?" Rose sat up, then stood unsteadily. Daniel took her arm and together they followed the others to the brow of the hill. From there they watched the slow approach of the weary oxen.

Jake rode in front and waved. "We got them all," he called.

"There's Lily." Rose straightened and pointed.

~

As Lily rode up the hill behind Jake, she saw Daniel coming to meet her, frowning. She lifted her chin. He came to her in the midst of the milling oxen and took Shadow's reins.

Jake turned back and greeted Daniel. "You can be proud of your daughter. Without her, we might not be bringing all these oxen back. I saw her from afar, riding like a wild one, keeping the oxen out of the buffalo. When Stephen fell from his horse, she cut right in and turned the beasts before they trampled him. I saw him fall but was too far away to help. She was the one who saved Stephen's skin."

Daniel was still frowning. "She could have been killed."

"But she wasn't. She was fantastic."

Lily's heart burst with pride. Her cheeks were pink, her eyes shining. "It wasn't really me," she said. "It was Shadow. She knew what to do."

Stephen had joined them. "But you stayed on her," he said, clapping Lily on the back, "which was more than I managed. And you handled her better than I ever taught you."

Jake nodded to her, one eyebrow lifted, his fierce, blue eyes bright with approval.

"All right." He raised his big voice to the group on the hill. "I know the oxen are tired, but find your own and hitch them up. I want these wagons circled up pronto."

Randall ran to Jake and drew him aside. Lily heard Jake exclaim, saw him rub his beard the wrong way, and break into a run, following Randall over the hill.

"Lily."

Lily turned at the sound of Rose's voice. The color drained from her cheeks. "Rose!" She swung her leg over Shadow, stumbled a little as she dismounted and ran to Rose. "What happened? You have blood all over you."

The minute Lily put her arms around her, Rose broke into sobs. Fear raced through Lily. "Rose, what happened? I felt you. I started to turn back, but I couldn't. We had to catch the oxen. Oh, are you hurt?" She moved her hands swiftly over Rose's body.

Daniel touched Lily's shoulder. "She's not hurt. But Cindy was run down by oxen and Rose was holding her when she died."

"Died! Oh, Rose." Lily almost staggered as the full weight of Rose's grief swept into her.

Rose lifted her head from Lily's shoulder, her face streaming with tears. She jerked herself away from Lily and seized Daniel by the shoulders. "You said God watches over us," she cried. "Why did He let Cindy die?" She shook him. "Why does He *let* the sparrow fall?

～

Late sun slanted across the wagon circle. In the center, a cook fire burned. During the afternoon, several of the men had gone to bring back meat from the buffalo Daniel shot, and spits of it were roasting over the flames.

Gabe and Bill and Nathan were gathered around the Merrill's wagon discussing how to repair the broken tongue. With Baby Beth in her arms, Mattie watched over Amelia, Little Nate, and Willy as they played by the Hollis's wagon. Jim rode up with Mrs. Dunin, disheveled and glaring, sitting awkwardly in front of him on his horse. Mrs. Shively turned the spits of meat, muttering, "The Lord giveth, the Lord taketh away."

Her knees drawn up to her chest, Rose sat against a wagon wheel, staring in front of her, numb, unseeing. She felt a touch on her shoulder.

Stephen knelt beside her. "Rosie, are you okay?" When Rose turned her head, he went on, "I came to see if you could help me. I took a tumble and scraped up my shoulder. Dr. Franz is busy, but said you might be able to clean it up for me."

Rose struggled to focus her eyes. "Of course. May I see?"

The sleeve of Stephen's blue denim shirt was shredded from shoulder to elbow. With careful fingers, Rose separated the tatters. "Oh my!" The raw flesh underneath was caked with dirt and dried blood.

"It's nothing really." Stephen shrugged. "But I thought maybe I should get it cleaned up."

"You certainly should." Rose got to her feet, wobbling a little. "Let me get some things from the wagon."

Stephen stood up with her and helped her climb in. She emerged a moment later with a bottle, a small jar, and some clean cloths. "Come over here." She went to the side of the wagon where the water barrel hung.

Stephen followed. "Maybe I should take off my shirt."

His lean, strong chest was white where the sun had not touched it, scattered with soft brown curls. Rose blushed. She turned away to the water barrel and wet one of the cloths. Carefully she wiped the blood and dirt out of Stephen's shoulder.

He looked down at her bent head as she worked. "You're so gentle … Rosie, I'm so sorry you were alone with Cindy when she died. It must have been really hard."

Rose couldn't answer. She turned to the water barrel to rinse out her cloth, biting her lip, then continued washing Stephen's wound.

"There," she said at last. "It's clean now. I'm going to pour some whiskey over it. I'm sorry. It will sting." She opened the bottle and poured some of its contents over the raw wound, catching her breath when Stephen winced. "Now I'll spread some calendula ointment on it to soothe it. Do you have a clean shirt?"

"Just one." Stephen looked ruefully at the torn one in his hands. "I guess this one's a gonner. Too bad. It was a good shirt, new in Council Bluffs."

Rose took it from him. "I can mend it."

"I don't think so; it's completely tattered."

"I can. Now go get your other shirt on to cover that shoulder and keep it clean."

Stephen didn't go right away. He stood watching Rose as she corked the bottle of whiskey and rinsed out her cloth. He touched her lightly on the back.

"Thank you, Rosie."

Lily lay in the dark wagon, curled around Rose. Rain drummed on the canvas cover. In the front end, Daniel snored softly.

Rose was heavy in her arms. When night came, Rose had begun to shake and cry again, and there was nothing Lily could do to comfort her. Finally, Dr. Franz had given her laudanum, and now she slept.

But Lily could not sleep. Her inner world was a turmoil of contrasts. Her spirit soared as she remembered the exhilaration of galloping after the oxen, her daring moment of cutting them off from trampling Stephen, Jake's defense of her and his praise. She wanted to remember only that. But there was also the tragedy of Cindy's death and Rose's pain beating into her, as it did still, even as she slept her drugged sleep.

Lily turned her head away from Rose. Why do I have to hurt so much when she hurts? Isn't it enough for one of us to be in pain?

I am sad about Cindy. And sad for Lydia and Bill, and Amelia who just lost her best friend and doesn't understand. But I don't feel it the way I do Rose's grief.

It's like an open door between us, and all she feels pours into me.

A door.

A door can be closed.

A shiver passed through her.

She imagined a door between Rose's heart and her own heart nestled against Rose's back. A sliding door, like the one between the dining room and Papa's study in the manse in Boston.

Without actually intending to, she slowly slid the door between their two hearts closed. Relief! A wave of guilt swept through her, but she did not open the door again.

Rose stirred in her sleep. "Lily, don't leave me."

Lily held her close. "I'm here. I'll never …"

She could not finish the sentence.

# Chapter 22

# *Partings*

Two days later the wagon train set out again. The wind was up with a cold, sharp edge. Lily and Rose walked silently, hand in hand beside the oxen, each absorbed in her own thoughts.

Images swirled behind Rose's eyes, overlaying the dusty track in front of her. Amelia and Cindy dancing to Gabe's fiddle, only three evenings before. Amelia's short dark braids bobbing, the setting sun making a radiance of Cindy's fair hair, their laughter, their little bodies light and lively. Cindy lying crushed in the dust. The open grave, Cindy's body wrapped in a pink blanket, lying inside. Amelia coming to lay Cindy's doll in the grave beside her. The cairn of rocks left behind as the wagon train moved away.

Lily, too, had somber images of the funeral, the heavy clouds and the fine thin drizzle, the awful feeling in the pit of her stomach when Jake threw the first shovelful of earth on Cindy's little body. These images mixed with those of the stampede, the speed, the light, the river ahead of her, Stephen rolling in the dust and bounding to his feet, the thunder of the buffalo. But mostly she thought about the door between her heart and Rose's. She had opened it again as soon as she woke the next morning; she could not bear to be separated from Rose for long. But she knew it was there, and that she could close it. The thought shook her with a strange excitement, waves of guilt, and an aching sense of loss. It would never be the same again.

She squeezed Rose's hand and felt an answering squeeze. They walked on in silence.

Later in the morning, Dr. Franz came to walk with them. "You did a good job with Stephen's scrape," he said to Rose. "I checked it just now and was very impressed that there is no infection."

Rose turned to look at him. "I'm glad. I tried to do it just as you taught me."

"You know, I could have done it myself, but I sent him to you because I wanted you to know that you could turn from death to care for the living."

"Oh!"

They walked on together. Inside her deep bonnet, Rose began to weep. She tried to hide it, but a sniffle and a sob escaped her.

Dr. Franz touched her shoulder. "It's hard, especially the first time, to be in the presence of death."

"I can't stop shaking inside."

"Yes, it was a shock for you."

He rested his hand on her back as they walked. After a while, he went on, "Death is a part of life for everyone, but especially for a doctor. You're a natural healer, Rose. You've had quite an initiation these last few weeks, first with Mr. Dunin's foot and then the birth and now death. I wish I had more time to train you, for you are gifted and the need is great."

Rose tightened her hand around Lily's.

Dr. Franz was silent a while, then spoke again. "Perhaps I can train you further. I've been talking to Jake and Stephen. Montview is a good-sized town a few hours' journey from where you'll be in Gold Creek. They have a school, which would be good for my boys, and they don't have a doctor. So I plan to settle there. I'm going to Denver first, to pick up supplies. The road from Denver to Montview goes by Gold Creek; I'll stop and see you on the way. And maybe later you can come to Montview and work with me for a while, then take your skills back to serve in Gold Creek. Would you like to do that?"

Rose had been working to regain her composure while Dr. Franz talked, but her breath was still a little ragged as she answered. "Yes, I would. Can Lily come, too?"

Lily turned to look at Dr. Franz, her eyes startled.

"Of course," he answered. "She would be welcome. But I sense Lily has a different path."

Rose's breath caught in a sob. "No."

The final week of the journey passed without further adventures. The people of the wagon train were weary of travel, but were used to the routine and had become increasingly efficient in the daily tasks of the trail. One day they made twenty miles.

Lydia stayed in her wagon most of the time, and often Rose heard her crying. Willy didn't run away any more, but clung to Lydia's skirts whenever they moved around camp.

The men of the four Ohio wagons talked excitedly about the treasure they were soon to gain.

Mr. Dunin became quite cheerful. At first Daniel feared he might have gotten hold of some whiskey at the road ranch, but soon realized that Clay was simply enjoying being lazy and having his wife do all the work. Daniel continued to try to convert him; they had long conversations, but Clay held out, saying he wasn't ready.

Mrs. Shively gave up lecturing everyone about the Sabbath, and she and her husband kept more and more to themselves. Judgment emanated from their wagon.

Almost every day, Daniel walked with Gabe. He shared his many worries about the twins and the task ahead of him, and was always comforted by Gabe's bright spirit and sweet gap-toothed smile, his simple words of faith and wisdom.

The twins felt the time coming when they would be leaving all their friends. Their friends felt it, too, and they almost never walked alone.

Regina got over her morning sickness, and emerged from her wagon to join them. "Brad says we can pay a nanny to take care of the baby, so we can still have fun. And he knows a way to not have any more. He can get something when we get to Denver. He's kind of excited about the baby. He hopes it will be a boy. Maybe it won't be so bad."

Mattie walked with them, carrying Baby Beth in a shawl slung across her shoulder, with Little Nate and Amelia scampering beside her. Amelia, lost without Cindy, attached herself to the twins who sang to her and played with her and gave her rides on Lucky's back.

Each afternoon, the twins took turns riding with Stephen. Lily always wanted to gallop, but Rose rode quietly beside him, and they talked. Stephen shared with her his plan for going to California. "When I finish this trip to Denver, I'm going to find some companions to travel with, not a train because we can go faster with just horses. Maybe I'll be there by fall."

"It's a long journey," Rose said softly.

"Yes. But once I've seen California, I'll be back to work on my uncle's ranch. And then I'll come find you and Lily in Gold Creek and hear your pa preach in your new church."

Day by day the mountains grew closer. Now the twins could see more detail, the wooded slopes, the cliff faces gleaming in sunlight after rain, the snow-covered peaks.

Then one evening Jake came to Daniel as he sat with the twins, Gabe, and the Hollis family around their cook fire.

"Sometime tomorrow," he said, "we'll come to the place where Gold Creek flows into the river. There's a road along the north side of it that will take you to the town of Gold Creek. This train's heading on down the river to Denver. So you'll want to leave us there. Your journey's almost over."

"Over!" Daniel exclaimed. "That's hard to believe." The twins looked up, eyes wide.

"I kind of hate to send you off alone," Jake went on, "but you'll be okay. You're experienced travelers now. And it's not far."

"He ain't going alone," Gabe spoke up. "Me and Sadie are going with him."

"What?" Daniel turned to Gabe.

"Yep. I been talking to Jesus, and He done told me why He called me to come West. You'll be needing a carpenter to build your church, and a friend to be by you in your new work."

"Gabe!" The twins clapped their hands.

"We're coming with you, too," Nathan said. "You're our preacher and we want to be in your church, wherever it is."

"I want to be near Rose when I have my next child," Mattie added. "And Amelia and Little Nate couldn't get along without their aunts Rose and Lily."

Daniel looked around the circle of his friends. "I'm touched … grateful," he stammered. "It would mean a great deal to me …" He broke into a huge smile. "You're really all coming with me?"

"We'll make your new church a little bigger," Nathan grinned.

"I'm so glad!" Rose pulled Amelia into her lap and kissed her.

"Yes!" Lily caught Little Nate up and held him, laughing, over her head.

"Well, well," Jake said. "Looks like I'll be losing three wagons tomorrow instead of just one. But that's good. Good you'll have old friends in your new church."

∽

The next day when the wagon train stopped for nooning where Gold Creek flowed into the river, the people came to say to good-bye.

"We'll miss you, Preacher."

"Thanks for all your sermons."

"Good luck."

Regina hugged the twins. "Maybe me and Brad will come visit you and show you our new baby."

Mr. Dunin waved from his jockey box. After all, he had never let Daniel baptize him.

Dr. Franz came to shake Daniel's hand. "You will do well with your church, I know. You truly speak the Word." He turned to the twins. "Good-bye, you two. Thank you for all your help, Rose."

Rose held tight to his hand. "Thank you for all you taught me."

He smiled at her with love. "I'll see you again. I'll be coming through Gold Creek before too long."

Even Mrs. Shively unbent herself to wish Daniel well in his new church.

Jake stood with his hands on his hips looking down at the twins. "You know, Preacher," he said to Daniel, "you didn't need to come West to find treasure. You brought it with you, two-fold." He touched Lily's bright hair. "Pure gold."

Impulsively the twins threw their arms around him; their heads came only to his chest. "We'll miss you, Jake."

"Here, here!" he laughed, his blue eyes bright. "You girls behave yourselves now."

He looked up, surveying the camp. "Ben, blow your horn. It's time to get moving."

One by one the wagons forded Gold Creek. Those staying behind watched them go, waving, calling good-bye.

Stephen on Fleet was last in line. He had just reached the edge of the creek when Rose called, "Stephen, wait!" She ran down the bank and caught hold of his foot in the stirrup. "Your shirt. I need to give you your shirt. Just a moment."

She ran back up the creek bank to her wagon, climbed in and returned with the shirt in her hand. Stephen dismounted.

Rose handed him the shirt. "It's all mended, but ..."

"Let me see. I can't imagine how you could have mended all those shreds." He unfolded the shirt. "Rosie, this is beautiful!"

Over the many seams required to bind the tattered sleeve together, Rose had embroidered a rose. Its vibrant red blossom curved over the shoulder and top of the sleeve. Its long stem extended down to the elbow with several branches and many green leaves. Stephen stroked the smooth, closely stitched embroidery with the tip of his finger. "This is amazing. I didn't know you could do stuff like this."

"I used to do quite a bit of it, in Boston. It's mended, but I didn't quite finish. There are still two leaves I didn't have time to fill in." She pointed to two leaves near the bottom of the stem, just outlined with the blue denim showing through. "I didn't realize our parting would come so soon… I'll miss you."

"I'll miss you, too. But I'll see you again when I get back from California."

"Good. Maybe then I can fill in the other two leaves—if you still have the shirt."

"Oh, I will. This is a treasure." He looked over his shoulder at the departing wagon train. "I have to go." He rolled up the shirt and put it in his saddle bag, then turned and took both her hands in his. "Don't forget me, Rosie."

She looked up at him smiling. "How could I forget you?"

Stephen tightened his hold on her hands, looked into her face for a long moment, half-opened his mouth as if he would say something more, then let go her hands and swung up onto Fleet. He turned in the saddle to look back at her. "Good-bye."

"Good-bye. Safe journey." Rose waved and watched him, one hand pressed to her heart, as he forded the creek, rode off after the wagon train, and disappeared around a curve in the river.

She turned and walked slowly up the bank. Lily put her arms around her.

"Well," Nathan said. "Looks like we should get moving, too."

Chapter 23

# The Last Miles

Gold Creek sang a loud, gurgling song for the three families traveling along its northern bank. Daniel rode ahead, feeling anxious and protective of his little tribe. The night before, he had led them off the trail and hidden them in a cluster of small evergreen trees. He and Nathan and Gabe had taken turns keeping watch, but the night had been peaceful with no greater threat than the howling of coyotes at dawn.

Toward noon they were stopped by a large flock of sheep crossing the trail in front of them. Two men on horseback and three dogs drove the sheep across a shallow ford in the creek and on up between the hills. Daniel rode up to the man at the back of the flock.

"Good day."

"Howdy."

"Can you tell me how far it is to the town of Gold Creek?"

"Not far. 'Bout five miles." He reined in his horse and looked over their small company. "You from back East?"

"Yes. I'm from Boston. I've come to serve a church in Gold Creek. You're welcome to come for services."

"A church, huh? Naw, I can't come. I'll be up in the high country all summer watching over these ones. Maybe next winter." He tipped his hat. "Good luck with the church. That town could sure use one." He waved and followed the herd northwest toward the mountains.

"Five miles!" Daniel exclaimed. "We could be there before dark."

"All right," Nathan said. "Let's get going."

"We need to stop for nooning," Mattie reminded them. "Let's go a little farther. There's some trees ahead where we can get out of the hot sun."

"Women." Nathan grinned at Daniel. "They always want us to be sensible and eat and rest."

"Nooning's important," Mattie insisted. "Jake never missed it."

When they reached the trees, Daniel was impatient. "Let's do a short nooning and get on."

Rose had opened their chuck box and was handing out lunch supplies to Lily. She turned to Daniel. "Papa, I have another idea."

"What then?"

"Look at us. We're filthy—our clothes, our hair, our faces, our wagons. Your beard and hair haven't been trimmed since we left Council Bluffs. Is this how we want to meet the members of our new church? The water is so clear and clean in this creek—"

"And deep enough to actually bathe in," Lily put in.

"Let's stop for the afternoon," Rose went on, "and bathe and wash our clothes. It's so warm they'll dry before evening. And then go into town tomorrow looking fresh and clean."

Mattie said that was a great idea. Nathan thought the creek looked inviting and arriving half a day later wouldn't matter much, and Gabe allowed as how a wash probably wouldn't hurt him.

Daniel felt his beard, rubbed his hand across his dusty brow and looked at his fingers. "Well …"

Close to their stopping place, the bank dropped steeply into a little cove, sheltered by willows and one big cottonwood. Once the lunch was packed up, Mattie and the twins gathered soap and towels, bundles of laundry, a couple of buckets, and clean clothes to put on after their baths. With the children scampering ahead of them, they made their way down the bank to the cove.

"We men can bathe right here," Nathan said, "and keep an eye on the wagons."

He sat down and started pulling off his boots.

"Shouldn't we guard the women?" Daniel asked. "What if some Indians came along?"

Nathan looked up, a boot in his hands. "Maybe we should. We can take turns."

"I'll go first," Gabe said. He sauntered down to the cluster of willows that shaded the women's bathing place and sat down against the cottonwood, his back to the creek.

The creek was cold and running fast. Daniel and Nathan plunged in, laughing, gasping, splashing each other. Later, well scrubbed and much refreshed, dressed in clean clothes, Daniel went to relieve Gabe.

"Everything okay?"

"Sounds like it. The kids are having a great time squealing and splashing."

"Papa," Lily called, "are you up there?"

"Yes."

"Throw down your dirty clothes."

Daniel got his dirty clothes and threw them down the bank, and then sat with his back against the cottonwood. Upstream he saw Gabe plunging into the creek and Nathan unyoking the oxen and leading them to the water.

Behind him it was quiet, except for the loud song of the creek. Daniel became uneasy. I don't hear anything. I'd better check. He got up and turned toward the top of the bank. But I shouldn't look. They might be— His head began to throb. He took a step. I should check. Hesitated. No. He stood still, listening, his heart pounding. No voices, no sound but creek song. Images rose behind his eyes of Indians silently swooping down on the twins and Mattie and the little ones, covering their mouths with strong, red hands, and dragging them away. He took three swift steps to the edge of the bank, parted the willows, and looked down into the little cove below.

Amelia and Little Nate squatted naked at the water's edge, playing in the sand. One of the twins bent over a low rock in the shallow water scrubbing clothes and passing them to the other twin, who stood knee deep in the creek swirling the soap out, then squeezing the clothes and piling them on a big boulder beside her. Their hair was loose, hanging wet down their backs, and their wet shimmies clung to them, revealing every detail of their shapely bodies. Mattie sat leaning against the bank nursing Baby Beth, her abundant white breasts bare, dappled with sun and leaf shadows from the tree above her. Daniel watched the baby suckle and tug on a strand of Mattie's long dark hair.

Silently he backed away, closing the screen of willows. His loins burned. His head ached. He reached around to feel the lump. It was gone, but he felt the same sick pain he had felt that first Sabbath after the river crossing. He sat down again, his jaw clenched, struggling with the burning in his loins, images of the twins' wet bodies, Mattie's full breasts. He could not even pray. I am damned for eternity by this evil passion, he thought in anguish. Even Christ cannot save me.

Later he was roused from his daze by their voices as they came up the bank. The children ran ahead. Mattie followed, her contented, sleepy baby in the crook of her arm. The twins, dressed in the blue gowns they had worn on the train, carried buckets of wet clothes.

Daniel got up. He took the buckets from the twins and carried them to the wagon, then crawled in and lay curled on the floor, sick with despair.

Outside he heard laughter and chatter as the twins and Mattie hung the clothes and played with the children. He heard Nathan's voice: "Come on out of there, Gabe. You must be clean enough now. You'll turn blue." Gabe's voice: "The dirt was pretty crusted on." More laughter.

Daniel uncurled and looked out. Gabe was coming out of the creek, dripping and shivering. One twin was sitting on a bucket while the other combed out her hair. It formed a bright golden halo of curls around her face, tumbling down her back. The image blurred. He saw Grace's hair, remembered loosening it on their wedding night—and what followed. His loins burned anew. He groaned inwardly and drew back. After a while he felt the wagon rock. "Are you all right, Papa?" It was Rose.

"I'm okay. I just have a headache."

Rose climbed in and knelt beside him. She stroked his head with her gentle hand. "Maybe it was the cold water. It made my head kind of ache, too. I'll make you some willow bark tea. Do you want to come out now? Lily's ready to trim your beard and hair. She's done Nathan's and Gabe's, and they look really good."

"I guess I could do that." Daniel climbed stiffly out of the wagon.

Lily, scissors in hand, gestured to the bucket. "You're next, Papa. Have a seat." Her hair was loose, wild and bright.

"Put your hair up," he said sharply. "Both of you. You're too old to be running around with it loose like that."

Rose looked at him, puzzled. "We will. We want to let it dry first."

Lily ran her fingers through her curls, fluffing them out even more. "It feels so good to have it clean and get all the dust and sand out. Come on, Papa, time for a trim."

During the long summer afternoon, they cleaned their wagons, scrubbed the sand out of their water barrels and filled them with fresh water from the creek. The clothes dried, and Mattie and the twins gathered them in. The children ran free. As evening came on, Nathan started a cook fire, and that night they had a feast, using up most of the rest of their provisions.

As they sat around the fire after eating, Lily said wistfully, "Our last night on the trail."

"But not our last night to eat together," Mattie said. "Wherever we make our home, you will all come and eat with us often."

"Mattie and I have decided not to do a homestead," Nathan explained. "We don't need that much land and don't want to be so far out of town. We're going to see if we can buy a couple of plats—two acres should be enough for a good garden and an orchard—and I'll see if I can get a job at the sawmill. We'll need a lot of boards to build our church and our houses, so they may need help."

"I wonder where we'll sleep tomorrow. Do you think they'll have a manse for us?"Rose asked.

Daniel frowned. "Probably not. They don't even have a church building yet."

"Maybe we'll still live in our wagon for a while," Lily said. "I wouldn't mind that. What about you, Gabe?"

Gabe's black eyes shone in the firelight. "Got something to show you," he said. "I didn't know what I was gonna do. My money's gone, and my food's just about gone. But I need to get a place to open my shop when I get to Gold Creek, and more tools, if I'm a'gonna help build your church. I asked Jesus. Then when I was getting my bath in the creek this afternoon, I found this." He drew something out of his pocket and held it out. The firelight glinted on the gold nugget in his palm.

There was a moment of stunned silence. Then Nathan said slowly, "That's a big chunk of gold."

"Gold? Is it really gold?" Lily asked.

Rose leaned forward and touched it with the tip of her finger.

Mattie laughed. "That's why you stayed in the creek so long! I was getting ready to tell Nathan to fish you out before you froze to death."

"I shouldn't a'stayed. I found it right away. Then I thought there might be more. But there weren't. Jesus done give me just what I needed. Just this one."

"Such faith," Daniel said softly. "Such faith brings forth miracles. This creek was not called Gold Creek for nothing, but it's been panned for years now. The Lord blesses you, Gabe."

"And He blesses you and your church, because that is what this is for, Daniel, to build the church. Jesus will help us, not just with this, but always." Gabe looked across the fire at Daniel and nodded. Then he slid the gold nugget back into his pocket.

"What will the church look like?" Rose asked.

"It needs to be big enough for lots of people," Lily said, "because Papa is such a good preacher, they'll come from miles around."

"It should have a steeple."

"And a bell."

Daniel sat in silence as they dreamed and planned. The gift of the gold nugget, Gabe's faith, the twins' trust in him, the love and support of Nathan and Mattie, all slammed up against his sense of the deep-rooted sin within him.

∼

They started early the next day. Daniel rode ahead. The twins walked together, leading the oxen, hands linked.

"Today we'll finally get there," Lily said. "I'm excited to see what the town will be like."

"And meet the people who are in the church," Rose added. "But, Lily, Papa doesn't look good. He's all tense."

"He's probably nervous about meeting his congregation."

"But he shouldn't be. He's such a good minister. Everyone loves his preaching. I wonder what's bothering him."

"Here he comes now."

Daniel rode up, dismounted, and fell into step beside the twins. "I need to talk with you."

"What is it, Papa?" Rose asked.

"I want you to understand that it is very important that I do well with this church."

"Of course." Lily looked over at him. "You always do well."

"Part of it will depend on you. People judge a minister by his family. So it is important that you behave yourselves."

Lily tightened her grasp on Rose's hand. Rose couldn't see her face because it was hidden by her bonnet, but she could feel Lily's surge of rebellion. She took a deep breath. "We will, Papa. We'll help you. That's why we came with you."

"I've been lax with you on the trail, but now it will be different. I want you to behave like good Christian ladies and set an example for the other women in the congregation. No riding astride, no dancing, keep the Sabbath, come to all the services, keep your hair *up*. No going off exploring on your own. Do you understand?"

Rose felt Lily's rebellion intensify. "Papa, it may be different there than in Boston," she said cautiously. "We do want to help you, but maybe we should wait until we get there and find out how things are."

"Sometimes," Lily blurted out, "we need to have some fun."

"We are not here on earth to have fun, but to serve Christ. And good Christian conduct is the same wherever we are."

Lily was squeezing Rose's hand so hard it hurt. Rose decided it was best to say nothing more.

"Do you understand?" Daniel asked again.

"Yes, Papa," Rose said. Lily didn't answer.

"Lily?"

"I understand." Lily's voice was dangerously quiet.

Daniel walked beside them a little longer. Rose sensed him scrutinizing them and was grateful their faces were hidden by their bonnets. Finally he mounted Shadow and rode ahead.

Lily exploded. "He just can't treat us that way! I'm not going to be tied down by his 'good Christian lady' rules. I'm not! We *are* good Christians and we help him all the time in lots of ways. We washed all his dirty clothes for him only yesterday. And he never even thanks us."

"Sometimes he does. I know he appreciates it even if he doesn't say so. Don't be upset. Let's just wait and see. Once we get there he's going to be busy with his church and can't keep track of us all the time. In the meantime let's do the little ladylike things that are so important to him. I don't know why he's so worried. That's not like him."

Daniel circled back, passed by their wagon, and dismounted to walk with Gabe. The trail curved, following the path of the river. As they came around the bend, the twins saw a woman ahead of them on the trail. She was walking slowly, leaning on a stout stick, bent under the weight of the big bundle on her back. She heard them coming, stopped, and turned to watch them approach. Rose waved. She waved back and waited until they came up to her. She wore a man's wide-brimmed hat and a faded brown gown, frayed at the hem. In her tanned, lined face, her eyes were startlingly green as she peered up at them from under the weight of her bundle.

"Good day," Rose greeted her.

"Good day to you," she responded. Her smile was wide, with several missing teeth.

"That's a big bundle you're carrying," Lily said, as she reined in the oxen. "Would you like a ride? We're heading to Gold Creek."

"That's where I'm heading, too. When I heard you coming I was hoping you'd offer. My old legs are tired." She loosened the straps across her chest that held the bundle in place.

Daniel and Gabe came up, followed by Mattie and Nathan and the children, who peered at the stranger from behind their mother's skirts.

"Good morning," Daniel greeted the woman.

"Morning." She shifted the straps off her shoulders and dropped the bundle to the ground behind her. Without her bundle, she stood straighter, small and wiry. Her black hair hung in a matted braid down her back. Wayward curls, streaked with gray, framed her face under her hat.

"I'm Reverend Daniel Wright on my way to serve the church in Gold Creek. Can we offer you a ride?"

"The preacher!" she exclaimed. "We been waiting for you. They sent us a letter saying you was coming, but it was a long time ago." She searched his face with bright inquisitive eyes. "Pleased to meet you, Preacher. I'm Isabel. Isabel Flannagan." She held out a lean, gnarled hand.

Daniel took her hand. "These are my daughters, Miss Lily Wright and Miss Rose Wright, and our friends Mr. Gabe Archen and Mr. and Mrs. Hollis and their children."

"Your daughters, eh? Twins I'd guess. Sweet and courteous they are. They already offered me a ride, and I said yes." She nodded to Gabe and the Hollis family. "Pleased to meet you."

"Let me help you up." Daniel took Isabel's arm and helped her up onto the jockey seat. "This is a heavy bundle," he said, as he heaved it into the wagon. "Have you been carrying it far?"

"Far enough. I've been walking pretty steady since early yesterday morning. That bundle's all my earthly possessions." Isabel settled herself with a sigh. "Can't say I'm sorry to set it down."

Rose and Lily exchanged a quick glance and climbed up on the jockey seat, to sit on either side of Isabel. Lily gathered up the reins, flicked them once, and the oxen set off again.

"Why are you carrying all your earthly possessions so far on your back?" Rose asked Isabel.

"Oh, it's a long story," Isabel sighed.

"Have you been in the Colorado Territory long?" Lily asked.

"Seven years. I came out here with my son, Ed's his name, back in '59 when they first found gold. Well, Ed didn't find much, but enough to set us up on a homestead out there on the plains." She waved her hand dismissively back over her head. "One hundred sixty acres you get, but you got to live on it for five years before it's yours. So Ed built us a little cabin and we got a few cows and started a garden. Wind, dust, grasshoppers. And one summer some cowboys ran their cattle over the garden and wrecked everything, so we near starved that winter." She shrugged.

"Then last year Ed got the notion he needed a wife and off he went back East, leaving me with only a hired man to help take care of it all. Came back with her last fall. Lucinda. I'm thinking, good, another woman to help out. But that woman, spoiled rotten she is, didn't know how to do the least thing, didn't want to learn and wanted me to wait on her hand and foot. Oh, I tried to be patient and teach her, but she whined about everything, the house, the weather, my cooking—but, mind you, she wouldn't lift a finger to cook anything herself. I talked to Ed. 'Tell her to shape up,' I said. But he's soft on her, wouldn't say a thing."

Isabel let out an exasperated breath. "Then, day before yesterday, she gets in a snit and says to me, 'Get outa here,' and I says 'Okay, I will.' So I packed up my stuff and left yesterday morning before she was out of bed. I expect she'll miss me when it's her as has to feed the cattle and tend the garden and do all the cooking and cleaning. But I'm not going back, and that's flat."

She turned to smile, first at Rose and then at Lily. "Now then, you got me going, you did. Being so kind and friendly."

"Do you have a place to stay when you get to town?" Rose asked.

"Don't know for sure, but Hannah who has the boarding house will probably find a place for me. She's an old friend. Came out here the same year we did. Her husband died of mountain fever the first year. Left her with two little boys. Hannah started out boarding a few folks in her cabin, did real well with it, and in a few years built the boarding house. She's expanded it three times, and her boys have grown bigger and help her. I can stay with her until I find work."

Isabel sighed and slumped. Lily guided the oxen around a boulder in the trail and they bumped along in silence for a while. Isabel's eyes had closed. She swayed dangerously. Suddenly she let out a snort and jerked her head up. Her eyes flew open, then closed again. Rose slid up close beside her and put an arm around her. With another sigh, Isabel rested her head on Rose's shoulder. After a moment she began to snore. Lily slid over to support her other side. The twins' eyes met over her head, alight with amusement.

Daniel, who had been riding beside the wagon listening intently to Isabel's story, gave them a nod of approval, and rode on ahead.

The trail curved away from the creek and widened into a dirt road. Here and there the twins saw an isolated cabin with a corral and garden. As they went on, they saw more cabins, scattered along the edge of the creek and out on the plains. When they came to a crossroad, Lily stopped the oxen. Daniel circled back, and Nathan and Gabe drew up beside them.

"We go straight, I think," Daniel said.

Isabel lifted her head and rubbed her eyes. "That's right. This is the Denver-Montview road. Gold Creek's just ahead."

They crossed the road and went up a long hill. From the top they looked down into a wide valley. The creek wound across it like a shining ribbon. On the far side, white peaks soared above rocky tree-covered hills. At their feet nestled a cluster of buildings, a town.

Isabel sat up straight and pointed. "That there's Gold Creek," she said.

# Part 3

# THE FRONTIER

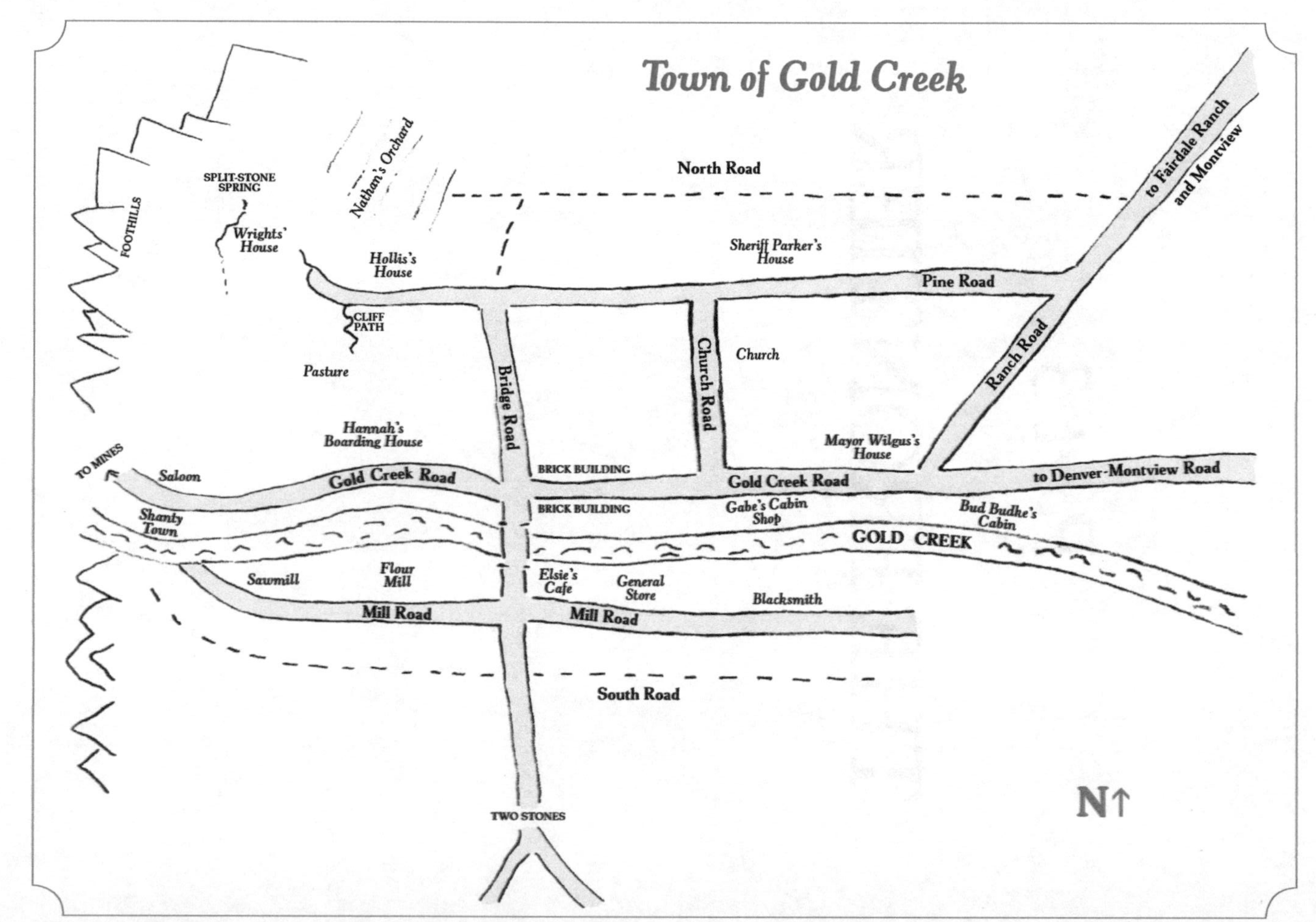

Town of Gold Creek
FOOTHILLS
SPLIT-STONE SPRING
Wrights' House
Nathan's Orchard
North Road
Sheriff Parker's House
to Fairdale Ranch and Montview
Hollis's House
Pine Road
CLIFF PATH
Church Road
Church
Pasture
Ranch Road
Hannah's Boarding House
Bridge Road
Mayor Wilgus's House
TO MINES
Saloon
Gold Creek Road
BRICK BUILDING
Gold Creek Road
to Denver-Montview Road
Shanty Town
BRICK BUILDING
Gabe's Cabin Shop
Bud Budke's Cabin
GOLD CREEK
Sawmill
Flour Mill
Elsie's Cafe
General Store
Blacksmith
Mill Road
Mill Road
South Road
TWO STONES
N↑

Chapter 24

# Gold Creek

The town was bigger than it had looked from the top of the hill. As they approached the center of town, the lots were smaller, the houses closer. Some were log cabins, some built of stone, some of boards. Most were surrounded by fenced gardens, pastures with horses and cattle, sheds and barns. A weathered sign on a post informed them they were traveling on Gold Creek Road.

Isabel was fully awake again, and, as they progressed into town, gave them a running commentary on the houses they passed and their occupants. Daniel rode close by the wagon, listening.

"That's Mayor Wilgus's place." Isabel pointed to a two-story house with glass windows to the right of the road. "The biggest place in town except for the boarding house and the saloon. And he lives there all alone. Takes his meals at Hannah's... Now that little stone house is the Widow Marlow's. Her husband and two sons were killed in the mine explosion two years ago, and her daughter's married and gone off. She takes in sewing and laundry... That log cabin down by the creek, that's Buddy Budke's. He's the butcher. He built it too near the creek, he did, and it got flooded last spring, but he's pretty well dried out now... The boarding house is a little farther on. That's where we should go first. Hannah will want to take care of you."

They passed by several vacant lots. "There's been talk," Isabel said gesturing, "of using one of those for a church or maybe a school."

"That would be a good location," Daniel observed with interest.

A little ahead of them, the road was cluttered with wagons and mules and ladders and a dozen or more men working on what looked like brick walls on either side of the road.

"What's going on there?" Daniel asked Isabel.

"Oh! Must be— I heard there was a rich man back East who was going to build stores and rent them out, so Bud the butcher, and Mr. Hill, the lawyer, and the Widow Marlow, would have shops together in the middle of town instead of us having to go to their cabins. They're building it fast. They hadn't even started last time I was in town."

Just a little farther on, the creek made a deep bend to the north coming close to the edge of the road. Across from it sprawled the boarding house, a large two-story structure with several wings added on at odd angles, and a big porch in front. A shingle hung from the front of the porch: HANNAH'S BOARDING HOUSE.

Four men in shirt sleeves sat at a long table on the porch, having their noonday meal. They looked up as Daniel, followed by the three wagons, drew up in front. Before Lily had quite stopped the wagon, Isabel brushed by her and jumped down with surprising nimbleness. She ran up onto the porch and through the open front door calling, "Hannah, Hannah, the preacher's here!"

One of the men stood up from the table and came forward. He was short and stout with bushy eyebrows and a bushy black beard. A gold watch chain looped across his substantial abdomen.

"Welcome," he greeted them in a booming voice. "Are you really the preacher?"

Daniel dismounted and walked up the steps to meet him. "I really am," he said smiling. "Reverend Daniel Wright, ordained Presbyterian minister."

"Jeremy Wilgus, mayor of this town." He held out a plump hand. "Glad you made it."

Daniel shook his hand. "Good to meet you. It's been a long journey, but we're finally here."

The other three men on the porch pushed back their chairs and came forward to meet Daniel. At the same moment, Hannah hurried through the door, wiping her hands on her apron, her face eager. She was tall and buxom, her blond hair wrapped in braids around her head, her cheeks pink, her eyes bright blue. Isabel hovered behind her. Hannah held out both hands to Daniel.

"I'm so glad you're here at last! I'm Hannah Anderson." She glanced around him at the three wagons at the bottom of the porch steps. "And this must be your family."

Daniel looked down at his companions. The twins had climbed down from the wagon and stood by the oxen, quiet and demure in their blue gowns. Gabe stood patiently by his mule. The Hollis family was descending from their wagon, Mattie with Baby Beth in her arms, Nathan swinging the little ones down. Daniel felt a surge of love for them all. "These are my daughters, Miss Lily Wright and Miss Rose Wright, and our friends, Mr. Gabe Archen from Tennessee and the Hollis family from Pennsylvania."

"Welcome," Hannah said with a wide smile. "You must all stay for dinner."

"Thank you, Mrs. Anderson," Daniel responded. "We would love to."

A tall, blond boy came through the door. "Ned," Hannah ordered him, "show these people where they can park their wagons, and take their beasts to the pasture."

Daniel started down the steps, but Lily spoke up. "We'll take care of the wagon, Papa." She picked up the ox lead and started after Ned, followed by Gabe and Nathan.

"Isabel," Hannah said, "tell Jim to bring another table out and some chairs. It's too hot in the house. Now Mrs. Hollis, you come on up and sit right here. Can I see your baby?"

Jim appeared, carrying two chairs. He was smaller than Ned and dark haired, his eyes the same bright blue as Hannah's. "Put them right here," Hannah ordered. "And bring these folks some water." She waved a hand at the four men hovering around Daniel. "Sit down, all of you. Here's a chair for you, Reverend. Now Mrs. Hollis, do tell me the names of your children."

While Mattie introduced the children to Hannah, the four men sat down again at the table with Daniel. Mayor Wilgus took charge. "This is Mr. Ken Hill, our town lawyer," he told Daniel. "And this is Mr. Aaron Jenkins who runs the sawmill, a great boon to our town. And this is Mr. Budke, our butcher."

Daniel leaned across the table to shake hands with each of them. Mr. Hill was of medium height and build with a small, precise mustache, smooth brown hair tied neatly at the nape of his neck, and wire-rimmed glasses enlarging his brown eyes. Mr. Budke was short and plump, bald with a fringe of red hair around his ears. He stuttered as he greeted Daniel.

"I'm the-the b-barber, too, if you need a-a hair c-cut."

"Butcher and barber both," Daniel said with a smile. "That's a dangerous combination." The men laughed. Mr. Budke blushed and looked around, pleased with the attention.

The third man, Mr. Jenkins, was tall and lean with pale blue protruding eyes and thin blond hair. He held his lips narrow and knots of tight muscle bulged over his jaw joints. Daniel felt an intensity in him that was both attractive and daunting.

When Gabe and Nathan and the twins returned, more introductions were made, Isabel and Jim brought another table out, and soon all were comfortably seated in the shade of the porch, enjoying an excellent meal.

After they had eaten and Hannah and Isabel were clearing the table, the mayor asked, "What can we do for you folks? Would you like a tour of the town?"

"We would," Daniel responded. "We all need to find places to settle."

"You're staying here tonight," Hannah said as she wiped down the table. "I've arranged for two rooms to be made ready with good beds, one room for the men and one for the ladies and the little ones. Isabel got here just in time to help me."

"That's very kind of you," Mattie said, smiling at Hannah. "We've been camping in our wagons for a long time now. A real room with beds sounds wonderful."

Daniel nodded. "That does sound wonderful, and the tour would be very helpful, but what's most important to me is to meet the people of the church. Do you know who these people are?"

"All of us here." Hannah straightened and pushed a wisp of hair back from her brow. "And Burt and Elsie Martin from the general store and their children, and Mr. and Mrs. Dodge from the bank and their two young ones, and the widow Marlow. Those are the church members. Other folks come sometimes to service on Sunday, and lots of people showed up when Reverend Jackson came through and preached here for a week. But then he went on and they fell away."

Daniel pulled his notebook out of his jacket pocket and wrote down the names. He counted them. "That's eleven. They told me there were twelve of you."

"There were," Aaron Jenkins said. "Craig Nichols was here for a while. But he got news of family trouble back East. Was gone in a day, on the stage. Left everything. People do come and go here, but, except for Craig, our church has held together well."

"Where do you meet?" Daniel asked.

"Here in the boarding house, in the dining room," Hannah answered.

"So." Daniel looked around the table. "Mrs. Flannagan guided us well—"

"Just call me Isabel."

The twins exchanged a quick amused glance. They were enjoying Isabel.

"What did you do when there were big crowds," Daniel asked Hannah, "like when Reverend Jackson came?"

"Then we meet outside under the trees by the river."

"Would it be possible," Daniel asked, "to gather all the church members this evening, so I can meet them and we can pray together?"

"Of course," Hannah replied. "They'll be eager to meet you. I'll send Ned around to tell them."

Daniel stood up. "Thank you. Thank you for everything, for your warm welcome, and the delicious meal."

"She's the b-best c-cook in t-town," Mr. Budke said.

"It's true," Mayor Wilgus declared. "As you can see." He laughed and slapped his rounded waistcoat. "I can take you on the tour now, if you're ready. I've got a big buggy with two seats. You can all fit."

The mayor's buggy was quite fancy, with shiny metal accouterments, a roof that shaded them from the sun, and two wide cushioned seats.

Mayor Wilgus took them first to see the brick buildings under construction. "Our town's growing fast," he said proudly. "These buildings will make a big difference. And the church—will you build one?"

"I hope so," Daniel said. "This summer if possible."

Mayor Wilgus nodded. "That, too, will draw people."

They skirted the construction area, going south across the wooden bridge that spanned the creek. "This is Mill Road," the mayor said as they turned off the bridge. "That's the flour mill there. Aaron Jenkins's sawmill is at the west end of the road where the river curves."

They drove east for a while as the mayor pointed out other landmarks—the general store, the blacksmith's shop, the brickyard, and some vacant lots. Then they returned across the bridge, and continued east on Gold Creek Road.

"Here's a couple of lots we thought might do for a church or a school," the mayor said, indicating the same lots Isabel had shown them that morning.

"Let's stop and have a look," Daniel suggested. The mayor pulled off the road and everyone got out.

"There's cactus here and there. Watch your step and look out for the children," the mayor warned.

They all scattered, looking over the two lots. Daniel walked slowly, stopping first in one spot and then another, gazing around, frowning. One lot was quite flat, the other sloped up to a low hilltop. The twins walked up the hill. Daniel saw them standing quietly, hands linked. "Papa," Lily called. "Come up here."

Daniel climbed the hill to join them.

"We think we should build our church here," Rose said.

"Because it's higher, and the church would be visible from all over town," Lily added.

"And there's a beautiful view of the river and the foothills. See?" Rose reached out to take Daniel's hand.

Gabe had followed. He gazed out over the river and hills. "Build it here. Look at the view!"

"What do you think, Nathan?" Daniel called. Nathan and Mattie and the mayor climbed the hill to stand beside them.

Nathan turned slowly. "I like it."

"So do I," Mattie said.

"I think this is it, Papa." Lily took his other hand.

"It feels just right," Rose said softly.

Daniel stood breathing deeply of the warm summer air. The town spread below him. The river sparkled in the afternoon sunshine. To the west the foothills rose steeply; their jutting rock faces intermingled with dark evergreens were vivid against the blue sky. A wave of wonder and excitement swept through him. It did feel right. He turned to Mayor Wilgus. "Can we reserve this lot for our church?" he asked.

"We sure can!" The mayor beamed and stroked his beard. "Now, you can have the lot next to it for your manse if you want, but before you decide, I've got a few other spots to show you. Let's get back in the buggy."

Mayor Wilgus headed the buggy uphill to a road that ran parallel to Gold Creek Road. "This is Pine Road," the mayor said. "There used to be a lot of pine trees up here, but they all got cut down for lumber and firewood." He pointed to a good-sized log house with a sod roof, set in the midst of wide fields to the right of the road. "There's Will Parker's place. He took two acres, doesn't grow much but hay. Has a wife and some kids. They don't come to church. He's the town sheriff."

"The town seems pretty peaceful," Daniel commented. "Doesn't seem there'd be much need for a sheriff."

"Just wait till Friday night," the mayor said grimly. "All the miners come down, fill up that miserable shanty town they've built at the bottom of the canyon, and spend their nights drinking and carousing at the saloon. There's fights. Will has his work cut out for him then."

Daniel felt a shiver of trepidation, realizing how little his decorous and affluent parish in Boston had prepared him for what might lie ahead.

Pine Road grew steeper as it approached the foothills. "Now up here," the mayor gestured, "to the northwest we have three more empty lots. We're aiming to put another road in soon along the back side of them to open up our northern area."

On the left side of the road a cliff dropped off. The twins, looking down, could see Shadow and their oxen in the pasture behind the boarding house.

"This top one we're coming to," the mayor went on, "is as far west as our township goes. The hill gets steep here, but it's a pretty spot and has water. There's a spring and a little stream. Nice view. Now here's the eastern edge, by this big rock, and it goes back"—he pointed— "to just past that cluster of junipers there."

The land sloped up gently at first, then steeply. The mayor drove the buggy up the last ascent and stopped. "Get out here and have a look. See what you think."

It was quiet except for the song of two meadowlarks calling back and forth. The little stream wound across the western edge of the lot and disappeared where the cliff dropped off to the south. It made no sound as it wove through the tall grass and an occasional clump of red-stemmed willows. All around the stream the grass was green, scattered with blue, yellow, and orange wild flowers.

The twins looked around, taking in the wide vistas, breathing in the smell of stream water, sun on dry grass, and a whiff of something else, a cool fresh scent that seemed to flow down from the mountains above. Their eyes met and they smiled at each other.

Daniel gazed up at the hills rising steeply above him. "I will lift up mine eyes unto the hills," he quoted softly.

Gabe and the twins followed the stream up to where it flowed out of the hillside between two vertical rock faces.

Lily peered into the narrow cleft between the rocks. "The spring must be behind here."

Rose stroked the smooth red face of the rock. "It looks as if these rocks had been one rock once, and something split them in two."

"It do look that way," Gabe said as he laid his lean brown hand against the warm rock.

"What could be strong enough to split a rock in two?" Rose wondered.

"Maybe the spring," Lily said, "though it's hard to imagine that this small flow of water could do that."

"Water can work miracles with its gentle strength," Gabe said with his sweet smile. "Like God's love."

The mayor's big voice broke the quiet. "Well, Reverend, what do you think of this piece? Very few lots have their own water, except down by the river. Even though this stream sometimes dries up by the end of the summer, there's a marshy spot over there that's probably another spring, so you wouldn't have to dig too deep to get a well."

He led Daniel over to look at the marshy spot.

"Mattie, come here," Nathan called. Mattie gathered up her little ones and joined him to walk down the road toward the lots just below.

Turning from the spring, the twins stood looking out to the east. Beyond the town and the scattered outlying homesteads, the plains flowed away as far as they could see, low undulating hills, dotted here and there with the blue of small lakes and streams. They walked a little farther down, and sat together, arms around each other, brows touching.

After a while, Rose said, "We could see the sun rise from here."

"And the stream and the spring," Lily said. "We wouldn't have to carry our water far."

"We could have our garden down there, where it's more level."

"This is where we should build our house, right here where we're sitting."

"Papa will like it here because it is quiet."

"Let's go," the mayor called out. "There's one more place I want you to see. Now where has Mr. Hollis gone?"

"They went down to look at those lots we passed on the way up," Rose reported.

As they drove down the road, Daniel looked back up at the hills. "That's a beautiful place," he said. "It's not too far from where we'll build our church."

"Less than a mile," the mayor said. "Fifteen or twenty minute walk. No time at all on a horse."

The twins, sitting in the back seat with Gabe, squeezed each other's hands.

When they reached the main road again, the mayor pulled up in front of a small cabin.

"This lot here by the river," he said, "is where Craig had his cabin. It's still here, mighty small as you can see, but solid. No one's spoken for it. It's too small for a family, but I was thinking it might be a good start for you, Mr. Archen."

The cabin sat near the road and the lot sloped down to the river's edge. It was a very small cabin and had no windows. A stove pipe jutted out through the roof. Gabe walked around it, looking at the foundation, the joints of the logs at the corners. "Looks sound," he commented. He paced out the length and width. "Eight by twelve."

"That's not much bigger than our wagon!" Lily exclaimed.

Gabe smiled his gap-toothed smile. "Bigger'n my cart. Can I see the inside?" he asked the mayor.

"No, I locked it up after Craig left." The mayor gestured to the padlock on the door. "Didn't want any of that mining riffraff to get in. I've got the key at home."

Gabe walked around the cabin again and stood behind it, looking down at the river. "I could sit out here of an evening and listen to the creek," he said thoughtfully. "I could build my shop onto the side of the cabin. And it's by the road, real handy to those new shops and right across from the church." He turned to the mayor. "I'll take it."

"Good," the mayor boomed. "I knew the right person would come along for it."

"What do I need to do?" Gabe asked.

"We just need to sign you on. Then I'll give you the key, and you move in."

"Thank you, Jesus," Gabe murmured softly.

"Good. Good." The mayor puffed up his chest and looked around at them, beaming. "We've got one of you settled already. Now let's get back to my place and get you signed up."

The mayor's house was spacious and comfortably furnished. He showed them around proudly, then led them to his office. There he pulled out a big chart, with a map of the town and all the lots laid out and numbered. He wrote Gabe's name on his lot and gave him the key to his cabin. Nathan decided to take the two lots downhill from the one with the spring. The mayor signed him up, too.

"Now what about you, Reverend?" he asked Daniel.

"I haven't decided," Daniel said, "Either next to the church, or up on the hill. The one on the hill's a little farther away, but pretty and peaceful. I'd like a few more days to decide."

"Sure, sure," the mayor said. He drew a gold watch out of his waistcoat pocket and flipped it open. "It's getting toward five o'clock. I should get you back to the boarding house so you have time to get settled in your rooms and ready for supper. Hannah's called the church meeting for seven."

~

That evening the members of the Gold Creek church gathered in the dining room of the boarding house. Aaron Jenkins, Ken Hill, and the mayor had taken their supper there, so Daniel had had time to get more acquainted with them.

Mr. Dodge, the banker, arrived in a fancy buggy with his wife, teenage son, and young daughter. Gerald Dodge looked to be about seventeen. Annabelle was just blossoming into womanhood. All the Dodges were elegantly dressed as if for a church meeting on the East Coast.

Burt Martin, owner of the general store, was short and stocky; Elsie, his wife, was short and plump. She had frowsy hair and a somewhat dazed look, which could be attributed to the four unruly, small children she had in tow—three boys and one little girl.

The widow Marlow was the last to arrive. She was small and bent with sad eyes and worn hands.

Lily and Rose watched as Daniel moved around the room greeting each one, speaking to each with the same concern and charm that had made him so beloved in his Boston church. "Papa's okay," Lily whispered. "He got over whatever was worrying him this morning as soon as he started meeting people and doing his church work."

"I hope so," Rose whispered back.

When all were gathered, Lily and Rose and Gabe, with their violins and flute, led the hymn, "The Church's One Foundation." Daniel led a long eloquent prayer. He read from scripture, several passages from the letters of Paul about the founding of a church, then set the Bible aside and spoke from his heart, meeting each person's eyes.

"Our Lord said to his apostle Peter, 'On this rock I will build my church.' I cannot tell you what joy I feel to finally meet you, whose call I heard from far across our vast country, and have hastened to respond to."

Lily looked at Rose and raised one eyebrow ever so slightly, but Rose, lost in her father's eloquence, did not notice.

"I look forward with much anticipation to entering with you into the marvelous adventure of building a church, to the praise of our Lord Jesus Christ. I am speaking now, not of a physical building, though that, too, I hope we will manifest before long, but of a congregation composed of faithful souls who come together to worship and serve Him and care for one another.

"And the rock on which this church will be built is you, who have been constant in your prayers and have held together through many trials. I am honored to be called to be your pastor. I'm not here to give a sermon tonight, but to get to know you, what your needs are, how I can serve you."

A stir moved through the small group. Hannah spoke up. "As I told you earlier, when Reverend Jackson was here we had crowds, over a hundred souls some days. But when he left, only Mrs. Marlow, who came to us for the first time then, has stayed with us. We want to reach those people again. I think some of them would come back if they knew we had a steady preacher here."

Daniel nodded. "I plan to spend the next two days visiting everyone in town and as far out as I can go to the homesteads, to personally invite them to worship with us on Sunday."

"We could print up some handbills and put them around," Burt Martin suggested.

"That's a good idea. Do you have a printing press in town?"

"Moses Sachs has one," Mrs. Dodge said. "He's a Jew." She curled her lip. "He won't come to church, but he'll print whatever we want—for money."

"Do we have money?" Daniel asked.

"I'm the treasurer," Mr. Dodge said. "We've been taking up collection. I checked it before I came. We have one hundred and eighty-seven dollars. But the handbills won't cost much. A penny a page."

"Thank you for serving as the treasurer. Have you chosen other officers?"

"Mr. Martin and I are elders," Aaron Jenkins said.

"Excellent. I hope you will work beside me as I get to know the town and its needs."

"We'd like to convert some of those miners who make so much noise every weekend," Mrs. Marlow said.

"And get rid of that saloon." Mrs. Dodge spoke emphatically. "And all the sinful activity that goes on down there."

"I don't think the town's ready for that," Mayor Wilgus said. "Too many people here have to have their drink. And Smythe looks out for the miners and the shanty-town riffraff, gives 'em a place to gather. If it weren't for the saloon, they'd be carrying on all over town."

Mrs. Dodge glared at him.

"I think the church building is important," the mayor went on. "It'll draw people. If we have a church with a steeple, folks'll believe we're a real town."

"If we had a building, maybe we could have a school," Elsie said. "My kids need schooling."

"All of that is important," Daniel said. "But first and foremost, we need to build a congregation."

The conversation became more lively and went on for another hour. Hannah and Isabel brought in cookies and cider. Mayor Wilgus brought up the matter of the church building again, saying that Daniel had liked the lot with the hill. They decided the Sunday service should be held there and that afterward they would have a picnic, and in the evening, a prayer meeting in the boarding house. Mr. Budke offered to take care of printing the handbill and young Gerald Dodge, eager to participate, offered to put them up.

They closed with a hymn and a prayer. After everyone had left, Daniel sat at a table in the dining room with Hannah and the twins and Isabel.

"This evening went well," Hannah said. "You were well received, I could tell. And it was lovely having the music."

Rose laid her hand on his shoulder. "You were wonderful, Papa."

"Things are really going to pick up now you're here," Isabel said. "The real reason people didn't come back after Reverend Jackson is that Mr. Jenkins killed 'em all off with his preaching. He holds his mouth so tight all his words come out dry and narrow. But you're a live one."

Hannah frowned. "That's enough, Isabel. Mr. Jenkins is a good and pious man and has worked very hard for us."

Isabel shrugged and glanced over at the twins, a mischievous gleam in her eye.

# Chapter 25

# *The Saloon*

After lunch on Saturday, Hannah asked Lily and Rose to gather some peppermint for tea for the evening meal. "There's lots of it down by the river. You know what it looks like?"

"Yes," Lily answered.

"Good. Here's a basket."

Delighted with their task, the twins crossed the road and scrambled down the bank to the water's edge. The summer afternoon was hot.

"Let's wade," Rose suggested.

They sat on the bank, pulled off their boots and tucked them behind a rock. Barefoot, skirts tucked up, they waded into the stream. The water was clear and cold, sparkling in the afternoon sunlight, its song loud as it swirled around rocks and tumbled over small waterfalls on its way from the mountains to the plains. Several ducks paddled in a quiet backwater. The twins watched them a while, laughing when they turned upside down, waggling their tails in the air. From the brush on the opposite bank, a red fox emerged, stared at them inquisitively, then trotted off through the willows on his own mission, his bushy tail a graceful arc behind him.

The twins wandered upstream, exulting in their freedom, in and out of the water, scrambling over rocks, gathering wildflowers from the bank. They found peppermint in abundance and soon had their basket full, but they continued farther upstream, curious to see what lay around each new bend.

They were sitting resting on the root of a big cottonwood when Rose held up her hand. "Listen!" They heard the sound of a piano playing, distant but clear.

"A piano!" Lily exclaimed. "Come on." She was already on her feet, reaching for Rose's hand to pull her up the bank. The basket of peppermint and flowers lay forgotten near the cottonwood root.

When they reached the top of the bank, they looked around in confusion. They had wandered farther upstream than they realized and the road above was completely unfamiliar. The boarding house was out of sight. Ahead of them was a jungle of shacks with rough-looking men moving around them.

"That must be the shanty town Mr. Wilgus was talking about," Rose whispered. "We mustn't go there."

Directly across the road, they saw a large building with more men milling around the front. The piano music seemed to be coming from an open door on the side. Gripping each other's hands tightly, the twins dashed across the road, around the building to the side door, and peered in.

They saw a spacious room with large comfortable chairs and a gilt-framed mirror on the wall. Several men sat around a low table playing cards. A full-bosomed woman in a low-cut red gown, her loose dark hair adorned with a red ribbon, sat at the piano playing a sad-sounding melody. She did not play very well. As they watched, her fingers stumbled and she turned away from the keyboard with a weary sigh.

"Ma'am." Lily stepped forward into the open door.

The woman came to meet them. "Well, hello there!"

Rose stepped up beside Lily.

"What? Two of you? Or am I seeing double?"

"No, ma'am," Rose said. "We're twins."

"Well, that's a relief." The woman passed her hand across her brow. "What can I do for you?" She looked them over from head to foot as they stood in the doorway. Their hems were wet and they were barefoot, but otherwise they looked quite proper in their high-necked gowns, their hair neatly pinned up with only a few stray curls broken loose around their fresh young faces. "You don't look like the kind of girls that would be looking for work here."

"No, ma'am," Lily said. "We heard the piano."

"We haven't been able to play a piano for a long time," Rose added hesitantly.

"We wondered—" Lily started.

"If we could play a little—"

"If it wouldn't bother anybody …"

The woman looked at them with an odd expression on her face. "You new in town?" she asked.

"Yes, ma'am. We just got here two days ago."

"We've come from Boston."

"We had a piano there."

"And we miss it."

"Well, I don't suppose it would bother anybody." She turned to the men playing cards. "Would it bother you if these young ladies played the piano for a little while?"

The men were absorbed in their game. One turned briefly. "Don't matter to me. You been playing." He returned his focus to the cards in his hand.

"So sure. Come on in," the woman said. "My name's Ella."

"Thank you, Miss Ella. I'm Lily."

"And I'm Rose."

"Here." She dusted off the bench for them. "You both play?"

"Yes, ma'am."

They sat down, looked at each other, eyes shining. Lily ran her fingers over the keys. "It's only a little out of tune."

"Let's play the Schubert," Rose said.

They were soon lost in their music. The men playing cards stopped and looked up, then came to stand by the piano. The twins proceeded from one favorite piece they had by memory to another, only vaguely aware that more and more men had gathered around them. When they finally paused and looked up, they were startled by loud applause. When the applause died down, one man said wistfully, "I haven't heard music like that since my ma died. She used to play classical."

Another asked, "Do you know any songs?"

The twins nodded. They knew lots of songs. Their music tutor in Boston had taught them songs for people to sing at parties. They'd never done it, because they hadn't come out yet, but they were well prepared.

"How about 'Oh, Susanna'?" Rose asked.

"Yeah!"

"That's a good one."

"We know that one," several voices answered.

They played "Oh, Susanna" and the men sang loudly and exuberantly. From there they went on to "Camp Town Races," "Sweet Betsy from Pike," and "Jimmy Crack Corn."

After "Jimmy Crack Corn," one man asked, "Do you know any hymns?"

"We know lots of hymns," Lily laughed. "Our papa's a preacher."

"Is your papa the new preacher that just came to town?" another voice asked.

The twins nodded.

"Do you know 'Amazing Grace'?"

In answer, the twins played the opening bars. The men sang and the big room was filled with their voices and the poignant longing of the hymn.

~

Daniel, Gabe, and Hannah were seated at a table in the boarding house dining room as Daniel spoke of his pastoral visits. He was weary after a long ride back from the outlying homesteads in the hot sun. Isabel came in with a pitcher of cool water.

"Thanks, Isabel," Daniel said. He drank thirstily, then continued his report to Hannah and Gabe. "Yesterday I talked with everyone in town or left handbills on their doors, and today I rode out onto the plains and talked with some of the homesteaders. Most people were friendly and many said they'd be here tomorrow. Some didn't have much use for church, but it's always that way. I think we'll have a good congregation tomorrow. I wish I'd had time to get up to the mine. That'll have to wait till next week. I need to stop now and prepare my sermon."

"Most of the miners are in town for the weekend," Hannah said. "Mr. Dodge has his Gerald putting handbills around. They'll see them at the general store and the blacksmith. He was going to put some up here, too."

Just then, Gerald came in with a bunch of handbills and set them on the table. "Hello, Reverend. I've put them up all over." His young face was eager for approval. "I even put one down in the saloon."

"Smythe will just tear it down," Isabel said.

"I know." Gerald twisted his fingers together. "But I thought some of them might see it before he did."

"I don't think your pa would have wanted you to go down there," Hannah said.

"It didn't seem like such a bad place. They were all singing, a big crowd of them, gathered around the piano, and Miss Rose and Miss Lily were playing."

"What?" Daniel leaped to his feet, knocking his chair over behind him. "Lily and Rose in the saloon?" He grabbed Gerald by the shoulder. "Are you sure?"

"Yes, sir." Gerald paled and drew back. "There's no mistaking them, sir. They're the prettiest … and look so much alike."

Daniel whirled to face Hannah. "I left them in your care."

"I sent them to the river to pick some peppermint," Hannah said. "I never dreamed they'd go down there."

"I've got to go get them, right now. God knows …" Daniel strode toward the door.

Gabe followed him.

Daniel ran down the road toward the saloon, muttering breathlessly as he ran, "How could they? … I'm going to lock them in their room … Good Lord, what could happen to them there?"

Before they reached the saloon, they could hear singing pouring out the open side door. Daniel charged forward, but Gabe caught his arm.

"Wait, Daniel. Look what your girls done for you. You wanted to talk to the miners? Sounds like there's a crowd of 'em in there, and a'singing a hymn to boot. All gathered. Go on in and invite them to the service tomorrow."

Daniel paused, let out his breath. "You're right."

Lily and Rose were having fun. Playing the piano again would have been enough, but the singing, the praise, the applause topped it. They had just played the last chord of "Rock of Ages" when they looked up and saw their father and Gabe standing in the open door.

"Uh oh," Lily whispered. They both lifted their hands off the keyboard and placed them on their laps.

"Let's do that one again," someone called.

Daniel came into the room and up to the piano. "That sounded great," he said into the sudden silence. "I'm Reverend Wright, the new preacher for the Gold Creek Church. We'll be having a service tomorrow at ten o'clock on the hill east of the new brick buildings. You're all invited. I'd be happy to have your good voices join us in song."

The men gathered around him. "Good to meet you, Preacher."

"We'll come."

"These your girls? They sure can make music."

"Yes, they are," Daniel said. "Miss Lily and Miss Rose Wright."

Lily and Rose, dumbfounded, turned around on the piano bench and bowed. The men applauded.

A door banged open at the back of the room and the applause was interrupted by an enraged shout. "What's going on here?" Smythe pushed through the crowd, waving a torn handbill. "First I find this." He crumpled it in his fist. "Then I hear hymns."

Lily and Rose went cold with shock. Fear ricocheted back and forth between them. Their thoughts tumbled. Mr. Smythe! Where did he come from?

Ella stepped in front of them.

Smythe stared at Daniel and Gabe. "Who are you?" he demanded.

Daniel drew himself up. "I'm Reverend Daniel Wright, pastor of the Gold Creek Church."

Smythe took a step toward him. "*Reverend!* What are you doing here? I don't allow any Christian crap in my establishment."

A low murmur ran through the crowd of men. Smythe came another step closer to Daniel.

"Christianity," he sneered, pronouncing each syllable separately. "I know it well. Brought up with it until it made me so sick I ran away. Sniveling Christianity." He raised his voice to a mocking falsetto. "God is love. Love your neighbor. Turn the other cheek."

The twins shivered at the hatred in his voice.

"But that same God," he spat out, "that God that is *love* is glad to damn you to burn in hell for all eternity if you so much as sip a drink or look sideways at a woman." He raised his voice to a shout. "Well, my business is drink and women, and you're not wanted here, preaching to my customers, and getting them singing hymns." He threw the crumpled handbill at Daniel's chest. "Get out!

"And who was playing those hymns? You, Ella?" He turned to her and saw the twins cowering behind her. He pushed her aside and stared at them. "You," he breathed. "You." He took a step toward them, thrust his head forward, his eyes narrow. His voice was dangerously soft. "I know you, meddling wretches. Did me out of my girl, you did, back there at Robinson's."

The room had gone deadly silent. Smythe took another step toward the twins. They were frozen, like prey ensnared in the gaze of a snake.

"I'd a mind to grab you that night, both of you, to make up for losing her, but you were too well guarded. Never mind, you're here now. Walked right into my lair."

He lunged forward and grabbed the twins by their wrists, jerked them to their feet. "I've got work for you. Just one night upstairs—I'll keep you busy— and you won't be playing hymns the next morning."

The room burst into commotion. Daniel knocked over the piano bench to reach the twins. Ella screamed, "No, Smythe!" Lily struggled, then cried out in pain as Smythe tightened his grip. Three men grappled with Smythe. Voices rose in protest—

"Let them go."

"They're not for here."

"They're the preacher's daughters."

Daniel bellowed, "Take your hands off my daughters!"

"Preacher's daughters," Smythe sneered. "I should have known." He threw them from him so suddenly and violently that they stumbled back against their father. Daniel thrust them behind him.

"How dare you?" he shouted at Smythe. "How dare you lay hands on my daughters? How dare you even *think* of involving them in your loathsome trade?"

The twins trembled in terror behind their father. Daniel was taller, but Smythe was compact and powerful. Both men were gathering themselves, muscles swelling.

Gabe put a hand on Daniel's arm. "He done asked you to leave," he said quietly into the tense silence. "Time to go now."

Daniel turned to Gabe and let out his breath. "Yes. Come Lily, come Rose." He seized his daughters by their wrists and walked toward the door. The men parted to let them pass. Gabe followed.

"Go!" Smythe shouted after them. "If I ever find you here again …"

As soon as they passed through the door, Daniel quickened his stride, dragging the twins after him. Lily stumbled and cried out.

"Papa, please," Rose begged. "You're hurting us, and Lily's cut her foot."

Daniel slowed down and looked at Rose. "I'm hurting you?"

"Yes." Rose was near tears. "You're holding our wrists right where *he* did, and he squeezed them so tight."

"I have to get you away from there."

"But you don't have to drag us. Papa, let go." Lily, too, was on the verge of tears.

Daniel stopped in the middle of the road and let go of the twins' wrists. They pulled their arms back and cradled them against their chests.

"What I want to know is"—Daniel's voice rose—"*what were you two doing in the saloon?*"

"The saloon!" the twins exclaimed. They stared at each other as realization flooded them.

"We didn't know—"

"—it was the saloon."

They were both crying now and shaking. Gabe stepped forward. "Easy, Daniel. These girls been hurt and scairt bad, and this ain't no place to be a'standing and talking."

A cart, heavily loaded with ore and pulled by two donkeys, rattled by, narrowly missing them. Gabe pulled them to the side of the road. Brushing back her tears, Rose bent down to examine Lily's bleeding toe.

"What happened?" Daniel asked, more quietly.

"You were pulling us so fast I tripped," Lily sobbed.

"Where are your shoes? Both of you, barefoot."

"We left them by the river." Rose stood up suddenly. "Oh! The basket. Hannah's basket with the peppermint. We left that too." She spun and started back toward the saloon.

"Where are you going?" Daniel grabbed her wrist. She winced and began to cry again.

"It's back there, across from the … the …"

"I'll git it for you," Gabe said. "Tell me where. Is it in the saloon?"

"No, down by the river, by the root of that big cottonwood." Rose pointed.

"Something else I want to know." Daniel's voice rose again. "What was that man talking about, that he knew you? Something about Robinson's ranch."

Gabe put his hand on Daniel's arm. "It sounds like there's lotsa stories. Let's git back to the boarding house. Your girls are crying. They're a'watching us from the saloon. I'll git the basket and catch up with you."

Daniel looked back at the saloon. A knot of men had gathered by the side door. "You're right, Gabe. Come Lily, Rose."

The way back to the boarding house seemed long to the twins, barefoot on the rough road, much farther than it had seemed as they waded in the creek on their way up. Daniel held them firmly by their hands, but walked more slowly. Gabe caught up with them with the basket. Gradually the twins' sobs quieted. When they came to the boarding house, Daniel released them to go down to the river and retrieve their boots. Alone for a moment, they stepped into the edge of the water, cooling their sore feet.

"The saloon," Rose whispered. "How could we have known?"

"Mr. Smythe ... Mr. Erickson! That's where we heard Mr. Smythe's name before. Remember? When Mr. Erickson came to dinner at Grandmama's house?"

"Yes. He told Papa Mr. Smythe ran the saloon ..."

"And the brothel."

"We don't really know what a brothel is."

"We need to find out," Lily said emphatically.

Daniel called from the top of the bank. Rose and Lily retrieved their boots and went up.

Gabe had gone ahead of them into the boarding house, and when Daniel and the twins came in, Hannah was waiting for them. "Come sit in the parlor. We can be private there. I need to know what happened. Isabel, bring water and bandages for Lily's foot."

After Lily's foot had been tended to, Daniel said, "I'm going to ask that question again. *What* were you doing in the saloon?"

The twins were sitting together on the couch. They took each other's hands. Rose started. "Papa, we didn't know."

"How were we supposed to know it was the saloon?" Lily demanded. "We never saw one before. It just looked like a nice house."

They went on to explain how they'd heard the piano, and Miss Ella had let them in, and the men had come to sing.

"When you came—"

"We thought it was really good that they were all together—"

"So you could invite them to service tomorrow."

"Then Mr. Smythe came." The twins fell silent. They moved closer together and put their arms around each other, feeling anew the terror of the moment when Smythe grabbed their wrists.

"What has he done to you?" Hannah demanded.

Daniel took up the story, told of Smythe's entrance, his rage against the handbills and the hymns, his vile words about Christianity, and how he had seized and threatened the twins.

"Good Lord!" Hannah exclaimed, when he finished. "It's no news that Smythe hates religion. But how did he know you?" she asked the twins. "Had you met him before?"

"That's what I want to know," Daniel said grimly. "What was he saying about some girl and Robinson's ranch?"

Speaking one after the other as was their way, the twins told the story of Robinson's ranch and Laura and Smythe and Jake.

When they had finished, Daniel groaned and rubbed his brow. "Where was I when all this was going on?"

"You were there," Lily said. "Remember we wanted to talk to Laura and you were dragging us back to the wagon circle? And we told you we had to talk to Jake?"

"And later," Rose added, "we heard Ben say he found you in a tepee talking to the Indians."

Daniel glared at them. "It seems I can't let you out of my sight for a moment."

"But look what they did!" Hannah exclaimed. "They saved that child from a life of the most abysmal slavery. And this afternoon— Maybe the good Lord used their innocence to gather the miners so you could speak to them."

"I'm glad you came when you did, Papa," Rose said. "Mr. Smythe really scared us."

"I'm glad Gabe was there, too." Lily dimpled, then giggled. "It wouldn't have been so good for your reputation as a preacher if you had gotten into a fight in the saloon only two days after you got here."

Everyone laughed then. Daniel said sheepishly, "No, it wouldn't. Thank the Lord you were with me, Gabe." He sighed. "Now that you girls are safely back here and all this is cleared up, I do need to prepare my sermon for tomorrow. I just need a quiet place."

"Why don't you go up on the hill where Mayor Wilgus took us the other day, where the little stream is," Rose suggested. "It's really peaceful up there."

"That's a good idea," Daniel said. "I think I will. I've been wanting to spend some more time up there."

Lily gave Rose's hand a quick squeeze.

"You can take a short cut through my pasture," Hannah said. "Just go all the way to the back. There's a gate there and a path that goes up the side of the cliff to Pine Road."

After Daniel left, Hannah said to the twins, "Thank you for getting the peppermint and the flowers."

"I'm afraid the flowers got wilted while we were in the saloon," Rose said.

Isabel had been standing quietly by the door. "They're fine," she said. "As soon as I put them in water they perked right up."

"Isabel," Hannah said. "I didn't know you were still here. Have you been listening to everything?"

"Yes, ma'am. I've taken a fancy to those twins. I needed to know what happened to them."

"You shouldn't be standing around listening when people don't know you're there. No gossiping about this, you hear? Not a word."

"No ma'am. My lips are sealed."

"Well, since you're here." Hannah turned to the twins. "Maybe you could help with something else." The twins nodded. "Isabel's cleaned herself up some since she came, but I can't have her working for me any longer with that matted braid and dirty hair. She'll need some help, it's gotten so bad. Would you be willing to help her wash and comb out her hair?"

Isabel reached over her shoulder and pulled her braid up under her nose. She sniffed it, wrinkled her nose, and grinned at the twins.

The twins dimpled. "Sure," Lily said.

Isabel's hair turned out to be quite a project. It took a while just to get the braid undone. Isabel hung her head down under the wash tub pump behind the boarding house while the twins soaped and scrubbed. Finally they got her settled on a stool in the late afternoon sunshine and set to work, each with a comb, tackling the tangles.

"Isabel," Lily said. "We want to ask you something."

"Sure—ow—what?"

"What's a brothel?" Rose asked.

Isabel turned around on the stool to look at them. "You don't know?"

"We sort of have an idea," Lily said slowly.

"But we don't really understand," Rose said.

"And we don't want to make any more mistakes like this afternoon."

Isabel gave them a long look. "Okay, I'll tell you."

The twins went back to work with their combs as Isabel explained.

"All these men here with no wives, they got no place to take their pleasure. You understand?"

"Yes."

"Okay. These men have no wives, and there's some as do have wives but like a change from time to time. So Smythe has some rooms and in each room he keeps a woman. The proper ladies in town call them soiled doves or fancy women. Anyhow, a man comes in, takes his pleasure with her, and pays Smythe.

And when he's done, another man comes. Smythe takes care of the women, gives them meals and a place to live. That's their job, how they live."

"That's horrible!" Rose exclaimed. "Miss Ella … does she?"

"Yes, she does. Now it's horrible for some of them, like it would have been for your friend Laura, if they're kidnapped or get into it because they've got no other way to survive. But there's some that don't mind it so much. They're fed and taken care of. And some like the attention from all the men."

"So a brothel is a place where …?" Lily asked.

"That's right. Smythe has his upstairs above the saloon."

"That's what he meant when he said, 'one night upstairs.'" Rose shuddered. "What if he kidnaps us, like he wanted to at Robinson's?"

"Now don't you worry, dearie, he can't touch you. All the town knows you by now, and they'd run him out for sure if he bothered you. There's plenty want to run him out anyway, and he knows that."

The twins were silent, attending to the tangles. Lily could feel Rose shaking inside. She felt a little queasy herself.

"Thanks for explaining," she said finally. She ran her comb smoothly through Isabel's hair. "I think it's all combed out now."

Isabel gathered up her hair and began braiding, her fingers moving swiftly. "Now don't you go telling your pa I told you all that, or he won't let me near you again, and then I'd be sad."

"Don't worry," Lily said with feeling.

"We'd be sad, too," Rose said.

Isabel kissed them both on the cheek and hurried through the kitchen door, tying off the end of her braid as she went.

## Chapter 26

# *The First Sunday*

Early the next morning, the twins woke to the sound of bird song floating in the open window of their room. They'd had the room and the wide comfortable bed to themselves since Nathan had moved his family to their new land on Pine Road the day before.

Lily stretched. "This is so luxurious. It's going to be hard to go back to our little straw mattress in the wagon tomorrow."

"Yes," Rose agreed. "But we'll be on our own land up on the hill. I love that place. I knew Papa would end up choosing it." She got up and leaned out the window. "It's a perfect morning, Lily. Come see. A perfect day for our first church service."

Lily rolled out of bed and came beside her. "It is. And we should get going. Gabe will be looking for us soon to practice the hymns."

They dressed with care in the blue-gray gowns with lace collars they had brought from Boston and kept, unworn, in the bottoms of their trunks until now. Daniel was already in the dining room, sipping coffee and frowning over his sermon notes.

The twins greeted him and found out what hymns he wanted for the service, then ate quickly and hurried out into the summer morning. They skipped and walked, hand in hand, down the road between the new brick buildings, deserted now in Sabbath quiet, and on to Gabe's cabin.

"I'm curious to see the inside," Lily said as they approached. "He's certainly very pleased with it."

"I think Jesus does watch over him," Rose said. "He just trusts, and everything works out for him."

Gabe was sitting on a chair outside his cabin, tuning his fiddle. "Here you are," he said smiling, getting up. "Come on in. Let me show you my new home."

The dirt floor of the small cabin was swept clean. There was a rude table and a chair, a round-bellied cookstove, a bed frame and some shelves. In the center of the back wall a big window, newly cut, let in light and the sound of the river.

The twins went to the window and looked out at the view of the river and the hills.

"This is lovely," Lily said. She turned and smiled at Gabe. "You've got a good home here."

Gabe smiled. "I sure do. We'd better git to practicing now. What hymns does your pa want for this morning?"

When they finished their practice, they walked across the road to the hill where the church was to be built. Hannah arrived in a big wagon filled with tables and benches from her dining room, and set to work putting up a picnic area with the help of Isabel and her two boys.

People were already beginning to gather, townspeople from both sides of the river and homesteaders coming in from the plains. The sound of their voices became a low roar, as they milled around, calling out, greeting each other. Bud Budke rode up on his mule. He dismounted and began directing the parking of wagons and buggies and carts, waving his arms, perspiring, and stuttering furiously. A crowd of miners walked up the road from the shanty town.

"My goodness," Hannah said, looking around. "This is as many as we ever got for Reverend Jackson. Here comes your pa. He looks mighty fine all dressed up in his Sunday clothes. He's a handsome man, your pa."

The twins nodded. "We think so, too." They watched as their father came through the crowd, stopping to greet people, shaking hands, pausing to listen.

"I brought my dinner bell," Hannah said. "When it's ten o'clock, I'll ring it. It's not a church bell, but it's loud."

Slowly Daniel made his way to the hilltop. Lily and Rose and Hannah, carrying her big bell, followed. When all was ready, Hannah rang her bell. The roar of voices quieted as Lily and Rose and Gabe played once through "Jesus Calls Us." Daniel lifted his arms. His strong musical voice rang out: "The Lord is in his holy temple. Let all the earth keep silence before him."

It was the first time Daniel had held a service for a group bigger than the wagon circle since Easter in Council Bluffs. The twins watched their father, marveling again at how he came to life, how his face shone as he shared his beloved gospel, how eloquently his words poured out. They watched the huge group of people standing on the hillside, captivated, silent except when they joined in singing the hymns. When the service was over, they saw how the people pressed around him, heard the murmurs of appreciation, even adoration.

Hannah came to the top of the hill and rang her bell again. "You're all invited to a picnic down where the tables are," she called out. "Bring your baskets and share, and if you don't have a basket, there's food there, compliments of the boarding house and Elsie's café. There's cider for all."

As the group flowed down the hill toward the tables, Lily and Rose began to realize that their father was not the only focus of interest and admiration. In spite of Hannah's attempts at privacy, the story of their adventure in the saloon the day before had spread through the town. After all, more than thirty men had witnessed the scene, and it was too good a story to pass up. The tale had grown, and there were already several versions afloat around the picnic tables.

Lily and Rose found themselves surrounded by admiring men.

"Got Smythe all riled up, did you?"

"You play the piano beautiful."

"Got us all together, you did, so you pa could meet us. Did your pa send you down?"

"You gonna come play for us again?"

Lily laughed and answered pertly, but Rose felt shy and confused by the press of men around her. She looked for her father, and saw him speaking urgently to Mattie, gesturing in their direction. In a moment Mattie made her way through the men and said to them, "Hannah wants you to help her serve cider. Can you come now?"

"Yes, we'll be glad to," Rose answered, breathless with relief. "Come on, Lily." She caught Lily's hand and tugged her through the crowd of men.

"Oh, good," Hannah said. "I need some help. Here are two bowls. You can each take one to serve from. Isabel'll bring you more cider when you run out."

The men followed them, but at least, to Rose's relief, they were on the other side of the table and had to keep moving as others came for cider. There were people all around them, and the twins overheard many snatches of conversation.

Behind them, Mrs. Dodge was talking to a woman they didn't know. "He took a great risk sending them down to that evil place to gather the miners for him. I certainly wouldn't—"

"Dolly, he did *not* send them," Hannah interrupted her. "You shouldn't be spreading stories that aren't true. They wandered in there, attracted by the piano, so innocent they didn't know it was the saloon." The women moved away and the twins didn't hear the rest of the conversation. They looked at each other, biting their lower lips.

Isabel brought her son and his wife over to meet the twins. Ed was lean and handsome with curly black hair and vivid green eyes like Isabel's. Lucinda was very pretty with big blue eyes and pale blond hair worn in an elaborate knot low on her neck. She leaned on her husband's arm and looked up at him from under long lashes.

After they had greeted the twins, Ed took Lucinda over to meet Mattie. He left her there and came back to Isabel. Though he drew her aside, the twins couldn't help overhearing their conversation.

"You've got to come back, Ma. Everything's falling apart since you left. Lucinda can't—"

"It's not a matter of can't," Isabel interrupted him. "It's a matter of won't. There's nothing wrong with her; she's young and healthy and smart. She's just spoiled rotten. You made a poor choice for a frontier wife, but you've got her now, and you'll have to shape her up. Best if you do before she starts having babies."

"There won't be any babies. She won't let me near her, cries and says she's tired. If only I had more money, I could hire help and build her a nicer house. Maybe then she'd be happy."

Isabel snorted.

"Ma, you've gotta come back."

"I told you no."

"Ma—"

"No! Seven years I've been out there with you. That's enough. You've got a wife now. Let her do for you. Besides I've got a job to do here, now the preacher's come."

More people came for cider and the twins were busy serving them. When they looked around again, Ed had disappeared, and Isabel stood a little way off, wiping her hands on her apron, as if she'd like to wipe the whole situation away.

The picnic lasted for several hours. Everyone seemed to be having a good time. People who hadn't seen each other for weeks, even months, got together to catch up. Groups settled around the tables and on the grass. Children ran and screamed. Daniel was busy the whole time, moving from group to group, sitting a while with each one. He forgot all about eating until Rose brought him a plate. The twins were busy, too, helping Hannah. Men kept gathering around them, "like bees around two blossoms," Rose heard Hannah say.

Lily was exhilarated, feeling for the first time the power of her beauty, laughing, responding to their jokes and teasing with her quick tongue, instinctively finding ways to tilt her head, to look out of the corners of her eyes, to enchant. Rose still felt shy, but became more at ease as she realized she could ask the men about themselves, listen to their stories.

At last, when the crowd began to disperse, Hannah called her helpers and loaded tables and benches and food into her wagon. The twins rode back with her, perched with Isabel between them, on a teetering bench.

Daniel and Aaron Jenkins walked together, engaged in earnest conversation.

That evening the prayer meeting at the boarding house overflowed the dining room and filled the front porch as well.

# Chapter 27

# Home on the Hill

Early the next morning, Daniel and the twins rounded up their oxen and yoked them to the wagon. Hannah came to meet them on the porch to say good-bye.

"Thank you so much for your hospitality," Daniel said. "How much do I owe you for these three days of room and board?"

"Nothing, nothing at all," Hannah said indignantly. "You're my minister, and I intend to take good care of you. You come on back for dinner this noon, you hear? And any time."

"Thank you," Daniel said. "You're very kind."

Isabel came to kiss the twins. "I'll be up to see you soon. You'll be wanting some help getting that garden in."

Daniel and the twins were leading their wagon out onto the road when Hannah called, "Reverend, wait a minute. I forgot. Mrs. Dodge, she's the postmistress, brought over some letters for you yesterday, two of them. I'll get them for you." She went back inside and was gone quite a while. "I'm sorry," she said when she came back. "I've mislaid them. I can't imagine what I've done with them. I'll look for them and give them to you when you come for dinner."

"Did you notice who they were from?" Daniel asked.

"Well, yes I did. One was from a Mrs. Adam Wright and the other from a Mrs. John Baker."

"Mrs. Adam Wright, that's my mother." Daniel frowned. "Mrs. John Baker? I don't place that name."

"That's Nell!" Lily exclaimed.

"Becky's sister, Nell," Rose added.

"Nell!" Daniel put his hand to his brow. "Nell, of course." He dropped his hand. "Do try to find them," he said to Hannah. "One may have news that's important to me."

A letter from Nell. News of Rachel. The twins, standing behind Daniel, struggled to contain their excitement. "But he'll never tell us what it says," Lily whispered to Rose.

"We'll know," Rose whispered back, "by his face."

Daniel seemed confused for a moment, then turned to the twins. "Come on now."

They had not gone far when Gabe joined them, riding on Sadie. "I thought I'd come help you set up your camp."

Farther up they passed Nathan's lots. The whole Hollis family came out to greet them. Nathan offered Daniel the use of his new plow, and Mattie and the twins hugged each other.

"I'm so glad we're neighbors," Mattie said. "We can share lots of things."

The twins turned back to wave as they went on up the road. As they passed the big rock that marked their eastern boundary, their land seemed to welcome them.

Daniel and the twins parked their wagon and set out with Gabe to explore their new home. As they walked, they discussed where the house and garden would go. Daniel wanted to put the house near the bottom where the land was level, but the twins wanted to put the garden there.

Rose took Daniel's hand and led him up to the place where she and Lily had sat the first day they visited the land. "This is where Lily and I thought we should build it. See how beautiful it is to look out over the plains."

Daniel stood and looked for a moment. "It is a nice view, but quite steep."

"Build your house into the hill," Gabe said. "Where I come from there weren't nothing but hills, so we built into them. Keeps the house warmer in winter when you have one side the wind don't blow on." He smiled at Daniel. "I been thinking about your house. I'm gonna build you a really good one."

They continued walking up toward the little stream where the land rose more steeply. "We'll fence off our pasture here," Daniel said, "where it's too steep to garden or build."

He rubbed his brow. "There's so much to do here, and what's most important to me is to visit my people and build the church."

"You'll have help," Gabe said. "Don't worry."

Daniel turned back toward the wagon. "Let's set up our camp down near the bottom. Then tomorrow I can make calls. Aaron tells me there's ranches between here and Montview I should visit."

"I wonder where Fairdale Ranch is," Rose said. "Stephen's family."

"I'll find out," Daniel answered her. "Stephen is a fine young man. I'd like to meet his family."

For the next four hours they worked hard. They settled the wagon in a level place and hung an India rubber sheet out from it for an awning. Isabel showed up and helped the twins dig out a permanent fire pit, and Gabe helped Daniel set up a tent Burt had donated for Daniel to live in.

"You girls will have the wagon to yourselves now," Daniel said as he and Gabe moved his trunk into the tent.

When the fire pit was finished, Isabel and the twins sat back on their heels and admired it. "This is going to be so much easier than digging a new fire trench every night," Lily said. "Even though we're still camping, we're luxurious now, with an awning and all."

"And I'll make you a table soon," Gabe promised.

When all was set, it was near noon.

"Don't forget Hannah's expecting you to come for dinner," Isabel said. "It's almost time." When Daniel stared to protest, she interrupted. "She'll be upset if you don't. She has a mind to look after you, and you'll learn when Hannah sets her mind—just come."

"Let's take our carpet bags," Rose suggested. "We can go to the store after dinner and stock up our chuck box. Maybe we can make some bread this afternoon."

Hannah still had not found the letters when they arrived for dinner. The twins watched Daniel, seeing his hope, his disappointment, noticing that he was so distracted he paid no attention to a long, stuttering account from Mr. Budke about how he planned to set up his butcher and barber shops next door to each other in the new brick building. He finished his dinner without seeming to notice what he ate, then left abruptly.

"If Hannah doesn't find that letter," Lily said to Rose as they crossed the bridge over the river on their way to the store, "Papa will never know. He can't write to Nell because Mr. Decker might see it."

"I hope she finds it," Rose said. "I hate to see him so upset. He wants to know so badly."

When they arrived at the general store, Elsie came to meet them and helped them find the supplies they needed. "The milk is fresh today," she said. "The Fairdale girls brought it in this morning."

"The Fairdale girls!" Rose exclaimed. "They must be Stephen's cousins."

"That they are," Elsie said. "Stephen used to come in with them sometimes last winter. But he went off again early March. How'd you know of Stephen?"

"He was an outrider on our wagon train," Lily answered.

"Fancy that, and then you coming right here where his uncle's ranch is." Elsie helped the twins pack up their supplies in their carpet bags as she talked. "Maybe he'll come back now that your wagon train's come through. Mr. Fairdale's right fond of him, glad to have his help on the ranch."

"He won't be coming for a while," Rose said. "He's going to California."

"California! That's a far piece. Dangerous journey, I hear. Maybe he'll never come back."

"How much do we owe you?" Lily asked.

"Mama." Elsie's little girl came running in, weeping, to cling to her mother's skirts. "Billy hit me."

Billy was right behind her. He planted his feet wide apart. "I did not. Tessy hit me first."

"Hush, now." Elsie lifted Tessy up onto her hip. As her gown pulled closer about her waist, Rose saw the bulge of the next child coming. "Nine dollars and seventy-five cents."

"I didn't," Tessy wailed. "I didn't never."

"Ach!" Elsie exclaimed in frustration. She set Tessy down and gave Billy a cuff on the shoulder. "Leave your sister alone. Run on, both of you. Can't you see I'm waiting on customers?"

Billy ran off, but Tessy still clung to her mother's skirts.

After Lily counted out the money, the twins picked up their bags and said good-bye to Elsie who was hoisting Tessy up onto her hip again.

"Come back soon," Elsie called after them.

"This bag is heavy," Lily commented as they started out.

"Mine, too," Rose said. "And it's uphill most of the way."

They followed Mill Road back to the bridge and stopped there to set down their bags and watch the water swirling underneath.

"We've got a ways to go yet," Rose said after a while. "We can change hands every so often."

They picked up their bags and continued, over the bridge, across Gold Creek Road, and on up toward Pine Road. The sun was hot and the bags grew heavier as the road sloped more steeply.

"We need a horse," Lily said.

"We should have brought Shadow," Rose agreed.

"We need our own horse. Papa will be using Shadow."

"Papa might not want us to have our own horse."

"So we won't ask him. We still have our money from Grandmama. When we find a good horse, we can just buy it. Once we have it, it would be hard for Papa to make us take it back."

"That's a good idea. Whew! Let's rest a little."

They had reached the corner where the road from the bridge met Pine Road. They sank down in the rough grass and stretched out their legs.

As they rested there, a man riding a shaggy brown horse and pulling a cart came out of a lane a short way down Pine Road. He stopped by the twins and dismounted. He was tall and heavy, and wore a soiled red-plaid shirt, a big black hat, and a wide belt with a gun on each hip. "You girls all right?" he asked.

The twins stood up quickly and caught each other's hands. "Yes, sir," Lily said. "We were just resting."

The man frowned. "You must be the preacher's daughters. I'm on my way up to talk to your pa. Get in. I'll give you a ride."

The twins looked at each other, hesitant. "Thank you, sir," Lily said. "But…"

"Get in," he said brusquely. "You look all tuckered out. You're right to be cautious, but I'll not harm you. I'm your neighbor, Sheriff Parker." With his finger tip he flicked a shiny medal on his chest that the twins hadn't noticed. He picked up their bags and threw them into his cart. "Hop up, now."

The twins exchanged another glance, then climbed in. The sheriff started his horse up before they were settled and they caught the sides of the cart to keep from falling. The cart was dusty, cluttered with tools and a half bale of hay. Rose sneezed.

The sheriff walked beside his horse, his gait heavy. "I hear you were down playing hymns in the saloon last Saturday. What was your pa thinking of? That's no place for young ladies. You stay away from there, you hear?"

"Yes, sir. We will."

The sheriff turned to look at them as he walked. His eyes were small and watery in his leathered face. "I've got to talk to your pa. That big crowd he had yesterday. I don't want any trouble."

"There wouldn't be trouble from a Christian gathering," Lily said indignantly.

"Innocent, aren't you." He looked them over as they stood jouncing with the movement of the cart, holding on to the sides. "Now I'll allow as there are some good Christian folk who actually do as they say you should do, some in this town, but there's plenty others, call themselves Christian, that make lotsa trouble, drinking and whoring and killing. Don't go trusting people just because they say they're Christian."

They passed the big rock and came to the wagon. Daniel, with Lucky hitched to a plough, was turning up the garden area, working with furious intensity.

The sheriff stopped his horse. Rose climbed quickly down. "Thank you for the ride, sir."

Lily handed down their bags, and jumped down after her. "Thank you, sir." She turned and called to Daniel. "Papa, Mr. Parker is here to talk with you."

The twins were back at the general store the next morning. Daniel had plowed a big garden area the afternoon before.

"Smooth it out and get it planted," he said, as he prepared to leave after an early breakfast. "Here's money for garden tools. Get a wheelbarrow, too, to move any rocks you find up where we're going to build the house. I'm heading out toward Montview to visit the ranches. Probably won't be back until evening."

He rode off. The twins cleaned up the breakfast dishes, then walked over to look at the garden. It was littered with clumps of sod and rocks.

Lily kicked a rock with her boot. "'Any rocks we find' he says. There's hardly anything *but* rocks."

"And the soil doesn't look very good." Rose squeezed a handful. "It sticks together like clay."

"Well, we'd better get going. This is going to take a long time."

They got their bonnets. Rose put the money in her apron pocket and they set out.

Burt was tending the store and helped them find shovels, rakes, trowels, and a wheelbarrow.

"Two of everything," he said smiling, as he rang up their purchases. "It must be nice to have a twin to work alongside of you."

The twins smiled back. "It is," Rose said.

"It's a good thing there's two of us," Lily added. "Papa plowed up a lot of garden and it's a mess, all rocks and clumps."

"There's always a number of fellows hanging around here," Burt said, "tired of the mines and looking for odd jobs. You might get a couple of them to help you. And you'll need some good rotted manure to loosen up that clay soil we got here. Hannah's got a big pile."

"Thanks," Rose said. "We'll remember that."

"You'll need a fence, too. Deer come down out of the hills and they'll eat your garden to the root if you don't keep them out."

"A fence. Papa didn't say anything about that," Lily said.

"Well, I've got posts and chicken wire, if you need them."

The twins loaded their tools into the wheelbarrow and started back up the road.

They walked a while, taking turns pushing the wheelbarrow. "Papa looked better this morning," Rose commented. "He was really upset yesterday about losing the letter. You could tell by the way he was plowing."

"Maybe that's why we now have such a big garden."

They were hot by the time they got back to their wagon. "It's already midmorning," Rose sighed. "We'll never get this done today."

When Daniel rode up to the wagon that evening, the first thing he noticed was that the area he had plowed the day before had been divided into two level terraces and smoothly raked out. Then he saw the twins. Lily was sprawled against a wagon wheel and Rose lay flat on her back in the grass beside her. Their eyes were closed, their green gowns smudged with mud. He dismounted and came closer. "Lily? Rose?" They smelled distinctly of manure.

Lily eased herself stiffly up from the wagon wheel. "Hi, Papa."

Daniel sat down beside her. "The garden looks good," he said. "You must have worked hard."

Rose stirred. "We did." She sat up slowly, bracing herself with her hands behind her. "But we couldn't have done it without a lot of help."

Lily sat straighter. "You said 'smooth it out' as if it were nothing. But it was all rocks and chunks dried hard as rocks and sloping—"

"And the soil was sticky clay."

"We went down to the store for tools and Burt said we'd need to put manure in to loosen it up."

"And Hannah had some."

"But we didn't have a horse and cart to bring it up."

"And those rocks were heavy to push up the hill in the wheelbarrow."

"It does sound like a big job," Daniel admitted. "Who helped you?"

"Gabe did. He said we didn't have to push the rocks up the hill because there'd be plenty there when he dug it out."

"So we brought him the rocks from the garden and he made those little walls so the garden wouldn't slope."

"And Isabel got four men who were hanging around the general store to come up and help us."

"You were working up here with four strange men?"

"Isabel was chaperoning us."

"Isabel!" Daniel passed his hand across his brow. "I'm not sure—"

"Papa." Lily was indignant. "We needed help. You have no idea how much work it was."

"I've talked with some of those men," Daniel said. "Who came?"

"Marcus and Benedict. They're brothers. They're really funny looking. They have these burly hunched shoulders and big noses, and their hair is cropped really short. They look so much alike we had trouble telling them apart."

"Mmm," Daniel said. "Now maybe you know what it's like when people can't tell you apart."

"And there was Harry, who speaks with a funny accent."

"And George, who doesn't speak at all. He's part Indian, Isabel says."

"So they all helped us. And Hannah loaned us a wagon for the manure, and we took the oxen down and brought it up."

"And unloaded it."

"And dug it in."

"And raked it out."

Rose flopped down into the grass again with a sigh.

"Be careful," Lily said. "You almost put your head on a cactus." Rose wiggled away from the cactus. Lily slumped back against the wagon wheel.

Daniel looked at them. "I don't suppose you have any supper ready."

"No." Rose sighed again. "We need to clean up before we can cook. We're all over manure."

"I'll get the fire going," Daniel said.

The twins went up the hill to the stream to wash. Then Rose rummaged in the chuck box and found some rice and beans already cooked that she heated up for supper. It was nearly dark when they sat down around the fire to eat.

"I didn't think about the manure," Daniel said. "It's good you got some. I noticed when I was plowing that the soil was rather dense. Good that Gabe helped you level it out."

"We need a fence," Rose said. "On account of the deer. Burt said so and so did Isabel. And remember Mr. Erickson? He said so, too. We'll have to put it up before we plant."

"A fence," Daniel sighed. "I'll see about that tomorrow. Did you pay the men?"

"Rose gave them each a dollar and we promised to make them some pies."

"Pies. You could make me one, too."

The twins didn't respond. Daniel scraped the last of the rice and beans out of his tin bowl and set it on the ground. He leaned back, supporting himself with his hands clasped around his knees. "I visited Fairdale Ranch today."

The twins perked up. "What's it like?" Lily asked.

"It's big," he told them. "Mostly a dairy ranch, but they raise some horses and chickens, too, and grow a lot of vegetables and fruit. Mr. Fairdale has three hired men. They all love Mr. Fairdale, say he is fair and kind and generous, and it's the best job they ever had… Have you got any bread?"

"No. We didn't have time to bake today."

"No bread?"

"Tell us more about the Fairdales."

"Did you meet Stephan's cousins?"

"I met them all, Mr. Fairdale, his wife, his daughters, and his son. Had dinner there. Mr. Fairdale is very well educated. He has a library I'm envious of, and kindly says I can use it any time, even borrow books. They invited us out on Friday to spend the day and the night. They have a piano in their living room. Mrs. Fairdale said to bring your instruments. Apparently Stephen wrote and told them about you."

"Friday!" Lily exclaimed.

Rose's eyes shone in the firelight. "I can't wait."

~

There were still two days to wait and much to be done. On Wednesday Daniel hired Marcus and Benedict, Harry and George to help him put a tall wire fence around the garden while the twins baked bread and the promised pies—an apple pie from the last of the dried apples in the barrel they bought in Council Bluffs and a peach pie from dried peaches Grandma Wright had given them. On Thursday Nathan and Gabe, Aaron Jenkins and Ken Hill came and helped Daniel fence off a pasture for Shadow and the oxen; and Isabel and the twins planted the garden.

By evening, all was finished. In the glow of sunset, Daniel and the twins led the four oxen and Shadow up to their new pasture.

"We've been here a week," Daniel commented as they walked. "Only a week ago we arrived, and we've accomplished a lot." He gave Shadow a final pat and closed the gate. "You girls have worked hard and done well. Tomorrow we'll have a break and make some new friends."

They walked slowly back along the little stream. When they reached the place where they planned to build their house, they sat down together, the twins on either side of Daniel. He put his arms around them. They rested in silence, watching the shadow of the mountains spread across the plains.

# Chapter 28

# Fairdale Ranch

At eight-thirty Friday morning, the twins, brimming with excitement, set out down the road to the store carrying their carpet bags packed with their instruments, their cloaks, music, and overnight necessities. Daniel had arranged for them to meet the Fairdale girls there and ride back to the ranch with them in their cart. He would come later on Shadow.

When the twins arrived at the store, the Fairdale girls were already there, and Burt was unloading the big cans of milk from their cart. Through the open door the twins could see the older girl at the counter with Elsie. The younger one stood holding the heads of two gray horses, one a little darker than the other.

"Hello," she greeted them. She had freckles across her nose and green-gray eyes, and though she looked about the age of the twins, she still wore her dark auburn hair in two long braids.

"Good morning," Rose answered. "What pretty horses." She and Lily went to stroke the horses' noses.

"What are their names?" Lily asked.

"This one's Dusk and this one's Dawn," she answered, touching first the darker then the lighter one. "And I'm Amy."

"I'm Lily."

"And I'm Rose."

"They're twins," Amy said, patting the horses. "Like you. Only easier to tell apart."

"Isn't it unusual for horses to have twins?" Lily asked.

"But they do sometimes, like humans." Amy looked at Rose and Lily, furrowing her brow. "You look *just* alike."

The older girl came out of the store, tucking her money packet into her waistband. Like Amy, she wore a blue denim skirt and a loose blouse of light-weight cotton with full sleeves. Her hair was smooth and dark and she had a quiet, demure air. "Hello," she said, smiling warmly. "I'm Julia. I've been really excited to meet you. Let's go home."

The twins climbed into the cart. It was much cleaner than the sheriff's cart.

"We brought pillows for you to sit on," Amy said, as she climbed in after them.

Julia swung up onto the seat in front and flicked the reins. As Dawn and Dusk started off, she turned around to look at the twins. "Now which one of you is which?" She had deep dimples in both cheeks when she smiled.

The twins introduced themselves. "We've been admiring your horses," Lily said. "They're really beautiful."

"Dusk is Julia's and Dawn is mine," Amy said, talking fast. "We used to ride their mother together when we were younger. Our father had a double saddle made for us. Then when she had Dawn and Dusk, Father gave them to us, and we've had them ever since they were born, and cared for them, and trained them and everything. They're five years old now and we can ride them now and use them to take us to the store like you see."

Julia turned around. "Slow down, Amy. My sister's a chatterbox," she said to the twins. "Do you have a horse?"

"No," Lily said. "We wish we did. Papa has a black one called Shadow, but he has her almost all the time. We rode her some on the way out. Stephen taught us to ride astride. We never had before."

"Stephen wrote about you in his letter." Amy bounced on her pillow. "He really likes you."

"We like him, too," Rose said.

"We miss him," Lily added. "He was a good friend."

They had reached the edge of town. Julia turned the horses off of Gold Creek Road onto a rougher road that angled north-east out onto the plains.

"How long does it take to get to your place?" Rose asked.

"About an hour," Julia answered, "on horseback. A little longer with the cart. Tell us about your journey. We came by covered wagon, too, but it was ten years ago and we don't remember very well."

Lily and Rose looked at each other for a moment. Wordlessly they agreed not to speak of some things—Cindy's death, Smythe and the road ranch, Regina's revelations; but that still left plenty of tales to tell. Lily did most of the talking, putting a humorous twist on her stories, so that soon they were all laughing.

The road branched, then branched again. They came to several intersections where tracks went off in four or more directions.

"Where do all these roads go?" Rose asked.

"Over here," Julia gestured to the right, "there's Hendrick's horse ranch, and that way, out a few miles Mr. Donegal has a big wheat farm, but some of these roads just go out into the plains and fade away."

"It's kind of confusing," Rose said.

"I guess it could be," Julia responded, "but we go this way so often I hardly have to guide the horses. The road we're on now—it's called Ranch Road—goes around our place and joins the road to Montview."

Farther on, they turned under a high gate onto a curving track, forded a wide shallow stream, and came to the ranch. Herds of cows grazed in neatly fenced pastures on both sides of the road. Dawn and Dusk picked up their pace. They passed more pastures, then drew up beside a large barn. Ahead of them were a big two-story house and a cluster of cabins.

Julia jumped down off the cart and unhitched the horses. "Come with us to take Dawn and Dusk to the pasture."

The twins followed Julia and Amy along a foot path between some outbuildings to a pasture where horses were grazing. The stream they had crossed earlier flowed across the far end. Julia opened the gate and led the horses in. Over by the stream, a tall gray horse lifted her head. Julia whistled to her, and she trotted over to them.

"This is Dawnstar, the mother of Dawn and Dusk," Julia said as she stroked Dawnstar's neck.

"She's beautiful," Lily breathed. She held out her hand and Dawnstar snuffled it.

Rose reached out to pat her side. She was tall and sturdy, her coat so light a gray that it was almost silver, and the blaze on her brow was in the shape of a star.

"She used to be our horse," Amy said. "We used to ride her everywhere, but we hardly ever do any more."

"Poor Dawnstar, she's been kind of neglected since Dawn and Dusk grew up," Julia said. "Mother rides her sometimes, but she has her own horse that she rides most of the time."

The twins had come closer, enchanted, and were stroking Dawnstar's sides, touching her silvery mane. "Could we ride her?" Lily asked.

"I think so," Julia answered. "I don't know why not. She'd love the attention."

"I know!" Amy gave a little jump. "Let's take them on a ride around the ranch. They could both ride Dawnstar—we still have that double saddle somewhere—and we could ride Dawn and Dusk and maybe Jonathan would like to come, too. Let's."

"We need to ask Mother," Julia said. "And she'll want to meet Lily and Rose."

"Come on, then. Let's ask her." Amy already had the gate open.

Dawnstar followed them to the fence. Lily and Rose lingered to give her one more stroke.

When they reached the house, Kate Fairdale came out onto the porch to meet them. Although she was dressed in a simple gown and apron, she carried herself with elegant grace. She wore her smooth dark hair in a knot of braids at the back of her head, and her gray eyes were kind and welcoming. "Here you are," she said. "I've been thinking you should be along soon."

Amy and Julia ran to embrace her. The twins, watching, felt a pang of longing and reached for each other's hands. Kate's quick eyes caught the gesture, and the look on their faces. She set her daughters aside and held out her hands to the twins. "Lily and Rose, I am so glad you could come. Please come in. Did you bring your instruments?"

"Yes," Rose said. "We left our bags in the cart."

"Mother," Amy burst out, "we want to take Lily and Rose for a ride around the ranch. They don't have their own horse, but they could ride Dawnstar. We still have that double saddle. Maybe Jonathan would like to go, too. Can we?"

"That sounds like a lovely idea," Kate said. "Why don't you get their bags and show them your room. Then we'll find the saddle and get you set."

As the twins followed Amy and Julia downstairs, Lily whispered to Rose, "We don't have our split skirts."

"Oh, no!" Rose looked down at her dark blue gown. "But Julia and Amy aren't wearing split skirts either."

"Maybe they ride side saddle."

"Let's watch and see what they do."

The four girls went back to the pasture and brought the horses to the barn where Kate was dusting off the double saddle. Amy and Julia saddled their horses. The saddles were not side saddles, nor was the double saddle Kate helped the twins settle on Dawnstar. They watched Amy and Julia closely as they bent over, reached between their feet and did something with their skirts so quickly that Rose and Lily couldn't quite make out what it was. Then Amy and Julia swung onto their horses—astride.

"What did you do with your skirts," Lily asked, "so you could ride astride?"

"I'll show you," Kate said. "You reach between your feet, take the center of your back hem, bring it through to the front and tuck it into your waistband." She demonstrated as she spoke. "Then when you get off the horse, you just untuck it." She loosened the front of her skirt with a flick of her hand. "Your skirt falls into place, and there you are, a perfect lady."

"Stephen said you had a trick with your skirt," Rose exclaimed, delighted. "But he didn't know what it was."

Kate raised one eyebrow. "It's a lady's secret." She led them to a mounting block by the barn door. The twins divided their skirts, and mounted Dawnstar, Lily in front and Rose behind.

Kate adjusted the stirrups. "I think that should work for you now," she said. She smoothed Dawnstar's neck. "Have a good ride."

"Thank you." Rose looked down at Kate, feeling a tug of yearning toward the warm, motherly woman.

Amy nudged her horse and rode ahead. "Come on, let's go. Let's find Jonathan." Julia and the twins followed. Dawnstar's gait was easy and smooth. Rose hugged Lily with excitement, and felt Lily's excitement flow back to her.

"Jonathan's down in the training corral," Julia said. "He's been breaking a wild horse that our foreman, Bernie, found last winter, separated from her herd and about to die. We named her Patches, and Bernie thinks she'll be a good cattle horse when she's trained. Jonathan's a good trainer, very gentle. He wins the horses' trust and then they'll do anything for him. He's just gotten Patches to the place where he can ride her."

In the training corral, Jonathan rode a small, sturdy paint, turning her first one way, then another. He looked up as the girls approached, swung down from Patches, swept off his hat, and bowed with a wide smile. "Lily and Rose, I presume. Welcome to Fairdale Ranch." His eyes were bright gray-green, his face tanned rose and brown, his hair a tumble of auburn curls.

The twins smiled back at him. "Thank you," they said in unison and mirrored his bow as best they could from Dawnstar's back.

"Jonathan," Amy burst out. "We're taking Rose and Lily on a tour of the ranch. Do you want to come?"

"Sure, I'll come. Go on. I'll get Patches settled and join you. Which way are you going?"

"We'll take the orchard path," Julia said.

It was a perfect summer day. Jonathan soon joined them on his tall chestnut, Brandy. They rode through the orchard where tiny green apples were forming, along the creek, past a deep inviting pool with a rope swing, through a wide area of open plains where they let their horses gallop. With the wind in their faces, the horse under them, the laughter and companionship of their new friends, the twins' joy overflowed.

∽

Daniel followed Andrew Fairdale around his cozy book-lined library. Andrew touched his books with a reverent affection that Daniel understood, often pulling one out and opening it to share a favorite passage, glancing up to meet Daniel's eyes as he read. Daniel found himself increasingly drawn to Andrew. There was a clarity about him—a light in his eyes, the way he moved with lean, quick grace, the way he spoke, his meaning shining through his uncluttered words.

But the present turn of the conversation was deeply disturbing.

Andrew had pulled down a well-worn volume. "Emerson. He's one of my favorites."

"Emerson!" Daniel exclaimed. "But he's a heretic, an ordained minister who has turned away from the church and has led many astray with his outrageous teachings."

Andrew smiled. "His teachings are indeed outrageous, which is why they delight me. He discards all authority, freeing us to turn inward to find the authority of our own truths."

"And that is exactly where he leads us astray. There is but one authority— the Holy Scripture, given us by God."

Andrew closed the volume of Emerson's essays and set it back on the shelf. He looked at Daniel, his eyes alight with challenge. "And how do you know that?"

"Because it says so in the Holy Writ. 'All scripture is given by the inspiration of God.' Second Timothy 3:16."

"But Daniel, you can't use scripture to prove that scripture is the word of God. It's a circular argument, don't you see?"

For a brief unsettling moment, Daniel almost did see. Then confusion roared through him, slamming shut all the doors of his mind except the one that opened onto a familiar corridor. "It's the very first statement in the Westminster Confession," he asserted, making a decisive slice through the air with his right hand. "That the Holy Scripture is most necessary. Other revelations of God are not sufficient. We receive this truth through faith."

"I acknowledge the necessity of faith," Andrew responded. "It takes faith to believe in a loving God when there is so much misery in the world. But do you really think that it is the word of God that we should dash babies' heads against stones—Psalm 137—or that we should stone a woman to death for adultery? What about the man who may have forced her, or even lied. He gets off scot-free. Is that the word of God?"

Daniel's eyes blurred. Behind them rose the image of Rachel's face as he had last seen it, bruised and swollen. He heard again Thomas's words that Ebenezer, in his rage, demanded that Rachel be stoned. When Daniel spoke again, his voice was husky. "Jesus said, 'Let he who is without sin throw the first stone.'"

"He did, and that was wise, but it doesn't change earlier words of violence that many devout Christians think they should act on. How could both be the word of God?"

Daniel was silent. From the next room the richness of a Mozart string quartet flowed in, Rose's flute playing along with the first violin.

"There is much evidence," Andrew went on, "that the Bible was written by many different men, some simply expressing the customs and prejudices of their time. Others are truly inspired, like the one who wrote the 139th Psalm, one of the most beautiful pieces of poetry in all literature. There is so much contradiction. There are even two different stories of creation in the very first two chapters of Genesis. What do you make of that?"

There was a moment of discord in the music, laughter, a burst of conversation, Jonathan's voice saying, "Let's take that part again."

Daniel could not speak, still seeing the image of Rachel's battered face. Andrew was silent, too, studying Daniel. The music picked up again, full and haunting. After a while, Andrew said gently, "What I'm saying doesn't negate the truths of Christianity. Jesus was a great man, a profound teacher. He—"

"Jesus was the Son of God, God himself!" Daniel interrupted. "If you think Jesus was only a teacher, how can you access his salvation? And without scripture you are lost. Where else can you find sure guidance for your life?"

"As I have said, I find the guidance of scripture somewhat inconsistent. But I am not without guidance. God reveals himself to me every day, every moment, in the beauty of nature, in the order of the stars, in the wisdom of the animals, in the words of all these great books, and of the people I meet and love. In your words also, Daniel, for you are wise in your path. I see the love you have for your God and your devotion to service, and I honor that. This valley is already the richer for your presence here. But I cannot follow your path; it is too narrow for me."

Daniel's heart contracted in a storm of outrage and fear for his friend. "'Enter ye in by the strait gate … for wide is the gate and broad is the path that leadeth to destruction,'" he quoted. "Andrew, if you go wide, you miss the path. The stream runs swift and clear to its destination only when contained by strong banks. Without the banks, it becomes lost in a marsh."

The music in the next room had stopped. There was a knock on the door and Kate's voice saying, "Andrew, Daniel, supper is ready."

"We're coming," Andrew answered. He touched Daniel's shoulder. "There are many interesting life forms in a marsh."

At supper, the families of the hired men joined the Fairdales and Daniel and the twins around the long table in the kitchen. The twins were introduced to Bernie, the foreman, and the two young families that lived in the cabins behind the big house. James and Sophia had two little daughters, four and three years old, and Luke and Molly had a baby boy. The twins took turns holding him. They cuddled him close, sharing the thought of their little brother.

After the meal, the young people gave a concert. Then Bernie and Jonathan, with their banjos, led folksongs and everyone sang along. Last of all Jonathan sang a comic ballad, mimicking different voices, until the whole room rocked with laughter. The twins went up to bed with Amy and Julia, replete with happiness.

Late that evening, Daniel rode back to Gold Creek. Andrew accompanied him part of the way, lest, as he said, Daniel miss a turn in the dark. But Daniel knew that Andrew just wanted to be with him as much as he, Daniel, wanted to be with Andrew. They did not speak of Emerson or scripture, but talked lightly of the events of the day and of their children.

"You have a family of fine musicians," Daniel noted.

"Yes. That's Kate's doing. She's an accomplished musician with piano, violin, and viola. She had Jonathan well started on cello before we left the East, and has taught the girls violin and viola since we got here. They all love it. Music is our favorite way to be together."

"Do you play?"

"No, I'm the appreciative audience. Your girls are also highly skilled. It's been such a treat to have them join us. I hope they can come often."

"Thank you. They would love that." They rode on in silence. Andrew carried a lantern, but they hardly needed it, as the moon was bright.

"It was fun to see your girls on Dawnstar, to have the double saddle used again," Andrew said after a while. "I heard them telling Kate how much they want their own horse. Perhaps we could work something out with Dawnstar. It seems a perfect fit."

"Maybe. I'd need to think about it."

When they reached the junction of Ranch Road and Pine Road, Andrew clasped Daniel's hand, said good night, and turned back. Daniel rode on alone, his heart and mind in tumult.

He had loved the day at Fairdale Ranch. The meals around the long table with the family and the ranch hands reminded him of meals at the Wright farm with his parents and brothers and their families. He thought of his time with Andrew in the library, of the music in the evening, and of his daughters.

He had met them as he arrived just before noon, coming back from their tour of the ranch, riding double on Dawnstar. The image of them returned to him with clarity. They had looked so happy, younger somehow than they had looked through all the difficulties of the journey and the recent week of getting settled. In his mind he saw them blissfully focused as they played Mozart, chatting vivaciously with Julia and Amy, laughing until tears came to their eyes at Jonathan's song. They've had a happy day, he thought. And even now are probably curled up in bed with Amy and Julia, whispering and giggling as girls do. They will want to go again.

But—maybe I shouldn't encourage it. The whole family is so attractive, but they're on the wrong path. What if my girls are subtly influenced? What if they are led astray from their faith? I am their father, responsible for their souls. I must be vigilant.

I should see if I can set up more connection with the Dodge family. Annabelle seems like a good girl. But not so lively as Julia and Amy … and in truth, I am not so very attracted to Dwight and Dolly. They're good people, devout, but ...

Damn! Why does Andrew touch me so? *I* could be led astray. No, never! My path is clear.

～

"I promised your father I'd have you home before noon," Kate said to the twins at breakfast. "But we still have a little time. Is there anything you'd specially like to do before you go?"

Rose looked up. "We'd love to see your garden. We just put ours in two days ago. There's nothing to see there yet but raked earth."

"And getting that far was a huge job," Lily said with emphasis.

"We have a really big garden," Amy said spreading her arms, "with herbs and flowers, specially roses, and lots and lots and lots of vegetables. We all work on it and we sell the vegetables at the store. My job is the tomatoes and squashes."

"We don't have any tomatoes or squashes," Rose said. "Isabel said it was too late to start them from seeds."

"Isabel? Isabel Flannagan?" Kate asked. "Isn't she the one who is homesteading out on the plains with her son?"

"She was," Lily explained, "but she's staying at the boarding house now. She comes and helps us a lot."

"Maybe we could give them some tomato and squash plants," Julia said, "if that would be okay with you, Amy. We have lots."

Amy considered. "We could," she decided. "We do have plenty."

When everyone had finished eating, they all walked out to the garden. Jonathan brought a wheelbarrow and a shovel and some burlap.

"It *is* big," Lily said, awed.

The garden was neatly laid out, with trenches between the rows for irrigation, and paths beside the trenches.

"Here are the herbs," Julia pointed out. "This is my part to keep. Mother's teaching me all about the medicinal herbs."

"Medicinal herbs." Rose looked over at Kate. "I'd like to learn about that."

"The next time you come," Kate promised, "I'll teach you, too.

Lily was still feeling impressed by the size of the garden. "I'm glad our garden isn't this big. We had enough trouble to do a garden less than half this size. If Isabel hadn't gotten Marcus and Benedict and a couple of others to help us, we'd still be raking it out. Papa plowed it, but it was all rocks and clumps."

"Marcus and Benedict," Julia laughed. "We know them. They flirt with us every time we come to the store."

"They *are* flirts," Lily said, tilting up her chin. "When I asked them how much they charged an hour, Benedict cocked his head to the side and closed one eye"—Lily mimed it—"and said they'd charge less if we'd throw in a kiss."

Amy and Julia started giggling.

"Lily!" Rose protested, blushing.

"They did," Lily went on, undaunted. "I said we didn't pay in kisses, but we'd bake them some pies. And Benedict, he just sighed and said he'd prefer kisses."

"I can understand that." Jonathan smiled, looking straight into Lily's eyes.

Lily's heart leaped. She dropped her eyes as the color rose in her cheeks.

"Come on and see my tomatoes," Amy urged. "They're this way."

When it was time for the twins to leave, Jonathan lifted a big box into the cart packed with four tomato plants, six squashes, and several herb plants—calendula, arnica, and chamomile—each root ball carefully wrapped in wet burlap. The twins went with Julia to the pasture to get the horses. Dawnstar came to the fence. They petted her and embraced her neck. "Good-bye Dawnstar," they whispered into her mane. She nickered after them as they closed the gate and walked away.

On the ride back to Gold Creek, Jonathan drove the cart, sitting backwards most of the time and teasing the four girls until they were aching with laughter. When they reached the Wright's land, Lily and Rose showed the Fairdales all around—the split standing stone with the spring, their wagon home, the fire pit they'd built, the oxen in the pasture, and the garden. All five worked together to plant the tomatoes and squashes and herbs, digging the holes, carrying water from the stream, patting the earth down around them.

Too soon it was time for them to leave. As the cart disappeared down the hill, Rose slipped her arm around Lily's waist and sighed. "I wish they didn't have to go."

They sat down together on the grass, brows touching. "Or that we could have stayed there," Lily said. "I love it there. I think yesterday was the most fun day we've ever had in all our lives."

"I think it was."

"Jonathan's so funny."

"I love Amy and Julia."

"Dawnstar."

"Yes."

Lily tightened her arm around Rose. "She's our horse. I know. We just have to figure out how to buy her without Papa knowing."

"We'll find a way."

"The music."

"And Mrs. Fairdale."

"Mama would have been like that."

## Chapter 29

# *Settling In*

In the next few weeks the twins settled into the pattern of their new life. Although camping with an awning and a permanent fire pit was easier than traveling all day and making a new camp each night, there was still plenty of hard work. They cooked hot meals for Daniel morning and evening, and made bread each day in their dutch oven. Aaron Jenkins came often to visit and brought them scraps from his lumber mill, so they were well supplied with firewood.

They made a dam in the little stream and dug out a pool big enough to dip their buckets. From there they carried water to a trough in the pasture, to their garden where they poured it carefully around their new little plants, and to the wagon to fill their water barrel for washing and cooking. Once a week, they loaded Lucky up with bags of laundry and led him to the river below Gabe's house to wash their clothes, then came back up the hill to hang them on lines strung from the wagon to the fence posts of the garden.

Almost every day, they walked down to the store. Gradually they added a few luxuries to their camp—some dish towels and pot holders, some new cooking utensils, a real broom to sweep out their wagon. One day they found Elsie setting out bolts of cloth and impulsively bought some blue denim and a light cotton with a print of little flowers to make themselves summer clothes.

"Though when we'll ever get a chance to sit and sew, I don't know," Lily complained. "I've never worked so hard in my life. It never ends."

"We worked hard for Grandmama learning all the things we had to know to enter society," Rose said.

"Yes, but then we came home and Becky fixed dinner *and* washed the dishes, and washed our clothes and cleaned our room and put fresh sheets on our bed—"

"Sheets," Rose sighed. "I wonder if we'll ever have those again."

The summer days were hot, with thunderstorms in the afternoons, sometimes with high winds that shook the canvas of their wagon and battered the small plants coming up in their garden. Once the wind was so strong that it tore the awning loose and blew down Daniel's tent. Often they met Amy and Julia at the store, and sometimes the Fairdale girls would come up to their camp. These visits were highlights for the twins. Julia and Amy kept inviting them to come to Fairdale Ranch again, but Daniel always had a reason for them not to go.

There were other bright spots in their hard-working days. Isabel came up almost every afternoon for a while to help them with whatever they were doing and make them laugh with her irreverent perspective. There were practice times with Gabe in his little cabin by the river, preparing hymns for prayer meetings and Sunday service, and visits back and forth with Mattie and the children. Baby Beth was growing and beginning to smile. Rose and Lily played with her, thinking of Rachel's child and wondering if he, too, were smiling now.

The stage came twice a week, from Denver to Montview, making a stop in Gold Creek, carrying mail, boxes of supplies, and a few passengers. One day it pulled in while Rose and Lily were shopping. Gerald Dodge came down from the post office to pick up the mail. He sorted through it as he stood at the store counter. "There's a letter for you," he said to the twins.

"Maybe from Grandmama," Rose said.

"Nope. This one's from a Miss Laura Russell in Ohio." He handed the envelope to Lily.

"Laura Russell?" Lily looked at the envelope, puzzled.

But Rose burst out, "It's Laura. Laura from Robinson's Ranch."

"Oh!" Lily caught Rose's hand. "Let's go out on the bench to read it."

They sat down side by side on the bench outside the store. Lily tore the envelope open and they bent their heads together to read. The letter was scrawled on rough lined paper:

*Dear Lily and Rose,*

*I hope this letter finds you well and settled in your new home. I hope you are really there, that nothing bad happened to you on your way, and that you get this letter.*

*Thank you, thank you for helping me. My aunt has talked with me very seriously and I understand now what you saved me from. How can I ever thank you? You are angels sent to me by God.*

*The stagecoach trip was hard. We never stopped, night or day, except to change horses. But the lady who was riding with us with her husband was kind to me. And we got there okay. My uncle met me because of the telegram and brought me here.*

*I live with him and my aunt and my cousins now and work hard on their farm. I am still sad, missing my ma and pa and my brothers, but my aunt and uncle are good to me. They are sad, too. I am doing okay.*

*Please write to me.*

*With much gratitude, Laura.*


The twins finished reading and hugged each other.

"She's all right. I'm so glad."

"I thought she would be, but we didn't know."


~


Gabe went right to work on his shop and soon had it up and open, a long board building attached to the east end of his cabin. The front was composed of two wide doors that opened onto the road. As he worked, he would smile and raise a hand in greeting to passers-by.

The gold nugget had given him a substantial account in the bank, more money than he'd had in all his life, and he was able to buy the tools he needed to make fine furniture as well as build houses. He was soon busy, but his first project was the table he had promised the twins. He brought it up one afternoon in his cart and set it up under the awning, a sturdy well-finished table with two benches.

In the evenings, the townspeople would see him on the hill across from his cabin pacing out the dimensions of the church, then later leveling the ground and beginning a stone foundation. Soon other men joined him in quiet working communion in the long summer dusk.


~


Nathan talked with Aaron Jenkins and arranged to work several hours each morning at the sawmill in exchange for the boards for his house. The rest of his time, he worked hard and steadily on preparing the ground and building the foundation for his new home. He and Gabe drew up plans for a sturdy three-room house with a view out over the plains, and Gabe came up often to help, teaching Nathan the skill of rock work.

Mattie had her hands full caring for the three little ones and the garden, and managing the basic housekeeping tasks in her wagon camp; but true to her word, she invited Gabe and the Wright family to share her cook fire once a week. Gabe and the twins brought food to share, and they all enjoyed again the intimacy of their companionship on the trail.

Within a few weeks, Gabe and Nathan had the foundation of the house prepared and the floor laid. The men of the church and a group of idle men from the shanty town joined them in a day of house raising. There was still much to be done to finish the inside, but the family was able to move in, much to Mattie's relief.

~

Daniel spent most of his days visiting his parishioners, sometimes sitting with them, listening to their dreams and difficulties, and counseling them with scripture and the wisdom of his own devout heart. Other times he rolled up his sleeves and helped them with a project—mending a roof, searching for a lost cow, splitting wood, lending a hand in a garden or orchard. After his long years of city living, he enjoyed using the skills he had learned growing up on the farm, and his parishioners appreciated his willingness to help with chores as well as advise them on spiritual matters.

The second Sunday, the congregation was almost as large as it had been on the first Sunday. As the weeks went by, some folks came and went, but the list of church members, watched over by Aaron Jenkins, continued to grow. Every Sunday Daniel performed baptisms, and every Sunday Gerald Dodge passed the collection plates and money came in for the building of the new church.

In spite of his ambivalence, Daniel often found himself stopping by Fairdale Ranch on his rounds. Andrew always welcomed him. They would sit on the wide porch and chat or Daniel would ride with Andrew, as he checked fences or oversaw the work in orchard, corral, and dairy. Kate always invited him to share a meal. The girls pestered him to let Rose and Lily visit again, but he put them off.

It's all right for me, he would say to himself. I won't be led astray. But they are young and impressionable.

Each afternoon on his way home from his rounds, he stopped at Gabe's shop to share the experiences of the day and go over the plans Gabe was drawing up for the church.

During the day, Daniel was happy to be doing his work again, engrossed in the building of his new congregation, but at night he dreamed of Rachel and woke afire with longing. He was beside himself with frustration that Nell's letter had been lost. Hannah finally confessed it must have gotten mixed up with some newspapers on the kitchen table and burned in the cookstove. Surely it had contained news of Rachel, maybe an address. If only he could write to her, hear back from her, know if she were well. And what of the child? How had the birth gone? Was she even alive? He felt he could not bear not knowing.

He tossed on his narrow mat, knelt with his brow against his trunk in the small tent and prayed, but found no ease for his troubled heart.

# Chapter 30

## *Fourth of July*

June rolled into July. Mayor Wilgus called a town fair and celebration for the Fourth of July.

At three o'clock that afternoon, Gold Creek Road was closed from Bridge Road to the road that ran next to the church lot, now called Church Road, creating a square enclosed on the north and south by the new brick buildings. People came from all directions and set up booths and tables around the square, or displayed their wares in the backs of their wagons—fruits and vegetables, flowers, crafts of all kinds. Some brought animals to sell. Along the north side of the square, Hannah and Elsie set up tables to sell bread and pies, coffee and cider.

Miners poured into the square from their shanty town. A group of men set up in front of the brick buildings with banjos, flutes, two fiddles and a drum, and played patriotic songs. People gathered around them singing.

Isabel and the twins sat on a bench near Hannah's table.

"This is a different crowd than the people that come to Sunday service," Lily observed.

"Sure is," Isabel agreed. "The sheriff's all antsy. He's deputized Marcus and Benedict. Look at them." The twins followed her pointing finger. Marcus and Benedict were slouching around the edge of the crowd, looking sheepishly uncomfortable with badges on their chests and guns on their belts.

"What about George and Harry?" Rose asked.

"Burt asked him the same. I heard him. Sheriff said he wasn't putting no badges on Injuns or foreigners. So they missed out.

"Now look who's coming." Isabel nodded toward the west end of the square. Smythe appeared, driving a large wagon. At the sight of him the twins caught each other's hands, feeling cold in the pits of their stomachs. Six women, brightly dressed in low-cut gowns, waved and smiled from the back of the wagon. The twins recognized Ella among them. As the wagon pulled into the square, the miners cheered. Smythe jumped down and, with the help of several men, set up a table and barrels of beer and whiskey. The women clustered around Smythe's table, flirting with the miners.

The twins watched in fascination as one of the men tapped a woman on the shoulder, then strolled off with her toward the saloon, his arm around her waist.

"There goes Kitty," Isabel remarked. "Getting her first job of the day. Those girls are going to be busy today, and especially tonight."

"Kitty? Do you know them?"

"Sure. I meet them down at the store sometimes. They have to eat like everyone else. I've met them all, one time or another. That young one there, who's hanging back, now that's a shame. She was brought up in the brothel, so I hear. Her mother wouldn't let Smythe touch her, but the mother died last winter. And now Smythe's selling the child. Lisbeth's her name. He shouldn't be. She's not twelve, if she's a day."

Lisbeth was standing behind Ella at the end of the table farthest from Smythe. She looked very young, her dark hair loose down her back, her ill-fitting orange gown cut so low her small, new breasts were almost entirely revealed.

Rose's heart ached for her. "That's awful."

"That's what would have happened to Laura," Lily said, shuddering.

A commotion broke out at the east end of the square, two men arguing about the placement of their wagons. As their voices rose, a crowd gathered, mostly men taking sides, yelling. The sheriff hurried over and plunged into the middle of it, waving his arms and giving orders. Marcus and Benedict followed. Lily saw them look at each other, shrug their burly shoulders, and slouch back to the edge of the crowd. The dispute rose to a crescendo, then abruptly quieted when Sheriff Parker fired into the air.

Rose looked back at Smythe's table. Smythe was standing with his arm around the shoulders of a young miner, grinning at the uproar. She saw Lisbeth, taking advantage of Smythe's distraction, duck down and dart behind the corner of the brick buildings.

Lily tugged at her arm. "Here come the Fairdales." Kate and Andrew and Jonathan arrived on horseback, Kate elegantly astride. Behind them, Amy and Julia drove the cart, laden with eggs and cheeses, vegetables, and big bouquets of roses. They were followed by Bernie driving a wagon with the other ranch hands and their wives and children. Rose and Lily ran to greet their friends.

"We're going to have a square dance," Amy announced. "Bernie's a great caller. Have you ever square danced? It's really fun."

Rose and Lily looked at each other, questions darting back and forth between them. "We haven't square danced," Lily said, "but we've danced. We can probably pick it up."

"Where's Papa?" Rose whispered to Lily.

"Over there." Lily tilted her head toward a group of homesteaders who were selling goats. Daniel was talking earnestly to a frowsy-haired woman wearing a goat-skin vest with big silver buttons.

"He'll notice for sure if we start dancing."

"He wouldn't dare drag us away here, like he did before, not with all these people."

"Maybe."

"It's worth a try."

Mayor Wilgus picked up his megaphone and bellowed through it. "Ladies and gentlemen, we're honored to have caller Bernie Turner, famed throughout our valley, here today to call some dances for us. Let's clear the center of the square and welcome Bernie Turner."

There were shouts and cheers. Bernie took the megaphone. "Find your partners, and shape up your sets."

The twins watched as the sets formed. Mayor Wilgus led Hannah to head up the first set. Burt and Elsie joined them, leaving Isabel in charge of the tables. From all around the square, men and women left their wagons and joined in.

"Look," Rose whispered. "Even Mr. and Mrs Dodge are going to dance."

"Marcus and Benedict are asking Amy and Julia," Lily giggled, "and they're going with them."

"Lily, will you dance?" Jonathan had come up beside them. He held out his hand to Lily. She caught her breath, her cheeks pink, and laid her hand in his.

Gerald Dodge was right behind him. "Miss Rose?"

Daniel was so absorbed in talking to the goat woman that he was only vaguely aware of the change in the music, but the goat woman started tapping her foot and looking over his shoulder, no longer attending to his words about salvation.

"Ah, look," she said. "They're starting the dances. Will ye dance with me, Preacher?"

Daniel turned around. Seven sets had formed in the middle of the square, and an eighth set was shy of just one couple.

"Come on." The goat woman grabbed his hand and tugged him toward the center of the square.

Daniel startled out of his bewilderment and pulled his hand away. "No … no, no thank you. I don't dance."

"Too bad," the woman said. A thin bearded man came by and she caught his hand instead and dashed off with him to join the eighth set.

Bernie gestured to the musicians. The music started, a lively tune that Daniel recognized, but couldn't place. Then Bernie started calling, and the whole square swung into motion.

Daniel stood stunned, little by little taking in the scene. All his parishioners were dancing, even Dwight and Dolly Dodge, whom he considered his most conservative. Smythe's women were dancing with some of the miners. He watched as Mattie settled her little ones by Hannah's table, then caught Nathan's hand and found a place in the dance. He saw Andrew whirling with Kate—and Lily and Rose. Both dancing. The people who were watching were stamping and clapping, singing along. The music swirled with the high whine of the fiddles. Everyone was smiling and laughing.

Gabe waved at him as he dashed by, fiddle in hand. Then he turned back. "Daniel, you look like someone done poured cold water on you."

"They're all dancing. All of them, my whole congregation. And my girls. I've forbidden them, and there they are defying me."

Gabe put a hand on Daniel's shoulder. "Maybe you forbid them too much. Dancing ain't a sin. Remember the scripture your daughters read you? It can be a way to praise God."

"But it leads to sin. Look at them! The men have their arms around the women. What will they do next?"

Gabe kept his hand on Daniel's shoulder. "There ain't no harm being done. Your girls are happy. See how they're laughing. They work hard every day and they're young. They need some fun. You can watch over them and I will, too. And Jesus watches over them always. Don't forget that." He gave Daniel's shoulder a final squeeze and moved off between the dancers to join the musicians.

Daniel found a bench by the Fairdale's wagon and sat down, hunched. He had an impulse to tap his foot to the music, but did not allow it.

∼

Lily and Rose climbed rebelliously into their wagon and sat facing each other on their trunks.

"Why did he make us come back? It's not even dark yet," Lily muttered.

"He did let us dance for a while."

"But now there's such fun music and singing, and here we are stuffed into our wagon. Who knows when there'll be another celebration as good as this one. Fourth of July only comes once a year."

"We could wait a little while," Rose suggested.

"Until he's asleep?"

Rose nodded. They could hear Daniel puttering around inside his tent, the rustle of his mattress, and a sigh. They waited. After a while, snores.

"Quietly, quietly," Lily whispered.

Without making a sound they climbed out of their wagon. It was almost fully dark now, but their feet knew the path to the road. Below them in the square between the brick buildings, lanterns were lit and the sound of the music and singing floated up to them. The lighter color of the road showed up in the dusk and they followed it down toward the square. As they passed the back of the first brick building, Rose caught Lily's arm.

"Hush! What's that?"

There were several carts of unused bricks parked behind the building. In the space between them and the back wall, there was movement and an odd choking sound. The twins froze, peering in the dim light. After a moment they made out a small hunched form and realized the sound was sobbing.

"It's Lisbeth," Rose whispered. "I saw her run back here this afternoon when Smythe wasn't looking."

Holding tightly to each other's hands, the twins approached her. "Lisbeth?" Rose called softly.

Lisbeth's head spun around, her eyes two dark pools of fear in the dimness. "No!" she gasped. "Don't tell him."

Rose came closer and held out her hand. "Can we help you?"

Lisbeth crossed her arms over her bare chest, clutching her shoulders. "No! Leave me alone." She stumbled to her feet, gathered up her skirts, and scrambled away from them into the darkness.

"Wait," Rose called after her. "We want to help you." But she was gone.

The twins stood still, clinging to each other's hands. Rose began to cry.

"She didn't want to … " Lily whispered. "I'm glad she got away."

"But where will she go?"

"I don't know, but at least tonight she won't have to …" Lily put her arm around Rose. "We'll watch for her. Maybe we can help her later."

"I wish she hadn't run away from us."

"She was scared we'd tell on her." Lily wiped Rose's cheeks with her hand. "Shall we go on?"

"I don't know. I don't feel much like singing now."

"We've come this far."

"Okay."

They went on along the side of the brick building and into the light of the square. It felt very different than when they'd left it only a little while ago. The Fairdales had left, and many of the homesteaders had also left or were packing up their wagons. Hannah's and Elsie's tables were gone. Most of the activity was focused around Smythe's table. Sheriff Parker stood alert at the edge of the crowd, his feet planted wide, one hand on the gun in his belt. Even the quality of the music had changed. The singing had become drunken shouting. The tune was familiar, but as the twins began to realize the import of the words, their cheeks burned. They hesitated at the edge of the light.

Gabe came up beside them. "Lily, Rose. I thought you'd gone with your pa. Where is he?"

The twins started guiltily. "He's asleep," Lily confessed.

"Ah!" Gabe looked at them for a long moment. They lowered their eyes.

"Come away." Gabe took Lily's elbow. "This ain't no safe place for you. I'll walk with you back to your wagon. I don't want no part of the music they're a'playing now." The twins saw he was carrying his fiddle in its case. He led them back up the road. They walked in silence in the growing darkness.

As they neared the wagon, Lily said, "Please don't tell Papa."

Gabe didn't answer. The twins grew tense. They walked on, past the big rock and onto the path to the wagon. Stars were coming out in the indigo sky above the black outlines of the hills.

"All right, I won't," Gabe said after a while. "But remember this. Your pa was wise to take you away before things went bad down there. He knows more of the world than you do. You must trust him. Do you understand?"

"Yes," Rose said softly. "Thank you for bringing us home."

# Chapter 31

# *Doctoring*

The summer afternoon was hot and still. Lily and Rose and Isabel sat at the new table in the shade of the awning, sewing. The twins had finally found time to cut out their denim skirts and Isabel was helping them sew up the seams.

"Papa wouldn't approve of us making more split skirts," Rose commented as she stitched.

"But he'll never notice," Lily said.

"Men," Isabel snorted. She grinned at the twins and waggled her eyebrows. "There's only one way they want to see a woman's legs apart."

It took a moment of stunned silence before the twins caught her meaning. Lily caught it first and began laughing. Rose's insides tilted into chaos. You could *laugh* about that terrible thing men do to women? But apparently you could, because Lily's laughter was spilling over into her and she found she was laughing, too.

Isabel's green eyes sparkled wickedly. "So, they don't like us sewing a skirt up like we're doing, 'cause then they can't get in so easy. That's the real reason men don't want women wearing bloomers."

Lily shrieked with hilarity. "Ow! You made me prick my finger."

"*I* made you? Stick it in your mouth and suck it. You don't want to get blood all over your new skirt."

Lily stuck her pricked finger into her mouth, giggling and snorting around it. Rose was still in a turmoil of laughter and confusion. "Isabel, Papa would have a fit if he heard you talking to us like that."

"Don't worry, dearie. He won't." Isabel picked up her needle again, suddenly serious. "I read your pa. He's a good man, heart of gold, the way he cares for all his people. But he's got this man/woman stuff all mixed up with his religion. And he takes his religion too seriously."

Lily stopped sucking her finger, wiped her eyes, and sighed.

Rose looked over at Isabel, puzzled. "I didn't think you could take your religion too seriously."

"Oh, yes, dearie, you can." Isabel nodded, her stray curls bobbing around her face. Lily and Rose began sewing again as they listened to her. "Yes, you can. Now I didn't say he takes his God too seriously. You're right—that you can't do. But the religion, the words you say about God, the things you get mixed up with the words about God, now that can cause trouble. Split up families, start wars even, if you take them too seriously."

"Hallo," a male voice called.

The three women looked up. A man came up the road toward the wagon. Rose saw a familiar battered hat, a beloved bearded face, and jumped to her feet.

"Dr. Franz!" she called, running to him. She caught both his hands, her face glowing with delight.

"Hello, Rose." Dr. Franz's smile welcomed her warmly. "Mrs. Anderson said I would find you up here. Lily, hello." He held out his hand to Lily as she came to meet him.

Isabel hurried up, bristling with chaperone energy. "Who's this?" she asked the twins.

"Dr. Franz, this is Isabel Flannagan. She helps us a lot. Isabel, this is Dr. Franz." Rose was breathless with excitement. "I've told you about him. He was our doctor on the wagon train and taught me so much. Dr. Franz, please come sit at our table. Would you like some water? You look hot."

"Thank you, I would. That's a steep path up the cliff. Good to meet you, Mrs. Flannagan."

"Just call me Isabel."

"Please sit here." Rose led Dr. Franz to the table and brought him water.

"I was coming into town," Dr. Franz said between sips of water, "and there was Gabe in front of his shop, waving at me. I stopped to visit and he directed me to Mrs. Anderson's boarding house. I'll be staying there for a while with my boys. She kindly offered me her parlor to hold a clinic, and said she'd get the word out that I am here for people who need help. I would like you to come and work with me, Rose, if your pa can spare you for a few days. Is he here?"

Isabel and Lily picked up their needles and resumed sewing. Rose just sat gazing at Dr. Franz.

"Papa's off seeing his parishioners," Lily said. "He visits them most days, all day. They love him and the church is really growing."

"That's what Gabe said. I'm not surprised. He's a fine pastor. What about it, Rose? Would you like to work with me for a few days or a week, whatever is needed? I brought you a big box of supplies from Denver."

"I'd love to," Rose answered. "I think Papa will let me. Would you mind, Lily?"

The twins looked at each other, suddenly realizing the next days would separate them. Rose held her breath. Lily's eyes softened.

"It'll be okay, Rose. I can take care of things here. Isabel will help, won't you?"

Isabel looked up. "Rose is gonna learn doctoring? That'd be really good. Sure I'll help out."

"We just need to clear it with your father then." Dr. Franz smiled at the twins. "I'm glad to see you both looking so well. You'd gotten rather tired and worn-looking on the trail." He looked around. "And this is a beautiful spot. You're still living in your wagon, I see, though this awning and table are a nice arrangement. Is your pa going to build you a house?"

"Yes," Rose said, "but the church is first."

The twins went on to tell Dr. Franz about the plans for the church, and news of Gabe and the Hollis family—the story of the gold nugget and Gabe's cabin, and the building of Nathan and Mattie's house.

"I want to see Nathan and Mattie," Dr. Franz said, "and especially that baby you and I delivered. Gabe said they were up here near you."

Lily put down her needle. "Just down the road. We'll go with you. We visit every afternoon, and it's about that time." She stood up. "Let's go now."

Dr. Franz and Rose stood, too.

"I'll stay here and do a little more on these *skirts*," Isabel grinned and raised one eyebrow, as she emphasized the word "skirts."

The twins giggled and kissed her, one on each cheek, then went down the road with Dr. Franz.

"What will she see?" Daniel asked Dr. Franz. "She's only a young maiden. She shouldn't be exposed to … She might have to touch their bodies."

Dr. Franz talked with him for a long time, sitting at the table under the awning that first evening. The twins had been sent away to water the garden and tend to Shadow and the oxen, but they did that very quickly, then slipped into the wagon without either man noticing. From there they could easily overhear the conversation. Dr. Franz spoke of the need in the community and how such service could be part of Daniel's Christian ministry, and Daniel finally relented.

The next five days Rose spent with Dr. Franz in the parlor of the boarding house.

Once the word was out that a doctor was in town, people came from all directions with sick children, sprains, burns, chronic illnesses, dog bites, cuts, and other misfortunes. One afternoon a group of miners came carrying a man with a broken leg. Dr. Franz put his hands over Rose's and guided her in aligning the ends of the fractured bones.

Elsie came to be checked; her baby was due in a month. Dr. Franz had Rose palpate Elsie's abdomen to feel the position of the baby. Its head was still high under Elsie's ribs. He explained to Rose and Elsie the risks of a breech birth and told Elsie he'd need to turn the baby.

"All my others came out fine," Elsie protested as she lay down on the table. "Just make sure it's a girl. I don't think I could stand another boy."

Again Dr. Franz put his hands over Rose's and guided her. Together they turned the baby's head down. After Elsie left, Dr. Franz gave Rose detailed instructions in how to handle a breech birth. "I hope that little one will stay put," he said. "But sometimes they turn around again."

Each day was an intense initiation for Rose. She bought a notebook at the general store and wrote down as much as she could of what Dr. Franz taught her. She prayed constantly to Jesus for help as she worked with the patients, slowed her breath, and taught them to slow theirs. Sometimes she wept in the spaces between patients. Then Dr. Franz would sit quietly with her, his hand on her back. "You will grow stronger," he told her. "I would not have you care less; your caring is part of your gift. But in time you will learn to hold all of it in the perspective of God's love, and give thanks each time that you can help."

In the evenings, she curled up with Lily, longing to tell her everything, to have her understand and share all her experiences. Lily listened, but Rose soon realized Lily could respond to her feelings, but could not take in all the details of what she was learning. Instead, Lily turned the conversation to the events of her own full day, doing all the work they usually shared. Rose held Lily tighter in her arms. A seed of desolation lay in her heart. How could it be? How impossible and yet true, that Lily didn't know everything she knew.

The miner whose leg Rose and Dr. Franz had set spread the word among his companions about Rose's gentle hands and beautiful blue eyes. Rose was familiar to them all. They'd all heard the tale of the twins in the saloon, and some had come to church services. Among themselves they started calling her Sweet Rose. On the third day of the clinic, several men showed up from the shanty town with rather insignificant complaints. Hannah overheard one saying to another, as they sat on the porch of the boarding house waiting for their turn, "I'd break a leg just to have her touch me." Hannah did not hesitate to speak to Dr. Franz, and it was decided that, after he left, all Rose's doctoring would be done at the boarding house under Hannah's supervision.

Late on the last afternoon of the clinic, a man in a dilapidated buggy pulled up in a cloud of dust in front of the boarding house and dashed into the parlor where Rose and Dr. Franz were packing up. His wife was in labor, he told them, had been all day and was like to die. Could they please come.

"Did you leave her alone?" Dr. Franz asked.

"Had to. There was no one."

It was a long, rough ride out to a homestead almost all the way to the Montview-Denver road. The woman lay on a straw pallet on the dirt floor of a one-room sod hut, exhausted, screaming with each contraction. The baby was breech. The husband hovered uselessly by the door, seeming torn between his concern for his wife and the impulse to run.

It was a hard delivery. Rose prayed to Jesus, and gradually was able to comfort and calm the frightened woman. Dr. Franz finally eased the child out with forceps, bottom first, and whipped the cord from around his neck as he emerged. A little boy, not breathing. Blood poured out of the woman.

"If it's between the mother and child," Dr. Franz said swiftly, grimly, "you save the mother. But maybe with the two of us we can save both. Massage her abdomen, like this." He guided Rose's hand. The woman winced and cried out. "Don't be tentative. We have to stop the bleeding."

He bent over the baby, suctioning his mouth and nose. After what seemed a heartbreakingly long time, the baby choked, then cried. Dr. Franz handed him to Rose. "Get him to nurse." Rose propped up the exhausted mother and guided the baby to her breast. Dr. Franz took over massaging the abdomen, reaching inside the mother as well as working with his other hand on the outside.

At last the bleeding stopped. The husband went to get water and Rose began cleaning up. They stayed the rest of the night, dozing, watching over the new mother and child.

As they rode to town in the dilapidated buggy the next morning, Rose sat in a daze of overwhelm and exhaustion, her mind still racing as she tried to grasp and remember all she had learned—the feel of the uterus hardening under her hand, the struggle to get the inexperienced mother's nipple into the groping baby's mouth, the impossible image of Dr. Franz's hand up *inside* the mother—all Dr. Franz had taught her as they worked and afterward as they watched together. Her head fell forward with a sudden jerk. Dr. Franz put his arm around her.

"Today you rest," he said. "This evening I will come and we will talk. You have done very well. Without you, we might not have saved the child."

~

Dr. Franz and his boys left the next morning. Rose went down to the boarding house to say good-bye. She watched, in a confusion of sadness and relief, as Dr. Franz climbed onto the jockey seat, flicked the reins over the oxen, and set the wagon into motion. She waved until it disappeared around a bend in the road. Then, without speaking to anyone, she turned away from the road, walked around the boarding house, across the pasture, and up the cliff path.

Will I really be a doctor someday, like Dr. Franz wants me to? she wondered as she climbed the steep path. How can I? How can I possibly learn it all? But Dr. Franz says I have a gift, and that my doctoring could be part of Papa's ministry. He said we might not have saved the baby without my help. I couldn't have done it without Jesus.

She stopped when she reached the top of the cliff. The early morning sun shone warm on her. Tears came to her eyes as she remembered the love and peace she felt when Jesus's healing flowed through her.

But Lily … How can I go down that path without Lily?

# Chapter 32

# *Dawnstar*

Thunderstorms ricocheted back and forth over the hills and the town, interspersed with brief periods of sunshine. In one such bright spell, Lily knelt in front of the fire pit, blowing gently on the young flames of her third attempt to light the supper fire. Daniel, just back from his rounds, sat leaning his elbows on the table, chin in his hands. Rose rummaged in the chuck box for soup makings. Just as Lily was adding larger sticks to the flame, lightning flashed across the valley. The sky grew dark again and thunder rumbled. In a moment the skies opened and rain poured down so fast and heavily that Lily couldn't even hear the hiss of the fire being extinguished. She jumped to her feet and ducked under the awning, already wet.

"Damn!"

Daniel's head snapped up. "Lily!"

"I don't care," Lily shouted in frustration over the beating of the rain on the awning. "You'd swear, too, if you'd been trying for an hour to light the fire and it kept raining like this. When are we going to have a *house*? Mattie and Nathan got here the same time as we did and Mattie has a house, and now she has a cookstove and she can keep her fire going and cook supper even when it's raining. I'm tired of trying to cook like this."

"It looks like cold supper tonight, Papa," Rose said. She studied the contents of the chuck box. "We have bread and some canned sardines. And mustard."

Daniel sighed. "No soup?"

"No! No soup." Lily stamped her foot. "How can I make soup when it keeps raining on the fire?" She pushed her wet hair back, leaving a smudge of soot across her brow.

"Never mind," Rose said. "We have food." She brought the bread and sardines and mustard to the table.

Daniel sighed again as he reached for the bread. The rain abruptly stopped. Lily shook her fist at the sky and sat down at the table.

"We'll have a house before too long," Daniel said. "The church is first, but that'll be up soon. I've been meaning to tell you. Tomorrow I'm going up in the mountains with a group of men to get logs for building the church. We'll be gone two or three days. I've arranged with Hannah for you to stay in the boarding house while I'm away." He spread some sardines on his bread.

"Two or three days?" Lily said. The twins' eyes met across the table.

"Yes. Hannah will look after you and feed you, and you can help her out a little in return. You'll need to come up to tend the garden, but you won't have to worry about the beasts. I'll be taking Shadow and all four oxen to haul the logs."

The twins' eyes met again. Lily lifted one eyebrow ever so slightly. "Okay, Papa."

～

After Daniel left the next morning, the twins packed their carpet bags with overnight necessities, their instruments, and money to buy Dawnstar. They had to wait until their father and the other men had gone up the canyon before they could go to the store to meet Amy and Julia. Once their bags were packed and the garden watered, they stood at the edge of the cliff where they could see the road below. They fidgeted, hoping the men would leave before Amy and Julia came. At last they saw a line of ox-drawn wagons and men on horseback heading west up Gold Creek Road.

Lily gave a jump of excitement. "Now. Let's go."

"Let's leave our bags here. We don't want to seem too— "

After a last-minute scurry, the twins set out down Pine Road toward the store, almost running. Mrs. Dodge was there, examining bolts of cloth, fingering each one, frowning over her glasses. Lisbeth, the girl they'd seen hiding behind the brick buildings on the Fourth of July, was at the counter paying Elsie for a big basket of groceries. When she completed her purchases, the twins approached her.

"Hello."

Lisbeth drew back a little, but smiled. "Hello," she said shyly. She was barefoot, dressed in a worn brown gown, frayed at the hem. Her cheeks were pale. There were dark smudges under her eyes, and purple bruises on her neck.

"I'm Lily, and this is my sister Rose. What's your name?"

Her smile widened a little. "Lisbeth. Aren't you the preacher's daughters? I—"

She stopped short, cowering. Mrs. Dodge charged over, grabbed the twins by their arms and pulled them away from Lisbeth. "You shouldn't be talking to her. Don't you know what she is?"

Lisbeth spun and darted away. Rose saw tears in her eyes.

"She's a child of God," Lily said loudly.

Lisbeth turned back for just a moment, stared at Lily, then ran out of the store, her big basket bumping against her legs.

"She's filth, that's what she is." Mrs. Dodge's eyes pushed forward in her face. She pinched her lips together.

"Now she isn't either," Elsie said from behind the counter. "She's a good child. She can't help where she is." Mrs. Dodge made a low guttural sound in her throat and turned back to the fabrics. The twins caught each other's hands, looking back and forth between Elsie and Mrs. Dodge. They barely noticed the sound of the cart pulling up outside the store.

"Lily, Rose!" Amy called delightedly as she and Julia came into the store. They both rushed to hug the twins.

~

As the cart rattled into Fairdale Ranch, Lily said, "We want to talk to your papa."

"I bet I know why," Amy said. "I bet you want to buy Dawnstar. I hope you do. Father was saying she would be the perfect horse for you. Then you can come visit us anytime, and we can go for rides together and have lots of fun. I know—"

"Calm down," Julia said, looking back from her seat in the front of the cart. "Is that why you want to talk to Father?" she asked Lily.

"Yes. Do you think he would sell her to us?"

"I think he will."

"But, Amy," Rose said. "Let *us* ask him."

"Of course." Julia frowned at her sister. "Don't butt in." She pulled the cart up beside the barn. Kate saw them from the porch and hurried to meet them.

"What a lovely surprise," she said as she embraced Lily and Rose. "We've been wanting you to come visit again. How long can you stay?"

"Papa's gone to the mountains," Lily answered, "with a bunch of other men to bring down logs for building the church. He said he'd be gone two or three days. We were supposed to stay with Hannah, but she said we could come here."

"If that's okay with you," Rose added.

"Of course it is. We're delighted. Come on in. Bring your bags. Oh, good, you've got your instruments. We'll make lots of music while you're here."

She led them into the house. Andrew was sitting at the kitchen table with Bernie. He looked up and smiled a welcome at the twins.

"Father," Amy burst out. "Lily and Rose want to talk to you."

"Amy," Julia muttered, pulling her back.

Andrew got up. "I'll be happy to talk with you." He turned to Bernie. "I'll meet you in the orchard in about half an hour. I need to see what these young ladies have on their minds."

"They want—" Amy started. Julia clapped her hand over Amy's mouth.

The twins grabbed each other's hands. "Sir," Rose started tentatively.

"We'd like—"

"We want to know—"

"If you'd be willing—"

"To sell us Dawnstar." They stopped and held their breath.

"Ah." Andrew smiled at them. "I've been thinking she'd be a good horse for you, and you would be good for her. I've actually discussed that possibility with your father."

"What did he say?" Lily asked.

"He said he'd think about it."

"I guess he did." Lily smiled brightly.

"We have money," Rose said.

"Well, well. But we need to ask Dawnstar."

"Ask Dawnstar?" The twins were first astonished, then delighted.

"Yes," Andrew said gravely. "I think she would want to be consulted about such an important change in her life, don't you? Julia, get me a couple of apples out of the pantry. We'll take her an offering and see what she says."

"Can we come, too?" Amy asked.

"Not this time. This time I'll go with just Lily and Rose. You might want to saddle up Dawn and Dusk. If Dawnstar agrees, I'll bet Lily and Rose will want to take her for a ride."

"Do you think she'll agree?" Rose asked.

"Let's go see." Andrew handed them each an apple, picked up his hat off the table, and led the twins out the door.

Dawnstar was grazing not far from the pasture gate. Andrew gave a whistle, and she trotted up to them. The twins reached out their hands to her, stroked her neck, leaned against her.

"Dawnstar," Andrew said to her. She looked straight at Andrew, her ears perked forward. The twins, standing on either side of her, watched anxiously. "These two young ladies would like you to be their horse, to ride you, and take care of you, and take you home with them. What do you think?"

"Do you think she understands?" Rose whispered.

"Watch."

Dawnstar turned her head and leaned it against Lily's shoulder, then bent it to the other side and pressed it against Rose. The twins held their breath in awe.

"I think you have your answer. Why don't you seal the agreement with the apples?"

First Lily and then Rose offered their apples. Dawnstar graciously accepted them. The twins put their arms around her neck, leaned their faces into her mane.

"There, that's settled," Andrew said. "I know you'll take good care of her."

Rose lifted her head. "How much does she cost?"

"Well." Andrew regarded them with his clear, gray eyes. "She's a fine horse, and in her prime. Ordinarily I'd ask a high price for her, but since you two and your father feel like family to us, I'll give you a deal. How about one hundred dollars with her saddle and bridle thrown in."

"We can do that," Rose said. "I have the money right here." She reached under the waistband of her skirt and drew out her money packet. Carefully she counted out one hundred dollars and handed it to Andrew. He tucked it into his shirt pocket.

The twins embraced their horse again. "Gold and silver, your hair and her mane," Andrew said. "Let's take her over to the barn. I'm guessing you'll want to go for a ride, and Amy's probably already mounted."

~

Two days later the twins rode their horse along the many branching paths back toward Gold Creek. Lily rode in front, Rose behind her with her arms around her waist. Beside them, Jonathan, Amy, and Julia rattled along in the cart, which was full of big milk cans, eggs, cheese, and butter for the store. There were also gifts from Fairdale Ranch for the twins—more herb plants and a box of jars of currant preserves.

Lily laughed and bantered with Jonathan. Rose rested her head against Lily's back. She was sleepy in the warm sun, rocked by Dawnstar's gentle gait, full of blissful memories of the last two days. They had not slept much, the four girls crowded into the big bed, whispering and giggling. And the days had been full. They'd gathered vivid red currants by the stream. Jonathan came along to protect them from bears, he said, but they all knew he just wanted to be with the twins, especially Lily. They'd learned how to put up currant preserves in the outdoor kitchen shed under Kate's guidance. Rose had spent hours with Kate and Julia learning about herbs. Long rides around the ranch and out into the plains, evenings of music and laughter, and Kate's warm mothering presence had filled the days with richness.

The afternoon of the second day, the four girls played in the swimming hole in the creek. Julia and Amy were both good swimmers. When Julia learned that the twins didn't know how to swim, she helped them stretch out in the waist-deep water and kick their legs, put their faces in and blow bubbles. A rope swing hung from the big cottonwood at the edge of the pool. Amy and Julia took turns climbing the tree, gripping the rope and swinging out, letting go at just the right moment to drop into the deep center of the pool. Lily insisted she wanted to try it—and she did. Rose thought her heart would stop when Lily swung out, dropped, and disappeared into the water. But in a moment she came up gasping and kicking her legs, and Julia was right there to pull her to shallower water.

Rose had wavered between longing and fear. Longing won. She swung and let go, slid through the water, felt her feet touch bottom and kick her to the surface where Julia's strong hand caught her. It was a breakthrough—to daring, freedom, sensuality. The lilt of the swing, the breathless moment of letting go, the cold caress of water, the deliciousness of the breeze drying her shimmy, the sun warm on her cold skin. She would never be the same again, and she could feel that was true for Lily, also.

The hollow thump of the horses' hooves on the bridge woke Rose. She lifted her head from Lily's back and looked around, sleepily confused.

"She's waking up," Amy teased.

"Did I fall asleep?"

"Way back by the road to Hendrick's Ranch," Jonathan said, laughing. "We've been watching to see you didn't slide off, but you're a good rider. You stayed on even when you were sleeping."

"I had Lily to hold on to."

"That would help." He smiled at Lily, his eyes warm and bright. Rose felt in herself the quiver that passed through Lily.

Elsie came out to meet them when they arrived at the store. "Thank the Lord you came," she said to Jonathan, putting her hand on her lower back. She was big with the child soon to come. "Burt's gone off on that logging trip, all the men have, and I don't know how I'd manage those big cans." She looked over at the twins sitting on Dawnstar. "Lord a mercy, you've got yourselves a horse. Look at you, both of you riding her. How're you doing that?"

"It's a double saddle," Amy explained, as she jumped down from the cart. "Dawnstar used to be our horse, mine and Julia's, and Father made a double saddle for us, and now Lily and Rose have her, and Mother adjusted the stirrups so they fit, and Father said they'd have to ask Dawnstar if she agreed and—"

"Amy, give me a hand with these cheeses," Julia interrupted her.

Elsie came up to stroke Dawnstar. "Well, aren't you fine. What you need now is a couple of saddle bags to carry your groceries home in. I've got some in the back of the store. Here," she said to Jonathan, "this way. I'll get the door for you."

The twins dismounted to help Amy and Julia with the cheeses and eggs. Jonathan shouldered one of the big milk cans, and they followed Elsie to the door of the cold room. The twins had never been inside before. Steps led down to a cellar room with a stone floor. Around two walls were shelves. The other two walls were lined with big chunks of ice.

"Ice!" Lily exclaimed. "How … where did you get ice?" She shivered. "It sure makes it cold in here."

"We cut it out of the river in winter. Down here it lasts pretty well, but it's going fast now it's summer. Put the milk cans here," Elsie told Jonathan. "When you get through bringing the cans in, be sure to shut the door."

When they came up out of the cold room, they found Isabel in the store. "Oh, there you are," she said to Elsie. "I've got a big order from Hannah. Three wagons came in yesterday, new folks coming to settle here." She grinned at the twins. "You're back, are you? I've kept your garden watered." She gave the twins a questioning look. "There's a fine-looking horse outside I haven't seen before."

"She's ours," Lily said.

"Yours?" Isabel's black eyebrows shot up.

"Yes." Both twins were beaming. "Come see her."

"Let me have your list first," Elsie said.

The twins went out with Isabel.

"Her name's Dawnstar," Rose said. "Isn't she beautiful?"

Isabel approached Dawnstar, tilted her head to look her over. She stroked Dawnstar's side. "A fine-looking horse, like I said. Now, did your pa know you'd be coming home with a horse?"

"Ssh," Lily said, glancing at Julia who was unloading the last of the cheeses. Julia went into the store. "Not exactly."

"Not exactly. What does that mean?" Isabel gave the twins a long look. "I figure that means he didn't know at all, same as he didn't know you were going off to Fairdale Ranch. How'd you come by this horse?"

"We bought her from Mr. Fairdale."

"With what?"

"Money we had from our grandmama."

"Oh, my." Isabel patted Dawnstar again and studied the saddle. "And a saddle for two. You're all set." She shook her head. "My, my. I do think I'll just happen to drop by your place when the men come back. I don't want to miss the look on your pa's face when he sees that horse."

Daniel was tired as he drove Hannah's wagon up to the boarding house. His body ached from the unaccustomed labor of two and half days of logging, but he was well satisfied. It had been good to work hard, sharing the labor with the men of his church. Remembering how they had parted at the sawmill, his heart warmed with a feeling of acceptance and comradeship.

Hannah waved to him from the porch as he drove in to return her wagon. "How did it go?" she called to him. "Come on up and tell me about it." She called back into the house, "Ned, come help Reverend Wright with the wagon."

Daniel handed the ox lead to Ned, then sank into a chair on the porch and stretched out his legs. Hannah bustled off and soon returned with a tall glass of cold mint tea.

"We did well," Daniel told her. "We have plenty of lumber for the church, maybe some left over. Aaron and Nathan will get right to work, cutting the boards. We've decided to have the church-raising bee a week from Saturday."

"That's wonderful." Hannah gazed at him, her blue eyes full of appreciation. "It's hard to believe it was only six weeks ago you got here. So much growth has happened. A week from Saturday. Praise the Lord!"

"The Lord's hand has guided us all. How have my girls been? Did they behave? Did they help you out?"

"They didn't stay here after all. Shortly after all you men left, they came to me with Amy and Julia Fairdale, saying they'd been invited out there for a couple of days. I said fine, and off they went. They got back this morning; Isabel saw them at the store."

Daniel's feet hit the floor, and he sat straight up. "The Fairdales? You let them go?"

"Of course. They really enjoy those girls. And the Fairdales are fine folk, finest in the valley, I'd say. But you know. Your girls won't get into any trouble out there." Hannah gave him a puzzled look. "What's wrong? Shouldn't I have let them go?"

"Well ..." Daniel leaned back in his chair again, frowning. "Of course the Fairdales are fine folk. But they're not church people. I've had long talks with Andrew. He's a transcendentalist. Doesn't hold the scripture sacred. Talks of Jesus as only a teacher. I worry ... well, Lily and Rose are very impressionable. I worry they might be led astray from their faith."

"I think it's all right, Daniel. I doubt those girls are talking religion. They just giggle and chatter like girls do. And have a lot of fun together. I don't think there's any harm done."

"Probably not," Daniel sighed. "It's such a responsibility."

"I know. I feel that way about my boys. But they're all growing up fine, your girls and my boys. The Lord watches over them, too. Don't forget that."

"That's what Gabe keeps telling me." Ned came around the corner of the house with the oxen. "Well, I'd better get going. Thanks for the tea. And spread the word about the bee." He went down the steps, unhitched Shadow, and took the ox lead from Ned.

Those minxes, Daniel thought as he headed up the road. The minute I turn my back, they're off. He remembered the way they'd looked at each other when he said he would be gone for a few days. They were planning it all along, he realized. He set his jaw. He didn't know yet quite what he'd say or do. But something.

They were in the garden when he came to the wagon. Wearing those men's hats instead of their sunbonnets, he noted disapprovingly. Isabel was helping them. In her disreputable hat.

They looked up and waved. "Hi, Papa," they called. They dropped their tools, ran to him, and kissed him on his cheeks. Isabel followed them.

"How did it go? Did you get lots of logs?" one of the twins asked.

"Here, we'll take the beasts."

"Did you get some for our house, too?"

"Sit down. Would you like some water?"

They always bewildered him when they talked so fast, one after another like that. For a moment he couldn't tell them apart, then figured it was Lily asking about the house, Rose offering him the water. Lily took Shadow's bridle and the ox lead from him; Rose handed him a glass of water.

"Thank you," he said, accepting it and sitting down on the bench under the awning. "Though I just had a glass of tea at Hannah's." He looked at them sternly. "She told me you didn't stay there at all, but went to Fairdale Ranch instead. I didn't give you permission to do that."

"Hannah did."

"We had a really good time."

"We learned how to make currant preserves and brought some home with us."

"And Mrs. Fairdale taught me about medicinal herbs and gave me some more plants."

Daniel was suddenly exhausted. He drank his water and got up. "I don't like you doing things without my permission. We'll talk more about this later. Take care of the beasts." He gestured toward the pasture, his gaze following his gesture. His arm stopped in mid air. His mouth dropped open.

A tall silver-gray horse stood looking over the gate, her ears perked forward, curiously surveying the scene below. Shadow noticed her, too. She lifted her head and whinnied. The gray horse answered.

Daniel slowly lowered his arm and turned to the twins. Their lips were pressed together, their dimples deep with suppressed laughter. Isabel stood behind them, her mouth drawn firmly down, but the corners of her eyes crinkling.

"Whose horse is that?" Daniel bellowed. Though of course he knew. He recognized the star-shaped blaze on her forehead.

"She's ours, Papa."

"That's Dawnstar."

"I can see that's Dawnstar. How did she get here?"

"We rode her."

"That's not what I mean and you know it."

"We bought her."

"From Mr. Fairdale."

"He gave us a deal."

"Because he said we were like family."

"I did not give you permission to buy a horse. Where did you get the money?"

"From Grandmama."

"Mr. Fairdale sold you a horse without my permission?"

"He said you'd talked about it. He must have thought it was okay with you."

"And you let him think that?"

"Well, yes." Lily bit her lip and looked up at him, her eyes wide. It was Lily. He knew that look.

"She's a lovely horse, Papa. Come see her." Rose took his hand.

Daniel shook her hand away. "I don't want you to have a horse."

"We need a horse." Lily's chin came up. "We can't go anywhere without one."

"I don't want you going anywhere. I want you staying right here where I know where you are, doing your work and keeping out of trouble. We'll take her back tomorrow."

"No, Papa!" a unison wail.

Daniel turned wearily away from them. "Settle the beasts and get back to work."

He opened his tent flap and ducked inside. It was stiflingly hot. He threw himself down on his mat. Good Lord, his body ached! I'm getting old, he thought. Can't work like I used to and not feel it. The horse. We'll take it back. But Andrew thought I'd given permission. He wouldn't have done it otherwise. It'll be very awkward. He groaned and turned his head from side to side. The tent was impossibly hot. He felt grubby, could smell his sweat. I need to talk to Gabe. I'll clean up and go talk to Gabe.

He searched in his trunk for clean clothes and emerged from his tent. The twins were back at work in the garden, heads close together. What are they plotting now? he wondered. Isabel was leaving. She waved to him as she started down the cliff path.

He trudged up the hill to the bathing place they had created in the stream behind the willows, cleaned up in the cool water, and went to the pasture for Shadow. She and Dawnstar had made each other's acquaintance and were standing nose to tail, flipping the flies off each other. He called Shadow to him, saddled her again. "I'm going to see Gabe," he called to the backs of the twins bent over in the garden.

He was glad of the horse under him. The twins walk everywhere, he couldn't help thinking. It's at least a mile to the store. They complain about carrying the groceries up the hill. But they're young, makes them strong. I can't have them owning a horse. It'll make them too free. They'll be out to Fairdale Ranch every other day, neglecting their work. I'd better take their money away so they can't do things like that again. Get Dwight Dodge to set up a fund for them at the bank, so it will be there in case of emergency, as Mrs. Lowell intended.

Gabe wasn't at his shop. Daniel rode on down to the store looking for him. There was quite a gathering in Elsie's café. Many of the men who had gone on the logging trip were there, Gabe with them. They had pushed several tables together and were drinking beer. Daniel had not yet been able to persuade Burt not to sell it. Elsie bustled around serving them.

"Preacher," they called. "Come on over."

Daniel went and sat with them. Matt Jackson, a lean-faced householder from down the valley, clapped him on the back. "We hear you've got a new horse. Elsie's been telling us. A pretty mare."

Elsie came up with a tray of drinks. "A really pretty one. And she'll sure make those girls' lives easier. I hate to watch them struggling with those heavy bags, knowing they have to carry them a mile up the hill in the hot sun." She set the drinks on the table and began picking up empty glasses. "I told them," she said to Daniel, "I have some good saddle bags they could put their groceries in. You want to look at them?"

"No," Gabe said. "I'm fixing to build them a little cart. I been planning it. They been wanting that horse a long time."

"Got her at Fairdale Ranch, I hear," another man said. "Fairdale raises good horses."

"Beer?" Someone pushed a glass toward Daniel. "Oh, forgot. The preacher doesn't drink."

"I'll bring you some sarsaparilla," Elsie said. "On the house. To celebrate your new horse."

The men went back to talking about the logging trip and plans for the church-raising bee. Daniel sat silent, sipping his sarsaparilla, his mind a whirl of frustration and anxiety. It would be impossible now, he realized, to return the horse.

# Chapter 33

# *The Church Raising*

In the week and a half that followed the logging trip, the town buzzed with anticipation of the church-raising bee. Mayor Wilgus was everywhere, showing the new families around and simultaneously promoting the church raising in his big voice.

Mr. Dodge took a handbill to Moses Sachs to be printed, and Gerald put them up all over town. Mr. Sachs, who had just started a weekly newspaper, The Gold Creek Tribune, put a notice in his column of up-coming events. But mostly the news spread by word of mouth. The men were asked to bring their tools, the women to make box lunches for two to be auctioned off at noon.

The day finally came, a hot July day, but with a breeze off the mountains and enough clouds to give occasional relief from the sun. Almost all the church members came with their families. Hannah and her boys set up a huge awning at the bottom of the hill, with long tables underneath. The women gathered there, watching over their children, catching up on news, and putting the finishing touches on their boxes.

Gabe organized the men into four teams, one for each of the walls, and moved from one to another, supervising. Even some of the homestead women were wielding hammers. Matt Jackson's wife, Jody, seemed as skilled as any of the men.

Mid-morning the whole Fairdale family arrived. Andrew and Jonathan joined the building crew, and Kate went to help Hannah prepare for the lunch. Annabelle Dodge had attached herself to the twins, and when Amy and Julia arrived, the five girls flowed back and forth between helping with the children under the awning, and going up to the hilltop to assist the men, fetching, clearing up debris, and watching in fascination as the church took shape.

At noon Hannah rang her big dinner bell. The men laid down their tools and everyone gathered under the big awning. Mayor Wilgus stood behind a table piled with brightly decorated boxes.

"Ladies and gentlemen," he boomed. "I have the honor of auctioning off these delicious box lunches, prepared by the ladies of our church. Step up, gentlemen. The lady whose box you buy will be your companion for lunch. Bid as high as you can, and then a little higher. The proceeds will go to buy glass for our church windows and a stove to keep us warm when the winter winds blow.

"Now ladies, when your box lunch gets sold, you come on up and take your gentleman to a place at one of these tables. Gentlemen, you won't know till you buy who your lady friend for lunch will be. But I know you'll eat well. The ladies of our church are fine cooks."

He picked up a box decorated with a rosebud and a pink ribbon. "What am I bid for this pretty box?" He held it up to his nose and sniffed, widened his eyes, and raised his bushy eyebrows. "Smells scrumptious, too."

The bidding began. Mayor Wilgus was in his element, egging the men on to bid higher. Gerald Dodge sat beside him, collecting the money. As each box was sold, the woman who had made it came to meet her lunch partner and take him to a place at one of the long tables. There were cheers and jokes. Lily and Rose, Amy, Julia, and Annabelle stood clustered together, waiting to see who would buy their lunches.

Jonathan came to stand near them. "Let me know which is yours," he whispered to Lily. Lily grinned and whispered back.

"Ooo!" Annabelle exclaimed. "That one's mine." She had painted her box blue and tied it with red and white ribbons. Ned Anderson bid the highest and she went to sit with him, blushing furiously.

One by one, the boxes were sold. Mayor Wilgus broke all the auctioning rules and threw in his own bids to keep the prices rising. He ended up with Rose's box. Aaron Jenkins outbid Jonathan and bought Lily's.

Rose and Mayor Wilgus sat at the same table as Lily and Aaron, across and down a little. Rose, overwhelmed to find herself sitting with the mayor, searched to find a subject of conversation.

"I noticed you have a new sign outside the town office," she began. "It looks fine."

Mayor Wilgus beamed. "You like it? 'Town Hall.' Doesn't that sound official?"

"Yes, it does."

"Gold Creek is really shaping up." Mayor Wilgus waved his arm, narrowly missing the bonnet of the lady on the other side of him. "Do you realize that it's only been three weeks since the brick buildings were finished and all the shops are full? I've got the town hall right in the middle, as it should be. And now we'll have a church with a steeple. It'll be the first thing people see when they come into town."

Mayor Wilgus sighed with contentment and bit into the sandwich Rose had made with her Dutch oven bread, cheese and butter from Fairdale Ranch, and lettuce from her garden.

All the time the mayor had been talking, Rose was distracted by an odd feeling from Lily. When Mayor Wilgus stopped to chew, she glanced down the table. Lily was tilting her head, smiling that certain way she had and looking at Mr. Jenkins out of the corners of her eyes. Mr. Jenkins was looking at her as if he had never seen her before.

Flirting, that's what she's doing, Rose thought in astonishment. With *Mr. Jenkins!* It upset her. She'd always been uncomfortable around Mr. Jenkins, and she didn't understand why Lily flirted, most of all why she would flirt with Mr. Jenkins.

"This is delicious," Mayor Wilgus said. "Did you make this bread?"

Rose nodded, pulling her attention back from Lily. She searched for another topic of conversation. "You must have more room in your house now that the town hall has moved to the brick building."

The mayor's mouth was full. When he finished chewing, he sighed. "I do, but I never should have built so big a house. I rattle around in it and go to Hannah's to eat because I don't want to sit there alone." He leaned toward her confidingly. "I was thinking I'd have a wife, you see, and a passel of young 'uns by now. But decent women here are few and far between, and all that are here are already married, excepting Hannah. I've asked her a dozen times if I've asked her once, but she says no. She likes her independence." He lowered his voice. "You know what I've seen? She's got pamphlets from that Susan B. Anthony in her parlor."

"Susan B. Anthony?" Rose was distracted by Lily. She was laughing, tossing her head, and Mr. Jenkins was laughing with her, actually laughing. Rose had never seen him unbend with anything more than a dour smile before.

"Yes. Susan B. Anthony. You don't know who she is?"

Rose shook her head.

"She's the one going all around the country, riding on the trains, standing up in front of crowds of people and saying that women should vote. Can you imagine that?"

Rose tried to focus. "No."

"Crazy, that's what she is. Voting's men's business. What would a woman want to do that for? The man's the head of the household. He votes for his whole family."

Rose was interested now. "But what if a woman doesn't have a husband? Like Mrs. Marlow, or Hannah? Or Miss Towry, who owns the ranch near Council Bluffs where we brought our oxen? I should think she'd want to be able to vote about things that affected her ranch."

Mayor Wilgus patted her hand. "Now don't you worry your pretty head about that. Women should just be married. That Miss Anthony's a good-looking woman in the newspaper pictures I've seen. She should be married instead of running around giving women like Hannah bad ideas about independence."

Laughter spilled down the table. Lily was being her most enchanting and entertaining. The people around her and Mr. Jenkins were laughing, too.

Mayor Wilgus looked across at her. "There now. Your sister's got Mr. Jenkins laughing. You don't see that often."

~

By evening the church was standing, all four walls up and the roof on. There were cheers when the steeple was erected. Hannah rang her bell, Gabe shouted "Alleluia!" and all the Presbyterians who didn't generally shout echoed him.

The next day, Sunday service and evening prayer meeting were held inside. There was no glass in the windows, there were no pews to sit on, but all the members of the First Presbyterian Church of Gold Creek were there celebrating their new home. The summer breeze blew through. Daniel stood behind his new pulpit, skillfully crafted by Gabe, read the scripture and preached the Word in his strong resonant voice, and Lily, Rose, and Gabe led the hymns as all sang "Alleluia!"

# Chapter 34

# *The House*

Gabe spread out his plans for the house on the table under the awning. Daniel sat beside him. Lily and Rose and Isabel leaned over his shoulders.

"Here's the main floor," Gabe said, pointing with his pencil. "Front door here, facing east and I'll build a porch out from it for you to sit out and look at the view. A window here, another window here on the south for the sun to come in in winter. Fireplace here. It'll be open on two sides with doors on both sides. It'll warm the living room and your room here, Daniel, north of the living room. Your room'll be big 'nough for both a bedroom and a study. I'll build shelves for your books." He turned to look at Daniel. Daniel nodded.

"Now here's a couple steps going up into the kitchen. I'll build a rock retaining wall here at the back. We'll put the cookstove here against it. Sink's here. We'll dig a cold room into the hill here, with a sturdy door. A door on the south side of the kitchen, here, opening to a covered wash area, with big sinks and a pump. Privy up here on the hill.

"You'll need a well. Burt says as how there's an old fellow named Enoch, lives up in the mountains, who's a water witch. I'll send a message up to him with one of the miners on Monday. Then we'll dig some trenches and lay pipe from the well to the kitchen and the wash area."

"That'll be real luxury," Rose sighed.

"No more than Hannah has," Isabel put in.

"Now for Rose and Lily." Gabe turned to smile at them. He drew a second paper out from under the first. "We'll put a stairway here, up out of the living room to a second floor under the eaves. The stove pipe and the chimney will both come through to warm you. I'll put a window here on the front so you can see out over the plains, and another one here on the west for air to move through. It'll open onto the hillside. You'll have grass growing right outside your window. The roof'll be sod, keep it cooler in summer, warmer in winter. And it will look like your house just grew out of the hill."

He turned to Daniel. "That's the plan. How do you like it?"

"Very much. It's carefully created. You've thought of every detail." Daniel frowned. "How much will all this cost?"

The twins continued to study the plans while Daniel and Gabe talked about the cost of the house. Gabe said he'd gotten so busy in his shop that he'd hired Harry to help him and he and Harry would contribute labor.

"Harry who talks funny?" Lily asked.

"He's from Russia," Isabel said. "It's a wonder he can talk English at all."

"Yup, he's from Russia," Gabe said. "He was a carpenter there and he's good."

Gabe went on to say Aaron Jenkins would contribute lumber and the only other costs would be sinks and pumps and pipes, the well, hardware for the fireplace, the cookstove, and glass for the windows."

"I love it," Lily said. "All of it, and especially what you've planned for me and Rose."

"I do, too," Rose put in. She hesitated, glanced at Lily. "I'm just wondering if our room will be warm enough, though, when it's really winter. Do you think you could put a grate in here by the east window?" She pointed. "Then heat from the fire downstairs would come up, too."

Lily raised her eyebrows, pressed her lips together to restrain a smile, and nodded ever so slightly at Rose.

Gabe considered. "Good idea." He took his pencil and marked his plans.

"What's gonna go right here?" Isabel asked.

"I was going to put a woodshed there, handy to the kitchen."

Isabel came around the table and sat facing Daniel and Gabe. "I was thinking," she said, her green eyes on Daniel's face, "that if you put in just a little room—I wouldn't need more than a space for a bed—then I could come live with you, and do for you like that one the twins talk about, Becky, did for you in Boston."

"Well," Daniel said slowly. He frowned and looked at Gabe. "I don't know that I need anyone more to do for me. My girls do fine."

The twins grabbed each other and almost jumped with excitement.

"Yes, Papa, yes!"

"We'd love that."

"Your girls won't be with you long," Isabel commented. "Pretty as they are, marriageable age, and a hundred and more men in this valley yearning for a wife."

"Marriageable age?" Daniel turned around to look at the twins. "How old are you?"

"Almost sixteen," Rose said.

"Sixteen," Daniel mused. "Your mother was seventeen when I married her."

"Will you, Papa?'

"Let Isabel live with us?"

"I'll help you chaperon those girls, too," Isabel said, "when you're away."

The twins, standing behind Daniel, grinned at Isabel.

"Well …" Daniel still hesitated. "What do you think, Gabe?"

Gabe looked across at Isabel. She had folded her lips together and her eyes looked sad and anxious. He turned to Daniel. "Isabel helps out here more'n you know. Your girls love her and she loves them. She do need a home. And it's true what she said, pretty soon your girls'll marry, and then you'll need someone to help you out."

"Well … well." Daniel cleared his throat. "Maybe. I need to think about it."

"You could put the woodshed here," Rose pointed, "next to the wash area. That would be handy to the kitchen, too."

Two days later the work on the house began. The twins' peaceful home was suddenly filled with men's voices and the crack of pick on rock as Gabe and Harry, Marcus and Benedict, and three other men from the shanty town began tearing the hillside apart. Daniel stayed home from his rounds and worked with them.

Rose cried out in dismay as her favorite sitting place in the midst of a patch of orange paintbrush was destroyed.

"It's okay, it's okay," Isabel said. "You've gotta crack some eggs to make an omelet. We can make it pretty again once the house is finished. There's more paintbrush up on the hill. We can get seeds and plant them around the porch or anywhere you want."

Isabel had come to help the twins in the garden, harvesting and weeding. The pole beans had done well and the carrots were ready. There were tomatoes and cabbages also.

"I saw you having a long talk with your son yesterday after church," Lily said to Isabel as they worked. "Was he still trying to get you to come back?"

"No, Ed's given up on that. He hired an Italian couple he found somewhere to take care of the place. He's going off again, this time to California, following some tale about a new gold field. He has the idea if he comes back rich, and builds that worthless wife of his a fancy house, then she'll be happy and love him. Fool! I told him he was a fool. The best thing he can do with that wife is divorce her and send her back East. She not only won't do any work, but she won't let him near her, be a proper wife to him in any way. But he's daft about her. And off he goes."

"Poor Lucinda," Rose said. "I wonder why she's so unhappy. Ed seems like a really good man."

"He's a charmer, like his pa was, but different. His pa was after any piece of tail he could find, never mind that he had a wife, me. And Ed, he's so faithful to that woman—ach! I just hope he doesn't get lost or starve to death or get killed running off after gold that may not even be there. All for a woman that doesn't deserve him."

"Do you worry about him?" Lily asked.

"'Course. Mothers always worry about their young 'uns no matter how old they get. But when they get a certain age, they don't mind you any more. There now, that row's picked clean. But there's lots of blossoms yet. We'll have more beans in a few days."

After the hill was dug out, Gabe and Harry set to work building the foundation and the retaining wall. The twins helped, bringing them rocks from the piles that had been thrown aside during the excavation. They became fascinated with the way Gabe's quick, skillful hands fitted the rocks together.

"Will you teach us?" they asked him.

So he did, kindly and patiently, as was his way. At first that process slowed things down, but by the end of the day the twins had gotten the hang of it and from then on the work went more quickly with their help.

Burt brought up sinks and pipes and pumps from the store. Aaron brought up wagon loads of lumber. Old Enoch came down from the mountain. He was thin and bent with a gray beard down to his waist, long gray hair flowing loose over his shoulders, and bright eyes peering out from under bushy eyebrows. He determined that the marshy spot near the eastern edge of the land, that Mayor

Wilgus had pointed out, was indeed a spring, and wouldn't take a lot of work to become a good well.

Day by day, the house took shape. Once the walls were up and the roof on, the twins helped Gabe and Harry pack the sod on top. They had saved it from the excavation, keeping it watered by the little stream. When the roof was covered, it did look, especially from the back, as if the house grew out of the hill.

The twins were delighted with their hillside window. When Gabe wasn't watching, they tried climbing in. It was easy. The sill was only knee high when they stood beside it and the window was plenty big enough for their slender, agile bodies to slip through.

"If we can climb in," Lily whispered to Rose as they stood together in their new room, "we can climb out."

"Ssh," Rose whispered back. "Papa's downstairs. Don't let him know."

They slipped back out.

"It may be a little harder when the glass is in," Lily said.

"But we'll be able to open it. Gabe said it was for the air to pass through."

"And with that grate in the floor that you suggested to Gabe, we'll be able to hear whatever's going on downstairs."

They grinned and hugged each other.

When mid-August came with three days of cold, drizzling rain, the twins begged Gabe to let them move in, even though he said the house wasn't ready yet.

"There's no cookstove," he said, "and I hain't trimmed out the windows or finished the shelves in the kitchen nor in your room or your pa's."

"But we can cook in the fireplace. That will work, won't it?"

"At least we won't have the rain putting the fire out."

Gabe rubbed his brow. "I guess it will be okay, but you're a'gonna have to put up with me and Harry hammering all around you."

Isabel came up that afternoon, wrapped in her ragged cloak. "The August rains," she said. "Happens every year around this time. But it'll be hot again. Summer's not over yet." She peeked into the little room off the kitchen. There was space for a bed and a small window looking out onto the pasture. "This looks mighty homey," she said, smiling widely. "I'm real glad your pa agreed. We're going to have to behave ourselves now, you hear? So he doesn't change his mind."

"We always behave ourselves," Lily said.

Isabel snorted.

Gabe and Harry moved the table and benches into the kitchen, Isabel helped the twins carry in supplies from the chuck box; and when Daniel came home that evening, wet and chilled, the twins had hot soup waiting for him. They sat around the table in their new kitchen.

"This is real nice," Daniel said with a contented sigh. "A roof over our heads and you can hardly hear the rain. Is there bread?"

Lily handed him bread. He dipped some in his soup and ate. "I've been talking to Mr. Jenkins," he went on between bites. "We're going to take a trip to Denver next week and meet with the Protestant ministers there to set up a Protestant council. The two Protestant ministers from Montview are coming, too. While I'm there, I'll pick out a stove for the church, a cookstove for our house, and order glass for the windows. I'll need to buy a buggy, too, now the weather's turning. Denver's the best place to get one."

"Denver's a long way," Lily said.

"Two day's journey and two days back. I'll be gone from Monday to Saturday. Burt will lead the prayer meeting on Wednesday and you and Gabe will help with the music as always."

The twins were looking at each other across the table. Daniel was beginning to be wary when he saw them looking at each other that way. "I want you two to stay here," he said firmly. "No running off to Fairdale's. Help Gabe anyway you can and finish moving in. Is that clear?"

"Yes, Papa," Rose said.

"Lily?

"Yes, Papa."

## Chapter 35

# *The Hay-in Celebration*

**M**onday morning, the twins watched from the cliff edge as their father and Mr. Jenkins rode off down Gold Creek Road toward the road to Denver. The rain had stopped and it was hot again.

"We can't go to Fairdale Ranch anyway," Lily said ruefully. "We've too much work to do. Gabe said he'd finish the kitchen shelves today, and there's another batch of beans to can."

"And cherries. Remember Amy and Julia are going to bring us another bushel of cherries, and a bushel of apples as well, to dry."

When Amy and Julia came by with the cherries and apples in their cart, they also had news. "We're bringing in the last of the hay this week," Julia said, "and we're going to have a big party Friday night to celebrate. Bernie's going to call some dances, and we'll sing and play games, bob for apples, and have a taffy pull. Of course you're invited. Father's invited the Dodges, too, Annabelle and Gerald, and lots of people from the town."

The twins looked at each other. "Papa said we were to stay here and help Gabe and move in," Rose said.

"But it's a party," Lily protested.

"Gabe's coming. He already said yes. And your friends Mr. and Mrs. Hollis and their children and lots of others are coming," Amy put in.

"Then we can go," Lily said. "If Gabe's going."

"Good," Julia said. "It's at three o'clock and all evening, and you can stay the night. We'll have lots of fun." She and Amy hugged the twins and went on down the road to deliver fruit to Mattie.

∾

On Friday afternoon the twins were part of a caravan of buggies, wagons, and carts that set out from Gold Creek to the Fairdale's hay-in celebration. Gabe and Isabel rode with the twins in their new cart. Gabe had driven it up only two days before when he came to work on the house. It was small and neat, painted blue with yellow trim. Even the spokes on the two big wheels were painted yellow, so they created a bright whirl of color when the cart was in motion.

Kate and Andrew Fairdale welcomed them when they arrived at the ranch. All their friends and neighbors were there. In the big grassy area between the main house and the cabins, the grown-ups gathered in clusters, visiting and watching the children. The little ones played in a big, clean horse trough filled with water, and the young people bobbed for apples, getting their heads wet, choking and laughing while the grown-ups egged them on.

Then Kate brought out taffy for the taffy pull. "All right, girls," she said. "This time you get to choose. Take your chunk of taffy and find a boy you want to pull it with."

Lily took hers without hesitation to Jonathan. Rose liked Ned Anderson best of the other boys, but knew Annabelle did, too. Gerald Dodge was looking at her hopefully, so she took her taffy to him. The others soon paired up. Annabelle did go to Ned, and Rose was glad because she knew how shy Annabelle was.

The couples began pulling. "Easy, don't break it," Kate warned. When all the taffy was pulled out so the boys stood in a line facing the line of girls, the taffy stretched between them, Kate said, "Okay, put your end in your mouth. You're going to eat your way to your partner. Hands behind your backs and don't let the taffy touch the ground. The first couple that completely eats their taffy and comes nose to nose with their partner will win a prize. Remember, hands behind your back."

There was a burst of laughter from everyone watching. Gabe picked up his fiddle and began playing, first a merry jig, then as the young couples began chewing, bending, and twisting, he imitated their movements with slides, stops, and bursts of melody, until it was all they could do to keep chewing and not giggle. Jonathan and Lily won. As their mouths touched, Jonathan let go his hands behind his back and hugged Lily. Everyone shouted and cheered.

"Uh, uh, hands behind your back," Kate reproved, laughing, too, as she brought them their prize, a peach pie for them to share at supper.

Rose stood watching. A shiver of anxiety passed up her spine.

The stars were bright between the boughs of the cottonwood trees by the creek. The night was warm and dark. Lily and Jonathan sat at the creek's edge cooling their feet in the running stream. Across the pasture they could hear the sound of music in the big barn and Bernie's song calling the dance. They sat close, not quite touching. Lily shivered, her whole body trembling inside with Jonathan's nearness.

"Are you cold?" Jonathan asked, his voice deep and soft.

"Not … not really. Just shivery."

He moved closer and put his arm around her. She leaned her head on his shoulder. Neither spoke.

After a while, Jonathan began kissing the tiny curls that always broke loose from her twist, kissing just the tips of those tendrils, so lightly, so exquisitely. Intoxicating liquid heat spread from her loins through her whole body. She held still, barely breathing.

Suddenly she felt Rose seeking her, anxious. No! No! Not now! Swiftly Lily slid the door between their hearts shut, and Rose was gone.

Lily felt Jonathan's hand under her chin, tilting her head up. He bent his head and touched her lips with his. Above and within her, stars spun.

Rose was dancing, dancing, lost in the joy of it. She loved the way the pattern unfolded, and the music—the swirl of the fiddles, the whine of the accordion, Bernie's sweet tenor calling the changes. And the swinging, whirling round and round. Gabe was her partner, the most fun of all the partners she'd had that evening, giving her extra fancy twirls between the moves, stamping his feet and jumping in counterpoint to the music. She was laughing with delight when she suddenly felt a frightening sensation sweep through her. Lily? Where was Lily? She lost her focus, stopped in the middle of a ladies' chain to look. She couldn't see Lily anywhere in the big barn filled with whirling dancers. Someone caught her hand and pulled her through the ladies' chain, and then Gabe was swinging her.

"What's wrong?" he asked.

"I don't know where Lily is."

"She's okay. Not far, I'm sure." He pushed her gently to do-si-do her corner.

Somehow she made it through the rest of the dance, but poorly. Her partners needed to push and pull her through the moves. She'd felt Lily for a moment. Something … and then Lily was gone and she couldn't find her, not anywhere in the big barn, or anywhere reaching out with her heart.

She fled from the barn before anyone else could ask her to dance and stood outside in the warm dark, her heart pounding with fear.

~

Later that night Amy and Julia, Rose and Lily settled into the big bed upstairs in the Fairdale house.

"Jonathan's sweet on Lily," Amy chanted, sing song.

"He sure is," Julia agreed.

"Are you sweet on him, too?" Amy asked.

Lily buried her face in her pillow and didn't answer.

"Are you?" Amy tried to pull the pillow away.

"Leave her alone," Julia said. "We should go to sleep now. It's really late and we'll have a lot to do tomorrow to clean up from the party." She pulled Amy away from Lily. After some giggling and tussling, Julia settled down next to Lily, having pushed Amy to the side of the bed. Lily hugged her pillow, uncharacteristically quiet. Rose lay on the other side of Lily, on her back, her arms crossed over her chest.

"Good night," Julia said. She snuggled down and drew the cover up over the four of them. "Sleep well." She and Amy soon slept. The twins could hear the shift and quieting of their breath.

But the twins did not sleep. Rose lay still, cold, even though the cover over them was warm. She had been so relieved when she saw Lily and Jonathan coming back to the barn. She had come back inside and joined the dance, but the joy of it was gone, even though she could see Lily whirling with Jonathan in the next set. Now Lily lay right beside her, but still Rose couldn't find her. She reached out with her heart—nothing. Fear curdled in the pit of her stomach. She turned on her side, waiting for Lily to curl around her, the curve of her back aching for that warm contact, waiting for Lily's cheek against her hair, Lily's good-night kiss. But Lily lay beside her, far away, hugging her pillow.

Lily thought she would never sleep again. Her body was aflame with liquid fire. I love him, she thought. I love him. This is what love feels like. She caught her breath, squeezing the pillow tighter. He is so handsome, and so much fun, and so gentle that the horses trust him. And plays the cello so beautifully. She relived again and again the sensation of Jonathan kissing the tips of her curls, and the deep kiss on her mouth. Afterward, they had lain down on the earth together, bodies touching, looking up at the stars, whispering words of love. Oh, the touch of his hand stroking her! She could hardly bear the intensity of her passion. *He is my true love. I will love him forever.*

Hours passed. She dozed, woke to become aware of Rose, still awake beside her. She opened the door a little and felt Rose's fear and grief, and her protective love of Rose awoke. *But I can't let her know about Jonathan, I can't. That's private, mine alone. I could make a little closet,* she thought. *No, it would take a big closet. I could hide everything about Jonathan inside, then open the door. I don't want to be all the way separated from her. I don't want her to be so sad.* She concentrated, creating the closet. *Yes, that would work.* She let out her breath, set the pillow aside and turned and curled around Rose, gently kissed her. Rose trembled. Lily felt her about to cry. *Don't cry,* she whispered without words. *I'm here.* Rose trembled again, sighed, and nestled back against Lily.

**Chapter 36**

# *Aaron Jenkins*

Daniel was pleased with his week as he jounced along the Denver-Montview Road on his way home in his new buggy. Aaron sat beside him.

They had talked a great deal during their week together, of theology, scripture, issues in the church, and some personal matters, but now they were silent and Daniel had time to follow his own thoughts.

He'd been surprised to learn that Aaron had started out to be a minister and had done one year of seminary. He'd run out of money and come West, knowing his skill with the sawmill would be needed. He was saving, he told Daniel, and hoping to return East again eventually to finish seminary.

"I thought you knew your scripture well," Daniel had said to him. "Why didn't you tell me before."

"I wasn't ready. There is so much more to know."

"Always," Daniel agreed.

Something else he had shared was occupying the forefront of Daniel's mind as they jogged along in silence. Aaron had told him he'd been thinking about it for quite a while. It was time he had a wife, he said, and he was attracted to Lily. He thought she felt warmly toward him, too. He'd asked Daniel's permission to begin courting her.

Daniel was taken by surprise. His first reaction was that Lily was too young. But was she? Isabel said she was of marriageable age. She was almost sixteen. Was she sixteen? He'd forgotten when the twins' birthday was.

He couldn't really imagine her with Aaron, but it would be a good match. Aaron was steady and pious, could offer her a good home, keep her clearly in her faith, and maybe in a few years take her back East. He had some misgivings imagining her as a minister's wife, but Aaron would settle her down. She was basically a good girl, just high-spirited. Rose would miss her, of course, but at first she wouldn't be far away, just down the road and across the bridge.

He'd told Aaron he would consider it, as he was doing now.

It would be a relief, he had to admit, to have someone else responsible for Lily. Whatever mischief the twins got into, he suspected Lily was the initiator. That's what Mrs. Lowell had told him. He imagined his home with just Rose to watch over and felt it would be considerably easier.

They reached the intersection of Gold Creek Road. As he turned the buggy west, his thoughts turned also. The Protestant council had gone well. It had been good to be with other ministers. He'd picked out the stoves and ordered the glass, accomplished all he had hoped for in the week. He wondered how the house was, if it was done yet and if he could sit in his new room to prepare his sermon.

At the juncture of Bridge Road, Aaron got down from the buggy, unhitched his horse from the back, and said good-bye. Daniel drove on home. Home it really was now with a house to call his own.

Gabe's cart was in front of the house and Daniel could hear the sound of hammers as he approached. The tent was gone. That must mean his room was done and Gabe and the twins had moved his things inside. He drove his buggy around the side of the house, unhitched Shadow, and took her to the pasture. Gabe's Sadie and the oxen were there, but he didn't see Dawnstar. He was frowning as he climbed the three wide steps to the porch and stepped in the door.

Harry and Gabe were working on the window trim. "Hello, Daniel." Gabe put down his hammer and came to greet Daniel. "Welcome home. We're almost done. Your room's all finished. Your trunk's in there and your mat, and there's shelves for your books."

Daniel looked around. "The house looks fine. Do you know where the twins are?"

"Probably on their way home now. Fairdales done had a big party last night. We all went, and they stayed overnight. They should be back soon."

Rage rose up in Daniel, the same rage and frustration that always assailed him when he felt he'd lost control of the twins. "I forbad them. I told them specifically not to go to Fairdale's, but to stay right here."

Gabe touched him on the shoulder. "They been here all week, a'working hard, not only in the house, moving in and fixing up, but over at Nathan's canning with Mattie. Then Elsie's baby came and Rose was down there helping, Lily watching the children. It was a big party last night, a hay-in celebration, and almost everyone in the valley went. I was there a'watching over them."

"But why didn't they come home last night?"

"They was gonna pick apples. They wanted to dry a bunch for me to thank me for the house."

"Well …" Daniel didn't know what to say. It was always like that. They sidestepped around him and then everyone defended them. Lily. If she weren't there, it would be different.

He walked through the main room, stepping over the boards and tools scattered on the floor, and opened the door to his room. It was finished, the floor swept clean. The summer air blew in through the open windows, one on the east and one on the north. His trunk sat under the east window, his mattress lay along the west wall with his pillow on top of the neatly folded blanket. The worn red pillow he'd brought from Boston, the pillow he knelt on to pray, was there, too. He picked it up and put it in front of the trunk.

There were book shelves on either side of the fireplace, wall to ceiling. He looked into the fireplace, saw ashes. The twins must have been cooking there. He closed the metal doors. Such a good idea of Gabe's to have one fireplace heat both rooms. Under the north window, Gabe had built a wide shelf that could serve as a simple desk. A small bench sat in front of it. Daniel thought with longing of the stuffed leather chair he had seen in Denver. He had almost ordered it. Maybe he still would. Send a message down with the next stage coach and have it shipped up with the stoves and the glass.

Hoofbeats. The twins' voices. He looked out his east window and saw them approaching the house. With a cart. So Gabe had built them a cart.

Daniel walked out on the porch to meet them. They jumped down from their cart and came to kiss his cheeks.

"Hi, Papa."

"How was your trip?"

"I thought I told you to stay home."

"We did."

"All week."

"Until yesterday."

"There was a party."

"Everyone went. Burt and Elsie even closed the store."

"We stayed overnight to pick apples—"

"To dry for Gabe."

Their rapid exchange confused him. He stepped back to look at them more closely, to distinguish them, and felt a wave of shock. Lily, it must be Lily, was bursting with radiance and beauty in a way he had never seen before. Her skin glowed, her eyes shone, even her hair seemed a brighter gold. She was bubbling over with a wild joy that frightened him. He looked at Rose. She seemed more subdued, tired, dark circles under her eyes. What had happened? He looked at Lily again. The thought hit him, crude, unwelcome. She looks like she's in heat! That settled it. He'd marry her off to Aaron as soon as possible. A husband to obey, maybe soon a child to care for. That would calm her down.

Lily laughed, even her giggles bubbling light. "Papa, you're staring at us."

"Did you see our new cart?" Rose asked, taking his hand. "Gabe gave it to us while you were gone. Come see."

"Not now." Daniel brushed Rose's hand away. "Take care of your horse and come in the house."

He turned back inside. Gabe and Harry had begun cleaning up. "All done," Gabe said, smiling widely. "Just in time for the Sabbath."

"Thank you, Gabe, Harry. It's good to have a house to come home to." Daniel looked around gratefully. "You've done a beautiful job."

The twins came in a few minutes later carrying a bushel basket of apples between them. When they came back from the kitchen, Daniel said, "Lily, I want to talk with you."

"Okay, Papa." She stood in front of him, questioning, Rose beside her.

"Just Lily," Daniel said.

Both looked at him, eyes wide with surprise.

"Just Lily?" Rose asked. She reached out for Lily's hand.

"Yes." Daniel realized his voice was probably unnecessarily stern. He felt guilty about Rose's look of consternation. "Just Lily. Rose, please go upstairs until we finish talking."

Rose hesitated, then let go of Lily's hand and climbed the stairs. Daniel heard her close the door at the top.

Lily stood facing him, frowning.

"Sit down." Daniel gestured to the two trunks sitting under the window. Lily sat down on the end of one of them; Daniel sat facing her, perched on the end of the other. "You've left your trunks downstairs."

"Yes. Gabe made us shelves to put our things on and said we could sit on these until we get furniture. Like we are. What is it, Papa?"

"Well …" Daniel cleared his throat. She was frowning, but still had that wild unnatural beauty that he found so upsetting. "While I was traveling with Mr. Jenkins, he told me that he was thinking it was time he married, that he was attracted to you, and asked my permission to court you. I —"

"*Mr. Jenkins!*" Lily exclaimed, "wants to … *court* me?"

"Yes." Daniel made his voice very stern. "And I have decided—"

"No! Papa, no! Are you crazy? Absolutely no!"

"I'm not crazy. He has a home and business and can provide for you well. He's a fine man, pious and mature, a good match."

"Not for me! I don't love him. I don't even like him. He's ugly. His eyes stick out like a fish's, and he has those lumps under his ears from holding his teeth so tight together. He's no fun. He hardly ever even smiles. And he's *old*. He's almost as old as you are."

Daniel winced. "You're being disrespectful."

"*You're* being disrespectful. Of me. Just foisting me off on some old man I don't even like. Why do you suddenly want to get rid of me? Don't you love me?" She sprang to her feet, tears in her eyes.

In her outrage she was even more dangerously beautiful. For a moment he had almost relented, but fear overrode. "Lily, you will obey me in this. I don't want to hear another word. He will be coming to call and you will behave yourself."

Lily whirled and ran up the stairs. Halfway up she turned. "Just so you know. I won't. I won't ever marry him. I'll die first." She dashed up the remaining stairs and flung herself into her room, slamming the door after her.

~

Rose was sitting by the grate when Lily slammed the door and burst into tears. Rose jumped up to embrace her.

"Did you hear?" Lily sobbed. "He wants to marry me off to Mr. Jenkins. He doesn't care about me at all. He just wants to get rid of me. Why? I thought he loved me." She clung to Rose, her sobs overwhelming her.

Rose grabbed a pillow from their mat and dropped it over the grate. She drew Lily over to the mat and sat down with her, her arms around her. "I heard. I couldn't believe it either. But you won't have to marry Mr. Jenkins. We'll see to that."

Lily's words came out between sobs. "Why does he want to get rid of me? I've been a good daughter to him. I don't understand."

"I don't either." Rose rocked Lily, her heart aching for her. "We'll make a plan. It won't happen, know that's for sure."

"How did Mr. Jenkins ever get such an idea?" Lily sobbed.

"You were flirting with him at the church raising, when he bought your box lunch. Remember?"

"Oh, that." Lily sat up and smeared the tears across her face with her hand. Rose handed her the handkerchief from her apron pocket. "I didn't mean anything. I was so disappointed he was the one who got my box lunch instead of Jonathan. He's such a bore. I was just trying to liven things up. So now he wants to marry me. Oh, no." Her tears overflowed again.

"Let's talk to Papa tomorrow and try to change his mind," Rose said. "And if we can't, then we'll have to make it so Mr. Jenkins doesn't want to marry you after all." She paused, biting her lower lip. "I have an idea." She whispered in Lily's ear. Lily started laughing. Rose whispered more. Soon they were both laughing, rolling on their mat in each other's arms, tears wet on their cheeks.

Daniel didn't know what to do. He sat in his room, leaning his elbows on his desk, his face in his hands. It was early afternoon, the quiet time of the Sabbath. The twins had just come to see him, both of them, clutching each other's hands. It didn't matter that he had sent Rose away the day before while he talked to Lily. She would tell Rose everything, of course, or Rose would just know somehow. The way they knew each other's thoughts always made him uneasy. He remembered Becky saying, "You can't get so much as a blade of grass between those two." Maybe that wasn't healthy. Maybe it would be better for them to be apart more.

They had begged him to reconsider the matter of Mr. Jenkins. They pointed out that Lily didn't like him, that he was old and dour, and that it would be miserable to spend the rest of your life with someone you didn't like. He had been touched, had been on the point of relenting, when Lily flared up and declared she wouldn't anyway, he couldn't make her. He hardened then and told them to go away, that he expected Lily to obey him and that was that.

He remembered hearing Lily asking, "Why do you want to get rid of me? Don't you love me?" and his heart contracted. Was it true he just wanted to get rid of her? Did he love her? He ached with confusion. He did love her, her brightness, her laughter, all the ways she took care of him. Her courage—he admired but feared it. And he didn't know what to do about that wildness, the way she had shone and bubbled the day before. He rubbed the back of his head, still expecting to feel the lump there. He couldn't control her. And that was intolerable. He was responsible for her, for her soul. She had to obey him. And he didn't know how to make her.

Footsteps on the porch, a knock on the door. He'd been so lost in his thoughts he'd not heard anyone approaching. He jumped up and looked out the window. Aaron's horse and buggy were tied up to the porch post. Another knock on the door. He hurried to open it.

"Aaron, come in. Come in. Welcome to my new house."

Aaron looked around gravely. "Very nice."

"Please sit down. We don't have chairs yet, as you see, but the trunks do for now."

"Thank you." Aaron lowered his lanky frame onto the very spot where Lily had sat the day before. Daniel sat opposite him, studying him. His eyes did protrude as Lily had said, but there was an eagerness in them today, and his mouth was softer than usual. He almost smiled as he said, "I came to see if I might take Lily out for tea at Elsie's this afternoon. Have you spoken to her? Is she in?"

"I have spoken to her," Daniel replied, his heart pounding with misgiving. "I believe she and Rose are resting. Please come and wait in my study, and I will call her."

He ushered Aaron into his study and gestured to the little bench in front of the desk.

"Lots of shelves for books," Aaron commented. "You need that chair we saw in Denver."

"Yes, I have decided to order it," Daniel said, deciding in that moment, embarrassed that he didn't have a better chair to offer Aaron.

He closed the door and returned to the living room. At the bottom of the stairs, he hesitated. What if Lily came down screaming her defiance? He would be humiliated in front of an elder of his church.

"Lily," he called.

The door at the top of the stairs opened. "Yes, Papa?"

"Mr. Jenkins is here and would like to take you out to Elsie's for afternoon tea." He waited, his jaw clenched, knowing that in spite of the closed door to his study, Aaron could hear everything.

"Okay, Papa. Just a minute."

Her voice was amiable, docile. He let out his breath in astonishment. He was sweating. He could hear a flurry of activity upstairs. Then the door opened and both girls came down. They looked just alike in their blue-gray Sunday gowns.

Daniel went to his study and opened the door. Aaron came out. There were a few pleasantries, of which Daniel could remember nothing afterward. Rose kissed Lily. Aaron took her arm, escorted her out the door, helped her into his buggy, and drove off. Lily had behaved like a perfect lady. Rose went back upstairs, and Daniel was left standing in the middle of the living room, shaking.

∾

The days shortened as August came to a close. Isabel moved into the little room off the kitchen and the twins were very glad of her help harvesting and preserving the last fruits of summer.

A big supply wagon came up from Denver with Daniel's chair and the stoves and the glass. Gabe went to work putting the glass in the windows of the church and installing the stove that would keep the congregation warm through the winter. Then he came to the house and put glass in the windows and hooked up the long-awaited cookstove. The twins were able to do their last canning in their own kitchen, and found to their delight that they could slip out of their hillside window almost as easily after the glass was installed.

Every Sunday at three o'clock sharp, Aaron Jenkins drove his buggy up the hill to pick up Lily. He paraded proudly through town with the buggy top down so everyone could see his lovely, fair-haired companion in her blue-gray Sunday dress with the lace at the neck. Sometimes he took her to Elsie's for tea, sometimes for a ride out onto the plains. On Sunday evening, after prayer meeting, the twins would retire to their room for long conversations, muffled by the pillow that kept permanent residence over the grate unless there was a reason to remove it.

Daniel didn't trust Lily's docility. It wasn't like her. He was uneasy, waiting for something, he couldn't imagine what. But there was nothing amiss that he could put his finger on.

Isabel watched closely each time Aaron came for Lily, a growing question in her eyes. One evening as she and the twins were preparing supper, she said to Lily. "You know, it's all over town that you and Mr. Jenkins are getting married. He was telling people down at the store today that he was going to marry you before Christmas."

"Before Christmas!" Lily exclaimed.

Isabel gave her a long look. "I'm thinking you're not planning on marrying him at all."

"No!" Lily made a face. "Absolutely not."

"I didn't think so. Can't see you two getting along. Then why're you going out with him every Sunday?"

"Because Papa makes me."

"Did you tell your pa you didn't want to marry Mr. Jenkins?"

"I sure did. But he doesn't care. He's got his mind made up. He just wants to get rid of me." Lily lifted her chin and tossed her head, but her voice broke and tears sprang to her eyes.

"There now." Isabel put her arm around Lily's shoulders. "I don't think it's that. He loves you, that I know, but he just doesn't know what to do with you sometimes. Maybe he hopes Mr. Jenkins will."

"Mr. Jenkins doesn't know anything." Lily sniffed back her tears.

"What are you gonna do then?"

"We have a plan," Rose said.

"A plan?" Isabel raised her eyebrows. "Oh, Lordy, I bet you do. Well you'd better do your plan pretty quick. Mr. Jenkins's got his pride, and there's no way you're not gonna offend him if you don't marry him, now that he's told everyone in town."

"We never said we would," Lily retorted. "It's his fault if he tells everyone."

"*We?*" Isabel put down the pan she was holding and set her hands on her hips. "Then my eyes weren't deceiving me when I thought I saw Rose go out with him one week and Lily the next?"

Lily bit her lip and looked at Rose. "Ooops," she whispered.

"Don't tell," Rose begged. "We do have to do it soon if he's talking before Christmas."

"What are you gonna do?" Isabel still had her hands on her hips, her green eyes fierce.

"If our plan works, Mr. Jenkins just won't want to marry Lily."

"Please don't tell Papa." The twins came to either side of Isabel, their blue eyes beseeching.

"All right. I won't. But if your pa finds out I knew and didn't stop whatever you're up to … Don't tell me what it is. I don't wanna know."

~

The following Sunday it was Rose's turn to go out with Mr. Jenkins. She and Lily sat in their upstairs bedroom waiting for him to arrive.

Rose sighed. "Isabel's right. We need to end this soon. It's getting out of hand, and spoils our Sundays."

"It really spoils our Sundays," Lily agreed. "And *he's* getting out of hand. Last time he kept sitting closer to me than usual and looking at me—I didn't like the way he was looking at me with his fish eyes. And he kept leaning over me. Ick!" Lily shuddered and shook her head.

"Poor man," Rose said. "He probably doesn't even know how repulsive he is."

They heard the sound of a buggy arriving and looked out their east window. "Here he is," Lily said. "Make sure he behaves himself."

"I'll try."

The twins came down the stairs as Daniel opened the door for Mr. Jenkins. Lily kissed Rose, saying, "Good-bye Lily," and Daniel watched approvingly as Mr. Jenkins ushered Rose out the door.

Mr. Jenkins seemed more agitated than usual, almost jovial in a nervous sort of way. He kept his hands on Rose's waist longer than necessary as he helped her into the buggy. He flicked his horse with his whip to set him going. He always did that. Rose didn't like it.

"I had a good week at the sawmill," Mr. Jenkins started out. "Fifty logs in makes about two hundred long boards at ten cents a board-foot. Mr. Ferguson's buying all of them to build his house down there on Mill Road across from the store."

Rose sighed inwardly. Another boring account of his week's business. She was beginning to let her mind drift, when he shifted closer to her. "I'm going to take you to my house today, so you can see your new home." He laid his hand on her thigh. Rose jumped and pushed his hand away.

They reached the junction of Bridge Road and turned down it. Sheriff Parker met them on the way up, pulling his dusty cart. He raised his hat. "G' day."

"Good day," Mr. Jenkins responded. They went on down Bridge Road. Rose found herself suddenly remembering her first meeting with Sheriff Parker, when he had told her and Lily, "Don't go trusting people just because they say they're Christian."

They turned onto Mill Road and headed west, passing the the flour mill. There was no one around, the road empty in Sabbath quiet.

Mr. Jenkins put his hand on her thigh again. Rose grabbed his wrist and threw his hand back at him. "Mr. Jenkins!" she said sharply.

"Now, now," Mr. Jenkins said, moving so close that when Rose slid away from him she was up against the strut of the buggy. "We're going to be married soon. You need to get used to this—and more." He put his hand back on her thigh, pressing her skirt down between her legs.

Rose pushed his hand away with all her force. "Stop!" she ordered.

"All right, all right. You're a shy young maiden. I'll be patient. I plan to talk with your father this evening to set the date for our wedding."

"Mr. Jenkins, you forget. I have not consented to marry you."

"But your father has consented, and you will obey him, of course. And after we are married you will obey me, as scripture commands."

Rose's back stiffened with defiance. Wait until Lily hears that, she thought.

"'Ye wives, be in subjection to your husbands.' Peter 3:1, Mr. Jenkins quoted. "And if you don't obey, I have the means to see that you do." He lashed his horse suddenly with his whip. The horse lurched forward, throwing Rose back against the seat. They dashed the last stretch to the sawmill.

Mr. Jenkins stopped the buggy in front. "Come now," he said, his voice gentler, coaxing. "I want to show you your new home." He jumped down and reached up for her.

Rose was both frightened and angry. "Mr. Jenkins, I can't go into your house with you without a chaperon. It wouldn't be proper. Papa would never permit it. I think we should go back to Elsie's for tea."

"Let me just show you around the outside. You can look in the windows. Then we'll go to Elsie's." Without waiting for her permission he lifted her down and set her on the ground in front of him. He kept his hands on her waist. She jerked free and stepped away from him.

The sawmill was the last building before the road dead ended into the curve of the river. It sat close to a small waterfall where the swift-moving current rushing down from the mountains could turn the wheel that powered the saw. In the yard beside it was a big pile of logs, neatly stacked, nearby a pile of curled pieces of bark. Rose could see a small log house with a slanting shed roof built onto the side of the mill.

Mr. Jenkins took her hand. "Come. The house is around back. I think you'll like it."

Rose pulled her hand away. "I shouldn't be here with you. Please take me to Elsie's."

Mr. Jenkins put his arm around her waist. He was trembling. A small drop of saliva hung on the corner of his mouth. He ran his tongue over his thin lips. "Just one little kiss, then we'll go."

"No!" Rose was struggling with him when a small dog, yapping loudly, its ears flying back, came tearing around the corner of the house. It dashed up to Mr. Jenkins and attacked his boot. Mr. Jenkins let go of Rose, drew back his foot, and aimed a swift, vicious kick at the dog. The tip of his boot caught the dog in its belly and sent it flying with a cascade of anguished yelps. It hit the edge of the pile of logs with a thud.

Rose froze in horror, her hands over her mouth. The dog twitched, moaned, and lay still. Rose ran toward it.

Mr. Jenkins grabbed her wrist. "What are you doing? Stay away. It's filthy."

Rose's rage gave her strength. "Let go of me!" She twisted her arm free and knelt by the dog, her hand on its side. A trickle of blood ran out of the corner of its mouth. It lay still, so still. Rose bent her head, swept back to the moment she'd held Cindy dead in her arms. That same stillness, empty eyes, trickle of blood.

Mr. Jenkins's hand gripped her shoulder. "Don't touch it."

Rose spun back to the moment, whirled and came to her feet. Mr. Jenkins drew back from the fury in her eyes. "You killed him! You just kicked him and killed him! How could you?"

Mr. Jenkins rubbed his hands nervously down the fronts of his thighs. "Good riddance. It's just a filthy cur from the shanty town. Wouldn't be hanging around here except that Nathan's been feeding it."

"He's one of God's creatures. Oh," Rose began to weep, "how could you be so cruel?" She turned back and knelt again by the still form of the small dog, her tears falling into its soft fur.

Mr. Jenkins shifted from one foot to the other. He rubbed his hands down his thighs again, clenched his jaw. Suddenly he lunged and pulled Rose to her feet. "I said don't touch it. Come away now. We'll go to Elsie's." He dragged Rose to the buggy, picked her up bodily, set her on the seat, and climbed up beside her.

Rose was still weeping, with rage as well as grief. "I don't want to go to Elsie's. Take me home. Right now. And don't whip your horse."

**Chapter 37**

# *Branding*

The following Sunday, Rose sat in front of the east window of the twins' bedroom, watching the road that led up to their house. It was twilight, the waxing moon just rising out of the plains. She was shivering with excitement.

Lily was out with Mr. Jenkins. Rose and Lily had overheard him talking to their father after the service that morning.

"I'd like to take Lily out this evening after prayer meeting instead of this afternoon, if that would be all right with you," he'd said.

Daniel looked up from gathering his sermon notes off the pulpit. "Why's that?"

"I have a customer who wants to talk with me this afternoon."

"You're doing business on the Sabbath?"

"I wouldn't ordinarily, but this man is planning to move here and build a big house, and he has to leave for Denver early tomorrow morning. Would it be all right with you if I take her out this evening?"

Daniel tucked his Bible and notes into his carpet bag. "I guess so. But just for a little while and only in a public place." He frowned at Mr. Jenkins. "She told me you took her down to your house last week, and wanted to take her inside without a chaperon. That wasn't proper. What were you thinking of?"

"I just wanted to show her her new home. I didn't realize ..."

"Well." Daniel was stern. "Take her only to Elsie's and have her back before dark."

The twins had discussed the change of plans that afternoon, curled up together on their mat for Sabbath rest.

"Even though he's changed the time, we've got to do it today," Rose said. "After last time, I can't stand to go out with him ever again."

"Definitely today," Lily agreed. "It will actually be even better in the evening. Twilight. It will seem more witchy." They giggled and rehearsed their plan again.

After prayer meeting that evening, Lily had hugged Rose before going out with Mr. Jenkins. "Watch for me," she whispered. "Remember the rhymes."

Now as Rose watched, the twilight deepened. The moon rose higher. Beneath her the house was quiet. Daniel was relaxing in the living room in his new chair. He'd started a fire, as the evening was chilly. Rose could hear him get up from time to time to poke it and add more wood. Isabel had gone to bed.

At last Rose heard the sound of hooves and the crunch of buggy wheels on the dirt road. In a moment the buggy came into view. Rose jumped up, crossed the room, slid swiftly through the hillside window, and stepped down to the cool earth outside. She gathered up her skirts, ran down the hill around the house, ducking as she passed the windows, and reached her hiding place in the shadow of the porch just as Mr. Jenkins stopped the buggy in front of the house.

"Thank you for the tea and scone," Lily said politely as Mr. Jenkins lifted her down. His hands lingered on her waist. He started to bend his head toward her, holding her tightly. It was time.

Rose dashed out from the shadow of the porch. Lily broke free from Mr. Jenkins and ran to meet her. They circled each other rapidly, then stood side by side facing Mr. Jenkins.

"Which one is Lily?" Lily asked.

They were dressed identically in their blue-gray Sabbath gowns with the lace at the throat.

"What? Well … I …" Mr. Jenkins stuttered.

"You don't know, do you?"

They began to circle him, peppering him with their words.

"You can't tell."

"One week Lily went, the next week Rose."

"If you marry Lily, she might be Lily—"

"Or she might be Rose."

"You'll never know—"

"Who's in your house."

"And if you make a mistake—"

"Then you'll be an adulterer—"

"And read out of church for your sin."

They circled faster, their moon shadows dancing eerily in the twilight. Mr. Jenkins spun from one to the other, reaching out awkwardly to grab them with his long arms, but they danced out of his reach, chanting in unison:

> "Rose, Lily, Rose, Lily
> You can't tell, can you, Silly?
> Lily, Rose, Lily, Rose,
> Which is which do you suppose?"

They changed direction, still chanting, circling still faster.

> "One week Rose, one week Lily,
> You didn't know, did you, Silly."

He lunged for them, but they were too nimble for him. "Stop!" he shouted. They stopped, just out of his reach, and shouted back,

> "If you take the wrong one of us into your bed,
> Sin and damnation will fall on your head."

He lunged again. Picking up their skirts, they ran, one around the south side of the house, one around the north, leaving Mr. Jenkins grasping at thin air, swearing.

They slipped through their hillside window and tumbled onto their mat, breathless, trembling, hugging each other, repressing their laughter.

Daniel looked up from his book. Moonlight shone in the darkened window. It's getting dark, he said to himself. Lily should be home by now. He thought he'd heard the sound of Aaron's buggy approaching, but they hadn't come in yet. He got up to stir the fire. There was shouting outside. He dropped the poker into the flames, hurried to the door, and was almost knocked backward by Aaron dashing in.

"Witches, that's what they are," Aaron cried "Possessed by Satan!" His pale blue eyes were wild and he flung his long arms around, nearly striking Daniel in the face.

Daniel caught his arm. "What's going on? Where's Lily?"

"She ran away, she and her unholy twin."

"Aaron, please, calm down. Come in. Tell me what's happened. I need to know where Lily is."

"I don't know and I don't care. She ran off, I said, she and that other one. Witches, that's what they are. Taunting me, deceiving me."

"Ran off where?'

"Up the hill there." Aaron gestured wildly.

"Aaron, please. Come sit down. Tell me. I don't understand what you're saying."

Aaron paced the room. "No! I'll not sit in your house again. Harboring those two evil, deceitful ..." He turned on Daniel. "You must have been in on it. Every Sunday you were here, watching me take them out, first one and then, the next Sunday, the other."

"What?" Daniel put his hand to his brow. "Are you saying they both went out with you, alternating?"

"That's what they told me, dancing around out there under the moon, mocking me because I couldn't tell them apart. Saying ..." He turned and gripped Daniel by the shoulders and shook him. "Saying if I married Lily they would still change places and make an adulterer of me. And you knew, standing there smiling each week when I came to take her out. You knew—"

"I didn't know. Please believe me. I had no idea—"

"But you were there each week, watching, smiling. Can't you tell your own daughters apart?" Aaron gave him another shake.

"Aaron, let go of me."

Aaron dropped his hands and stood in front of Daniel, fists clenched, eyes protruding so far that for a brief hysterical moment Daniel feared they might pop right out of his head.

He drew in his breath. "Please believe me, Aaron, if what you say is true, I had no idea. I usually can tell them apart, but I suspected nothing. I wasn't looking closely. What do you mean, they both ran away? Rose is upstairs in bed."

"That's what you think." Aaron laughed wildly. "No, she's out there on the hillside somewhere with Lily, both of them probably communing with Satan. A fine minister you are, breeding witches in your own home."

"They are not witches. I can hardly believe what you're saying. If it's true, then they are extremely mischievous, ill-behaved young girls, but they're not witches."

"Mischievous young girls—no! They taunted me, dancing in the moonlight, chanting verses. Evil, evil. And I, courting in good faith, with your approval."

He raised his fists. "I should have guessed. One week she'd be so saucy, the next week quieter— But you! How can you guide a church when you can't control your own daughters? I'm humiliated, made a mockery of in front of the whole town." He gasped. "I can't stay. They'll all laugh at me." He stared at Daniel, flung his arms out, spun, and dashed back out the open door.

Daniel stood stunned in the middle of the room, hearing Aaron's running feet pound across the porch, down the drive, his shout at his horse, the crack of his whip, and the buggy careening away down the road.

～

Rose and Lily sat very still by the grate, biting their lower lips. For a moment only. Then Rose shoved the pillow back over the grate.

"Quick," Lily whispered. "If he finds us here, he'll guess about the window."

They ran silently across the room, slipped out the window, one after the other, and sat down in the grass outside.

"Where shall we go now?" Rose asked.

"Hush! Papa's coming up the stairs."

They flattened themselves on the ground, holding their breath. "Rose," they heard him call. They heard his footsteps in their room. "She's not here," he muttered. "Then where is she?" He went down the stairs again and in a moment they heard his voice out on the hillside, calling their names.

"He's worried about us," Rose whispered.

"No, he's mad. We're gonna to catch it."

"He mustn't find us here."

They scrambled to their feet and ran down around the house and in the kitchen door. Isabel peered out of her room. She was in her nightgown, her black braid hanging over her shoulder, her green eyes round. "Ooo. You're in for it now."

"Shh." Lily made pushing-away gestures with her hand. Isabel disappeared back into her room.

Lily stepped to the kitchen door. "We're here, Papa," she called.

～

Daniel's mind was a whirl as he raced up the hill. Aaron had gone crazy. That in itself was shocking. The most steady elder of his church, the one he had thought would soon be his son-in-law. And the twins had had some part in driving him there. Where were they? His heart pounded in panic. He'd been sure Rose had gone to bed. And Lily—

When he heard Lily's voice and saw them both standing safely in the kitchen door, his panic flipped to rage.

"What have you done?" he bellowed. He stormed into the kitchen, seized them by their wrists and dragged them into the living room. "Sit here," he commanded, pushing them down onto the hearth bench. "You have some explaining to do."

The twins sat silent, clutching each other's hands, looking up at him as he stood over them, their blue eyes wide.

"Don't give me that innocent look," he raged. "Mr. Jenkins is very upset. He told me you'd *both* been going out with him, alternating, deceiving him— and me— then just now mocking him because he could not tell you apart." His voice rose. "Is that true?"

"Yes, Papa."

They looked just alike, sat in the exact same attitude. He didn't know which one had answered. His rage and frustration rose.

"He also told me—" Daniel stopped and swallowed. He could barely control his voice. "That you threatened him with *adultery* if he married Lily, by changing places. Is that true?"

They both nodded.

Daniel almost choked. "You shouldn't even speak of such things, much less— How could you? Wicked, wicked girls!"

"We had to be sure he wouldn't want to marry Lily."

There. That was Rose, the one on the left. Then Lily was the one nearest the hearth.

"You did that?" Daniel raged on. "You confess to all of it? After I asked you, after I told you the very day we arrived here, how important it was that I do well with this church, after I asked you to behave in a seemly manner, never dreaming you could disgrace me so. Don't you realize you've just humiliated one of the elders of my church? He asked how I could guide a church when I couldn't control my own daughters. I can't think of any worse judgment on my ministry."

"I can," Lily said, lifting her chin.

Her words were goad to his long guilt. His rage became a red haze in front of his eyes.

He seized her wrist and jerked her to her feet. Hardly realizing what he was doing, he grabbed the poker from the fire where he had dropped it earlier. "Enough of these childish games, deceiving everyone with your likeness. I'll mark you, I'll brand you, so you can never do it again." He slapped the red hot poker across the back of her hand.

She screamed. The smell of burning flesh struck his nostrils. Her face went white. Her eyes, round with shock, filled with tears.

"Papa, you hurt me!" she cried, pulling her wounded hand away from him.

With her words, the red haze cleared, and Daniel stared back at his daughter, as much in shock as she over what he had done. The poker fell from his hand back into the fire.

Rose moved. Daniel and Lily stared into each other's eyes, so caught up in their gaze that for a moment neither realized what she was doing. Then Lily cried, "Rose, no!"

But it was too late. Rose had ducked between them, seized the poker from the fire and laid it across the back of her own hand. She gasped as her flesh sizzled. The poker fell with a clatter to the stone hearth.

Isabel burst into the room. "Who's screaming? What happened?"

The twins had collapsed onto the bench, sobbing, shielding their wounded hands against their chests. Daniel stood before them, the poker at his feet, his face as white as theirs.

Lily looked up, gulped back her sobs. "We accidentally burned our hands."

"Burned your hands? Let me see." Isabel bent over the twins. "*Both* of you? The *backs* of your hands? Dear Jesus, these are bad burns. Come with me right now. The sooner we get them under the pump—" She jerked her head toward the kitchen.

The twins got up shakily, and ran to the kitchen, their feet quick on the three steps. Isabel turned to give Daniel a long look, then hurried after them.

Daniel fled to his room. He dropped to his knees on his red pillow, leaned his brow against his trunk, and wept.

Rose and Lily lay on their backs on their mat, side by side. Lily's hand burned with pain. Isabel had held both their hands a long time under the pump, then treated them with calendula ointment from Rose's medicine bag, and bandaged them. Still the burn was so painful that she wanted to cry. "I never thought Papa would do something like that," she said, her voice wobbly. "He's stern sometimes but he never … he never *hurt* us before."

Rose turned her head so that her brow touched Lily's. "I don't think he meant to. He lost his temper. I think he felt sorry right away. I saw the look on his face. We *were* really bad, teasing and deceiving Mr. Jenkins, and Papa too, the way we did. I didn't realize it would get them so upset."

"They deserved it. Both of them. Papa didn't listen, no matter how I pleaded. And Mr. Jenkins is a really horrible man, more horrible than we knew at first. But your plan worked. We'll never have to go out with him again. It was worth it. You got the worst of it last week, seeing him kill that dog."

"The dog saved me." Rose curled on her side and began to cry. "I think Mr. Jenkins was planning to drag me into his house and ravish me."

Lily curled around Rose. "He deserved everything we did and more. He's the one who is evil. Calling us witches. He went crazy. Oh." She shuddered. "I can't imagine anything more horrible than being married to him." Rose was still sobbing. "Does your hand hurt?"

"Yes. And the poor dog. It was like when Cindy died."

"Oh, Rose." Lily held her closer and stroked her hair with her good hand.

They were quiet a while, then Lily asked, "Why did you burn your hand? Was it because you thought we should share the punishment?"

"No. Because I didn't want us to be different."

A chill passed through Lily. "But we are different."

"No."

"Of course we are. In lots of ways. You play the flute; I play the violin. You're going to be a doctor, and I, I just want … to live on a ranch and ride horses."

"I like to ride horses."

"But we're different. We always have been. Maybe we forgot sometimes when we were younger because everyone treated us the same. But inside we knew."

"No."

"Don't be silly."

"I don't want us to be different. You're part of me. I want us to still be just alike and be together always."

Lily uncurled herself from Rose and sat up, suddenly angry. "We can't be together always. I want to get married and have babies. You'll want to get married someday, too."

"No, I won't. I just want to be with you." She turned on her back and looked up at Lily.

Lily felt Rose's longing wrap around her, squeezing her. "Don't cling to me," she said sharply. Rose went still. Lily could feel her shock and fear. It was too much. She slammed the door between their hearts shut.

Rose sat up and grabbed Lily's shoulders. "Don't," she cried in anguish. "Don't cut me off."

"I have to. I can't bear anymore to feel all that you feel. My own feelings are enough for me to manage. You have to let go of me. I'm *not* part of you. I am myself."

Rose's hands shook on Lily's shoulders. She caught in a quick breath and held it, her eyes filling with tears. Slowly she let go of Lily's shoulders and sank back down on the mat, curling away from Lily, pulling her quilt over her head.

Lily lay down, too, on her back, on the very edge of the mat, so as not to touch Rose. Of course Rose would know when she shut the door. Had she always known? Thinking of it, Lily realized she had, from the very first time Lily had found the door, after the stampede, when Rose, even in her drugged sleep, had cried out, "Lily, don't leave me."

The moon floated over the house and shone in the hillside window. Rose began to cry, deep, desolate sobs. Lily lay listening, her throat constricted. Finally she couldn't bear it any more. She kept the door closed, but curled her body around Rose. Gradually Rose's sobs subsided and she slept. Lily lay long awake, her heart burning as fiercely as her hand.

Daniel wept and pushed his brow against the edge of the trunk hard enough to hurt himself.

How could I have done that? Burned my own child? How could I? But how could they have done what they did? They drove him crazy. Aaron must have been unstable all along and I never knew. Calling them witches! What did he mean, that they danced and chanted? What did they do? What stories will he spread through the church? I am ruined!

I had hoped God would forgive me if I did well with this church, but now…

He pounded the trunk with both fists. Now I have sinned further, harming my child, both my children. Why did Rose …?

I don't understand them. I'm not fit to be a father. What do I know about young girls? If only Grace had not died. If only Rachel were here. She taught young girls at the orphanage. She'd know what to do.

At the thought of Rachel, passion flamed through him. He ached with longing and writhed with shame. *Dear God, I am riddled with sin. How can you abide me? I have burned my child and now I burn …*

He caught back his sobs. Burning. Lily was burning, too, in heat, that day she came back from the Fairdales. What had happened to do that to her? Dear God, has she … ? He saw her again, her face radiant, heard her bubbling laughter, and burned with shame for her.

Then all the burnings were confused inside him. The back of his head ached. Burning shame suffused and engulfed him. His mind hazed over. He struggled in the haze to pray. Could not. Exhausted, he finally dozed, slumping down against the side of the trunk, the red pillow a lump under his hip.

In his dream he stood on the wide front steps of the River View Presbyterian Church in Boston. All the elders of his church were around him. They were stoning Rachel. She lay bloody and broken in the courtyard below them. Daniel seized their arms to prevent them, cried out to them to stop. But when he looked down, he saw he held a stone in his own hand.

He woke shaking with horror, crumpled over the red pillow. He stumbled to his feet, looking wildly around the dark room—the trunk in front of him, the pale square of the window—struggling to remember who and where he was. Finally he made his way unsteadily through the house to the privy. As he passed through the living room, he heard Rose's sobs. Her desolation arrested him, seared his own desolate place, exacerbated his shame. He went on through the kitchen and out into the autumn night.

The moon had set. The hills rose up dark above him. Only the faint light of the stars showed him the path. After he'd visited the privy, he sat down on the hillside, his knees drawn up to his chest. Below him the town was dark, the plains dark beyond, the sky vast, deep with stars.

Scenes of the night tumbled in his mind—Lily leaving decorously with Aaron after prayer meeting, Aaron charging through the front door, Lily's face when he burned her hand, Isabel's long look. I got it all wrong, he thought in misery. Aaron is not who I thought he was, pious, stable. Daniel shuddered, remembering Aaron's shouting, his wild eyes, his hysteria about witches. Maybe the twins knew something I didn't. Lily did plead with me, but I wouldn't relent. They were just trying to chase him away. They succeeded! At what price to me, to the church? He groaned. They deserved to be punished, but not injured. And only a moment after I burned her, Lily protected me, lying to Isabel. But Isabel knew. Will she talk? He groaned again and bent his brow against his knees.

The stillness of the night enfolded him. After a while he lifted his eyes to the blazing stars. His heart opened in awe, and for the moment all shame and worry were erased by an immense wave of love for his God. Love, incomprehensible, flowed back to him from the stars, from the high arc of heaven. A spiral of wind swirled up from the valley, unexpectedly warm in the chill night, touching his cheek, gentle as a caress. He sighed, a long deep sigh, released his drawn-up knees, and stretched out on his back, surrendered.

# Chapter 38

# Reconciliation

Daniel sat at the kitchen table with a cup of coffee while the twins and Isabel prepared breakfast. There was a knock on the kitchen door. Isabel opened it and Nathan came in. Daniel stood up to greet him. "Nathan, good morning, come in. Have a seat. Would you like some breakfast?"

Nathan sat down on one of the benches. "Thanks, I've already eaten, but I could use a cup of coffee. Good morning Lily, Rose, Isabel."

"Good morning," Lily and Rose answered. Isabel nodded and smiled, busy turning the bacon.

Lily brought him a cup of coffee. "Thanks," he said. "What happened to your hand?"

Daniel's stomach clenched. He reached for his coffee, bumped his cup, and slopped dark liquid across the table. Rose came with a cloth to wipe it up.

"You've hurt your hand, too," Nathan noted. "Both of you. How did you do that?"

"We were taking a tray of bread out of the oven," Lily said. "It got stuck. When we pulled at it, it came loose all of a sudden and we bumped our hands on the top of the oven."

"That's too bad," Nathan said. "That must've hurt."

"Isabel took good care of us," Rose said, as she finished mopping up Daniel's coffee.

Isabel came to refill Daniel's cup. As she bent over, she met Daniel's eyes, gave the slightest nod. In a rush of relief Daniel knew that she wouldn't talk, that his family stood solidly behind him. His hand shook as he lifted his cup to his mouth.

"What brings you here so early?" he asked Nathan. "Is your family okay?"

Nathan smiled. "My family is fine. But I have news. This morning just at dawn, Aaron Jenkins came banging at the door, calling for me. All upset. He looked awful, like he hadn't slept all night. He had the deed to the sawmill in his hand and a contract he wanted me to sign. Said he was leaving this morning on the stage, never coming back, wanted me to buy the sawmill. I could pay him off in installments through Mr. Dodge—that's what the contract was. He wanted me to come with him to Ken Hill's to sign it, make it legal, but Ken doesn't open his office until nine. The stage doesn't come until eleven, so there's time."

"Leaving!" Daniel exclaimed. He put his cup down carefully so his shaking hand wouldn't spill it again.

"Yuh. I was pretty surprised, too, because he'd been telling me that, since he was gonna marry Lily, he planned to stay here a while longer before going back East to seminary. But something changed his mind all at once. Did you decide after all not to have him marry Lily?"

Daniel nodded, unable to speak.

"That must be it then. He was talking it up so, he probably couldn't face being turned down, what people would say. Well, I'm relieved." Nathan leaned his elbows on the table. "I've been worried about him marrying Lily, thinking I should talk to you about it, but I've been so busy all day at the sawmill and evenings putting my orchard in. Daniel, he's not all he seems. He's got a bad temper, a violent streak. Last week he killed my dog, the little runaway from the shanty town I was taming to bring home for my kids. I went down Monday morning last week, and it was lying there by the pile of logs, dead."

The handful of utensils Rose was carrying to the table clattered to the floor. She turned to the sink with a small incoherent sound. Lily scooped up the utensils and brought them to her, put her arm around Rose. "It's okay. We can just rinse them off."

Nathan paused, momentarily distracted, then turned back to Daniel. "He said it attacked him, but it was just a pup. He'd bite my boot sometimes in play. I was pretty upset. He was a good dog, and I was fond of him. But even more, I was worried about Lily. Men that are violent with animals can be hard on their wives. I just never thought it was a good match for our Lily anyway, she being so bright and he so much older and kind of grim."

Daniel still couldn't speak.

Isabel bustled up to the table with a plate of bacon. "Sure you won't have a bite to eat?" she asked Nathan. "I've got some eggs coming up."

"No, no thanks. I thought you'd want to know, Daniel, Aaron being an elder of the church and all. Also I wondered if you would look over the contract before I sign it."

Daniel finally found his voice. "Yes, yes, of course." He pushed back his chair. "Let's go to my study."

Nathan got up and followed him.

"Don't you want breakfast, Papa?" Lily called after him.

"I'm not hungry."

∼

After Nathan had gone, Daniel looked around for the twins. "Lily, Rose," he called.

The door opened at the top of the stairs. "Yes, Papa?"

"Come down. We need to talk."

"Just a minute."

He paced the living room, waiting for them. The poker, cold and gray now, still lay on the hearth. With a stab of guilt, he picked it up and hung it on its hook beside the fireplace.

After a moment, the twins came down the stairs. "Sit here," he directed them, gesturing to the bench by the hearth where they had sat the night before. They sat side by side, hands clasped, silent, looking up at him. He drew his leather chair up and sat down facing them. He took a long breath, held it, let it out slowly.

"I'm sorry, Lily, that I burned your hand. And that you, Rose, burned yourself. You both behaved badly and deserved to be punished, but not injured. You made me very angry and I lost control. For that I apologize."

The twins remained silent. Daniel studied them, not sure who was who. Both wore bandages on their hands, but, he noted, one had her right hand bandaged, the other her left. He tried to remember which of Lily's hands he had seized and burned the night before, but could not. It had all happened in such a haze of rage. He shook his head slightly, trying to penetrate his right/left confusion, and gave up.

"Last night," he said sternly, "you confessed to changing places with Mr. Jenkins, to teasing him for not being able to tell you apart, to threatening him with … " Daniel could not say the word, deeply shocked that his daughters had said it, and in such a way. "Why? Did you not realize how that would disgrace me? Did you not care?"

The twins remained silent. Then one spoke up. "We told you, Papa. We had to make him not want to marry Lily." That was Rose then.

"But that way? That disgraceful way?"

"What else could we do?" Lily's chin came up. "I begged you. I told you right off I could never marry him. But you wouldn't listen. If you'd only listened, you could have told him politely no, and all this wouldn't have happened. Why did you want me to marry him anyway?" Tears came to her eyes. "It felt like you just wanted to get rid of me. Don't you love me?"

Daniel took a deep breath. "I do love you. But you seem so ... wild recently. I thought to put you in the care of a good and pious man for your own protection."

"But I am already in the care of a good and pious man—you. What do you mean I'm wild? I'm not. We work really hard all day, every day, to take care of you. We cook for you, tend the garden, keep the house clean, wash your clothes, clean up after you. We come to every church service and prayer meeting and practice the hymns so there will be good music.

"We didn't have to come with you, you know. We could have stayed in Boston with Grandmama and not have anything harder to do than learn French and math and read philosophy, with Becky taking care of everything else. But we came with you, because we knew you'd need us. Where would you be without us? Half-starved and grubby, more than likely." Lily caught her breath. "I'm not wild. I'm very hard-working and responsible, and you don't appreciate it or ever even say thank you."

"What about this wild prank you've played the last few weeks and last night."

"That was my idea," Rose said.

Daniel stared at her in shocked amazement. The fantasy he'd built like a castle, that Lily was the mischievous one, Rose the more biddable, crumbled, the dust of its collapse fogging his mind. "You?"

"Yes." Rose lifted her chin, but her lips trembled. "I didn't want you sending Lily away."

Daniel rubbed his brow. His hand strayed to the back of his head. Abruptly, he asked, "Lily, have you ... are you still a virgin?"

The twins were clearly shocked. "Yes!" Lily said, emphatically. "Why would you think I wasn't?"

"Because ..." Daniel was lost. He couldn't tell her it was because she looked as if she were in heat.

Rose interrupted his bewilderment. "*I* might not be if Mr. Jenkins had had his way, if Nathan's dog hadn't defended me. Your good and pious man took me down to the end of the road, to his house alone, and was about to … Then he kicked the poor dog and killed it." Her voice caught in a sob.

"You were the one he took down there? You saw him kill the dog?"

Rose nodded, near weeping. "Mr. Jenkins was really horrible. He put his hands where he shouldn't. He said I'd have to obey him and if I didn't … then he whipped his horse."

"He would have beaten me," Lily said. "Like Mr. Decker did Rachel."

Daniel froze. The room went silent. Rose stared at Lily, her eyes huge. Lily stared back, biting her lower lip.

"Mr. Decker?" Daniel finally managed to say. "What do you mean, like Mr. Decker?"

The twins' eyes locked. Daniel could almost feel the words flying silently back and forth between them. Then Lily raised one eyebrow ever so slightly and Rose nodded, almost imperceptibly. She turned to Daniel.

"Papa, we know."

"What do you mean, you know?"

Their words poured out.

"We know about you and Rach … Mrs. Decker."

"Why you had to leave Boston."

"Why we came here."

"What?" Daniel spluttered. "What do you mean? How do you …?" Shock and fear ricocheted through him.

"We were hiding in your study the evening you confessed to Mr. Peabody that you were the father of Rachel's … Mrs. Decker's baby."

"You were hiding? How dare you!"

"We were worried about you."

"Because you were so sad."

"And we wanted to know what was wrong."

Daniel's chest was so tight he could hardly breathe. "Where were you hiding?"

"Under the table in the corner, with the red cloth over it."

"Later we heard Becky and Nell talking, Nell telling how she helped Mrs. Decker run away."

Daniel slumped back in his chair, his heart pounding, his head aching, burning with shame. To have them know! "Have you told anyone?" he asked, his voice hoarse. "In Boston? Here?"

"No."

"Of course not."

"You knew, and you came with me? You knew, and you pulled me out of the river?"

The twins got up in a rush and knelt on either side of his chair.

"We had to—"

"Because you're our papa."

"You needed us."

"And we needed you."

"We couldn't bear for you to go away and never see you again."

Daniel buried his face in his hands. He felt their gentle touch on his shoulders.

"Don't feel so bad, Papa."

"Everyone makes mistakes."

"And God forgives them."

"Maybe it wasn't even a mistake."

Daniel sat straight up in his chair. "How can you say that?"

"She escaped from Mr. Decker because of you."

"Maybe it was God's will for you to come here and build the church."

Daniel shook his head no, no. He looked from one daughter to the other. Their blue eyes were soft and compassionate.

"Do you understand now?" he asked, suddenly trusting them, trusting their love, longing to unburden his heart. "Do you understand why it is so important that I do well here, to redeem myself?"

"Papa." It was Rose, her brow furrowed. "Of course you want to do well, because that's how you are, but you're already redeemed."

"What do you know of such things?"

"We know what you taught us," Lily said. "Don't forget, we've been listening to your sermons, your prayers, all our lives, ever since we were old enough to sit still in church."

"And you taught us," Rose went on, "that God is love, and it's His love that redeems us, because Jesus died for us, because we'll always make mistakes. I guess I made a mistake in my plan for Mr. Jenkins. Maybe we could have done it a better way."

Daniel slumped down in his chair again. "It looks like I made a mistake insisting Lily should marry him." He sighed and closed his eyes, resting his head against the high back of his leather chair. The twins knelt quietly beside him, their hands on his shoulders.

After a while Daniel sat up. "Promise me something."

"What, Papa?"

"That you'll stop pretending to be each other, that you won't deceive that way ever again."

The twins shared a long look. "Okay, Papa," Lily said.

Rose nodded. "We promise."

Lily spoke up. "We need a promise, too. Promise you'll never make us marry someone we don't want to marry, ever again. Promise we can choose the husbands we want."

Daniel looked from one to the other. "I promise," he said.

# Chapter 39

# *Autumn*

Aaron Jenkins left town that same day. Nathan came by on his way home for lunch to report to Daniel that he had signed the contract, and had gone with Aaron to his house to pick up his trunk and a big pile of boxes.

"He must have been preparing for weeks and never told me," Nathan said. "His house was all packed up."

Or he stayed up all night packing, Daniel thought.

"He left his furniture, gave me his horse and buggy—a welcome gift. I've needed both for a while, though the horse will need some loving attention before he'll be worth much. Everything else Aaron packed up. The stage would only take his trunk, so he asked me to leave all the boxes at the post office until he had an address to send them to. Mrs. Dodge isn't too pleased. So he's gone, and I am the sudden owner of the sawmill." Nathan rubbed his brow. "I wasn't expecting that. I don't know how I am going to manage both the sawmill and my new orchard."

"Did he say anything?" Daniel asked. "Why he was going?"

"Not a word. He had nothing to say at all except directions about his possessions and details of the contract. He was even more tense than usual. It must be about Lily."

That's what everyone in town seemed to think when the news got around. Daniel listened to the talk, fearful of hearing of witches and chanting in the moonlight, but finally after several days began to relax. It seemed Aaron had not raved to anyone but him.

After about a week, Burt Martin, now the only elder, came with Mayor Wilgus and Ken Hill to talk with Daniel about the matter of electing a new elder. They decided that since the church had grown, they should choose not one, but three new elders. That Wednesday at prayer meeting, Daniel asked for nominations.

"You should be an elder," Lily said to Hannah, as she and Rose sat with Hannah on the church steps after prayer meeting. "You know everyone and do almost as much as Papa to keep the church going."

"Only men," Hannah said. "Didn't you know that, all the years you've been a preacher's daughter?"

"No," Rose said. "Papa never talked to us about such things when we were in Boston."

"Only men?" Lily asked. "That's not fair. We're part of the church, too."

"We sure are." Hannah pinched her lips together. "But we can only nominate men, and only men can vote. That's how it is now. But someday it'll change."

When the nominations were in, the election had been held, and the votes counted, Ken Hill was chosen to take Aaron's place, and, much to their surprise, Gabe and Nathan were elected to become the two additional elders.

"Happy birthday," Rose whispered to Lily.

Lily turned sleepily to hug her. "Happy birthday to you." They nestled together, waking slowly as early morning sun slanted in their east window.

"Sixteen today," Rose sighed. "If we were back in Boston, Grandmama would be preparing our coming-out ball."

"Yes. It would have been a good party, but still I'm glad we're here."

"I don't suppose we'll have any celebration. Papa can't even remember how old we are, much less our birthday, and I don't think anyone else knows."

They lay quietly together, brows touching, memories of past birthdays flowing between them. Becky waking them with kisses and presents, the parties at Grandmama's with birthday cake and candles.

"Well, it's Sunday," Rose said finally, "so we can rest this afternoon. And I like the hymns Papa chose for today." She kissed Lily and got up, slipped off her nightgown and began to dress, singing softly,

> *"Come ye thankful people come,*
> *Raise the song of harvest home."*

After prayer meeting that evening, Isabel went off with Hannah. The twins stayed behind to help their father close up. As they waited on the church steps for him to bring the buggy around, they saw a slender figure emerge from the shadow under the west window and slip away into the darkness.

Rose caught Lily's arm. "Who was that?"

"I don't know." Lily peered after the disappearing form. "A woman; she had long skirts. Or maybe a girl. She was small."

Daniel pulled up in front. "Hop in." He was smiling at them. The twins stowed their instruments in the back and climbed up onto the buggy seat on either side of Daniel.

He flicked the reins and started down the road. "Hannah has invited us over for a while this evening."

The twins were puzzled. Usually Daniel was tired at the end of Sunday and they went straight home.

When they arrived at the boarding house, Ned came out to meet them. He gave the twins a wide grin. "I'll take care of your buggy, sir," he said to Daniel. "Go on in."

As they entered the dining room, the twins were startled by a shout of "Happy Birthday!"

All their friends were there—the Hollis family, Gabe, Isabel, and Hannah, Burt and Elsie and all their little ones, the Dodge family, and Mayor Wilgus. And the Fairdales.

"A party after all!" Lily exclaimed.

"How did you know?" Rose asked Hannah.

"Isabel told me."

Lily and Rose turned to Isabel, question in their eyes. "Ah," she said. "You don't remember. I wormed it out of you long ago, when we first met."

Hannah and Isabel had made two big cakes, each with a spiral of sixteen candles. After the twins had greeted everyone and received many hugs and birthday blessings, Hannah called them up to the table to make their wishes and blow out the candles.

"We mustn't tell our wish," Lily whispered to Rose, "not even to each other." She closed her eyes and wished to marry Jonathan.

Rose nodded, but her heart contracted. *I wish,* she thought as she drew in her breath, *that Lily and I could be together always.* But when she blew, two candles remained lit.

"You'll have to wait two years for your wish to come true," Amy called out.

"And Lily will have to wait one," Elsie said.

Lily looked around the circle of her friends. She smiled into Jonathan's eyes, her heart pounding with love. He smiled back at her as if he knew her wish.

After the cake there were presents. Elsie gave them a shiny new cook pot with a tight lid. The Dodge family gave them a box of writing paper. "For all the letters you send to your grandmother," Mrs. Dodge said. Gabe gave them each a small wooden box, Rose's with a rose carved on the lid, Lily's with a lily. Kate and Andrew gave them a new bridle with bells on it for Dawnstar. Amy and Julia gave them hand-knitted hats and mittens, Rose's deep pink and Lily's white.

"Now we'll be able to tell you apart," Amy crowed. "Promise you won't switch them."

"We won't," Rose promised.

As they drove home after the party, Daniel said, "I didn't know it was your birthday. I'm glad Isabel knew. It was a good party." The twins sat on either side of him; Isabel nodded in the back.

Rose leaned against Daniel. "You should remember, Papa. After all, our birthday was the day you became a father."

"It's just dates I forget. I do remember the day you were born. We never expected two of you, so we had only one cradle. When I finally persuaded your mama to lay you down, we had to put you both in the same cradle. The next day I hurried out to get another cradle, but when we separated you, you cried and cried until we put you together again. I don't think you've slept a night apart since."

"We haven't." Rose reached for Lily's hand, but Lily was on the other side of Daniel.

Lily hunched her shoulders and said nothing.

The days shortened and the nights grew colder. The twins got out their long flannel nightgowns and wool vests. The grasses of the plains turned red, tan and brown, purple and gold, a kaleidoscope of color. The little stream above the house almost stopped running; even Gold Creek ran low. The cottonwoods along its edge turned brilliant yellow against the deep blue of the autumn sky.

The twins and Isabel spent their days gathering in the last of the harvest, digging compost into the garden as they cleared it, storing squashes and potatoes in the cold room, canning the remaining tomatoes and beans. The pantry shelves were bright with rows of clear glass jars of peas, beans, tomatoes, carrots, cherries, plums, and currants. Two big barrels, one of dried apples, one of dried peaches, stood along the back wall alongside barrels of flour and cornmeal.

When their harvest was in, the twins went to the Hollis orchard to help Nathan and Mattie plant the saplings of apple and peach trees that the Fairdales had given them. In return, Nathan gave them an apple tree and a peach tree that they planted on either side of the walkway that led up to their house.

A big box arrived on the stage addressed to the twins, late-coming birthday presents from Mrs. Lowell. There were two long, hooded coats made of thick blue-grey wool, a down comforter and pillows, and fine linen sheets. There was also a check included in her letter of birthday wishes, and instructions to have a "proper bed" made.

One of the new arrivals in town was a small wiry man called Red because, one would suppose, of his bristly red beard. His head was quite bald. He and his big-boned wife and their two strapping sons built a cabin on Mill Road between the flour mill and the sawmill and set up a logging business. He needed more oxen, so Daniel bargained with him for a winter's worth of firewood in exchange for Bo and Buff, Lad and Lucky. The twins were distraught at losing their companions of the trail, but were somewhat mollified when they met Red and saw how well he treated the oxen. He led them away, and returned a few days later with a big wagonload of wood, cut and split.

Wolves howled in the hills at night. Sheriff Parker came around one evening to talk to Daniel. "You'd better get a stable up for your horses. Once the snow comes and the deer get scarce, the wolves'll be down looking for other prey. I'll give you a hand. You'll be needing some hay, too. I've got lots for sale." So Red came with another load, this time of logs, and Daniel and Gabe and the sheriff built a stable, with room for the two horses and hay for the winter, and a stout door to keep out the wolves.

<h1 style="text-align:center">Chapter 40</h1>

<h1 style="text-align:center">Gleaning Day</h1>

On the first Saturday in October, the Fairdales offered a gleaning day. Anyone in the valley could come and glean the last of the fruit from their orchards. It was apparently a yearly tradition, a gift from the Fairdales to those who had less abundance. It was also the occasion for the last big picnic before the snow fell.

Folks came from the town and all over the valley. Gabe and several other musicians set up at the edge of the large grassy area between the big house and the cabins, and struck up a tune. The women sang along as they helped Kate set up tables for the picnic. Children tumbled on the grass. Daniel moved from group to group, listening, sharing the gospel.

The twins went to the orchard with Jonathan and Amy and Julia to help with the last gathering of the fruit. "We don't keep any of the gleaning," Julia said. "We help gather it and then give it to folks who don't have much. We're so lucky we have plenty."

The orchard was full of people, laughing and calling to each other, filling their baskets from fruit on the ground, some climbing into the trees to gather the last apples in the high branches. Andrew and Bernie moved among them, watching over the safety of both trees and people.

Jonathan caught Lily by the hand. "Come with me. I want to show you something." Lily glanced over at Rose who was lifting a little boy out of the lower branches of a cherry tree. Swiftly, she slid the door between their hearts closed. Jonathan tugged at her hand and they slipped away. Once out of the orchard, they ran, still holding hands, laughing for no other reason than that they were together. They stopped, panting, at the top of a low knoll. Jonathan put his hands on Lily's shoulders and turned her slowly around.

Just below them to the north, the stream wound its way through golden cottonwoods. To the east the plains stretched out to faraway hills. To the south a wide meadow separated the knoll from the big house and the barn and the cluster of cabins. To the west, was the orchard, the trees in neat rows, the paths between dwindling to points. The warm autumn sun shone down on them. The muted voice of the stream floated up to them.

"Do you like this place?" Jonathan asked. A light wind ruffled his auburn curls. He looked down at her, his eyes soft with love.

Lily felt his question was important, but didn't quite understand why. She was holding her breath, her heart pounding from more than running. "I do," she said, so softly that Jonathan bent his head to hear her.

"Father said I could build a cabin here. If … Lily, will you marry me?"

Her heart leaped. "Yes! Yes!"

He picked her up off her feet and whirled her around, set her down and kissed her. Kissed her again. With joy overflowing, she wrapped her arms around him, pressed against him.

"It will be our own place," he said, when they could speak again. "Just you and me. I'll start now and when it's finished, I'll come and ask your father's permission. Let's keep our pledge a secret until then. Maybe by this time next year we'll be wed."

They sat down on the grass, sharing dreams and plans, their arms around each other. It was different, Lily noticed, than sitting with Rose. His body was lean and strong. Her brow did not touch his, but rested on his shoulder. Different, but also sweetly familiar, as if she had always known him, always known the way she would fit with him, the curve of his arm around her, the bones of his shoulder, the way his lips touched her hair.

~

Rose lifted the small boy down out of the cherry tree. As soon as his feet touched the ground, he ran to show his treasure, a cluster of cherries, to his mother.

She looked around for Lily. The orchard, full of laughing, calling men, women and children, was empty. "Do you know where Lily went?" she asked Julia.

"She's with Jonathan. I saw them running together, holding hands." She tilted her head to look into Rose's face. "Don't worry. He'll take good care of her."

Rose walked slowly to the edge of the orchard. She reached out with her heart, but knew before she did that she would not find Lily. Lily had told her about the door between their hearts after the night of the burning. It had been a relief to hear in words what Rose had known since the stampede, but had not dared to admit to herself. Lily had said she would keep the door open most of the time, but wanted to be able to close it sometimes for privacy. But even when it was open now, even when thoughts and feelings flowed freely between them, Rose knew that Lily held something back. She knew that at least some of it was about Jonathan.

Rose did not understand the need for privacy between them. She searched in her own heart for a door, but there was none, only the open reaching for connection to her twin, the other part of her soul.

~

That night Lily told her. They sat together on their new bed with the down comforter and linen sheets their grandmama had sent them for their birthday. Rose loved the sheets and the light warmth of the comforter, but had mixed feelings about the bed. She liked that it was up off the floor on the sturdy frame Gabe had built for them, but it was much wider than the narrow mat they'd had before. Sometimes Rose woke in the night to find Lily wasn't touching her.

"I have a secret," Lily said, her voice bubbling. "But I have to tell someone. I know I can trust you."

"You can." Rose's heart ached with dread. She already knew, but didn't want to know, longed for Lily to confide in her, and cringed away from the confirmation of her fear. The words came.

"I'm going to marry Jonathan." In the dim light of the one candle in their room, Lily's face glowed. "He asked me today and I said yes. He's going to build us a cabin on the knoll above the stream. Oh, Rose, I'm so happy! I love him so."

Rose sat silent, her hands clenched in her lap. Lily's words poured over her.

"He'd been planning to ask me for a long time, but Mr. Fairdale told him to wait. Then he was really worried when the talk went around I was going to marry Mr. Jenkins, but I told Jonathan I never would have, because I have loved him, too, from the very first day I met him." She sighed. "I never knew it would be like this, to love like this. It is the most heavenly feeling in the world."

"I'm glad for you," Rose finally managed to say. "Jonathan's a fine man, and lots of fun. He ... he suits you."

"He said he's going to start building the cabin right away and when it's done, he'll ask Papa, and then we'll tell everyone and set a wedding date."

"Do you think Papa will say yes?"

"Of course he will. He promised, remember? That day after he burned my hand, he promised we could choose our husbands."

Lily flopped down on the comforter with a long sigh. After a moment, she asked, "Rose?"

"I'll miss you."

"Oh, Rose." Lily sat up to hug her. "I won't be far away. You can come visit often. You'll always be my sister. And it won't be right away. Winter's coming and he won't be able to do much on it until spring. But maybe by this time next year we'll be married. That's what he said. Come now." Lily pulled Rose down beside her and wrapped her arms around her. "I'm here now. And we should go to sleep. Tomorrow's Sunday, and we have to be up early to work on the hymns. Oh, I don't know if I can sleep. I'm so excited."

Rose got up to blow out the candle, then lay down beside Lily. They had placed their new bed beside the hillside window. Crisp night air flowed in with the smell of earth and grass. She pulled the comforter up over them. Lily nestled around her, and, in spite of her excitement, fell promptly to sleep. Rose lay long awake, looking out onto the hillside and the stars, cherishing the warmth of Lily's body curled around her, the touch Lily's soft breath on her neck. Tears clotted in her throat.

# Chapter 41

# *Lisbeth*

W inter came early with heavy wet snow, bending the saplings in Nathan's orchard to the ground. The last gold leaves swirled down from the trees, and the cottonwoods by the creek raised their bare black branches, stark against the gray sky. For a few days the sun came out and the snow melted, then it snowed again.

On the heels of the second storm, Dr. Franz came to town, driving a tired horse and a storm-battered buggy. He had been to Denver for supplies and stopped at Coal City to do a clinic on his way. He was settled in Montview, he reported, his practice already busy and his boys doing well in school.

For the next three days, Rose worked beside him in Hannah's parlor, setting aside her grief and confusion to pour herself into praying, healing, and learning. She filled more pages of her notebook with the treatments for frost bite, croup, mountain fever, and other ailments common to winter. Between patients, she shared with Dr. Franz what she had learned of medicinal herbs from Mrs. Fairdale and reported on what she had done since he had last been there—her postpartum visits to the woman on the plains, the birth of Elsie's baby, and the minor cuts, burns, and colds she had treated when called on.

When another storm threatened, Dr. Franz cut his clinic short and packed up and left, anxious to get back home to his boys before he got snowed in.

It snowed and snowed. The hillside window in the twins' room was soon covered over. The people of the valley huddled in their houses. At first Jonathan and Amy and Julia brought milk to the store in a sleigh, but then the snow became too deep for the horses to get through, and the twins didn't see them for weeks. Many cattle died. The baby Rose and Dr. Franz had delivered the summer before, out by the Denver/Montview Road, died of croup, but Rose did not find out until spring.

It was the worst winter anyone could remember, folks said to each other when they could get out between storms and gather in Elsie's café to commiserate.

One bitter Wednesday evening, Gabe stayed behind to help Daniel and the twins close up after prayer meeting. When they stepped out of the warm church, the stars were bright and high, the whiteness of snow reflecting their light. They hardly needed the lantern Gabe carried.

"It's cold," Lily said, pulling up the hood of her thick, warm coat.

"Very," Daniel agreed. "Blest we are to have a warm house to go home to." He turned to lock the door of the church.

"Please." A small voice spoke out of the shadow of the church steps. "Please, sir, before you lock up … Could I stay in the church tonight to keep warm? Just for tonight? I won't hurt anything. I'll be gone in the morning."

"What?" Daniel turned, startled.

A slender figure rose up hesitantly beside the steps. "They said maybe you would let me, that the church is a sanc … sanctuary."

Daniel held out his gloved hand. "Come here." Her hand was bare and she could hardly stand she was shivering so. Daniel drew her up onto the steps. "Who are you? What are you doing here?"

"It's Lisbeth!" Rose and Lily exclaimed together.

"Lisbeth? Hold up the lantern, Gabe." Daniel put his hand gently under Lisbeth's chin and tilted her face up into the lantern light. Her eyes were dark with fear.

"What are you doing here?" Daniel asked her again. "Why are you out alone in the cold without even a coat. Why aren't you home?"

"I don't have a home."

"No home?"

"Lisbeth." The twins came to either side of her. "Did you run away?"

Daniel released her chin. She turned her face to Rose. "I had to. I can't go back."

"Papa, look at her. She's freezing cold," Rose exclaimed.

"She can't stay in the church all night," Lily said. "The stove will go out and she'll freeze to death."

"Wait a minute," Daniel ordered. "You know this girl?"

"Yes, she's Lisbeth."

Daniel put his hands on Lisbeth's narrow shoulders. "Lisbeth, why have you run away?"

Lisbeth shrank away from him and bent her head. "Because …" she stammered.

"Papa," Lily interrupted. "Her home is the brothel, and she's running away because Smythe makes her …"

Daniel felt a jolt of shock. "The brothel? This child?"

Rose put her arms around Lisbeth. "She's freezing, Papa, and I am, too. We need to take her home with us where it's warm. We can talk there."

"Rose is right," Gabe said. "It's too cold to stand here and the child's so chilled she's in danger."

Daniel nodded. "Come, then."

As they went down the steps, Lisbeth bent and picked up a bundle wrapped in a blanket.

"I'll carry that for you." Gabe took it from her and put his other hand under her elbow to steady her.

They walked around the church to the hitching area. Shadow and Dawnstar and Sadie were huddled together by the back wall.

"She can barely walk," Daniel exclaimed, as he saw Lisbeth stumble.

"She's too cold," Gabe said. "She can ride on Sadie." He lifted Lisbeth onto Sadie's back. "I don't have no saddle for her," he explained to Lisbeth, "but she's very gentle." He took off his coat and wrapped it around Lisbeth.

Daniel watched, frowning with concern. "Let's go. Let's get her home." He swung up onto Shadow. The twins mounted Dawnstar, and the little procession started off.

The fire was bright on the hearth when they came in.

"Lord a mercy!" Isabel exclaimed when she saw Lisbeth. "Get that child to the fire." She hurried over, took Lisbeth by both hands, and seated her on the bench in front of the hearth. "Lisbeth, dearie, I'm so glad you're here. Me and the twins have been wanting to help you for months, but we didn't know how. Have you run away then? It's high time. Just you sit here and get warm. I'll bring you something hot to drink."

The twins hung up their coats and sat down on either side of Lisbeth, wrapping their arms around her. She looked from one to the other, shivering, then put her hands over her face and began to sob. Isabel came with a cup of hot cocoa and stood in front of her holding it, waiting. Daniel drew up a chair. Gabe settled himself cross-legged in a corner of the hearth, his black eyes glowing with compassion.

When Lisbeth's sobs finally quieted, Rose handed her a handkerchief out of her apron pocket, Lily stroked her hair, and Isabel gave her the cup of cocoa.

"Does anyone else want cocoa?" Isabel asked.

"I think we all do," Daniel answered. "It was a cold ride home." He pulled his chair closer to Lisbeth. "Can you tell us your story now?" he asked gently, struggling to stifle his outrage so as not to frighten her. "How did it come about that the brothel was your home? Did Smythe kidnap you?"

"No," Lisbeth said. She had almost stopped shivering, sipping the cocoa and leaning into the twins' arms. "My mother worked for Smythe. She wasn't … We're from a good family. We're Spanish." She straightened her back and lifted her head. The firelight shone on her fine, delicate features. "Indians burned our ranch and killed my father and all our people. Only my mother and I escaped. I hardly remember. I was little. We had nothing, nowhere to go. For a long time … I don't remember very well." She took another sip of cocoa. "Then we came here. Smythe was just starting up his … He gave us a place to live. It was different when Ginny was there. She took good care of us, all the women."

"Who was Ginny?" Daniel asked.

"Smythe's wife. But she died, and then he turned mean."

"I didn't know he'd had a wife." Daniel looked over at Isabel.

"I knew her," Isabel said. "She died five, six years ago. Kicked by a horse. Smythe took it hard. Things have gone down over there since."

"And now?" Daniel turned back to Lisbeth.

Lisbeth's lips trembled. "Last winter my mama got a bad disease from one of her … customers, and died. Then Smythe said he was short of girls, and I'd have to work for my food and bed."

Daniel let out an angry exclamation. Lisbeth stopped and held her breath. "Go on," Daniel said.

"My mama never would have let him." Lisbeth struggled with her tears. "I didn't know what it would be like. I tried to run away before, but he found me. But now I have to get away because … because …" She hid her face in her hands again.

"Because what?" Rose asked.

"Because I have a baby inside me. I wasn't sure until … this morning. I felt it move. I told Smythe, but he said I could work anyway. But I'm afraid they'll hurt it, ramming on me like they do."

Daniel drew in his breath. He looked uneasily at the twins, but they were holding and comforting Lisbeth, who was weeping again. "Do you know who the father is?" he asked.

Lisbeth shrugged her hunched shoulders. "How would I know? So many of them came."

Daniel pushed back his chair and paced the room. "He should be shot, to treat an orphaned child like that." He turned to Lisbeth. "You are safe here."

"He'll come looking for me."

"Don't worry. Tonight you are safe. We'll figure out something for the future. We'll make sure you don't have to go back to him."

Gabe had been sitting quietly in the corner of the hearth, listening intently. He stirred and leaned forward. "I have an idea," he said.

Everyone turned to look at him.

He hesitated, his eyes on Lisbeth. "I could marry you."

The room went silent with amazement.

"I know I'm old enough to be your pa," Gabe went on, all his loving energy focused on Lisbeth. "And kind of funny looking, don't have all my teeth. But I can give you a snug home and a name for your baby. I'd treat you kindly. And as for that other business—I figure you had more'n enough of that. You'll have your own bed. I can sleep in my shop, and when spring comes, I'll build a new room on my cabin just for you and your babe."

Lisbeth's hands flew to her mouth, her large dark eyes filling with tears again. "But why would you? If you're not going to make me ..."

"Ah!" Gabe's voice ached. He came and knelt in front of her. "Lisbeth, I'll never make you, I promise."

"But if you're not going to ... why?"

Gabe sat back on his heels. His sweet smile spread across his face. "'Cause," he said, "soon as I saw you in the lantern light, I knew Jesus wanted me to take care of you. Seems like the best way to do that, things being like they are, is to marry you." He paused. A wistful expression came over his face. "And besides, it gets kind of lonesome sometimes. It'd be nice to see a pretty face across the table. And I've always wanted a little one."

"But ..." Lisbeth struggled with her next words. "I would disgrace you. You know what they say about me, the ladies in your church, that Rose and Lily shouldn't talk to me because ... because I'm soiled."

Gabe's black eyes flashed. "Anyone who calls my wife soiled will have me to deal with."

That seemed to be too much for Lisbeth. She bent her face into her hands and wept again. The twins held her close.

"Do it, Lisbeth."

"You'll never be sorry."

"Gabe is the kindest man in the world."

Daniel sank slowly into his chair. "That would be a good solution. Once you were married, Gabe would have authority over you, and Smythe couldn't touch you." He leaned forward to touch Lisbeth's shoulder. "What do you think, Lisbeth?"

Lisbeth lifted her face from her hands and looked down at Gabe kneeling in front of her. Her soft full lips parted in a smile, even as tears glistened on her cheeks. "I will," she said. She held out her hands to Gabe and he took them in his. "I will. I'll marry you. I'll work real hard for you. But I don't know your name."

Everyone laughed. A wave of relief swept through the room.

"My name's Gabe." He looked up at her smiling widely, his eyes shining. "Gabriel Archen. And I'm the luckiest man alive to have won such a beautiful bride."

They all sat around the table in the warm kitchen the next morning. Isabel and the twins served up a hearty breakfast of oatmeal, eggs, and pancakes. A little color had come into Lisbeth's face and she ate hungrily.

"You should do that marriage today," Isabel said soberly. "Smythe'll be looking for her, and it may be that some saw you bringing her here last night. He won't let her go easy."

"I've been thinking that, too," Daniel said. "We could have the ceremony here this morning if you're ready."

"I'm ready." Gabe looked happy.

Lisbeth nodded.

"I'd like to have Mr. Hill here to take care of the legal part," Daniel said, "and to be a witness, but I don't want to leave Lisbeth unguarded while I go fetch him."

"I'll go," Isabel said. "You and Gabe should both stay here." She got up from the table. "I'll go right now. You girls clean up."

"Let's make a wedding cake," Lily suggested, "and have a celebration."

They all got up from the table. "Come to my room," Daniel said to Gabe. "I want to talk with you."

The three girls cleared the table. "I'd like to lend you a pretty dress to get married in," Rose said, "and do up your hair. As a married woman, you should wear your hair up." She picked up a lock of Lisbeth's rich, dark hair. "You have such beautiful hair, so long and thick."

"Smythe always made us wear it down, even the older girls like Ella."

"You don't have to do what Smythe says ever again," Lily said hugging her. "What kind of cake would you like for your wedding?"

Lisbeth shrugged, smiling a little. "I don't know. No one ever made me a cake before." She frowned. "I'm worried. I don't know how to cook very well. I want to take good care of Mr. Archen."

"You can learn," Rose assured her. "We had to. We were older than you when we started." She moved things around in the pantry. "How about a peach cake? We have some dried peaches we could cut up and put in."

"That sounds good."

As the twins mixed up the cake, Lisbeth sat twisting her fingers together. "I've been wondering." She hesitated. "Do you think …?" She stopped, blushing.

"What is it?" Rose asked.

Lisbeth's words came out in a tumble. "I want to be baptized. I watched your pa baptize people … through the church window, and wanted so much for him to do it to me. Do you think he would?"

"I know he would. We saw you there once," Lily said. "Why didn't you come in?"

"I couldn't have!" Lisbeth looked shocked. "They never would have let me."

"Papa would have," Rose said. "He always says whoever truly seeks Christ is welcome. Some of the miners aren't too virtuous. One of them may even be the papa of your baby. But they come."

"It's different with men."

"You're right, it is." Lily nodded. "It's not fair."

Once the cake was in the oven, the girls went to Daniel's door. "Papa," Lily called. Daniel opened the door. "Lisbeth wants you to baptize her."

Daniel smiled and held out his hand to Lisbeth. "Come," he said, and guided her to sit on the bench in front of the hearth. "Tell me."

Gabe came to sit beside her.

Lisbeth sat straight, her big eyes fixed on Daniel's face. "I used to come when you had services, when it wasn't so cold. I'd hide until everyone went in, and then come to the window and listen, to the music and the words. I watched you baptize people and it seemed like … like they'd be different afterwards, and I wanted that, too."

"I wish I had known. I wish you had come to me sooner. Are you ready, then, to commit your life to Christ?"

"I am." Lisbeth's face was very serious and at the same time filled with hope.

"Then of course I will baptize you. It is always a blessed day when a new soul comes to Christ."

There were voices outside. Isabel came through the door, followed by Mr. Hill and Hannah. "I brought Hannah, too," Isabel explained, "so we'd have another witness. It smells good in here. What are you girls cooking?"

"We're making a wedding cake." Rose took Hannah's and Mr. Hill's coats and hung them on the hooks by the door.

Daniel shook Ken Hill's hand. "Thank you for coming. I assume Isabel told you what was afoot. You are welcome, too, Hannah, always. Please sit down. I have a few preparations to make."

"We do, too," Rose said. "We want to dress Lisbeth up pretty for her wedding."

Gabe glanced down at his clothes. "I'm wearing my prayer meeting clothes. Best I have, but they're a bit wrinkled from sleeping in."

Lisbeth smiled at him, a hint of laughter in her eyes. "You look fine to me."

Upstairs Rose opened her trunk and pulled out the pink silk gown. "I knew there was a reason to bring our pink silks. She can wear mine." She shook the wrinkles out of the gown and held it up against Lisbeth. "It's a little big, but we can fix that. It will look lovely on her."

Lisbeth touched the smooth silk with awe. "It's beautiful." She turned to her bundle on the floor. "I have some pretty things, too. They'll go perfectly." She undid her bundle and took out a black lace shawl embroidered with pink roses and a large mother-of-pearl comb. "These were my mama's. She was wearing them when we ran from the fire and kept them safe and hidden from Smythe. She never wore them for the johns. She gave them to me when she was dying." Lisbeth bit her lower lip, tears coming into her eyes. "I'd think she'd like for me to wear them today."

The twins set to work adorning their friend. When Lisbeth came down the stairs a little while later, trailing the pink silk, draped in the black lace shawl, her hair caught up elegantly with the white comb, Gabe stood up slowly, his eyes wide. "Oh, my," was all he could manage to say.

The ceremony was simple and touching. First Daniel baptized Lisbeth. She knelt before him as she spoke her words of commitment to Christ, as he touched her head with water, saying "Elizabeth Lucia del Valle, I baptize you in the name of the Father, the Son, and the Holy Spirit." The marriage ceremony followed. The twins had witnessed many weddings in the church in Boston, but none had touched them as this one did. They held each other's hands tightly as their father spoke the time-honored words: "For richer, for poorer, in sickness and in health, to love, honor, and cherish …" At the end, Gabe kissed his bride gently on the cheek.

They were gathered around the table sharing the wedding cake when they heard pounding on the door. Lisbeth gasped, "It's him, I know," and tried to stand, but was in the middle of the bench between Gabe and Rose.

Daniel rose slowly from his chair at the end of the table. "It probably is. Don't be afraid. We're here with you."

Everyone stood, the benches scraping on the floor. Daniel went down the three steps from the kitchen to the main room. Ken Hill and Hannah followed him. The twins stood on the steps, clutching each other's hands. Gabe, beside them, put his arm around Lisbeth's shoulders. Isabel glared from the rear.

The pounding continued. "Open up. I know you're in there," Smythe's voice roared. Before Daniel could reach the door, it burst open and Smythe surged in. A blast of cold air came in with him.

"Come in," Daniel said calmly, though the twins could see his fists were clenched. "Please close the door behind you."

Smythe kicked back with one foot and slammed the door. His head swiveled from side to side, and his eyes narrowed as he took in each person in the room. He focused on Lisbeth. "I thought I'd find you here. Hiding behind the preacher and his girls. All dressed up, too. Well, the party's over."

He strode toward her, but Daniel put his arm out to the side, blocking him. Daniel's voice was quiet and controlled. "We are celebrating her marriage to Mr. Archen this morning. All these people are witnesses, and Mr. Hill has drawn up the legal papers, to be registered today in the town hall."

Smythe stopped, his shoulders hunched, his eyes so narrow only slits of pale brown could be seen between his lids. He looked Gabe up and down and curled his lips. "Married? To that skinny old goat?"

Lisbeth's head came up, her eyes flashed. "He's not—"

But Gabe interrupted her. "It's okay." He was laughing. Lisbeth gazed at him, startled, then began to laugh, too. It was the first time the twins had heard her laugh. Their laughter was so infectious that soon everyone was laughing. Everyone but Smythe.

He drew back toward the door, turning his rage on Daniel. "Laugh. I'll have the last laugh. You'll be sorry. Taking my girls. There's not room enough in this town for both of us. And I was here first. Trust me. I'll not rest until you—you and your meddling twins …"

His voice trailed off. He spun on his heel, and went out, slamming the door behind him.

In the silence that followed the banging of the door, Hannah said, "I'd like a little more of that peach cake."

They went back to the table, laughing again, sharing their triumph, and ate all the rest of the cake except one piece that the twins insisted Lisbeth keep.

Ken Hill stood. "I'll go now and get this marriage registered at the town hall. Wilgus'll be amazed and pleased." He shook Daniel's hand. "There's been good work done here today, a soul baptized for Christ and one less girl in Smythe's damnable brothel. You know," he said, tucking his briefcase under his arm, "that's how we can close his brothel. Just win over the girls for Christ and get them married to good men." He nodded to Gabe and went out.

Gabe took Lisbeth's hand. "The sun's out," he said, "and it's warmed up some. I wanna take you to see your new home, and then go to the store and git you some cloth for a coat."

"I need to change first." Lisbeth went upstairs and came back down in her worn brown gown.

"Get some cloth for a new gown, too," Hannah said. "She's outgrown that one, and it's tattered."

Gabe examined Lisbeth's gown. "You're right. I will."

"Bring the cloth back here and we'll help you make it up," said Rose. She took her coat down from the hook by the door and held it for Lisbeth. "You can wear my coat. It's still cold."

As they went off together, Lisbeth riding on Sadie, Isabel looked out the window after them. "Looks like Mary and Joseph on their way to Bethlehem, 'cepting she's riding on a mule instead of a donkey." She turned from the window. "And she's already in love with him. Looks at him like he's the prince of the world."

"He *is* a prince," Rose said. "He may not look like it, but inside he is."

"He sure is, dearie. She's a lucky girl."

Two hours later, as Isabel and the twins were about to serve up dinner, Gabe and Lisbeth returned with a bundle of cloth.

"Let's see," Lily said. She helped Lisbeth unwrap the bundle.

"The dark brown wool is for my coat," Lisbeth explained. "See how thick it is. It will be really warm. And this rose-colored linsey-woolsey is for my gown. Isn't it pretty? Elsie helped us pick it out and she gave me this lace to trim it with." Her cheeks were pink with pleasure. "I never had such nice stuff before." She looked gratefully at Gabe.

"I didn't take her inside o' the house," Gabe said. "She saw the outside, but then I remembered how I'd left it. I didn't know when I went out last night that I'd be a'coming home with a wife. Could she stay with you for a few days until I clean it up and put in a floor? I don't want our baby crawling on a dirt floor."

"Of course she can stay," Rose said. "It'll give us time to make her new clothes."

After dinner Daniel retired to his study, and Isabel and the girls went to work, measuring and cutting. Once the coat was cut out, they sat around the table stitching the seams as the short winter afternoon darkened into evening.

"Gabe took me to the bank before we went to the store," Lisbeth said. "I didn't know Mr. Dodge was the banker. He seemed kinda nervous when Gabe said I was his wife. Because I know him, I guess. He comes real regular to the brothel. He never came to me, though. He likes Kitty and Candy."

"Mr. Dodge!" the twins exclaimed in unison.

"Yes." Lisbeth looked confused.

"But he's married."

Isabel looked up from her sewing. "Remember I told you that there's some that are married that like a change from time to time? He's one."

"But isn't that adultery?"

"Yep."

"But he's a Christian."

"You're not supposed to commit it."

"It's in the ten commandments."

"I know. I know." Isabel fixed her green eyes on the shocked twins. "Not all Christians obey the ten commandments."

Lily took a breath. "Sheriff Parker told us that. But Mr. Dodge!"

Lisbeth had stopped sewing and turned her head away.

"Does Mrs. Dodge know?" Rose asked.

"Sure she does." Isabel started sewing again. "Maybe not with her head. I bet her head doesn't know. But she knows with her body. Every woman knows in her body when her husband's been astray, the first time he touches her after. It was that way with me and my Micky before he got done in in a bar fight.

A handsome, charming devil he was, but always straying. At least I knew with my head, too. It's easier that way."

"Oh!" Rose said. "Maybe that's why Mrs. Dodge is so mean and judgmental to Lisbeth." Lisbeth made a small sound and turned her body away from the table. "What is it, Lisbeth?"

"I've done bad. How could I know which one was married, committing … what was that word?"

"Adultery," Rose said gently. "You couldn't know unless they told you."

"They didn't talk much." Lisbeth covered her face with her hands.

Rose put an arm around her. "It's all over now. Jesus understands you didn't know. And you've been baptized, all your sin washed away."

"I wish I could forget."

Isabel shook her head slowly. "Some things you can't forget, much as you wish you could. But they make you wiser, more understanding of others. And today you began a new life."

"And we're making you new clothes," Lily said.

Lisbeth sighed and turned back to her sewing. They stitched in silence.

"Smythe's the one who really did bad," Isabel said after a while, "forcing you to do that work like he did. It's sad. He never would've done that before Ginny died."

"What was he like before Ginny died?" Rose asked.

"I used to come into town for a day or two to get provisions and take a break from the homestead," Isabel said, as she pushed her needle in and out through the thick cloth. "I'd stay at Hannah's, help her out a little in return. Sometimes I'd meet Ella at the store and we'd have coffee together at Elsie's café. We got to be friends. Ella's a good woman."

"She tried to protect us from Smythe that day we went in there," Lily said.

"Yes, she would. Over time, she told me a lot about Smythe and their life there. Some she heard herself, and some she got from talking to the other women." Isabel tucked a stray gray lock of hair behind her ear and continued sewing as she told her story.

"Seems he was the youngest of eight. His mother was fed up with kids and especially him, 'cause he was lively and mischievous. She was strict Baptist, always beating him for most anything he did, yelling at him he was sinful while she beat him. Story is he got that scar on his face from his ma whacking him with an iron skillet. So he grew up angry and hating religion and ran away when he was fourteen.

"He got a job working in the stables of a fine household. The woman of the house—she wasn't married—took to him. He must of been a good-looking boy. He's still good looking when he turns on the charm. She took him for her lover, educated him, dressed him up fine, took him about with her to concerts and plays, got him thinking he was something special. Then she got tired of him and sent him off."

"He still has some of those airs," Lisbeth said.

"Next he got a job on a steam ship on the Mississippi," Isabel went on. "That's when he met Ginny. She was a runaway, too. She could sing and dance and was part of the show they put on for the passengers. Smythe was bold and asked her to dance, and pretty soon became part of the show, a fancy dancing pair."

"I remember them dancing," Lisbeth said. "Everyone would shout and cheer and he'd swing her right off her feet."

"I saw them, too. They were fine. Then 'round about '58," Isabel continued, "he heard news of the gold find here and he and Ginny came to start a saloon. Me and Ed came just a year later and it was thriving. They'd have parties in that big room with the piano, and give shows, some of the men doing a piece, and him and Ginny dancing. Lots of music. After a bit, a couple of professional fancy women came and offered to work there."

"Suzy and Belle," Lisbeth put in.

"So that was the start of the brothel. Smythe built on a second floor with rooms for the women, and others came, some professionals like Suzy and Belle, some like Ella and your ma who had no place else to go. Ella said it wasn't bad then. Ginny took good care of the women, got 'em pretty clothes and something to keep 'em from having babies, checked all the men for disease."

"Ginny was good to me, too," Lisbeth said. "I was only little, but she'd hold me in her lap and sing to me sometimes when my mama was busy."

Isabel nodded. "She was a bright thing. Ed and I would go to their shows sometimes. She was so pretty, red-gold hair and always smiling. And Smythe was gone on her; you could tell by how he looked at her. She was never part of the brothel. He kept her to himself.

"Just before she died there was some talk that a customer, Bud his name was, had a big crush on her and kept asking Smythe to let him take her upstairs. Smythe got real angry at him. The day Ginny died, she'd gone up on the mountain to help a sick woman with a baby. Smythe went into a rage, thinking she'd gone to visit Bud who lived up that way, too, but she hadn't. Ella said she never would have. She loved Smythe as much as he did her. She was just helping that sick woman.

"It was when she came back from that trip, that she was kicked by her horse as she was stabling it, and she died."

"She wasn't," Lisbeth broke in.

"Wasn't what?"

"Kicked by her horse. Smythe killed her."

"Killed her?" Isabel's head snapped up. The twins froze. All three stared at Lisbeth.

"He trampled her. With his horse."

"How——? That's not what Ella said."

"I … I saw it. My mama's room looked out over the stable. She came riding in real fast, him after her, yelling. She rode her horse into the stable … he just waited for her. When she came out, she ran for the back door, and he just … rode over her."

"Dear Jesus!" Isabel exclaimed.

"I ran and hid. I told my mama and she said I should never tell anyone …" Lisbeth pressed her hands to her mouth. "And now I have. I didn't mean to. Don't tell. Don't tell, or maybe he'll kill me." Lisbeth tensed with fear, her eyes wide and dark.

Isabel reached across the table and touched Lisbeth's arm. "We won't tell. But what happened next? Ella told me as how they had her laid out in the big room with all the women weeping around her."

Lisbeth drew her hands down from her mouth. "Yes. I was there with my mama. All the women were talking about her and crying. Candy said she was so kind, how the last thing she'd done was help that woman up on the mountain. Then Smythe—his face got white pale, all twisted, and he let out a roar that scared me so bad I hid my face against my mama. When I looked out again, he was gone and all the women huddled together."

Lisbeth laid her head on the table and wept. Rose stroked her hair. Isabel sat very still with her mouth slightly open. "That makes sense, that makes sense," she said finally. "In a jealous rage he killed the one he loved most, maybe the only one he ever loved, and then finds out—no wonder he's turned so sour. Ah, dearie, it's okay to cry. 'Tis a sad story."

"Sad and scary," Lily murmured. She slid close to Lisbeth and put an arm around her. "Don't worry. We won't tell. But I'm more scared of him than ever now, knowing he could kill."

Isabel looked around at the three girls. "Okay. We've got a secret to keep to protect Lisbeth, to protect all of us. I'd like to go to Sheriff Parker, but we couldn't prove anything, and it's been years. Lisbeth kept her secret all this time. Can you two keep a secret?"

The twins' eyes met, their own secret between them. "We can," Lily said.

"And one other thing," Isabel added. "No talk about Mr. Dodge. The last thing poor Mrs. Dodge needs is for that to come to her through gossip."

The three girls nodded.

~

Saturday evening, just after supper, when the family was gathered around the hearth, the lamps lit, Gabe came. He looked tired but very pleased with himself. "I got my cabin fixed up, and I'm set to take my wife home. Would you all like to come and see?"

"Yes, let's." Lily jumped up. "Did you get the floor in?"

"I did." Gabe grinned. "And more. You'll see." He went to Lisbeth and kissed her hand.

Lisbeth got up, suddenly shy. "I'll get my things."

"We'll help you," Rose said.

Gabe and Daniel sat by the fire and talked until the girls returned with Lisbeth's bundle, bigger now with the new gown inside.

Rose took Lisbeth's coat down from the hook by the door. "This is what we've been doing," she said to Gabe as she helped Lisbeth into it. "Doesn't she look pretty?"

Gabe had been generous with the cloth. The coat was long and full with a hood that tied snugly around Lisbeth's face. The deep brown of the fabric matched her eyes.

"She does." Gabe tilted his head to one side, surveying her. "I got me the prettiest wife in all the Colorado Territory."

"And it's warm," Lisbeth said, looking gratefully at Gabe.

Daniel, Isabel, and the twins bundled up, and they all walked to Gabe's cabin under the cold winter stars, the snow squeaking under their feet.

Gabe had left a lantern lit inside, and the light flowed out when he opened the door. He picked Lisbeth up in his arms and carried her over the threshold. He gently kissed her cheek as he set her down. The lamplight shone on the new wood floor. The little potbellied stove had been polished and warmed the small room. A length of dark red cloth hung in front of the window. On the west wall was a wide new bed frame, topped with a mattress and a down comforter.

"This is real homey," Isabel commented.

"I made the bed nice and wide for you and the babe," Gabe said to Lisbeth. "And I made myself a sleeping nook in the corner of the shop." He opened the door he had put in between the cabin and the shop and showed them.

Lisbeth stood silent in the middle of the room.

"How do you like it?" Rose asked.

"It looks fine."

Rose put an arm around her. "Maybe you should take off your coat. You're home."

"I'll help you." Gabe came and took her coat and laid it on the bed with her bundle.

"We'll go along now," Daniel said, "and let you two get settled."

Lisbeth turned suddenly and clung to Rose and Lily. "Thank you so much for helping me. I'll miss you." She hid her face in Rose's shoulder. Gabe watched, his brow furrowed with concern.

Rose held her close; Lily stroked her hair. "We'll see you every day," Rose assured her. "And tomorrow in church."

"Come on." Daniel opened the door. Cold air flowed in. "Let's go. Good night, Gabe and Lisbeth."

The twins kissed Lisbeth and followed Daniel out the door. Isabel gave her a hug and came out last, closing the door behind her.

As they walked home, Isabel said, "She's scared. Scared to be alone with a man, even though he's told her she's safe. She's been hurt so bad."

"And scared to go to church tomorrow," Rose added.

Daniel looked over at Rose. "I'll do what I can about that."

Lily and Rose waited for Lisbeth by the church door, watching through the window. Down the hill and across the road, they saw the door of Gabe's cabin open and Gabe and Lisbeth come out. It was snowing again, a fine, drifting snow. Gabe took Lisbeth's hand and tucked it into the fold of his arm, then walked with her across the road and up the hill. Other parishioners arrived and stared at them. When Gabe stopped to speak to some of them, gesturing to introduce his wife, Lisbeth stood bravely beside him, but even from a distance the twins could feel her fear.

As soon as they came through the door, the twins hugged Lisbeth. Then, all at once, the back of the church became a lively scene. Mayor Wilgus arrived and congratulated Gabe in his booming voice. Burt and Elsie came in with their five children, Nathan and Mattie right behind them with their three.

Nathan clapped Gabe on the shoulder. "How did the floor come out?"

Elsie stopped to admire Lisbeth's coat. "You did a beautiful job on that," she said to the twins. "Did you make up the gown, too?"

Lisbeth shyly undid her coat so Elsie could see the gown. "Lovely," she said. "Stop it, Billy. Let go, Tessy." A sigh of exasperation. "Go with Annabelle now."

The Dodges had come in. Isabel emerged from the children's room and she and Annabelle took the little ones away. Mrs. Dodge lowered her eyes. Mr. Dodge glanced nervously at Lisbeth and hurried his wife to their pew, followed by Gerald with the collection basket.

Mattie held out her hands to Lisbeth. "I am so happy to see you here, and hoping you and Gabe will come visit us soon."

Hannah bustled in with her sons. "Good morning, everybody. Lily and Rose, you should be starting the music. Go sit down, all of you. You're blocking the doorway."

In the flurry that followed, Gabe led Lisbeth to a pew and sat close beside her, and Lily and Rose went to the front and began playing "Jesu, Joy of Man's Desiring." The congregation flowed in. Daniel took his place behind the pulpit. Even as the service began, there were whispers and many curious glances directed at Gabe and Lisbeth.

Daniel opened his Bible. "Our scripture this morning is Luke 7:1-7, the parable of the lost sheep." The sanctuary was hushed as he read the story. When he finished reading, Daniel looked up from his Bible, his eyes moving over his congregation. "Today," he said, "we welcome a new member to our fellowship, Mrs. Gabriel Archen. Thursday was a blessed day when she came to me, confessing her commitment to Christ and asking to be baptized. Mr. Archen has taken her under his protection. Thursday morning, I baptized her and married them in a small ceremony in my home, witnessed by Mr. Hill, Mrs. Anderson, Mrs. Flannagan, and my daughters, Miss Rose and Miss Lily."

A stir moved through the congregation. Daniel waited until it settled, then spoke again.

"Some of you know Mrs. Archen as Lisbeth. She has fled from an unspeakable slavery, right here is this town, imposed on her, child that she is, against her will. Wednesday night she came here after prayer meeting, seeking the sanctuary of the church, shivering with cold because she dared not come in. I learned that for months she had hidden outside the church window to hear the Gospel, afraid to be seen, so greatly did her soul hunger for salvation, so much did she fear the judgment of you good people. Had I only known, we could have rescued her sooner and spared her much suffering."

Daniel paused and looked around fiercely. "I want it to be clear, that as long as I am pastor of this church, anyone who truly seeks Christ is welcome here. I do not want to hear again of someone hiding, afraid to enter. We are all sinners, daily sin against God's holy will. 'Judge not that ye be not judged.' And we are all Christ's ministers. It is not up to me alone to seek the lost and bring them into the fold. I ask you to be vigilant, guarding against your own sinful ways, your judgments. Join me in seeking out those who are ready to receive Christ's salvation, *no matter who they are or what their past has been.*"

He paused again. There was not a sound in the sanctuary. Daniel's voice softened. "I call on all of you, especially you ladies, to welcome Mrs. Archen and assist her in her transition to her new life."

Everyone turned to look at Lisbeth. Her head was bent, her cheeks crimson. Gabe put his arm firmly around her shoulders. Daniel drew in a long breath and proceeded with his sermon on the lost that are found.

It took some time for Lisbeth to feel comfortable in the church and the society of the town. Hannah, Elsie, Mattie, Isabel, and the twins were her staunch supporters. It didn't hurt that Ken Hill's idea was whispered in the inner circles of the church. And everyone loved Gabe. As the snow melted and people began coming to the shop again, they found Lisbeth handling the cash register and taking orders. Then her sweet, gentle ways won her friends on her own account. By the time her baby was born in the spring, no one seemed to remember its source, and simply welcomed little Lucia as Gabe's child.

# Part 4

# THE NEW LIFE

## Chapter 42

# *Rachel*

At last the days lengthened, the sun grew warmer, and the snow began to melt. The ice broke up in the river and its song grew loud, its waters running swift and high. People emerged from their houses and greeted one another on the roads, and Isabel and the twins began to plant their garden.

One lovely May morning, the twins hitched Dawnstar to their cart and went to the store a little later than usual. They finally had all of the garden planted, and were feeling easy and happy in the warm sunshine. There were lots of folks in the store, and they took their time, visiting as they bought their groceries.

Just as they were loading their bags into the cart, the stage coach arrived. Gerald hurried by them to meet it and pick up the mail. The twins stopped to watch.

The driver jumped down from his high seat and opened the door. The first person out was a tall, thin man who hurried into the store without speaking to anyone. Next a young woman alighted with a sleeping baby in her arms. She got out carefully, cradling the baby's head against her shoulder with her hand. The driver pulled several bags out of the coach and set them on the ground beside her. The twins stared, their mouths open in astonishment.

The driver climbed up to the top of the coach, swung a trunk down, and dropped it with a thump in the dusty path. The woman sat down on it, rocking her child.

"It's Rachel!" Lily whispered. "How could it be?"

Excitement and joy welled up in the twins, then fear. "But she mustn't —" Rose whispered back.

"No. Quick."

They approached Rachel. She was clearly exhausted. Her face was pale, there were dark circles under her eyes, and her fine clothing was wrinkled and stained.

"Good morning, ma'am," Lily said.

Rachel lifted her head. Her weary face broke into a wide smile of recognition. As she turned to greet them, her sleeve brushed the baby's feet. One small shoe fell onto the ground. Rose bent to pick it up. As she handed it to Rachel, she whispered, "Pretend you don't know us."

Rachel looked confused for a moment, then nodded, but her face still shone with relief. The child stirred on her shoulder and whimpered. "Hush," she murmured, and shifted the baby into the curve of her arm. It pressed its face against her bosom.

"Welcome to Gold Creek," Rose said aloud. "Can we help you?"

"Thank you," Rachel answered, dropping into the pretense. "Yes. I've had a very long journey and need a place to rest and feed my baby. I've heard there was a boarding house here. Could you direct me?"

"Hannah's," Lily said. "It's a good place, clean and comfortable. We have our cart. We'd be happy to take you there." She held out her hand. "My name is Lily Wright, and this is my sister, Rose."

"Good to meet you, Miss Lily, Miss Rose. We'd be very grateful for a lift to the boarding house. My name is Mrs. Decker." She looked down with tender pride at the child in her arms. "And this is Joshua."

The twins' eyes met in delight, the thought flashing between them: It *is* a boy. They bent over to look at him. "He's so sweet," Lily murmured.

"He is, he's a very sweet child," Rachel said, "but the trip has been hard on him. He's cried a lot. I'm glad he's sleeping now."

While they talked, there was a bustle of activity around them. The stage driver unloaded several large boxes. Burt came out of the store to get them, followed by Elsie, trailing Billy and Tessy. The stage driver and Gerald exchanged packets of mail.

Elsie came up to greet Rachel. "I'm Elsie Martin," she said, holding out her hand. "Welcome to town. Have you come to stay?"

"I hope so," Rachel answered. "I'm a schoolmarm. I heard you didn't have one here and came to offer my services."

"A schoolmarm!" Elsie exclaimed. "Oh, we need you. Lots of kids here in this valley, and no school. They're not learning 'cepting what their parents can teach them, and most of us too busy. These here are Tessy and Billy, two of my five. I got two older boys—heaven knows where they are—and a new baby. A schoolmarm. You'll be mighty welcome. But you look tuckered out. Where'd you come from?"

Rachel smiled at the children. "Boston," she answered.

"Boston, now that's a far piece. It's a brutal trip, coming by stage, especially with that little one. I've got a café in back, if you'd like some refreshment."

The thin man emerged from the store and climbed back into the stage. The driver hopped up onto his high seat. "Bye, Mrs. Decker," he said, looking down at her. "Hope it works out for you here." He nodded to Burt, flicked the reins, and pulled out onto Mill Road.

"Thank you," Rachel said to Elsie, "but Miss Rose and Miss Lily have kindly offered to take me to the boarding house. I'd like to get settled."

Elsie nodded. "Hannah'll take good care of you."

Gerald stood with one foot on the bench by the door, sorting through the packet of mail. "Miss Rose, here's a letter for your pa."

"Probably from Grandma Wright." She took the letter and slipped it into her apron pocket. "Gerald, could you help us lift Mrs. Decker's trunk into our cart?"

A few minutes later, Lily spoke to Dawnstar, and drove the cart out onto the road. The baby had started crying when Rachel climbed up onto the seat between the twins. She propped him onto her shoulder and patted his back.

"Rach … Mrs. Decker," Rose began.

"Please call me Rachel. I said you could, long ago. Do you remember?"

"Yes. We need to talk with you before we go to Hannah's."

Joshua cried louder. "All right." Rachel shifted him. "Hush now, sweetheart. But first I need to take care of Joshua."

"Let's go down here a little farther," Lily said as they crossed the bridge. She turned off the road and guided Dawnstar along soft grass by the river's edge. "There's a nice place under the trees. It's pretty private."

She stopped the cart under a big cottonwood, its new green-gold leaves unfurling in the spring sunshine, rippling in the light breeze off the water.

Rachel looked around. "This is lovely."

Soon they were settled under the cottonwood. When she had changed Joshua's napkin and put him to her breast, Rachel leaned back against the trunk of the tree with a long sigh. "There. I can talk now."

The twins were bursting with questions.

"How could you come here?"

"What about Mr. Decker?"

"Mr. Decker died in March," Rachel said quietly. "He had another one of his spells, and that time it killed him."

"He's *dead?*" Lily asked.

"Yes. Nell wrote me and I came back to Boston. I was away visiting my aunt." She stopped. Color rose in her cheeks. "I went there to have Joshua. Mr. Decker didn't want a child."

"We know," Rose said.

Rachel looked up, startled. "You know?"

"That's why we want to talk to you," Lily said. "We know about you and Papa."

"Oh!" She turned her face away from them and closed her eyes. "There was talk then, after I left?"

"No," Rose said. "We only knew because we overheard Papa confessing to Mr. Peabody, and later Becky talking to Nell. So we know why you had to run away and why the Presbytery sent Papa here."

"The Presbytery knew then?"

"Yes. Mr. Decker told them. But they kept it a secret."

"How awful! How awful for your father."

"It was," Lily said. "But he's done really well here. Everybody respects him and he wouldn't want … Well, if anyone knew …"

"Oh!" Rachel hunched her shoulders and bent her head. "Maybe I should go away."

"No." Rose touched her shoulder. "You're free now."

"Papa can marry you," Lily said.

"You just need to pretend you don't know him. Then he can court you—"

"And marry you. And you and Joshua can come live with us and be part of our family."

Rachel half-laughed, half-sobbed. "You have it all figured out. But what if he doesn't want to marry me? Perhaps he's planning to marry someone else."

"You came all this way, not knowing?" Rose asked. "But he wouldn't marry anyone else. He loves you. We know."

"We've prayed for you," Lily said, "but we never dreamed— I'm glad Mr. Decker died. It serves him right. We heard Nell say how he beat you."

Rachel began weeping softly, hanging her head, folding the shawl closer around her baby. The twins sat beside her, longing to embrace her but not quite daring. They smoothed her back with gentle hands.

"You know then," she said after a while. "And still you welcome me."

"Of course."

"We're so glad to see you, and Joshua, our little brother."

"Papa will be so happy."

Rachel lifted her head. "I sent him a letter, telling him I was coming. Do you know if he got it?"

Rose frowned. "I don't think so. We pick up all the mail and I haven't seen it."

"He would have been really excited," Lily said. "We would have known."

"Wait a minute." Rose reached into her apron pocket. "Is this it?"

Rachel looked at the letter in Rose's hand. "Yes. I sent it days before I left, and it took longer to get here than I did. So he doesn't even know I was coming. Oh, dear."

"He'll be happy. We know he will."

Rachel straightened and sighed. Joshua had fallen asleep. She shifted him off her breast and laid him in her lap. His rosy lips were still parted, his long lashes dark on his round cheeks. The twins hung over him, adoring.

"He's beautiful," Lily whispered.

"I think he looks like Papa," Rose said, "except for his eyes being brown like yours."

Rachel traced his cheek lightly with her fingertip. "I think so, too." She sighed. "Is there anything else we need to speak of?"

"I don't think so," Lily said.

Hannah welcomed them warmly and showed Rachel to a pleasant room at the back of the house, looking out onto the pasture. The twins stayed with her for several hours. She didn't feel she could rest until she was clean, she told them, so they played with Joshua in the parlor while she bathed in the big tub of hot water Ned and Jim carried into her room. Joshua warmed to the twins, his solemn stares blossoming into smiles, and then laughter when the twins chased him, as he crawled rapidly around and under the furniture in the parlor.

At noon Hannah brought lunch to the room; Rachel didn't feel ready yet to meet new people. Afterward, the twins helped give Joshua a bath and Rachel let them dress him in clean clothes. When they left, Rachel was stretched out on the bed, nursing Joshua, almost asleep as she thanked them for their help and murmured good-bye.

~

Daniel rode slowly up the hill toward home, enjoying the soft air of the late May afternoon. He had stopped by Gabe's, as he often did at the end of his day, and Gabe had told him that a young woman, a widow with a baby, had come to town, a schoolmarm wanting to start a school. Elsie had met her, was excited about the school and had spread the news. Daniel was pleased with the idea of having a school in his parish. She could hold her classes in the church until a school house could be built.

He dismounted and led Shadow up the path toward the pasture. As he passed the house, he heard one of the twins call to the other, "Here comes Papa." She waved to him from the porch. "Hi, Papa." There was excitement in her voice.

What now? he wondered. Are they up to something? Then he reminded himself that they'd been very responsible and well-behaved all winter, ever since their talk after the Aaron Jenkins affair. He noticed as he passed that the garden was all in. They worked hard, he thought with appreciation.

He stopped to clean up in the wash area outside the kitchen. As soon as he came through the door, the twins were waiting for him, bursting with some news. They caught him by his hands and led him to the living room.

"You have a letter," one told him.

"You'd better sit down to read it," the other said.

He stood in front of his chair. "What? Is it bad news then?" The way they were smiling, it didn't look like bad news. "You act as if you know what's in it."

"We do."

One of them took an envelope out of her apron pocket and handed it to him. The return address said "Mrs. Ebenezer Decker." He closed his eyes, opened them, and looked again. Slowly he sank into his chair.

"Open it," one of the twins urged.

Trying to control the shaking in his hands, he opened the envelope and spread the letter out on his knee. A faint fragrance floated up to him, her fragrance. The letter was written on fine linen paper with a purple flower design along the left border.

*Dear Daniel,*

*I hope this letter finds you and your daughters well. I am glad to finally be able to send you news, having learned your address from Nell, who got it from Becky.*

*My aunt received me kindly when I fled from Mr. Decker, and our son was born May 9th, just a year ago now. He is a fine healthy boy, sweet-tempered and agreeable.*

*We stayed with my aunt until last March, when I received a letter from Nell telling me that Mr. Decker had died from one of his spells and his lawyer wanted me to come back to Boston to settle his estate. With his help, I have sold the house, given Nell and John a pension, and am now preparing to leave in a few days to come to you, to bring you your son, and myself, if you will have me.*

*It has been a long year. I have missed you sorely and rejoice in the hope that I may see you again soon.*

*Your devoted friend, Rachel*

The twins had been so quiet as he read that he had forgotten they were there. Unbelieving, he read the letter through again. Then joy surged through him. "Rachel!" he exclaimed aloud. He remembered the twins then, and turned to them. "Rachel is coming with her son."

They were beaming at him, all but exploding with excitement.

"How did you know?" he asked then. "You said you knew what was in the letter."

"Because she's here."

"She came on the stage today, the same stage that brought her letter."

"We were there when she arrived—"

"And we took her to Hannah's."

Daniel sprang out of his chair. "She's at Hannah's? Now?"

"Papa, wait." They grabbed his arms from either side and pulled him back down into his chair. "She doesn't want to see you until tomorrow."

"Until she's rested."

"And Papa, you have to be discreet."

"Discreet! *You're* telling *me* to be discreet?"

"You don't want the whole town to even guess about you and Rachel."

"Oh!" Daniel rubbed his brow. "Yes. Yes, you're right."

The twins were kneeling beside his chair. He looked at them more closely and saw that it was Rose who was speaking to him. "It's okay, Papa. We have it all figured out. We told her right away to pretend not to know us. Then we talked with her and we made a plan."

Lily took it up. "You don't know her. You never met her before. She came here to be the schoolmarm."

"She's the schoolmarm Gabe was talking about?"

"Yes. Tomorrow you go call on her, to talk to her about coming to church and about her school. You see how pretty she is so you court her—properly—and then you can marry her, and no one ever needs to know that you're Joshua's real papa."

"Joshua? That's his name?"

"Yes." Rose was smiling. "He's very cute. You'll love him."

Daniel couldn't sit still. He got up abruptly, brushed the twins aside, and strode toward the door. Again they caught him by the arms.

"You mustn't go see her until tomorrow."

"I won't."

"Supper's almost ready."

"I'm not hungry."

He crossed the porch in three strides, ran down the steps, around the house, and onto the hillside. He ran straight up, leaped over the little stream, and on up and up. He stopped finally, out of breath, heart pounding, and turned to look back over the valley and the little town down below nestled on its western edge. His house, just below him, its sod roof melting into the hillside. Soon she would come to live there with him, his wife. And a little boy named Joshua, his son.

Rachel. Her image filled his heart, her wide dark eyes, her full breasts. Fire raced through him as he remembered laying his face against their softness and smoothness. It's all right, he told himself. I will marry her. It's not a sin to love your wife.

Then the realization came. God had forgiven them, He must have forgiven them to bring them together again. Daniel choked on a sob. In all his prayers he had never dreamed, never dared to pray for this, that she would come to him with their son, free, that he could marry her.

He turned and flung himself face down on the breast of the hill, the rough grass against his cheek, and wept. It seemed that the earth rocked him, the wide sky enfolded him. His gratitude was so deep he could find no words to pray, but knew that God understood his tears. Forgiven and gifted beyond all hope.

~

"You're taking the buggy, just to go to Hannah's?" Lily asked. The twins had come out to say good-bye to him.

"Well, I thought I might take Rachel to see the church, and maybe for a tour of the town."

"Papa, be careful."

"Please be careful."

"We don't want you to be sent away again."

"We like it here."

Their upturned faces looked young and vulnerable in the morning sunlight. What had it cost them when he had been sent away the first time? He hadn't really thought of that before.

"I'll be careful. I like it here, too."

"You look very nice Papa." That was Rose.

Lily tilted her head. "You really do."

Daniel smiled down at them, feeling them to be allies, co-conspirators. He flicked the reins on Shadow's back and started off.

He drove slowly. The euphoria of the night before had subsided into the sober reality that he must indeed be careful. He reminded himself that he and Rachel had kept their secret for months in Boston. They could do it again. But he didn't like deceit, and he would have to deceive those he was closest to— Gabe, Nathan, Andrew. No one must know.

He kept going slowly, holding Shadow back. She danced a little, letting him know she wanted to get moving. Once they were married, he thought, it would be easier. He would adopt Joshua and everyone would just accept them as a family.

As he turned down Bridge Road, his stomach flip-flopped. Would Rachel be able to carry off the pretense? In Boston she had been sheltered by being Ebenezer's wife, but here? He didn't know. He realized that, in many ways, he didn't know her at all. Their relationship had been so focused on Ebenezer's abuse and their own swift passion, intensified by guilt and secrecy. What would she be like now?

Hannah was sweeping the front porch when he arrived. "Come on in, Reverend," she greeted him, setting her broom aside. "It's always good to see you."

"And good to see you. How are things at Hannah's boarding house this morning?"

"Busy." She tucked a stray blond wisp behind her ear. "But that's how I like it."

"I hear you have a new boarder, a lady come to town to be a schoolmarm."

"Yes. A lovely young lady, a widow, with the cutest baby boy."

"So I heard from Lily and Rose."

"She created quite a stir at supper last night. Mayor Wilgus was beside himself offering her tours, plans to build a school house, you can imagine. Mr. Budke was stuttering so badly you couldn't understand a word he was saying, and Mr. Hill never took his eyes off her, peering at her through those spectacles of his. It's not often a pretty young single woman shows up in town."

Daniel felt a surge of jealousy. She's mine, he almost said. Instead he said, "I came to call on her to invite her to prayer meeting this evening, and to chat with her about her plans for a school. Is she in?"

"She is. She's resting in her room, but I know she'd like to meet you. She was asking about what kind of church we had in town, and about you. I told her you were a mighty fine minister." She smiled at him. "Have a seat in the parlor. I'll tell her you're here."

Daniel sat down on the edge of the couch. He was sweating. He could feel the trickle running down inside his blue linen shirt. Footsteps. Hannah came through the parlor door, followed by Rachel, her child on her hip.

He stood.

"Mrs. Decker," Hannah said. "This is Reverend Wright. Reverend, Mrs. Decker."

She was even more beautiful than he remembered, her bosom fuller, her cheeks smooth and pink with no bruises, her dark eyes wide. Her smile was so full of joy and welcoming that he had to struggle to contain himself. She stepped forward and held out her hand.

"I'm glad to meet you Reverend Wright."

Her slender hand in his. She was managing the pretense. He must, too.

"I'm glad to meet you, Mrs. Decker. And this must be Joshua. My daughters are enchanted with him."

"Your daughters were very kind to me yesterday. They are lovely young ladies. And they definitely won Joshua's heart."

Daniel bent his head to smile at Joshua. Joshua half-hid his face against Rachel's shoulder, then shyly smiled back. Daniel's heart ached with love. My son! He was still holding Rachel's hand.

"Sit down now," Hannah ordered, as was her way. "Can I bring you some tea?"

Rachel withdrew her hand and seated herself gracefully on the couch, settling Joshua on her knee. Daniel was in a daze. Somehow he found the chair Hannah indicated and sat down.

"I'd love some tea," Rachel was saying. "Do you have more of that mint we had last night?"

"We do. Fresh out of the garden. How about you, Reverend?"

"That sounds good to me, too."

Hannah bustled away. As soon as she was gone, Daniel leaned out of his chair, holding out his arms. "Rachel."

She held up her hand, palm out. "No, Daniel," she said softly. "We must be careful. The door is open."

He sat back, almost missing the chair. Although she would not embrace him, her eyes were full of tears and that special look of love that he remembered. He found the chair with his sit bones, but still leaned forward to her.

"I can't believe you're really here. And free! That wicked Ebenezer—dead of his own intemperance."

"Don't call him wicked. He was brutal to me, to be sure, but it's sad, really. I think he loved me, but just couldn't bear the passion that can be part of love. I pray for his soul that he may have more peace now than he knew in his life."

Joshua wiggled in her lap. She set him down and he dropped to his hands and knees and took off across the room.

Daniel watched him with wonder. "He crawls fast."

Joshua reached the far end of the room, pulled himself up on a chair, and crowed loudly.

"Look at you!" Rachel called to him, laughing with pride and delight. She turned to Daniel, hesitant, color rising in her cheeks. "Daniel, is it all right that I came? Are you glad?"

"Glad!" Daniel was out of his chair, kneeling in front of her. "There is no greater gift God could have sent me."

He was reaching to embrace her when they heard Hannah's brisk footsteps approaching. He scrambled for his chair. Rachel smothered a smile as he almost missed it a second time.

Hannah bustled in. Daniel saw with a sinking heart that there were three cups on the tea tray. She pulled up a low table, set the tray on it, and settled herself on the couch beside Rachel.

"Now where's that little boy? Oh, there he is." Joshua had hold of the chair leg and was starting to drag it. "Such an active little fellow."

She poured tea and handed each of them a cup. "Tell us," she said to Rachel, "what are your plans for a school?"

Rachel sipped her tea. "This is so delicious. No, Joshua!" She was up and across the room in a flash, catching his little fist just as he was about to pull the cloth off a table with a lamp on it. She brought him back, took some nesting metal cups out of her apron pocket, and settled him at her feet with the cups. He began banging them on the wood floor.

That boy will need some discipline, Daniel thought.

"About the school." Rachel turned to Hannah. "I'm assuming most of the school-age children will be needed to help out at home during the summer. I was thinking that I would spend the next couple of months visiting the families, getting to know the children, gathering supplies. Then start the school in the fall. We'll need a place. Mayor Wilgus was enthusiastic about building a school house, but I would need to know first how many families are interested."

"You could use the church," Daniel began. "We have a children's room behind the sanctuary—"

Joshua banged his finger between two of the cups and started to cry. Rachel scooped him up. "Hush, sweetheart." She looked over at Daniel. "I'm sorry. It's hard to talk with a baby around."

"I'd be happy to take you there, so you could see if it would work for your school," Daniel continued.

Joshua pulled at the lacing on the front of Rachel's dress. Daniel stared.

"I need to feed him," Rachel said, restraining both his little hands with one of hers. "Then we could go. Would you mind waiting just a little while?"

Daniel tore his eyes away from her bosom. "No, no. That's fine. I can wait."

"Once he's fed, leave the baby with me," Hannah said. "It's been years since I've had a baby boy to play with. Then you can see the church without distraction. Would you like some more tea while you wait, Reverend?"

Daniel was still trying to get his mind off Rachel's bosom. "Yes. Yes, thank you."

"That's settled then," Hannah said to Rachel. "You go feed him, then bring him down to the kitchen. I've got Annabelle helping me today. Between the two of us, we'll keep him out of trouble."

~

Daniel felt as if he were in a dream as he guided the buggy down Gold Creek Road. Rachel sat beside him, a russet shawl wrapped around her shoulders, a matching hat covering her dark hair. He could hardly keep his eyes on the road. "It rejoices my heart to see you looking so well," he said. "I can't tell you how worried I've been, remembering how I last saw you, not knowing all this long year and more, how you were."

Rachel turned to him. "That was a bad day, that last day you saw me. But I escaped, thanks to John and Nell. And my aunt was kind. I hardly knew her, you know. She was the wife of my uncle, my guardian after my parents were killed in the carriage accident. He sent me off to a finishing school and I never returned to his home, just went straight from school to teach at the orphanage. He's dead now, but she wrote to me when I was in school, and, bless her, was there to offer me a refuge in my time of need."

"I feared you would die in childbirth."

"As you see, I didn't."

"I wanted so to be with you, to care for you, to hold our child."

"We are here now." She touched his hand. "Tell me how it has been for you. I was devastated to learn from Nell that you had left Boston. She didn't say so, but I knew you had fled from disgrace, and I the cause."

"No, I was the cause. But thanks to God's grace, I was given another chance."

"Yes. Mrs. Anderson says you have created a miracle, building the church so fast. Clearly you are well-loved here, as you were in Boston."

"It has gone well. The Lord has blessed my efforts. And now—Rachel, God must have forgiven us. I have prayed and prayed for forgiveness. He must have forgiven us to send you to me, you and Joshua, and you free."

"God is love," Rachel said softly, "and love forgives."

They jogged along between the brick buildings. Several people waved and called, "Good morning, Preacher," and stared curiously at Rachel. She nodded her head in greeting.

"Tell me," she said, "how was your journey?"

"We had many adventures. At one river crossing, I became unconscious from hitting my head on a rock and would have drowned if the twins hadn't pulled me out. And there was a stampede when a herd of buffalo crossed our path. One child died. But that was our only loss. We had a good guide. How was your journey? The plains are beautiful, aren't they? Did you see the stars at night?"

"I saw almost nothing on my journey. The windows of the stage coach were coated with dust. We could only get out for a few minutes when they changed horses. Then the immensity of the plains terrified me. It still seems so different … so wide, so few trees, and the mountains … Do you like it here?"

"Yes, I do. I like riding all over the valley to visit my people, being outdoors, helping them with their homestead tasks. I helped bring the logs for the church down from the mountains with the men in my parish. I like the openness of the land. And the people. It's different than in Boston. People share and care for each other, because they need each other, because life is harder and they don't have as much. I hope you'll like it, too, when you get used to it."

"And your daughters? How do they like it here?"

"They like it. They just told me that this morning." Daniel smiled. "Along with telling me to be discreet in courting you."

"They've grown up so much. When I knew them in Boston, they were sweet, but in spite of their years, seemed more like children than young ladies. But yesterday—they were so quick to see the situation and warn me. And so helpful."

"They're good girls, but high spirited and sometimes mischievous. I'm glad you're here now, to help me guide them. They need a woman."

Daniel turned up the road to the church and stopped the buggy in front. "Here's the church. We built it last summer. It's already full on Sundays. We may need to expand it soon."

"What a beautiful spot."

"Come, let me show you the inside." Daniel climbed down and reached up to help Rachel down. Feeling her waist in his hands, he almost embraced her, but remembered that they stood on the hill in view of the whole town. Trembling with repressed desire, he offered his arm instead and led her up the steps to the door. He fumbled in his pocket for the key.

"You keep the church locked?" Rachel asked.

"I wish we didn't have to, but there are some in town, one man mostly, the saloon keeper, and those who follow him, that don't want us to have a church, and might get in and do damage."

Daniel swung the door open. Inside, it seemed dim after the brightness of spring sunshine. Light slanted in through the high arched windows along the sides and the round window over the altar. Rachel walked down the center aisle, brushing her fingertips over the smooth wood of the pews. "It's lovely," she said. "Simple but elegant. I like the shapes of the windows, and you must have had a good craftsman to do such a fine job on the pews."

"Gabe Archen. He designed the church and guided the church raising. He's still working on the finishing touches."

"You don't have an organ."

"Not yet. For now Rose and Lily lead the hymns with their violin and flute, and Gabe also plays violin."

Rachel wandered down to the front of the church, examining the raised platform and the carved pulpit. "Did Mr. Archen make the pulpit, too?"

"Yes. He is a dear friend. I'll take you to meet him soon. Here's the children's room." Daniel opened a door in the front corner of the sanctuary and led Rachel in. There was very little in the room, only two chairs and an oval braided rug that covered most of the floor. Two windows, one on each side, looked out onto the open plains.

"We don't have much for the children yet. The mothers take turns reading Bible stories and singing hymns with the ones that are old enough." Daniel closed the door to the sanctuary. "Rachel—"

He held out his arms and she came into them, pressed against him, warm, yielding, sweet beyond his wildest fantasies. Her bonnet fell off as she tilted her head up to meet his kiss. Dizzy with pent-up longing he kissed her, kissed her more deeply, and drew her down onto the thick rag rug.

She pulled away from him. He groaned and pulled her back. But she was saying, "No. No, Daniel."

"It's all right." He could barely speak. "No one can see."

She sat up. Her hair had come loose and tumbled over her shoulders. "We must not."

"Why?" He thought he might die of the intensity of his longing.

"Because we aren't married."

"We will be. Soon." He reached for her again, but her hand in the center of his chest held him back.

"You haven't even asked me to marry you."

Daniel sat up then. "But … but you came. You're free. I assumed …"

Although she looked stern, her eyes were laughing. "There are some things one shouldn't assume."

He stared at her, stunned. "Dear God," he muttered. He held out his hands. "Rachel will you marry me?"

Her soft lips parted in a wide, sweet smile. "Yes."

"Then come." He pulled her to him.

"No."

"Now what?"

She twisted free of his embrace. "We're not married."

"But we will be. As soon as I can get a preacher here. Tomorrow. Please come. I've waited for you so long."

"No."

He released her then. "You've changed. You never said no before."

They sat facing each other on the rag rug.

"I *have* changed. I can tell you about it, but you will never know what I have been through, this last year and a half, since I found I was with child. I will not endure that again, the fear, the shame. And then I was protected from the worst of it by Mr. Decker's name. I believe you intend to marry me, but you are mortal. Should I conceive again, and anything happen to you before we wed, I would be in far worse condition than before. And I have Joshua to think of."

Daniel's passion ebbed. "I'm sorry," he said at last. "You're right. I could never know. I only wanted to give you my love, never to cause you pain. And I have caused you so much. How can you forgive me?"

"Ah!" She reached out to touch his face. "It's past now, and all will be healed. Joshua will have his father, and we will be wed. Then I will be yours, to love and cherish as much as you desire, as long as we both shall live."

She stood up and gave him her hand. "We mustn't linger with your buggy outside for all the town to know how long we've been here unchaperoned." She pinned up her hair, straightened her gown, and put on her bonnet.

Daniel was silent as he locked the church door and helped Rachel back into the buggy. "Forgive my impatience," he said, as they drove back toward the boarding house. "It is blessing enough that I have you here with me, that I know that you and Joshua are well. I will wait for the rest."

Daniel called on Rachel every day, and took her all over the town and the valley, to meet the families with children. On one of their excursions, they stopped by Fairdale Ranch. Amy saw them coming and ran to spread the news, so that when they arrived the whole family was gathered to meet them. Even though Daniel tried to act formal with Rachel, he saw the smile that passed between Kate and Andrew and knew by the way they welcomed her that they guessed his feelings for her.

They went for tea at Elsie's café, and people gathered around to meet her, to ask her about her school, to watch curiously how Daniel looked at her, how he took her hand when they stood up to leave.

One week after Rachel arrived, Mayor Wilgus proposed to her. She told him she was promised, and the word was out. All the town knew to whom she was promised. The townspeople gossiped about how their minister had completely lost his heart, anyone could see by the way he looked at her, and it was a good thing, it's better for a minister to be married, and she was clearly a quality lady.

Two weeks after Rachel arrived, Daniel announced their betrothal after Sunday service. As he left the church, Mayor Wilgus approached him. "I thought I was being too hasty," he said with a deep sigh, "asking her only a week after meeting her, but you got ahead of me." He sighed again. "Well, I couldn't lose to a better man. I know you'll be very happy." He shook Daniel's hand and looked as if he might cry.

"You may yet find a good wife," Daniel tried to assure him. "There are new people coming all the time. Someone will have a sister or a daughter who will be just right for you. Pray to the good Lord to send you a wife."

"I have, I do, I will," the mayor sighed.

The wedding was to be held a week and a half later, on a Thursday. The Presbyterian minister in Montview, Reverend Caldwell, would arrive the night before, stay at the boarding house, and perform the ceremony the following morning.

A flurry of preparations began. Rachel and Daniel decided to make it a small wedding, with only the original members of the church and a few close friends invited. The twins helped Rachel make the invitations, then delivered them around the town on Dawnstar. Rachel and Hannah walked in Hannah's garden, choosing the flowers for the bridal bouquet.

"I must have a decent bed," Daniel said to the twins at breakfast one morning. "I can't ask Rachel to sleep on that old mat of mine on the floor."

"You'll need a trundle bed for Joshua, too," Lily said.

"And a rocking chair for her to rock him," Rose added.

"Yes. All of that. I'll go today and talk to Gabe."

Daniel took Rachel with him when he went to see Gabe. Lisbeth was there, sitting in the rocking chair Gabe had crafted for her, rocking her newborn daughter. Rachel sat near her while the men discussed the details of the bed.

Daniel overheard fragments of their conversation. They spoke of their babies, as women will.

"Her name is Lucia," Lisbeth said, her voice soft and shy. "Gabe doesn't mind that she's a girl."

Later he heard Lisbeth saying, "I was scared, but Rose helped me so much."

And Rachel. "How lucky that you had such good help. I was scared, too, but my aunt was even more scared, so I had to be brave."

As they rode back to the boarding house, Rachel remarked, "Lisbeth seems so young to be a mother, so much younger than Gabe. Though they are clearly devoted to each other."

Daniel told her the story of Gabe and Lisbeth.

"That's terrible!" Rachel exclaimed, "to treat a child like that. I'm glad you were able to help her. And Gabe—what a sweet gentle soul he is. No wonder you love him. How does Smythe get away with such evil? I've heard folks speak of him, but I've never seen him. I don't even know where the saloon is."

"It's around the bend in the river at the mouth of the canyon. Smythe was very angry when he lost Lisbeth to us. He threatened me, saying the town wasn't big enough for both of us. He hates religion. But so far he leaves us alone. I don't know what he could do."

Reverend Caldwell arrived the evening before the wedding. Hannah set aside a table in the dining room for a pre-wedding supper for Reverend Caldwell, Daniel's family, and Rachel. Daniel couldn't take his eyes off Rachel, still barely believing that they would really be married the next day. Reverend Caldwell was genial, congratulating Daniel on the beauty of his bride.

But after they had finished eating and Hannah had brought a second round of tea, Reverend Caldwell cleared his throat and frowned. "Reverend Wright, there is a matter that concerns me. And it is well that your family also hear my concern. It has come to my attention that there is a man in your parish, a very influential man, who does not attend church and who is an outspoken transcendentalist, an atheist. I understand he is well-liked and holds parties on his ranch, with *dancing,* and that most of the people in your parish attend these parties. That you and your daughters are often guests there.

"Surely you realize how dangerous this is? Either he must be converted, brought into Christ's fold, or you must warn your congregation to have nothing to do with him."

Daniel felt a surge of protest, thinking of Andrew's clear, gray eyes, feeling his love for him, even though Reverend Caldwell expressed in words his own worry.

"He's a good man," Hannah broke in. "A fine man. His whole family are fine people. It's true he doesn't come to church, but he doesn't speak against it. His hired people come."

Reverend Caldwell glared at her, a look that said it was not appropriate for a woman to speak.

Daniel quelled his protesting heart. "Believe me," he said, "I share your concern. I have spoken often with Mr. Fairdale about his relationship to Christ and to scripture, so far to no avail. But he is not an atheist. He is devout in his own way."

"His own way! There is only one true way. Do not be led astray by his wealth, his culture, his fine ways. Make no mistake, unless he receives Christ as his savior, he and all he influences will burn in hell. Burn in hell!" Reverend Caldwell thumped the table. "For all eternity. Do you understand?"

The twins stirred, and Daniel knew that under the table they were reaching for each other's hands. Rachel looked across at him, a question in her dark eyes.

"He is a kind man, and generous," Daniel could not help saying. "There are many in my parish who get through the winter without scurvy because he shares his fruit with all comers in the fall. His ranch supplies milk and cheese and eggs and produce for the whole town. It would be hard to cut him off."

"But cut him off you must if he will not be converted. It doesn't matter how kind and generous he is. He's on the wrong path, a path that leads to hellfire and damnation. And any who follow him, who listen to his fine words and are led astray, will also be damned. You must guard your flock well against this wolf in sheep's clothing."

Hannah pushed her chair back and left the table.

Daniel took a long breath. "Thank you for sharing your concern. The Fairdales will be coming to my wedding tomorrow. I ask that you welcome them and trust me to attend to this matter as I see fit. I would not have my wedding day marred by controversy or the Fairdales made to feel unwelcome the first time they come to my church."

"He is invited to your wedding? You are in this further than I knew." Reverend Caldwell rapped the table with his spoon. "Very well, I will respect your wishes, but once your wedding is over, do not delay in taking action."

He stood, becoming genial again. "Well, well, we should all get some sleep. Tomorrow is a big day. Good night, Mrs. Decker, Miss Rose, Miss Lily." He nodded, bowed slightly to the ladies, and left the room.

A moment later Hannah came storming in. "You're not going to do that, are you Reverend? Cut off the Fairdales? There's no harm there. Mr. Fairdale doesn't push his theology on anyone. He never speaks of it. And how he acts, the way he runs his ranch, the way he treats his people, is more Christian than most in this valley. Reverend Caldwell doesn't even know him."

The twins were standing, hands clasped, their eyes on his face. "You wouldn't, would you, Papa? Mr. Fairdale is your friend."

Daniel sighed. "Please don't worry. The Fairdales are an integral part of this valley. Even if I chose to, I couldn't isolate them. To try would only turn people away from the church. Let it go. I didn't want to get into an argument with Reverend Caldwell on the eve of my wedding. And he is right, we should all get some sleep."

As he walked across Hannah's pasture toward the cliff path in the spring twilight, the twins trailing behind him, he found he was angry. He wanted to think only of his wedding, the soft look in Rachel's eyes when he kissed her hand, but his mind was taken up with Reverend Caldwell's words. Of course he was right. The Fairdales were a danger. Hadn't he thought so himself and tried unsuccessfully to keep the twins away from them? But he had thought only of his daughters. His whole congregation was in danger. He remembered them all dancing at the Fourth of July celebration while Bernie's clear voice sang out the calls and the fiddles swirled. And there had been other parties with dancing. He had even allowed his own daughters to dance. Had he himself been entranced and grown soft on what he knew was right?

Just this evening he had spoken up in defense of the Fairdales and assured Hannah there was nothing to worry about. As she had assured him. It was true that Andrew did not speak of his beliefs or press them on anyone.

The evening was sweet and soft, and tomorrow was his wedding day. Daniel sighed and let his shoulders relax as he walked. Perhaps there really was no danger as long as he kept the church strong and spoke the gospel clearly to his people each Sunday, each Wednesday evening.

# Chapter 43

# *The Golden Summer*

The summer that followed was a golden summer for Daniel. It began with the wedding and the moment Rachel looked up at him, her dark eyes soft with love, and said, "I do."

Morning sunlight flooded the church. Rachel wore a gold silk gown and looked more beautiful than he had ever seen her. His friends and family were all around him, the twins smiling with tears in their eyes. Gabe played a piercingly sweet melody on his violin, and everyone sang the hymn, "O Perfect Love."

The rest of the day was a joyous celebration, with lunch in the boarding house, speeches, congratulations, laughter. Reverend Caldwell was gracious and kept his promise, although Daniel did notice him frowning when Kate and Andrew embraced him and the twins greeted Julia and Amy exuberantly after the service.

By late afternoon, everyone had dispersed. Daniel brought his buggy around to the boarding house to bring Rachel and Joshua and their possessions home. Isabel had a simple supper prepared, and they all sat together around the table in the kitchen, Daniel at one end, Rachel at the other with Joshua in her lap, the twins on either side. Isabel brought bread to the table, set her hands on her hips, and said, "A fine family you've got here, Preacher."

"It is indeed," Daniel replied, his heart full of gratitude. His loins burned with thoughts of the night ahead. That burning had been distracting him all day, but he reassured himself. It's all right. She will be my wife. It's all right to cherish your wife.

When supper was over, it seemed to take forever for Rachel to settle Joshua. When at last he was asleep, Daniel carried his little bed into Isabel's room where he was to spend the wedding night. Isabel touched his shoulder.

"Preacher, if I may be so bold, you might want to wait a little before you get too cozy. Gabe and them are getting together a chivaree. Folks in this town won't feel you're properly married without one. Come dark, there'll be a crowd and a racket around here fit to wake the devil. I've got some cookies to give them, but you'll need to come out and let them see you before they'll go away."

Daniel sighed. A chivaree, of course. "That Gabe," he said.

"Better Gabe than some of the others. He'll make it a short one. He won't run you out on a rail or dump you in a horse trough like they do sometimes."

"I hope not." He smiled at her. "Thanks for the warning. We'll be ready."

So he had to wait a little longer. Isabel went into her room with Joshua, and the twins slipped away. Daniel sat in the living room with Rachel, holding her hand, reminiscing about the day. Just as it got dark, they heard the voices of a crowd of people coming up the hill, the sound of Gabe's fiddle playing a wild and rollicking tune. Soon the crowd was all around the house, and the sound of the fiddle was drowned out by the banging of pots and pans, a drum, singing. All the people of Gold Creek, it seemed, were out there. Joshua woke up and cried, and Isabel brought him to Rachel.

"Go on out," Isabel urged them. "They won't go away 'til you greet them."

Rachel set Joshua on her hip, Daniel took her hand, and they stepped out onto the porch. They were greeted with cheers and shouts. "Daniel, Rachel. Chivaree! Chivaree!"

Hannah appeared at the kitchen door with a basket of muffins, and she and Isabel and the twins moved through the crowd handing out treats. The banging on pots subsided as the revelers consumed cookies and cakes. Friends and neighbors came up on the porch to congratulate Daniel and Rachel.

"All blessing to our preacher and his wife," Mayor Wilgus boomed in his big voice.

"Alleluia!" Gabe shouted. He waved his arm, struck up a tune on his fiddle, and led the crowd back down the hill.

When they were gone, Joshua had to be settled again. Finally all was quiet. Daniel led his wife into the bedroom and shut the door. "At last," he murmured, as he took her into his arms, "I can love you in peace and safety."

She did not answer, only drew his head down to kiss him. Dizzy with longing, he took her hand and led her to their bed and the deep, sweet fulfillment of his long desire.

∽

In the days that followed, Daniel swam in a euphoria of love. Everything about Rachel delighted him—the grace of her movement, the sound of her voice, the dark wave of her hair where it rested against her cheek, the luminous whiteness of her soft breast revealed as she nursed Joshua. He was awed by the skill and tenderness with which she cared for their son. Coming home each day he could hardly believe his good fortune knowing she would be there, her face lighting up as she came to greet him with a kiss. Most of all he cherished the warmth of her body curled in his arms each night.

At last the burden of his guilt and unmet lust was lifted. Rachel welcomed him as often as he came to her, returning his love with such tenderness and passion he sometimes feared God could not sanction the intense bliss that he felt. When he whispered his misgivings to Rachel, she assured him, "It is good. It is God's gift and blessing to us." And he dared to believe her.

Having a lively toddler in the house certainly required some adjustments. The room that had been Daniel's study and retreat now became a nursery and family bedroom, with Joshua's napkins, baby clothes, and toys filling the shelves intended for books. The boxes of Daniel's books that had finally arrived from Boston were still piled in the corner, providing a mountain for Joshua to climb on, and Daniel had to retreat to the church to study and prepare his sermons.

But he didn't mind. He was enchanted with his little son. Joshua was a bright, adventurous child, and, though shy at first, soon warmed to his tall new papa. Before long he would run to meet Daniel, still unsteady with his first steps, and hold up his arms saying, "Up, Papa." Daniel would scoop him up, toss him in the air, causing Joshua to shriek with laughter, then set him on his shoulders and give him a ride around the house. Sometimes Daniel would get down on the floor and tussle with Joshua. "It's good to have another man around the house," he would tell his son.

The church almost doubled in size that summer. New settlers poured into town, filling the boarding house, camping along the river. Mayor Wilgus gathered teams to open roads and added new plats to his map. North Road, which had been just a grassy track, was cleared all the way from Ranch Road to the edge of Nathan's orchard, and more roads were created across the river, south of Mill Road. Mayor Wilgus was in his element, showing the newcomers around and filling in their names on his map.

Daniel welcomed each family. His days were long, as he visited the newcomers. He worked beside them to open a garden, set a foundation, or fence a pasture, taking every opportunity to share the gospel. His joy and love poured into his sermons. By mid-July the church was overflowing, with no more room in the pews and people standing in the aisles and the back of the church.

"We done outgrown our church," Gabe said one evening after prayer meeting as he and Daniel and the other elders sat with Hannah around a table in the boarding house. "We need to expand it. I been working on a plan."

"It's time we had an organ," Hannah said. "Mr. Dodge says we have enough money in the church treasury now."

"An organ. That would be fine," Burt Martin said.

"Do you realize how amazing this is?" Hannah exclaimed. "Before Reverend Wright came we were only twelve, and now we grow so fast we need to enlarge the church only a year after we built it. The Lord blesses your ministry, Reverend, and all of us."

"What do you think, Preacher?" Gabe asked. "Shall we do it? Expand the church and buy an organ?"

Daniel's heart swelled with happiness. He felt blessed indeed. His church thrived beyond his fondest dreams. "If the money is there, let's do it," he said, looking around at all of them, smiling. "My daughters will be delighted. They've been begging for an organ. I don't know that they've ever played one, but they're fine pianists, and will learn quickly."

"Sure they will," said Nathan.

"I have a catalogue from a place in Denver that sells organs," Hannah said. "It's got pictures. We can choose one, and I'll order it. It says they deliver."

"Tell me the size and I'll put it in the plans," Gabe said. "Then all we'll need to be complete is a bell."

Enthusiasm was high the day of the church-expanding bee. A large crowd gathered to work, with many of the new settlers joining in. Gabe guided teams of men to move the east wall out and extend the sanctuary north into the area that had been the children's room. The workers continued the following week, building a whole new wing behind the sanctuary with two rooms for the Sunday School and a comfortable study for Daniel. After all the dust had settled and Gabe had built shelves, Daniel finally unpacked his books.

The organ arrived on a stormy afternoon, wrapped in india rubber in the back of an open wagon. A crowd gathered, standing in the rain to watch Nathan and the delivery man carry it into the sanctuary to the place Gabe had prepared for it. Then they surged into the church to listen as Rose and Lily sat in front of it, pumped the pedals and reverently touched the keys, calling forth its voice.

The crowning glory for the church came only two weeks later.

Daniel was in his study when a stout man in a dusty hat came to his door. "I got a delivery here for Reverend Wright, Gold Creek Presbyterian Church," he said.

"I'm Reverend Wright," Daniel said, pushing back his chair and standing. "But I wasn't expecting anything. What is it?"

"Dunno. It's heavy. Where d'you want it?"

Daniel followed the man out to the front of the church. There, in a wagon even dustier than the man's hat, was a crate.

"Set it up here on the porch," Daniel directed him. "Do you need a hand?"

"Nope. Got it." The man grunted as he carried the box up the porch steps and set it down. "Sign here."

He produced a stubby pencil out of his overall pocket, and Daniel signed.

"G'day," the man said as he climbed back up on his wagon. He flicked the reins over the back of his swaybacked horse and drove off.

Daniel turned to examine the crate and saw he would need tools to open it. What can it be? he wondered. He walked down the hill and across the road to Gabe's shop.

Gabe came with a crowbar and pried the crate open. When the sides fell apart, the sun gleamed on a shiny bronze bell.

"A bell!" Daniel exclaimed.

"Praise the Lord," Gabe said. "Where'd it come from?"

"I have no idea." Daniel was stunned, then exultant. "A bell! You were saying that was all we needed for the church to be complete."

Gabe ran his work-worn hand over the smooth surface. "It's a beauty."

Daniel picked up the bell and Gabe set the clapper swinging. The bell rang out sweet and loud. Daniel and Gabe looked at each other and began laughing. Gabe kept ringing.

Heads popped out of the brick buildings. People came running from all directions.

"What's this? What's this?" Mayor Wilgus exclaimed, puffing from his dash up the hill. "A church bell. Perfect. Where did it come from?"

No one knew.

"Let's h-hang it r-right aw-way," Bud Budke stuttered.

Gabe was already running to his shop for more tools. By sunset the bell hung in the steeple. It seemed the whole town had gathered to watch Gabe climb up and set it in place. "Alleluia!" he shouted as he shimmied down.

Bud Budke pulled the bell cord and rang the bell loud and long.

That evening as Rachel and Daniel prepared for bed, Daniel said, "I wish I knew who sent the bell. It is a generous gift. I would like to thank that person."

"You can," Rachel said as she took the combs out of her hair, letting it fall around her shoulders and down her back in a shining cascade. "It's from me."

"You! How?"

"Mr. Decker left me a small fortune, which is now in a bank account in Boston. I knew how much you wanted a bell, so I asked my trustee to pick out a fine one and send it. But don't tell anyone." She shook her hair back and smiled at him. "I don't want people to think you married me for my money."

The town soon became used to the sound of the church bell. Bud Budke eagerly took on the role of bell ringer. He trudged up the hill from his little cabin by the river early every Sunday morning and rang the bell to announce the Sabbath. Then he rang it again just before the service and on Sunday and Wednesday evenings to announce prayer meeting.

Isabel told the family that she'd heard by the grapevine that some of the miners hated the bell because it woke them up on Sunday and gave them headaches after their Saturday nights of drinking.

"Maybe then they won't drink so much," Rose said.

Isabel snorted. "Unlikely."

There were many visits to Fairdale Ranch during the long summer. Rachel had become very fond of Kate. "I've never had a friend like her before," she told Daniel, "so wise and warm. I can share my thoughts with her, and she understands."

Joshua, too, enjoyed Fairdale Ranch. He had a high time playing with the ranch hands' children—James and Sophia's two little girls, and Luke and Molly's boy, Johnny, who was just Joshua's age. There was a sandbox, a swing hung from the big willow by the barn, often a trough full of clean water for them to play in. Molly watched over them so Rachel could drop Joshua off with the other children and be free to enjoy her conversations with Kate.

The twins, of course, were always delighted to go. As soon as they arrived they would run off with Amy and Julia. Several times they came to dinner with wet hair, and Kate told Daniel that Julia had been teaching them to swim in the creek. He wasn't quite sure how he felt about that, but they looked so happy he decided not to interfere.

He worried at times about Reverend Caldwell's warning. One afternoon, as he and Andrew sat talking in Andrew's library, Daniel tried again to persuade him to accept Christ as his savior. For the first time he saw a flash of anger in Andrew's eyes.

"Let it be, Daniel," he said sharply. "You have your path and I have mine."

"But I love you," Daniel protested, "and would not see you lost for all eternity. All your good works, and they are many, will not save you if you don't accept Christ's sacrifice."

"What good I do on this earth," Andrew replied, "is not to win some prize in the hereafter, but because it is the right thing to do here and now. As for the rest, I trust in God's love."

There was a sternness in his answer that silenced Daniel. Not wanting to harm their friendship, he brushed aside his worry and let it go.

It soon became a tradition for the whole Wright family to spend every Friday at Fairdale Ranch. The young people took long rides on their horses. They brought out their instruments and spent hours playing together. One afternoon Jonathan asked Daniel to come see the cabin he was building. Daniel and Andrew stayed and helped for a while, then all three took a refreshing dip in the creek.

Kate and Rachel walked together in the garden, worked side by side in the kitchen. Sometimes Kate gave Rachel a piano lesson, helping her regain the skills she had learned in finishing school.

Best of all for Daniel were the conversations with Andrew. They took to loaning each other books, reading them during the week and discussing them when they met again. Daniel had never had such an exciting mind to dialogue with. He loved the way Andrew's eyes would light up with challenge, the sword play of their words. They laughed, parried, and listened to each other. Even though Daniel had given up trying to convert Andrew, he felt triumphant at times when it seemed Andrew understood his position. He didn't realize that his own position was softening, opening as the clear air of new ideas blew into the locked corners of his dogma.

Usually the twins spent Friday night at the ranch and came back in the morning with Amy and Julia and the milk cart. If one twin looked bright and happy when they came home and the other twin more withdrawn, Daniel was too busy with the church to notice.

# Chapter 44

## *Forbidden Love*

The golden summer ended abruptly for Daniel one afternoon in early September when young Jonathan Fairdale rode up to the Wright home on his tall horse, Brandy.

The twins and Isabel were in the garden, Rachel and Joshua were napping in the bedroom, and Daniel was reading in his leather chair. He heard the sound of hooves approaching, got up from his chair, and stepped to the window to look out.

He watched as Jonathan stopped by the garden. The twins ran to meet him. He swung down from his horse and took one of them in his arms and kissed her. On the mouth. Daniel stiffened in outrage. How dare he? Which one was it? Lily? It must be Lily. Then Jonathan turned to the other twin and kissed her cheek. Isabel had straightened from her work and greeted him. Fine chaperon Isabel, allowing that!

They talked for a few minutes, while Lily—was it Lily?—clung to Jonathan's hand. Then Jonathan led his horse up toward the pasture and disappeared from view. Isabel and the twins clustered together. They seemed excited, hugging each other, gesturing. The sound of their voices floated up to Daniel, but he couldn't hear what they were saying.

Jonathan came to the front of the house and up the porch steps. He was all dressed up in new blue jeans and a red shirt, his face shining, his auburn curls neatly combed. He seemed bursting with happiness. Daniel felt a stab of envy for his youthful beauty and vitality.

The front door was open to let the afternoon breeze through. Jonathan paused at the threshold. "Good afternoon, sir."

"Come in," Daniel said sternly. He held back his outrage over the kiss he had witnessed, waiting to see what Jonathan would say.

"Thank you, sir. If you are not too busy, I would like to talk with you."

Daniel gestured to the bench by the hearth and pulled his leather chair up opposite it. "I'd like to talk with you, too," he said. "I couldn't believe my eyes just now when I saw you kissing my daughters in the garden. How dare you?"

"I'm sorry, sir. I guess I was ahead of myself. Because I've come—" Jonathan hesitated, blushed, then blurted out, "I've come to ask you for Lily's hand in marriage."

Daniel sat straight up in his chair. "What?"

"Yes, sir. I've loved her from the first day I saw her and she loves me, too. And I've—"

"No! Impossible!" Daniel was on his feet. "How long has this been going on?"

Jonathan stood, too. "What do you mean, impossible? We've been promised for a year. You've seen the cabin I've been building for her, and my parents are very pleased—"

"Your father has known all along and said nothing to me?"

"No, sir. Father said it was up to me to speak to you. I wanted to ask her right away as soon as I met her, but Father thought it would be best for us to wait a year for me to build the cabin and for Lily to get a little older. Then when you almost married her to Mr. Jenkins, I had to ask her and she promised me last fall at the gleaning. She loves me, too. We are meant for each other. What do you mean impossible?"

Daniel held up his hand, palm out. "Silence!" He turned away and paced up and down, while Jonathan stood pale and frozen by the hearth.

Daniel could barely think. *This has been going on a year and I never saw it? I never thought of Jonathan that day Lily came home from the hay-in looking as if she were in heat. I thought one of the homesteader men who go to the Fairdale parties had gotten to her. Jonathan! I didn't know they even saw each other when the twins went off with the girls. He was always in the corral or working on his cabin. Of course they made music together but ... I've been too lenient allowing them to visit Fairdale Ranch, and now it's come to this.*

Daniel stopped pacing. He looked over at Jonathan and was touched with pity by the look on his face. "Sit down," he said, more gently.

Jonathan sat, gripping the bench with both hands. Daniel lowered himself into his leather chair and leaned forward. "I'm sorry," he said. "But I cannot allow Lily to marry you."

"Why not?" Jonathan's voice was choked.

"Because she is Christian and you are not. Nor is your family. I cannot allow her to be led astray from her faith, as she surely would be if she married you and went to live with you on Fairdale Ranch. I've had long talks with your father, trying to persuade him to accept Christ as his savior, the Bible as the word of God, and he is unrepentant."

"What do you mean we're not Christian?" Jonathan's face flushed with indignation. "My father is the most Christian man I know. He is the kindest— every person, every animal on our ranch is cared for. I've never seen him do a single cruel thing, and that's more than you can say for a lot of the folks who come to your church."

"He *is* a kind, good man. Do you think I do not love him? And fear for him that he will be lost for eternity, he and all your family? I cannot risk Lily coming under his influence and being eternally damned."

Jonathan pounded the bench. "What kind of God do you worship that would cause someone so pure and beautiful as Lily to be damned? Or my father, or mother, any of us? God is love and we love each other. How can we be lost?"

Daniel struggled to control his voice. "Jonathan, there is much you don't understand, cannot understand, having been brought up as you were. Suffice it to say I forbid you to marry Lily. That's final. I am sorry to disappoint you—"

"Disappoint me!" Jonathan jumped to his feet. "You just ruined my life." He ran out the door, his feet quick and loud on the porch steps, and disappeared around the corner of the house.

The door opened at the top of the steps, and Lily and Rose came running down, Lily screaming, "No! No, Papa, no!"

Daniel turned in confusion. They had been in the garden and now they were coming down the stairs from their bedroom, but they hadn't come through the house, had they? He didn't have time to sort it out because Lily grabbed his shoulders and shook him.

Rose stopped at the foot of the stairs, white-faced and still, clenching the bannister.

Lily gave her father another shake. "How could you?" Her eyes were blazing with fury.

"Lily, calm down."

"Calm down?" Lily's voice rose. "You promised. After Mr. Jenkins you promised we could choose whom we marry. I choose to marry Jonathan. How could you send him away?"

Daniel disengaged himself from Lily's grasp. "I didn't promise you could marry whomever you wanted. I promised I would not make you marry someone you didn't want."

"It's the same thing. I will never marry anyone but Jonathan. Why, why did you send him away? He's the perfect husband for me. I'll never love anyone else."

"Because." Daniel tried to quiet his voice. "Jonathan is not a Christian, nor is his family Christian. You must marry a Christian man. I am your father, responsible for your immortal soul—"

Lily stamped her foot. "You are *not* responsible for my immortal soul. Only God is. *You are not God.* And just so you know, my immortal soul is fine."

The sound of clattering hooves came through the open door as Jonathan galloped by on Brandy.

"No!" Lily raced out onto the porch calling, "Jonathan, Jonathan, wait." But Jonathan tore on down the road, head bent. Lily ran down off the porch and around the house.

"Daniel." Rachel's voice. He turned. She stood at the bedroom door, closing it behind her, her finger to her lips. "What's all this yelling? You'll wake the baby. What's going on?"

Daniel groaned and sank down in his chair, leaning his head in his hand. "Jonathan came to ask to marry Lily. I had no idea. Did you know he was courting her?"

Rachel went to sit on the arm of Daniel's chair. "I knew."

"You knew, and you didn't tell me?"

"Ah, Daniel." She stroked his hair. "You see everyone in your parish so clearly and look right past your own daughters."

"Why didn't you tell me?"

"I thought you knew. It was obvious. And there was always so much else you wanted to talk about. It's been a busy summer with the church. You didn't tell Jonathan no?"

"Of course I did. Had I known, I'd have put a stop to it long ago."

"Why?" Rachel bent her head to look into his face. "They are very well suited and clearly love each other."

Daniel threw off Rachel's gentle hand, stood, and started pacing again. "The Fairdales aren't Christian. I never should have let the twins visit. I knew that from the first. I've been negligent. But no more."

Rachel started to say something, but there was another clatter of hooves. Daniel's head snapped around as Lily raced past the house, bareback on Dawnstar.

Rose let out an incoherent cry, and turned and ran up the stairs.

"Lily!" Daniel strode out onto the porch. "Lily, come back," he shouted. Lily ignored him, kicking Dawnstar into a gallop.

"Lily!" Daniel ran down the porch steps, but Lily was already far down the road, a cloud of dust rising behind her. Daniel shook his fist at her, suffused with helpless rage. He spun around and found Rachel standing beside him. "I'm going after her," he said. "I'll not have her defying me like that."

Rachel touched his arm. "Let her go. Let her ride out her grief. She'll be back."

Daniel let his arms drop to his sides. He drew Rachel close, resting his cheek against the top of her head, his anger fading.

"All right." He sighed heavily. "All right, but there will be no more visits to the Fairdales."

∼

Lily clung to Dawnstar's mane as they galloped down the road. There had been no time to saddle up. She had to catch Jonathan. Even in the midst of her grief and rage, she felt the exhilaration of the swift ride, the ripple of Dawnstar's muscles between her thighs. Her hair came loose, her hairpins scattering behind her.

She leaned low over Dawnstar's neck. I love him, I love him, her heart beat in rhythm with Dawnstar's pounding hooves. How could Papa say no? He promised. What does he know about my immortal soul? Nothing. Or he would know my soul and Jonathan's are one.

She sent out a silent call. Jonathan, wait for me. I'm coming. Oh, he can't hear me like Rose does. Rose … She hesitated. Dawnstar slowed. Rose's grief poured into her. She's crying for me, Lily realized, but I can't hold it now. Swiftly she slid the door between their hearts closed.

If only Jonathan could hear me like she does. Lily reached the end of Pine Road and swerved onto Ranch Road, leaning with Dawnstar, still galloping, although Dawnstar was breathing hard. Far ahead she saw Jonathan, just at the top of a rise.

"Jonathan," she called. "Jonathan!" It was too far. He would never hear her. But he turned and saw her. She let go of Dawnstar's mane with one hand and waved. He waved back and galloped toward her.

They slowed their horses only when they were close. Jonathan dismounted and held up his arms. Lily slid down into them.

"Don't go away," she sobbed. "Don't let him send you away."

"Lily, I had to go. I was so angry I was afraid I would hit him."

"You didn't say good-bye to me."

"I didn't want to say good-bye." He was holding her close, kissing her hair, her cheeks, kissing away the tears. "I never want to say good-bye to you." Lily clung to him, feeling her heart would break with love.

Two horses pulling a wagon came over the top of the hill and started down toward them. Jonathan looked up, circled Lily's waist with his arm, and guided her and the horses off to the side of the road.

The man driving the wagon was smartly dressed, wearing a wide brown leather hat with a feather in the band. Lily hid her face against Dawnstar, not wanting to be caught with her hair coming loose and her cheeks smeared with tears, not wanting to be seen unchaperoned way out on the plains in her lover's arms.

"Howdy," the man said, slowing his horses. "You young uns need help?"

"No, thanks, Mr. Henderson," Jonathan said. "We're just resting our horses."

"Resting your horses, are you?" Mr. Henderson gave them a knowing smile. "I see." He flicked the reins and the wagon moved on.

Lily was burning with embarrassment. "We shouldn't be standing here in the road. If Mr. Henderson tells Papa—"

"I know a place," Jonathan said. "Follow me." He lifted Lily back onto Dawnstar, mounted Brandy, and led Lily a short way up the road. There, a track branched off to the right, one of the many confusing side roads Lily and Rose had learned to pass by on their way to Fairdale Ranch.

Jonathan turned onto the track and Lily followed. It went straight for a short distance, then down a slope that hid them from the road. A little farther on, in a stand of cottonwoods, it faded away. Lily heard the sound of running water.

Jonathan dismounted and lifted Lily down. "I have a favorite place just a little upstream," he said. "Let's go there."

They set off, hand in hand, leading their horses, stepping softly between the trees. A narrow break in the willows led to a little glade by a swift running creek. The grass at the edge was still green, even that late in the summer. One huge cottonwood grew at the edge of the water, its roots spreading down the bank and out into the grass. Except for the narrow path that led in, the whole clearing was surrounded by willows, sheltered and still except for the laughing rush of the creek.

Lily stood holding Dawnstar's halter, drinking it in. "This is beautiful," she said softly.

"I found this place a few years ago," Jonathan said. "I've been wanting to bring you here."

They led their horses to the creek to drink, tethered them, and turned into each other's arms.

"Lily, Lily," Jonathan murmured. She felt his hand under her chin, then his lips against hers. Tingling heat poured through her. She pressed close against him.

Jonathan released her lips and held her a little away from him, smoothing her tousled hair. "I don't know which is sweeter," he said, "kissing you or looking into your eyes. Lily, how can we persuade your father?"

They sat down on the grass. "We can't," Lily answered. "I know him. When he gets stubborn about religion, nothing can change him."

"I'm stubborn, too. You're my promised wife and my love. I can't let you go."

Lily drew in her breath. "We could elope."

Jonathan stared at her, gripped her hands. "Would you?"

"Yes."

"We will then."

Lily trembled. It was outrageous. Her father would be mortified. And she didn't care. Anger, defiance, freedom flared through her. And love. "I just want to be your wife, be with you always, have your babies, never leave you."

"You will." Jonathan kissed her again, his mouth warm on hers. Sweet. She had never dreamed such sweetness. They lay down on the soft grass by the creek's edge, lost in kisses, touch, their bodies blending in passion.

After a while Jonathan sat up. "We must stop," he said huskily. "I cannot contain myself much longer and it would not be right, before we are wed."

Lily sat up, too. He touched her face, cradled her cheek in his hand. "We must marry soon. Let's plan. Will Rose help you?"

"She will help me." Lily sobered at the thought of Rose. "She is sad because she will miss me, but she will help me."

"When? When can you escape?"

Lily pushed back her hair and tried to gather her thoughts. Her loins ached. It was hard to focus. "Monday," she said. "On Monday morning Papa does a prayer meeting for the homesteaders out past the Denver-Montview Road. He leaves early and doesn't get back until afternoon. I'd still need to get past Rachel and Isabel, but I can do that. I'll find a way."

"Monday morning then. Have Rose bring you here. I'll meet you and we'll ride to Montview and find a preacher."

"Not Reverend Caldwell. He'd never do it. He'd just curse us with hell fire and damnation and drag me back to Papa."

"There's a Methodist minister Father likes, Reverend Haywood. We could go to him."

"Are you going to tell your parents?"

"I can't. They love you and want us to be married, but Father would never go against your papa. Once we're married, they'll be happy." He paused. "Maybe we should stay away for a little while. I know. There's an abandoned shepherd's cottage up in the mountains. I've been there with Father a couple of times when we went logging. We can get married and then go there for a few days for a honeymoon. I can go up there and fix it up, put some supplies in." He caught Lily in his arms and rolled her on the grass. "It will be perfect. It's a beautiful place. Mountains all around. I'll think of some story to tell my parents about why I'll be gone for a while."

They kissed again until Jonathan moaned. "I need to get you home now."

Lily stood slowly. The afternoon had grown cool and the sun was low. They led their horses out of the glade. The glade of love, Lily called it in her mind. When they reached the track, they mounted and rode slowly side by side. The main road was deserted. The sun dropped behind the hills, and they picked up their pace. Riding beside Jonathan in the gathering twilight, Lily felt at peace. This is where I belong, she thought, beside him always.

Soon they were climbing the hill on Pine Road. When they reached the big rock that marked the eastern boundary of the Wright property, Lily reined Dawnstar in. "Go now, before anyone sees you."

Jonathan rode Brandy close and reached over to squeeze her hand. "Until Monday."

"Until Monday."

～

Rose lay face down on her bed, her fists clenched under her chest. She had cried a long time, then, worn out with grief, slept. When she opened her eyes, her head was turned toward the window that looked out onto the hill. She could see the tops of summer-browned grasses, their heads bent, heavy with seed, swaying gently in the light breeze that came through. Higher up on the hill a meadowlark sang. From the slant of the sun's rays, she knew it was late afternoon.

Below her she could hear the sounds of the family—Joshua banging the wood blocks Gabe had given him to play with, Isabel clattering around in the kitchen getting supper. She knew she should be down there helping, but even though her tears had passed, she lay still, immobilized with grief. When Lily rode away she had felt as if her insides were torn out. For a little while she had shared Lily's rage and exhilaration, the motion of her body as she rode. Then came the dead silence of the closed door between their hearts. Although the door had been closed at other times, in that moment Rose knew with devastating certainty that Lily was gone, gone in a way she hadn't been before. Even if she came back to live in the house, sleep in the bed with Rose, it would never be the same again.

"When's the preacher getting home?" Rose heard Isabel ask.

Rachel's quiet voice answered, "Soon, I think. He's down at the church working on his sermon."

"And that Lily?"

"I don't know."

There was a howl from Joshua. Rose knew what had happened. It wasn't the first time he'd banged his fingers between the blocks.

Rose sat up slowly, listening to the gentle murmur of Rachel soothing Joshua, another clatter from the kitchen.

"Well, as soon as he gets back, supper's ready," Isabel announced.

Footsteps on the porch, then Daniel calling, "Rose."

Rose got up, pulled aside the pillow she'd put over the vent to keep the family from hearing her sobs, and dropped down to peer through the opening. She saw Rachel go to greet Daniel with a kiss. Joshua toddled over to hug his legs, saying, "Papa, up."

Daniel brushed them aside. "Where's Rose?" he demanded.

Joshua started to whimper. Rachel picked him and set him on her hip. "She's been in her room all afternoon."

"All afternoon?" Rose cringed at the disapproval in his voice.

"Since Lily left," Rachel answered. "She was upset—"

"Is Lily back?"

"Not yet."

"I should have gone after her. Do you know what I just heard?" Daniel's voice rose. "Not an hour ago there was a knock on my study door. Mr. Henderson came to tell me he saw Lily and Jonathan standing in the middle of Ranch Road, *kissing.*"

Rose felt a chill go down her spine.

Daniel went on, his voice even louder. "You shouldn't have dissuaded me from going after her. How can I face my congregation when word of that gets around? Where's Rose?"

Rose slid the pillow back over the vent and opened the door at the top of the stairs. "I'm here, Papa."

"Come down. I want to talk with you."

Rose went down the stairs, but hesitated at the bottom.

Daniel strode over to her. "Where's Lily?"

"I don't know, Papa."

Daniel gripped her shoulders. "Don't protect her. You two always know where the other one is. Where is she?"

"Papa, I don't know. I don't know anymore." Grief surged up in her. She felt tears sting her eyes.

Daniel was watching her. His voice softened. "Why not?"

"I can't explain." In spite of herself, Rose's words came out with a sob. She backed away from Daniel up two of the steps behind her. "But I don't know where she is. I can't hear her anymore."

Rachel stepped between them and laid her hand on Daniel's arm. Joshua on her hip was staring at his father, his lower lip trembling. "Gently, Daniel," Rachel said. "Rose is not to blame."

Daniel softened, looking from one to the other of them. He reached out to touch Joshua's hair. "No, I suppose she's not. I just hoped she could tell me how to find Lily." He began pacing again. "I can't have her out there with Jonathan, unchaperoned, doing God knows what, disgracing me. I should get out a posse to go find her."

"She'll be back," Rachel said. "Give her time. It was a heavy blow you dealt her this afternoon. She's probably at the Fairdales' by now. They'll bring her home."

"Sure they will," Isabel said. Rose looked over to see her standing in the door to the kitchen. "And supper's ready." She glanced at Rose, her green eyes full of compassion. Rose drew in a ragged breath. Isabel knows, she thought. Isabel always knows much more than anyone thinks.

Daniel was still pacing. "The Fairdales. All this trouble is because of them."

"Maybe it's not the Fairdales," Rachel said, "but you yourself who are the cause of this grief. Perhaps you should reconsider Jonathan's request."

"*What?*" Daniel spun around and faced Rachel with such intensity that Joshua hid his face against her shoulder and began to cry. "I told you," he said furiously. "I'll not have her marrying into a non-Christian family. Don't you understand?"

Rose trembled for Rachel, but she stood calm and straight, cradling her child's head in her hand, her wide dark eyes looking straight into Daniel's. "Daniel, you're frightening your son. Supper is ready. Isabel has made us a fine soup. Let's sit down and eat. If Lily hasn't returned when we finish, I'll go with you to Fairdale Ranch and see if she's there."

Slowly Daniel's fists unclenched. His shoulders sagged. Rachel took his hand and led him toward the kitchen. "Remember," she said, "you told me you needed a woman to help you with your daughters. I'm here. Please trust me. Give her a little more time."

Rose followed them into the kitchen. Isabel served up soup and cornbread. Rose didn't think she could eat, but the soup was good, and she found she was hungry. She was finishing her second bowl, when she felt Lily return. The door between their hearts was open again, at least partway. Lily was excited and happy. Rose could feel that much.

A few minutes later Lily stood in the kitchen door. Her hair was disheveled, tumbling loose around her shoulders, bits of leaves and grass caught in her curls. Daniel pushed back his chair so abruptly that it fell over with a crash. Joshua started to cry again.

"Where have you been?" Daniel bellowed.

Lily took a step into the room. Her chin lifted. "I went to say good-bye to Jonathan. We've been betrothed for a year. I needed to say good-bye."

"Mr. Henderson came by the church to tell me you were standing in the middle of the public road with Jonathan," Daniel roared. "Kissing!"

"Uh, oh," Lily said.

Rose held her breath.

Daniel rubbed the back of his head, still roaring, "Running around with your hair loose down your back like a . . like a tart."

"Daniel!" Rachel's voice cut through the shocked silence. "Please sit down. Lily, get yourself some soup and sit down also. Let's have some civility as we eat."

To Rose's amazement, Daniel righted his chair and sat. She and Lily exchanged an astonished glance. Lily went to the stove, got her soup, and took her customary place at the table. Isabel passed her some cornbread.

Rachel took Joshua into her lap and put him to her breast. No one said anything.

When the silent meal ended, Lily and Rose began clearing the dishes. Daniel stood. "Lily." His voice was stern. "Come with me. I want to talk with you."

Lily gave Rose a quick glance and followed Daniel. Putting down the dishes in her hands, Rose went to the steps that separated the kitchen from the living room and sat there, watching, her heart beating fast.

Lily sat on the bench in front of the hearth, her spine straight, her chin lifted. Daniel pulled up his leather chair and faced her. "What do you have to say for yourself?"

Rose quaked at the anger in his voice.

"Nothing, Papa," Lily answered.

"Well, I've something to say to you. I'll not have you running around with your hair down, kissing young men in the public road, disgracing me. From this moment on, until I tell you otherwise, until you have shown me you know how to act like a respectable young lady, you will go no farther from this house than the garden. And there will be *absolutely* no visits to Fairdale Ranch. Nor do I want you to ever see Jonathan again. Do you understand?"

"Yes, Papa."

Rose watched in awe. Lily was so calm, so docile. Though her chin was up. Daniel looked bewildered by her docility. "Do you understand?" he asked again.

"Yes, Papa. Is there anything else?"

"Go to your room and put your hair up."

"Yes, Papa." Lily stood, lifted one eyebrow as she glanced at Rose, and went up the stairs.

Daniel strode out the front door. Rose knew he would soon be running up the hill behind the house as he did when he was distressed.

"Go on," Isabel said to Rose. "I'll get the dishes."

Rose gave her a grateful look and ran up the stairs after Lily.

Lily was spinning round and round in the center of the room, her hair flying. Rose saw she had piled pillows over the vent. She grabbed Rose and whirled her.

"I'm getting married," she sang. "Monday. We're going to elope. Let Papa lay down his laws. I'll be gone."

When she let go, Rose staggered, unbalanced by the sudden whirl and even more by Lily's news. She sat abruptly on the bed. Lily whirled again and landed beside her.

"I'm so happy." She hugged Rose. "I love him so. I can't wait to be married." She giggled. "I almost was. Isabel is right about split skirts, why men don't like them. If I hadn't had it on …"

"Lily!" Rose whispered.

"It's okay. We didn't. Jonathan is honorable. But I wanted to so much."

Rose drew away, unable to hide her shock.

Lily pulled her back and kissed her cheeks. She held Rose close, rocking her. "I know you don't understand. It's only because you haven't found your true love yet."

Rose could feel Lily's heart beating fast against her. The door between them was wide open. Lily's joy and excitement, even the strange aching in her loins, rushed into Rose. She gasped and wriggled free.

Lily took her hands. "We need you to help. You will, won't you?"

"Of course." For the first time Rose wanted to close the door, but had no idea how. Her own feelings of fear and loss, colliding with Lily's jubilation, caused her to reel with confusion. She tried to steady herself. "How do you want me to help?" she asked.

"Monday, after Papa's gone to do his prayer meeting out east, we need to slip away without Isabel or Rachel seeing us. There's a place on the way to Fairdale Ranch, where we went after Mr. Henderson saw us. Jonathan will meet us there. Then when you come back, somehow keep everyone from knowing that I'm gone at least until night. Can you?"

"I think so," Rose answered slowly. "I think we can slip away okay. It may be harder to pretend you're not here. Papa will be furious when he finds out. It will be awful."

Lily sobered. "I'll be gone and you'll have to take it. I guess I'm asking a lot of you. But I'll die if I can't marry Jonathan. I don't know what else to do."

"I'll manage," Rose said. "He'll be angry, but he gets over it. It will be okay."

She wanted Lily's happiness, but desolation swept through her. The thought of leaving her with Jonathan and coming back alone was far more terrifying than the threat of Daniel's rage.

~

On Monday morning the Wright kitchen was full of activity. Daniel sat at the end of the table, his Bible open beside him, sipping coffee and scribbling in his notebook. Rachel sat at the other end of the table nursing Joshua. The twins and Isabel were preparing eggs and pancakes for breakfast.

Rose dropped an egg on the floor.

"Uch," Isabel said, "an egg wasted."

"I'm sorry." Rose got a rag from under the sink and knelt down to clean it up.

"You feeling okay?" Isabel asked, kneeling beside Rose with another rag.

Rose lifted her head. Isabel looked straight into her eyes, and Rose felt her knowing, her caring. "I'm okay," she said. She got up and carried the slimy rag to the sink. "Just a little tired. I didn't sleep well last night." But it wasn't fatigue that had made her drop the egg. She was shaking inside, in terror of the day to come.

Lily touched her shoulder. "I'll do the eggs. You set the table."

"We need to move along," Isabel said. "Remember we're canning today."

As they ate, Rachel said, "Mattie has invited us down there to do the canning. Nathan's going to move the stove out into the shade of the barn, so it won't be so hot."

"That'll be better than heating this place up," Isabel said. "Today's gonna be another scorcher."

Daniel was still writing as he ate. He looked up from his notes and over at Lily. "Remember, you're not to leave the house. I'm sure there is plenty of work you can do in the garden while the others are canning."

"Yes, Papa." Lily said. That was about all she had said to him for the last two days. Rose could see that their father was suspicious of her docility, but what could he say? She hoped Lily wasn't overdoing it.

Daniel pushed back his empty plate, folded his Bible, gathered up his papers, and stood. "A day of canning," he said, looking around at the four women. "Give thanks for God's bounty as you work."

Rachel walked to the door with him, Joshua on her hip. Daniel kissed her good-bye and rumpled Joshua's hair. A few minutes later he rode past the house on Shadow and headed down the road.

Lily squeezed Rose's hand tightly. "Let's get this kitchen cleaned up. Then I'll help you load the cart. There's more beans to pick. I can work on that after you go."

As they washed the dishes side by side at the sink, Lily whispered to Rose, "I forgot about the canning. It will be perfect. Everyone will be gone. But how will you get away?"

"I don't know," Rose whispered back. "I'll think of something."

While the twins cleaned up the kitchen, Rachel and Isabel gathered bags of vegetables, baskets of fruit, and canning jars. Then Rose brought Dawnstar and the cart down to the kitchen door. When all was loaded, Rachel and Joshua and Isabel climbed in, and Rose led Dawnstar down the road. Lily waved to them from the porch.

Rose's hand trembled on the bridle. The shaking inside her had grown worse. She was glad she had her back to Rachel and Isabel. How will I get away? she wondered. The canning is such a big job. I'll be needed. Especially since Lily won't be helping. She remembered Lily packing her carpet bag the night before, her joy and excitement as she chattered about Jonathan. I'll have to think of something. I can't let her down.

Mattie came out to greet them. "Here you are. Nathan's got the stove going. Come on back. Where's Lily?"

Rose and Isabel looked at each other, not knowing what to say, but Rachel spoke up. "There're more beans to pick. She's working on that."

Rose's mind was racing as they unpacked, her hands trembling as she unhitched the cart. Then all at once the words came. "I'm sorry. I need to go for a little while. Jody Jackson spoke to me at prayer meeting last night. She's due next month and is afraid the baby's turned wrong. I forgot we were going to be canning today. I promised her I'd come by." She cringed inside at her lie.

"Both of you gone," Mattie said. "More work for the rest of us."

"Never mind," Isabel said. "We'll manage. You go make sure that baby's gonna come out right." She gave Rose a sharp look, then boosted Joshua out of the cart. "Come on, young man. Let's go find Baby Beth."

Rose led Dawnstar to the mounting block and climbed on, bareback. "I'll be back as soon as I can," she called. "I'll stop by the house and bring the beans Lily's picking."

Swiftly she rode to the house. Lily came out onto the porch to meet her. She was dressed in the denim split skirt and the flowered blouse they had made the summer before, her hair neatly coifed. She looked beautiful, radiant, bursting with excitement. She gave a little spin on the porch, then ran down to walk beside Dawnstar to the stable.

"I'm all ready," she said breathlessly. "My bag's outside the window on the hill. Let's saddle up quickly before someone comes."

They had saddled Dawnstar together so many times, each knowing her part, that they had her ready to go in just a few minutes. Lily ran to fetch her bag. Rose leaned her head against Dawnstar's flank. Will we ever saddle Dawnstar together again? she wondered. Something went cold and still inside her. I mustn't ask.

As they tied Lily's bag to the back of the saddle, Rose said, "We'd better not go down Pine Road or North Road. Someone will see us. We can cut through Nathan's orchard. Let me ride in front. I know a way across the fields to Ranch Road."

"Good idea," Lily said.

The trees in the orchard were still young, only five or six feet tall, but well leafed out. Rose guided Dawnstar down the long aisle between the rows, then cut between the trees, angling across the orchard toward the open prairie. As they emerged into the next aisle, they were greeted by a child's high voice, "Hi, Aunt Lily. Hi, Aunt Rose." Amelia came running toward them, followed by Little Nate—followed by Isabel, walking more slowly, holding Baby Beth by one hand, Joshua by the other.

Rose pulled on the reins.

"No!" Lily whispered in her ear. "Keep going."

Rose nudged Dawnstar, but then had to stop her completely because the children dashed in front of her.

"We're running the rows," Amelia announced. "Come on, Little Nate." She tore off, braids flying, with Little Nate close behind her.

"Now," Lily urged. But it was too late. Isabel left the two little ones, stepped up, and seized Dawnstar's bridle.

Her green eyes swept the horse, the twins, Lily's bag strapped behind the saddle with the neck of her violin sticking out.

"Rose," she said. "That doesn't look like your doctoring bag to me. And unless my eyes deceive me, it looks like you've got some other baggage behind you, something your pa specifically didn't want leaving the house."

Rose, caught in her lie, felt her face burn. Lily squeezed her tight from behind.

For a moment, no one spoke. The children came up to clutch Isabel's skirt and stared at the twins, eyes and mouths wide open.

"Running away, are you Lily?" Isabel asked. Her voice had softened. "I thought something was afoot."

"Please, Isabel," Lily begged, "don't tell. Let me go. I'll die if I can't marry Jonathan. Papa lied. He promised we could marry whom we wanted, then he broke his promise. He said he'd never let me see Jonathan again."

Isabel pressed her lips together, but her eyes were kind. "Whether I tell or whether I don't, your pa's gonna notice pretty quick that you're not there. And Rose'll take the brunt of it. Go on then. But don't tell me where you're going."

"Thanks, Isabel," Lily breathed. "Go, Rose."

Rose set Dawnstar into a canter, through the orchard, across the fields, and onto Ranch Road. Her heart was like a cold stone in her breast. She could feel Lily's anticipation, her thoughts of Jonathan. She doesn't even care that she'll be leaving me, Rose thought. She tried to burn into herself the sensation of Lily close against her, Lily's arms around her.

"Just over this rise," Lily said, "we'll go right on the track that crosses the road. There's a twisty pine where we turn."

They rode up the rise. A little farther on Rose saw the twisty pine standing alone at the crossroads.

"There," Lily pointed.

Rose turned Dawnstar. Everything felt unreal, as if she were moving in a dream.

"Just a little farther, down this hill, into the cottonwoods," Lily directed her.

Jonathan was waiting at the edge of the cottonwoods, his hat in his hand, Brandy beside him. The morning sun shone on his auburn curls. He hurried to meet them, beaming with welcome.

Dawnstar had barely stopped moving before Lily dismounted and ran into his arms.

Still mounted, Rose watched as they embraced. Finally she dismounted and began untying Lily's bag. Her hands were clumsy. The knots wouldn't undo.

"Here, let me help." Jonathan had the bag off in a moment. One stray piece of rope was left hanging. Rose brushed at it ineffectively. Her throat constricted. She could barely breathe.

Jonathan and Lily were chattering as they secured Lily's bag with Jonathan's behind Brandy's saddle. "I've made you a comfy seat with blankets here in front of me," Jonathan said, "so I can hold you in my arms as we ride." More chatter. Rose's ears roared. She could no longer hear what they were saying.

Then she felt Lily's hand on her arm. "Good-bye, Rose." Lily's hug, her kiss. "Thank you so much for helping us."

Jonathan's kiss on her other cheek. "Thank you, Rose. We'll bless you all our lives. You'll be my sister now."

"Don't cry," Lily said. "I'll see you again soon. You'll come to visit often."

Was she crying? Rose didn't know. All she could feel was the ache in her chest.

"Let me help you up." Jonathan lifted her onto Dawnstar. Automatically, she took the reins in her hands.

Through the blur of her tears she watched Lily and Jonathan mount Brandy and start off. Dawnstar followed without prompting, up the little hill, along the track. When Lily and Jonathan reached Ranch Road, they turned right toward Montview. Lily waved and blew a kiss.

Rose sat a while by the lone twisty pine, then turned left, back toward Gold Creek, the saddle empty behind her.

## Chapter 45

# *Cut Off*

"Before I can marry you, I need to talk with your fathers," Reverend Hayward said. He looked across his desk at Lily and Jonathan sitting opposite him.

Lily's heart sank. "But," she protested. "The reason we're here is because Papa has forbidden us to marry."

"How is that?" Reverend Hayward's kindly face was concerned. "He forbade you?"

Jonathan spoke then, pouring out their story—how they'd been promised for a year, how happy Jonathan's parents were with their betrothal, the shock of Reverend Wright's refusal, and the reasons he gave.

Reverend Haywood's eyes were warm with sympathy. "Brother Wright is very strict with dogma," he said. "Andrew Fairdale is the best Christian I know. He doesn't say the words, but he lives the way. 'By their fruit ye shall know them.' I can't imagine, Miss Lily, that you would be led astray from Paradise by living at Fairdale Ranch. But I need to think about this. Reverend Wright is a colleague and a friend. I don't like the idea of going against him."

He pursed his lips and was silent a while. "Go on home," he said. "I have much to attend to in the next few days, but I'll come to Fairdale Ranch on Saturday and talk with both your fathers. We'll see if we can find a solution."

Lily wept as they rode slowly out of Montview. "I can't go home. Papa said I could never see you again. He might lock me up or marry me to some other man like he almost did with Mr. Jenkins. He broke his promise and I don't trust him anymore."

Jonathan held her close, his arm warm around her waist. "I have an idea," he said. "Let's go to the cabin. Father says we don't need a minister to connect to God. We only need to open our hearts. We can pray to God to marry us. We can make our own wedding, say our vows to each other. Then we'll be married in the sight of God, and no one can separate us." He guided Brandy off the road and turned Lily to face him. "Will you marry me that way, Lily?"

Lily's heart leapt. "Yes!" she said. A huge smile broke through her tears.

~

The cabin was in a mountain meadow with wildflowers all around. They carried their bags inside, tethered Brandy, then walked hand in hand to a high grassy knoll. Mountains upon mountains spread below them, purple-blue in the twilight. Lily knew most of the marriage words and they made up the rest. When Jonathan kissed her at the end of ceremony, Lily felt it was the most sacred moment of her life.

Their marriage bed was a straw mat by the hearth in the cabin. There the urgency of their kisses found fulfillment at last, and Lily experienced the shock and joy of being entered, becoming one with her beloved.

In the days that followed they laughed and loved, wandered in mountain meadows, dreamed by sparkling streams, and loved again.

On the fourth day they rode slowly down the mountain trail toward Fairview Ranch. Jonathan's arm circled Lily's waist. She leaned back against him, delighting in the feel of his lean body moving with Brandy, as the horse made his way down the steep slope. Late afternoon sun sent their shadow ahead of them.

Lily was brimming with bliss. I'm completely changed, she thought. I'm a woman now, a wife, and I know what love is. Maybe soon I'll be a mother. Maybe there's already a baby growing inside me.

The path leveled out. They were down out of the foothills approaching Fairdale Ranch. Brandy picked up his pace. Jonathan bent and kissed her cheek.

"Father may be angry," he said. "And Reverend Haywood, too, since we didn't go home as he told us to. But we are truly married now, no matter what."

They passed under the high gate that marked the boundary of Fairdale Ranch, forded the stream, and followed the road between the pastures. Amy saw them from the garden. "Hi, Jonathan, hi Lily," she called, then gathered up her skirts and ran toward the house to spread the news. They could hear her calling as she ran, "Jonathan's back and Lily's with him, riding on Brandy, and she has her bag on the back with her violin sticking out, and ..." Her voice faded away as she disappeared inside.

When they reached the barn they met Andrew and Bernie coming in with a wagon load of hay. Andrew jumped down from the wagon and approached them. Lily could see right away that he was angry.

"What have you done?" he asked Jonathan. "You told me you were going camping to get over your grief about Lily, and now I see you riding in with her. Her father has been frantic, searching for her."

"Father—" Jonathan began.

But Andrew cut him off. "Dismount and take care of your horse. I'll meet you in the house. We need to talk."

He watched as they dismounted. Jonathan untied Lily's bag and handed it to her, then led Brandy into the barn. Lily felt suddenly alone, not like a woman anymore, but like a child about to be punished.

Andrew turned to her. "Go into the house. Kate will look after you."

As Lily walked slowly up the porch steps, Amy burst out, followed by Kate and Julia. They led her into the house. Amy and Julia hugged her. Julia asked, "Are you okay?"

Kate was stern. "We've been worried about you. Where have you been?"

Lily lifted her chin. "I'm okay. Jonathan has been taking care of me."

"Have you been with Jonathan all this time?" Kate asked.

Andrew had come to the door and stood listening. Lily blushed. "Yes."

"Sit down, Lily, Kate," Andrew said. "Amy, Julia, leave us." Amy hovered in the doorway. "Amy, go."

The girls left. Andrew shut the door between the living room and the kitchen, and seated himself. Jonathan came in and sat by Lily on the couch. Lily reached for his hand, her heart thumping. She loved Andrew and Kate and was upset at displeasing them. She had never seen them angry before.

"All right, Jonathan," Andrew said. "You owe us an explanation. A week ago you came home angry that Reverend Wright refused to let you marry Lily. I shared your disappointment and your anger for the reason he gave and let you go off to be with your grief, even though it's haying time. The day you left Reverend Wright came, much distraught that Lily was missing. I now hear that you have been together, somewhere, since then. You deceived me, and you, Lily, have caused your family much anxiety and distress."

Lily held tight to Jonathan's hand. Jonathan looked straight into his father's eyes.

"Father, I am sorry to deceive you. But I didn't know what else to do. I couldn't let Lily go and have her father prevent me from ever seeing her again. She is my true love. You know. I've built the cabin, and you and Mother were so happy Lily would be my wife. But I knew you wouldn't go against Reverend Wright, so the only possibility was to elope."

"Elope!" Kate exclaimed. "Are you married then?"

"Yes." Jonathan turned to look at Lily, love and pride in his eyes. "We got married last Monday evening."

"Who married you?" Kate asked.

"God," Jonathan answered.

"God!" Kate exclaimed.

"Yes. We went to Montview to ask Reverend Haywood to marry us, but he wouldn't without talking to you. He said he would come here on Saturday and told us to go home. But we were afraid Reverend Wright would never let Lily go again, and that he'd come here looking for her, as he did. So we went to the shepherd's cabin."

"What do you mean God married you?" Kate demanded.

Jonathan turned to Andrew. "You said once we don't really need ministers if we open our hearts to God. So we prayed to God to marry us. Lily knows the marriage words. We said them to each other. In the sight of God we are married."

"Oh, Andrew," Kate said. "Sometimes you go too far. You *do* need a minister to be married." She looked at Jonathan and Lily, a frown between her brows. "And then you behaved as if you were married?"

"Yes," Jonathan answered.

The room was silent. Lily could feel her heart thumping. She was glad Jonathan's hand was warm and strong around hers, because Kate and Andrew looked stern and she was afraid.

"What a fine mess," Kate said finally. "Triggered by our dear Daniel being so fearful about salvation and so narrow … And you two." She shook her head, sudden tears in her eyes. "Young love can't be stopped. But we must get you properly married soon because— Did you say Reverend Haywood was coming here tomorrow?"

"He said he would," Jonathan answered, "to talk to Father and Reverend Wright. But Reverend Wright already said no."

"The situation has changed," Andrew said. "We must send word to him at once. I'll see if James can take a letter." He got up and left the room.

Kate stood. "Jonathan, you will sleep in your cabin tonight. Lily, I will put you in Jonathan's room upstairs. Under the circumstances I think it's best that you not sleep with the girls. And until you are properly married, by a minister, you and Jonathan will not sleep together. Come, I'll get you settled."

Lily felt a pang when Jonathan let go of her hand. Not long afterward, she stood alone in Jonathan's room upstairs under the eaves. There was only a desk in the corner and a narrow bed along the wall. He'd already moved most of his possessions to the cabin in preparation for her joining him there.

She was suddenly desolate at the thought of sleeping alone in that little room. If only Rose were with her.

Maybe she'd come, Lily thought. James is going. I'll send a note. She ran down the stairs into the kitchen where Kate and Julia were helping Sophia prepare supper. "Did James leave yet?" she asked.

"I'm just fixing him a bite to eat along the way," Sophia answered.

"I want to send a note to Rose," Lily said.

Kate looked up from the carrots she was peeling. "There's paper and a pencil over there on the shelf by the door."

"Thanks." Lily found the paper and pencil and sat down at the kitchen table.

*Dear Rose, Please come back with James. Get away from Papa if you possibly can and come. I need you. Bring my pink silk. I'm getting married tomorrow. Love, Lily.*

I hope that's true, she thought as she folded the note.

James came into the kitchen, his hat in his hand. "I'm off," he said. Sophia handed him a packet of food.

"Please, James," Lily said, jumping up from the table. "Would you give this note to my sister?"

"Sure." James smiled at her. "I'm the mailman tonight, a letter from Mr. Fairdale to your pa and now a note to Miss Rose. She'll be glad to hear from you." He took the note, patted Sophia's shoulder. "I should be back before dark."

Lily watched him tuck her little note into his pocket as he departed. She stood in the midst of the kitchen bustle longing for Rose, the warm comfort of her body, the constancy of her love. Only then did it occur to her that she could have opened the door between their hearts and called her. The door had been closed ever since they'd said good-bye on Monday. She slid it open. At first she couldn't find Rose, then felt only a vague sense of her. Maybe she wouldn't have heard me. Oh, I don't want to lose connection with her. I hope she can come. Papa will never let her. I hope she can escape.

～

Rose sat on the floor of the living room, playing with Joshua to keep him out from under foot while Rachel and Isabel prepared supper in the kitchen. Rose and Joshua piled his blocks into towers which he then gleefully knocked down.

Suddenly she felt a stirring in her heart. Lily? She lifted her head. *Where are you, Lily?* she called silently. But there was no answer, only the sense that Lily wanted her.

Joshua knocked down his tower with a crash. "Do it again," he said. But Rose hardly heard him. She was on her feet, turning from side to side, all her senses reaching out to that whisper in her heart, searching, searching. A stirring only, nothing more.

"'Gain. Do it again," Joshua insisted.

Rose fled up the stairs to her room. She heard Joshua's wail, then Rachel saying, "What's the matter? Where's Rose?"

The bedroom window was open to the warm late afternoon. Swiftly, Rose slipped through and ran out onto the hill. "Lily," she called, "Lily." No answer, only the feeling that Lily was lonely and needed her. She shouldn't be lonely, Rose thought. She's with Jonathan. Has anything happened? Rose ran as far as the spring coming out of the split rock. There she stood, turning again, heart aching, calling. She wanted to get Dawnstar and start riding, anywhere, to find Lily, put her arms around her and comfort her. She started toward the pasture where Dawnstar was grazing, but then the connection with Lily was gone, snapped into silence, and with it the tenuous thread that might have guided her.

Rose dropped down onto the rough grass, drew her knees up to her chest, and buried her face in her skirts. Anguish, like cold darkness, swept through her. The last days had been a nightmare, reaching futilely for Lily's hand, tossing sleepless in the empty bed, turning to share and finding herself alone. She felt as if half of herself had been torn away and she bled from a mortal wound. How long can I bleed, she wondered, before I die?

The whole family had been shaken. Daniel came back from Fairdale Ranch that first night, sat her on the bench by the hearth, raging and questioning her, demanding until she couldn't hold out any longer and confessed to taking Lily to meet Jonathan.

"Where are they?" he shouted at her. Rose didn't know. She thought then that he might strike her, but Rachel intervened, and he gave up questioning her.

Still he raged, pacing and threatening what he would do to Lily when he saw her again, until Joshua wailed and Rachel stamped her foot and insisted Daniel be quiet.

In the days that followed he fretted about what people would say if they knew his daughter had run off, and told them not to speak of it, though Rose knew he had gone to Gabe for comfort. Rachel was stretched thin trying to calm Daniel and dealing with Joshua, who responded to the family tension by becoming fussy and clingy.

Only Isabel seemed to remember Rose and to comprehend how shattered she was. Rose would often feel her keen, compassionate gaze, and once when Isabel found her sitting hunched and weeping in a corner of the garden, she wrapped her arms around Rose and rocked her. "I know you miss her something awful," was all she said, but Rose was comforted by her understanding.

Now Isabel was calling her. She came out the kitchen door and looked up onto the hill as if she knew where Rose would be. "There you are," she said. "Sitting up there all by your lonesome. Come on down now. Supper's ready. We're not going to wait for your pa. He may be late."

Rose came slowly down the hill, part of her still listening, still hoping for a whisper of connection. She was relieved Daniel wasn't home yet. Even though he'd stopped shouting, his anger filled the house with tension.

They had just sat down to eat when they heard a horse approaching. "There's Daniel," Rachel said, jumping up.

But it wasn't Daniel. It was James from Fairdale Ranch. He'd come, he told them, to let them know that Lily was there and safe, and to bring a letter from Mr. Fairdale to Reverend Wright.

"Reverend Wright's not here," Rachel told him. "There was a cave-in up at the mine and two men died. He's been gone all day. I don't know when he'll be back."

"Well," James said. "Give him this when he comes. Mr. Fairdale said it was very important." He handed an envelope to Rachel. "And there's a note for you, Miss Rose, from your sister," he added, taking the note out of his pocket.

The little piece of paper shook in Rose's hand as she opened it. Lily *had* been calling.

"What's that runaway rascal got to say?" Isabel asked.

Rose scanned the note quickly. "She wants me to come. She needs me. And to bring her some things." Rose looked up at James. "She suggests I ride back with you. Would you be willing to wait a few minutes?"

"Sure, Miss Rose."

"Rose," Rachel said. "Your papa—"

"Lily *needs* me," Rose interrupted. "I'll be just a moment, James."

She dashed up the stairs to her room before Rachel could say any more. *Lily, I'm coming,* she called silently. She searched through Lily's shelves. She found the pink silk, a clean shimmy, and, amidst a tangle of hair ornaments on the top shelf, Lily's favorite comb. *She's getting married tomorrow? I thought they were getting married the day they ran away. What happened?*

Swiftly she packed Lily's things in her carpet bag. *What do I need? My hairbrush, my nightgown, my flute.* Her heart raced as she packed.

In a few minutes she was downstairs again, her bag in her hand. Rachel was offering James coffee. *No!* Rose thought. *I need to get out of here before Papa comes back.*

"Thank you, ma'am," James answered. "But if Miss Rose here is ready, I need to be getting on home."

"I'm ready," Rose said. "I just need to saddle Dawnstar." She raced out the door and up the hill to the pasture. She wasn't used to saddling Dawnstar without Lily, and everything seemed to take agonizingly long. At last she was mounted. From her vantage point on the hill she saw Daniel coming along Gold Creek Road past the boarding house.

She rode down to the house where James was mounting his horse. Trying to sound calm she said, "Let's go this way. I know a short cut across the fields that will take us to Ranch Road."

"A short cut, eh?" James looked uncertain. "You sure?"

"Oh, yes. I go that way all the time."

"Lead off, then."

Rose led him back up the hill and into Nathan's orchard, cutting northeast through the trees. James stopped to make an adjustment to his saddle. Rose was frantic. *If Papa comes up Pine Road before we get behind Nathan's barn—.* She urged Dawnstar forward. At last James was moving again, catching up with her.

"You in a big hurry?" he asked.

Rose looked back. Daniel was in sight, coming up the hill. *Don't let him look this way,* she prayed.

"I'm eager to see Lily," she answered and kicked Dawnstar into a gallop. It wasn't until they reached Ranch Road that she slowed down. Her heart was still racing.

~

That night she lay in Lily's arms in the narrow bed under the eaves at Fairdale Ranch, drinking in the dear familiar feel of Lily's body wrapped around hers. But it wasn't the same. Lily smelled different.

Nothing was the same. When Rose arrived at Fairdale Ranch and came to the kitchen where the family was gathered around the long table, Lily looked as if she already belonged there, part of the family, sitting between Jonathan and Julia. Lily had jumped up to hug her, everyone had greeted her warmly, but she felt like an outsider, a guest.

Now she lay snuggled against Lily as Lily poured out her adventures, the cabin in the mountains, the marriage ceremony.

"You're already married?" Rose asked. "What about tomorrow?"

"Jonathan said we didn't need a minister, but Mrs. Fairdale says we do, and she wouldn't even let me sleep in the cabin with Jonathan until a minister marries us. So we're going to have another wedding tomorrow. Reverend Haywood is coming, and Mr. Fairdale wrote to Papa and told him to come, too."

"Papa! He won't let you marry Jonathan."

"He has to. Because we've been together and I might be … Mr. Fairdale wrote it all to him."

Rose cringed at the idea of her father appearing. She had just run away from him.

But Lily didn't seem too concerned. "I'm so glad you could come," she said, kissing Rose's cheek. "I wanted you to be with me the night before my wedding. It would be awful to have to sleep alone here tonight."

Pain ripped through Rose. She already knew the agony of sleeping alone and realized Lily would never know it. She would have Rose that night, and ever after Jonathan.

The door between their hearts was only partway open. Rose tried to shield Lily from her anguish but didn't know how. Lily held her closer.

"Rose?"

"I'm okay."

"I think I may have a baby growing inside me."

Rose's belly knotted. "You mean … Jonathan …?"

"Yes."

The feelings that flooded through the half-open door shook Rose to the bone. "You did that?"

"Oh, yes!"

Rose could hardly bear the tumult of sensation that swept into her from Lily. *Dear Jesus*, she whispered inwardly. She tried to slow her breath. Finally she asked, "Did it hurt?"

"Just for a moment. And then it felt like … like nothing I've ever known. Bliss. You know that part of the marriage ceremony where it says to love, honor, and cherish? I think that's what cherishing means. And I wanted him to do it again and again, and he wanted to, so we did. And now maybe … When my baby's ready to be born, will you come and help me?"

"Of course."

"You're trembling."

"I'm cold."

"Oh." Lily pulled the blanket up around them. "Snuggle up. You'll be warm now. I'm so glad you're here." She kissed Rose's cheek and curled her body closer around her.

Gradually Rose let her muscles relax. Pretend, she told herself. Pretend this isn't the last time.

～

This is the last time, Daniel resolved as he rode under the high arch and along the road between the well-kept pastures of Fairdale Ranch the next morning. I will bring my daughters home and we will never come here again. Too much harm has come to my family because of the Fairdales. Under the resolution, grief rose like a tidal wave for all he would lose—seeing the light in Andrew's clear gray eyes, the deep conversations, the music, the family gathered around the long table. He set his jaw.

It had all gone wrong because he had not listened to his conscience, had not heeded Reverend Caldwell's warning. He should have stopped all visits to Fairdale Ranch after that very first time, over a year ago, when he learned that Andrew wasn't a Christian. But he'd been seduced by Andrew's intelligence, his library, the music, the beauty of the ranch, all of it, and the twins, young and impressionable, had fallen the hardest. He'd even taken Rachel there, and now Kate was her closest friend. He just needed to get his family back under control. He clenched his jaw tighter.

Rachel sat silent beside him in the buggy, Joshua on her knee. They had quarreled the night before and his heart still ached with the memory of that.

She had given him the letter from Andrew as soon as he arrived home. He read it, threw it on the floor and erupted with all the frustration, rage, and fear of disgrace he had struggled with since Lily ran away. He couldn't remember now what he'd said, but Joshua had begun to wail, and Rachel had called Isabel to take him for a walk. She picked up the letter. "May I?"

As she read, he continued storming. "I'm going right away to bring her home. I'll lock her up. I'll not have her defying me like that. Where's Rose?"

When he learned that Rose, too, had disobeyed him and gone to Lily, he started out the door. But Rachel caught his arm and drew him back. He remembered her gentle touch, and wished he had not thrown it off.

"Please, Daniel," she'd said. "You've had a long day. It must have been hard up there at the mine. I've saved you some supper. Please come back. It's late now. I'll go with you tomorrow."

So he had come in and eaten. As he ate, she tried to reason with him. "We really don't have much choice. She must marry Jonathan now. They've been together as man and wife for five days."

"I don't care. I'm bringing her home. Whatever marriage they did has no validity."

"But what if she is with child?"

"She can't be."

"Of course she can. We may not know for a month or two, but by then it will be too late. Do you think the ladies of our church can't count to nine?"

"Then I'll marry her immediately to someone appropriate. Gerald Dodge has always admired the twins."

"Gerald Dodge! He wouldn't suit her. Besides it's Rose he's attracted to."

"That's beside the point. Don't you understand? This is not even a matter of life and death; this is a matter of eternal salvation or damnation. She's gone far astray, but in time she can be brought back."

Rachel's fists were clenched on the table. "Daniel, you can't force her. She's already shown you that. The only graceful option we have is to go tomorrow and bless her marriage, and, as far as the church is concerned, just say they preferred a quiet ceremony at the ranch."

"*Bless* their marriage! I cannot."

Joshua was wailing. Isabel came in carrying him. "I'm sorry, Rachel, but this young man needs his ma and his bed."

"Thank you, Isabel, I'll take him now." Rachel took her child, held him close and rocked him. Over his head, she met Daniel's eyes. "Please reconsider."

Rage stormed up in him again. "I cannot. Will you, too, defy me? I must attend to God's will and safeguard my daughter's salvation."

Rachel's eyes had blazed then and her voice snapped like a whip. "Maybe it is not God's will you are attending to, but Daniel's." She carried Joshua into the bedroom and closed the door. Later that night, when he reached for her, she had turned away from him for the first time in their marriage.

Reverend Haywood's buggy was parked by the barn. Daniel recognized his white horse. He tied Shadow to the hitching post and lifted Rachel and Joshua out of the buggy. He held Rachel close for a moment. "Help me," he begged. "Please stand by me. I need you."

She looked up at him with her dark, clear eyes. "I do stand by you, Daniel. But we must listen to God's guidance."

He wasn't quite sure what that meant, but was comforted by her hand in his as they walked up the wide steps to the porch.

"Go on in," she said, giving his hand a squeeze. "I'll take Joshua around to find Molly and Johnny."

Reverend Haywood, Kate, Andrew, Lily, and Jonathan were gathered in the living room. Andrew came forward to greet him. Reverend Haywood shook his hand. Lily kept her head bent and wouldn't look at him.

"Please sit down, Daniel," Kate said. "Can I bring you any refreshment?"

"No, no thank you." Daniel sat down. A moment later Rachel slipped in, kissed Kate and Lily, and drew up a chair close beside him. There was a moment of awkward silence.

"I'm glad you've come," Reverend Haywood spoke up. "I was just saying I wanted your agreement before I marry these two."

"You don't have it," Daniel said. "I've forbidden this marriage. I've come to take my daughters home. Where's Rose?"

"She's with Julia and Amy," Kate answered. "We didn't think it suitable for her to be part of this conversation."

Reverend Haywood cleared his throat. "We've been discussing it, Brother Wright. Since Lily and Jonathan have said their vows to one another, in all sincerity, in the presence of God, and have lived together as man and wife for these last five days, it seems wise to seal their marriage. What God has joined together, let no man put asunder."

Daniel felt rage rise in him again and struggled to contain it. "What God has joined together! Their joining has come, not from God, but from unseemly lust. You see what comes of your free-thinking ways?" he said to Andrew. He saw the hurt in Andrew's eyes but couldn't stop. "These two young people have been led into sin and fornication. Their so-called marriage has no validity. Lily is coming home with me."

Jonathan leaped to his feet. "It does have validity, sir. Reverend Haywood agrees."

Lily was on her feet also, standing beside Jonathan, her chin up. "And what's more," she said, "it has been richly consummated."

Daniel stared at her, burning. Slowly he stood to face his daughter. "Whore," he said.

The room went dead silent. Lily looked as if she'd been slapped in the face.

Jonathan took a step toward Daniel, fists clenched. "How dare you call my wife a whore!"

Andrew stepped quickly beside him and laid a hand on his shoulder. "Easy, son."

Lily's cheeks flushed. Her eyes glittered with tears. She shot her words straight at Daniel. "Let he who is without sin cast the first stone."

All eyes turned to Daniel. Rachel was beside him, her hand holding his tight. He swayed. The room blurred. Was it over now? Would everyone know? How could she betray him so?

"There now," Reverend Haywood said. "Those were wise words of our Lord because we are all sinners, all in need of His blessed blood to cleanse us. Please sit down, everyone. Let's have a moment of prayer."

Outside the window that opened onto the porch there was a scuffling sound and a muted exclamation. Andrew strode to the window and looked through. "What's this? I told you girls to stay away." The three girls emerged from their hiding place below the window sill. Rose swung her legs over the sill, ran to Lily's side, and wrapped her arms around her. Julia and Amy stood in the window hanging their heads.

"Go to your room," Andrew ordered them, "and stay there until I call you."

Amy and Julia disappeared from the window. Andrew turned to Rose. "Rose, we thought it best for you not be involved in this."

"But I am," Rose said, her voice quavering. "Lily is part of me."

"Let her stay." Rachel spoke in her soft voice. "What happens with Lily deeply affects her."

"Please, everyone sit down," Reverend Haywood said again. He turned to Daniel. The prayer seemed forgotten for a moment. "Brother Wright, under the circumstances, I do believe it best for these young people to be formally wed today. Even though she lives here, she will surely come to church and bring her new husband. Will you not reconsider?"

Something snapped inside Daniel. He barely kept his voice under control. "I have, in this moment, reconsidered. Lily, you are no longer my daughter. I cut you off. Nor are you welcome in my church, or in my home. Marry whom you please. I'm done with you. Andrew, I regret that I can no longer be your friend, nor can I allow my family to mingle with yours." He tried to ignore the look on Andrew's face, Kate's startled movement. "Your lax ways have caused too much grief to me and mine. Rachel, get Joshua. Rose, come. We are going home."

Rose still had her arms tightly wrapped around Lily. She lifted her chin. "No, Papa. I'm staying with Lily."

"I will stay, also," Rachel said. She released his hand and looked up at him. "Lily is about to be married and needs her family with her. She needs you, too. Please, relent, stay and give her your blessing. Do not cut off those who love you."

The rage drained out of Daniel, leaving behind grief and a numbing sense of isolation. "You, too?" he murmured. He turned away from her toward the door, his shoulders bent. "I cannot."

# Chapter 46

# *Desolation*

Rose stirred. The morning sun slanting in the eastern window had awakened her. She lay still a moment, confused. A chill began at the center of her body and spread through her. Slowly she rolled onto her back and stretched out her hand. Nothing. Only the empty bed, the sheets cold where no one had slept. She let out a brief, incoherent sound. In a swift movement she turned her back on the emptiness, curled into a ball, her eyes tight shut. A sob caught in her chest, but could not come through.

Unbidden, a memory floated behind her closed eyes. An evening on the trail, long long ago it seemed. In the center of the wagon circle, a fire burned. Seth was playing his accordion and the people of the wagon train were gathered around singing. Lily sat across the circle from Rose, the firelight bright on her hair.

Rose remembered how in that moment she realized for the first time that she loved Lily. How strange she had not known before. Was it because they had been one and you can only love what is other? Was that the moment they ceased to be one? That moment so long ago?

Later that evening as they walked hand in hand to their wagon, Rose stopped Lily, took both her hands and said, her heart aching with tenderness, "You know, I just realized I love you."

Lily frowned. "Of course," was all she said. She dropped one of Rose's hands. Still holding the other one she continued walking toward the wagon. Rose remembered the shocking thought—she doesn't understand. A cold sliver of fear pierced her heart. She covered it with protest. Of course she understands. Lily understands everything I feel.

That was only the beginning. In the last year as Lily slipped farther and farther away, the sliver of fear had penetrated deeper. And now, no longer a sliver, it spread to engulf her. The thought of going on without Lily was crushing, impossible, utter terror.

Downstairs she heard the bedroom door open, Joshua babbling and Rachel talking to him as they passed through on their way to the privy. Then the sounds of Isabel stirring up the cookstove.

I should get up, Rose thought. I can't. I can't.

Daniel's voice floated up through the vent as he crossed the living room into the kitchen. "Good morning, Isabel. How soon till breakfast? Remember it's Monday. I need to leave soon for the prayer meeting out east."

Slowly Rose uncurled and sat on the edge of the bed. Monday. A week ago, only a week ago, she'd taken Lily to meet Jonathan. She had to get up. She'd promised Lily she'd take her trunk to her today.

The floor was cold under her bare feet. I have to pack all her things. How can I tell what's mine and what's hers? Our books, our music. How can I divide them? They're just ours. Even our clothes. She pulled her feet up off the cold floor and hugged her knees to her chest.

Across the room, the shelves Gabe had built on either side of the window were filled with their mingled possessions. One side was supposed to be for Rose, the other for Lily, but they had never paid attention to such a division.

Somehow she had to separate out what was Lily's, take it to Fairdale Ranch, and be back before Papa returned from his prayer meeting.

Daniel had been stern the day before, sitting Rachel and Rose on the bench by the hearth, delivering his orders from his leather chair.

"You understand you are never to go to Fairdale Ranch again. Either of you, for any reason. And Lily is not to come here. Or any of the Fairdales."

Rachel had answered, "I will obey you in this for now, Daniel, but it is all wrong. I trust in time you will realize that and open your heart to Lily again."

"You heard how she betrayed me."

"No one knew. It was only your guilt that heard her words as betrayal." She drew in her breath to say more, but Daniel cut her off.

"Enough!"

Rachel was quiet, but Rose, sitting close to her, could feel her rebellion.

"Rose," Daniel said. "Do you understand?"

Rose had nodded.

I understood, she thought now, but I didn't say I agreed.

She stood, gazed a moment at the confusion of hers and Lily's clothes, then pulled on one of the dark blue dresses they had worn on the train, faded now from many wearings and washings. Rose gathered a fold of the skirt in her hand. Maybe it was the one Lily had worn. They had still been one then. She finished dressing, brushed out her hair and twisted it up, longing for the touch of Lily's gentle, skilled hands. Then she opened the door and went downstairs.

After Daniel had left, Rachel asked, "Are you going?"

"I promised her I would. Before Papa told me I couldn't. She'll need her things."

"Would you like me to help you pack them up?"

"No." Rose turned and climbed the stairs.

She began. Some things were easier. The box Gabe had made for Lily with the lily carved on top. The other dark blue dress. She started a pile on the bed. The white knitted hat and mittens Amy and Julia had made for Lily. Her boots, scuffed a little differently than Rose's. One of the green linsey-woolsey dresses they had worn on the trail, frayed at the hems, mended here and there. Rose chose the least tattered one for Lily. Lily already had her pink silk. The blue grey Sunday dress with the lace at the throat. Their silk shimmies from Boston. Rose divided them, three for each of them. Their hair combs. She worked faster, separating all the rest of their possessions arbitrarily. She found the money packets Grandmama had given them, divided the remaining money and put one packet on top of the pile. One pillow.

When everything was sorted, she carried armloads downstairs and packed them into one of the trunks. She took a long blue coat off the hook by the door, laid it on top, and shut the lid. Rachel rearranged the mat that had made a couch out of the two trunks.

"Your papa will notice right away a trunk is gone."

"Let him," Rose said. "It's hers."

When she went back upstairs to find her boots, the stark emptiness of the room hit her like a blow in the belly. I can't stand it, she thought. I can't come back to this.

All at once her grief turned to anger. I won't. I won't come back. I'll stay with Lily. They have two rooms in their cabin. I know I can't sleep with her any more, but at least I can see her every day and help her with her house.

Swiftly she packed her carpet bag. Her thoughts flew faster than her hands, rage burning in her chest.

I hate Papa. I'll never come back. He can just get along without me. I hate him. How could he treat Lily that way? How could he say I could never see her again? She is part of me. I'll die without her.

Rose slipped her packed bag out the window onto the hillside and climbed out after it. In the stable she hitched Dawnstar to the cart, hid her bag under her cloak in the front of the cart, and brought it around to the front of the house. Isabel and Rachel helped her load the trunk. Rose kissed them good-bye. Isabel held her tight, then set her back to look into her face, her green eyes sharp and questioning.

"Be sure to be back before your papa," Rachel said. "He's just beginning to calm down. I don't want him to get angry again."

Rose gave Rachel another kiss, climbed up on the seat of the cart, and set off.

An hour later she reached Fairdale Ranch and pulled up in front of the big house. Molly came out with Johnny on her hip.

"They're all over in the orchard getting in the apples," she told Rose, "except Miss Lily. She's up in her new home, settling in. Go on up. She was hoping you'd come."

"Thanks." Rose guided Dawnstar around the barn and up the new path that led to Jonathan's cabin.

It was quiet up there, except for the soft sigh of a light wind in the grasses and the muted voice of the creek in the valley below. The cabin was nestled, neat and snug, into the side of the knoll near the top. The sun glinted off the new glass in the windows.

Rose drove the cart up to the little porch on the front of the cabin. She sat a moment, remembering Jonathan carrying Lily over the threshold after their wedding, the family gathered calling out blessings, the rending feeling in her chest.

The door was open. Rose could hear Lily inside humming a Bach minuet. A moment later she came out on the porch to shake out a little rug.

"Rose." She smiled, welcoming. "You came."

She dropped the rug and ran down the steps from the porch. Rose jumped off the cart and into her arms. Lily's kisses. Lily's arms around her. For a moment Rose was whole again. Then Lily drew back.

"Does Papa know you're here?"

Rose shook her head. "I waited till he was gone to his prayer meeting."

Lily looked into the cart. "You brought my trunk. Good. Let's take it in."

She let go of Rose and greeted Dawnstar, stroking her neck and scratching behind her ears. "Dawnstar will be your very own horse now," she said. "Jonathan gave me a horse for a wedding gift. She's beautiful, a palomino. Her name is Sunshine. She's young and still kind of frisky, but Jonathan will help me train her. I rode her a little while yesterday in the corral." She opened the back of the cart as she talked. Rose still stood where Lily had left her, bereft, the embrace too brief to solace all the loneliness of the last week.

"Come on," Lily said. "Grab an end." She pulled the trunk toward the open back of the cart. Rose recovered herself and went to help. They carried the trunk into the cabin and set it down.

Lily spread out her arms. "This is my new home. Isn't it beautiful? Jonathan thought of everything."

The main room of the cabin was simply furnished. Rose recognized two rocking chairs that had been in the big house. There was a new couch along one wall. I could sleep there, Rose thought. One end of the room was a kitchen with a table and two chairs, a sink with a pump, and a cookstove. Lily caught her hand.

"Come see my kitchen. We even have running water. See." She swung the pump handle up and down and water poured out, bright and clear. "I love my cookstove. And look at this. Jonathan made cupboards with doors, and Mother gave us some dishes." She opened a cupboard, revealing a stack of pretty china.

"Mother?" Rose asked, an ache in her voice.

"Yes. Mrs. Fairdale says I am to call her Mother and Mr. Fairdale Father, because I'm part of the family now." She whirled around in the middle of the kitchen. Her joy and excitement cascaded through Rose.

"Come see the bedroom."

The bedroom opened off the main room. There was a wide bed, a wardrobe, a window looking out over the plains.

Rose looked at the bed. She sleeps there with Jonathan. And they … She couldn't think of that.

Lily was still bubbling. "Jonathan made the bed big enough for us and a babe, when we have one." She gestured toward the window. "And in the morning the sun comes in. Don't you love it?"

"It's very nice," Rose said. It was—clean and new and cozy.

Lily smoothed a wrinkle on the coverlet of the bed with her left hand. The gold ring shone on her finger. A wave of desolation went through Rose. She belongs to Jonathan now.

"Help me unpack the trunk." Lily danced back into the main room. Rose followed.

"I think I brought everything," she said. "It was hard to know what was yours and what was mine."

Lily lifted the top of the trunk. "Oh, good, you brought a coat." She pulled it out and laid it on one of the chairs. "Music." She picked up the pile of music and handed it to Rose. "You keep the music. They have so much here. You'll need it for church." She glanced back at the chest, then said, "I can get the rest of this later. You should go soon so you'll be back before Papa gets home."

Rose stood holding the sheaf of music. "I'm not going home," she said. "I brought my bag. I want to stay here with you. I can help …"

Her voice trailed off. She'd never seen that look on Lily's face before. Then the words came.

"No, Rose. You have to go back. I don't want you to stay here. This cabin is just for me and Jonathan. Don't you understand? We're married. We need our privacy."

"I could sleep on the couch," Rose said. But even as she said it, she knew it was all wrong. Everything was wrong. The look on Lily's face, her eyes bright and angry, her whole body tense.

Rose set the music down on top of the trunk. She stepped forward, caught both of Lily's hands. "Please, Lily. I can't go back. Papa says I can never see you again. I can't live without you. You're part of me. I'm all torn when we're apart. I'll die without you. Let me stay."

Lily shook her hands free with a slight push, pushing Rose away from her. She stamped her foot. "I'm *not* part of you. I told you that before. I am myself. And you are you. You won't die. That's ridiculous. Don't hang on me. I'm married now. I need to be free to love Jonathan. Don't you understand?"

The door between their hearts slammed shut.

Rose stood a moment staring at her twin. Nausea swept through her.

She spun and ran out the open door and down the steps, hurled herself up onto the cart, flicked the reins on Dawnstar and turned her, flicked the reins again to signal her to go fast. They careened down the path. Just as they passed the big house, Julia and Amy came around the barn carrying a basket of apples between them.

"Hi, Rose," they greeted her.

Rose kept going, her head bent, her eyes stinging with tears. She hit a bump in the road and the cart jounced behind her.

"Rose, wait," Julia called. She shouted something else, but Rose couldn't hear her. There was a roaring in her ears, filling her body with darkness.

Lily's words. Don't hang on me. I'm married now. *Lily pushing her away.*

She drove blindly, between the pastures, under the high gate, out onto Ranch Road. After a while she came to the lone twisted pine tree, and impulsively turned, so quickly that the cart tipped onto one wheel. Down the path she had taken Lily a week ago, down the hill into the trees. There she pulled Dawnstar to a halt and tumbled off the cart onto the ground.

She curled up in the grass under the cottonwoods. The sobs came, horrible racking sobs, tearing her chest open, taking her breath, shaking her whole body.

Lily gone. The touch of her hand, the smell of her hair, the sound of her voice, her laughter, the way their eyes met to start a new phrase of music, her kisses.

Inside empty swirling darkness.

Fairdale Ranch gone. Lily had it all—the pool in the creek with the rope swing, Amy and Julia, the music, her own horse, the garden, Mrs. Fairdale for mother. And Rose cut off from it all.

She cried until she lay exhausted on the ground.

Dawnstar shifted her feet and bent her neck to nudge Rose. Rose uncurled and looked up at the big head hanging over her, the silver mane. She reached up to touch the moist muzzle. Dawnstar lifted her head and sniffed, then started to walk past Rose deeper into the trees. The cart caught on a fallen tree limb. Dawnstar jerked it, but that only wedged it more firmly. She snorted and looked back at Rose.

Rose's whole body ached. She crawled forward, pulled herself up on a low branch and leaned against Dawnstar's neck. "What is it, Dawnstar?" she asked.

Dawnstar pulled again on the cart. Some of the branches on the limb snapped, but the cart remained stuck. Rose became aware of the sound of running water.

"Poor Dawnstar," she said, stroking the horse's neck. "You're thirsty. I drove you so hard and left you hitched." She undid the tracings of the cart. Dawnstar shook herself and started off toward the sound of water. Rose followed. Just a short way through the trees, they came to the creek. It was a small stream with a bright voice and a lively flow, shallow, but with a few deeper pools.

Rose sat down, leaning on one hand, head bent, and looked into the creek, watching the ripples, the little bursts of foam. In the quiet pools, brown rocks on the bottom blended with the reflections of clouds and trees. It was cooler there by the water, and she shivered. My cloak is in the cart, she thought, but it seemed too much effort to get up again and get it. Dawnstar finished drinking, let out a whooshing sigh and moved off a little to stand quietly in the shade.

Rose stared at a particular swirl of water around a gray rock, a swirl that was always moving, yet always the same. Time passed.

A cool breeze came up making Rose shiver again. She pushed off the ground and got up to find her cloak. When she got to the cart, she saw that the back was still open. She stiffened with shock. Her bag was gone.

The cloak was still there. A corner of it had caught between the front wall and the seat. But the bag was gone, fallen out somewhere along the road.

"No," she moaned. "No." Her mind raced through the things she had put in her bag that morning. Her shimmies, her skirt, her hairbrush, her nightgown, her favorite comb with the blue ribbon wound through—*her flute!*

Forgetting her cloak, she dropped to the ground and lay still, curled up tightly, fists clenched.

It doesn't matter, she thought at last. I'll never play again anyway. How can there be music without Lily?

The afternoon moved on. Rose lay amid the dry grasses and fallen leaves, cold, still. The sun slanted lower through the cottonwoods, the shadows lengthened. Dawnstar came and nudged her. Rose stirred and came back from dark depths to the trees around her, the cart beside her. She was deeply chilled. She pulled herself up on the side of the cart and freed her cloak from where it was caught under the seat. As she wrapped it around herself, she began shaking. She leaned against Dawnstar's warm side.

I should take her home, she thought.

An image of the bedroom stripped of Lily's belongings rose behind her eyes.

No. I can't. I can't go back.

The cart looked hopeless, stuck over the fallen tree limb. Rose bent and made a futile attempt to pull the limb out from under it, but some of the branches had caught in the spokes and it wouldn't budge. She threw her arms out in a gesture of despair.

I can't go home. But night's coming. There's wild animals, wolves, mountain lions. And bad, rough men. Fear tightened in her belly. She'd never been alone outside at night, never been alone ever, until Lily … Grief surged up like a tidal wave. I just want to die.

Dawnstar pushed her head against Rose. Rose stroked her. "I can't go home," she told Dawnstar, "but you should. Rachel will take care of you."

She slapped Dawnstar's flank. "Go home. Go on home."

Dawnstar nuzzled her and stood solid.

"Go!" Rose pushed her. She didn't move.

"Do what you want then. You're free." Rose turned away from her and walked back to the creek. She sank down on the bank, and returned to staring at the ripples, the foam, the swirl around the gray rock, the reflections in the pools. She leaned forward and dipped her hand into the nearest pool.

It's deep enough. If I lay face down. And cold enough. She bent toward the water.

Then it seemed that the rounded shapes of stones in the bottom of the pool blending with cloud reflections shifted, and she saw the face of Jesus looking up at her. His deep eyes looked straight into her soul.

She gasped and drew back. Covering her face with her hands, she whispered, "Forgive me ... dear Jesus, please forgive me." She rocked back and forth. "Help me ... I'm lost ..."

She looked again into the water, but saw only rocks and reflections. Terrified by what she had almost done, she pushed herself to her feet and stumbled away from the creek. Dawnstar still stood patiently by the cart. Rose leaned against her and buried her face in the silver mane.

The quiet of the wood was broken by the soft thud of horse hooves approaching. Rose spun away from Dawnstar and looked around wildly for a hiding place. The sound of the horse came nearer. She dived behind a low patch of willows, drew up her feet, wrapped her arms over her head, her heart pounding.

Dawnstar whinnied and the approaching horse answered. Then she heard a familiar voice. "Dawnstar, here you are. Now where's our Rose?"

Gabe.

The fear ran out of Rose and left her trembling. Gabe came straight to her. "There you are." Dry leaves crunched as he sat down beside her and laid his hand on her back. His gentle touch set her tears flowing again.

After a while he asked, "What's a'grieving you?"

"She sent me away."

"Lily?"

"Y . . yes." Rose's words spilled out between sobs. "I took her trunk and asked to stay with her, but she said no ... go back ... don't hang on me ... I need my pri ...privacy."

"Ah."

"And I left the back of the cart open after we took Lily's trunk out, and my bag fell out and I've lost my flute."

"Your flute. We'll find it. You was gonna run away from your pa and go live with Lily?"

"I was, but now she doesn't want me. She pushed me away. She was part of me, and now I'm all torn."

Gabe was silent a while. His hand was warm on her back. "Rose," he said. "Lily's not part of you. You two has been real close. 'Course you miss her bad. But you're you, all here. Ain't no one else like you. You're our Rose. Come, let's go home now. Your folks are a'worrying."

"I can't. I can't bear it without her."

Again Gabe was silent, his compassion pouring through his hand. Then he said, "Elsie came up to your house this afternoon when I was there, a'looking for you. Her baby, little Mandy, is sick. That fellow that you bandaged up a few days ago, the one what sprained his shoulder, he'll be back a'wanting you to check on it, put more of your ointment on it. And winter'll be along soon. Winter's hard on babies. Lisbeth and I, we're a'counting on you being by to help us take care of our Lucia. We need you, Rose. Lots of folks need you. You're the only doctor in Gold Creek."

Rose lay quiet under his hand.

"Your pa would miss you."

Rose uncurled and sat up in a fierce rush.

"Papa! Look what he did to Lily. And now he says I can't ever see her again, or go to Fairdale Ranch or see Amy and Julia or Mrs. Fairdale. And if I go home he'll just yell at me."

"Ah, Rose, he loves you and he loves Lily. He's all mixed up, worrying about you two and your salvation and the Fairdales, but Jesus is watching over him. He'll come 'round."

Rose drew her knees up to her chest. "Maybe." She pushed a stray lock of hair back from her face, brushed a few leaves off her dress. "How did you find me?"

"Your blue dress showed up pretty good in the willows."

"But how did you know to come here? Why were you looking for me?"

Gabe laid his warm hand on her back again while he told her that her pa was having a fit about her going to Fairdale Ranch, but didn't want to go get her after all that had happened. So Gabe offered to go. Her pa loaned him Shadow. He followed her cart tracks, and saw the skid marks where she turned by the twisty pine.

"After that it was easy, Dawnstar coming to meet us."

He smiled. Gabe's sweet, gap-toothed smile was hard to resist. Rose felt a faint echo of it on her own face.

"I need to get you home now," Gabe said. "Sun's down and it's getting cool." He stood, took Rose's hand and helped her up. "Your hand's mighty cold and you look all tuckered out. Isabel'll be getting your supper on. She was fixing a good-smelling soup when I left. Some hot vittles and a warm bed'll put you right again."

As he talked he led her out of the willow thicket. She followed, his hand warm around hers, too weary to resist, weak with relief that she was no longer alone with night coming.

"What's this?" Gabe stopped by the cart, bent and looked under it.

"It's stuck. I couldn't get it loose."

Gabe got down on his knees and broke the branches that were caught in the spokes. "Heist her up a bit," he directed Rose.

Rose lifted the back end, Gabe gave a pull, backed up and pulled again, and the limb came free.

"There now," he said as he hitched Dawnstar up to the cart. "Let's be on our way."

It was almost dark when they reached the house. Just as Rose expected, the minute she and Gabe came through the door, Daniel jumped from his chair and stood over her shouting, "Where have you been? I told you not to go to Fairdale Ranch ever again."

Gabe cut in. "Daniel, I need to talk with you. Let's go out on the porch. I got something on my mind."

Daniel looked back and forth between Rose and Gabe, started to say something, seemed to think better of it, and followed Gabe out. Then Isabel and Rachel came to embrace her. Isabel washed her tear-stained face with warm water, brought her a bowl of hot soup and some cornbread, and sat with her while she ate. Joshua came and snuggled in her lap until Rachel took him off to bed.

When they were alone Isabel asked, "You were planning to run away and stay with Lily?"

Rose nodded. "How did you know?"

"I keep an eye on you. What happened?"

"She didn't want me." Rose stopped eating. Grief welled up.

Isabel laid her hand over Rose's. "That Lily."

"Don't tell anyone. That I was going to run away. That she didn't want me."

"I won't."

"And I lost my bag. It fell out of the cart somewhere along the road with all my things in it. My flute."

"Oh, it'll show up. Somebody'll find it and know it's yours. You're the only one in Gold Creek with a flute."

When Rachel came back and heard about the lost bag, she brought Rose one of her nightgowns and a hairbrush. Isabel brushed out her hair and braided it.

"Ah, poor lamb," she said. "You're still shivering. You get on up to bed now. Get under that fancy comforter your grandmama sent you. That'll get you warm."

Rachel held her close and kissed her. "I'm so glad you're home. We were worried."

Rose climbed the stairs and opened the door at the top. The room felt bleak and cold, lit only by moonlight shining in through the east window.

Still shivering, she pulled off her blue gown and slipped into Rachel's nightgown.

She was about to climb into bed when she heard her father's voice, then Gabe's. They were still talking out on the front porch. She pulled the comforter off the bed, wrapped it around her and crept to the open window to listen.

"Trust Jesus," she heard Gabe say. "He's watching over her. She's not a child anymore, Daniel. She's a woman grown and a doctor. Folks need her and she needs to do her work. She's bad heartbroken right now, having Lily gone. Doing her doctoring will get her mind off it."

"But what if she goes to Fairdale Ranch when she's out on her horse? She doesn't obey me. She went today."

"To take Lily her clothes and all."

"But I forbade her, and she defied me. What if she goes again and gets led astray like Lily did? Lost for all eternity?"

"She'll not be lost. Don't you see your own child? I ain't never knowed a body held so close in the bosom of Jesus as that one. Haven't you heard how she prays to Him when she does her doctoring, calling on Him to come and help her?"

"No. I didn't know she did that."

"She does. And He comes into her hands and she brings His peace and love to the one she touches. That's why she doctors so good and they all love her.

I heard her praying like that when our Lucia was born, and Lisbeth let go being scairt and brought her babe out fine."

Rose heard Daniel clear his throat and shift in his chair. "Well …"

"Let her go," Gabe said. "And let her see her sister. God made 'em twins. It's not for you to separate 'em."

Daniel cleared his throat again. "I'll consider it."

Rose heard a chair scrape on the porch. "I need to be getting on home," Gabe said. "Lisbeth'll be looking for me."

As they said their good nights, Rose slipped away from the window and climbed into her bed. Outside on the hill, coyotes took up their song, calling back and forth to each other. Rose wrapped the comforter closer around her, thinking how dark the woods would be by then, how cold the creek.

She was exhausted, but far from sleep. Gabe thinks Jesus is holding me in his bosom. He must be, because as soon as I prayed for help He sent Gabe to me. Gabe said once his mama named him after an angel. He really is an angel, though he doesn't look like the angels in the pictures. She thought of his gap-toothed smile, his lanky hair, his frayed hat brim, and felt her love for him create the beginning of warmth inside her.

She curled on her side. The window framed the dark shape of the hillside, and high above a ribbon of stars. The fresh cool smell of earth and grass flowed in.

I'm glad I'm home, she thought. Gabe is right. I'm needed here. I feel like I can't bear it without Lily, but I have to. I have to be strong. Tomorrow morning I'll go see Elsie and baby Mandy.

She turned to her other side. The moon had risen higher, but still sent a pale path across the floor. Gabe said I should pray. I should. I need to thank Jesus for saving me … from committing a terrible sin.

She slipped out of bed, pulling the comforter with her, and knelt, hands over her heart, head bent. No words came, but after a while she felt the peace of His presence enfold her. She let out a long sigh. "Thank you," she whispered and climbed back in bed and slept.

The next morning, shortly after Daniel left, Amy and Julia came to the front door. Rose and Isabel were cleaning up the kitchen, Rachel was sitting at the table working on plans for her school while Joshua noisily investigated a bottom cupboard filled with pans. In a lull in his banging, Rose heard Julia call, "Hello."

She dropped her dish cloth and ran to the door. "Amy, Julia, I'm so glad to see you." She hugged them tight.

"We're glad to see you, too," Julia said. "We miss you already."

"We know we're not supposed to be here," Amy said. "We waited on the bridge until we saw your papa go into the church. But we had to come because we needed to bring you your bag. It fell out of your cart when you rode by us so fast yesterday. Why didn't you stop and talk?"

"My bag?" Rose saw it then, on the porch just behind Julia. Relief flooded her. "Oh, thank you!"

"It fell out right in front of our house when you hit that bump. I called to you, but you didn't seem to hear." Julia picked up the bag and handed it to Rose.

Rose hugged the bag to her chest. "It feels heavier than it was."

Julia nodded. "When we told Lily that you'd dropped it, she brought down some things she said you should keep. Like the music, and *The Pilgrim's Progress*, because we have lots of music and Father has *The Pilgrim's Progress* in his library. Lily said that was one of your favorite books."

"It is." Rose opened the top of the bag and looked in. There was the music on the top, and it seemed other things had also been added.

"Lily said to tell you she's sorry," Julia added. She tipped her head to look into Rose's face. "She didn't say what for."

Rose felt her cheeks flush. She turned away a moment to set the bag down. When she could look at them again, she said, "Won't you come in? Have some tea?"

"We can't," Amy said. "Your papa said we couldn't and Father says we have to obey him. How can your papa be so mean?"

"Amy," Julia interrupted. "Father says we're not to talk that way about him. But she's right, we shouldn't come in. We'll miss you, Rose. Maybe you can meet us at the store sometime and we can have tea at Elsie's café."

"I can do that," Rose said. "I'll miss you, too."

"We should be going," Julia said. "Come meet us soon at the store."

Rose stood on the porch and waved as they drove away, then went back into the house and carried the bag up the stairs to her room.

The sight of the empty shelves, the one pillow on the bed assaulted her anew. She carried the bag over to the bed and tipped out its contents. Besides the music and the book, Lily had given back a favorite comb set with tiny sapphires, a treasure from their Boston days that they had taken turns wearing. Rose could almost feel the memory of Lily's silken hair in her hands as she twisted it up and set the comb to hold it.

Suddenly she was angry. Is this comb supposed to make up for her shutting the door and pushing me away? She doesn't even care that I'm alone. She couldn't bear to sleep alone even one night. She calls me when she needs me, then sends me away and shuts the door. Well, I can shut the door, too.

Could she? She had never tried. She looked inside and found that she could. She slid it shut. There. It's double shut now.

A sob caught her unaware, tearing through her and flinging her down onto the bed. She curled up in a ball amongst her scattered possessions, hugged the pillow to her chest, and let go into her grief.

She didn't hear the footsteps on the stairs or the sound of the door opening. Arms gathered her in. Isabel rocked her. "There, there. I know it hurts terrible to have her gone. But you still have the rest of us. We're real glad you came back. We love you and we need you."

Rose couldn't quite understand how such a skinny little woman as Isabel could enfold her as she did, but she rested her head gratefully on Isabel's shoulder. Gradually her sobs subsided.

"That's a girl now," Isabel said, wiping Rose's cheeks with the corner of her apron. "Like I said, we need you, 'specially now Lily's gone. There's a load of harvesting left to be done, and then more canning, and Joshua to keep track of 'cause Rachel's busy with her school. I'm about to head out to the garden. Will you come help me now?"

Rose drew in her breath and straightened. "First I need to go down and see Elsie. Gabe said baby Mandy is sick. After that I'll help you."

Being needed was what kept Rose going in the weeks that followed. She bent her head and worked.

There was plenty of work—the garden to be harvested and manure and compost dug into the beds as they were cleared, the last of the vegetables to be canned, meals to prepare and clean-up afterwards, the house to keep clean,

Joshua to be tended. With Lily gone and Rachel busy with her new school, the work that had once been shared by four women now fell on the shoulders of Rose and Isabel.

Once a week, Rose held her clinic in the parlor of Hannah's boarding house. Her reputation had spread through the valley and she was usually busy the whole day. In between clinics, it was not unusual for someone to come knocking on her door or looking for her in the garden, begging her to come quickly. A child had fallen off the roof, a man had cut his leg chopping wood, a boy had been bitten by a dog. Then Rose would drop whatever she was doing, saddle Dawnstar and ride out with her medicine satchel in the back of the double saddle. Mattie was pregnant again, and having trouble with morning sickness. Rose checked in with her everyday, sometimes taking Joshua and staying a while to help with the children.

There was also music to prepare for the prayer meetings and Sunday services.

Everywhere she went people asked her about Lily. The Sunday morning following Lily and Jonathan's wedding, Rachel had suggested that the family have a consistent answer to the questions that were sure to arise about why Lily was not in church. Daniel, still lost in his rage, didn't want to discuss it, but Rachel insisted, saying, "We might as well tell the truth, because it is sure to come out anyway." So they agreed to say simply that Lily had gotten married and would be away for a while. It did not take long for word to get around that Lily had married Jonathan Fairdale. There were many opinions about why she and her new husband didn't come to church. When Daniel frowned and refused to discuss it, folks turned to Rose with their questions.

"When's Lily coming back?"

"Was your pa upset she married a Fairdale?"

"Do you miss her?"

"Why doesn't she bring her new husband to church?"

Their questions and comments, not unkindly meant but often thoughtless, pierced Rose like burning arrows. She never knew when they would come or from what quarter. She dreaded going to church, and took to starting the organ early and, after the service, continuing to play until the last parishioners had gone.

She prayed every night, but wasn't able to find again the peace that had comforted her on her first night home and often went to bed feeling abandoned even by Jesus. Only when she prayed with her patients did she feel Him surely with her.

It was hard to eat. She helped Isabel prepare meals, but when she sat down with the family, the food stuck in her throat. Even that short respite from work left her prey to the grief that always lurked above her like a dark ravenous beast ready to tear her asunder. She ate little and quickly, then excused herself to find a new chore.

Rose worked. Each task was like a length of cord wound around her, binding her together for that moment. But all that she did, except for the clinic, she had always done with Lily. It was impossible not to turn to her countless times a day, to share a thought, to reach for her hand, only to find emptiness.

## Chapter 47

# Dr. Franz's Invitation

One afternoon in late September, Rose was in the midst of preparing supper when she heard a knock on the front door. Drying her hands on her apron, she hurried to the door and opened it to find Dr. Franz beaming at her.

Her heart lifted. "Dr. Franz!" she exclaimed. "Come in, come in." She clasped both his hands in hers and almost pulled him across the threshold. "I'm just fixing supper. Can you stay and eat with us?"

"Thank you," he said. "I would be happy to stay for supper. I've been looking forward to seeing you." He settled himself at the kitchen table. He'd been to Denver, he told her, for supplies and was planning to stop a few days in Gold Creek and hold a clinic.

"I'm so glad you've come," Rose said. "I have so many questions. Mattie's been having a hard time with morning sickness, and I haven't been able to help her much. There's a boy across the river with a dog bite that's festering in spite of everything I can do, and Mrs. Marlow has arthritis. There's so much I don't know. Maybe you could do some house calls with me."

Rose stopped talking to stir the potatoes in the big iron skillet. When she turned back to Dr. Franz, she saw a frown on his face.

"Have you been ill?" he asked.

"No, no. I'm fine."

"You look tired."

Rose bit her lower lip and held her breath as traitorous tears threatened in response to his kindly concern.

"I'm a little tired," she admitted. "There's a lot of work this time of year."

"Where's your family? This house was full of people last time I was here."

"They'll all be back soon. Rachel took Joshua out to play on the hillside. She's teaching school now, so she doesn't have time to play with him until late afternoon. Isabel's up in the pasture watering the horses, and Papa should be along any minute. Would you like some coffee?"

"Yes, thank you. And Lily?"

Rose turned her back to him to pour the coffee.

She brought the coffee to Dr. Franz and said, trying to keep her voice light, "Lily got married a few weeks ago. To Jonathan Fairdale. She's living out at Fairdale Ranch now."

"Married!" Dr. Franz exclaimed. "I didn't know she was going to get married. Was it sudden?"

"They'd been betrothed for a year, but Papa didn't know. He … he didn't want them to marry. So they eloped. They love each other. I think she's happy. But don't tell anyone they eloped, or that Papa disapproved. There's enough gossip."

"I won't." Dr. Franz was frowning again. "You miss her," he said. It was a statement, not a question. "You said you think she's happy. Don't you visit?"

"No, not at all. Papa forbids it. He was very angry. We don't go to Fairdale Ranch at all anymore." In spite of herself, Rose choked over her last words and tears filled her eyes.

"I see," Dr. Franz said.

Isabel bustled in the kitchen door with an armload of firewood and dropped it with a crash into the wood box by the stove. "Dr. Franz," she said, dusting off her hands and holding out her right one to him. "Good to see you. You staying for supper?"

"Good to see you, too, Isabel," he said warmly. "Rose invited me and I accepted."

"Well, we'd better get it on then, Rose. Your pa's coming up the road, and Rachel's on her way in with the babe. Good, you've fried the potatoes." She lifted a lid and peered into a pot at the back of the stove. "And the cabbage looks done. I'll get the bacon on. You set the table and slice up some tomatoes and we'll be ready in a jiff."

After dinner the family lingered around the table with Dr. Franz. Joshua dozed in Rachel's lap. The conversation had been lively and pleasant. Daniel shared news of Gold Creek, and Dr. Franz spoke of Montview and his boys. No one spoke of Lily. Rose felt a lightness in her heart that she hardly recognized.

She even found herself laughing when Dr. Franz described the mischievous adventures of his younger son, Sam.

As Isabel got up to clear the plates, Rachel asked, "Would you like some tea? We have fresh herbs from the garden."

"That sounds very nice," Dr. Franz replied.

"I'll make it." Rose got up and went to the stove to put the kettle on.

Dr. Franz leaned his elbows on the table. "I have a proposal to put to you," he said to Daniel. "It's an idea I've been turning over for more than a year, ever since we were on the trail together and I first saw how gifted Rose is."

Rose turned away from the stove, watching him, eyes wide, startled.

"Now that I'm well established in Montview," Dr. Franz went on, "I'd like to invite Rose to come and spend some time with me, a month, maybe six weeks, so I can give her more consistent training than I've been able to just stopping by every few months. Then she can come home and bring her skills to serve Gold Creek." He looked over at Rose. "Would you like to do that?"

Rose's heart jumped a beat; she couldn't tell if it was fear or excitement. She reached out with her left hand, groped a moment in the space beside her, then let her hand fall back into the folds of her apron. Dr. Franz was watching her, compassion in his eyes, and she knew he had seen the gesture and understood it. Her cheeks grew hot.

"The widow lady who lives across the road from me," he went on, "has a room in her house where you could stay. We could work together every day, and in the evenings study my medical books. What do you think?"

"We can't spare her," Daniel said. "She's needed here. And I'm not sure it's a good idea for her to continue working as a doctor. It's not women's work."

"Actually, there are many women doctors," Dr. Franz said, "especially out here in the West, filling an important role in their communities, as Rose does. In some ways they're better suited than men to be doctors, being nurturing by nature. Did you know there's a school back East in Pennsylvania specifically for training women doctors? The Female Medical College they call it. But it's far away and expensive. I can train her closer to home."

"We need her here," Daniel said, as if he hadn't heard Dr. Franz's words. "My wife's teaching school, and someone has to care for Joshua and keep the household running."

Isabel turned around from the sink. "I can do that. The garden's mostly put to bed, the canning done. That little boy of yours is a rascal, but there's just one of him. I can keep up with him."

"Who's going to play the organ for church?"

"I will," Rachel said. "Let her go, Daniel. We'll manage. It's an important opportunity for her."

Rose stood listening. Her breath came quickly. She suddenly felt what it would be like to be away, away from everything that reminded her of Lily. To be with Dr. Franz. To learn. To pray all day as she worked and feel Jesus with her.

"Well, Rose," Dr. Franz said, smiling at her, "everyone's had their say but you. Would you like to come study with me?"

A fresh wind blew through her. "Yes," she answered, her voice coming out more strongly than she expected. "Yes, I would."

"I'll have to think about it," Daniel said.

The kettle boiled and Rose poured hot water over the herbs in the teapot.

Daniel shifted in his chair, dismissing the issue. "Tell me," he said to Dr. Franz, "about the churches in Montview. How many are there now? What kind?"

"There are three churches. A Presbyterian. You know Reverend Caldwell."

"Yes, he married us."

"My boys and I go to the Methodist church. Reverend Haywood is a fine pastor. I think you know him also."

Daniel nodded, his lips tight. "And the other?"

"There's a new Catholic church."

"Catholic! I didn't know the papists had gotten a foothold there."

Rose poured the tea and brought cups to her father and Dr. Franz. Rachel got up quietly and left the kitchen, carrying her sleeping child. When Rose took the tea pot back to the stove, Isabel caught her eye. She lifted her chin, with a little nod and a wide smile. Rose felt a surge of excitement. I'll go, she decided. If Papa won't let me, I'll run away.

She and Isabel began clearing the table and washing the dishes. Daniel continued talking, ignoring the issue of Rose leaving, chatting animatedly about how the church had grown, and sharing news about Nathan and Mattie and Gabe.

After a while Dr. Franz stood up. "I need to get back to the boarding house. It's been a long day of travel. Thank you for supper. Please also give my thanks to your wife." He touched Rose on the shoulder. "I'll be starting my clinic at nine tomorrow morning. Will you join me?"

"Yes, of course," she responded quickly, before Daniel could say anything. She smiled at Dr. Franz. "Have a good rest."

"Daniel, will you walk with me?" Dr. Franz asked. "It's grown dark and I didn't bring a lantern."

Daniel nodded and got up.

After the two men had left, Rose hugged Isabel. "I'll go," she said. "I'll figure out a way to persuade Papa. Or maybe Dr. Franz will." She laughed suddenly. "If I were Lily, I'd tell Papa I was going anyway, and then even if he'd decided to let me go, he'd get mad and forbid me. But I'm not Lily." Her laughter wobbled toward a sob and then came back to laughter. "I'll be more subtle."

Isabel laughed with her, then looked seriously into her eyes. "A change will be good for you. Just seeing Dr. Franz has brightened you up."

"It has. Are you sure you can manage without me?"

"'Course we can."

~

A week later, on the first Saturday of October, Rose packed her carpet bag, sorted through her satchel of medical supplies, and dressed in her split denim skirt and flowered blouse.

Isabel came up to her room to say good-bye. "I'm heading out to Fairdale Ranch for the gleaning," she said. "Any message you want me to give Lily?"

Rose shook her head.

"No? Okay. You have a good trip, dearie." Isabel took Rose into her arms. "Learn lots. We'll miss you, but I'm glad you're getting this chance."

"I'll miss you, too." Rose hugged her tight. Isabel turned back at the bottom of the stairs to wink and throw Rose a kiss.

When Dr. Franz drove up to the house in his buggy, Rose was ready. She carried her bags down the stairs. Daniel took them from her and loaded them into the buggy. Rose kissed her papa on the cheek, hugged Rachel, picked up Joshua and nuzzled him, then climbed up on the seat beside Dr. Franz.

Daniel and Rachel, with Joshua on her hip, stood on the porch and waved as they drove away.

~

Lily picked up a table cloth from the pile beside her, unfolded it, and flipped an end to Kate. She and Kate and Julia were setting up tables for the gleaning.

"We're lucky again," Kate said, as she caught the cloth and she and Lily spread it over the table. "It's a beautiful day for our party."

It was. The sky was the deep blue of Rocky Mountain autumn, the cottonwoods by the barn gold in the early sunshine.

Lily lifted her head to drink in the freshness of the morning—then stilled.

*Rose?* She reached out with her heart. Nothing. Yet for a moment there'd been a whisper, a breath, as if Rose called her. Lily bit her lip. *Rose?* she called again. No answer, and now even that subtle whisper was gone.

Lily turned away from the table and pressed the back of her hand against her mouth. It had been that way ever since the day she'd sent Rose away. No response to her calls. She never meant for that to happen, never dreamed that Rose would close the door. Now she knew how Rose had felt when she, Lily, had closed the door. She hadn't guessed it would hurt so much.

"Here they come," Julia said. Lily could hear the first wagons pulling up by the barn, laughter and greetings, Andrew's deep voice welcoming his guests.

Julia touched Lily's shoulder. "Let's hurry up and finish these tables." Lily took a deep breath and returned to her task.

As soon as the tables were done, she slipped away and ran up the hill toward her cabin on the knoll. Halfway up, she stopped. *Rose?* She sent her call out, searching, searching. *Please answer. I miss you.* No answer. The wind whispered in the dry grass. A babble of voices floated up from below.

Lily looked down and saw Hannah's wagon unloading by the barn. There was Isabel in her outrageous green gown with the purple trim. Lily's heart leaped. "Isabel," she called, and ran back down the hill. She tried to weave through the crowd to Isabel, but was surrounded by friends, neighbors, parishioners. They caught at her, greeting her.

"Lily! How are you?"

"We miss you."

"When are you coming back to church?"

She responded as briefly as she politely could and pressed forward to Isabel.

Isabel grinned broadly. "There you are, you rascal." She opened her arms and Lily ran into them. She hugged Isabel tight, burying her face against Isabel's shoulder, drinking in the soap and lavender smell of her.

When she lifted her head, Isabel set her back a little, searching Lily's face with her keen, bright eyes. "I need to have a look at you. First time I've laid eyes on you since I caught you riding off behind Rose pretending to be her doctoring bag." She stroked Lily's cheek with her work-gnarled hand. "You're looking mighty fine, Mrs. Fairdale."

"You look fine, too." Lily felt laughter bubbling up. "You look beautiful."

Isabel snorted.

Lily looked past Isabel, searching. "Did Rose come with you? Or Rachel … Papa?"

"No." Isabel pressed her lips together. "No, dearie. They didn't come. Not yet."

"How is Rose?" The question stuck in Lily's throat. She'd never had to ask before.

"Well, Rose … she's been working hard. She misses you."

"I miss her, too. I was thinking I'll come to town soon and see if she can meet me, maybe at Elsie's."

"Now you'll have to wait for that. Rose is gone for a while."

"Gone!" Lily gripped Isabel's shoulders. "Where?" Fear dropped like a cold stone into the pit of her stomach.

"It's okay," Isabel said. "Dr. Franz came by and he's taken her off to Montview to teach her doctoring. They just left this morning. Must've driven right by your gate on the way."

**Chapter 48**

# *Rachel Speaks Up*

After Dr. Franz's buggy disappeared over the brow of the hill, Daniel paced to the edge of the cliff where he could look down on the town below. Hannah's wagon, full of people, was pulling out from the boarding house, joining a stream of carts and buggies and riders on horseback, all moving in the same direction. He walked back to Rachel, who was sitting on the porch steps with Joshua.

"Do you know what's going on?" he asked. "It looks as if half the town is heading east."

"It's gleaning day at Fairdale Ranch," Rachel answered. "Haven't you heard everyone talking about it? It's apparently a big event, the last picnic of the season. Did you go last year?"

"Gleaning day." Daniel frowned. "Yes, we went last year. That was when Lily, unbeknownst to me, promised herself to Jonathan. No, no one's spoken to me about the gleaning day." He brushed past Rachel and went inside.

The house felt empty. He missed Rose already, though she'd been silent and sad of late. He remembered how she and Lily had filled the house with their laughter and chatter. The thought of Lily brought a sour taste to his mouth. If only she hadn't spoiled everything.

He sank into his leather chair with a sigh. Rachel and Joshua came in. Joshua ran to the bedroom where Daniel could hear him dumping out his box of blocks. Rachel came to stand beside him. He put his arm around her hips and leaned his head against her bosom.

"So, Rose is gone for a while," he said. "Will you really be able to manage without her? She did a lot of work."

"She did." Rachel smoothed his hair. "More than she needed to. I think it was her way of trying to forget how much she missed Lily."

Daniel felt a surge of irritation at the mention of Lily, then a longing for comfort. He drew Rachel down into his lap. He still couldn't get over how sweet

433

it was to hold her, how perfectly she fit in his arms. But since Lily's wedding, something had changed. She still responded to him as a wife should, but there was a reserve that hadn't been there before. He held her tighter, soothed by her warmth. He didn't want to hear any more about Lily or face the guilt he kept repressing over separating the twins. Dr. Franz had spoken sharply to him about Rose's grief, how it was bad for her health and important for her to have a change of scene and new learning to involve her.

The house felt too quiet. Even Joshua had stopped banging his blocks and was humming the special song he sang only to his tiger, a rag doll-like creature with black button eyes and fur of orange and black yarn that Rose had crafted for him over the summer.

"Where's Isabel?" Daniel asked.

Rachel lifted her head from his shoulder. "I gave her the day off. She's gone with Hannah to the gleaning."

Daniel stiffened. "I didn't give her permission. I don't want anyone in my household going to Fairdale Ranch. Haven't I made that clear?"

Rachel jumped out of his lap and stood facing him. Her eyes flashed. "*I* gave her permission. She needs a day off. We don't own her, you know. She serves us voluntarily and generously. I don't know what we'd do without her to care for Joshua, now that I'm teaching all day."

Daniel pinched his lips together. To his surprise, Rachel suddenly knelt in front of him and took both his hands in hers.

"Daniel, please. Please soften your heart. Let go of this terrible anger toward Lily and the Fairdales. It's poisoning you. I'm not surprised no one spoke to you of the gleaning. People know. They know you have cut off Lily and the Fairdales, and they're troubled. It's poisoning Rose. Can't you see how thin and sad she's become? Haven't you heard her crying at night? It would be hard enough for her to have Lily marry and move away, but for you to forbid them to see each other … I don't understand you."

"Enough! I don't want to speak of this anymore." Daniel tried to pull his hands away, but Rachel held them tight.

"I'm not done. I've been silent long enough. Do you know what Lily said to me after her wedding? She told me that the whole year she'd been betrothed, she'd dreamed of her wedding, in the church, with music and flowers, and *you* marrying them. She wept telling me. She said she couldn't believe that you would cut her off, and even forbid her to come to church. How could you do that? All the hired people come—Bernie, and Luke and James and their families. They're not lost because they live at Fairdale Ranch. And Lily probably would have brought Jonathan to church with her. She thought you'd be happy to have her marry him since you were such good friends with Andrew."

"Enough, I said." Daniel jerked his hands away. "I was mistaken to cultivate that friendship. I've told you that. I deeply regret it. Don't you remember what Reverend Caldwell said? That unless Andrew received Christ as his savior, he and all he influences will burn in hell?"

Rachel sat back on her heels, rubbing one hand over the other. "And I remember what you said—that Andrew is not an atheist but devout in his own way. Also that the Fairdales are an integral part of the valley, and that many people survive the winter without scurvy because he shares his fruit in the fall. As he's doing this very day."

She leaned forward to touch his knees. "I want to go. I want to be there for the gleaning. I miss Kate. I miss Lily. I miss the whole family and all the joys we shared there, the music, the laughter. Joshua misses Johnny. Let's go. I know we'd be welcome. Everyone is just waiting, longing for you to let go of this poisonous rage that possesses you."

Joshua stood in the doorway, hugging his tiger. "Go Fairdale? See Johnny?"

That was too much for Daniel. He leaped out of his chair, towered over Rachel who still knelt on the floor. "Poisonous! Is that a word a wife should use for her husband?"

"Not for you, my dear." Rachel looked up at him, her eyes dark and troubled. "Only for your anger." Joshua crept to her side and hid his face against her shoulder.

Daniel felt rage rising in him. "Poisonous?" he said again, his voice terrible.

Rachel still knelt at his feet, cradling Joshua with her arm. Her lips trembled and there were tears in her eyes, but she held his gaze unwavering. "You don't believe me? Feel how you are right now."

Shocked, he felt his stomach clenched, his heart pounding, his right leg twitching, the rage burning through him. Burning.

He turned and ran up the three steps to the kitchen, knocked over the chair at the end of the table in his dash for the door. Up the hill he ran, up and up, higher than he'd ever gone before. He topped the ridge and saw below him a tiny valley nestled in the hollow below the rising of the next ridge.

He flung himself down the slope into its shelter and dropped to the earth.

His run up the hill had burned away the rage and he was trembling now, remembering Rachel with Joshua in her arms kneeling at his feet. Those two, dearer than anything on earth to him. He had almost kicked them. What if he had? What if he had hurt them? He'd be no better than Ebenezer. Maybe Rachel was right. Maybe it *was* poison, this rage that made him forget himself and hurt those he loved. Like Lily. Burning her hand.

He rolled over onto his belly, his cheek against the earth.

Images of Lily rose before his eyes. Lily riding in with the oxen after the stampede, her hair loose, her eyes shining. Lily's face, rapt, bent over her violin. Lily kneeling by the fire pit, blowing the coals into life. Lily glowing with new love, frightening him with her beauty. Lily carrying Joshua on her back, bouncing him as he laughed with delight. Lily, as he had last seen her, tears of outrage in her eyes, saying, "Let he who is without sin …"

What if? An alternative past arose in his mind. He saw himself welcoming Jonathan, marrying him and Lily in a church wedding with music and flowers, Lily radiant in a white gown and veil, all the congregation celebrating. Visits back and forth with the Fairdales continuing in all their richness, the golden summer unfolding into a golden autumn.

But I cannot. The Fairdales are a danger. Reverend Caldwell was right. No man cometh to the Father but by Christ. He is the Way, the Truth and the Light. And Andrew will not accept Him as his savior.

Daniel propped himself up on his elbows, pressing his hands to his head.

Is that a reason to cut him off? Shouldn't I remain his friend and keep witnessing? What about my family?

Swamped by confusion, he prayed. *Dear Lord, help me.*

He listened, his heart aching, and then heard God's beloved voice answer, *Let go of your anger, my son. Only then can I guide you.*

He waited, his heart pounding, but there was nothing more. Anger, he thought. That's the problem. That's what Rachel said, too. I mustn't be angry. I just need to be clear and firm.

He stood, brushed himself off, and climbed the short rise to the top of the ridge. Far below he could see the roofs of the town and the vast prairie stretching out to the east. From this height he could even see the ranches, the Henderson Horse Ranch, and beyond that, like tiny specks, the barn and the big house of Fairdale Ranch, the stream encircling it like a shining thread.

They're having the gleaning there today, he thought, and Rachel wanted to go. I can't allow that, but she needs a day off, too.

He started down the ridge toward his home, planning. I'll take her and Joshua up the mining road in the buggy and we'll have a picnic in the mountains by the stream. It's beautiful up there. Joshua can play in the water. Maybe we'll make a house for his tiger out of sticks.

The descent took longer than he expected. When he reached the house at last, the kitchen door was closed. He opened it and stepped in. "Rachel," he called. His voice echoed back to him.

"Rachel?" he called again. He went down the three steps from the kitchen to the main room. The door to the bedroom was open, the front door shut. There was no answer. Rachel and Joshua were gone.

# Chapter 49

# *Rose Returns*

Here we are," Dr. Franz said, as he drove the buggy up to the house. It was dusk, a fine snow blowing in the wind. The light flowing out of the windows was warm and welcoming.

Rose's heart beat fast in a mixture of anticipation and trepidation. Home again. She was eager to see Isabel and Rachel and Joshua, uncertain about her papa. But what she wanted most was to see Lily running out to greet her, her arms open, and knew that would not be.

Dr. Franz tied his horse to the porch post and lifted Rose down from the buggy. The wind caught at her skirts as she ran up the steps. She pushed the door open. Inside, the fire was bright on the hearth. Her father sat in his chair with Joshua in his lap. In the kitchen, Rachel and Isabel were preparing dinner. The rich odors of onion and venison and cornbread mingled with the smell of wood smoke.

Isabel was the first to see her. "Here's our Rose!" she exclaimed, hurrying down the steps from the kitchen, wiping her hands on her apron. She caught Rose in her arms and held her tight. Rachel was right behind her.

Daniel set Joshua down and crossed the room to her in long strides. As soon as Rachel let her go, he took her in his arms and held her close. "Rose, we've missed you," he said, a catch in his voice. Rose looked up at him and was startled to see tears in his eyes.

"I'm home now, Papa," she said, "to stay." He still held her close. She never remembered him holding her that way before.

"I'm glad," he said at last, then released her to welcome Dr. Franz.

Joshua pulled at her skirts. "Up, Wose." He held up his little arms.

She scooped him up and kissed his sweet neck. "We'll have to teach you how to say *R*," she told him. "Otherwise you make my name sound sad."

She looked around the living room. "You have a couch," she noted.

"Yes." Rachel smiled. "After you took Lily's trunk, we only had the one, and it looked odd. So I put the two mats together and made a cover, and Gabe made us a frame."

"It looks really nice," Rose said. "I like the warm, red color."

Before long they were gathered around the supper table, Daniel at the head, Rachel at the foot with Joshua in her lap, Rose and Dr. Franz on one bench, and Isabel across from them on the bench nearest the stove. *Just as we were before*, Rose thought, *when Dr. Franz came to get me. These suppers are like parentheses around my journey. As if that journey never happened. But I know it did, because I'm changed.*

"How did our Rose do?" Daniel asked Dr. Franz. "Was she a good help to you?"

"Of course." Dr. Franz turned to smile at Rose. "She was an excellent help and an excellent student. You now have a fine doctor to serve in Gold Creek."

"Tell us. What did you learn?" Rachel asked Rose.

Rose set down her soup spoon. "Mostly I learned by working with Dr. Franz. We delivered three babies, set the broken leg of a man who got run over by a cart. It wasn't near as bad, Papa, as Mr. Dunin's foot. We took care of people with winter flu, which started early this year, and treated a woman who burned her hand. And many more." Rose paused as images of all the patients they had seen swirled behind her eyes.

"In the evenings," she went on, "I studied Dr. Franz's books, and he taught me from them. He ordered me a copy of his medical manual and it arrived just before I left, so I have it now to study and refer to."

"You know lots already," Isabel said proudly.

"No, Isabel. I'm just beginning. There's so much to learn, I'll never learn it all. And they keep finding out more."

"Who did you stay with?" Rachel asked. "Was it a comfortable place?"

"The Widow Summers." Rose smiled and glanced at Dr. Franz. "Though I don't think she'll be a widow much longer. Her house is right across the road from Dr. Franz. I had a pleasant room with a window and a comfy bed. And she was very kind to me."

"She's not going to be a widow much longer?" Rachel raised an eyebrow as she looked at Dr. Franz. "Do you have anything to do with that?"

"Well, yes." Dr. Franz wiped his mustache with his napkin and emerged with a wide smile. "She's a fine woman and good to my boys. So we're set to be married at Christmas. Then my boys and I will move into her house and I'll fix my house up to be an office. It will be good to have a complete family again."

"What's been happening here?" Rose asked.

"My Ed came back from California," Isabel said.

"Oh, good," Rose said. "Did he find much gold? Is he going to build a fancy house for his wife?"

"He didn't find much. Just enough to pay for the stage and the train to take them back East."

"Back East?"

"Yep. Lucinda insisted. He gave it all up, all that him and me worked for, for seven years out there, with the dust and the grasshoppers—the cabin, the garden, the cattle, everything. He sold it to the Italian couple who've been looking after that worthless wife of his and running the place while he was away. So they're gone. Don't know if I'll ever see him again. He wanted me to come with them, but I can't stand that woman, and I've got my place here."

"More news," Daniel said. "We've had a wedding. A most surprising one."

"Who?" Rose asked.

"Bernie Turner married Ella."

"Ella from the br ... from Smythe's?"

"The same."

"How did they even know each other? Bernie?"

"Bernie is a good Christian man," Daniel said. "Never misses church. But I didn't know he was spending Saturday nights down at Smythe's before the Sunday services."

Rose was shaking her head in disbelief. "Ella?"

"Apparently he's been seeing her for years," Rachel said. "When he confided in Lily, she asked him why he didn't marry her. He told her he didn't think he could because of her profession, but he knew she hated it and loved him. Then Lily reminded him about Lisbeth—"

"So," Daniel broke in, hurrying past the mention of Lily, "he came here just two weeks ago and told me and Rachel the whole story. I made him promise to pray for forgiveness and not to go to Smythe's again except to bring Ella to me. They came on a Saturday evening. I baptized them both and married them, with Rachel and Hannah and Mr. Hill for witness. They spent the night at Hannah's—she got up a little celebration for them—then came to church on Sunday morning. They're living out at Fairdale Ranch now."

"Ella was shining," Rachel said. "She thought she'd never get away from there. Smythe doesn't pay them, we found out, just gives them board and room. So she never had a way out. Lily did a good deed, encouraging Bernie."

"She had to sneak away," Isabel said. "She's been there a long time and Smythe counts on her to play the piano and keep the place up. He came over here with a gun Sunday afternoon, raging worse than he did when Lisbeth got married. But the preacher was out, and after he yelled and screamed at me and Rachel, he left."

Rose shivered. "With a gun? Weren't you scared?"

"We were," Rachel said. "When your papa came back he went and talked to the sheriff, and the sheriff went down and warned Smythe."

"Sheriff Parker says not to worry," Daniel said. "I was pretty upset about Smythe threatening my women folk, but he said Smythe would never dare hurt them or me. He knows the whole town would turn on him. There's nothing he can do."

Rose wasn't so sure. She remembered Smythe almost attacking Daniel in the saloon, his face livid when he came looking for Lisbeth, his threats. "Be careful, Papa. He really hates you."

Daniel patted her hand. "Don't worry. Just rejoice with us that there is one less woman caught in that dreadful slavery."

He turned to Dr. Franz. "Are you going to do a clinic tomorrow?"

"No, I'll just stop the night at Hannah's, then head on back tomorrow to my boys. Rose can do a clinic when she gets settled." He patted Rose on the shoulder. "She can handle whatever comes up." He stood. "I should go on down to Hannah's now before it gets too late."

After Dr. Franz had said his goodbyes and left, Rose helped Isabel clean up the kitchen.

"Are you sad about your son?" she asked.

"Sure I am. But he's besotted with that worthless woman. I can't see him being happy with her. She has some idea he can work in her father's store. Don't think he'll like that. Maybe he'll be back some day. Meanwhile, I've got my family." She put her arm around Rose's shoulder and gave her a squeeze. "I'm sure glad you're back. We missed you bad."

"I'm glad to be back . . though ..." Rose concentrated on the pan she was scrubbing. "It still feels so odd not to have Lily here. Have you seen her?"

"I have. I saw her at the gleaning. She said she misses you. She was hoping you and the family would come to the gleaning. But your pa's still stubborn."

"He always is." Rose handed the clean pot to Isabel to dry. "But he seems different than when I left. Gentler."

"Yeah. He and Rachel had a big row. Over Lily and the Fairdales. I don't know much about it. Just that he ran up the hill like he does, and when he came back Rachel and Joshua were gone. It scared him. Rachel told me that much. She'd just taken the boy for a picnic by the river. Your pa's been different since. I guess he realizes how important his family is."

"I wish he'd remember Lily is part of it."

Isabel put down her dishtowel and took Rose in her arms. "Don't you fret, dearie, he will. It just may take a while. He's stubborn, like I said." She brushed a loose lock back from Rose's brow. "Now you're tired. It's a long trip from Montview. You go on to bed. I'll finish up."

She lit a candle and handed it to Rose.

Daniel was settled in his chair by the fire, reading. He looked up as Rose came through.

"Rose," he said. "Sit down a moment. I have something to tell you."

When Rose was seated on the bench by the hearth, Daniel went on. "While you were gone, Gerald Dodge came and asked me if he could court you."

"*Gerald?*"

"Yes. He's a good man, Rose, and solid. He's started partnering with his father and will eventually manage the bank. He will give you a good home and treat you well, I know. He said he'd loved you from the first time he saw you."

"No, Papa."

"Rose, you should consider it. I know I promised ..."

"No." Rose took a deep breath. "I know Gerald is a good man. But I don't love him. Please tell him kindly no. I don't want to get married. I have my work to do."

"I was afraid of that. I told Dr. Franz women shouldn't—"

"Jesus called me to be a doctor." Rose stood. "It's been a long journey. I want to go to bed now." She went to Daniel and kissed his cheek. "I'm glad to be home. Goodnight, Papa."

Her room was just as she'd left it. She set her candle on the headboard of her bed and sat down. Across the room, the shelves she had shared with Lily still had big bare spaces.

Grief rose in her like flood waters.

It had been easier in her room at the Widow Summer's place, because she had never shared it with Lily. But here—images flooded her. She and Lily slipping in and out of their hillside window, lying on their bellies by the grate to eavesdrop on the family below, curled on their straw mat plotting the demise of Aaron Jenkins's courtship, whispering to each other in their Sunday afternoon quiet times. Every corner of the room exhaled the absence of Lily.

Rose caught her breath, pressing back the grief. I need to do something about this room, she thought. She sat looking at the empty spaces on the shelves on either side of the window, then decided. I'll put my clothes and personal possessions on one side and my apothecary on the other. Tomorrow.

She undressed and slipped into bed. Wind blew snow across the window pane, a soft shushing sound. She dropped into sleep, then suddenly woke, trembling with fear. An image had come behind her closed eyes, dream or prescience she did not know—Smythe's face in a swirl of snow, leering in triumph.

## Chapter 50

# Lily Reaches Out

Lily sat on the edge of her bed, her stomach roiling. Ew, she thought, maybe I'm going to throw up. She ran to the kitchen, grabbed a bucket from under the sink, then stood holding it, not sure.

This is the third day I've felt like this, she told herself. Maybe … maybe it's morning sickness. Maybe— A thrill of excitement ran through her in spite of her nausea.

I'll go ask Mother, she decided. She might have some herbs that will help. Maybe she'd know how you know if … She stood a moment more with the bucket in her hand, then set it on a chair and returned to the bedroom to dress.

Jonathan had left earlier, kissing her good-bye before he went down to do the milking. "I'm sorry you're not feeling well," he said. "Go back to sleep. I'll get breakfast at the big house."

The winter morning was crisp, the long grasses white with frost, as Lily hurried down the hill. Kate was in the kitchen studying her cookbook. She got up to embrace Lily. "How are you doing?" she asked. "Jonathan said you weren't feeling well."

"I'm a little better now," Lily said. "I went back to sleep after Jonathan left. But it's the third day I've waked up feeling like this. I'm wondering …"

Kate smiled. "I've been wondering, too." She pulled out a chair for Lily and sat beside her, holding her hands. "You have a look about you and it's been a long time since I've seen your napkins on the clothesline."

"Oh." Lily put her hand on the side of her face. "I didn't think about that."

"You didn't? How long has it been since you bled?"

"I don't know. I never paid much attention. Rose always knew and had everything ready. I did bleed once right after we got married. I remember because I wasn't prepared and stained the bed and was so embarrassed when Jonathan saw. But that was the only time."

Kate's smile grew broader. "You got married in September, and it's December now. And your tummy's upset. I think you've got a baby on the way."

"You do?" Lily caught her breath. Then she smiled, too, as a rush of excitement coursed through her, along with another wave of nausea.

"I do. So we need to take really good care of you." Kate got up and went to the stove. "I'm going to make you a tea to ease your nausea. You must rest a lot, especially during these early months. And you must eat."

Kate bustled around the kitchen, putting on the kettle, looking through her box of herb packets, pulling a tin of crackers out of the cupboard. She set some out on a blue plate and put it in front of Lily. "Here, start with these. Dry crackers usually help settle the stomach. Take little bites."

Lily sat watching Kate, hugging herself with excitement. Then she had to loosen her arms because her breasts were tender.

"I think it's best not to tell Jonathan yet," Kate said. "Wait a little longer to be sure. It'll be a secret just between you and me."

"I want to tell Rose." Tears came to Lily's eyes as she felt the closed door between their hearts. Before, Rose would have just known; she might have known even before Lily.

Kate sat down again beside Lily. "Can't you? It seems you two don't need to be together to communicate."

"Not any more. It's all changed since Papa …" The tears spilled over. "I can't hear her anymore. I didn't even know she'd come back from Montview until Julia told me." Lily put her head down on the table and began to cry. Kate stroked her head.

"Don't misunderstand," Lily said between her sobs. "I love living here. I love Jonathan and having you for my mother and being part of the family. But I miss my other family." Another sob shook her. "I miss Rose."

"I'm sure you do," Kate sighed. "I'd like to shake that stubborn father of yours. It's not right to separate you two."

"I'd like to kick him," Lily said between her teeth. But even as she blamed her papa she knew deep down that it was she who had pushed Rose away. She sobbed anew.

That evening Lily was crying again. Jonathan, sat beside her, very concerned, his arms around her. "What is it, sweetheart?" he asked.

Lily didn't know how to answer. She felt weak and shaky and upset, and she wasn't used to feeling that way. She certainly wasn't used to breaking down and crying twice in one day. She was excited about the baby, but also awed and frightened. It felt impossible that Rose did not know, unthinkable not to share it with her, terrifying that Rose might not be with her to help her when the time came. She *needed* Rose.

"I miss Rose," she managed to blurt out.

Jonathan's arms tightened around her. "I'll take you tomorrow. We'll go find her, and if your pa gets in the way, I'll knock him down."

Lily pressed her face into Jonathan's shoulder. "I do want to see Rose." She'd stopped crying and even felt a bubble of laughter rising up. "But I don't think you should knock my papa down. That would only make matters worse."

Jonathan smoothed her back. "You're probably right. It's just that I've wanted to knock him down ever since he said I couldn't marry you. But we showed him; we're married. It's high time we defied him about you and Rose. I don't want you to be sad."

Lily nestled closer into Jonathan's arms, comforted by his love and concern. He was right. It was time to defy her papa. *I'll go and find her*, she resolved. *I want to tell her about the baby. I want to see her. It's been months.*

"I'll go," she said aloud. "I can go with Amy and Julia when they take the milk to the store." She looked up at him, mischievously. "They're less likely to knock him down."

Jonathan chuckled. "Amy might."

Lily laughed, too. "I'll go on Monday when Papa goes out east to his prayer meeting. Then there'll be no danger."

The following Monday Lily bundled up in her blue hooded coat and hurried down to the barn where Luke was loading the milk cans into the cart. Kate came out with some pillows and a blanket. "I'm not sure it's good for you to be jounced around just now," she said privately to Lily. "Wrap up well and sit on these pillows. How's your tummy?"

"Better today," Lily answered. "I'm excited to go to town. I want to do some shopping at the store, maybe get some cloth for baby clothes."

Julia and Amy came around the corner of the barn. "Let's go," Julia said as she climbed up on the seat of the cart.

Amy scrambled in beside Lily. "Let me have one of those pillows."

It had been a dry month, but very cold. The road was frozen hard and rutted. As the cart bumped along, Lily felt nausea arise and hoped she wouldn't be sick. I'm going to find Rose, she thought to calm herself. I'll hold her in my arms and ask her to open the door between our hearts again. And I'll tell her about the baby. I don't want to be separated from her anymore.

"After we go to the store," she said aloud, "I'd like to go up to my house. I want to see Rose."

"What about your father?" Julia asked.

"He's not there on Monday."

"I want to see Rose, too," Amy said. "And we need to tell her about Stephen, that he's coming back to stay and sends his greeting to her. We were wondering how we could tell her, but now we can." Amy bounced with satisfaction.

As it turned out, they didn't need to go up to the house. Lily was looking at fabric, dreaming of baby clothes, while Amy and Julia were settling accounts with Elsie, when the bell over the door rang, and Rose came in.

Lily turned. Rose stopped just inside the door. Their eyes met. Lily took a few steps toward Rose, held out her arms. Rose hesitated by the door, then crossed the room to Lily.

Lily held her close. She felt so thin, even under the heavy blue coat that matched Lily's. She didn't melt into Lily the way she always had, but held herself stiff, slightly resisting Lily's embrace.

Lily felt a wave of panic. "Rose," she whispered. "Please open the door to your heart. I miss you so much. I don't want to be cut off from you anymore."

Rose pulled back a little. She had tears in her eyes. Lily felt tears in her own eyes.

"I can't," Rose said. "I can't find it." She pulled farther back. Lily let her go.

Amy came running up, caught hold of Rose and whirled her around. "Hi, Rose. Here you are. Lily's come to see you. We were going to go up to your house after the store, but now we don't need to because here you are."

Rose freed herself from Amy. "Were you?" she asked Lily.

Lily nodded. There was a terrible lump in her throat. Rose looked pale, her cheek bones prominent, dark shadows under her eyes. Her face was no longer like the rosy face Lily saw in the mirror each morning. Lily touched Rose's cheek. "Are you all right? Have you been sick?"

"I'm all right."

Amy was standing beside them, looking from one to the other, her brow wrinkled. "There's no problem telling you apart now," she said. "Rose has gotten thin, and Lily's been blossoming."

Lily turned to Amy, startled. Had Mother said anything?

Julia came over. "Rose, we were hoping to see you." Lily watched with a pang of jealousy as Julia embraced Rose. It seemed Rose melted more into Julia's arms than she had into Lily's.

"Come, Amy," Julia said, taking Amy by the arm. "Let them have some time together."

"But I didn't tell her about Stephen yet—"

"Later," Julia said firmly.

Lily couldn't take her eyes off Rose's wan face. "Are you sure you're all right? You look tired."

"There's been a lot of mountain fever." Rose still held herself away from Lily and spoke to her almost formally. Then she seemed to break. "Kitty died. Kitty in the brothel. Suzy came for me, but I couldn't save her. Then the whole Dodge family got it."

For a moment their thoughts met in the old way, sharing an understanding of how mountain fever might have spread from the brothel to the Dodge family.

"I've been up all night with Gerald." Rose's voice caught. "He died just before dawn."

"*Gerald* died?" Lily felt sick with shock.

"Yes."

"Oh, Rose. What about the others? Annabelle?"

"Gerald was the last to get it. It took him so fast. All the others are recovering, but there's no food in the house. I came to get some for them. I need to get back. Mrs. Dodge is beside herself."

Rose turned away toward the counter. Elsie hurried to help her. "Did you say Gerald died? Ah, poor Dolly. She'll take it hard. And her just getting over the fever herself. What do you need?"

Lily followed Rose. "Can I help you?" She stayed beside Rose while Elsie brought her the groceries, and packed them into Rose's carpet bag. "Let me come with you."

"No." Rose gave Lily a swift, stiff hug and hurried out the door.

~

Rose closed and barred the stable door and started across the hillside. Low in the sky, the silver sliver of a new moon shone pale in the last light of day. The cold stung her nostrils. She had been with the Dodge family most of the day and was limp with grief and weariness.

As she followed the path toward the house, she passed the place where the spring split the two standing stones. It was frozen, a glitter of white ice, knobby, as if arrested in the act of bubbling.

Impulsively, she dropped down onto the cold earth beside the spring. She remembered the day she and Lily had first found it flowing between the two rocks that looked as if they had once been one. She drew her knees up to her chest and bent her head down onto them. *The water separated them, she thought, and now that it's frozen, it pushes them even farther apart.*

A silent wail of anguish twisted through her. *I know why Lily came to find me. She's with child. I could see it right away. I wanted to hug her. I wanted to open the door, but it hurts too much. I can't let her in again. I can't. I'm frozen like the spring.*

## Chapter 51

# *Winter*

Winter bore down on Gold Creek and the epidemic of mountain fever grew worse. Rose was stretched to her limit. She held a clinic twice a week for all the other ills and accidents that winter brought, and the rest of the time rode out to the homes where the fever had struck. Sometimes whole families were afflicted and she stayed all night to tend them. With her prayers and tender, skillful care she was able to save most of her patients, but some died. Rose was deeply affected by each death, grieving, questioning herself in the night. If only she'd done something different, gotten there sooner.

Isabel watched over her with growing concern, trying to make sure she ate and rested. Daniel watched her with love and pride. Everywhere he went, folks spoke of her with awe. Doctor Rose, they called her, and sometimes Sweet Rose. Daniel saw that she carried out another part of his ministry, as Dr. Franz had said she would.

As winter wore on, tension built between the church and the saloon. One Saturday night, soon after New Year's, Gabe woke to the sound of drunken shouts and saw lantern light across the road at the church. Suddenly the church bell clanged. Men emerged from their houses and ran or rode to the church. Sheriff Parker was there in short order, charging down the hill on his horse. The three men, who had a ladder up against the steeple and were yelling about stealing the damn bell, were too drunk to realize they'd been surrounded until it was too late. Sheriff Parker, with the help of numerous eager volunteers, handcuffed them, marched them up to his ranch, and locked them in one of his outbuildings. In the morning he let them go, and told them not to be seen in Gold Creek again. So the affair ended, but not the talk and outrage about it.

Mrs. Dodge, hard hit by the death of her son, emerged from her grieving with a fierce vendetta against the saloon. She gathered a group of like-minded women from the church and formed a temperance union, whose goal was clearly not only temperance, but shutting down the saloon. They met weekly and put

450

pressure on Daniel to preach against drink and on Mayor Wilgus to make Gold Creek a dry town. Mrs. Dodge even swallowed her prejudice sufficiently to approach Amos Sachs to have bills printed about the evils of alcohol, which she and her ladies put up all around.

Temperance became the talk of the town, discussed over kitchen tables, at Elsie's café, in the store, in the boarding house—and in the saloon. Mayor Wilgus was against it, as was Elsie who had a good business selling wine and beer in her café. Many were strongly for it. Daniel was supportive of temperance, but urged restraint, being reluctant to set neighbor against neighbor.

Then on a Saturday night, late in February, after a dry month with no snow on the ground, a fire broke out in the shanty town across from the saloon. A man too drunk to know what he was doing spilt oil on his cook fire and set his shack ablaze. Driven by a cold wind, the flames leaped the narrow spaces between the shanties.

Daniel was waked by the sound of the church bell ringing, Bud Budke calling all the town to help. A moment later Ned Anderson was at the door, breathless, telling Daniel to come and bring buckets and asking Rose to go to Hannah's, where they were taking men who were burned.

When Daniel reached the shanty town, men had formed a bucket brigade, passing water up from the river. He took a place in the line near the blaze. Suddenly out of the swirling smoke, Smythe appeared.

"Get out of here," he snarled. "I'll handle this. These are my people. I don't need any *Christian ministers* butting in." He pushed Daniel in the center of his chest.

A burst of flame exploded near them. Its roar drowned out the rest of Smythe's words.

"Fool," Daniel shouted back. "Fight the fire, not me. Your own place is in danger."

But Smythe had disappeared into the smoke and confusion.

By dawn, when the blaze was at last extinguished, there was nothing left of the shanty town but smoldering rubble. Five men had been seriously burned, one man was killed when his cabin collapsed on him, and fourteen men were homeless.

Daniel moved among the men of the church, asking each to take in a homeless man. A few hours later, when he stood behind his pulpit with a burn on his cheek to deliver his Sunday sermon, he minced no words about the dire effects of drunkenness.

In the following weeks, men of the church joined with men of the shanty town to clear the rubble and rebuild. Within a month, eight small, sturdy cabins in a neat row along the road replaced what had once been a tumble of barely habitable shacks. Touched by the warm hospitality and help of the church, many of the men converted.

The church socials were Hannah's idea. "There needs to be another place for those men to go on Saturday nights besides the drunken orgies at the saloon, or we may lose them again," she said to Daniel. "We can push back the tables in my dining room and have a party. Everyone will enjoy it." Daniel was all for it and the word went out. The first Saturday night at Hannah's was a huge success. Almost everyone in town came, bringing food and musical instruments. So a new tradition began. After several weeks, Hannah actually persuaded Daniel to let her invite Bernie to come and lead a square dance.

"Papa's come a long way," Rose said to Isabel as they made their way down the cliff path to the dance. "I wish I could laugh with Lily about it. She's sure to know. I know she's laughing."

# Chapter 52

# *Snowstorm*

Rose felt dizzy as she started down the stairs from the brothel. She had waked that morning with a pounding headache and felt worse as the day wore on. Finally, admitting to herself that she was sick, she closed her clinic and was on her way home when Suzy from the brothel caught up with her. Candy had something awful happening in her woman parts. Could Rose please come?

So Rose had pushed aside her headache and followed Suzy to the brothel. Because of all the births she had attended, she was used to seeing women's parts, but she had never seen anything like this—running sores and a sickly stench. "You've gotten a bad disease from one of your customers," she told Candy. Stifling her nausea, she did what she could, bathing the afflicted parts with soothing calendula tea. "I don't know how to treat this," she confessed. She turned to Suzy and Belle. "If you can, take her to Montview to Dr. Franz. He'll know what to do." Then she left.

The stairs seemed to undulate in front of her. She had gotten only as far as the landing, where the stairs turned at a right angle, when she heard men's voices below. Smythe and his bartender, Brick. Rose had seen Brick only once before when she had come to care for Kitty, and he had terrified her. He was a huge man with a hard, red face and stubbly beard. It was said he kept a cudgel behind the bar and clouted any man who was unruly. Rose had treated some of those head wounds.

She drew back, looking around quickly. Built onto the side of the landing, there was a closet without a door, filled with fancy dresses and high-heeled shoes. Stumbling over the shoes, Rose ducked down behind the dresses, shrinking away from the odor of stale sweat and cheap perfume.

Smythe was in a rage. "Another one sick. It's Saturday and only two girls."

"If you work 'em all night," Brick said, " and give 'em shorter shifts, two will do. We don't get that many men anymore."

"No, we don't." Smythe's voice rose. "Not since they started having *church socials*"—Rose could hear the scorn in his voice—"over at Hannah's. Saturday night. That's my night. They all used to come here. It's his fault. That damn preacher. And if it wasn't for him and his meddling twins, I'd have three more girls upstairs."

"Three?"

"Yeah, Ella and Lisbeth and that girl I went all the way to Robinson's for, only to have them snatch her away." Hate filled his voice. "If it weren't for him, that church— Before he came it was nothing. Now there's the goddamned bell splitting our heads every Sunday morning and"—he raised his voice to a mocking falsetto—"the Ladies Temperance society."

Brick gave a dry laugh.

"Laugh," Smythe snarled. "They mean to close us down, run us out of town."

"Naw. Wilgus'll never go for it."

Smythe seemed not to hear him. "I'll kill him, that preacher. I'll kill him. He's ruining me. I was here first. It's my town. He's gotta go."

Brick laughed again. "You want him dead? No problem. I'll take him out for you. It'd be easy. He rides around by himself all over the valley. All I'd need to do is catch him in a lonely place and plug him one. Bam! Or better, drag him off his horse and beat him good. It'd be a pleasure."

Rose cringed, retreating farther back behind the dresses. Her head ached fiercely and her heart beat so fast she feared she might faint.

"No, no." Smythe lowered his voice. "We can't do it that way. Remember when the sheriff came? That time after Ella ran off, and I took my gun up to the preacher's house? He said that if anything happened to the preacher or any of his kin, they'd know it was me and he'd string me up without a question. He means it, too.

"No, I gotta make it look like an accident. Thanks for your offer, but *I* want to do it, personally. It's between him and me. I've been thinking on it. A lonely road, like you said."

The two moved on. Rose heard the door to the bar open and close. She crawled out of the closet shaking violently, she couldn't tell whether from fear or the fever that was swiftly overtaking her. Clinging to the railing, she somehow made it down the stairs. I must warn Papa, she told herself over and over again. The big room was empty. She hurried across it and out the side door, where long ago she and Lily had peeped in, seduced by the sound of a piano. Dawnstar was tethered just outside.

It was late afternoon, April and springtime, but cold. Rose shivered in the sharp wind, and gathered her cloak closer around herself. Her hands shook as she tied her medicine bag onto the back of the double saddle. Mounting took all her strength. "Take us home," she told Dawnstar. As Dawnstar moved forward, Rose swayed in the saddle and almost fell. Her eyes darkened. She let go of the reins and clung to Dawnstar's silver mane.

Later she had only confused memories. Dawnstar carrying her through the town. Isabel's concerned cries. Rachel and Isabel carrying her into the house. The brightness of the fire hurting her eyes. Then blackness, searing agony in all her limbs, her throat dry and aching. An urgency pushing at her. Papa, I must tell Papa. A horror pressing down on her, but what she had to tell him was swept away.

Hands tended her. A cool cloth on her brow. A blanket over her. But she was too hot. She thrashed and cried out. Later she opened her eyes. It was night. She was lying on the couch in the living room. The fire had died down. Isabel dozed beside her in the leather chair. Then fever swept her away again. White bones— were they hers? —bleaching on the plains.

Lily. Lily was sad. She was with child and wanted to tell Rose, but Rose ran away from her, would not listen, would not open the door. Long ago. So long ago she had lost Lily. *Lily, Lily, I'm sorry. I was angry. But I love you. Lily, where are you?* The door of her heart opened. Her cry echoed down a long corridor with a closed door at the end, echoed back to her unanswered.

When Daniel and Rachel returned from church the next morning, Isabel was kneeling by the couch where Rose lay, her face in her hands, weeping. Rachel set Joshua down and ran to kneel beside her.

"What is it? Is she ...?"

Isabel lifted her head, her cheeks streaked with tears. "She still breathing, but she's gone away. I can't get her to answer me, not even to lick the drops of water I put on her lips. And she's so hot."

Daniel stood by the door, his hat in his hand, his heart contracting with fear. Moving methodically, he hung his hat on the coat rack, took off his coat and hung it, then walked to Rose's side. She lay pale and still, her breath barely discernible. He bent and laid his hand on her brow, then recoiled, shocked at the heat.

Joshua came to look also. Rachel drew him away.

Isabel was still talking, pouring out her grief to Rachel. "I've been bathing her to keep the fever down. I didn't know what else to do. I never knew she'd gotten so thin. Poor lamb, she's naught but skin and bones. She's been wearing herself out taking care of everyone and grieving for Lily all this long winter. I shoulda taken better care of her, made her rest more. She's been calling for Lily, calling and calling her name—and then it was like she just gave up, and now ..." Isabel broke down into tears again. "Poor, poor lamb. Poor dear lamb."

Rachel looked up at Daniel. "She's been calling for Lily. You need to go get her right away. Maybe Lily can bring her back."

Daniel straightened. "No," he said. "I don't want Lily here."

Rachel leapt to her feet and gripped Daniel's arms. "*When* will you let go of this craziness? What if she dies, and you never brought Lily to her? How would you feel then?" She actually shook him. "Can't you see? She's been dying of grief ever since you forbade her to see Lily, and now she may actually die. Maybe only Lily can bring her back. Please go, Daniel, go now. Bring Lily before it's too late."

Her grip on his arms was painful. He pulled away from her. Fear and guilt swirled in him and morphed to anger and denial.

"She won't die. She'll come through. She's young and strong."

"So was Gerald, and he died in one night from the fever. Will you go?"

"I told you I have a wedding this afternoon. Way out on the plains. I need to leave soon."

Joshua stood looking up at his parents, his chin trembling.

"Skip the wedding." Rachel was almost screaming at him. "Don't you understand? Rose may be dead before you come back."

Joshua began to cry. Isabel picked him up and carried him into the kitchen.

Daniel stiffened. "I told you, she won't die. The Lord is watching over her. Get me some bread and cheese to eat as I go. I need to leave now."

He really didn't need to leave immediately, but he suddenly couldn't bear to stay. Rose's still form on the couch terrified him. Rachel's anger, even though he knew deep down the righteousness of it, outraged him. How dare she shake him? He had a wedding to do. He couldn't skip that. It was a new family in the area. They'd built a fine big house out on the plains and invited guests from as far away as Denver. They would be influential in the valley.

He turned away from Rachel and went into the bedroom to change into riding clothes. He packed his best suit and his Bible in his bag. When he walked back through the living room, Rachel was kneeling by the couch, a bowl of water beside her, bathing Rose's brow with a blue cloth. Isabel had pulled herself together to calm Joshua. She came out of the kitchen with Joshua on her hip and a bundle in her hand.

"Here's food for your journey. Pray for our Rose and come back as soon as you can. We need you here."

Daniel softened. Faithful Isabel. "Thank you, Isabel," he said. "I'll be back before dark. Take good care of her."

He did not say good-bye to Rachel, but stepped out the door, closing it firmly behind him.

It was beginning to snow. Damn, he thought. Snow. It's April. This crazy Rocky Mountain springtime, sweet and warm one day and snow the next. Maybe I should take the buggy. No, that would just slow me if it keeps on snowing. Shadow and I will do okay. He swung his bag over his shoulder and strode up the hill to the stable.

Once he was on the road, his anger subsided, and he regretted being so harsh with Rachel. He recalled his last glimpse of her, kneeling by Rose, the tender way she was bathing Rose's face, the blue of the cloth. He sighed. I should have said good-bye to her. I'll be gentle with her when I get back.

He had by now crossed Mill Road and passed the last few houses on the south side of town. The open plains lay before him. He rode on, turning his mind to the wedding and how he would arrange the ceremony.

After a while he came to a place where long ago some capricious force of nature had deposited two huge boulders in the middle of the plains. They had become a landmark, known to the locals as Two Stones. The road divided around them.

Daniel stopped there and pulled out the scrap of paper given him by the young groom. "At Two Stones take the left fork," he read. The snow was coming down harder. Wishing he'd thought to wear a scarf, he turned up the collar of his coat and set off down the left fork.

Daniel gave a final blessing to the young bride and groom and stepped out of the warm, festive house into a blizzard. As he made his way to the stable, wind whipped snow into his face. It was already up to his ankles and coming down thick and fast.

"We've got a cold, wet ride ahead," he told Shadow as he led her out into the storm.

At first he couldn't see the road, only the white expanse of the plains. Then, as he looked more closely, he could see a slight indentation ahead of him, and remembered that when he had come the road had still been bare. The snow was just beginning then, melting on the warmth of the bare dirt even as it accumulated on the grasses.

He glanced back at the house to get his bearings, pulled his hat down to shield his face, and set off. It's well I didn't stay much longer, he thought. It would be easy to get lost in a storm like this, out here on the plains with the snow too thick to see the hills. Shadow seemed as anxious as he to get home, and moved along at a brisk pace. Soon the house was far behind them, and Daniel and Shadow were enclosed in a white world.

As he rode, Daniel thought of Rose, remembering how hot her brow had felt under his hand. She won't die, he told himself. He felt his heart contract. She mustn't die. She's so full of light, so sweet. Maybe I should have gone for Lily. Maybe she's dying of grief and it's my fault. No. I did what was right. But alone in the whiteness, he was less sure of himself. He remembered Rachel's anger, her blazing dark eyes. He nudged Shadow. "Hurry up."

Shadow moved along steadily, but Daniel became increasingly anxious. He could see nothing ahead or around him, only snow. The slight indentation that had marked the road had disappeared and the late afternoon light was fading. What if we get lost? he asked himself. I don't know where we are.

They rode on and on in the whiteness.

After a while, Daniel noticed that Shadow also seemed anxious. She tossed her head, and snorted, picked up her pace. Then Daniel began to feel a prickling in the back of his neck, as if he were being followed. Don't be ridiculous, he told himself. Who would follow me? No one but a fool would be out in a storm like this.

Suddenly he saw a dark shape loom up on his left. He reined Shadow in and held her still, his heart beating fast. The shape did not move. Daniel loosened the reins and approached slowly. A gust of wind blew the snow aside for a moment, and Daniel let out a sigh of relief.

"It's only Two Stones," he told Shadow. "Two Stones," he repeated. "That means we're on the road after all, and close to home." He patted Shadow on the neck. "Good girl. You found the way."

They had gone only a few paces forward when Daniel heard a soft whir by his ears. Then something tightened around his shoulders and he was pulled sharply backward. Shadow neighed and reared and Daniel fell hard onto the ground, striking his head. He lay shocked, the breath knocked out of him, dizzy from the head blow.

"Gotcha." Daniel knew that voice. He opened his eyes and looked up to see Smythe on his massive brown stallion, towering over him.

"It's perfect," Smythe gloated. "You alone and the snow to cover my tracks. They'll find you later, trampled by your horse. Such a sad accident."

Daniel tried to move, but his head spun and he almost fainted from a wave of nausea. He was vaguely aware of Shadow behind him.

Smythe's voice was smooth and evil. "You don't look so good. Hit your head hard when you landed, didn't you. I heard it. Never mind. I'll put you out of your misery."

Daniel twisted and found himself tangled in the rope that had lassoed him. He struggled with it and pulled it off.

Smythe was still talking. "I have you now. Bruno will trample you and all the world will think it was an accident. It will not be the first time—" To Daniel's astonishment he heard Smythe's voice catch in a sob. "Not the first time," Smythe sucked in his breath and went on, "his hooves have tasted blood. Call on your God to save you—if He can."

The stallion pranced, his hooves dangerously near where Daniel lay. A jolt of fear cleared Daniel's head. He truly means to kill me, he realized. He let out a cry, a wordless prayer to heaven. Strength surged through him. He sprang to his feet. Shadow was near, dancing in agitation. He took a step toward her. The rope caught at his ankle. He kicked it away. One foot in the stirrup.

"No you don't," Smythe shouted. He drove his stallion hard against Shadow, leaned to the side and grabbed Daniel's arm as he reached for the saddle horn. Shadow laid her ears back, snaked out her long neck, and bit the stallion on the rump. He squealed and reared high on his hind legs, his front legs pawing the air. Smythe, off balance from his grip on Daniel's arm, fell to the ground, pulling Daniel down with him. Daniel jerked free of Smythe's grasp and rolled away from him. The stallion's great hooves came down on Smythe, crushing his chest.

Smythe screamed, a hideous gurgling scream. The stallion reared again, whirled and fled, disappearing into the thickly falling snow.

Daniel crawled to Smythe's side. Smythe was gasping, writhing. Blood pulsed from his open chest.

Daniel took Smythe's hand. "Even now," he pleaded, "it is not too late. Call on Christ for forgiveness. You can yet be saved."

Smythe turned his head toward Daniel, his face contorted with agony. "Go to hell," he snarled. He caught a tortured breath.

Then it seemed to Daniel that a soft light surrounded them, growing brighter. He looked for its source, but saw only curtains of falling snow. Smythe stirred. He opened his eyes and lifted his head, a look of incredulity on his face. "Oh!" he exclaimed. His head fell back and he lay still. The blood stopped pulsing from his chest. The agony and the snarl were gone from his face, leaving it smooth and serene.

Daniel bent over him. "He's gone," he whispered. "Lost. For all eternity. I could not save him." Grief overtook him as he looked at the peaceful face.

Daniel wept. The light brightened around him and he heard God's voice. *Do not weep, my son. He is not lost. His soul was sorely wounded, but he has come home to Me and is at rest.*

"Home to Thee?" Daniel exclaimed, tilting his face up into the light. "How could he be with Thee? If any man deserved to go to hell it is this man, who has sinned in every way possible and denied Christ even at the end."

*He has been in hell. Now he has come to Me to be healed.*

"But … but …" Daniel was still looking up. Snow melted on his cheeks. The light slowly faded leaving dusk behind. Daniel bent his head and found himself kneeling in blood-spattered snow, Smythe dead before him.

He touched the still body. Not lost? If *he* is not lost, then no one is. "How can that be?" he asked God, but the light was gone and God did not speak again.

**Chapter 53**

# *Epiphany*

Shadow bent her neck and nudged Daniel. He lifted his head. He had no idea how long he had been kneeling there. The blood-stained, trampled snow around him was filling in with a fresh layer of white. Smythe lay dead before him. Curtains of falling snow surrounded him. It was growing dark.

Shadow nudged him again. He reached up and stroked her neck. "What is it, girl? Time to go home?" He looked down at Smythe's body and shook with shock. "What should I do with him?" he asked his horse. "What must I do?"

Shadow tossed her head, her message clear. It was no time of day to be sitting around in the snow. It was time to go home. She stamped a foot.

Daniel stood slowly. His legs were cramped and cold, his trousers wet.

"What must I do?" he asked again. "I need to go home. Rose ..." He looked again at the dead body. Smythe's head had rolled to one side. The wound in his chest was ghastly. "I can't leave him here," he said aloud, still talking to Shadow. "But how can I get him onto your back?"

*Help me, God,* he prayed. *Help me. I don't know what to do.*

Then he felt another surge of strength and understood that the strength that had come to him before, when he lay helpless on the ground with Smythe approaching to trample him, had also been an answer to prayer. God is with me, he realized, and even in the horror of the moment, he felt comforted.

He bent and gathered Smythe's body into his arms, pushed down into the earth with his strong legs and straightened. The body almost fell apart as he lifted it, the chest hanging strangely, the head dangling. Barely controlling an impulse to retch, Daniel somehow heaved it up onto Shadow. He stood a moment breathing hard. The body started to slide. Quickly he caught it and pushed it back up, balancing it precariously on the saddle. With trembling hands he fumbled in his saddlebag for the coil of rope he always carried there, pulled it out, and tied the body securely in place.

His hat lay a few paces away, half buried. As he put it on, the surge of strength drained out of him as quickly as it had come. His head pounded. He swayed and caught hold of Shadow for support.

"Come, girl," he said to her, taking her reins. "I'll walk beside you. Lead us home."

The act of walking calmed him. He still couldn't see the road under the snow, but trusted Shadow to find the way.

As he walked, he struggled with God's words to him. Smythe was with God? Home with Him? He'd been in hell, but now God was healing him? *Smythe?*

His theology was blown to smithereens. If a man like Smythe did not go to hell, then what is hell? God said he'd been in hell. What does that mean? That hell is here on Earth? That it is here on Earth that we burn from our sins?

A gust of wind blew snow into his face. He let go of Shadow's reins, looped them up, and wound his fingers in her mane. His head swam as he remembered his own agonies, burning with rage, burning with lust. Maybe it's true, that hell is here. But there are also times of bliss. He remembered those times, too.

I have seen it all, agony and bliss, in myself, my family, my parishioners. Are heaven and hell both here on Earth? Then what about afterwards? What is heaven that we should strive for it?

*I am confused*, he prayed. *What shall I teach my people now?*

In his aching, opening heart he heard the answer: *Teach them that I am Love.*

Even though he could not see it, it seemed then that the light that had surrounded him at the moment of Smythe's death was still with him, like a golden bubble protecting and embracing him. His heart swelled in awe and gratitude, and, all at once, he knew what heaven was. It was being connected to God, whether on Earth or afterward—and hell was being separated.

He glanced over at Smythe's body. He'd been in hell, God said. But at the very end he saw. He lifted his head and exclaimed. And when he died his face was peaceful.

A fragment of Scripture crossed Daniel's memory. "I am found of them who sought me not."

As he walked on, more Scripture flowed through him. "The mercy of the Lord is from everlasting to everlasting … He hath not dealt with us according to our sins nor rewarded us according to our iniquities."

"Whither shall I go from Thy Spirit and whither shall I flee from Thy presence … if I ascend up into heaven Thou art there; if I make my bed in hell, behold, Thou art there."

*Never leave me,* Daniel prayed to his God.

And it seemed that God answered, *I never will.*

Daniel felt such ecstasy that he wanted to kneel in the snow, but Shadow plodded on, drawing him forward.

**Chapter 54**

# *Fateful Night*

A building loomed up out of the snow, then another. They had come to South Road and were back in town.

Daniel emerged from his ecstasy with a jolt. *What do I do now?* he asked himself. *What if someone sees me with a dead body on my horse? What shall I do with him?* Shadow picked up her pace, knowing she was near home, pulling Daniel along, his fingers still wrapped in her mane. Soon they crossed Mill Road. Daniel could see lights in the store. On they went, across the bridge and up the hill.

*I'll take him to Sheriff Parker,* Daniel decided. *And then home. I hope Rose is all right. And Rachel. I never should have left her as I did.* Anxiety swirled up in him. He walked faster.

When they reached Pine Road, Shadow turned up the hill toward home. With all his heart, Daniel wanted to follow, but he had a dead body on his horse. He picked up the reins and, with difficulty, turned her down the hill to Sheriff Parker's place.

Sheriff Parker opened to his knock and peered out into the snow. "Evening, Preacher," he said. "What brings you out in this storm?"

Daniel took a deep breath. His head was spinning again. He'd left Shadow at the bottom of the porch steps and felt unsteady without her beside him.

He hesitated, then blurted out, "Smythe is dead."

"*What?*" The sheriff stepped out onto the porch and gripped Daniel's shoulder. "What happened? How'd you know? Did'y kill him?"

"He tried to kill me. We struggled. He fell off his horse, and his horse—that huge stallion—trampled him."

"Good God, man. Are you all right?"

Daniel nodded.

The sheriff clapped his hand to his brow. "Smythe dead? That'll change the town. Where is he?"

"Here." Daniel gestured toward Shadow.

"Wait a minute. Let me get a lantern and my boots."

A few minutes later the two men stood together by Shadow. The sheriff lifted his lantern. "Got him bad," he commented.

Seeing the mutilated corpse again, Daniel felt his stomach roil. He swallowed. "I didn't know what to do with him," he said. "I couldn't just leave him in the road."

"Could've. He didn't deserve any better. How'd you get him up on your horse?"

"The Lord gave me strength."

The sheriff looked Daniel over, raised one eyebrow. "Must've. Well, bring your horse around. We'll put him in my cart, and I'll take him down to the saloon. Let those folks deal with what's left of him."

Daniel led Shadow around to the barn. Together they untied the ropes and lifted Smythe's body down into the cart.

"How'd it happen?" the sheriff asked. "You said he was trying to kill you. What'd he do?"

Briefly Daniel described the lasso, the fall, Smythe's gloating. When he spoke of how Shadow bit the stallion's rump causing him to rear and throw Smythe, he realized as he said it, "She probably saved my life." He stroked her neck in gratitude.

"Mares never did tolerate being pushed around by stallions," the sheriff noted. "So, he got what he was fixing to dish out. You sure you're all right. You look kind of peaked."

"I'm okay. I need to get home. My daughter's got the fever."

"Sweet Rose? The doctor girl? You go on then. I'll handle the rest. Take good care of that girl. She's a treasure."

It wasn't more than a half mile from the sheriff's place to his home, but Daniel was grateful to ride. He found he was shaking. Seeing Smythe's body again in the light of the lantern had reawakened his shock, and the sheriff's words about Rose renewed his anxiety. She *is* a treasure, he thought. She mustn't die. And Rachel. He was swept with longing to hold her in his arms, ask her forgiveness. "Hurry, Shadow." He nudged her with his heels and she broke into a canter. Straight to the house he rode, dismounted and ran up the porch steps. At the door, he stopped himself, took a breath and entered quietly.

Hannah sat in the rocking chair with Joshua asleep in her arms. She caught Daniel's eye and put her finger to her lips. Isabel knelt on the floor by Rose, her head down on the edge of the couch. When she heard Daniel come in, she looked up, her face drawn with grief and weariness.

Daniel took a hesitant step into the room. "How is she?" he asked softly.

"The same," Isabel answered.

Daniel walked to the side of the couch and looked down at Rose. He didn't dare touch her again. It seemed as if she hadn't stirred since the last time he'd seen her.

He glanced around the room. Why was Hannah there holding Joshua? "Where's Rachel?"

"Gone," Isabel said.

"Gone! Where?"

"She took Dawnstar and went to Fairdale's to get Lily."

"But she's only just learning to ride. She's never gone there alone. All the way to Fairdale's in this storm?" Daniel's voice rose. "When? When did she leave?"

Isabel seemed near tears. "Right after you did. She took the boy down to Hannah so I could tend Rose, said she wouldn't be gone more than a couple of hours, just to Fairdale's and bring Lily right back. I'm feared she's lost with the snow and all those twisty little tracks that cross the road and don't go nowhere."

Terror rose up in Daniel. "You let her go?" he shouted.

Joshua stirred and moaned in Hannah's lap. Hannah raised her hand, palm out. "Don't wake the boy. We just got him quiet."

Isabel rose stiffly from her knees. "I couldn't stop her. She was sure Rose would die if Lily didn't come. And so she may." Isabel's voice broke with a sob. "So she may. She hasn't stirred for hours. Hardly breathes."

Hannah spoke quietly. "Rachel is probably at Fairdale's, safe and sound, and them just waiting for the storm to pass to bring her and Lily."

"She wouldn't have waited," Isabel said.

Daniel felt torn in so many directions he thought he might explode. He wanted to sit by Rose and pray with all his heart for her to be healed. He wanted to ride pell mell to Montview and fetch Dr. Franz. He wanted to bring Lily back. Most of all he wanted to find Rachel, hold her safe and close.

He flung his arms out wildly in a gesture of desperation. "I must go find her."

"Wait." Isabel came to him and touched his chest. "You have blood on your coat. Are you all right? What happened?"

"Smythe ... I'll tell you later. I have to go find Rachel, bring Lily."

He whirled and rushed out the door, leaving it open behind him.

Shadow stood patiently at the foot of the porch steps, her head hanging.

Daniel swiftly mounted, then bent to stroke her neck. "We're not done yet, girl. We've more miles to go." Feeling her weariness, he felt his own. "I know you're tired. I am, too. But we must go." He turned her back down the road. In his urgency he wanted to gallop all the way to Fairdale's, but knew he must ride her gently.

The snow was falling less thickly, only a few flakes now, drifting down on the wind. The clouds were breaking up, and he could see the black shape of the hills against the sky.

It had grown colder. He searched in the snow for any sign of hoof prints, but it was dark. Only the faint shine of the stars that were emerging and the whiteness of the snow gave enough light for him to find his way.

I should have brought a lantern, he thought. I'll never find a trace of her like this. What if she's lost, like Isabel says? She could freeze to death before we find her. What if a mountain lion takes her? His stomach clenched, and he felt sick with terror. She must be at Fairdales', he told himself. He nudged Shadow to go faster, but the snow was deep and she was weary. She cantered a few paces, then fell back into a plodding walk.

The bubble of light that he'd felt around him after Smythe's death was gone. He felt chilled and alone. The outline of the hills to the west helped him keep his bearings, but his inner landmarks were all upside down. He never doubted his vision. The new understanding about heaven and hell was already rooted in him. Now, as he rode, the implications of it rushed in on him, assaulting him from every side.

If heaven and hell were on Earth, and the afterlife for everyone—everyone, even Smythe—was to return to God to be healed, then—

Then there was no reason to shun the Fairdales, no reason why Lily shouldn't marry Jonathan. No reason, no reason at all to separate Rose and Lily.

I've done it all wrong, he groaned inwardly.

Words came back to him:

Jonathan. "What kind of God do you worship that would cause someone as pure and beautiful as Lily to be damned?"

Gabe, speaking of Rose. "She'll not be lost. Don't you see your own child? I ain't never knowed a body held so close in the bosom of Jesus as that one."

Lily. "You're not responsible for my immortal soul. Only God is. You're not God."

Andrew. "What good I do on this Earth is not to win some prize in the hereafter, but because it is the right thing here and now. As for the rest, I trust in God's love."

Rachel. "Maybe it is not God's will you are attending to, but Daniel's."

They were all trying to tell me, he thought, and I wouldn't listen.

Most damning were Rachel's words that afternoon. "She's been dying of grief ever since you forbade her to see Lily."

He grew cold with remorse. It was true. All winter Rose had been withering, and he had seen it and done nothing. He knew with certainty that if she and Lily had still been close, she would not have faded so. It was all his fault. If he had not refused to let Lily marry Jonathan, had not cut off the Fairdales, had not cut off his own daughter and forbidden her to see her twin, then none of this would be happening. Rose would not be ill, Rachel would not be lost.

But I thought I was doing the right thing, he protested to himself, to God.

How dark it was. It seemed that he had been plodding along in the night forever. At last he came to the arch that led into Fairdale Ranch. The stars were bright now, the clouds dispersing. The road lay clear before him between the neat fences. As he neared the house, the memory of the last time he'd been there caused him to writhe with shame. How can I face them? What about Lily? Then all else was overwhelmed with his anxiety about Rachel. What if she wasn't there?

She has to be. She just has to be.

He dismounted in front of the house and looped Shadow's reins over the porch railing. Light poured out of the unshaded window. He stopped on the porch and looked in.

All the family was gathered there in the living room—Kate and Andrew, Amy and Julia, Lily and Jonathan, and another young man, a stranger. He was talking, and all the rest were listening.

Daniel saw with shock that Lily was big with child. She was blooming, beautiful. An ache moved through him, and he knew that he loved her, that he had missed her sorely.

The strange young man, at second glance, was not strange. Daniel knew him, knew him quite well, but couldn't put a name to him. The young man gestured, and everyone laughed.

Rachel was not there.

Daniel knocked loudly.

Everyone turned at the sound. Andrew came and opened the door.

"Daniel!" he exclaimed. "Daniel, come in." He held out both hands. Daniel reached for them. Andrew's clasp was warm and strong. He drew Daniel into the warmth and light and closed the door behind him.

Lily was on her feet, eyes wide. "Papa!"

Jonathan went quickly to her side and put his arm around her.

Kate came to greet him. "Daniel, you're welcome. We've missed you."

Daniel could not speak. The warmth after the long, cold ride, the welcome he did not deserve, overwhelmed him.

Andrew looked into his face. "Is anything wrong?"

"Rachel," Daniel stammered at last. "Have you seen Rachel?"

"Rachel?" Kate asked. "No, we haven't seen her. What's happened?"

"Rose." Daniel's words came out in short bursts. He was shivering with cold and fear. "Rose is sick. Calling for Lily. Rachel left to get Lily. Hours ago. I was gone. Didn't know. She hadn't come back when I returned. After dark."

"Rose is sick?" Lily interrupted. Her eyes went distant. "Oh," she cried out. "She *is* sick. No, Rose, don't. Wait for me, Rose. I'm coming." Her eyes focused again. "I have to go right away. Now. She might die. Jonathan—" She turned to him.

"I'll take you," he said. "In the sleigh. I'll go hitch up Brandy. Get your coat. Mother, get blankets and pillows for her. It's cold." He dashed out through the kitchen. Daniel heard the back door slam.

Kate ran up the stairs. Julia brought Lily's coat and helped her into it. It was too narrow to button over her big belly. Lily began to cry, "Rose, Rose." Julia put her arms around her.

Andrew stood close beside Daniel, his hand on Daniel's shoulder. "Tell me about Rachel."

"I don't know anything more. Isabel said she went to bring Lily. But you haven't seen her. She must be lost. The snow was so thick. She's never come here alone." His desperation poured through his words.

"We'll find her," Andrew said. "Amy, go quickly. Get Bernie and James and Luke. Tell them to bring lanterns and guns."

Amy, who had been staring with her mouth open, her head turning from one to the other, sprang into action at her father's command. She raced out through the kitchen and ran smack into Jonathan who was coming in the back door.

"The sleigh's ready." Jonathan went to Lily and took her hand. "We'll go as fast as lightning."

"Wait a minute." Kate came hurrying down the stairs with her arms full of blankets and pillows. She handed them to Jonathan. "Wrap her up warm. That coat doesn't cover her anymore."

Lily turned to Daniel, her eyes bright with angry tears. "It's your fault," she cried. "If you hadn't kept us apart, I would have known. I would have taken care of her. If she dies, I'll never, ever forgive you."

Jonathan tugged at her hand, and she ran with him out through the kitchen. The back door slammed again.

~

Rose walked alone, barefoot, across the plains. It was night and the stars were bright. As far as she could see there was no one, no sign of life but the tall grass that brushed her skirt.

Far ahead there was a light. It grew brighter and brighter as she hurried toward it, a clear white light like no light she had ever known.

Then she saw that the light emanated from a crystal castle set on top of a green hill. Flowers were scattered in the grass and sheep grazed there, pure white against the green. All was bathed in the light from the castle.

Her heart opened and she knew. Heaven. She didn't look where her feet were going. Her gaze was on the crystal castle and the light pouring out of it, illuminating all with such beauty and peace she felt her heart would break with joy. She ran toward it, reaching out her arms.

Suddenly she stumbled. Dark water swirled around her ankles, tugged at the hem of her skirt. She looked down and saw that she stood at the edge of a wide, deep river, running swiftly, separating her from the green hill on the other side.

She staggered back to the shore and looked up again. A door in the castle opened. Jesus stepped out, and came down the hill toward her, holding out his hands. Light radiated from Him. She looked into His deep eyes, and, heedless of danger, plunged into the river. Waist-deep she foundered, caught by the current, and was swept under into darkness.

He came to her swiftly then, walking across the surface of the turbulent water. "Not yet, beloved," He said tenderly, as He gathered her up into His arms. "Not yet." He carried her back to the shore of the dark plains, set her on her feet, and embraced her.

Then it seemed that it was not Jesus but Stephen who held her close, cradling her head against his shoulder, as he had when he pulled her out of another river. Long ago. Stephen. It was sweet to be in his arms, as it had been then.

A voice called. *Rose.*

Stephen released her. "Lily's calling you."

*Lily!* she shouted. The doors were open.

Lily's voice floated across the dark plains. *Rose, I'm coming.*

Stephen caught her hand. They ran back across the dark plains toward a light that beckoned to them. It was not the pure white light of Heaven, but a warm, golden glow.

It was the lamp on the mantelpiece. Rose's eyes opened. Isabel bent over her. "Lily's coming," she told Isabel. Then she closed her eyes again, turned on her side, and slept.

~

Again, Daniel rode alone in the night. Now he carried a lantern, but it only magnified the darkness around him.

Stephen rode ahead of him. The strange young man that he knew but couldn't place turned out to be Stephen Fairdale, outrider on the wagon train and Andrew's nephew. As the men gathered by the barn, he had approached Daniel.

"It's good to see you again, sir. I'm so sorry to hear about Rosie being sick and your wife being lost. I'll ride with you to search for her. With all of us looking, we'll find her for sure."

Daniel knew him then. He was the only one who had ever called Rose "Rosie." He had matured over the last two years. His shoulders had broadened, his beard filled in, but his kind blue-gray eyes, now warm with compassion, were the same.

Once the men were mounted and ready to go, Andrew set out his plan. "Daniel and Stephen, you ride on the west side of the road, following any tracks or paths that lead toward the hills. Luke and James, you go straight down Ranch Road, looking to each side. Bernie and I will search east of the road, down toward the creek. Keep calling. There's a good chance she'll see our lanterns and come to us. Whoever finds her, bring her to the road, and shoot three times into the air. Keep signaling until we're all gathered. Let's go."

Daniel had felt heartened as they rode together through the ranch and under the arch. Then they spread out. At first he could see the lanterns scattered across the plains, hear their calls growing fainter with distance. But now he was alone again. Stephen, with his well rested horse, had galloped on ahead. Shadow moved frustratingly slowly.

He felt as if he'd been riding alone in the snow and the night forever. Weariness bore down on him. How will we ever find her? he despaired. It's ten miles by the road between Gold Creek and Fairdale Ranch, and all the wide plains on either side. She could be anywhere. And if we don't find her before daylight, she'll freeze to death. A sob shook him. If she is lost, if Rose dies and Lily never forgives me … What does it matter that I have built a thriving church if I have destroyed my own family?

Shadow was walking more and more slowly. Finally she just stopped and hung her head. Daniel sat in the saddle, his own head hanging. His arm ached from holding the lantern. For a few minutes he gave in to his sobs and despair. Then he lifted his head, took a long breath. "Rachel," he called. "Rachel."

His voice faded away into the vastness of the night.

Far ahead of him he saw Stephen riding back toward him. Daniel felt a rush of hope. Maybe he found something.

But when Stephen reined in beside him, it was only to ask, "Are you all right, sir? I didn't mean to leave you so far behind."

Daniel felt like an old man with the young man coming to check on him.

"My horse is weary," he answered. "We've ridden many miles today. Did you see anything?"

"No, but look." Stephen gestured to the east. "The moon is rising. That will give us more light, especially with the snow. Don't lose hope, sir."

Just as Daniel turned toward the east to see the moon, three shots rang out. A pause. Three shots again.

Daniel's heart leaped, beat so intensely that he almost passed out.

"They've found her!" Stephen exclaimed. "Come on, sir." He beckoned and set off at a gallop.

Daniel felt as if he were in a dream. Somehow he got Shadow into motion again and galloped after Stephen toward the sound of the shots. As if in a dream, he saw the dark shapes of horses and riders, lanterns swinging, as they converged on the silhouette of a man on horseback standing still against the white snow.

As he got closer, Daniel saw that it was Andrew astride his tall bay, holding a slumped form in his arms. Beside him, Bernie held the reins of Dawnstar, her saddle empty.

Daniel was seized with dread. *Is Rachel injured? Dead?*

Snow flew up from Shadow's hooves as he pulled her to a stop beside Andrew's big bay. He dismounted, dropped his lantern in the snow, and took the last two paces to Andrew's horse.

"Here you are, Daniel," Andrew said. "She's all right, mighty chilled, but all right."

Daniel held up his arms and Rachel slid down into them. He folded her close. His voice broke. "Rachel."

She lifted her head. Her face, outlined by her black scarf, was as white as the snow. "I'm here, Daniel."

Daniel held her closer. "Thank God, thank God," he sobbed, then broke down completely.

Luke and James rode up. The men made a quiet, respectful circle around Daniel and Rachel.

After a while, Andrew said, "Come, Daniel. We need to get this lady home where it's warm. Why don't you take her on Dawnstar. She's got the double saddle."

He turned to the other men. "Bernie, the rest of you, go back to the ranch and tell the women that Mrs. Wright is found and safe and that I'm riding to Gold Creek to see her and Reverend Wright home."

Rachel lifted her head from Daniel's shoulder and spoke out. "Someone must go to Montview and bring Dr. Franz to Rose."

"Dr. Franz?" Stephen said. "Did he settle in Montview then? I'll go. I'll go right away."

"Lily?" Rachel asked.

"Lily should be with Rose by now," Andrew told her. "Jonathan took her in the sleigh as soon as we heard Rose was ill."

Andrew dismounted and led Dawnstar over to where Daniel stood, with his arms around Rachel, struggling to control his sobs.

"Mount, Daniel," Andrew said. "I'll lift her up in front of you so you can hold her close and warm her."

~

Home at last. Daniel dismounted stiffly from Dawnstar and helped Rachel down. Andrew rode up beside him, leading Shadow. "I'll take care of the horses," he said. "You go on in."

Light shone out around the closed shutters. Daniel took Rachel's arm to help her up the steps, but she brushed his hand away.

She had sat silent in front of him on the ride home. He held her with one arm around her waist, but she had not leaned back against him. He could feel her shivering, and feel her anger.

"I'm sorry," he had said as they rode. "I should have gone for Lily. I'm sorry you got lost. Please forgive me, for that and all the rest."

But she had not answered, and now she hurried up the steps ahead of him.

Inside, the twins were curled together on the couch. Isabel dozed in the leather chair and Jonathan sat by the hearth.

Isabel startled awake and rushed across the room to embrace Rachel. "Thank the Lord you're found," she exclaimed, even in her excitement keeping her voice low. "Ach, you're so cold. Come to the fire. You, too, preacher. Let me take your coats."

"How is she?" Rachel asked softly.

"Blessed be, her fever broke. She knew Lily was coming before she ever got here. 'Lily's coming,' she said to me, and when I touched her she was cool. Now Lily's here and she's sleeping. Don't you worry. She's gonna come through."

All the time she was talking, she pulled the rocking chair up close to the fire and led Rachel to sit down.

"Joshua?" Rachel asked.

"He's sleeping, too, in my bed. Hannah brought him back. He missed you bad and let us know, but between the two of us we got him quiet."

Daniel still stood by the door, dazed with relief and exhaustion. He couldn't take his eyes off Lily and Rose. Lily was curled around Rose, her arm around her, her face nestled in Rose's curls, just as he had seen them sleeping together countless times in the wagon. A knot deep in his gut let go, a knot that had been there, he realized, ever since the day he had forbidden them to see each other.

Isabel bustled over to him. "Now, preacher, what are you doing just standing there? Come in. Give me your coat. What's this—blood? You said something about Smythe before. What happened?"

Daniel, still dazed, passed his hand over his brow. Isabel gave him a sharp look. "Never mind now, we'll hear the story later. You're shaking with cold. Come sit." She tugged him toward his chair.

Jonathan stood by the hearth, clearly uneasy, shifting from one foot to the other, chin up, chest defiant. Daniel went to him and held out his hand.

"Please sit down. You are welcome here."

Jonathan mumbled, "Thank you, sir," and sat. But Daniel still couldn't sit. He walked softly to the couch and bent over to look in Rose's face. Her lashes were dark on her pale cheek, her face peaceful.

Lily turned her head slightly to look up at him. "Don't wake her, Papa." Their eyes met. Lily's filled with tears.

Hardly daring, Daniel reached out to touch her hair. "Lily, I'm sorry. For everything. Please forgive me."

Lily's lips trembled. She pressed them together, gave a little nod, and turned her face back into Rose's curls.

The front door opened quietly, and Andrew came in. Daniel went to him. There was so much he wanted to say to this beloved friend, so much that it rose up and choked him. All he could finally get out was, "Forgive me."

Andrew did not answer with words, but simply embraced him.

Isabel came bustling out of the kitchen with two steaming bowls in her hands. "I've had a stew on the back burner and it's good and hot. Here, Rachel. I know you haven't eaten all day. This'll warm you." She handed a bowl to Rachel. "Preacher, when are you going to sit down? You look plumb tuckered out. And I bet you haven't eaten either since that bread and cheese I gave you at noon."

Andrew led him to his chair and at last he sank into it with a sigh. Isabel gave him a bowl of stew.

"Jonathan," she said, "bring a chair out of the kitchen for your father."

Soon everyone was settled in a circle around the hearth with bowls of stew.

"Where did you find her?" Daniel asked Andrew.

"She came out of the trees down by the creek, leading her horse, walking wobbly the way people do when they're near death with cold. Glad we found her when we did. Much longer ..."

Rachel looked over at him. She was still shivering slightly but color was coming back into her face. "I sure was glad to see your lantern, hear your voice."

"Tell us," Isabel said. "What happened to you?"

Rachel took another bite of stew before she answered. She had been eating hungrily.

"I got lost," she said simply. "I got as far as Ranch Road okay, but then the snow was so thick I couldn't see the hills, or the road. I let Dawnstar go, hoping she'd find the way to the ranch, but she took me down a hill to the creek. I thought maybe it was the one that flowed out of the ranch, and if I followed it, it would take me there. I dismounted to lead Dawnstar, but the willows were too thick. After that I don't remember anything until I saw the lantern and heard Andrew calling me." She shuddered.

Daniel sat hunched in his chair, terror sweeping through him again. How nearly he had lost her. If Andrew hadn't helped … The bowl of stew was warm in his hands, but he couldn't eat.

Isabel was looking over at him with sharp questioning eyes. "What happened with you, Preacher? If I'm not mistaken, you've got a story to tell. You came in here all wild-eyed, blood on your coat, saying something about Smythe, before you dashed out again. And you still don't look so good. Eat now. You need some vittles."

He looked around the room. Jonathan watched him, wary. Rachel's eyes were huge and dark in her pale face. Lily sat on the edge of the couch, pressed close to Rose. Andrew waited quietly, question in his clear, gray eyes.

Daniel felt he could not speak. But he had to.

"Smythe is dead," he said.

It was as if an electric current passed through the room. Stunned silence.

"Smythe dead?" Isabel exclaimed. "Is it his blood on your coat then, or yours?"

"What happened?" Andrew leaned forward in his chair.

"Papa, are you all right?" Lily asked.

Rose stirred and mumbled.

"Hush," Rachel said. "Don't wake her. Daniel, tell us."

So, haltingly, shaking again from the memory, he told them how Smythe had attacked him, how they'd struggled, how Smythe had died with the light around him. "And then," he said, "God spoke to me."

The room was silent, all eyes on him.

"What did God say?" Andrew asked.

"That Smythe was not lost, not lost, but home with Him in heaven. Smythe."

No one moved.

"Light was all around me, like Paul on the road to Damascus. And then I knew. I've had it all wrong. About salvation." He looked at Andrew. "And I've caused great harm to those I love most. To you. All of you. I pray you can forgive me." He met Lily's eyes, then turned to Rachel.

She got up from her rocking chair, came to him, and sat down in his lap. As he wrapped his arms around her, bent his head over her, she reached up and stroked his cheek. "Oh, my dear," she said. "Oh, my dear. It's all right now. Don't grieve."

~

The moon sailed high across the sky. In the preacher's house on the hill everyone was asleep—Rachel snuggled in Daniel's arms, all the reserve of the last months melted away; Lily curled around Rose, pouring her love through the open doors of their hearts; Isabel stretched out on the edge of her narrow bed because Joshua was sprawled in the middle; Jonathan and Andrew rolled up in blankets by the hearth.

Below, in the saloon at the mouth of the canyon, no one slept. Suzy, Belle, and Candy packed their few personal possessions, and, before midnight, had taken Smythe's buggy and the mare that used to be Ginny's, and disappeared into the night. Brick also was busy. In the gray light before dawn, he swept the cash register clean. Then he hitched his horse to Smythe's wagon, pulled it up to the side door of the bar, loaded Smythe's entire liquor supply, and threw his cudgel on top. Before sunrise he was gone, his tracks going east in the new snow, covering those of the women who had fled before him.

### Chapter 55

## *The Next Day*

Sheriff Parker was up early the next morning. He got on his horse and rode through the fresh snow down to Mayor Wilgus's house. "Come with me," he said. "Got something to show you."

The two men rode down Gold Creek Road in the early morning quiet.

"What's up?" the mayor asked.

"You'll see."

The front door of the saloon stood open. Sheriff Parker stuck his head in. "Halloo," he called. There was no answer. The bar was empty. They walked through, called up the stairs. Still no answer.

"I have a feeling," the sheriff said, "there's no one here."

"How strange," the mayor said. "What about Smythe? He wouldn't leave the door open like this. Where is he?"

"Follow me."

The sheriff led the mayor into the big room where he and Brick had laid Smythe out and covered him with an old blanket the night before. He plucked back the blanket. "Here he is."

The mayor paled. He coughed, pulled a silk handkerchief out of his vest pocket, and covered his mouth and nose. "My God!" he said, and coughed again. "What happened to him?"

"He tried to kill the preacher yesterday. Fell off his horse in the fight, and his horse, that big stallion, trampled him. The preacher brought him to me last night."

"My God." The mayor choked behind his handkerchief. He drew back farther, waved his hand at the corpse. "Cover him up, for God's sake. What are we going to do with him?"

The corner of the sheriff's mouth twitched as he pulled the blanket back over Smythe. "Don't know. I thought the folks here would tend to him, but it looks like they all lit out."

"Something's got to be done with him. We can't just leave him like that." The mayor choked again.

"I'll ask the preacher. Let's take a look around."

The two men walked through the whole building. Everywhere there were signs of hasty departure, drawers left open, beds stripped of linens. Smythe's room behind the bar was in disarray. They returned to the bar and contemplated the empty shelves. "Been looted," the sheriff commented. "It's a stinking place. We should burn it to the ground."

The mayor was recovering. "No," he said. "It's a sturdy building. Big. We could clean it up and turn it into an inn. We need an inn in this town. Hannah's place isn't big enough for all the people coming."

"It'd take a lot of cleaning. Let's check out the barn."

The stallion stood exhausted in the stable yard, his head hanging, his saddle askew.

"Come here," the sheriff said to the mayor. "Look at his forelegs. Blood all over 'em. I didn't doubt the preacher's story, him being who he is, but here's proof. Have a look. You'll be a witness that's how Smythe died."

The stallion shied as they neared him. The sheriff approached him slowly, took his reins, patted his neck. The mayor kept his distance. "That's a dangerous animal. Yes, yes, I see. Blood for sure."

Rose woke to morning sunshine coming through the east window and the sound of voices in the kitchen.

She sighed and stirred. Her body felt light, empty, almost as if it weren't there. She rolled to her side. She was tired, so tired. Weak. But also strangely peaceful.

She heard Lily's laughter in the kitchen. That was it. Lily had come. Peace moved through her, and she drifted away.

When she opened her eyes again, Lily was standing nearby with her arms around Jonathan. "I don't know how long," she said. "Until I'm sure she's okay."

There were other voices. Mr. Fairdale's. Mr. Fairdale is here, Rose thought in wonder.

"I hate to leave you now that I've found you again," he was saying. "But it's spring, calving time, everything to be done on the ranch. You'll come soon. We'll talk. There is much to catch up on."

Her father's voice. They were in the room near her, but out of sight. "How can I ever thank you for your help last night. Without you—"

"Don't think of it. All's well now."

Their voices faded out. The next time she woke, Lily was bending over her.

"Hi, Lily," she whispered. Her voice felt strange to her, as if it came from far away.

Lily kissed her brow. Rose could feel a smile moving through her body, touching her lips.

Lily smiled back. "Isabel has some tea for you. Could you drink a little tea?"

She drank some, supported by Lily's arm around her shoulders, then lay quietly holding Lily's hand. She was awake enough now to wonder. She was so weak. What was wrong with her? Why was she lying on the couch? Vaguely she remembered the pain, the fever, something else. Fear raced through her. She struggled to sit up. "Papa. I have to tell Papa."

"Rose, don't." Lily put her hand on Rose's chest and gently pushed her back down. "What's wrong?"

"I heard Smythe—" Rose's heart was racing. "Telling Brick he's going to kill Papa. On a lonely road. Where's Papa?"

"It's okay, Rose. Papa's right here. He's fine. And Smythe is dead. We don't have to worry about him any more."

Rose's head spun. "Dead? How?"

Lily bent over and put her arms around Rose. "I'll tell you the whole story later. Please rest now. You've been really sick. Papa's safe. Everything's okay."

Everything *was* okay with Lily there. She slept again.

Joshua stood by her bed. "Wose, you can hold my tiger." He thrust it at her, then ran to the kitchen calling in his high, shrill voice, "Wose is awake."

Rachel's voice. "Yes, hush. She needs us to be quiet."

Joshua, just as loud. "But she's awake."

Later Dr. Franz knelt beside her. "Hello, Rose. I hear you got the fever. I'd like to check you out." Rose felt a rush of happiness. Dr. Franz. Now she would be okay. He'd know what to do. She felt his kind, wise hand on her brow, the cool stethoscope on her chest.

He left her and went to the kitchen. To the accompaniment of Joshua playing in the pan cupboard, she heard him tell Isabel, "She must eat a little every hour or two. Give her the tonic three times a day. Isn't there a room upstairs? She should be moved there if Lily can stay with her. There's too much going on down here. Half the town is out front. And even this little one ..."

Lily's voice. "I'll stay with her. But someone will need to carry her up."

Another voice, one she hadn't heard for a long time. "I'll carry her."

A young man knelt by her couch. Blue eyes, a beard. He didn't have a beard before.

"Hi, Rosie," he said.

"Stephen." She felt herself smiling. "I dreamed about you." She moved her hand toward him.

He took her hand. "I've been dreaming about you for two long years." He was silent, just looking at her. Then he bent and kissed her hand.

When he lifted his head, he spoke more lightly. "I was real worried when I heard you were sick. You have to get well now. You promised me, you know, that you would fill in the last two leaves on the shirt you embroidered for me."

She remembered. "Yes," she said. "I will."

"I'm going to carry you upstairs now where you can be quiet and rest. Lily will stay with you. Okay if I pick you up?"

Rose nodded. He gathered her into his arms and stood. "You're so light," he said. She rested her head on his shoulder. As she had in her dream.

Like the wind rushing down from the mountains, the news of Smythe's death swept through the town, carrying before it a debris of shock, rejoicing, rumor, fear.

"Smythe is dead."

"He tried to kill the preacher."

"Did the preacher kill him?"

"He wouldn't have."

"There was blood on his coat, Hannah said."

"Trampled by his horse."

"That stallion is dangerous, running wild through the town."

"The fancy women are gone."

"Someone stole all the liquor."

"Is the preacher okay?"

Daniel and Andrew were talking in the kitchen over morning coffee, when Gabe knocked on the front door. Daniel opened the door. Gabe seized him by the shoulders. "Are you all right?"

"Yes, yes. Let's step outside. Rose has been sick." Daniel gestured toward the couch where the twins were still sleeping.

Gabe looked around Daniel and saw them. He smiled. "Lily's here. That's good."

They went out onto the front porch. "What happened?" Gabe asked. "The mayor came by my place, all shaken up, saying Smythe tried to kill you and he's dead, trampled by his horse. The mayor wanted me to make a coffin right away."

"It's true," Daniel said. "It's a long story."

"The word's out, and the town's a'buzzing," Gabe said. "Some are a'saying Smythe killed you. You're gonna have a mob up here real soon wanting to see if you're alive." He frowned. "Tell you what. I'll set Harry to making the coffin, and then come back up here. I'll get Nathan to help. We'll meet them and turn them back. What'll we tell them?"

"That I am well. And that we'll bury Smythe this afternoon."

The town people gathered in the café, stopped each other on the road, knocked on each other's doors. Before long, as Gabe had predicted, a crowd moved up the hill to the preacher's house. Gabe and Nathan stationed themselves by the big rock at the edge of the property, answered the people's questions, and turned them back. There was quite a stir when Jonathan and Andrew Fairdale emerged from the house and rode out through the crowd.

Word flowed back down the hill. The preacher is okay. Doctor Rose is sick. The Fairdales were there. Miss Lily, too. Smythe will be buried this afternoon.

There was much discussion about where Smythe would be buried, but that soon became clear. A crowd gathered to watch Marcus and Benedict dig a grave in the cemetery south of the river. It was a balmy spring afternoon, the sun warm, the ground muddy with melting snow. Looking more like his usual jovial self, the mayor directed the digging. The sheriff pulled up with the coffin in his cart.

When Daniel appeared, sitting pale and tall on his horse, a murmur ran through the crowd. A woman's shocked voice could be heard. "He's not going give him a *Christian* burial, is he? Not Smythe."

Dolly Dwight ran to Daniel and stood by his stirrup, looking up at him. "Why have you come? That man doesn't deserve even a prayer. And he shouldn't be buried here next to decent folks."

"No," someone else shouted. "Throw him out onto the hills for the wolves." More voices were raised, agreeing.

Daniel's voice rang out. "Enough!"

The crowd fell silent. Something had changed in the preacher's presence; there was a pallor, a sternness, yet also a tender openness, a light around him. Some remembered that only yesterday he had fought for his life.

There was no sound but the scrape of shovel on hard earth and an occasional grunt as Marcus and Benedict continued digging.

Daniel gazed out over the crowd, meeting each person eye to eye. Finally he spoke. "God is love."

The people stirred.

"He is our Father, we are His children," Daniel went on, looking down at them from his seat on horseback, speaking in such a way that each person felt the preacher spoke directly to him. "He loves us as a father loves his children. John Smythe, whom we bury here today, is also His child and loved by Him. Shall we scorn him whom God loves?"

Daniel swept his gaze over the faces turned up to him. "God's mercy is beyond our comprehension. We are all sinners, we all stray from the path. All of us are in need of His mercy, all are lost without His love. Judge not."

The crowd remained silent as Marcus and Benedict climbed out of the grave, leaned on their shovels, and wiped their brows. The mayor nodded to the sheriff, who drove the cart to the graveside. Marcus and Benedict lifted the coffin out, tied ropes around it, and lowered it into the earth.

Daniel dismounted, handed Shadow's reins to Gabe who stood beside him, and, Bible in hand, walked to the grave. "Let us pray," he said.

The people bowed their heads.

# Chapter 56

# *Rose and Lily*

Spring blossomed in the valley, and little by little Rose grew stronger. Lily stayed with her and cared for her tenderly. When she curled around Rose at night, it was as comforting as ever, but also different. Rose felt the firm bulge of the unborn child and, sometimes, its movement against her back.

After a few days, Rose was able to come downstairs to join the family for meals. In the mornings, she sat in the rocking chair on the front porch in the spring sunshine, while Lily sat beside her sewing tiny garments for her baby. Soon Rose asked for her embroidery materials and began decorating the little clothes. Lily had never been much interested in embroidery and was glad to have Rose do that part.

"I think it's a boy," Lily said. "So don't make too many flowers. Maybe animals."

"I think it is, too," Rose agreed. "How about horses?"

"Perfect for a Fairdale."

After the drama around Smythe's death had died down, the town people realized they had almost lost their beloved doctor and came bringing gifts— a pot of chicken soup, a loaf of bread, a crocheted afghan, a basket of eggs.

Amy and Julia came every morning after their delivery to the store. Lisbeth came often, with little Lucia on her hip. One morning as she sat with Lily and Rose on the porch, she shyly confided that she was with child again.

Rose looked up from her embroidery, startled.

"But I thought," Lily said, "Gabe … that he … had his bed in the shop."

"Last winter it was so cold," Lisbeth said. "He is always kind and gentle to me, so I wasn't afraid. I love him. I wanted to be a proper wife to him."

Rose felt a rush of anxiety. Her heart beat faster.

"He'd never been with a woman before," Lisbeth said. "It wasn't like at the brothel, not at all. It just made me love him more. And he's so happy. Maybe that's what it's for, besides making babies. To make your husband happy."

"I think it is," Lily said. "It's that way with me and Jonathan."

Rose pricked her finger, and put it to her mouth. Her mind was a tumble. Maybe, after all, it wasn't like the dogs they'd seen rutting in Council Bluffs. Maybe the brothel was like the dogs, and marriage was different. She sucked her pricked finger. "When will your baby come?" she asked.

"I don't know for sure. Sometime in the fall."

"We'll have lots of babies," Lily said. "Mattie's will be very soon, and then mine and then yours."

Hannah came, full of news. A new doctor, Dr. Ira Barkley, had come to town, an older man with a spinster daughter. They were staying at the boarding house and planning to settle in Gold Creek. Mayor Wilgus had no sooner set eyes on the daughter than he'd asked her to marry him.

"She's not young," Hannah said, "but still comely. At first she said no, she'd come to keep house for her father. But then the mayor told her he had a big house and her father could live with them, and sweet-talked her, and brought her flowers—from my garden—and now she's said yes. So the mayor will have a wife at last, which is a relief. He'll stop pestering me."

When Hannah had told Dr. Barkley about Rose, she went on to report, he'd been doubtful at first. A young maiden acting as doctor for the town? A woman? What did she know?

"I had to bite my tongue," Hannah said, "over him thinking a woman couldn't be a doctor. I did tell him how Dr. Franz had been training you for two years and how you saved so many lives last winter. He's been talking to some other folks and seems to be changing his mind. He's a good man, I think, and it might be well for you to have some help. He'd like to call on you. I told him I'd ask you."

Rose felt a wave of relief. Another doctor to share the work. Someone new to learn from. She'd been concerned that she still didn't have the strength to do her clinics. "Yes, please tell him to call. I'd like to meet him."

The next morning, Dr. Barkley strode up the cliff path from the boarding house and came to sit on the porch with Lily and Rose. He was a tall, lanky man with a beak nose, kind, dark eyes, and gray hair. They began with pleasantries about the weather, but soon he was asking Rose about her practice. Rose told him about her training with Dr. Franz, her clinics, and about the terrible epidemic of mountain fever the last winter. He asked what treatments she had used, nodded as she answered. Their conversation deepened into more detail and an exchange of strategies for various maladies.

Rose was excited to have someone to talk to about her work. She liked the new doctor and he seemed more and more impressed with her knowledge as their conversation continued.

"I hope we can practice together," he said as he stood up to leave. "You are much loved in this town. I wish you a speedy recovery. Please let me know if you need anything."

Stephen came often to visit in the evenings after the day's work on the ranch. He brought the shirt Rose had embroidered for him and watched in awe as she filled in the last two leaves. One evening he asked to borrow Daniel's buggy and took Rose for a short ride onto the plains. It was the first time she'd been out since her illness, and she was thrilled to see how rapidly spring was returning to the valley. During the long winter she had often felt that spring would never come.

It had always been easy for her to talk with Stephen. Their friendship, nurtured on the trail, felt unbroken by the two years he had been away. But something was different now. They shared their adventures and thoughts and laughed together as they always had, but Rose could not forget the tenderness with which he had carried her up the stairs, or his presence in her dream. On the trail Stephen had been a carefree youth, eager to explore California; now he had matured and was settling down to be a partner on his uncle's ranch. And there was an expression in his eyes when he looked at her that said more than his words.

～

"I have to go home soon," Lily said to Rose as she brushed out Rose's hair. "Jonathan misses me, and I'm afraid my house will be an awful mess if I don't get back to take care of it." They sat on their bed in the upstairs room. Soft spring air flowed in through the open window.

Rose didn't answer. A shiver went through her at the thought of Lily being gone again, the empty bed, the loss of her constant companionship and loving care. Rose still felt weak, unsure of being able to take care of herself.

"Isabel and Rachel will look after you," Lily said, hearing her thought.

Rose felt Lily's deft hands looping up her hair and pinning it securely. Lily turned to sit facing her, and took Rose's hands in hers.

"I'll miss you," Rose said.

"I'll miss you, too." Lily leaned forward to kiss Rose's forehead. "But we can see each other often, now that Papa's finally come around. He was so mean to keep us apart."

Anger flared up in Rose. "It wasn't Papa who kept us apart," she blurted. "I would have come to visit you every day in spite of him. He couldn't have stopped me. It was you. You pushed me away." She pulled her hands out of Lily's.

"Rose, don't." Lily's lips quivered. "I didn't … I didn't mean … It was just at the very beginning. I needed to be with Jonathan. To get used to being married. Then I came to look for you and *you* pushed me away. That day in the store."

"Three months later. When you needed me. Because you were with child. Until then you didn't care."

"You knew then?"

"Of course I knew. The minute I saw you."

"I did care. I missed you. I wanted to share the baby with you."

"And be sure," Rose snapped, "I'd be around to help you give birth."

Lily was clearly shocked. She pulled her rejected hands back against herself. Rose was shocked, too. Why should all the feelings of anger, grief, and rejection pour out now, when Lily had tended her so lovingly for the last two weeks?

They faced each other, both angry, both hurt, each feeling the other's anger and hurt.

"I'm sorry," Rose said. Her hands were clenched in her lap. "You came when I needed you. Thank you for being here and taking care of me."

How strange to say such a thing to Lily. To thank her. There had never been the need for such words before. Caring for each other had been second nature.

Rose looked into Lily's eyes, bright with angry tears. Her heart constricted. All the pain and desolation of the winter felt as real as when it had happened. And now Lily was going away again. At that moment the gulf between them felt wider and more turbulent than the river between her and Heaven. She turned her head away.

Lily folded her lips together and held her breath. Slowly she let it out. She tilted her head to look into Rose's face. "Rose," she said, hesitantly, "I want to be close to you again. I've missed you horribly. I love Jonathan very much, but it's not the same with him. He wants to understand, but I have to explain things to him. There will never be anybody who knows me like you do."

Rose nodded, but still didn't look at Lily.

"It's just that our closeness …" Lily's voice trembled. "Needs to be different than it used to be."

Rose squeezed her hands so tightly together that they hurt. "How different?"

"Partly," Lily's voice steadied, "because I need to go home and we don't live together anymore, or sleep together, or do everything together. But we can still call to each other when something is important. And visit often, sometimes stay the night. And make music as we used to. Maybe even ride Dawnstar together again after my baby comes. I do want to share the baby with you."

Rose's heart began to ease. "I want you to."

Lily went on, her words tumbling over each other, as she felt Rose softening.

"I've been thinking about this a lot. It used to seem that we were the same, part of each other, when we were children. But it was never really true. We've always been different, even more so now that we're grown up."

A tear dropped onto Rose's clenched hands. "I know. You're a wife and I'm a doctor."

"That's true," Lily said, "but not what I mean. Our difference is more than our roles. You have always been more gentle and nurturing, and I've been more adventurous. We've complemented each other. I miss your gentleness. Do you miss me, my wildness?"

Rose lifted her head and saw in Lily's face Lily's longing, that matched her own longing to be close again. Rose held out her hands. Lily caught hold of them. They looked deeply into each other's eyes. Rose felt the smile she saw opening on Lily's face reflected on her own. Then they rolled down onto the bed, hugging each other.

After a while they sat up, side by side, arms around each other, brows touching in the old way.

"What about the doors?" Rose asked.

"I want to keep them open," Lily said, "especially now that we live apart, so we can share things and know how the other is." Lily's arms tightened around Rose. "It was so awful when I couldn't reach you and then found out you were dying. I could see you going into that river, and thought I'd lost you forever."

"Jesus didn't want me to die yet."

"You see, that's another way we're different. I believe in Him, but Jesus doesn't talk to me the way he does to you."

"But you said you wanted your privacy, because you're married," Rose said, coming back to the matter of the doors.

"Yes. Here's what I learned to do. Make a closet for the private things about me and Jonathan, but still keep the door open."

"That's what it was. I felt there was something, even when the doors were open. I don't know if I can do that. When I closed the door in my heart last fall, I couldn't open it again. It was frozen shut. Until the fever split it open."

"I'll show you. It's easy." They sat silent a little while.

"I see," Rose said. "But I don't have any private stuff."

"You will," Lily said. Rose could feel her smile. "Stephen loves you."

# Epilogue

As spring opened into summer, the town grew. New buildings sprang up along Gold Creek Road east of Gabe's shop and on South Road. The church also grew. Daniel's deepened experience of God's love overflowed into his ministry, and the people of the town responded, holding him in awe for his eloquence and compassion.

One of the new buildings on South Road was Dr. Barkley's office, with a waiting room and two treatment rooms. On the door of one of the treatment rooms was a sign that said "Dr. Rose Wright." After Rose and Dr. Barkley had worked together assisting Mattie's birth, Dr. Barkley was eager to practice with her.

Friday visits between the Wright and Fairdale families resumed. All rejoiced in their reconnection. Kate and Rachel sat at the kitchen table and walked in the gardens, sharing woman lore. Joshua played boisterously with little Johnny. The young people, now joined by Stephen, rode their horses and made music together. Daniel, still unsettled about his theology, was deeply grateful for his conversations with Andrew.

Stephen worked every evening building a cabin at the foot of the knoll, near a curve in the creek. Each week, when the Wright family came, he took Rose to show her his progress. His courtship was gentle, but persistent. Gradually Rose let go of her fears and opened her heart to the sweetness of first love.

In mid-August, Lily gave birth to twin boys. As the family sat around adoring the newborns, Lily said, "I knew it was a boy. Jonathan and I couldn't decide which grandfather to name him after, but now …"

"Andy and Danny," Amy pronounced.

Later Rose and Lily sat together on the wide bed in Lily's cabin, each holding a baby boy. They looked into each other's eyes with wonder.

"Twins," Rose breathed. "Do you think they'll be like us, and understand and hear each other?"

"They already do," Lily said.

On a blue-sky day in September, Rose and Stephen were married by Daniel in a big church wedding. Rose wore a white gown and veil, and the Fairdale family made music. After the wedding, Rose went to Fairdale Ranch to live with Stephen in her new home at the foot of the knoll, only a few minutes' walk from Lily's and Jonathan's cabin.

So Lily's and Rose's lives were intertwined again, though in a new way. Each tended her own house and cared for her husband. Rose rode off several days a week to her clinic in Gold Creek and was often called, night or day, to attend a birth. But otherwise they shared, as they had before, work in the garden, music, rides in the double saddle on Dawnstar, romps in the creek, and now the care of two beloved baby boys.

Also from Heather Starsong

*Never Again*

*Leaves in Her Hair*


~


www.heatherstarsong.com

# About the Author

Heather Starsong grew up in New England and graduated summa cum laude from Boston University in 1957 with a Bachelor of Arts in Comparative Literature.

She has been a dancer since childhood, especially fascinated with the connections between healing, art, and spirit. She has explored and taught many forms: creative dance, liturgical dance, dance therapy, yoga, ceremonial dance, Rolfing® and Rolf Movement,® Continuum, and most recently Argentine Tango.

Although her career has been focused on body language, she has loved and told stories all her life. In 2007 she began to write her stories. *Leaves in Her Hair* was published in 2009, *Never Again* in 2015.

She is presently semi-retired from a long career of teaching dance and yoga and practicing Rolfing. She lives in Boulder, Colorado, and enjoys writing, dancing, hiking in the high country, and spending time with her grandchildren.

Find out more about Heather Starsong on her web page: www.heatherstarsong.com.

www.ingramcontent.com/pod-product-compliance
Lightning Source LLC
Chambersburg PA
CBHW030644120726
47905CB00001B/44